POINT OF NO RETURN

JOHN P. MARQUAND

Point

of No Return

LITTLE, BROWN AND COMPANY · BOSTON

EIGHTEENTH PRINTING

The lines from "Easter Parade" by Irving Berlin are quoted
by permission of Irving Berlin Music Corporation. Copyright
1933 Irving Berlin.

The lines from "School Days," words by Will D. Cobb, music
by Gus Edwards. Copyright 1906 and 1907 by Gus Edwards
Pub. Co. Copyright renewed. By permission Mills Music, Inc.,
and Shapiro Bernstein and Co., Inc.

The quotation on page 222 is from "The Boston Evening
Transcript" from *Collected Poems 1909–1935* by T. S. Eliot,
copyright, 1936, by Harcourt, Brace and Company, Inc.

The lines beginning "When I was one-and-twenty" are from
A Shropshire Lad by A. E. Housman. Reproduced by permission of Henry Holt and Company, Inc.

The lines from Rudyard Kipling's "If" are quoted by permission of Doubleday & Company, Inc.

PRINTED IN THE UNITED STATES OF AMERICA

6109

To B. F. H.
with love

Contents

PART THREE

PART ONE

I

Thy Voice Is Heard thro' Rolling Drums
— ALFRED LORD TENNYSON

CHARLES GRAY had not thought for a long time, consciously at least, about Clyde, Massachusetts, and he sometimes wondered later what caused him to do so one morning in mid-April, 1947. It was a mental accident that reminded him of certain passages on telepathy in *Man the Unknown,* the book by Alexis Carrel which everyone had been reading before the war. For a month Charles had read snatches of *Man the Unknown* each morning on the train, after finishing the headlines and the financial page of the *New York Times.* In fact he had done this while going through one of those self-improving phases that sometimes still overtook him — although he had begun to doubt, even before the war, that you could materially better your general cultural deficiencies by thirty minutes' reading every day. He would probably have done as well for himself by doing crossword puzzles or pondering on the financial difficulties of the New York, New Haven and Hartford, or by simply staring out of the window at Rye, Harrison and Mamaroneck. Still he had those hopeful moods occasionally. When he looked at the sets of Conrad and Kipling around the fireplace of the knotty pine library and at those newer books that Nancy kept buying and at the older ones of his father's that had come from Clyde, he could still feel that he, too, might become familiar with the world's great classics, provided he could get things sufficiently straightened out at home so that he could have a moment by himself without Nancy's coming in to take up some problem or without Bill's interrupting with his algebra. At least he had not yet lost his old desire to read, though Nancy said he had. He had read *Man the Unknown* all the way through, sometime around 1935, and now in 1947 he could still remember that it had something in it about telepathy.

In Charles's own experience when something was about to happen to you, particularly anything rather unpleasant, you always had a vague sort of a preview of what was coming. It was like those previews that flashed before you in the darkness of a motion picture theater — *"It's one way or the other, Clifton — Take it or leave it — Darling, I can't leave you, but I must — Don't fail to see next week the struggle between love and duty."* At any rate, he did not feel the way he should have felt that morning. When Nancy waked him up, he had a slight headache — nothing that would not pass, however, when he had some coffee.

"Are you awake now?" Nancy asked.

"Yes," he answered, "naturally I'm awake. It's a terrible morning, isn't it?"

"If you'd only remember," Nancy said, "not to take anything to drink after dinner. I've learned it long ago and I don't see why you can't."

It always annoyed him when Nancy got on the subject of alcohol, because she invariably made it seem as though alcohol were a problem. She was always saying to people that she and Charles, when they were just quietly at home, enjoyed each other's company so much that they did not need a cocktail — which sounded well enough but was not strictly true, particularly when Nancy got started on the household bills.

"I hate sitting around with a lot of people," he said, "just talking after dinner. I can't take four hours of steady conversation after I've been talking all day."

"Now, darling," Nancy said, "who was it who wanted to go to the Cliffords'?"

"All right," Charles said, "who was it?"

"I told you," Nancy said, "that we didn't have to go to the Cliffords'. They had us in January and we had them and everything was square and now we'll have to have them again."

"Well, we don't have to have them right away," Charles said. "Let's try not to think about it now. She's the one who gets me

4

down. You know, when I see the whole picture I can't help feeling sorry for Bradley Clifford."

"Everybody's always sorry for him," Nancy said. "I wish you'd start feeling sorry for yourself."

"I do," Charles said, "right at this moment."

"And I wish you'd feel sorry for me."

"I do," Charles said. "I do feel sorry for you and for everybody else who lives in this bedroom town and in fact for everyone else in the world. That's the way I feel at the moment."

"Darling," Nancy said, "don't be so broad-minded. You'll make me cry."

"Is Bill awake?" Charles asked.

"Yes," Nancy said. "He doesn't have your troubles."

"He doesn't have to stay up all night," Charles said. "Is he out of the bathroom?"

"Yes, dear," Nancy said. "There's no excuse for you to lie there. You'd better get up or there'll be the usual morning marathon."

"Is Evelyn up?" Charles asked.

"She's up and she's studying her geography," Nancy said. "And besides, she doesn't use your bathroom."

"All right," Charles said. "All right."

"And don't go to sleep again," Nancy said. "I have to go down and cope with the coffee."

"What?" Charles asked.

"You heard me," Nancy said. "You're always better when you have your coffee. Now don't go to sleep again."

"What's happened to Mary?" Charles asked.

"She went to spend the night with her sister in Harlem," Nancy said. "She won't be back until tomorrow afternoon."

"Are you sure she's coming back?" Charles asked.

"Oh, yes, she's coming back," Nancy said. "She's left everything in her room."

"All right," Charles said. "All right. Is it raining?"

"Yes," Nancy said. "It's raining hard, and the windshield wipers on the Buick hardly ever work."

"Well, that makes it swell," Charles said. "It's nice it's come to our attention."

"I thought that might wake you up," Nancy said. "You'd better wear your herringbone suit. It came back from the cleaners yesterday. I've put your ruptured duck on it."

She was, of course, referring to the gold emblem which had been issued to ex-soldiers and sailors by a grateful government, but there was no reason why she had to call it by its GI name, as though she had been in the service, too. Also there was no reason why she should keep inserting it in his buttonhole. The emblem placed him in a youthful category to which he did not belong. He was not sure how well it looked at the bank, either.

"Never mind it," Charles said. "I'm not running for any office." He checked himself because he knew exactly what she would say before she said it.

"Oh, yes, you are," she said, "and don't you keep forgetting it. You're right in there polishing apples."

"All right," he said, "I'm not forgetting." There was no way to forget, since most of his life had been spent polishing some apple or other. If you had to earn your living, life was a series of apples.

"And don't forget," and Nancy shook his shoulder, "to put two hundred into the housekeeping account. It's down to twenty dollars and I'm going to draw on it today."

"What," Charles asked, "again?"

"Yes," Nancy said, "again and again and again. I thought you'd like some cheerful news, darling."

"All right," Charles said. "It's a hell of a morning, isn't it?"

"And don't forget that herringbone," Nancy said, "and don't take that thing out of the buttonhole. No matter how well Roger Blakesley looks, he hasn't got a duck."

"No," Charles said, "that's right. He was too bright to get one."

"And remember we're going to the Burtons' Friday night," Nancy said. "Don't forget to tell Mr. Burton you're looking forward to it when you see him." Nancy was good at putting details into useful order.

When Charles was in the bathroom shaving he disassociated

6

himself from the activities of the moment and though he had always heard people say that you had your best thoughts while shaving, all that he usually thought about at such a time was that he was in a hurry. Now that he looked in the plate-glass mirror in the baked-enamel medicine cabinet — the expensive cabinet that Nancy had induced the architect to install instead of a cheaper fixture — the brushless cream on his face, the battered safety razor he was holding, and in fact the entire bathroom gave him a transient feeling. He had been moving about in the last few years from one set of plumbing appliances to another, in Pullmans, hotels, in ships' heads and in Quonset huts, but he was still paying for this unfamiliar bathroom.

The house had been a thirty-thousand-dollar house before the war, not including extras and there had been a number of extras. It had been more than they could possibly afford, but then the house itself had never looked expensive. Nancy had wanted everything to be right and she had always dreamed about the right sort of bathroom. Those were the days when there was no shortage in materials and when there were all sorts of catalogues. You could have fixtures in colors and you could select from a dozen built-in showers. You could have it done in tile or any way you wanted — and then there were all those waterproof wallpapers. Charles had wanted the one with fishes but Nancy had wanted the one with sailboats and after all he was doing it for Nancy and the children.

He should have felt at home in that bathroom because the architect had drawn and redrawn it, and he and Nancy had quarreled over it twice; but now, although the building of the house and the bathroom and all those struggles with copper pipes and automatic gas heaters were a part of the comparatively recent past, the memories seemed as hazy as those of childhood. The whole house now seemed to belong to him only vaguely. It was the same way with the branches of the oak tree that he saw outside the window.

It was, as he had said, a hell of a morning. The sky was leaden and the air was full of the pervasive, persistent sort of rain of early spring. The water was soaking into the frostless ground and was

7

dripping from the bare twigs of the oak tree, giving them a purplish silver tinge, and the buds on the branches were already swelling. He was thinking of the family bathroom in Clyde, Massachusetts, which everyone had used before his father had added others in 1928. He was thinking of its white walls, its varnished floor and its golden-oak-framed mirror — not a specially designed bathroom but one that had been installed in what must have been a small bedroom once at the end of the second-story hall. For a second this recollection had been so vivid that the tree and the rain had not seemed right. Trees and the rain were different in Clyde, particularly at that season in the year. April rain was colder in Clyde. It generally came with the east wind, so it would beat hard on the windows; and the house, in spite of the hot-air furnace, was always damp and chilly. There were more elms than oaks in Clyde, and in April there was hardly a hint of spring.

His herringbone suit had a slight benzine odor which showed it was just fresh from the cleaners. He had worn it very little though it was four years old and now it was tight in the waist and shoulders, but not too tight. It was not a bad-looking suit at all and in fact it made him look rather like one of those suburban husbands you often saw in advertising illustrations, a whimsically comical man who peeked naïvely out of the corners of his eyes at his jolly and amazed little wife who was making that new kind of beaten biscuits.

There were ten minutes left for breakfast and it was important to keep his mind on the immediate present, yet when he went downstairs that memory of Clyde hung over him in a curiously persistent way, almost like a guilty secret, not to be discussed. Clyde had always bored Nancy and he could not blame her much. Nancy had come from upstate New York and he seldom wanted to hear about her home town either.

"Darling," Nancy used to say, "we never saw each other in either of those places, and thank God we didn't."

She was absolutely right. Thank God they hadn't, or they might have misunderstood each other. He had first seen Nancy in a partner's outer office in a law firm downtown on Pine Street, the firm of Burrell, Jessup and Cockburn. He could remember the exact, uncompromising way that she sat behind her typewriter and the exact amount of attention she had given him, not a bit more than was necessary and that was not very much.

"Mr. Jessup's in conference and he won't be free for half an hour," Nancy had said. Nancy was always able to keep track of time as readily as a railroad conductor. That was the way he and Nancy had met and that was all there had been to their meeting.

"You needed a haircut," Nancy told him later, "but not very badly, and the way you held your brief case showed you weren't one of those bond boys, and you didn't have a handkerchief in your breast pocket."

"Well," he had told her later, "you didn't look so lovable either."

"Darling," Nancy said, "that's one of the nicest things you've ever told me. I spent a long time cultivating just that look."

When he came down to the dining room, Nancy was sitting in much the same posture, very straight in her bleached oak chair. Instead of a typewriter she was manipulating a toaster and an electric percolator, and there was a child on either side of her — their children.

"Don't trip over the extension cords," Nancy said. "Billy — "

His son Bill rose from the table and pulled out his chair for him, a respectful attention on which Nancy insisted and which always made Charles nervous.

"Well, well," Charles said. "Good morning, everybody. Hasn't the school bus come by yet?"

"It's not the school bus," his daughter Evelyn said. "It's the school car. Why do you always call it a bus?"

"It ought to be a bus," Charles said. "You kids ought to be going to a public school."

Nancy was looking at him critically as she always did before he went to town.

"You've forgotten your handkerchief," she said.

That idea of hers that every well-dressed man should have a corner of a handkerchief peeking from his breast pocket he often thought must have been a hangover from Nancy's earlier days, but then perhaps every woman had her own peculiar ideas about male dress.

"Now listen, Nance," he said, "never mind about the handkerchief."

It surprised him that she let it pass.

"Evelyn, pass your father his coffee," she said.

"And don't look cute when you're doing it," Bill said.

"Mother," Evelyn said, "won't you tell Bill to stop that, please?"

"Yes," Nancy said. "Stop, Bill, and go out in the kitchen. Put the eggs in and watch the clock."

There was no necessity for listening carefully to the voices of Nancy and the children. He could go on with his orange juice, toast, and coffee as though the conversation were a background of words issuing from a radio. He had heard the program again and again.

"You've got to leave in five minutes," Nancy said. "The roads will be slippery."

Charles pulled his watch from his vest pocket, the one that Nancy had given him just before they were married, and glanced at it.

"And remember," Nancy said, "you'll have to go and get the Buick out. Something seems to be wrong with the automatic choke."

"Didn't you send it down to be fixed?" Charles asked.

"Yes," Nancy answered, "but you know what they're like at that service station. They just look at the carburetor and don't do anything. I wish you'd go to that new Acme place."

"Acme. I wonder what acme means exactly," Charles said.

"Why, Daddy," Evelyn said. "Don't you know what acme means? It means the top of everything."

It startled him to have Evelyn tell him something which he should have known himself and which, of course, he would have known if he had put his mind on it. The trouble was that he had not been back long enough for broken links of habit to be wholly mended, and everything at home still seemed to have sprung ready-made out of nowhere. There was something in Berkeley's theory of philosophy — as he had learned it at Dartmouth — that there was no proof that anything existed except in the radius of one's consciousness.

Before the war, Bill had been nine and Evelyn had been six, and now Evelyn was able to look up acme in the dictionary. He was in a ready-made dining room, though he had been responsible for its having been built in 1940. He and Nancy had bought the bleached chairs and table and sideboard and had agreed that the walls should be done in pickled pine because they had wanted it to look light and modern. The glazed chintz draperies still had their original luster and the begonias and ivy and geraniums in the bow window looked as though they had just come from the florist, because Nancy had made an intensive study of the care and feeding of household plants. There were no finger marks or smudges on the table or the chairs and the light carpet was just back from the cleaners without a smudge on it either. It was amazing how beautifully Nancy could keep a house with only one maid to help her.

"You'd better get the Buick now," Nancy said. "There's no use killing ourselves getting to the train."

The rain gave the blue gravel near the garage a metallic sheen. The water on the lightly whitened brick of the house — he believed it had been called Southern Brick — made the variegated color look like new plastic, and the leaves of the rhododendrons and the firs near the front door glistened like dark cold water.

The Buick started easily enough, though it was a 1940 car. It reminded him of a well-preserved old gentleman with an independent income, cared for by a valet, and he did not see how Nancy could have kept it looking so well considering all the bundles and the children it had carried.

"Move over," Nancy said. "I'll drive down."

She adjusted a little cushion against the small of her back and took the wheel. She had on one of those transparent, greenish rain capes over her greenish tweed suit. She pulled her gloves deliberately over her engagement and wedding rings, but then she had fixed it so there was plenty of time. She had always said that she was never going to have any man of hers get ulcers running for the train.

When they were out of the drive and safely through the gates marked Sycamore Park, he glanced at her profile. The rain had made her hair, where it showed at the edges of her green felt hat, moist and curly. They always seemed much more at peace when she took him to the station than at any other time and for some reason it was always the friendliest moment of the day. He and Nancy were alone together, undisturbed by all the rest of the world.

"You didn't forget your reports, did you?" Nancy asked.

"No," he said. "I've got them."

"Have you still got that headache? There's an aspirin in the glove compartment."

"It's all right," he said. "It's gone."

"Well, that's good," she said. "Darling?"

"What?" he asked.

"It's nice driving you to the train again. It's sort of like coming back to where we started."

He looked at her again. She was looking straight ahead of her, but she was smiling.

"Yes, I know what you mean," he said. "It's funny, when I came down there to breakfast this morning the whole place seemed ready-made."

"Ready-made?" she repeated.

"Yes," he said. "Just as though I'd never done anything about it."

"I know," she said. "I'm too efficient."

"That isn't what I mean," he said.

"It's all right," she answered, "as long as you don't mind."

He was never nervous when she was driving. She had a peculiar gift of being able to divide her concentration, which permitted her to drive and at the same time balance the household budget or quarrel artistically or give intelligent answers to the children's questions about God and the life hereafter. The casual way in which she spoke told him that she was thinking very carefully about what she was saying.

12

"I wish I could stop coaching from the sidelines, but I can't help it, can I?"

There was no use answering because of course she knew what he would say, but still he answered.

"Hell, no," he said. "Of course you can't."

"Someday you're going to say you don't like it. I'm afraid of that."

There were drawbacks, he was thinking, to knowing anyone too well, and yet there was no way to avoid this. There was no actual chance for decent concealment when you knew someone's voice as well as he did hers. It was all part of the relationship that was known as love, which was quite different from being in love because love had a larger and more embracing connotation. It was a shadowy sort of edifice built by habit, without any very good architecture, but still occasionally you could get enough impression of its form to wonder how it had been built.

"Darling," she was saying, and her voice broke briskly into his thoughts, "why don't you ask Burton what the score is? Aren't you tired of waiting?"

The question made him edgy because that phrase about the score was as out of place as her allusion to the ruptured duck. She might just as well have said, Why not go and ask Burton what's cooking, and he was very glad she hadn't. The car had stopped at the Post Road for the red light. They were almost at the station.

"That would be stupid," he said. "Naturally he knows I want to know."

"Well, can't we get it over with?"

"It will get over," Charles said. "Everything does."

"Well, if we just had the cards on the table," Nancy said. "If you just said to him — "

"Now don't tell me what to say to him," Charles said, "because I'm not going to say anything."

The light turned green and the car moved forward.

"Well, I hope Roger Blakesley likes it. Do you know what Molly told me yesterday?" Nancy asked.

Charles moved uneasily. They were going down the main street.

13

A gift shop had opened there and also a new antique shop on the corner and he wondered why he had not noticed either of them before.

"She said Roger's so glad you're back and settled down."

"Well, that's swell," Charles said. He had observed that Roger Blakesley had lately been assuming the attitude that Charley had only just returned from the service and was still getting adjusted. He was very glad they were reaching the station. "If the officers and directors want him, they'll take him."

"And you'll have to resign," Nancy said.

"The next thing," Charles said, "you'll be asking me to think of the children." He began to laugh. " 'Thy voice is heard thro' rolling drums, that beat to battle where he stands; thy face across his fancy comes, and gives the battle to his hands.' Alfred Lord Tennyson." They were stopping at the last light and the station was just ahead of them and there were still three minutes before eight-thirty. "This whole business sounds like Tennyson. It's exactly as contrived."

"All right, why is it so funny?" Nancy asked.

"I didn't say it was funny," Charles said. "I said it was contrived. The little woman kissing her husband good-by. Everything depends on this moment. He must get the big job or Junior can't go to boarding school. And what about the payments on the new car? Good-by, darling, and don't come back to me without being vice-president of the trust company. That's all I mean."

Nancy threw the car into gear.

"Don't say that," she said.

"Why not?" Charles asked.

"Don't say it," Nancy said, and her voice was louder, "because maybe you're right."

"Now wait a minute—" he began, but she did not let him finish.

"Because if you say that—" she said, "if you mean that—maybe it isn't much but it's all we have. Maybe it isn't much, but then maybe we aren't much and if you feel that way there won't be anything any more."

14

It was a discordant instant of revelation and it broke unpleasantly into the morning. He thought of Clyde again, and Clyde was suddenly more real to him than the car in front of the station. He was thinking of peaceful voices saying that you often had moments of doubt or disappointment, that you often wondered whether what you were doing was worth while. The solution was to continue doing the best you could and everything would turn out all right in the end.

"Now listen, Nance," he began, and then for some reason he felt as deeply moved as if he were saying good-by to her for good. "Let's not get so emotionally involved."

"Involved with what?" Nancy asked.

"With each other," he said. "Let's get some sense of proportion."

"Don't talk about proportion," Nancy said. "There isn't any time."

It was only one of those minor partings, but he was leaving her again.

"If you're not taking the five-thirty," she said, "call me up. Good-by."

"Good-by," he said. "I'll make the five-thirty all right."

II

A Moment, While the Trumpets Blow

— ALFRED LORD TENNYSON

SHORTLY BEFORE the outbreak of the European war, Charles had
begun taking the eight-thirty. This was a privilege that had raised
him above the ruck of younger men and of shopworn older ones
who had to take the eight-two. It indicated to everyone that his
business life had finally permitted him a certain margin of leisure.
It meant that he was no longer one of the salaried class who had to
be at his desk at nine.

The eight-thirty train was designed for the executive aristocracy,
and once Mr. Guthrie Mayhew, not one of the Mayhews who lived
on South Street, not George Mayhew, but Guthrie Mayhew, who
was president of the Hawthorn Hill Club and also president of
Mayhew Brothers at 86 Broadway, had even spoken of getting an
eight-thirty crowd together who would agree to occupy one of those
club cars with wicker chairs and card tables and a porter, to be
attached to the eight-thirty in the morning and again to the five-
thirty in the afternoon. Mr. Mayhew was a public-spirited man who
always enjoyed organizing small congenial groups. He had suggested the idea first to Tony Burton and they both had decided
that they did not want it to be an old man's car. They wanted some
of the younger fellows, too, who were coming along, and they
wanted it informal. You could play bridge or gin rummy or pitch
if you wanted, or else you could merely sit and read; but the
hope was, if you got a congenial group aboard, both young and old,
coming not from all walks of life, because there was only about
one walk of life on the eight-thirty, but from different business
atmospheres — brokers, lawyers, doctors, architects, civil engineers,

and maybe even a writer or two from as far away as Westport, if you could get one — it was the hope that if you could get such a crowd together, you could have some good conversation going to and from the city.

You could have an interchange of ideas on all sorts of subjects, and goodness knows there was a lot to talk about in these days, a whale of a lot, Mr. Mayhew said. There was the New Deal, and Mr. Mayhew was broad-minded about the New Deal. He wanted some New Dealers aboard that car, if you could get them, who would stand right up on their hind legs and tell what the New Deal was about. That car would be a sort of open forum, Mr. Mayhew said. They might even find some newspaperman. They could talk about the Chinese war and about Hitler and Mussolini and the whole European mess. It ought to make the ride to New York a real occasion to which everyone could look forward, because there were a lot of interesting people going to New York if you only got to know them, and in Mr. Mayhew's experience about everything came down to just one thing — knowing and understanding people, and somehow you kept being shut away from people. That, roughly, was Mr. Mayhew's idea, but naturally it had evaporated after Pearl Harbor. Charles remembered Mr. Mayhew's idea vividly, if only because it had come up at the same time that Mr. Burton had suggested that Charles call him Tony.

Charles could still recall the glow he had felt on this occasion and the sudden moment of elation. Mr. Burton had been shy about it in a very nice way, as an older man is sometimes shy. Charles remembered that Mr. Burton had fidgeted with his onyx pen stand and that first Mr. Burton had called him "feller." It had all happened one evening when they had stayed late talking over the Catlin estate, which was one of the largest accounts in the trust department.

Mr. Burton had just made one of his favorite remarks, one which Charles had heard often before. It had happened, Mr. Burton had said, that when he was a sophomore at Yale he had studied Greek. He never knew just why he had hit on Greek, but the result showed that a concentration on any subject trained the mind.

"Now you'd think, wouldn't you," Mr. Burton said, "that the

orders of Greek verbs would be a long way from banking. Well, I can only tell you that Greek verbs have taught me more about corporate figures than anything else I ever learned at Yale."

Though Charles had heard this before, he had been pleased that Mr. Burton had touched upon the subject of his Greek studies for it showed that everything was going smoothly.

"Yes, sir," Charles had said. "I'm just beginning to see that everything fits into banking somewhere."

"Everything," Mr. Burton had said. "Everything. You see banking basically is only knowing how to use extraneous knowledge. I like to think of banking as being not only the oldest but, well, the most basically human business that there is in the world, for it deals with all the most fundamental hopes and aspirations of human beings. In fact, I don't like, honestly I don't, to think of banking as a business or even as a profession. Banking — it may startle you a little that I say this, but I'm right, I know I'm right — banking, for a good banker, is an art. The last of the arts, perhaps, but the oldest of the professions."

Charles had heard Mr. Burton advance the idea several times before but he did not interrupt.

"Now you may remember," Mr. Burton had said, "that Mrs. Burton and I took a little trip in 1933. You hadn't been with us long then, but I don't believe that you or anyone else will forget how tense things were in 1933, and now and then I found I was getting a little taut, so when things eased up I decided to go away somewhere to get a sense of perspective. That was when Mrs. Burton and I went to Bagdad. You ought to go there sometime."

Charles could not imagine what had ever made Mr. Burton want to go to such a place, unless it had something to do with Burton's *Arabian Nights,* and he wondered also what connection it had with all the reports that lay on Mr. Burton's mahogany roll-top desk. Mr. Burton had placed his elbows on the desk, had linked his fingers together and was resting his narrow chin on them, and there had been nothing for Charles to do but listen.

Well, it appeared that it had been a very interesting trip to Bagdad. The cruise ship had stopped at Beirut and from there everyone who wanted to take the side trip, including Mr. and Mrs. Burton, had embarked on buses that were as comfortable as the Greyhound buses in America, and after a night in quite a nice French hotel in Damascus, where Mrs. Burton had bought from a real Arab the rare rug that was now in Mr. Burton's library, they had proceeded in these buses at dawn right across the desert. It had been hot, but there was plenty of ice water and the seats were comfortable. Toward evening the buses had stopped at a place called Rutba Wells right out in the middle of nowhere. It was a mud-walled fort like something in the story *Beau Geste,* except that, fortunately, it was run by the British and so was sanitary.

After a very good meal of soup and fried chicken, Mr. and Mrs. Burton had played a game of darts, that British game, right in that mud-walled fort; and then in the cool of the evening they had proceeded right across the desert to Bagdad, and there it was at dawn — a city on a muddy river, spanned by a bridge of boats. They had stopped at the Tigris Hotel, right on the river, large and not uncomfortable, though one strange thing about it was that the water from the bathtub came right out on the bathroom floor and then drained through a hole in the corner.

The first morning he and Mrs. Burton had gone to the museum to see the treasure from Ur, parts of which looked like something in a case at Cartier's. You got a lot out of travel if you kept your eyes open. There had been a man in the museum, a queer sort of British archaeologist, who showed him some mud bricks that were actually parts of an account book. When you got used to them, you could see how they balanced their figures; and on one brick, believe it or not, there was even an error in addition, preserved there through the centuries. This had meant a great deal to Mr. Burton.

That clerical error in mud had given him an idea for one of the best speeches he had ever written, his speech before the American Bankers' Association in 1936 at the Waldorf-Astoria. Mr. Burton had opened a drawer and had pulled out a deckle-edged pamphlet.

"Take it home and read it if you have the time," he said. "I dashed it off rather hurriedly but it has a few ideas. It starts with that mistake in addition."

The pamphlet was entitled *The Ancient Art of Banking, by Anthony Burton, President, the Stuyvesant Bank, Delivered before the American Bankers' Association, May 1936.*

"Why, thanks very much, sir," Charles had said. "I certainly will read it." It was not the time to say that he had read the speech already or that for years he had made a point of reading all Mr. Burton's speeches.

"Look here, feller," Mr. Burton said, and he had blushed when he said "feller," "why not cut out this sir business? Why not just call me Tony?"

That was in 1941 but Charles still remembered his great joy and relief, with the relief uppermost, and that he could hardly wait to hear what Nancy would say.

"You know, Charles," Mr. Burton had continued, "Guthrie Mayhew and I have quite an idea. We're going to get hold of Tommy Mapes on the New Haven and see if he can't get us a special car on the eight-thirty. How about getting aboard? My idea is to call it the *Crackerbarrel.*"

"Why, thanks," Charles had said. "I'd like to very much, Tony."

He had worked late that night and he could not remember what train he had taken home, but Nancy had been asleep when he got there.

"Nance," he said, "wake up. I've got something to tell you. Burton's asked me to call him Tony." And Nancy had sat bolt upright in her twin bed.

"Start at the beginning," Nancy had said. "Exactly how did it happen, and don't leave out anything."

They must have talked for a long while, there in the middle of the night. Nancy had known what it meant because she had worked downtown herself.

"Now wait," she had said. "Let's not get too excited. Who else calls him Tony?"

"I don't think anyone else does," Charles had told her, "except the officers, and old Jake when he speaks of him."

"Who's old Jake?" Nancy asked.

It surprised him that Nancy did not know, for she usually kept everything straight, but when he told her that old Jake was a day watchman in the vault who had been there when Mr. Burton had first started at the bank, Nancy had remembered.

"Darling, we ought to have a drink of something, shouldn't we?" she said, but it was pretty late for a drink. "Darling, I knew it would happen sometime. I'm pretty proud of you, Charley."

It was only a week later that they found out that Mr. Burton had also asked Roger Blakesley to call him Tony and they never could find out whom Mr. Burton had asked first.

Tony Burton always boarded the eight-thirty at Stamford and it occurred to Charles that it might be a good idea to walk through the cars and to sit by him if the seat beside him should be vacant. He had nothing particular to say to him, but it might be a good idea. He even went so far as to think of a suitable conversational subject and he decided on the action of the market. He knew it would be a risky subject, to be approached cautiously, because Tony Burton was always careful to say that he was not interested in stock-market gyrations. The Board was convinced, and Charles was too, that the general situation predicated a long-term rise and that the present slump was a temporary adjustment and not the beginning of a bear market, no matter what the statisticians might conclude, unless a drastic change appeared in the foreign situation.

The station was crowded and damp, but in spite of the crowd the atmosphere was restful. You had a feeling that the rush of commuters was nearly over for the day and that of the whole army that had marched to the city only the rear guard was left. The men in the station gave an impression of executive leisure, appearing as if they did not have to arrive anywhere at any particular time, but as if nothing of importance could happen until they did arrive. Their mail would be open and waiting and everything else would be waiting. In the meanwhile, they gathered about the radiator near the ticket windows, talking about the weather, and the waiting room was almost like a club where everyone was on a first-name basis.

As Charles moved to the newsstand to buy the *New York Times* he noticed that Mr. Mayhew was wearing a new gabardine raincoat. He nodded to Courtney Jeffers of the New York Life and to Rodney Bishop in the General Foods sales department and to Bill Wardwell in Eckert and Stokes. Curiously enough, it was all more familiar than home because it was all a part of the city to which they all were going, something more important than any suburb, a part of life that was more genuine.

There was a sort of preoccupation today, almost a feeling of suspense. He had just bought the *New York Times* and had turned away from the newsstand when he saw that he was face to face with Roger Blakesley. Roger was wearing a blue, pin-striped suit, double-breasted and carefully pressed, in Brooks Brothers' most conservative tradition. His dark brown hat went very nicely with his cheviot overcoat. He was polishing his rimless glasses with a fresh handkerchief and his face, which had grown plumper and more rotund lately, was fresh and shining.

"Why, hello, Charley," Roger said.

"Hello," Charles answered, and then he went on because one had to say something. "Are you still using that electric razor, Roger?" It must have been the smoothness of Roger's cheeks that made him say it.

"Frankly, yes," Roger said. "My beard is just the thing for it, and besides" — he put on his glasses and laughed — "it makes me feel like a putting green." It was just the sort of thing that Roger would have said and his broadening smile showed he was pleased with it.

"Or a bowling green," Charles said.

"All right," Roger said, "a bowling green, as long as you don't cut it too fine. That was a swell party last night, wasn't it? I couldn't tear myself away."

"Neither could I," Charles answered, and they both smiled.

"Listen, Charley," Roger asked, "will you have any time on your hands today?"

"Not much," Charles said. "How about lunch?"

"I can't make it," Roger said. "I have a date with Tony at the University Club. After that Mapes is coming in, but we've got to check up on that Catlin thing sometime before we meet the attorneys."

There was a roaring sound outside and everyone was moving. The eight-thirty was coming in.

"We can go over it on the train if you want to," Charles said. "I've got the papers here."

Roger Blakesley patted his shoulder.

"Boy, I simply can't," he said, close to Charles's ear because of the roaring of the train. "Tony wants me. He's saving me a seat."

Charles raised his voice.

"There's a lot more to banking than you think, isn't there?" he said. "It's an art, isn't it?"

Roger laughed and linked his arm through Charles's.

"Charles," he said, "you're always subtle in the morning. Well, I'll see you in the studio."

"All right," Charles said. "Don't mix your colors wrong, Roger."

Roger had not heard him. He was already bounding up the steps of the third coach. Roger was always quick on his feet and this sort of thing had been going on long enough for Charles to understand its shades of meaning. He was reasonably sure that Tony Burton had not asked Roger to sit with him, and he was not even entirely sure that Tony Burton had asked Roger to lunch at the University Club, even though Tony Burton tried to lunch there when he could on Tuesdays.

Charles found a seat by a window and opened the *New York Times* to the financial page. There was nothing like competition. His mind had been working more alertly since he had met Roger Blakesley and everything assumed a new significance. They were both assistant vice-presidents in the trust department now, but they had both worked almost everywhere in the bank, except the vaults. Either could handle customers about as well as the other. They both were very bright boys, but he had never worried about Roger much until lately. There would have been no reason to do so now if Roger had gone to the war instead of using that period to make himself useful. The financial page was dull but Charles put his mind on it.

Roger had a quick way of jumping at facts without examining them first. His own memory was far more retentive and reliable than Roger's and Tony Burton undoubtedly knew it. Charles knew more about the trust accounts than anyone in the bank, more about the limitations under the wills and about the lawyers and the specific family situations. His mind was working smoothly now that he was on the train.

When the train pulled into the lower level of the Grand Central Station, habit made Charles move instinctively, almost oblivious to his surroundings. Without consciously noticing the polished marble of the lower level or the starry vault of the concourse on the upper level, he was aware of the changing spaces, for habit had made him a proprietor of that station and all the streets around it. Habit made him move instantly to the broad stairs on the right and he ran up gently and easily, for no good reason except that he had always taken them at a run. On the upper level he turned sharp right again, walking past the parcel checkroom to the ramp on the left and past the heaps of newspapers by the doors and out to the corner of Forty-second Street and Vanderbilt Avenue.

Whenever he emerged from the station and set foot on Forty-second Street, he experienced in varying degrees a sense of coming home. Sometimes this feeling was one of deep gratitude and more often only one of boredom, but whenever he arrived there, all those other times he had reached Forty-second Street somehow added themselves together into an imponderable, indivisible sort of sum. His mind was adjusted to the traffic, to the drugstores and the haberdasheries, to the Lincoln Building and the Park Avenue ramp. He belonged to New York, and conversely New York belonged to him, if only because so much of his life and energy and thought had been spent within its limits.

It did not matter that he had not been born and raised there, because New York belonged almost exclusively to people who had come from other places. New York in the end was only a strange, indefinable combination of triumph, discouragement and memories. It did not matter what the weather was there, or the season of the year, or whether there was war or peace — he was always able to lose himself in the city's abstractions. The place was changing—new stores, new façades, new plastics—without his being able one jot to influence that change, but still the changing place belonged to him. The only institution in the neighborhood that had not been altered much was the Stuyvesant Bank, which had been given its name when Murchison Brothers had first started the business on lower Broadway in the early 1800's. It had moved uptown long since, but almost from the beginning of its history the Stuyvesant had been what it still was, a family bank.

It was essentially the same, Charles often thought, as it had been when he had first entered it with his father on a trip to New York when he was twelve years old. It was too late now to recall the circumstances which had caused that trip, but it must have been one of those times when some transaction in Boston had put his father temporarily in a genial and opulent mood or they never would have come to New York or stopped at the Hotel Belmont. Another sign that something must have gone exceptionally well was that his father had brought his cigar case, and what Charles could remember most clearly about the trip was the rich smell of heavy Havana tobacco. It was always a good sign when his father took his cigar case from the back of his upper bureau drawer. Charles remembered very clearly the oak woodwork in the downstairs room of the Belmont where they had breakfasted after driving in a taxicab from the Fall River Line pier. There was no need, his father had said, to bother taking the elevated or the subway. They had breakfasted on grape-fruit with a red cherry in the center, oatmeal and cream, kippered herrings and scrambled eggs, and after consuming a pot of coffee his father had lighted a cigar.

"It's a great town, New York, when you get to know it," his father had said, "and everyone ought to get to know New York." It was pathetic, Charles sometimes thought, that desire of his father's to be a man of the world. It was not unlike Tony Burton's desire to be a great cosmopolitan, and their efforts achieved approximately the same measure of success. "Now straighten your tie. We're going to the bank to cash a check, and pull your stockings up."

It was God's truth, and not a very palatable one, that Charles wore black ribbed stockings and knickerbockers, purchased at Setchell's on Dock Street at Clyde. He was old enough to be painfully embarrassed at the way his stockings kept slipping down and he tried to change the subject.

"What bank?" he asked.

"Let's see," his father said, and he pulled a letter from his pocket. "The Stuyvesant Bank. It's just a few blocks from here."

Even in 1916, banks were beginning to be imposing, and Charles was disappointed when he first saw the Stuyvesant, for anyone could see that it was a bank in a former private dwelling, a big New York corner house of somewhat sooty brick and brownstone. A doorman in a black chauffeur's uniform stood on the sidewalk near what had been the front door, and once they were inside the impression of being in a house still remained, though all the ground floor had been remodeled to make room for the tellers' cages. One side was for ladies. Here in an open fireplace a little fire was burning, and near by was a desk behind which sat a white-haired gentleman whose duty it was to give the ladies advice and help, just as Mr. Cheseborough did now. There were the same mahogany roll-top desks by the windows, and other desks in the distance under electric lights. Charles could remember staring at the flight of stairs leading to the vaults in the old house cellar while the teller read his father's letter and asked his father whether he wanted it in fives or tens.

"That's a good bank," his father had said when they were out on the street again. "A family bank, without any funny business. It stood up through the panic of 'ninety-three."

That old house of the Stuyvesant was still an asset. It was still a family bank, whose doorman could greet depositors like the doorman of a club, and inside there was always a studied atmosphere of leisure. One had a reassuring suspicion, as one entered, that the Stuyvesant had handled the same family accounts for generations and that an effort had always been made to think of individuals as well as the size of their deposits. Superficially the Stuyvesant was more like Brown, Shipley, 123 Pall Mall, in London than like an American bank, and it paid to keep it that way.

Year after year there had been talk about a new building, not necessarily a modern one but something Colonial and bright like that brick effort of the Bank of Manhattan on Madison Avenue — but the directors had always in the end turned down such proposals. It paid to keep the Stuyvesant in that ugly old brownstone mansion with its floor plan about the way it had been when the Stuyvesant had first moved there. Though adjoining houses had been added and though its interior had been refinished and its exterior occasionally sandblasted and cleaned in the rough beauty-parlor treatment given to old houses, it paid to keep everything looking essentially the same. It paid to keep the open fire that burned real logs and to encourage tellers and investment counselors to be patient with confused old ladies and genial with arthritic old gentlemen. It paid to have a foreign department which could take great pains about letters of credit and perhaps advance allowances to depositors' grandchildren overextended while traveling on the Continent. It paid to have kindly tax experts seemingly willing to waste hours over minor problems of bewildered clients.

Other banks, larger ones, were constantly advertising their friendly services and pointing out the almost insoluble personal complications faced by anyone who owned property in this period of economic change and regulation, but the Stuyvesant seldom advertised. It was a matter of deeds rather than words at the Stuyvesant, and it paid. The wills of deceased depositors were proof enough that the Stuyvesant had been an institutional friend through life. The Stuyvesant had been named as executor and trustee in hundreds of wills. The employees of the Stuyvesant understood rich clients and knew all the pains and drawbacks of being rich, although they were not rich men themselves. They had to deal familiarly, almost jovially, but always scrupulously with large sums of money, while living usually on modest salaries.

If you were successful at the Stuyvesant you ended by developing a priestly, untouchable, ascetic attitude. You learned to think of your own financial life and your own problems as something apart from those other financial complications. If you did well enough to become an executive in the Stuyvesant, and this required a long time and an arduous apprenticeship, you found yourself solving the problems of individuals who had difficulty living within incomes approaching a hundred thousand dollars a year. You found yourself spending the working day discussing the investment of huge sums of money, only to get home yourself and to worry because the butcher's bill had risen some twenty dollars above the previous one. You had to debate the purchase or the sale of controls in business enterprises and then return home yourself to decide whether or not you could afford to buy a motor lawn mower, or a ready-made or a tailor-made suit. In time this gave you a split personality since you had to toss your own problems completely aside and never allow them to mingle in any way with those of clients and depositors when you reached your desk at the Stuyvesant. At your desk you had to be a friend and confidant, as professional as a doctor or a lawyer, ready and with an intelligent perspective for almost anything. Anthony Burton had once said that this attitude was one's responsibility toward society. Though personally Charles had never felt like a social worker, he felt this responsibility. He was already forgetting Nancy and the children, already assuming his business character, when he said good morning to Gus, the doorman on the sidewalk outside the Stuyvesant.

"Is it wet enough for you, Mr. Gray?" Gus asked.

"It has to rain sometime," Charles said. "Are you a grandfather yet?"

"No, not yet," Gus said, "but any minute now."

Then Charles said good morning to Joe inside the door. The bank was scrupulously neat and cleared for action. He could hear the click of the adding machines in back and he could see the new pens and blotters on the depositors' tables as he walked past the tellers behind their gilded wickets and turned to the right past the foreign department to the coatroom. When he had hung up his coat and hat, he looked at himself in the mirror. Though his herring

28

bone suit was a little tight, it was adequate, and he automatically straightened the coat and adjusted his tie. His slightly freckled face was moist from the rain and his sandy hair, though it was carefully trimmed, needed brushing, so he went to the washroom. He had learned long ago that you did not neglect exterior details when you sat out near the vice-presidents' desks by the front window.

Though you seldom talked of salaries at the Stuyvesant, your social status was obvious from the position of your desk. Charles occupied one of the two flat mahogany desks that stood in a sort of no man's land between the roll-top desks of the officers and the smaller flat-tops of lesser executives and secretaries crowding the floor of the bank outside the cages. A green rug extended from the officers' desks, forming a neat and restricted zone that just included Charles's desk and the one beside it which was occupied by Roger Blakesley. Charles could see both their names, Mr. Blakesley and Mr. Gray, in silver letters, and he was pleased to see that he had got there first from the eight-thirty, a minute or two ahead of Roger and Mr. Burton and ahead of everyone else near the windows.

Mr. Burton's desk, which had the best light, was opened already and so was that of Mr. Stephen Merry, the oldest vice-president, and so were all the others except one. This was the desk of Arthur Slade, the youngest vice-president of the Stuyvesant, who had died in a plane accident when returning from the West Coast six months before. The closed desk still gave Charles a curious feeling of incompleteness and a mixed sense of personal gain and loss because he had been more friendly with Arthur Slade than with anyone else in the Stuyvesant — but then you had to die sometime. Once Arthur Slade had sat at Charles's own place but that was before Mr. Walter Harry, who had been president when Charles had first come to the bank, had died of an embolism and everyone had moved like players on bases — Burton to Harry, Merry to Burton, Slade to the vacant roll-top — and so on down to Charles himself. The Stuyvesant was decorously accustomed to accident and death and now it was moving time again and it was so plain where one of two persons might be moving next that it was embarrassing. Any observing depositor and certainly everyone employed in the bank, right up to the third floor, must have known that either Mr. Blakesley or Mr. Gray would move to Arthur Slade's desk by the window. Undoubtedly they were making side bets out in back as Charles used to himself when he had first come there from Boston. Undoubtedly the clerks and the secretaries and the watchmen had started some sort of pool.

Charles pulled back his mahogany chair and sat down, glancing coolly at all the desks in front of him. Miss Marble, his secretary, had already arranged his engagement pad and now she was standing beside him with his morning mail. She reminded him of Nancy as Nancy had looked when he had first known her — a front-office girl, an executive's private secretary, as neat as a trained nurse, whose private life, like his own, was temporarily erased. In spite of that crowded room, for a few hours he and Miss Marble would be almost alone, dependent on each other in a strange, impersonal, but also an intimate relationship. As soon as he said good morning to Miss Marble, his whole mind set itself into a brisk, efficient pattern.

"There's nothing on your calendar," Miss Marble said, "before the meeting, but Mrs. Whitaker has just called you."

"You mean she's called this morning already?" Charles asked.

"Well, not Mrs. Whitaker," Miss Marble said, and she smiled sympathetically. "Her companion called. Mrs. Whitaker's very anxious to speak with you."

"All right," Charles said. "Get her for me in five minutes," and he picked up the letters.

Then Roger Blakesley and Anthony Burton came in from the coatroom and Charles nodded at them and smiled. Roger walked to his own desk at once and Miss Fallon, his secretary, was there, but Anthony Burton stopped for a moment. As he did so, it seemed to Charles that the whole bank was watching them and Mr. Burton must have been aware of this too, but he was more used than Charles to being watched. He stood straight, white-headed and smiling, dressed in a pearl-gray double-breasted suit with an expansive, heavy, gray checked necktie. He had that air of measured deliberation which eventually always covered the features and the postures of bank officers and corporation lawyers. He was slender and athletic, almost young-looking considering that he was close to sixty-five, though Charles could never think of him as having been a young man. Charles always thought of him as unchanging, a measured, deliberate, constant quantity, like a Greek letter in a mathematical formula.

"I didn't see you on the train," Mr. Burton said.

Charles glanced at Roger Blakesley's desk. It was an opportunity but it was also a time to be careful.

"I didn't see you either," Charles said. "Mrs. Whitaker is after me."

It was better to do it that way. It did no harm to have him know about Mrs. Whitaker.

"Well, as long as she's after you and not me," Mr. Burton said. "We'll see you at dinner Friday, won't we?"

"You can count on it," Charles said. "Absolutely," and he laughed and Anthony Burton laughed.

"Yes," Mr. Burton said, "I suppose we can, Charley. How are Nancy and the children?"

"They're wonderful," Charles said. "They keep me out of trouble."

"Nancy's a great girl," Mr. Burton said. "You boys are getting together at eleven, aren't you? I'll be there."

He smiled and nodded and walked over to his desk in the corner.

Charles could not help but wonder whether Mr. Burton had weighed every word of that conversation as carefully as he had. For a second he wondered whether there might be some implication between the lines, but he could not think of any. It had simply been a bland routine conversation, friendly and nothing more. It could not very well have been anything else with Roger's desk right beside his own.

"Mrs. Whitaker's on the telephone now," Miss Marble said, and Charles picked up the desk telephone, speaking softly as one always did in the bank.

"Good morning, Mrs. Whitaker. This is Mr. Gray."

He could recognize a particular tone in her voice. It was the gracious, informal tone that she was in the habit of using when she wanted to make a pleasant impression on people who handled her affairs. It kept one at arm's length, though at the same time giving a pretty little picture of her capacities for universal understanding, democracy, and kindliness.

"Oh, Mr. Gray," he heard her say, "it's so nice to hear your voice."

It was difficult for Charles to respond properly to this remark because he was not at all glad to hear Mrs. Whitaker's and he had heard it a great deal lately, yet he had learned long ago never to be brief with a large depositor, particularly when the Chase, the Guaranty, and the National City were all making overtures for the Whitaker account.

"You sound well and happy, Mrs. Whitaker," Charles said.

Occasionally he was astonished at his own adaptability. He never sounded like himself when he spoke in those hushed tones at his desk. He sounded instead like a doctor or a diplomat, and now he was also a loyal friend of the Whitaker family, who could allow himself the least bit of jovial familiarity.

"Hewett and I are so dreadfully worried, Mr. Gray," Mrs. Whitaker said. "That's why it's so nice to hear your voice."

He could not tell whether it was a further act of graciousness or a lapse of memory that made her refer to Mr. Whitaker as Hewett and he could not recall that she had ever done such a thing before.

"Why, I'm sorry," Charles said. "What have you to be worried about?"

That was it. What did she have to be worried about?

"We have to sell something, Mr. Gray," Mrs. Whitaker said. "We have to sell something right away. We literally haven't got a cent of money."

At least he was able to smile since Mrs. Whitaker was not there and the strange thing about it was that her tone of desperation was completely genuine, as genuine as though she had to sell some piece of furniture to pay the grocer. One part of him could smile but another part was honestly sympathetic. This was one of the things that the bank had taught him.

"Oh," Charles said, and he was about to add that he was sorry, but he checked himself because he had learned that it made depositors angry if you became too actively sorry.

"And we simply don't know what to sell," Mrs. Whitaker said. "We've been going over it and over it."

"I know," Charles said. "It's always difficult to make up one's mind."

"We would like to sell something that has a loss to it," Mrs. Whitaker said, "but there literally isn't anything. Everything shows a profit. Why don't you ever leave us anything with losses?"

Charles drummed his fingers softly on the desk and raised his eyes to the baroque ceiling with its new indirect lighting. It was a wonderful conversation and he wished he could tell Nancy about it but he knew enough not to gossip about clients, particularly large clients.

"Well," he said, "I see what you mean, but the object usually is to show a profit. Most of our friends like it better that way. There are still advantages to having a profit rather than a loss."

"Are there?" asked Mrs. Whitaker. "I know it's so if you say so, but you've simply got to help us, Mr. Gray — anything you decide on — you will help us, won't you?"

"Of course I will," Charles said, and his voice was gently reassuring. "That's what I'm here for. Let me see, you have a number of short-term governments."

"I know. Mr. Whitaker doesn't want to sell those," Mrs. Whitaker said. "He refuses, absolutely."

"Oh," Charles said. "Why does he?"

"Because his father always said that you mustn't be a bear on the United States," Mrs. Whitaker said. "He says that we must back up the government no matter what it does. If we don't back up the government, where will we be? I believe that, don't you?"

"I wouldn't say it would be disloyal," Charles said. "Short-term governments are about the same as cash. That's the way they're generally used."

"Suppose we try to think of something else," Mrs. Whitaker said. "There must be something else."

"Yes," Charles said. "I'll tell you what I'll do. I'd better get a picture of the whole situation. If you're not well enough to come in yourself, I could send Mr. Joyce over to see you."

"I don't think Mr. Joyce has the experience, do you?" Mrs. Whitaker said. "I know he's a charming young man, but he is still rather immature and he's always so, well, so indefinite. And Mr. Thingamajig, what's his name? The one Mr. Burton turned me over to the last time I came in, when you were out. He was indefinite too, and besides I thought he was a little *chétif*."

"Whom do you mean?" Charles asked. "I can't exactly place him from your description."

"That round-faced, pussycat man with glasses," Mrs. Whitaker said. "The furtive, pussycat one."

"You don't mean Mr. Blakesley, do you?" Charles asked.

"That's it," said Mrs. Whitaker. "Mr. Blakesley."

Charles glanced across at Roger Blakesley, who was busy dictating.

"I know him pretty well," Charles said. "I wouldn't say he was a pussycat."

"It's a compliment to you, Mr. Gray," Mrs. Whitaker said, "that Hewett and I both want you to help us, and we simply have to find a hundred thousand dollars somewhere. It isn't asking too much for you to come over, is it?"

"No," Charles said. "It's rather hard for me to get away but I think I can arrange it."

"You see, we've decided after all to buy that ranch," Mrs. Whitaker said. "Albert's fallen in love with it, and I think Mr. Whitaker has too, a little. You'll come at five, won't you, when we can all be quiet at teatime, and tell us how unwise it is?"

"I suppose it depends on the ranch," Charles said. "Why, yes, I think I could arrange to come at five."

"But don't say it's too unwise," Mrs. Whitaker said. "You're so New England sometimes, Mr. Gray. Don't be too uncompromising, will you? Just say it's a little bit unwise."

"All right," Charles said. "At five. I'll remember. A little bit unwise."

"And Mr. Gray."

"Yes," Charles said.

"I adore New Englanders. Father came from Maine."

"Maine's chief export is character," Charles said.

"Do you know," Mrs. Whitaker said, "your voice sounds just like Father's when he was in a disapproving mood. You won't be too Olympian, too disapproving, will you?"

"Oh no," Charles said. "Only a little disapproving. I'll see you at five, Mrs. Whitaker."

Charles put down the telephone and rang for Miss Marble. He would have to call up Nancy and tell her he could not take the five-thirty train, but it was already ten-fifteen and Nancy would be at the chain store. Before he forgot, it would be well to tell Miss Marble.

Down there on the floor of the Stuyvesant you worked with the privacy of a goldfish. There might be certain sheltered corners in the neighborhood of the officers' desks, but there was no shelter at the edge of the green carpet where Charles and Roger Blakesley were stationed. They sat there in a kind of advanced bastion, barring the way to the higher executives, like a knight and a bishop on a chessboard, Charles sometimes thought, pieces expendable in a pinch, who had to pay for their own errors and for others' but who always must protect the rooks and the king and queen. Of course there was an outer ring of pawns in front. Individuals like Tom Joyce, his assistant, at his smaller desk well off the carpet, or Holland just behind him, or Miss Marble, were all protecting pawns. There was no physical railing to guard any of them from the customers.

Old Joe, who stood just inside the door, in a neat business suit instead of a uniform, was in the most exposed position, with duties roughly like those of a floorwalker in a department store. He was the one who helped with the counter checks and the deposit slips, who directed traffic and estimated the preliminary situation. It was he who decided that our Mr. Joyce or our Mr. Holland or, if it seemed justifiable, our Mr. Gray or Mr. Blakesley would be glad to help you.

Charles often wondered why this system of everyone's working in the open should exist. It might have been a part of the great tradition, stemming from the medieval days of the goldsmiths and the moneylenders, that all the workings of a bank should be as visible as the wheels and mainspring of a glass-enclosed French clock. It was perhaps a tradition that was deeply rooted in human suspicion regarding money and those who handled it. There must be positively no deception, everything open and aboveboard and nothing up the sleeve. If anyone had money in a bank, it seemed that he had an inalienable right to see the bankers sweating over it. Then, too, it established confidence to see a roomful of well-dressed, capable individuals sitting behind desks, reading, answering telephones, or moving in fixed orbits, according to their rank. You grew used to being an exhibit, of course, through time and training, and it was surprising how through sheer self-discipline you could avoid making mistakes of fact or even of judgment. You learned a lot about a certain kind of person there and certain facets of human nature. Granted that the clientele of the Stuyvesant was well above the average and that a high balance must be maintained for a checking account, you still met fools and rascals, and you encountered fear and hopelessness and avarice. Sometimes it seemed to Charles that all human behaviorism was mixed in some way with money.

"That's all now, Miss Marble," he said, and he saw that Tom Joyce was coming over to his desk. It was his habit to come over in the morning to see if there was anything Charles wanted.

Charles must have looked much like Tom Joyce when he was twenty-six or -seven. Tom Joyce had come there fresh out of the Harvard Business School but had only worked at the Stuyvesant for about a year before he was drafted. He had returned there from Europe in 1946 as a captain of artillery to take his old place in the trust department about the time that Charles himself had returned, and now he was one of the bright young men, as Charles had been when he was twenty-six. New York had given Tom Joyce the same veneer and the bank had given him the same watchful manner. He made mental notes for future reference, he was careful, he was steady, he was giving his full attention to the business. He had so much promise that Charles would have liked to give him his place if he should be moved up. The only thing that interfered was age and lack of maturity. Tom Joyce was still too eager and impatient, as he had been once himself, too anxiously, openly competitive, without as yet the finished capacity for concealing his likes and dislikes. That was one trouble with being young and one that Charles was planning to point out when an opportunity arose.

"Good morning, Colonel," Tom Joyce said. It was a little joke between them that was wearing rather thin, and besides military experience did not help at the Stuyvesant.

"That will do, Captain," Charles said. "Never mind the war."

"Don't you ever mind it?" Tom Joyce asked.

"I'm too busy to mind it this morning," Charles said, "but I'll tell you what. We'll talk about it if you'll come out some Sunday."

"That'd be swell," Tom said.

That was his trouble, overeagerness, but it was very pleasant to have anyone look at him as Tom Joyce did, pleasant and at the same time a little sad.

"It won't be as swell as all that," Charles said. "How do you like it here downstairs?"

"It's swell," Tom said.

It was a reflection of his own early enthusiasm, his own desire to sacrifice to get ahead, staring back at him over a gap of fifteen years.

"Banks are filled with nice boys, particularly up in front," Charles said. "We're all delightful fellows."

"There are quite a lot of bastards, too," Tom said.

Charles thought, before answering, that this was indiscreet as well as overeager.

"There are everywhere," he answered, "and sometimes it pays to be one."

"You're not one," Tom said.

"Thanks," Charles answered. It was not the conventional way to talk near the front desks of the Stuyvesant. "I'll tell you what I want right now, Tom. I want the Whitaker security list and I want everything on Smith Chemical. Tell them I'll be upstairs this afternoon to look things over."

"Yes, sir," Tom Joyce said. "I'll get them right away."

Nevertheless, he still lingered by the desk and his slowness made Charles look up at him sharply. Charles was about to ask what else he wanted but stopped when he saw the other's face and the guileless admiration in it. It was exactly the way he had looked at Arthur Slade in the old days.

"I've been thinking about Smith, too," Tom Joyce said. It was strange how easy it was to forget that subordinates could sometimes think. "The first quarter earnings were off again."

"Yes," Charles said.

"I met a friend of mine yesterday," Joyce went on. "He has a brother on the floor. He said — "

"Run along now," Charles said, "and never mind what friends' brothers on the floor say — never."

Sometime, he was thinking, he would have to have a talk with Joyce. He would have to make him see that the trust department was a great machine not governed by anyone's individual judgment but by the collective decisions of committees and boards. It might be possible to speak out in meeting and to influence the committee's decision, but that was all. When it came to trends, and the drop in Smith might indicate a trend, the conditions of industries and individual companies were being watched by a dozen subordinates. It was all very well to notice them but it was no use thinking you were a Napoleon running the trust department.

There was nothing more futile or more stultifying to sound investment judgment than being swayed by what other people said. It was one of the first things he had learned when he had started with E. P. Rush & Company in Boston and he had learned it again and again and perhaps he was still learning. The truth was that people who knew anything never said a word. The mere fact that they were in a position to know guaranteed their silence. Personally, he had never obtained a word of useful information from them except by indirection. You had to work it out yourself. You had to read between facial lines and between the lines of all the financial reports, but in the end it all depended on yourself. There were certain rules, of course, but in these days even rules were flexible because they were influenced by personalities. If you were a good investment man, in the end you had to depend upon yourself. You had to have a sense of the whole financial balance coming from an accumulation of fact, and that accumulation developed as slowly as a stalagmite in a cave, drop by drop. He was thinking as he read the financial reports on the desk before him that they were all written by stupid little people and that no man in a high category would ever dare write one because there were always famines, the wind and the tide.

At any rate he had developed sufficient ability to concentrate so that he could block off the mechanical sounds and the sounds of voices and footsteps. He was also able to break off from abstraction to immediacy. When he heard Joe speak to him, he was able to lay down his papers instantly and still to remember for future reference exactly where he left off.

"Mr. Gray," Joe said, "here's a gentleman to see you."

Joe had not said there was a gentleman who *wanted* to see him. There was no opportunity to ask who he was or what he wanted. The gentleman was right there.

III

The Business of America Is Business

— CALVIN COOLIDGE

CHARLES often wished that he was a back-slapping type like Roger Blakesley. Roger had a habit of cultivating acquaintance and contact as scientifically as a market gardener could start young tomatoes in flat boxes and tend them until they grew into vines. It was related to the extrovert, the Dale Carnegie practice of making everyone your friend and being a friend to everyone. Charles had never been good at using personal liking for business purposes, yet naturally he had developed some sort of technique since he was continually dealing with people.

Charles could see that the man whom Joe had brought to his desk was eight or nine years older than he, and this would place him in his early fifties. It was always hard for him to recall, when he met anyone of this age suddenly, whether he had ever known him before, because fifty is a period in life when time begins altering faces in all sorts of disagreeable and incongruous ways. Charles knew instantly that he was not a salesman and that he was not connected with any gainful occupation. Michael Cavanaugh, the bank detective, had once told Charles that he could always tell from one look whether a man had been in jail or not but he could not explain how he could tell this. Charles could not tell either why he knew his visitor was not a businessman, except that his face was not smooth enough, his manner did not have that sort of breezy assurance, his clothes lacked uniformity. He had lumpy intellectual features, deep-set eyes and heavy, muscular hands. His shoulders were broad and his coat fitted badly. He was not in business, and at the same time Charles was certain that this man did not want to see him about money. His face with its rather untidy gray hair might have been that of a college professor or some minor employee from a Washington bureau or, finally and most probably, that of a crank, imbued and intoxicated with a social economic theory. You had to be very careful handling anyone like that. He gave Joe a quick questioning glance but there was no help in Joe's placid, pleased expression.

"Good morning," Charles said carefully.

The stranger answered in a nasal, twanging voice.

"Well," he said, "if it isn't Charley Gray."

Charles tried hastily to recall where or when or in what phase of his life they could have met. It might have been at Dartmouth. It might have been in Boston. It might have been somewhere in the war — they all looked different out of uniform.

"Charley," the stranger asked, "don't you remember me at all?"

It was one of those unpleasant moments that you could do nothing about and it was better not to try. This unknown from his past had an outdoors and at the same time an indoors appearance. His mouth was large. There was a patch of stubble at the left of his chin which he had missed in shaving.

"Come on," the stranger said. "I could tell you anywhere, Charles. The child is father of the man."

"Did I know you when I was a child?" Charles asked.

"No, you didn't," the other said. "You knew me when I was thirty-two. My God, Charley, I'm Malcolm Bryant."

Then, of course, he remembered. The deep eyes, the large mouth, the heavy hands — everything came together into sudden focus. He had been thinking of Clyde that morning and there in front of him was Malcolm Bryant, who, of course, had been locked untidily away in memory. It was not an entirely agreeable experience, for it illustrated how easily one could forget things that one once was certain could not possibly be forgotten.

He found himself shaking hands again with Malcolm Bryant and Malcolm was saying that he had dropped in to cash a government check and the cashier had asked him if anyone in the bank could identify him. Then he had looked across the room and there, by God, was Charles. At least the business of the check was useful because it placed everything on a routine basis. Charles initialed the check and gave it to Joe to cash and asked Malcolm Bryant to sit down in the visitor's chair beside him.

"How's Jessica?" Malcolm asked.

"I don't know," Charles said. "I haven't seen her for quite a while."

"What?" said Malcolm. "Didn't you marry Jessica?"

"No," Charles said. It seemed to him that the tellers were unreasonably slow.

"How's Clyde?" Malcolm asked.

"I don't know, Malcolm," Charles said, and, though it was the truth, the bareness of his answer made him feel uneasy.

"Aren't your family still living there?"

"My father's dead," Charles said. "My mother's living with Dorothea in Kansas City."

"Oh," said Malcolm, "so Dorothea's married."

"Yes," Charles said. "She married a man named Elbridge Sterne who was a metallurgist at Wright-Sherwin. He's in Kansas City now."

"Oh," said Malcolm. "Elbridge," and he must have remembered Elbridge Sterne. "What about the old house?"

"I guess it's still there," Charles said. "We sold it. I haven't been there for a very long time."

"A ghost town," Malcolm said. "A vital sort of ghost town. That's the way I described it in the introduction. Haven't you seen my book on Clyde?"

"No," Charles said.

"You've never seen it?" Malcolm said. "It's the best thing the foundation ever got out. I'll give you one."

"Why, thanks, Malcolm," Charles said.

"*Yankee Persepolis,*" Malcolm said. "That's what I called Clyde — Persepolis."

Charles wished Joe would come back with the cash.

"Why Persepolis?" he asked.

"Where the Persians worshiped memories," Malcolm said. "I

42

stopped off there in 'thirty-five on my way to India and looked in on the University of Chicago dig. I was studying some dog worshipers in India."

The dog worshipers made Charles more comfortable.

"So you're still on primitive man, are you?" Charles asked.

"Yes," Malcolm said, "but don't forget all man is primitive. You ought to know that. You're primitive."

"Yes," Charles said, "I suppose I am."

"And so is Clyde," said Malcolm. "Primitive, like any other social structure."

Charles glanced uneasily at Roger Blakesley's desk. Roger could not help but overhear the conversation.

"I don't know much about anthropology," Charles said, "except what I learned from you, but it always seems to me you people over-simplify."

"Man only has a few basic behavioristic patterns," Malcolm said, "that are constantly repeated with silly variations. You can't over-simplify. That's the beauty of it."

Charles laughed. Joe was moving toward them with Malcolm's money and Miss Marble had also appeared.

"It's eleven o'clock, Mr. Gray," Miss Marble said.

"Here is your wampum, Malcolm," Charles said. "You'd better count it."

"It's paper," Malcolm said. "It has less intrinsic value than shell money. It's symbolism. Where are you going?"

"I have to go to a meeting," Charles said.

"How about lunch?" Malcolm said. "Come on over to the Harvard Club."

Charles glanced meaningly at Miss Marble.

"Have I a luncheon engagement, Miss Marble?" he asked.

"Why, no," Miss Marble said. "Not today, Mr. Gray."

It was very obtuse of Miss Marble and now there was no reason for him not to have lunch with Malcolm Bryant.

"Well, thanks," Charles said, "if you don't mind lunching early. Can you make it twelve-thirty?"

43

"Meet me there at twelve-thirty," Malcolm said. "Good-by, Charles."

The depositors' room off the vaults had just been refinished and redecorated and Tony Burton had called the conference there because he wanted to see how everything looked. The vaults themselves, starting with the barred anteroom with its uniformed attendant at the gate, always reminded Charles of the prison scenes in films showing the brave wife on a visit to her erring husband at Sing Sing. There was an efficient smell of oil on all the glittering steelwork, and down the narrow, brightly lighted passages he had a glimpse of the safe-deposit boxes and the private cubicles where individuals could examine the contents of these boxes in an antiseptic seclusion almost as complete as the privacy of the Great Pyramid. Even the gentle sound of a ventilating system added to the impression of inexorable security.

The Stuyvesant was a small bank, but its vaults were completely modern, shock-proof, dust-proof, and time-proof, the acme of safety, the ultimate citadel of property and possession. Put your family jewels in the vault, leave your heirlooms for a modest sum, your priceless papers and mementos, your bond and stock certificates. The Stuyvesant would guard them, and if, for any reason, you did not wish to descend to the vaults yourself, walking the slightly slippery steel floors to your safe-deposit box, if you found it tiring clipping coupons and filling out all those troublesome federal forms, why not let the custodian service of the Stuyvesant do it for you? Why not leave such fatiguing details of ownership to the oversight of careful, conscientious experts? For a purely nominal sum the Stuyvesant would do it for you. Call today yourself and consult one of our officers.

Hugh Garrity, an old Second Division veteran of World War I, dressed now in a Confederate-gray uniform, was on duty at the gate, and Mr. William Poultney, who led clients to their boxes and put both clients and boxes into the private alcoves, was seated watchfully, like a Sing Sing warden but also like a kindly hotel clerk, at his desk behind the bars. Hugh Garrity, and Mr. Poultney too, both wore an air of lynxlike alertness, which was to be expected since the bank officers were making this unaccustomed use of the new room.

"Good morning, sir," Hugh said, and he saluted in that heavy, half-formal way common to all civilian guards. If he had been a dog, Charles thought, he would have slowly wagged his tail. Charles waved his hand to William Poultney and it occurred to him that William Poultney still owed him fifteen dollars, but it was not the time to mention it. Somehow there never did seem to be a suitable occasion for taking up this detail.

"William," Charles asked, "do you use an electric razor or a safety razor?"

William Poultney looked startled and passed his hand carefully over his smooth and rather heavy jowls.

"What's the matter?" he asked. "Don't I look shaved?"

"You look beautiful," Charles said. "I was just thinking of something else."

He was thinking of Roger Blakesley's electric razor, but Mr. Poultney still looked startled. It was seldom in order to joke in an eccentric way down there in the vaults. Besides, William Poultney had a thorough and conscientious mind and he approached every subject carefully.

"As a matter of fact, now you bring it up, I have this shaving problem licked," William said. "The truth of it is, the razor doesn't matter. It's the soap. I use a brushless cream. You just rub it on and there it is."

"Well, well," Charles said. "But you have to get it off later, don't you?"

Hugh Garrity smiled sourly.

"The whole secret is the lather," Hugh Garrity said. "Get a good heavy lather and swab it on your face with a big brush — " His face froze suddenly and he stiffened to attention and Charles saw William Poultney square his shoulders and he heard a light, quick step behind him. It was Mr. Anthony Burton, coming down for the conference.

"Hello," Tony Burton said. "What's the discussion?"

45

Tony Burton was smiling, but even so there was a faint atmosphere of constraint. After all, they were on their way to a conference.

"I don't know how the subject came up," Charles said. "We were talking about shaving and electric razors."

He was relieved to see Tony Burton smile and he remembered what Tony often said about the bank — that everyone in it was part of one big family.

"I wouldn't have one of those damned electric razors in the house," Mr. Burton said. "My wife gave me one for Christmas and it blew out half the fuses. Come on, Charles."

Charles had a vicious fleeting thought, which he immediately dismissed, that it might be appropriate to say that Roger Blakesley used an electric razor. It was one of those small matters that could possibly count for something, but as he weighed the question he was appalled at his own small-mindedness, and he followed Mr. Burton to the depositors' room without speaking.

That subterranean room, like most bank interiors, had formerly been decorated with dark paneled walls and indirect lighting, with an oval table, and chairs, until someone had hit upon the idea that the Stuyvesant was old enough to have a tradition and the room, in which large customers met with officers and attorneys, ought to have some of that tradition. Thus some interesting prints and pictures now adorned the walls, old prints of Broadway, the Seventh Regiment marching down Fifth Avenue in the Civil War, framed pieces of Continental currency, ancient lottery tickets, century-old advertising broadsides, and a shelf with the first account books of the Stuyvesant. The State Street Trust in Boston, Tony Burton used to say, went in for ship models and now they had so many it made him seasick. He did not want to go as far as this but at the same time it did not hurt to show that the Stuyvesant had a past.

The group had already gathered in the room with a past, although the material under discussion at this routine meeting was to deal essentially with the future. Stephen Merry was there, wearing his new oversize tortoise-shell glasses, and Roger Blakesley with his rimless glasses, and Alfred Brock from trust administration and Tom Joyce and two other men from the trust department. When the door was closed everything was friendly, because they were one big family.

"That was an awful rain last night," Steve Merry said. "Our cellar leaked again."

Then they all sat down and talked for a few moments about cellars and the difficulties of subsurface drainage and Tony Burton began to tell about his own cellar and heating plant until he checked himself and said they had better get to work.

Charles sat listening attentively with his eye on Roger Blakesley as Tony Burton took the meeting over. Since it was a routine conference, he knew most of the subject matter already — the general money situation, the holdings in new accounts, the stability of certain industries. Roger Blakesley, it seemed to Charles, was talking more than usual and trying almost too hard to contribute useful ideas. Charles could follow the discussion with no difficulty and at the same time think of Malcolm Bryant upstairs. He remembered, too, that he must have two hundred dollars transferred to the housekeeping account for Nancy, but his watchfulness never flagged. No matter how dull and how meaningless it was, you had to be very careful at a meeting. You had to remember the arguments and the way the minds had worked around the table. At any moment Tony Burton was apt to ask your opinion.

It was only after half an hour that anything came up of an unusual nature. It came so entirely out of the blue that he had to think carefully back to what had led up to it. Somehow the thread of the meeting and its purpose had been dropped and Tony Burton had embarked on an extraneous subject, and it was most unusual for Tony to stray from the agenda. Suddenly he had announced, out of a clear sky, that a new depositor, with whom Charles was not acquainted, was applying for a six months' loan of three hundred thousand dollars. He was a man named Godfrey W. Eaton who was the head of a substantial company manufacturing tiling. Roger Blakesley had seen him first and he had taken him to Stephen Merry and afterwards to Tony Burton. The bank had investigated Mr. Eaton through all the ordinary channels and now all his business life was down on a memorandum that sounded like the dossiers of a hundred other people whose names had come up at loan conferences.

Mr. Eaton was from the Middle West, where he had owned a number of small factories, and Mr. Eaton had obviously done well for himself because now he owned two apartment buildings free and clear, was a director of a chain of stores, and a part owner of a sugar refinery. He was obviously one of those adroit people who could move from one enterprise to another. The purpose of the loan was for additions to a tile plant. Part of the collateral was in government bonds and part in stocks. It surprised Charles that the officers had not given him the loan at once, particularly since it appeared that Mr. Eaton was a director of the Pacific Investors Trust and thus indirectly controlled several large accounts at the Stuyvesant which were not his own. If Mr. Eaton were disappointed personally, the disappointment might go much further, but recently Tony Burton and Stephen Merry had been exhibiting an unusual slowness in making decisions.

"I wonder why he didn't go to his own bank," Charles said, "not that it's any of my business."

Clearly Roger Blakesley was delighted by the question.

"Because I met him first, Charles," Roger said, "and I'm selling him on the personal service of small banks. I met him playing golf. I've seen quite a good deal of Godfrey Eaton. He's a friend of Sam Summerby — you know, Tony — Sam Summerby from Baltimore."

Perhaps it was Charles's imagination, perhaps he was becoming unduly sensitive, but it seemed to him that there was a slight rustle around the table. It seemed to him that everyone was watching them, and he realized that Roger had made a very good point. He knew that Roger was implying, without being obliged to say it, that he had brought in a very nice piece of business to the Stuyvesant, which was more than Charles had done lately. He was implying, without having to say it, that he brought in new business because he got around and sweetened contacts and played golf with people like Samuel Summerby, and everyone knew the Summerby Corporation. He was implying, without saying it, that it was too bad

Charles played a very poor game of golf, and it seemed to Charles that he was called upon to give some sort of answer.

"Are you on a first-name basis with him, Roger?" he asked.

It was a small and sordid little contest. He was implying, without having to say it, that several times in the past Roger had been too prematurely friendly.

"Of course I am," Roger said. "I've known Godfrey Eaton for a year. Everybody at the club knows Godfrey."

"What club?" Tony Burton asked. "Where does Eaton play golf?"

"Why, the Seneca Club," Roger said. "I've got in the habit of playing there lately instead of at Oak Knoll. It's a sportier course."

Mr. Burton nodded and made a note on a memorandum pad. The meeting had turned into a club's committee on admissions.

"I rather liked him myself," Tony Burton said. "He's breezy, but he has an agreeable personality. But Charles has put his finger on it. Why should he come around to us?"

"Because he likes us," Roger said. "He told me he liked you very much personally."

"Why shouldn't he?" Stephen Merry asked. "I like Tony personally."

Roger Blakesley laughed.

"As a matter of fact, I do too," he said. "That's why the Stuyvesant is a great bank. Everybody likes Tony."

"I'd love Tony myself," Charles said, "if he'd lend me three hundred thousand dollars. That's the way it is. Love and money."

The officers laughed. Even the younger men around the table smiled, and Mr. Burton picked up a piece of paper. "He's putting up enough," he said. "There's only one security I question."

"What?" Roger Blakesley asked.

Mr. Burton frowned at the paper he was holding, and he looked very handsome there at the head of the table as everyone's eyes moved toward him.

"Here's an unlisted company from a place called Clyde, Massachusetts — a block of five thousand shares at twenty dollars a share."

That was how Clyde came into the conference room, suddenly, out of nowhere. It came because Tony Burton's mind had been on a

49

loan when he should have been discussing trust business. It came like an unexpected gust of wind through an open window, except that there were no windows in the conference room — nothing but scientific air conditioning.

"I remember that five thousand shares," Roger Blakesley said, "but he has enough without it, hasn't he? We ought not to disappoint him. He's just the sort of person who in different ways controls a lot of business."

"The Nickerson Cordage Company, Clyde, Massachusetts," Mr. Burton read. "Five thousand shares. Now of course we don't want to disappoint Mr. Eaton, but has anyone here ever heard of the Nickerson Cordage Company? Wait a minute — " Tony's glance had turned toward Charles. "Clyde. Let's see. Charles, didn't you come from a place called Clyde?"

Mr. Burton had a good memory. As far as Charles could recall, he had only mentioned Clyde to him once and that was years ago when the Burtons were going to take a vacation trip to Maine. Mr. Burton had shown him a road map marked by the AAA and Charles had told him that Clyde was a pretty place, that he did not know about accommodations now but that he had once lived in Clyde.

"Yes, sir," Charles said. "I was born there but I haven't been there for quite a while."

"Well, what about the Nickerson Cordage Company?"

"They used to make rope," Charles said, "and twine and fish nets. They were near the Wright-Sherwin Company in Clyde." Charles cleared his throat. It did not seem appropriate to say any more, but Mr. Burton was still listening.

"They used to build a lot of sailing ships in Clyde," Charles said, "and they needed ropes for them."

He could see as he spoke the sheds of the Nickerson Cordage Company beside the river, a small and shabby plant, and he could remember the smell of tar and hemp that came from it. Mr. Burton was still looking at him and it seemed necessary to go on.

"I didn't know it was incorporated," Charles said. "It must have grown."

"If Godfrey Eaton has money in it, it must be good," Roger said.

He spoke as an authority, as a golf partner and an intimate personal friend of Mr. Godfrey Eaton.

"Well, we'll leave this for now," Mr. Burton said. His voice was resonant and agreeable, but it seemed to Charles that it had changed slightly.

Charles relaxed in his leather-seated mahogany chair. It was peculiar that the name of Clyde should have cropped up at the table. Things happened all at once. You thought of a name or a face and then it would appear.

"I remember Clyde," Stephen Merry said. "The road to Bar Harbor used to go through it but it's by-passed now. It's a pretty little town, something like Wiscasset in Maine. Nice houses but not much of a hotel. Elm trees. I never knew you came from there, Charles."

"Well," Charles said, "that was quite a while ago."

Mr. Burton picked up another paper but it seemed to Charles that he was still disturbed about the Nickerson Cordage Company.

"Never mind it now," he said. "It's getting on towards lunch time."

Charles only half heard him. The mention of Clyde was taking his attention from the meeting. It was not that he was daydreaming, it was not that he was not listening carefully. He could see the faces about him very clearly and the papers on the table and the inevitable memorandum pads and newly sharpened pencils that were conventionally on every conference table, though you hardly ever used them except to draw squares and pictures if you did not smoke. It was only that he found himself wondering how he had ever got into that conference room and whether he really wanted to be there, and he wondered whether anyone else around that table had ever shared those thoughts. Certainly their faces did not show it, though they had all arrived there as he had, through some sort of accident, if only because banking was a dignified and fashionable pursuit and there wasn't much else but business when you finished college.

Charles glanced at his watch, not surreptitiously as one usually did at conferences but deliberately. It was ten minutes past twelve, and he was relieved because that situation with Roger was beginning to be difficult. They were both of them showing off before the bank officers like college boys running for manager of some team, although they were both assistant vice-presidents. They were doing it in a very nice way, and of course they both were justified, but he was glad when it was over. In five minutes everyone was standing up, looking almost carefree because there would be a breathing spell for lunch.

"I didn't know the Eaton thing was coming up this morning," Roger Blakesley said.

Probably, under the circumstances, it was right to hover around Tony Burton and to show eagerness and zeal, but at the same time it might be possible to go too far.

"Speaking of electric razors," Charles said, "there was a story in the war — " He had decided that he would bring up electric razors after all.

"What's that about electric razors?" Roger asked quickly.

"There was a story in the war," Charles said, "about someone who brought one to Port Moresby in New Guinea and there weren't any outlets at Moresby."

Charles was pleased to see that Tony Burton looked amused.

"Do you use one of those damned things, Roger?" Tony Burton asked.

"Of course," Roger said. "When you get the hang of one, you never want anything else."

"Don't you?" Tony Burton said. "Well, I wouldn't give one houseroom."

IV

I Remember, I Remember, the House Where I Was Born

— THOMAS HOOD

THERE HAD BEEN times in the past when Charles was embarrassed because he was not a Harvard or a Yale graduate as the New York banks he dealt with most were full of Harvard and Yale men, but in recent years he no longer felt any particular handicap. He had lunched at the Harvard Club often enough to find his own way to the checkroom and Malcolm Bryant had left word at the door that he would be at the bar.

Charles found Malcolm at once, standing beside a middle-aged man who wore a tweed coat and gray slacks. The sight of a tweed coat in the city made Charles slightly uneasy for it showed that Malcolm's friend, like Malcolm, belonged in some category where correct dress was not necessary. The tweed coat meant that he had just dropped in casually from the country and that he was a teacher or writer or something, and though it was a relief occasionally to meet personalities like this, still it was an effort in the middle of a crowded day to shift to them from people like Tony Burton and Roger Blakesley.

"Hello, Charley," Malcolm said. "This is Guy Lake. Mr. Gray, Mr. Lake."

Mr. Lake shook hands with Charles unsmilingly. His brown hair was closely cropped. His face was thin and studious.

"Malcolm says you're a banker," Mr. Lake said. "Malcolm says he picked you up somewhere at a desk. It's been quite a shock to Malcolm."

"It was quite a shock to me, too," Charles said. "I still haven't got over it." He smiled. At least he was able to deal with people.

Experience had finally taught him to watch and wait and to find out what people were like.

"What'll you have to drink, Charley?" Malcolm asked.

At first Charles thought of saying that he would not have anything, but this would have been needlessly austere so he said that he would like a sherry.

"That's the boy, Charley," Malcolm said, and he waved one hand at Charles and put the other on Mr. Lake's shoulder. "You know when I was doing that job on *Yankee Persepolis,* Guy — "

"Yes," Mr. Lake said. "I know when you were doing it."

"Well, Charley was right there. That's where I met Charley."

"I know," Mr. Lake said. "You've been telling me."

Charles picked up his glass and wondered uneasily just what Malcolm had been telling him.

"That's right," Malcolm said. "I've been telling you — and he never read it. What do you think of that? It hurts me. It really hurts me."

"If it hurts you, you'd better take another drink," Mr. Lake said. "Alcohol kills pain."

"That's a very good idea, Guy," Malcolm said. "Two more bourbons and plain water. In fact it hurt me so much that I went right to the store and bought him a copy."

"What," said Mr. Lake, "is that thing still in print?"

"You're damned well right, it's still in print," Malcolm said. "Where's that book? I had it here."

"You left it at the other end of the bar, sir," the barman told him.

"Oh yes," Malcolm said. "Well, get it for me, will you?"

"Are you going to give it to him?" Mr. Lake asked. "You ought to make him buy it. It shows you're an amateur."

"He wouldn't buy it," Malcolm said. "Do you buy Guy's books, Charley?"

Charles smiled again.

"No," he said, "but I suppose I should."

There was nothing more difficult than standing at a bar with people who were a little tight and only being able to drink sherry.

The barman had passed Malcolm an academic-looking volume in a plain dust wrapper with *Yankee Persepolis* printed on it — *A Social Study* — MALCOLM BRYANT.

"There you are," Malcolm said.

"Why, thanks, Malcolm," Charles said. "Thank you very much." Malcolm put his hand back on Mr. Lake's shoulder.

"Charley's a nice boy, Guy," Malcolm said. "You see why I like him, don't you? He has that repressed quality."

"It's too bad you haven't got some of it yourself," Mr. Lake said.

"Oh, I wouldn't put it that way," Malcolm said. "It's healthier to be an extrovert — happier. Are you happy, Charley?"

"Frankly, no," Charles said. "Not at the moment, Malcolm."

Mr. Lake began to laugh.

"You'd feel happier if you had another drink," he said. "How about another drink?"

Charles was trying to remember what it was he had once liked in Malcolm and he thought it was largely that Malcolm had been an older man who had been very decent to him. There was still that gap in age as they stood there in front of the bar.

"How about lunch?" Charles asked. "I haven't got much time, Malcolm."

"Now that's what I was saying, Guy," Malcolm said. "It's control rather than introversion. It's control and environmental influence. We once went through an intense emotional experience together, something that must have shaken us both. Sex has a way of doing that. And now he asks about lunch. That's what I call control. Get me another bourbon and water."

"You'd better get lunch, Malcolm," Mr. Lake said. "I've got to be going now. I'm glad to have met you, Mr. Gray," and he shook hands and walked away.

Malcolm Bryant scowled and shook his head.

"He's a conceited bastard, isn't he?" he said.

"I didn't have a chance to find out," Charles said, and he knew he never would find out.

"Well, he's a conceited bastard," Malcolm said. "He's an ornithologist. We were on a trip once in the Orinoco."

"Oh," Charles said, "I remember. You used to talk about the Orinoco." He had been bored and ill at ease, but suddenly it all was different. "So you got to the Orinoco, did you?"

"Yes," Malcolm said. "I got there."

Up to that moment, it had been hard to remember much about Malcolm Bryant but now everything was beginning to be clearer. The mention of the Orinoco gave Charles a slightly guilty but at the same time a pleasant feeling. It brought him back to a time when he had been able to consider seriously regions like the Orinoco as places he might conceivably visit. He had never been able to understand Malcolm's interests or activities. He had only known him as an eccentric person, engaged in pursuits that demanded a queer accretion of knowledge.

Malcolm had always talked about foundations and fellowships and expeditions and surveys, and part of his life had sounded as dry as dust and part of it unintelligibly exotic. As they stood by the bar, he gave Charles an impression of being removed by virtue of his own brains and ability from all ordinary obligations. The fact that he was older brought back to Charles a familiar callow feeling, one partly of admiration and partly of envy, though envy was not exactly the right word. He had never envied Malcolm Bryant as much as he had mistrusted his influence. He was thinking again that people like Malcolm Bryant fitted into no reasonable category. They were pampered, preposterous creatures who lived an artificial life, who did not understand or want to be like other people.

"I guess you have to have a Ph.D. to go to places like that," Charles said. "You have to know about bugs or snakes or rubber, I suppose."

Malcolm was regarding him in his old friendly, detached way, as though he were examining a strange human specimen.

"Yes," Malcolm said. "It's better to have a Ph.D., but it's more important to think of a project. Then you sell that project to somebody and they give you the money and you go. That's why I'm going to New Guinea tomorrow."

"Oh," Charles said, "are you going to New Guinea?"

"Yes," Malcolm said, "for the Pacific Investigation Institute. They had to have an anthropologist. Walter Sykes was going — you know,

Sykes at the Peabody, who did that work on the Micronesians. He's overrated, if you want my personal opinion, and he keeps harping on the Haynes method. His kidneys gave out last week and so they went around to the Birch Foundation and the Birch found me."

"Oh," Charles said. It was like groping in the dark in an unfamiliar room that was filled with odd odors and awkward pieces of furniture. "You mean you just pack up and go?"

"It isn't any problem," Malcolm said. "I have an assistant. He's doing all the work. The only thing that is going to be interesting is the circumcision rite. All the rest has been pretty well covered, but I hope to get in on that. You see, it's about the proper time of year." He stopped, as though he took it for granted that Charles understood everything he was saying.

"Oh," Charles said. "Do they like strangers to see things like that?"

Malcolm looked at his glass and set it back on the bar.

"It all depends on how you handle the head men," he said, "and head men are all about alike. Well, I suppose we ought to have some lunch. What is it, son?"

One of the club attendants had interrupted them. It was a telephone call for Mr. Bryant.

"Oh," Malcolm said. "I'm sorry, Charley. That will be about the penicillin. Just wait for me in the other room, will you? I won't be a minute."

Charles walked into the other room and sat down in a red leather chair. The snatches of talk he heard were reassuring and a part of his own language. No one, in this other room, was talking of head men or of circumcision, but about the weather and the news from Washington. Charles drew a deep breath and opened the book which Malcolm Bryant had given him. It was published, he saw, by a university press, but even university presses had bright accounts of their books' contents inside the dust wrapper.

"*Yankee Persepolis*," Charles read, "appears as the final and considered summation of part of a study made some years ago of a typical New England town, its culture, and its social implications. This volume has been written by Malcolm Bryant, in general charge

57

of the survey. Mr. Bryant, fresh from the study of the Zambesis of Central Africa, has applied, in broad principle, the methods of research which he developed and perfected there. The result of this, his concluding volume, is a brilliant and exhaustive case history which can serve as an adequate text . . ." Charles's attention had wavered. His eye traveled without reading down to the last paragraph. "Malcolm Bryant, though stemming from the Middle West, took his doctorate at Harvard University, is at present a Fellow of the Birch Foundation, and is widely recognized through his papers in scientific journals and as a lecturer."

That was all there was about Malcolm Bryant and it conveyed very little to Charles. The book, as he glanced at it, was written in an abstruse and awkward way, adding up to something that he could not possibly read continuously, though he knew the book was about Clyde. The first chapter was entitled "Yankee Persepolis, Its Geography and Population" and the second "Social Structure," with a number of charts and drawings which Charles could not understand. Turning the pages hastily, Charles could see the names of streets and neighborhoods and buildings, thin and inartistic parodies of real names. Johnson Street was called Mason Street, the North End was called Hill Town, Dock Street was called River Street, and so it went, down to the names of families. The Lovells were obviously called the Johnsons and the Thomases were called the Hopewells, in a chapter entitled "Family Sketches." It was not difficult to perceive, in spite of these clumsy concealments, that Clyde was Yankee Persepolis. It was like looking at Clyde through a distorted lens or seeing Clyde through rippling water, with small things assuming portentous shapes.

"For the purposes of distinction," Charles read, "it will be well arbitrarily to define the very definite and crystallized social strata of Yankee Persepolis as upper, middle, and lower. These will be subdivided into upper-upper, middle-upper, and lower-upper, and the same subdivisions will be used for middle and lower classes."

Charles turned to the middle of the book. Even that quick perusal brought him back to the time when Malcolm Bryant had been studying Yankee Persepolis. He could remember Malcolm's voice and Malcolm's alien figure on the main street, but it was curiously shocking to find that period preserved in print.

"Typical of a lower-upper family," Charles was reading, "are the Henry Smiths — father, mother, son and daughter. Like other lower-upper families, they dwell on a side street ('side streeters'), yet are received on Mason Street. Mr. Smith, with investment interests in Boston, whose father owned stock in the Pierce Mill, is a member of the Sibley Club, also the Country Club, but is not a member of the Fortnightly Reading Club, belonging only to its lower counterpart, the Thursday Club. Though a member, he has never been an officer of the Historical Society or a Library trustee. His wife, Mrs. Smith, was Miss Jones, a physician's daughter (middle-upper). She runs their home in the lower-upper manner, with the aid of one maid (middle-lower) coming in daily from outside. The son Tom, a likable young graduate of Dartmouth, works ambitiously in the office of the Pax Company and is thinking of leaving for a job in Boston. He and his sister Hannah are received by the upper-upper but are not members of the committee for the Winter Assembly. They are, however, in a position to move by marriage to middle-upper or possibly upper-upper status. There is even talk that in time Tom may be taken into the Fortnightly and he is on friendly terms with the daughter of Mr. Johnson (upper-upper) though there is little prospect of more than friendship. Hannah is occasionally squired by Arthur Hopewell (upper-upper) but here, too, the prospect of marriage both recognize as small. . . ."

Charles felt his face redden, because it was easy enough to read between the lines. It was his own family there in black and white, starkly indecent, without trimming or charity. He was Tom, that likeable young graduate from Dartmouth. It was indecent and infuriating, but he still read further.

"Let us examine a typical day in the Smith family (lower-upper). The rising hour is seven. Tom starts the coal fire in the kitchen range. Mrs. Smith arises to prepare breakfast, the maid Martha Brud (middle-lower) not appearing until eight. Hannah does not assist at this function because of a parental effort, very marked in the lower-upper and continuing through the middle group, for social

59

advancement, especially of the marriageable daughter. The distinction in this regard between son and daughter seems definitely marked."

There it was in black and white, devoid of tone and shading, but Charles could see the rest between the lines. He could remember Malcolm coming in to call and talking of the Orinoco River and even helping with the dishes and giving his father an Overland cigar. He might have called it pacifying the head man, and he must have rushed to his notebook before he could forget.

"The ancestral motif is as marked in this group as it is in the upper-upper. The same importance is attached to the preservation of the heirloom and the decoration of the grave. Thus over the mantel of the Smith parlor is jealously guarded a primitive oil painting of a sailing vessel captained by the Smiths' ancestor, Jacob Smith."

He could clearly recall Malcolm's interest in that picture and the satisfaction in his mother's voice as she had explained it to him. He himself owned the picture now and every word he read seemed to him a crude breach of hospitality. His eye was still on the page when he heard Malcolm Bryant's voice.

"All right, Charley," Malcolm was saying. "Let's go in and have some lunch." Malcolm was standing in front of him with his hands in the side pockets of his coat. "So you've been looking over the opus, have you?"

Charles stood up with the book under his arm and tried to look calmly placid, especially as he saw that Malcolm was regarding him with detached, scientific curiosity.

"Yes," Charles said, "I was just glancing through it. It's funny I never heard of it before."

"It's a professional sort of book," Malcolm said. "Everybody has to publish something."

"It's like all sociological books," Charles said. "It's a little over my head. It has a queer style."

"It isn't meant to have style," Malcolm said. "Scholars suspect anything with style."

"It has a lot of facts," Charles said, "but it doesn't sound much like Clyde."

They were already at the door of the long dining room and the clatter of dishes and voices were all about them so that Malcolm had to raise his voice.

"My God," Malcolm said. "It isn't meant to be Clyde. It's only meant to represent a characteristic social unit. Let's not wait on ourselves. Let's get a table at the end."

"All right," Charles said. "You're paying for it. I can't. I'm a likable Dartmouth boy."

Malcolm looked startled but he laughed.

"So you read that piece, did you?"

"I just glanced at it," Charles said. "There wasn't much time to go over it."

"It's funny — " Malcolm began, but he had no time to finish. The headwaiter was leading them to a table at the end of the room, and Charles was looking over the tables and faces of the diners because his training had taught him that it was worth while to recognize people. He smiled and waved his hand to a vice-president of the Guaranty Trust Company and he was back in his own life again — just out from the Stuyvesant for lunch with an unconventional acquaintance, an anthropologist who was going to New Guinea.

"You don't have to have the regular lunch," Malcolm said. "Order anything you like."

"Oh no," Charles answered. "The regular lunch is fine, thanks. I haven't got much time."

He unfolded his napkin and glanced out of the window at the traffic on Forty-fifth Street.

"That book — " Malcolm said, pointing at it — Charles had been carrying it and he had put it down on the table beside a small basket of rolls — "I thought everything was pretty well scrambled in that book, but you picked yourself out, didn't you?"

"Yes," Charles said. "The Smith family."

"I'm afraid it made you sore," Malcolm said. "Get it out of your head that it's personal."

Charles took a sip of water.

"I wouldn't say I was sore," he said, "but of course it's personal and I can't say that I like the idea."

"What idea?" Malcolm asked.

"The idea," Charles said, "of someone like you coming there and treating us like guinea pigs. As far as I can remember, we were pretty nice to you in Clyde."

"Now, listen, Charley," Malcolm answered. "A social survey hasn't anything to do with friendship. Besides, it was twenty years ago."

"That's right," Charles said. "It was quite a while ago."

"Just remember," Malcolm said, and he looked hurt, "it hasn't got anything to do with friendship, Charley. I wish you'd get it into your head that I liked a lot of people there. I liked you, for instance, God knows why."

"I used to like you, too," Charles said. "God knows why, and up to a certain point."

"What point?"

"Oh, never mind," Charles said, "but I'll tell you something — " And then he stopped.

"Go ahead. What is it, Charley?"

"A year or two after you went away, I tried to look you up in New York but you weren't there." He stopped again and fidgeted in his chair. "I thought you might get me on that trip you used to talk about, that one to South America." It was something he had never told anyone, although he had nearly told it once to his son, and now the only thing to do was to laugh about it, and he laughed. "You have a lot of queer ideas when you're that age."

"By God, I might have taken you," Malcolm said. "That would have been funny."

"Yes," Charles said, "it would have been," and he straightened his shoulders and took another sip of water. The sounds of the room came back, the voices and the gentle clatter of china. Malcolm had lighted a cigarette and was blowing smoke through his nose.

"You might at least," Charles said, "have put us in middle-upper instead of lower-upper."

Then they were silent for a minute, but it was not a constrained silence.

"Did you ever get married?" Charles asked. "You were always talking about marriage."

"Never mind it," Malcolm said. "Women always forget me when I go away. What happened about you and Jessica?"

"Never mind it now," Charles said.

"All right," Malcolm said, "what's happened to you since? I mean since I used to know you."

It was a blunt question but it offered opportunity, which came very seldom, of saying what you thought, to someone whom you would probably never see again.

"That's quite an order," Charles said. "Why do you want to know?" It was exactly as if a blank questionnaire had been thrust in front of him.

"Because I always liked you, Charley," Malcolm said, "and I'm interested in people, academically."

"That's it," Charles said. "Academically. But I don't believe you know very much about people. You know about custom and form and habit, but those are all results and not causes. I don't believe you know as much about people as I do."

"Now listen," Malcolm began, "I only asked you because I was genuinely curious. When you see someone whom you haven't seen for years — "

Charles interrupted him before he could finish and he was beginning to enjoy the conversation.

"Why don't you say what you really mean?" Charles asked. "You mean you want to fill in the end of a case history about likable Tom Smith from Dartmouth." He shrugged his shoulders. "You and that bird man in the bar were talking about it before I came in, weren't you? I don't mind. I rather like being a part of case history."

"That's true," Malcolm said. "I was telling him, Charley, you've got a damned tough mind."

"I have to have one," Charles said. "I've cultivated it, I suppose. There are a lot of tough minds in New York."

"Oh no," Malcolm said. "You haven't cultivated it. You've always had a tough mind, Charley, and a sensitive disposition. Clyde was full of minds like that."

"Never mind Clyde," Charles said. "Go ahead and ask me questions."

"All right," Malcolm said. "Never mind Clyde. What have you been doing, Charley?"

Charles looked at his plate. It was empty. He had finished the main course of the lunch without knowing what it was and now the waiter was taking away the plate.

"Well," he said, "I met someone in Boston once who asked me to look him up in New York. That was when I was working in E. P. Rush & Company. I got a job in the statistical department at the Stuyvesant and I did well enough so I held it through the depression. I married a girl who worked downtown in a law office. We have two children, and we've built a house in the suburbs that I'm still paying for, and now there's a vice-presidential vacancy. It rests between me and another man, who has a tough mind too. That's about all I've been doing."

Malcolm had lighted another cigarette, cupping his hands carefully around the match as though he were in a wind.

"I always said you were a nice boy, Charley."

"Thanks," Charles said. "Thank you, Malcolm."

"Of course you haven't filled in many details," Malcolm said. "For instance, do you love your wife?"

"I thought you'd ask that," Charles answered, "and the answer is yes. I love my wife. I love my home and my children."

"I thought you would. You're an essentially monogamous type." Malcolm Bryant sat there looking at him. "So you've been to the war." It was that discharge button that Nancy had put in his coat lapel.

"Yes," Charles said. "I'd forgotten about the button."

"I was in the war, too," Malcolm said. "In the OSS."

"As long as it wasn't the OWI," Charles said. "As a matter of fact, I saw the Orinoco." He paused a moment. "From the air."

"On your way to Africa?"

"Yes," Charles said. "It was one of those missions, before I was assigned to the Eighth. I was only good for staff work — the bank, you know."

"And now you're back don't you ever feel restless?"

"No," Charles said, "I'm not restless. I didn't like the army. Most civilians don't."

"Well, let's put it another way. Don't you ever get to wondering what everything's about?"

"Naturally, but what's the use in wondering? I'm doing the best I can."

"Let's put it still another way," Malcolm said. "Do you ever wonder whether everything is worth while?"

"It's a little hard to answer that one," Charles said. "I'm just Tom Smith from Dartmouth, trying to get along."

Malcolm must have known that he would not say any more, yet Charles had inadvertently told a good deal. He could almost see himself as Malcolm must have seen him, and this unexpected mental picture was close to his own impression of himself without the customary apologies and excuses.

"You're still thinking about that book of mine, aren't you?" Malcolm asked.

"Your categories and groupings bother me," Charles said. "I like individuals, not groupings. It doesn't make any difference where anyone comes from, it seems to me."

"Now look here, Charley," Malcolm said, "whether you like it or not, everybody's in a category."

"Yes," Charles answered, "but you're trying to put me in a category and keep out of one yourself. It isn't really fair. There weren't so many classes. Clyde's a pretty democratic place."

"I thought you said never mind Clyde," Malcolm told him. "Just remember that no matter what sort of system he lives under, man still stays the same."

"Do you mean to say that a political system doesn't change the mental habits of individuals?" Charles asked. "What about fascism? What about communism?"

"It doesn't matter," Malcolm answered. "All ideologies arise from instincts. You can't change instincts. Man is always the same."

It was getting to be one of those conversations that would never get anywhere and it was too heavy a one for lunch.

65

"Well, it's nice to know it," Charles said, "even though the left wing doesn't agree with you. It must be nice to sit there and be able to talk like God Almighty."

Malcolm pushed the end of his cigarette carefully into the ash tray.

"Charley, do you believe in God Almighty?"

"Yes," Charles said, "I think I do. It may be early habit. Yes, I do, since you ask me."

Malcom leaned his elbows on the table and Charles saw that his coat fitted him very badly.

"Well, if you were to pin me down to it, so do I," he said.

It must have been the mention of God that made Charles think of time. He looked at his watch and it was a quarter after two.

"I've got to go," he said, and suddenly he realized that he had found out nothing, or almost nothing, about Malcolm Bryant.

"Don't go," Malcolm was saying. "We've only just begun to talk."

Charles pushed back his chair. "You've got to be taking off to New Guinea," he said.

They were both walking side by side between the tables and he was sorry that it was over.

"I wish you hadn't made me talk about myself all the time," he said.

They were out of the dining room and Charles had tossed his brass check on the coatroom counter when Malcolm put his hand on his arm.

"Charley," he said, "you've got a lot of guts."

"How do you mean, guts?" Charles asked.

"Saying what you do," Malcolm said, "doing what you do, takes guts. You're a very nice boy, Charley."

"I wish," Charles said, "you'd stop calling me a nice boy."

"Well, you are," Malcolm said, "and it takes guts to be your type, these days. Good-by, good luck, Charley."

"Put me down in Category E," Charles said. "Good luck, Malcolm, and thanks."

"Thanks for what?" Malcolm asked.

"Since you ask me, I don't exactly know," Charles said, "but thanks."

V

Everything Fits into Banking Somewhere

THOUGH COMMON SENSE told Charles that he should hurry, some other inner impulse made him walk with perverse slowness, as you did when you tried to hurry in a dream. The sun had finally broken through the clouds and the sky was almost entirely blue and when he reached Fifth Avenue he came to a stop. He saw the sunlight hit the wings of a plane that must have risen from La Guardia Field just a minute or so before, and in spite of the noise on the Avenue he could hear the drumming of the motors. The green lights were on and he watched the steady flow of the traffic as though the sight were new to him — yellow cabs, green-and-white cabs, and the new buses, so different from the old ones with the open tops. The sun was still high enough to shine through some plate-glass windows on a display of men's colored shirts — maroons, blues, salmon pinks and canary yellows. He still could not get used to colored shirts even though they were quite the thing now to wear at the country club on Sunday.

Everything was changing and Fifth Avenue was changing too, in spite of all the efforts of the Fifth Avenue Association; but then Fifth Avenue had always been in a state of flux, with old buildings coming down and new ones going up, the old ones crumbling into rubble and being poured into the wreckers' trucks. It was always changing, but the spirit of it was still as young, confident, and blatant as when Henry James had written of it long ago. It still conveyed the same message that it had when he had walked along it on that first visit with his father. The motion of it had the same strength and eagerness, so different from the more stately motion of Piccadilly and the Strand.

"On the Avenue, Fifth Avenue . . . you'll be the grandest lady in the Easter Parade.". . . . He had gone with Nancy to that musical show and it must have been in the winter of 1934 when they still lived in a walk-up apartment on West Eighteenth Street. They had paid Mrs. Sweeney, whose husband was a policeman, a dollar to sit listening for the baby, and they had not been to the theater once that year or the year before. 'Thirty-four had been bad enough, though nothing to 'thirty-three. They had gone to dinner in a small French restaurant and had taken the bus up Fifth Avenue and had walked across to Broadway. When the chorus had sung that song about Fifth Avenue he had been holding Nancy's hand, just as he used to when he took her to the Capitol before they were married. . . . "You'll be the grandest lady in the Easter Parade." . . . He must have been deathly tired because he had dozed off in the darkness in the middle of it and she had dug her elbow in his ribs and he still remembered her whisper.

"Wake up. Don't waste your money sleeping."

It had been quite a while, in fact not since he had been upstairs at the Stuyvesant, since anyone had made a remark to him about staying out too long at lunch; and there was never the slightest criticism now that he was downstairs, at a desk near the front window. There was still the inner compulsion never to be late, but at the same time it was your privilege. Tardiness could be excused on the assumption that you were having a business lunch with a client. Nevertheless, Charles knew that Miss Marble and Joe had been wondering where he had been, and it did not help to see that Roger Blakesley was busy at his desk already. Charles repressed an instinct to hurry and hang up his hat and coat but instead he walked slowly past the desks and stopped where Miss Marble was typing and asked her if there was anything new.

"Nothing new," Miss Marble said. "I called up Mrs. Gray and told her you couldn't catch the five-thirty. She said to remember that you're going to the country club tonight."

"It isn't tonight, is it?" Charles asked.

"You didn't tell me to put it on the calendar," Miss Marble said, "but Mrs. Gray said to remind you."

"Well, call her again and tell her I'll meet her there," Charles said. "I'll get there as soon as I can, but I'll be late."

He stopped in front of the washroom mirror to see that his tie was straight. His short, sandy hair was in order and he looked competent and carefree. It was time to put the luncheon out of his mind. Malcolm had said that he was a nice boy, Charley, and he was not a nice boy any longer. He did not look the way he had at Clyde, though even there his mother had always said that he had the Gray high cheekbones and the Gray pointed chin. The roundness had gone out of his face. There were wrinkles at the corners of his eyes and his mouth was tighter but there was no gray in his hair. It was not the face that he used to have but it still looked young.

"Charley," he heard Malcolm Bryant saying, "it takes guts to be your type, these days. Good-by, good luck, Charley."

He was still not sure whether or not Malcolm Bryant had been laughing at him. Businessmen were not on the pinnacle they had once occupied. It was hard sometimes to tell the difference between strength of mind and habit.

The tellers' cages would close at three and already, as was usual in the afternoon, the pace was growing more leisurely. There were always new problems in the morning but these grew old by afternoon, fitting with still older problems into a symmetrical design so that you had a sense of everything running smoothly, a sense of teamwork, if you wanted to call it that, or what Mr. Burton called a meshing of the gears. You could think of the whole system of capital, of rates, discounts, markets and production, as running without interruption, like the traffic on the Avenue.

Charles had devised a system that permitted him to examine every trust account personally at least once a month, and now Miss Marble brought to his cleared desk the ones which he was to review that day. As he thanked her and settled himself in his chair, he glanced across at Roger Blakesley. Roger's desk was heaped with piles of papers. It was a habit of Roger's to shove a great many papers around in the afternoon, especially toward closing time.

"Hello there, Charley," Roger said. "Everything's backing up on me."

Charles knew this was not true but it gave the picture that Roger wanted, a picture of heavy and unremitting labor.

"You're back early," Charles said. "I thought you were going to have lunch with Tony."

"He canceled it," Roger said. "Something came up the last minute." Roger took off his glasses and polished them. When his glasses were off, his blinking eyes gave him a vacant, guileless look. "Are you going to the country club tonight?"

"Yes," Charles said, "but I'm afraid I'll be late."

"Who was that bird you went to lunch with?"

There was no privacy. Everyone heard everything, particularly Roger.

"A man I used to know," Charles said, and then some impulse made him explain it further. "He's an anthropologist."

"A what?"

Then Charles knew that it would have been better not to have mentioned it. It was just the sort of thing that Roger would remember.

"An anthropologist."

"He looked like a teacher in business school," Roger said. "One of those 'if you can't do, teach' boys."

As far as Charles could tell, everything in Roger's career had stemmed from his stay at the Harvard Graduate School of Business Administration, where business was the oldest of the arts but the newest of the professions. He had to admit that Roger used his academic background adroitly, extracting the last drop from it. Roger was always saying it was a great place, the Harvard Business School. When you studied under the Case system, you became aware of practicality and theories at the same time. It was a proving ground, the Harvard Business School, and it paid to keep up with it afterwards. If you were to ask Roger, but you did not have to ask him, this proving ground was directly accountable for the record he had made at the Guaranty before he had come to the Stuyvesant. He had been asked to come to the Stuyvesant and before accepting, of course, there had been certain reservations in his mind, but he had never regretted the step after taking it. There were fine fellows at the Stuyvesant, like Tony Burton and Steve Merry, and good boys like Charley Gray, fellows who always stuck together without getting out the old stiletto and inserting it between the shoulder blades.

Charles began on the first account. It was the Burrell School for Negroes in Tennessee, founded by the late Charles Burrell, the moneys for which were administered by Mr. Burrell's old bank, the Stuyvesant, in conjunction with Mr. Burrell's old law firm, Burrell, Jessup and Cockburn. Charles would have to meet with Mr. Cockburn the first of the week and the meetings were never agreeable. The trouble with institutional accounts of late had been that all institutions were screaming for more income, although they continued demanding a margin of absolute safety. Mr. Cockburn always wanted to lower the bond holdings and to increase the higher-yielding preferred list. That million-dollar fund had been beautifully invested. Even in the depression, income had held up well, and now the market was considerably above the book value.

Charles was in the middle of the security list when he realized that Miss Marble was waiting by his desk.

"It's twenty minutes to three," Miss Marble said. "Mr. Selig is coming in at a quarter of — the one who wants to open an account. I thought you'd like to see the credit department memorandum."

"Selig?" Charles repeated, and his mind darted swiftly away from the investments of the Burrell School.

"The matter that Mr. Burton asked you to take up," Miss Marble said. An anticipatory quiver in her voice showed that Miss Marble was interested. He had been asked yesterday to do that job and now he understood why Tony Burton was not yet back from lunch. He always seemed to be the one who was picked for unpleasant interviews.

"Thanks," he said, and he took the memorandum. "Does Joe know I'm to see him? You'd better check again with Joe."

His eye traveled over the memorandum. He had learned to read office memoranda quickly and to pick the salient details out of the dull verbiage.

"Burt J. Selig," he read, "is part owner of the Teddy Club and the La Casita night club, owns real estate at . . . and also in Miami,

71

was indicted for income-tax fraud but indictment was quashed
. . ."

There was no use going any further because everything had been decided. It seemed to Charles that there was no reason for a personal interview and that the matter might have been settled as well by letter, except that Tony Burton had disapproved of anything as permanent as a letter. Charles's desk had just been cleared except for a pile of Moody reports when he saw Joe moving from the door accompanied by a thin, dark man who wore a bluish-purple overcoat and a lightweight gray felt hat. Except for the shimmering sheen of the overcoat and the violently brilliant polish of his shoes, Mr. Selig was quietly dressed. His tie was dark, like his suit; his face was tanned, probably by the Miami sun, into a smooth meerschaum color. When he took off his hat, as he did when he approached the desk, Charles saw that his forehead was high and that his close-cropped dark hair was receding from his temples. His eyebrows, which might have been trimmed, formed a straight, almost Grecian line. His eyes were gray, his jaw was heavy, but there was nothing heavy about his step.

"This is our Mr. Gray," Joe said. "He will take care of you."

Mr. Selig held out a carefully manicured hand.

"I'm happy to meet Mr. Gray," he said. "My name's Selig, Burt Selig."

"Yes, I know," Charles said. "Mr. Burton asked me to see you and I have all the details. Won't you sit down, Mr. Selig?"

He wondered for an instant where Malcolm Bryant would have placed Mr. Selig in his social scale, for Mr. Selig must have moved fast from group to group in combinations more complicated than any in Clyde or New Guinea. His voice had undertones of lost accents. His face had a look of things written on it that had been partially erased and of preparation for new writing. It was a face of a type that Charles did not know, but it was as marked and distinctive as a soldier's or a doctor's — positive, alert and confident.

"A nice little place you have here," Mr. Selig said. "Very nice."

"It's just a small bank," Charles answered.

"Yes," Mr. Selig said. "That's what draws me to it, Mr. Gray, particularly for Mrs. Selig. I know some lovely people banking here, some of my best friends. My friend Alf Fieldstone banks here. Do you know Alf?"

"Yes," Charles said, "I've met him."

"A very nice fellow, Alf," Mr. Selig said. "He likes La Casita. Have you been to La Casita, Mr. Gray?"

"I tried once," Charles answered, "but there was a long line waiting."

"Well, any time," Mr. Selig said, and smiled.

"Thanks," Charles said.

"Well," Mr. Selig said, "I suppose you've looked me over. I hope I've passed through the line-up by now."

He paused and smiled, but there was no need to give any answer.

"I'm used to being looked over," Mr. Selig said, "in my position."

"Well," Charles said, "anyone in business always gets looked over."

"Yes, that's right," Mr. Selig said. "How long have you been here, Mr. Gray?"

"Quite a while."

"I suppose it takes time to work up anywhere in a business like this. Nothing can move fast."

"That's right," Charles said, "it takes time."

"I wouldn't want any son of mine working in a bank," Mr. Selig said. "So little action."

"It all depends on temperament," Charles answered.

"Yes," Mr. Selig said. "Everybody has a different temperament. I ought to know."

The best way to hurry an interview was to wait, but he was sure that Mr. Selig ought to know.

"Well," Mr. Selig said, "what's the story? Do you want my account or don't you?"

Many people believed that banking was a matter of dull routine but whatever it might be to the boys in back, up front you could never count on monotony or even on a restful moment. It was necessary, as soon as Mr. Selig asked that question, to change from an investment consultant into a man of the world. It was necessary to

73

remember that he was in a very responsible position, representing in his own person the prestige and dignity of the Stuyvesant and at the same time protecting the inviolate sanctity of its officers. Suddenly, with hardly any time to prepare, he had to change from book values to diplomacy and to draw smoothly on a store of conventional phrases, which were deceitful but which had to stick.

"Our officers have been over that question very carefully," Charles said, and the smoothness and the consoling tone of his voice reminded him of a hotel clerk saying nicely that there was no room for a certain guest. "We would value your account in a great many ways, Mr. Selig, but we really feel that you will be better off in another bank. You said yourself this is a small bank, and smallness has its difficulties." Charles smiled at Mr. Selig and felt still more like a hotel clerk. "I hope you'll understand, Mr. Selig, sorry as we are to turn away profitable business." Charles smiled again. "Mr. Burton asked me to tell you personally that this is a purely business decision."

Of course he was using Mr. Burton's name unofficially but still it had a soothing sound, even if it did not have the desired effect.

"So the answer is no, is it?" Mr. Selig asked.

"I'm afraid so," Charles said, "for the time being. We're very sorry."

Something made Charles sit up straighter and something made him feel that it would be unwise to shift his glance from Mr. Selig, for a film had seemed to drop over Mr. Selig's eyes. It was as though Mr. Selig had tried to suppress an impulse which he had been unable to conceal and for a second Charles had a sense of something close to physical danger.

"So I'm not a nice enough guy to play with you, is that it?" Mr. Selig said.

Charles spoke slowly and very carefully. You had to go on with the act and make no rash statements. You had to be glib and still say nothing.

"There's nothing personal intended," Charles said. "We often find the needs of some depositors are better filled by other banks."

"I'm not used to being given the run-around. Why didn't they say that the first time I came in?" Mr. Selig asked. He had not raised his voice but there was a difference in his accent.

"I'm sorry you put it that way," Charles said. "Mr. Burton was very impressed by your references. We never like to disappoint our friends, Mr. Selig."

"So you're fronting for the crowd, are you?" Mr. Selig asked.

"If you mean I'm out in front," Charles said, "I suppose I am. Mr. Burton asked me to attend to the matter, but of course if you're not satisfied — "

"How much do they pay you for doing it?" Mr. Selig asked. "Ten grand a year?"

Mr. Selig was looking at him curiously, in a way that reminded Charles of Malcolm Bryant.

"That hasn't anything to do with your account, has it?" Charles asked — but still, he was fronting for the crowd. He liked the expression "fronting for the crowd." Mr. Selig was looking at him with a new sort of interest.

"Guys like you fascinate me," Mr. Selig said. "I don't see why you do it, for that money."

"I suppose I think I'm underpaid," Charles said. "It's human nature."

Mr. Selig lowered his voice.

"How would you like twenty-five grand a year?"

"What for?" Charles asked.

"For what you're doing here," Mr. Selig said. "Fronting for the crowd."

It was something, after all it was something. At least it meant that he had not done his job badly.

"Thanks," Charles said. "I'm afraid I couldn't use it, but I appreciate your asking."

"You guys fascinate me," Mr. Selig said. "Money everywhere and you don't want money."

"Maybe we get too used to it," Charles said. "Maybe we get tired of seeing so much of it around."

"That's what fascinates me," Mr. Selig said. "All of it around, and you don't take it. Well, no hard feelings."

They both stood up and shook hands.

"Oh, no," Charles said. "Not at all. We're very sorry, Mr. Selig."

"It takes poise," Mr. Selig said. "I wouldn't have the poise."

"I wouldn't call it poise," Charles said. "I'd call it temperament and timidity. Good-by. We're sorry, Mr. Selig."

There was no flagging in the bank's activity, but Charles was conscious of a ripple of excitement, of curious glances from the cashiers' cages and the smaller desks. They were all like good little boys and girls who had witnessed one of their number having it out in the school yard with a naughty boy from the street. The adding machines were still clicking and whirring with the typewriters, the cashiers were still thumbing through their currency, but beneath it there was a flurry, a sense of the unusual. Mike Cavanaugh, the bank detective, was moving toward him, not hurriedly but quietly as though he were only making his afternoon rounds, and Roger Blakesley had turned in his swivel chair.

"How was he?" Mike Cavanaugh asked.

"He was a perfect gentleman," Charles said. "He asked me if I was fronting for the crowd."

Then Roger Blakesley asked whether Mr. Selig was mad, but Charles had no time to answer. Mike Cavanaugh had stiffened to attention and Charles saw that Mr. Burton had come in, still in his overcoat, just back from lunch.

"Has Selig called?" Tony Burton asked.

"He's just left," Charles told him.

"Well, I'm glad I missed him," Tony Burton said. "How did he take it?"

"His feelings were hurt," Charles said, "but then mine would have been. I wouldn't say he was angry at me personally."

"There aren't any complications, then?" Tony Burton asked.

"No," Charles said, "I don't think so."

"This sort of thing always worries me," Tony Burton said. He began to move away to the coatroom.

"Oh, Mr. Burton," Roger Blakesley said, and Mr. Selig and possible complications left Charles's mind. Roger sounded like a model student speaking in one of the classes at the Harvard Business School.

He was being careful not to call the president by his first name right in the middle of the bank.

"Yes, Roger," Tony Burton said, benignly, like a kind teacher.

"Have you got time to see me for a minute?"

"Yes," Mr. Burton said. "If it's only for a minute."

Charles had rung for Miss Marble and Miss Marble was bringing back the trust folders. He was careful to show no undue anxiety but such a request of Roger's, at such a time, might have implications. Ordinarily, either he or Roger Blakesley, because of their position, would have risen and walked over to the president's roll-top desk without asking for any sort of appointment. That request of Roger's meant that he wanted to see Tony Burton privately and perhaps about something personal. It might even mean that Roger, like himself, was getting tired of waiting and that Roger was going to step over, as Charles had often dreamed of doing in the last few weeks, and ask right out about the vice-presidency. It was not like Roger, but it was possible — on the grounds that this sort of waiting was bad for general morale.

Mr. Burton had left his coat and was settling down at his desk and Roger Blakesley had risen.

Anxiety and self-inflicted suspense were useless and unprofitable, but there was nothing one could do. Charles was back in his personal world again, his little narrow world, and the trust accounts were facing him. It was time to be going through them, because it was after three o'clock, but something discordant moved him beyond the control of ingrained habit and system. Ordinarily his ability to concentrate enabled him to forget his own problems by plunging into a good page of figures on a balance sheet, but now he could not keep his attention on the trust accounts. His eyes were on a list of common stocks — American Can, American Cyanamid, American Tobacco B, American Telephone and Telegraph. Through wars and rumors of wars, in the midst of panic and depression, out of the maze of taxes and social change, through all the welter of a cracking tradition, American Tobacco B and American Tel and Tel stood, with occasional lapses, like the precepts of early life, like the

77

granite peaks of a half-submerged continent, serene above a swirl of hostile seas. Other securities might go sour, but not Telephone and Tobacco — or not very sour. Still, though he was surrounded by those trusted symbols, his thoughts kept wandering off at tangents.

Roger Blakesley was over by the front windows, his chair pulled close to the president's desk, talking very earnestly. Charles could not forget what Nancy had said that morning — that he could go to Tony Burton and put his cards on the table. Even though he dismissed it as just the thing a woman would suggest, still Nancy had good judgment. She understood as well as he did the routine and jealousies and discipline of an office, and besides there was the question of personal dignity. It was humiliating, considering his position, to sit, day after day, waiting for Tony Burton to tell him what was on his mind, when he had probably made his choice already. It was humiliating to have one's life and a good part of one's future depend on one man's eccentricity, but that was the way it always was.

Charles had often thought that it was fortunate for Tony Burton that he seldom needed to make quick decisions. Tony Burton had told him himself that he liked to mull over problems and fuss with them, particularly problems of personnel, but he usually did what he decided in the first place, from sheer intuition and instinct tempered by training and experience. All his talk of mulling and weighing and balancing was vacillation, if you wanted to use a harsh word for it. There were also the qualms that always surrounded a definite negative. That probably was what was delaying Tony Burton — the certainty that no matter what he did someone would be hurt.

It would obviously have ruined everything if Charles had endeavored to end the suspense by talking it over with Tony Burton. It was against all convention and Tony would instantly have put him in his place, but still it was possible to consider such an impossible scene. He could even frame just what he would say.

"Listen, Tony," he would say, "let's face the facts. Maybe you're removed from office politics, but everybody here in the bank knows that you are considering proposing either Blakesley or me for this vice-presidency. Maybe you don't know, but you ought to, that they're making bets on it in the washroom. It isn't dignified. It isn't fair to Roger or me to keep us waiting. We're both of us making monkeys of ourselves running around and polishing apples. You know everything about me, Tony. I've been around here long enough. Of course, I was out in the war, but you approved my going, or you said you did, and I'm about the same as I ever was in spite of it. I know it's hard to step on somebody's face, but this thing has been going on for months, ever since Arthur was killed, and I'm tired of staying awake at night, and Nancy's getting tired, too. How about it, Tony?"

It was not a bad speech, either, even though it was out of his usual line and beyond the realms of discipline. In fact the words were so vivid in his mind that he seemed to be saying them right now at the far corner by the window, but of course he would never say them. He was at his desk and out of the corner of his eye he saw that Roger Blakesley was back again, leafing through a pile of papers with his left hand while he scribbled with his right on a memorandum pad. It may have been that Roger also had been dreaming of a talk with Tony. He could even make a savage, unkind parody of Roger's possible speech, which Roger would have called an "approach."

"Listen, Tony," Roger would have said (that is if he had said anything), "how about you and me doing a little mind reading? You've got one of the best poker faces I've ever seen. I love your inscrutability, but let's unscrute, shall we? That's a pretty good word, what? I always knew I should have been an English professor and not just a poor dumb bank boy. . . . Well, to get back to it, Tony. I know you're hot and bothered, and I don't want to bother you and I know old Charley doesn't. Why, Charley's the grandest guy I know. You and I don't want to hurt old Charley, especially after the war, and you don't want to hurt me, but you couldn't hurt me, Tony, the way I feel about you. It's just a little matter, Tony, and Charley and I can take it, though maybe Charley's more brittle than I am. I never take things hard, Tony. Let's help each other out and let's get an extra on the street . . ." That was the way Roger would do it, because Roger had the sales technique. If it made Charles impatient sometimes, he was broad-minded enough to know that a lot of people liked it.

The shades on the front door were drawn already, showing that the bank was closed to depositors, and there was the inevitable air of relaxation now that they were no longer on public display. Voices were louder. There was a snatch of laughter. People were assuming more comfortable positions and far in the back of the room, in that region where there was not so much to gain or lose, he saw some of the boys moving toward the washroom to smoke a cigarette. If he had wished to have that talk with Tony Burton, now would have been the time, but he still sat at his desk with the trust accounts in front of him. The tension was beginning to undermine his judgment and self-control but if they wanted to keep him waiting, he was not going to show that it bothered him. Just then his desk telephone rang with its specially contrived device to avoid undue noise. It was Miss Sumner, Tony Burton's secretary.

"Oh, Mr. Gray," Miss Sumner said. Her voice was sweet with the assured authority of being the dean of all secretaries, the repository of all secrets. "Mr. Burton wants to know if you can see him for a moment."

There were some reactions you could not control and in spite of himself his heart was beating faster. He deliberately finished the page of his report before he rose, and when he was on his feet he looked at Roger Blakesley.

"Yes, Sugar," Roger was saying over his own telephone, which meant that Roger was speaking to his wife. "I'll be there on the five-thirty, Sug. Yes, I'll pick up the prescription."

Roger's concentration on his conversation was not misleading. Charles was sure that Roger knew exactly why Tony Burton wanted to see him for a moment.

Tony Burton looked very fit, in spite of his white hair and his roll-top desk which both conspired to place him in another generation. For years Charles had accepted him as a model willingly, even though he realized that everyone else above a certain salary rating also used Tony Burton as a perfect sartorial example, and he was pretty sure that Tony himself was conscious of it. Charles never rebelled against this convention because Tony had everything one should expect to find in a president of a first-rate bank. It was amusing but not ridiculous to observe that all the minor executives in the Stuyvesant, as well as the more ambitious clerks, wore conservative double-breasted suits like Tony Burton's, at the same time allowing undue rigidity to break out into pin stripes and herringbones, just like Tony Burton's. They all visited the barber once a week. They all had taken up golf, whether they liked it or not, and most of them wore the same square type of wrist watch and the same stainless-steel strap. They had adopted Tony Burton's posture and his brisk, quick step and even the gently vibrant inflection of his voice. In fact once at one of those annual dinners for officers and junior executives when everyone said a few words and got off a few local jokes about the bank, Charles had brought the matter up when he had been called upon to speak. Speaking was always an unpleasant ordeal with which he had finally learned to cope successfully largely from imitating Tony. He remembered standing up and waiting for silence, just as Tony waited, with the same faint smile and the same deliberate gaze.

"I should like to drink a toast," he had said, "not to our president but to everyone who tries to look like him. When I walk, I always walk like Tony, because Tony knows just how to walk; and when I talk, I always talk like Tony, because Tony knows just how to talk; and when I dress, I always dress like Tony, in a double-breasted suit. But no matter how I try, I cannot be like Tony. I can never make myself sufficiently astute."

It was the one time in the year, at that annual dinner, when you could let yourself go, within certain limits, and Tony Burton had loved it. He had stood up and waited for the laughter to die down and then he had spoken easily, with just the right pause and cadence. He had said that there were always little surprises at these dinners. He had never realized, for instance, that there could be a poet in the trust department, but poetry had its place.

Poetry could teach lessons that transcended pedestrian prose.

"And I'm not too old to learn," Tony Burton had said, "and I'm humbly glad to learn. Sometimes on a starlit night I've wondered what my function was in the Stuyvesant. I'm very glad to know it is that of a clothing dummy. It's a patriotic duty. It's what they want us to be, in Washington."

That was back in 1941, but Tony Burton still had the same spring to his step, the same unlined, almost youthful face, and the same florid complexion; and he had the same three pictures on his desk, the first of Mrs. Burton in their garden, the second of their three girls standing in profile, like a flight of stairs, and the third of his sixty-foot schooner, the *Wanderlust* (the boat you were invited on once every summer), with Tony Burton in his yachting cap standing at the wheel. Time had marched on. All of the girls had come out and all were married, and the *Wanderlust* had been returned by the navy in deplorable condition, but Tony Burton had no superficial scars.

No matter how well Charles might know him, in that half-intimate, half-formal business relationship, he still had a slight feeling of diffidence and constraint. It was the same feeling that one had toward generals in wartime or perhaps toward anyone with power over one. There was always a vestige of a subservient desire to please and to be careful. You had to know how far to go, how long to laugh, and how to measure every speech.

Tony Burton looked up and smiled and waved his hand with the circular motion at the wrist that everyone had tried to imitate.

"Sit down, Charley," he said. "Have a cigarette and relax."

No matter how much you might pretend, it was no time for relaxing, and Tony Burton must have known it. It must have been a little hard for Tony, trying to be friends and always being faced by that line of demarcation. It might have been different, Charles was thinking, if he had inherited money of his own instead of being dependent on a job. It might have been different, even, if he had received some attractive offer lately, if he had known that there was something waiting for him elsewhere with the same salary, instead of knowing that times were tight and uncertain.

Everything was uncertain and there was nothing to do but to wait. He shook his head when Tony Burton offered him a club cigarette from his gold case. There was the unwritten rule of no smoking on the banking floor — even though Tony Burton suggested it be broken.

"What's on your mind, Tony?" he asked. There was nothing to do but wait, while Tony Burton laid his cigarette case on the desk in front of him. From where he sat Charles could read the engraving on its gold surface, done in script in three different specimens of girlish handwriting. "To America's most representative daddy, Gladys, Olivia, Babs."

"The girls gave it to me on Father's Day," Tony Burton said. "I didn't know I was a representative dad."

"I didn't know you were either," Charles answered, "but it must be nice to know."

There was nothing to do but wait, but it was clear already that they were not going to talk about the future or they would not have begun with the cigarette case. At the same time, it was also clear that Tony Burton did have something on his mind. Charles glanced at his cool and placid features, set in assured, easy lines etched by a career in which everything had always worked out right. From the very beginning Tony Burton could have had no doubts about anything. From the very beginning he must have known that he would end where he was sitting.

"I don't like being representative of anything," Tony Burton said.

"I don't see how you can help it very well," Charles said.

"How do you mean, I can't help it?" Tony Burton asked.

"Sitting where you are," Charles said, "you've got to represen That's all I mean."

"Well, I was thinking the other day," Tony Burton said, "t' you're pretty representative yourself."

"I hope I am, Tony," Charles answered. "I try to be, in bus' hours." He did not like the conversation because he did not *l* where it was leading, although he understood that this was part of Tony's technique.

"We ought to call this place the House of Representatives," Tony Burton said, "but it isn't a bad shop, is it?"

"No," Charles answered, "it isn't. I'm glad to be back in it, Tony," and Tony Burton smiled at him, almost as though they were friends.

"Well," Tony said, "speaking of representatives — " and he paused and Charles sat motionless. For a second he thought that he had been wrong and that they were coming to the point at last, but only for a second. "How did you represent things to Selig?"

"I told him he would be happier elsewhere," Charles said. "I told him there were too many complications."

"Why didn't you tell him that we'd have room for him in the quite near future?"

"Because he wouldn't have believed it," Charles said. "He had to know, not that he hadn't guessed already."

"Did he take it?"

"Yes," Charles said, "he took it."

Tony Burton leaned back and clasped his hands behind his head.

"He has a lot of good connections. That's the trouble with life these days. There's no pattern. You don't know where you're at any more. The girls keep going to La Casita. It's a damn funny world, isn't it? It's getting curiouser and curiouser."

"A man told me at lunch today," Charles said, "that no matter what the world is doing, man remains the same."

Tony Burton unclasped his hands from behind his head and placed them on the arms of his chair.

"Well, let's forget it, Charley. There's one other thing."

"Yes, sir," Charles said. He knew it was the other thing that Tony Burton wanted to talk about and he knew that informality was over. It was time to be a bright young man again and to call Tony Burton "sir."

"About that loan."

"Which loan, sir?" Charles asked.

"The one we were talking about this morning. That cordage company. You said you were born up there. What's the name of the place?"

"You mean Clyde?" Charles answered. He had never dreamed

that Clyde would come into the conversation again, yet now that it had, it seemed inevitable. All day, from the moment he had arisen in the morning, Clyde had been behind everything.

"Yes," Tony Burton said, "that's it. Clyde. Somebody ought to see that company and it just occurred to me" — he raised his hand from the right arm of his chair and rotated it slowly from the wrist — "it just occurred to me if you've lived up there and know the background, you'd better go up for a day or two and look things over, just quietly. Talk to people. Find out from the bank. Nothing is secret about any business in a small town."

"No, sir," Charles said. "Everybody in Clyde knows about everything."

"Well, if you want to, take the midnight, or take the plane up to Boston tomorrow morning. Stay as long as you like and see if you can get some figures."

Charles nodded slowly. He did not want to speak for a moment. He was going up to Clyde and he could not help it. He was going back to where he had come from because Roger Blakesley had seen Mr. Burton for just a minute.

"I envy you getting away for a while," Tony Burton said. "You're looking a little tired, Charles."

"Do you want to come along?" Charles asked.

"I wish I could," Tony Burton said, and he laughed, "but I'm the representative dad."

Charles's thoughts were moving smoothly again. For an instant he thought of refusing. He even began to invent a possible excuse, but a refusal or excuse would have been as bad as going.

"Do you mind if I ask you a question, Tony?" he asked.

"Why, no, of course not, Charley," Tony Burton said.

"Did you think up this idea yourself?"

It was dangerous, impertinent, and out of order, but from the slight narrowing of Tony Burton's eyes and from a faint look of surprise, he knew that Tony Burton understood, and that was all he wanted.

"Why, no," Tony Burton said. "Now that you mention it, it wasn't entirely my idea."

At least Tony Burton understood, if he had not before, why Roger had suggested it. It was an opportunity to get Charles Gray away for a while, out of sight and out of mind in a crucial period. Charles had to admit that it was clever of Roger Blakesley.

"I suppose Roger ought to go," Tony Burton said. "It's his responsibility, but he doesn't know Clyde. How about riding back with me on the five-thirty?"

"I can't," Charles said. "The Whitakers want to see me at five. They're very short of money."

Tony Burton frowned. He was thinking, obviously, of dignity and convention.

"Why can't they come down here like other people?" he asked.

"Mrs. Whitaker hasn't been well," Charles said, "and so I thought — " He did not have to tell what he thought because Tony knew. They both knew the size of the Whitaker account.

"All right," Tony Burton said. "Let's see, you'll be back by Friday, won't you? Remember you're coming to dinner on Friday."

"I wouldn't miss it for the world," Charles said.

When their glances met, there was no doubt that Tony Burton knew what he meant. He smiled in a paternal way, far removed from any trouble of Charles's but still with sympathy.

"Well, relax and have a good time, Charley," he said, and he leaned forward and slapped Charles's knee.

"That's the second time," Charles said, "that you've told me to relax."

"Well, do it," Tony Burton said. He seemed to be speaking from a great distance, from Olympian heights of security which Charles would never reach; or he might have been speaking from the deck of the *Wanderlust*, with a wet sheet, a flowing tide, and sailors in white drilling pulling on the braces. He sounded like a doctor in his office, giving sound advice to a nervous patient.

"Go ahead and relax, Charley. I'll see you Friday," and then his voice had a note of kindly promise in it. "Just you and Nancy are coming, and you and I'll have a good long talk about the whole situation here on Friday."

VI

We're Both Doing What We Do Very Well

THE APARTMENT BUILDING on Park Avenue where the Whitakers
lived was one of those co-operative structures built in 1926 on an
unstable foundation of high mortgages. Charles could recall as he
walked under the green awning off the street through the travertine
marble doorway into the travertine marble hall that the Whitakers'
equity on the fifteenth floor of the house had cost them originally
two hundred thousand dollars. He could also recall a later period
when equities in nearly all co-operative apartments had dropped
from nothing to a minus quantity, and when tenants had frantically
endeavored to avoid their upkeep and mortgage charges by giving
away their equities and even paying prospective tenants handsome
bonuses for taking them off their hands. That was the period when
people used to say the purchase of a co-operative apartment was
like buying the hole in a doughnut.

This particular building, Charles remembered very well, had
gone through the financial wringer in the year of 'thirty-three.
There had been a time when its lawyers, agents, and even its uniformed attendants had worn the worried and courteous expressions
that he had observed on the faces of all persons dealing with white
elephants, but it was different now. It seemed to Charles that the
hall attendant who ushered you to the elevator and who looked,
even in his light blue uniform, something like Tony Burton wore
an expression of unctuous triumph, and he was justified. God was
in His heaven again. The building was solvent again. If you were
in one of those brackets, with which Charles was academically familiar, it cost very little to live in a co-operative apartment now,

when so much of the annual expense could be written off on the income tax as interest charges. On the whole the Whitakers had done very well because they had held on with faith in the ultimate victory of righteousness.

The hall attendant was looking now at Charles questioningly, particularly at his worn pigskin brief case. People, of course, who entered from the street with brief cases fell into a dubious professional category and were not always people whom tenants would welcome. No matter how beguiling their superficial appearance might be, a brief case always meant that such individuals were not calling on tenants for purely social purposes. They might be insurance agents or even a Fuller Brush man, or a server with a summons. Charles could understand and even sympathize with the doubt. He himself was like the attendant. He could feel the vague bond of fellowship that came of being an employee.

"Is Mrs. Whitaker expecting you?" the attendant asked. He might conceivably have asked the same question, Charles was thinking, but he certainly would have called him "sir" if it had not been for the brief case.

"Yes, I have an appointment with Mrs. Whitaker," Charles answered. "Call, if you like — Mr. Gray." If he had been carrying a a small black bag, he might have been taken for a doctor and there would have been no question.

"Oh, no," the attendant said, — "if Mrs. Whitaker's expecting you. The elevator to the right."

"Yes," Charles said, "I know," and then it annoyed him that he had said he knew, because there was no reason for it except some subconscious one to make it clear that he had been to the Whitakers' before.

The street door opened. An elderly lady in a mink coat had entered. Her gray hair beneath her ineffective little hat had a fashionable bluish tinge. In front of her, pulling at a leash, was a toy poodle, cut to resemble an Airedale. Its fur was also bluish gray.

"Good afternoon, Mrs. Gorham," the attendant said. "It turned out to be a beautiful afternoon, after all, didn't it?"

"Yes, spring is almost here," Mrs. Gorham answered.

"Hello, Bobo," the attendant said, and he leaned forward eagerly to address the poodle. "How's it outside, Bobo?"

It was not clear whether or not Bobo had enjoyed it outside. He was pulling Mrs. Gorham also to the elevator at the right.

When Charles followed them into the small mahogany lift, neither Mrs. Gorham nor Bobo looked at him until he asked the elevator man for Mrs. Whitaker's apartment, please. Then when Mrs. Gorham saw his brief case she looked away and they rode in stony silence, both denizens of different worlds, both thrown together in that moving car against their wills.

Charles was very conscious of the fact that he belonged in a different world whenever he entered the Whitakers' apartment. When he handed the butler his hat and coat, he knew that he understood the whole place very well, academically but not practically. It was an environment in which he could move gracefully, without tipping things over, but one in which he would never live.

The hall was filled with all sorts of objects which he knew had come from the house on Fifth Avenue belonging to Mrs. Whitaker's father, that canny Yankee from Maine. The Isphahan runner in the hall, and the heavily gold-framed pictures on the walls of Corot-like landscapes and of Oriental ladies with guitars on Moorish roof-tops, all told their tale of an art collection acquired in the eighties and nineties when such things were an essential part of a businessman's background. Above the small refectory table that held a silver tray for visiting cards there was even a portrait of Cyrus J. Smedley, Mrs. Whitaker's father, still dominating those possessions. It was a three-quarters portrait of an elderly man in a high-lapelled dark business coat, a high waistcoat, and a large cravat. He had a lantern-jawed, wary look, and a sort of assurance that belonged to another generation. He was dyspeptic and dangerous looking, and Charles was always acutely aware of his presence. If the old man had been alive, he often thought, he would never have needed the services of the trust department of the Stuyvesant. His general taste in furniture might have been terrible, but it must have been impeccable in blue-chip securities. There must have been a time, Charles was also thinking, when Mr. Whitaker had been obliged to face Cyrus J. Smedley and to tell of his intentions, in a Victorian sort of way, and it made Charles feel sorry for Mr. Whitaker.

It was obviously going to be another family conference because the room at the end of the hall was set for it, a large room that looked small because of the piano and the Bouguereaus and Alma-Tademas on the wall, the Italian chairs, the overstuffed sofas, and the maze of silver-framed photographs on the tables. The family had all been waiting for him, although he was certain that he was there right on the dot of five. Mrs. Whitaker, in a dark tailored suit, was seated on a sofa in front of the fireplace, amazingly upright in spite of the sofa's yielding upholstery. She was obviously prepared for the interview because she was holding a tablet on her knee with questions written on it. She always wrote down questions. Mr. Whitaker was standing near the fireplace in a suit that was too tweedy for him, looking round and red and uncomfortable. Their son Albert, who had risen when Charles came in, looked more like his mother than his father. You could see that he had kept his figure by conscientious outdoor exercise, and he had kept his hair, too, though it was gray at the temples.

Albert's wife as usual looked very bored. Though she and Charles had never exchanged more than a word of greeting, it always surprised him how clearly she could tell him what she was thinking without saying a word, not that she cared whether he knew or not. She was telling him simply by perching on the edge of one of the Italian chairs that she was bored by having to be there, that she was too young, too pretty, too blond, to be there, that she hated the stuffy furniture and her family-in-law, and that she was bored by Albert, too. She was telling him that she wanted to get away somewhere and have a Martini, that she wanted to play a rubber of bridge or something, that only necessity had brought her to this place and that he mustn't think that she liked it, or that she liked him either. She knew just what he was, a tiresome man from the bank, called for one of those damned family conferences that Mother Whitaker was always having. She knew just where he belonged and there was no need for any introductions.

"I hope I'm not late," Charles said.

"Oh, no," said Mrs. Whitaker. "I know we can count on your never being late. Sit down here beside me, Mr. Gray, so we can read things together."

Charles sank down beside her on the sofa. He wished that he could sit upon it as straight as Mrs. Whitaker.

"Albert," Mrs. Whitaker said, "get Mr. Gray a little table."

"Oh, I don't need a table," Charles said. "There won't be anything to sign."

"You'll need it to put things on," Mrs. Whitaker said, "the things out of your brief case. It's always so reassuring to see you with a brief case. I can't imagine how you'd look without it."

"That's true," Charles said. "I don't believe you've ever seen me here without it."

"You'd look, well, almost naked without it," Mrs. Whitaker said. "I remember what Father always used to say."

"What did he use to say?" Albert asked.

"You were too young to remember Granddaddy well, dear," Mrs. Whitaker said. "I wish you could have seen him, Mr. Gray. Hewett, doesn't Mr. Gray remind you of Papa?"

"Well, not altogether, Ellie," Mr. Whitaker said.

"I don't mean altogether, Hewett. I mean partly. He has the same expression sometimes, when we're getting down to brass tacks, as Papa used to say. Papa always used to say when you do business with someone, be sure he does business."

"I understand what he meant," Charles said. "Shall we get down to brass tacks?" and he reached for the catch of his brief case where it lay across his knees.

"Hewett."

"Yes, Ellie," Mr. Whitaker said.

"Perhaps Mr. Gray would like a Scotch and soda."

"Oh, no, thank you," Charles said.

"Well, I'd like one," Albert said. "Come on, Dad. How about it, Dorothy?"

"Well," Dorothy said, and her voice was coldly sweet, "I might have one if Mother Whitaker doesn't mind."

"Of course I don't mind, darling," Mrs. Whitaker said. "Why on earth should I mind? Mr. Gray and I will have some tea when everything is over. Won't we, Mr. Gray?"

"Why, yes," Charles said. "That would be very nice." He saw Dorothy glance at him. She was telling him as plainly as though she had spoken for God's sake to get on with it, and he hoped that he was telling her when he glanced back at her that, for God's sake, he wanted to get on with it, that he didn't like sitting there any more than she did, that he was only present as she was because he had to be.

"Now," said Mrs. Whitaker, "let's begin at the beginning. Let's begin by having you scold us, Mr. Gray, because we all need a good scolding."

"About what, Mrs. Whitaker?" Charles asked.

"About the ranch," Mrs. Whitaker said. "I know how it must look with the world the way it is, but it's really for Albert's sinus. Albert and Dorothy are just back from Arizona. You can tell it by looking at them, can't you?"

Charles looked up at Dorothy and their glances met again.

"Albert," Dorothy said sweetly, "why don't you show him the photographs? That's what you brought them for, wasn't it?"

"Oh yes," Albert said. "If you have to be out there, you might as well have some sort of place and not stay at a hotel. We saw this one fifty miles out of Tucson. These are just snapshots but they'll give you an idea, and Dorothy's crazy about it. She needs some sort of place."

Curiously enough he could feel their uncertainty as Albert handed him the photographs and he knew that they were anxious for his approval. The photographs were mountain and desert views with low buildings of the Spanish hacienda type in the foreground, corrals, patios, galleries, a swimming pool. They represented an exotic life pattern which the Whitakers must have known was entirely out of his experience, but still they wanted him to approve.

"If you really want it," Charles said gently, "I don't know why you shouldn't have it. Is a hundred thousand the asking price? If you really want it, you'd better give me the agent's name."

"He does really want it," Mrs. Whitaker said. "If you could call up the agent it would be sweet of you, Mr. Gray. It would sound better than having Albert do it."

"Of course," Charles said, "you'll have to use a little capital, but I don't see why you shouldn't."

He was opening the brief case, taking out the folders and spreading them on the table. There was no earthly reason why they shouldn't, any more than there was any earthly reason why he should not have bought a three-dollar book if he had really wanted it, or an overcoat if he really needed it, but it hardly mattered as much to them as a new overcoat would have mattered to him. It was not a conventional way of looking at the problem and he wondered what they would have thought if he had presented it to them in this light.

"That's all that bothers me," Mrs. Whitaker said. "Papa always said never to touch capital. It always was his rule."

That was what clients like the Whitakers were always saying. No matter what capital might grow to, you must never touch your capital.

"Things are a little different now," Charles said, "with the tax rate the way it is in the higher brackets."

He saw that Dorothy was watching him. She was bored and telling him wordlessly to get on with it, but at the same time it looked as though she understood what he would have to go through. It would be necessary to discuss the tax structure again.

"But don't you think," Albert Whitaker was asking, "that there's going to be a twenty per cent reduction across the board?"

"They're talking about it, but I wouldn't count on it," Charles said.

"If they're going to reduce taxes," Albert said, "the only sensible, democratic way would be to reduce them across the board."

"I know," Charles said, "but I'm afraid that isn't the way a politician's mind works. But there's no reason why you shouldn't sell some of these short-term governments. They scarcely yield any income at all after taxes."

He was speaking quickly, easily, just as though their problems were his own, dealing in millions just as though they belonged to him. He explained painstakingly item after item on the list.

"You make everything seem so reasonable, Mr. Gray," Mrs. Whitaker said. "I really don't know what we'd do without you."

The Whitakers were as helpless as the soft Manchu descendants of the hardy Mongols who once sat in their moldering Peking palaces, surrounded by Chinese attendants and estate stewards, before they were overtaken by the Boxer rebellion. Somewhere along the way the Whitakers had lost their ability to cope with any present exigency. Their life had taken from them all the ordinary drives of ambition, hope and fear.

"You could always find someone else, Mrs. Whitaker," Charles said, "and he might be better."

"No," said Mr. Whitaker. "You're the only one who's ever seemed to make Mrs. Whitaker understand."

"I don't know why you say that," Mrs. Whitaker said. "I've always been taught to supervise my own affairs, and Mr. Gray knows it."

"Yes," Charles said. "I'm developing a great respect for your general judgment, Mrs. Whitaker."

"I do hope they appreciate you at the bank as much as we do," Mrs. Whitaker said.

"I hope they do, too," Charles answered, and he picked up some of the papers on the little table in front of him as a hint that he had been there for nearly an hour. He wanted very much to catch the six-thirty.

"Well," Albert said, "if everything's settled perhaps Dorothy and I had better be pushing off."

Dorothy rose from the edge of her chair, gracefully, without pushing herself from it.

"It stays light so long," she said, "that I keep forgetting what time it is," but Mrs. Whitaker had picked up the pad from her knee.

"I thought you told me that you didn't have any engagement until dinner, dear," Mrs. Whitaker said. "Now that Mr. Gray's here, I did have a few other questions, but if you want to run along — "

"Oh, no," Dorothy said. "We're really in no hurry."

She smiled at Charles — a ghost of a smile — and sat down again and folded her hands carefully in her lap. She did it brightly and cheerfully, without a hint of resignation, but Charles was sure he knew what she was thinking. Oh, God, she was thinking, here it goes again, the same damned questions.

Mrs. Whitaker's mind was always filled with unshaped, broad-gauge thoughts that mingled confusingly with little ones. There was still that matter of trying to settle a little more on Albert and of balancing the gift against inheritance taxes. She knew, as Charles had so often said, that these were really legal problems and she had nothing at all against Mr. Stone who handled them, but she did value Mr. Gray's opinion and her father had always said that two minds were better than one.

It seemed to her that the government, which she had always been taught was created to protect people and the things they owned, was making a deliberate effort to discourage people who had a little something. For some reason, no one seemed to appreciate any longer what people in her position were doing. What would charities do without people in her position, what would the government do without the taxes, what would business do without the money of people in her position? She knew that she had said all these things before, but she did wish that Charles would take a copy of Mr. Stone's last letter to read, and, when he had time, consult with Mr. Stone.

Then there was the question of the place on Long Island. With wages rising the way they were, she wondered if Charles would mind sometime looking over the books that Mr. Stone was keeping, because she knew, although it was not in his sphere, that he would have some suggestion for cutting down. Then she wanted to know what Charles really thought of the Atchison, Topeka and Santa Fe Railroad, and besides there were several other questions, but now tea was coming in and perhaps they had better put most of it over until another day, but while they were having tea she would like to look over the security list with Albert. It was high time that someone gave it attention beside herself because she was tired of having everyone expect her to do everything alone.

"Nothing's been changed since last time," Charles said.

"I know," she said, "but I would like to look at it with Albert for a minute if you wouldn't mind waiting, Mr. Gray. Why don't you take your tea and talk with Dorothy?"

Charles rose and picked up his teacup. Dorothy had moved to a window with her highball glass in her hand. She stood there straight and beautiful, smelling faintly of Chanel Five, looking out on Park Avenue, and she smiled cordially at Charles.

"I'm sorry it's taken so long," Charles said.

"Why don't you take a drink?" she said. "I would."

"Oh, no," Charles answered. "I don't believe you would."

"Well, maybe I wouldn't," she said, and she smiled again and glanced toward the sofa where Mr. Whitaker and Albert stood looking over Mrs. Whitaker's shoulder.

"I didn't know," he heard Mrs. Whitaker saying, "that we had so many shares in Homestake Mine."

Dorothy had turned toward him again. Her beautifully molded, made-up face and the wind-blown look to her hair had an impermeable sort of completeness. It made him nervous that there was so little wrong about her. There was nothing wrong about her delicate hands and her pointed red fingernails, nothing wrong about her silk print dress or her diamond clip or her straight, lithe figure or her nylon stockings, but still there was something baffling.

"What do you do," she asked, "when you aren't doing this?"

"I go home," Charles said. "It looks as though I'm going to be late tonight."

"You make me curious," she said. "You really do."

"Why?" Charles asked.

"You make me curious because I can't picture you as doing anything but what I see you doing."

"Well," Charles answered, "now you mention it, I've been thinking about the same thing about you."

Her lips curved in that same faint smile.

"That's because we're both doing what we do very well," she said, "but it takes a lot of trouble, doesn't it?"

"Well," Charles answered, "sometimes — yes."

"Do you ever wonder whether it's worth it?" she asked.

"Yes," Charles said, "occasionally. I suppose everyone does."

"That's the question," she said. "Is it worth it? I'm glad you're curious about me. I didn't know you were."

"I am," Charles said, "academically."

"You know," she said, "we ought to have a long talk sometime."

Charles squared his shoulders. He could not imagine how he had become involved in such a conversation and nothing would have been more unwise than having a long talk with Dorothy Whitaker sometime.

"I'm very glad you suggested it," Charles said. "It's an interesting idea."

"It would be a lot of fun." Her smile grew broader. "If we could sit in a bar some afternoon and get quietly tight and talk — "

Charles found that he was laughing. The beauty of it was that it was so impossible that there was nothing at all to worry about.

"You see," she said, "I'd find out what you used to be and how you got the way you are."

"It wouldn't be worth it," Charles said. "I've always been about the same."

"Oh, no," she said, "nobody ever is. We can't help working on ourselves."

He had a momentary picture of her working on herself, sitting before her mirror with her lipstick and her powder base, and brushing back her hair.

"Not on ourselves," he said. "Everyone works on us. Everyone wears us down."

"If you're tough enough," she said, "you don't have to be worn down."

Charles found himself laughing again.

"All right," he said, "what did you use to be?"

She shook her head slowly and her smile had gone.

"Nicer," she said, "quite a good deal nicer."

"Oh, Mr. Gray," Mrs. Whitaker was calling, "could you come over here for a minute?"

"Good-by," she said. "Good luck."

"I see you have a question mark in pencil after Smith Chemical," Mrs. Whitaker was saying.

VII

Shadows of the Evening

THE SIX-THIRTY from the upper level of the Grand Central was a good train, express to Port Chester and never crowded. Though it would get him home late for dinner, he welcomed the opportunity of riding on it because he could be reasonably sure of not having to talk to anyone and it gave him an opportunity to go over all the events of the day, the people he had seen, and what he had done well or badly. As the train moved out of the station into the dark beneath Park Avenue, Charles laid his brief case on the vacant seat beside him and took out the book, *Yankee Persepolis,* that Malcolm Bryant had given him. He laid it on top of his brief case and then looked at the headlines on the front page of the *New York World-Telegram.*

The headlines had the same disturbing quality as his personal thoughts for it seemed that nothing was in order that day with himself or with anything else. They were still arguing in Moscow over German reparations, which everyone must have known could never be collected. There were terrorist bombings in Palestine and the news was bad in Turkey and there were student riots in Cairo. It often seemed to him that Cairo students never had time to study. All that foreign world kept slopping over its borders like water spilling untidily out of a shaking dish.

He was thinking, for no good reason, of Shepheard's Hotel in Cairo as he had first seen it from the jeep that had brought him in from the army airfield in the desert. He remembered the beige façade and the robes and the red caps of the dragomans and the khaki shorts of the British and colonial officers crowding the terrace and their caps and tam-o'-shanters that somehow made them look like grown men pretending to be Boy Scouts at a children's party. It all made no particular sense, since neither he nor anyone at headquarters had ever found why he had been sent to Cairo. Then he thought of the field at Prestwick and of the uncompromising Scottish streets of Glasgow. Then he was thinking of the main street in Clyde, of the brick sidewalk and a display of elastic bandages and digestive powders in the windows of Walters's drugstore, and the tools and galvanized pails and hickory bushel baskets in front of Harrison's hardware store which was only a few doors further down the street, just before you came to Bates's grocery. There was no reason to think of Clyde and Shepheard's and of some dingy pub in Glasgow all at the same time, except that everything was closer together than it used to be.

He could hear the creaking, complaining sounds of the train and he was aware of the dim tunnel lights moving past the windows in an even sequence of light and dark that was punctuated now and then by a blue electric flash when some locomotive lost contact with the rail. Although his thoughts had no appreciable pattern, he knew that they were all symptoms of his own uncertainty.

The people he had seen that day and the things that he and they had said had no disturbing connotation in themselves. Taken separately, they were all elements that he might encounter in any working day. The trust conference, the interlude of lunch, the activities of Roger Blakesley, his words with Mr. Selig, his talk with Tony Burton and his conference with the Whitakers, were manifestations that he had encountered often in slightly different forms, yet taken all together they achieved a different stature. Even the question of competition, of his having been outmaneuvered, though he was keenly conscious of it, was not what disturbed him. There was something more in the sum of all of it that lay within himself.

For some reason Clyde kept coming into it, and for some reason he kept seeing events in terms of Clyde; and all the things he had done that day were like things he had done in Clyde, on a different projection and a wholly different scale. Actually he was not very different from what he had at one time been. But nicer. He remembered the word "nicer." The train was out of the tunnel, moving by the lighted tenements of uptown New York whose unshaded windows gave abrupt glimpses into other people's lives.

When he had stood by that other New York window watching Dorothy Whitaker's tapering fingers with their brightly polished red nails as she held her half-empty glass, he might again have been calling on Jessica Lovell at the Lovell house in Clyde. Granted that Jessica was a wholly different person, there was that same indirect involvement. It was true that if you weren't tough enough, contact with other people wore you down.

"Tickets," the conductor was saying. He had not noticed the conductor walking through the car. You had to have some sort of ticket for everything and it was generally one-way. Then he remembered that he had used up the last of his commutation ticket that morning.

"I'll have to pay you," Charles said. He could not remember when he had last forgotten a ticket. "How much is it to Clyde? . . . I'm sorry. I was thinking of something else."

Charles picked up the book from the top of the brief case and began to turn the pages.

"For the purposes of distinction," he was reading again, "it will be well arbitrarily to define the very definite and crystallized social strata of Yankee Persepolis as upper, middle, and lower. These will be subdivided into upper-upper, middle-upper, and lower-upper . . ."

Since he was late, he had to take a taxi. The taxi starter, who sorted the clientele, putting those who were going in the same general direction into the same cab, was standing at the far end of the platform, a lay figure silhouetted against the headlights of the cars.

"Sycamore Park," Charles said, and the starter called out his words above the rumbling of the train that was leaving.

"Sycamore Park. Anyone else going to Sycamore Park?"

The night air was fresher and it smelled of spring, and there was a vacancy of sound after the train had left. The train seemed to have carried away everything that Charles had been thinking. Everything connected with the city, Smith Chemical, Telephone, American Tobacco B, and short-term governments, was gone with the train. He was going home again, and no one else was going to

Sycamore Park. He was returning to the basic reason for everything for which he had been working.

As he sat in the back seat of the taxicab he still thought about Clyde. They used to play hide-and-seek in the old back garden of the Meader yard in the spring, just when it was getting dusk — he and Melville Meader and Earl Wilkins and all the rest of the crowd along Spruce Street. There was a better chance of hiding, just when it was dusk. You could hide downstairs in the barn or back of the carriage shed or anywhere in the garden. There was always that indecision, that rushing about, until you heard "five hundred, coming, ready or not." Then you tried to sneak back without being seen. The best way was to dodge around the carriage house and then to the corner of the barn where you could watch the back porch, which was home, until everything was clear. There was always an uncertainty, a wondering whether you could make it, and then that dash for home. If you got there safely, all the other incidents were behind you. There was a triumphant, out-of-breath feeling, a momentary impression that nothing else mattered, when you called out "Home Free!"

Sycamore Park had been developed in 1938 on the forty-acre grounds of an old estate and the subdivision had been excellently managed by the local real estate firm of Merton and Pease. As Mr. Merton had said, it was a natural, and he had never understood why someone had not dreamed it up long ago — not too far from the shopping center and the trains, and yet in the neighborhood of other larger places. Every place had its own acre, and no house was to be constructed for a cost of less than thirty thousand dollars. It would have been wiser, perhaps, never to have gone there but to have bought a smaller place.

It would have been wiser, easier, and much safer. He had not at that time been moved up in the trust department and in 1939 all he had was twenty thousand dollars in savings, part of which was in paid-up life insurance. He could never analyze all the urges that made him lay everything on the line in order to live on a scale he could not immediately afford, discounting the possibilities of illness or accident and relying on possibilities of promotion. He only remembered having had an irrational idea that time was of the essence, that he would always stay on a certain business level if he did not take some sort of action, and Nancy, too, had shared that feeling.

The sight of the house at Sycamore Park still gave him qualms of uneasiness. Its whitened brick, its bow windows, still reminded him of what might have happened and of what he would have done if things had turned out differently. Those worries were all top-secret between Nancy and himself, to be shared with no one else. Yet, no matter what, that house was his and hers, a tangible achievement of the past and a sort of promissory note for the future.

When he had paid the driver and the car had driven off, he stood for a while at the end of the flagstone path that led to the green front door. The light from the ground-floor windows sharpened the outlines of the ell and roof, and his imagination enabled him to put the rest of it together in the dark — the yard, the lawn and trees, the garage and the flagstone terrace by the windows of the library. Now they were even talking at odd moments about selling and getting something larger, but nothing would ever be the same as that particular house. No other house of theirs would ever have the sleepless nights, the hours of argument, spent over it. There was too much of him connected with the house ever to view it objectively. He was thinking of the copper gutters and of the way the conductors drained over a part of the lawn. It would be necessary to have a dry well dug for the conductors; and then there was the broken latch on the garage door, and the oil burner needed a new lining of firebrick; and then there was the weather stripping around the living room windows, and there was something still wrong with the gas water heater. Then there was the mortgage. Then there was the part of the cellar that he was going to turn into a workshop for himself and Bill, now that you could buy lathes and drills again. Those were the species of thoughts that came over him as he stood there by the door, and they were a relief after everything else.

The hall, when Charles entered, seemed what the architect had called gracious and welcoming. At the left came the dining room; the living room was opposite, then the stairs, and the pine-paneled library at the end. Once he had thought this ground plan was entirely original until, to his amazement, he had found it repeated in all the other houses at Sycamore Park. The hall furniture was what made it undeniably their own hall, for the furniture, though Nancy had kept changing it, came from other incarnations, from apartments in New York, from the little house in Larchmont. The four rush-bottomed chairs they had bought once on a vacation trip and on which no one could sit were good antiques that never fitted well with the reproductions that Nancy had bought before she knew better. They still stood, with the gilt mirror and the console table, like parts of older civilizations, waiting to be absorbed into another way of life.

It was strange the way a family developed habits. For instance, no one seemed to use the living room much, although it was the largest and most comfortable room in the house. The children as usual were in the library listening to the radio — no longer learning parchesi and reading the *Wizard of Oz*. Instead they had progressed imperceptibly to the outer edge of childhood, a strange, transient region. Bill was sprawled on the sofa in a manner which he must have copied from some older boys. He was wearing a pullover sweater and his gray flannel trousers had worked halfway up to his knees, showing stretches of bare shin, and garterless knitted socks that wrinkled above those laceless moccasins that all the boys were wearing. His face seemed to have outgrown itself, like his body, so that his nose looked too big for his eyes, and he had a crew cut which was very unbecoming.

Evelyn sat sideways in an armchair. Instead of being nervous, petulant, and slender, as she had been when she was seven and eight, Evelyn was almost fat. He could imagine she would be pretty someday for she had Nancy's tranquil features and Nancy's chin and mouth, yet it was hard to believe that Nancy, when she was thirteen, could have looked like Evelyn, that Nancy could have worn a little girl's plaid dress or that Nancy's light brown braids had ever been so untidy.

When they saw him they both jumped up, clumsily yet with a puzzling sort of co-ordination. There had been a time when he had taken it for granted that they were fond of him, but now he found it very reassuring to realize that they were still glad to see him, even though their feelings toward each other were undergoing some adolescent change. Evelyn still kissed him like a little girl, winding her arms tight around his neck, but Bill simply stood there grinning at him, with his wrists dangling out of the sleeves of his sweater.

"Hello," Charles said. "How about turning that radio off?"

"It's going to be over in a minute, Daddy," Evelyn said, "and then there's going to be Eddy Duchin."

"Well, never mind Eddy Duchin," Charles said. "Turn it off. I'm tired."

Bill switched it off and there was a silence that was almost embarrassing to Charles. It was obviously incredible to both Bill and Evelyn that anyone could exist who could bear to miss Duchin.

"What's the matter?" Bill asked. "Don't you want to hear it, Pop?"

"Not right this minute," Charles answered, and he put his arm around Evelyn's shoulders. "You're getting to be a big girl, aren't you?"

"Don't," Evelyn said. "You tickle."

"Where's Mother?" Charles asked.

"She's gone to the club," Bill answered. "The Martins took her and she left the car. She said for you to go up there when you've had supper."

"Your supper's in the oven," Evelyn told him, "but I'll get it."

"Why do you have to go out?" Bill asked. "Why don't you just stay here?"

"Because he's on the committee," Evelyn said. "And don't forget to shave."

She sounded just like Nancy.

"Don't worry," Charles answered. "I'll put on a black tie and everything."

"Mother laid your clothes out," Evelyn told him. "Daddy, why don't you use lotion?"

"What?" Charles asked.

"After-shaving lotion. Don't you want to be like other people?" Charles started to laugh, but a desperate, tragic note in her voice stopped him.

"Do you really think that would help?" he asked, and she nodded without speaking.

"All right," Charles said, "I'll tell you what I'll do. If you really think so, I'll buy some of it tomorrow."

It must have been worrying her, because she smiled the triumphant smile of someone who has been through a considerable ordeal and who has been brave enough to speak frank thoughts.

"Oh, Daddy," she said, "you don't have to do it if you don't want to."

That expansive mood was still with Charles as he sat in the dining room eating warmed-over corned beef hash and string beans and drinking a cup of bitter, warmed-over coffee. Now that it was spring, he found himself saying, they would take the car some Saturday soon and drive away out in Connecticut for a picnic. It would be a cooking picnic, if they could find a place somewhere near a brook where they could light a fire. When he was their age, he was saying, they often went for picnics down on the beach and they always built a fire of driftwood because there was always a lot of dry wood on a beach. Bill was saying that he wished they had a sailboat, but Evelyn was saying that of course they couldn't afford a sailboat, and Charles said that perhaps they could sometime. Then Bill was saying that he had been with some of the boys to the airport that afternoon watching the Piper Cubs, and Charles said that maybe Bill could take flying lessons sometime, if he wanted, when he was seventeen or eighteen. This brought the conversation around to the war, and Charles was telling them again, as he had before, that he had not done anything much in the war and that a great many people in the Air Force were on the ground all the time, repairing the planes and briefing the crews who were going on missions. Then Bill was asking him if he had ever been on a mission, and Charles said that he had been, twice, but not doing anything, just there to see what it was like. He had never thought that their talk would end that way after beginning with shaving lotion.

"What was it like?" Bill asked.

Charles pushed his plate away. He would never be able to tell Bill what it was like, even if he wanted to. He was thinking that he had been about Bill's age after the last war and that he had always wondered what it had been like.

"It was cold . . ." he said. "If I'm going to the club, I've got to get dressed . . . It's all over anyway, Bill. All of it's all over."

He must have spoken sharply without having intended to because they were quiet when he stood up, but Bill followed him to the stairs.

"Do you mind if I come up with you?" he asked.

"No," Charles said, "of course not, as long as we talk about something else."

His brother Sam had been old enough to go to the last war.

While he was putting his studs in his shirt, he kept looking at Bill, who sat on the edge of the bed, and wondering whether he could ever have looked like Bill when he was fifteen. It did not seem possible that he could have ever been a gangling sight like Bill, so awkward or so immature.

"I don't want you sitting around wishing you'd been in that war," Charles said.

"Well, just the same, I do," Bill answered.

"It doesn't do any good to wish," Charles said. "I kept wishing I'd been to the first one and that's why I went to this one and it wasn't a very good idea."

"Why wasn't it a good idea?" Bill asked.

"It didn't help anything," Charles said.

"How do you mean," Bill asked, "it didn't help anything?"

"Never mind," Charles said. "It didn't. It was a luxury."

"A luxury?" Bill repeated.

The subject was not worth discussing. Bill was too young to understand him.

"When you do something that you don't have to do, it's generally a luxury," Charles said. "You've got a lot of other things to think about, Bill. I want you to go to college, and I want you to have more opportunities than I've had."

"What sort of opportunities?" Bill asked.

They were on ground where they could never meet.

"I want you to be able to see more things and do more things than I ever have," Charles said. "I'd like you to have some sort of profession, something you'll be proud and happy doing." He was pulling on his black trousers and it occurred to him that it was an undignified position from which to deliver a pontifical speech.

"Aren't you happy," Bill asked, "working in the bank?"

"Yes," Charles answered, "but that hasn't anything to do with you. What do you want more than anything else?"

"I want to go to Exeter," Bill said.

Charles did not answer. It was an anticlimax, but he could understand it. It was a disappointment, but he could understand it. It meant that Bill was like himself. When he was that age, he too had usually wanted something small and definite.

"Dad, is there any chance of sending me to Exeter?"

"Why, yes," Charles said, and he put on his coat. "I think so, Bill. I think there's a pretty good chance, if everything turns out all right. Do you know where the keys to the car are? I ought to be going now."

Not since he had left Clyde had Charles ever felt as identified with any community as he had since he had been asked to join the Oak Knoll Country Club. They were in a brave new world involving all sorts of things of which he had scarcely dreamed after they had moved to Sycamore Park. This cleavage between past and present, Charles realized, was a part of a chain reaction that started, of course, with one of those shake-ups in the bank. Charles had known that he had been doing well. He had known for a year or so, from the way Mr. Merry and Mr. Burton and particularly Mr. Slade had been giving him little jobs to do, that something was moving him out of the crowd of nonentities around him. He was aware also that Walter Gibbs in the trust department was growing restless. There had been a premonition of impending change, just like the present tension. One day Walter Gibbs had asked him out to lunch and had told him, confidentially, that he was going to move to the Bankers' Trust and that he was recommending Charles for his place. Charles was not surprised, because he had been a good assistant to Walter Gibbs, and he was glad to remember that he had been loyal to his chief, ever since the old days in the statistical department.

"Charley," Walter Gibbs had said, "a lot of people around here have been out to knife me. You could have and you never did, and I appreciate it, Charley."

He had known, of course, for some time that Walter Gibbs was not infallible, that he was fumbling more and more over his decisions and depending more and more on Charles's support, but Walter had taught him a lot.

"Slade keeps butting in," Walter had said, and then he went on to tell the old story which Charles had often heard of conflicting personalities and suspicions. Walter had felt that frankly he was more eligible for a vice-presidency than Slade, and the truth was he had never been the same after Arthur Slade had been selected.

"If they don't like you enough to move you up," Walter had said, "it's time to get out, Charley."

God only knew where Walter Gibbs was now. He was gone like others with whom you worked closely once and from whom you were separated. Walter Gibbs was gone with his little jokes and his bifocal glasses and the stooping shoulders that had given him a deceptively sloppy appearance. He was gone with his personality that would never have permitted him to be a vice-president of anything.

Charles was ready, not surprised, when Tony Burton, though of course he did not call him Tony then, had called him downstairs and had asked him if he knew what was coming, that he had been with them for quite a while and that they had all had an eye on him ever since he had done that analysis on chain stores. Even if you were prepared for such a change there was still an unforgettable afterglow, and an illuminating sense of unrealized potentiality. It was a time to be more careful than ever, to measure the new balance of power, and not to antagonize the crowd that you were leaving. One day, it seemed to Charles, though of course it was not one day, he was living in a two-family house in Larchmont that smelled of cauliflower in the evenings, stumbling over the children's roller-skates and tricycles, taking the eight-three in the morning, keeping the budget on a salary of six thousand a year. Then in a day, though of course it was not a day, they were building at Sycamore Park. The children were going to the Country Day School. They were seeing their old friends, but not so often. Instead they were spending Sundays with Arthur Slade. There was a maid to do the work. He was earning eleven thousand instead of six, and he was an executive with a future. New people were coming to call; all sorts of men he had hardly known were calling him Charley. It was a great crowd in Sycamore Park and he was asked to join the Oak Knoll Country Club. They were a great crowd in Sycamore Park.

It would have made quite a story — if it could have been written down — how all those families had come to Sycamore Park. They had all risen from a ferment of unidentifiable individuals whom you might see in any office. They had all once been clerks or salesmen or assistants, digits of what was known as the white-collar class. They had come from different parts of the country and yet they all had the same intellectual reactions because they had all been through much the same sorts of adventures on their way to Sycamore Park. They all bore the same calluses from the competitive struggle, and it was still too early for most of them to look back on that struggle with complacency. They were all in the position of being insecurely poised in Sycamore Park — high enough above the average to have gained the envy of those below them, and yet not high enough so that those above them might not easily push them down. It was still necessary to balance and sometimes even to push a little in Sycamore Park, and there was always the possibility that something might go wrong — for example, in the recession that everyone was saying was due to crop up in the next six or eight months. It was consoling to think that they were no longer in the group that would catch it first, or they would not have been at Sycamore Park — but then they were not so far above it. They were not quite indispensable. Their own turn might come if the recession were too deep. Then no more Sycamore Park, and no more dreams of leaving it for something bigger -- only memories of having been there once. It was something to think about as you went over your checkbook on clear, cold winter nights, but it was nothing ever to discuss. It was never wise or lucky to envisage failure. It was better to turn on the phonograph — and someday you would get one that would change the records automatically. It was better to get out the ice cubes and have some friends in and to talk broad-mindedly about the misfortunes of others. It was better to go to the club on Tuesday evenings and to talk about something else — and that was where Charles Gray was going.

Charles was frank enough to admit that the Oak Knoll Club was not as good as the older country club at Hawthorn Hill. Charles's knowledge of people in the bank and his acquaintance with Hawthorn Hill clients had taught him that the Oak Knoll Club was intended for a definite sort of person, either one who could not afford the Hawthorn Hill dues or one who had not had the edges polished off. It was all very well to say that the Hawthorn Hill Club was meant for old men and older dowagers and that the Oak Knoll was a young man's club. That was what the Sycamore Park crowd always said, but any one of them would have dropped Oak Knoll like a hot potato if he had been asked to join Hawthorn Hill and could afford a share of stock. It was reassuring to Charles to recall that several members of Hawthorn Hill had spoken to him casually about joining it someday when he got around to it. Cliff Dunbarton, who kept his polo ponies and his hunters at the stable at Hawthorn Hill and who had come to Charles several times at the bank to ask him about investments, had once invited Charles and Nancy to the house for a drink, when he had met them walking on Sunday, and had said that any time Charles wanted to get into Hawthorn to let him know. Tony Burton himself, who was a member, had said only last year that it might be a good idea for Charles to think about getting into Hawthorn Hill, as long as Charles was a confidential advisor to so many of its members. It might even be a good thing for the bank to have him in there When Charles had pointed out that he could not possibly afford the initiation fee or the purchase of the necessary share of stock, Tony Burton had said that there might be some way to wangle it, but it had either gone out of Tony's mind or there had not been any way, for the subject had not been brought up again.

Charles could not help wondering that night, as he drove between the stone gateposts of the Oak Knoll Club, whether Tony Burton had said the same thing to Roger Blakesley. Cliff Dunbarton certainly had not done so because it was clear from certain bitter remarks of Roger's about not having time to suck up to the Dunbartons that the Dunbartons had so far not bothered to know the Blakesleys. Charles had enjoyed assuring Roger that the Dunbartons weren't bad at all when you got to know them — not bad at all, only stand-offish.

It was true that in some sections of the town Oak Knoll was referred to as the "Monkey Cage," and now that Charles was a member of the House Committee he could see what was meant, but at the same time they all enjoyed themselves at Oak Knoll, and even some of the Hawthorn Hill crowd still kept their memberships. You did not have to worry so much about the furniture at Oak Knoll. If you wanted, you could drink a little more. You could be more relaxed, within reason — but not if you were a member of the House Committee. When Charles was hanging up his hat and coat in the men's coatroom, the first person he saw was Cliff Dunbarton, who looked more relaxed than usual.

"Why, hello," he said. "If it isn't Mr. Gray."

"That's right," Charles said. "The name's Gray," and he was tempted to add, "Fancy seeing you here," but he did not know Cliff Dunbarton well enough to be familiar and besides it was not up to him to belittle a party at Oak Knoll. Still they smiled at each other and he wished very much that he could be more like Cliff Dunbarton, happy wherever he was and not caring a damn about anything — but then, Cliff Dunbarton could afford it.

"Margie's away," Cliff Dunbarton said, and Charles realized that he must be referring to Mrs. Dunbarton. "She never can stand this place. Margie isn't what you'd call democratic, but this is quite a party."

"I wouldn't know," Charles said. "I just got here – but it must be if you say so."

"I've always kept my membership here," Cliff Dunbarton said, "out of community spirit. Frankly, Charley, there are some very amusing types and hurry-come-ups in this place. I've got to get around more. I'm having a wonderful time. How about having a drink, Charley?"

"I'd like to a little later, but not right now," Charles said. Obviously Cliff Dunbarton was quite tight or he would not have called him Charley.

"Have you got a pencil and a piece of paper?" Cliff Dunbarton went on. "There's a little number I was dancing with out there and I want to write her name down before I forget it."

Charles took a fountain pen from his inside pocket and tore a leaf from the back of his small black notebook.

"Where does she live?" he asked.

"She's a very nice little number," Cliff Dunbarton said. "Her name is Sherrill or Merrill or something, and I never would have met her if I hadn't come here. She lives in that new development. What is it? Something about a tree."

"Every new development is something about a tree," Charles said.

"Don't interrupt me. Let me concentrate." Cliff Dunbarton placed the notebook page against the wall and began writing slowly. "Bea Merrill. She asked me to call her Bea. I wish I knew what her husband's name was. She lives in that new, young-executive development. I remember the name now — Sycamore Park.'

"That's right," Charles said. "She's Mrs. Tom Merrill."

"How do you know?"

"Because I live there," Charles said. "I live in Sycamore Park."

"By God," Cliff Dunbarton said, "that's right. Of course you do. You're the only person I've ever heard of who lives there."

"Except Bea," Charles said.

"Except Bea." Cliff Dunbarton began to laugh. "Well, thanks for the pen, Charley, and don't let the sycamores fall on you."

Perhaps Roger Blakesley was right, perhaps it was a waste of time to have anything to do with people like the Dunbartons, but it was pleasant to realize that he was the only person living in Sycamore Park whom Cliff Dunbarton had ever noticed. Yet though it was pleasant, he had a feeling of disloyalty. They were a great crowd in Sycamore Park, and he was on the House Committee of the Oak Knoll Club.

The Oak Knoll Club had been making one of its frequent drives for new members at just about the time the houses were being finished in Sycamore Park. A committee of good mixers had been formed for the purpose of the drive, known as the "Stir Up Committee," and its members had taken Saturday afternoon off and Sunday to go calling in a body on new Sycamore Park residents. Bill Forbush, the president of the club, who could play around any course in the eighties, and J. P. Swiss, who had once been an All-America tackle, and Walter Crumm, who had one of those one-man bands, which he played in his rumpus room, using his hands, feet, mouth, nose, and even his cranium, had dropped everything in order to get that committee going. Charles had only seen them in the distance, getting out of their station wagons at the eight-thirty, until they called on him.

He and Nancy were still hanging pictures in the new house and at first Charles had not been sure what they wanted, because a great many people he had never known before had been calling recently to see whether he needed insurance or to ask for contributions for Bundles for Britain, but when they trooped into the new pine-paneled library, they said their only purpose was to welcome Charles and Nancy into the community. Mr. Forbush said that his own son Rex was in the same class at the Country Day as Charles's boy Bill, and Mr. Swiss picked up a small plated-silver cup off the mantel, a trophy awarded to Charles for winning the quarter mile at Dartmouth; and they all talked about football and skiing, while Nancy was in the pantry getting something for them to drink. When Nancy had suggested this, Charles remembered that they all three had exchanged wordless glances and then Mr. Forbush had said that it would be a very good idea just to have a touch of something as long as it was the end of a long, hard Saturday afternoon. When Charles had gone out to help Nancy with the tray, he observed on his return that the three callers were pacing about the room, unobtrusively examining the furniture and exchanging low monosyllables, but when each had his glass everything was very cordial and there was an atmosphere of friendly confidence.

Charles had told them that he had given up track in his freshman year, that he had never been good enough for the varsity, and that he had never done much with golf. Mr. Forbush told Nancy that she ought to make that man of hers take it up. It would keep him from fussing around the house, and there was a fine professional at the Oak Knoll Club. Then Mr. Crumm asked why they didn't join the Oak Knoll Club. Nancy had looked a little startled, and Charles had said that they had never done much about clubs and right now the house and moving and getting settled had cost a good deal more than they had expected. Mr. Swiss had said that everything always did, but it was not the cost, it was the solid satisfaction that you got out of things that mattered. Regular exercise and fresh air and friends were what mattered. Now why didn't the Grays come around to Oak Knoll next Tuesday night and look the crowd over?

Then Mr. Forbush drew a deep breath. Seriously he didn't want to be a salesman, he said, and urge anything on the Grays, who looked as though they had minds of their own, particularly Mrs. Gray. They had really just come around to get to know the Grays and to welcome them into the community, but now they were all there, just friends together, he did want to say a few things about the Oak Knoll Club, because it was his special hobby, his baby. He remembered that when he and Mrs. Forbush first came to this town they came here cold, years ago, not knowing many people, and at first he didn't know whether he and Mrs. Forbush would fit in, particularly Mrs. Forbush. There were too many snooty people with too much money, all wrapped up in their own affairs, but then he found that there were a lot of regular human beings around, people who were busy, without too much money and without any side, and they were all in the Oak Knoll Club. Now they had heard of the Hawthorn Hill Club, hadn't they, where you had to wait for someone to die before you got in and where you had to mortgage your house to buy stock and pay initiation fees? Well, there were real human beings at Oak Knoll. It was just a simple building, made for people just like the Grays, one big old room with a few comfortable chairs, locker rooms with a few plain showers, a little bar and a kitchen where they tossed up simple meals, but a mighty nice eighteen-hole course and some good tennis courts, and they were raising money for a swimming pool. There was something for every member of the family there, and nobody complained about children having a good time. Everybody had a good time. Oak Knoll was a democratic club, for self-respecting people. The best friends he ever made, he made right there at Oak Knoll, boys like Swiss and Crumm and girls like Mrs. Swiss and Mrs. Crumm. They got up their own entertainments and made their own good times at Oak Knoll, and were they good times! You ought to hear Crumm and his one-man band and you ought to see Ma Epping do conjuring tricks. Did the Grays know any parlor tricks? Well, it didn't matter if they didn't. He didn't either, but the main thing was that the members made Oak Knoll and Oak Knoll didn't make the members.

Somehow once you started, you kept going to Oak Knoll, to the Tuesday dinner dances and the Saturday pick-up suppers, nothing elaborate, no lace parasols, not many chauffeurs in the parking lot, but somehow, he didn't know why, you got to think of it as a second home. What was it Daniel Webster said about Dartmouth? It's a small place, but we love it. Yet at the same time, he did not want the Grays to think for a minute that Oak Knoll welcomed all the rag, tag, and bobtail you always found in the suburbs. Actually, there was a pretty strict committee, who gave prospective members a good going over, but the Grays needn't worry their heads about formality, now that he and Swiss and Crumm had seen them and had sat with them in their gracious home. Well, he hadn't meant to run on so long about Oak Knoll. Someone should have stopped him. Yet seriously, why didn't they come and just look the crowd over at Oak Knoll? He would love personally to give them a card for two weeks. Come to think of it, he had a card right in his pocket and if anybody had a pen he would sign it now — and now they'd better all be going, but before they left how about making a date for the Tuesday night dinner dance at Oak Knoll? They would all personally guarantee that the Grays had a good time, and the Grays would meet all the crowd.

This had all happened before the war but war's aftermath had not changed the spirit of Oak Knoll. When Charles stepped out of the coatroom, though he felt tired, he knew he ought to dance, being a member of the House Committee. His ear for music was bad and, in spite of having gone once furtively for a course of lessons at the Arthur Murray studio, he had never developed an interesting technique, nor had he ever entirely mastered that basic Arthur Murray step, and he always had a feeling that he was back at his senior high school dance at Clyde or at a Dartmouth prom, both unwelcome memories. Nevertheless, he could see it was a good Tuesday night party, with a big enough crowd to make it more than break even financially. The tables had been cleared away from the big room and Sol Blatz and His Orchestra from Stamford were playing in one corner. The sight of Mr. Blatz, with his dark, waving hair and his languidly moving arm, reminded him that he must write Mr. Blatz a check.

The first girl he noticed was Bea Merrill, in the arms of Mr. Swiss. Mr. Swiss had put on weight in the last few years. His face was red and he was talking rapidly. Then he saw Cliff Dunbarton cut in on them. Then he saw Mr. Forbush dancing with Dotty Jack, the Jacks who had bought the stucco house, the one that had been hard to sell, near the entrance to Sycamore Park. Then he saw Nancy. She was dancing with Cyril Renard, who sold life insurance downtown. Cyril had been talking to him lately about a new endowment policy, and he hoped that Cyril would not bring the subject up again that night. He edged his way carefully across the floor and Nancy saw him and smiled. They looked as though they had been dancing for quite a while, and Cyril always wanted to change his partners quickly for business reasons.

"Hello, Cyril," Charles said. "I'm going to take Nancy off your hands."

116

"Don't put it that way," Cyril said. "Nancy and I were talking about you and education. Where's Bill going to college?"

Charles knew that Cyril was thinking of one of those educational policies which would both send the children to a proper school and you to a hospital if you needed it, and pay damages, too, if the dog bit the milkman.

"Charley, you and I ought to have a long talk sometime," Cyril said.

"All right," Charles answered. "Sometime, Cyril." He put his arm hastily around Nancy and began to dance.

"Thank God you've come. I've been dancing with him for ages," Nancy said, and then she gave him a little squeeze. "Is there any news?"

"Nothing much," Charles said. "I can't talk about it here, Nancy."

"There's that Dunbarton dancing with Bea Merrill."

"Yes, I see," Charles said. "Did he dance with you?"

"Yes, he danced with me. It was very gracious of him. He acts like someone in a settlement house."

"Oh, don't say that," Charles said. "Cliff's all right."

"Oh, you call him Cliff, do you?"

"Occasionally," Charles said. "There's no use being sensitive about people like Cliff."

"Well, as long as he doesn't feel he has to exercise seigniorial rights."

"What?" Charles asked.

"Oh, nothing. All those horsy people are highly sexed. What have you been doing all day?"

"I was stuck in the Whitakers' apartment."

"Oh," Nancy said, "the Whitakers. Did anything else happen?"

He knew he would have to tell her about Clyde and that he was going away tomorrow but he did not want to tell her then, to the sound of Mr. Blatz and the saxophone.

"Did you say anything to Tony Burton?"

"No," Charles said, "not exactly."

"How do you mean, not exactly?"

"What I say. Not exactly."

"Roger Blakesley's here tonight. Have you seen him?"

"No, but I've seen him all day."

"He looks exuberant."

"Oh," Charles said, "does he?"

"You look a little tired, darling."

"Well," Charles said, "I am tired."

"Did the children get you your supper?"

"Yes," Charles said. "Thanks for leaving the car. Whose table did you sit at?"

"Oh, the usual crowd," Nancy said. "They all missed you."

"Well, what's all this about Cliff Dunbarton?"

There was no time to answer. Someone had clapped him on the shoulder and they separated. It was Christopher DeMille, who lived two doors away from them and who wrote advertising copy.

"Hello, beautiful," Christopher said. "Are you two quarreling?"

"No," Nancy said. "We're having a second honeymoon."

"You ought to see Bess and me," Christopher said. "Bess and I always get fighting here on Tuesday nights. There's something in the atmosphere."

Charles moved away carefully over the dance floor. He could not imagine why anyone would think that he and Nancy had been quarreling.

VIII

We're All in the Same Boat — Eventually

THEN CHARLES DANCED with Bea Merrill. Even though he did not enjoy dancing this was always something of an adventure — not that it was not expected of him and of other husbands, because of poor Tom Merrill. Charles had observed that everyone was beginning to refer to Bea's husband as "poor Tom," and this had no reference to his financial status because he was doing very well. Instead it must have arisen from the rumor that the Merrills were not getting on, and of course this was Bea's fault and not poor Tom's. Other wives were beginning to say that Bea was beginning to be talked *about* instead of simply *over*. You talked *over* couples, they said, like the Sellers and the Kendricks, wondering how they ever could get along together, or afford new cars on their incomes, but you talked *about* Bea, not that Bea was not a sweet, generous girl, but discontented, restless, and full of high spirits, even when Tom was always giving her everything she wanted, like a diamond clip at Christmas time.

It was even intimated by some of the men that Bea had what was known as hot pants, a vague condition that made wives check over afterwards whose husbands had danced with Bea on Tuesday nights — not that anyone was told not to dance with her as Bea was part of the crowd and no one wanted to hurt poor Tom. Besides, most of those stories about Bea, other wives said when they got together, were spiteful stories invented by jealous people, and certainly they were not jealous of poor Bea. Why should anyone be jealous of a kindhearted, restless little thing with a high voice who did not know what she wanted? It was true there was a story about Bea and a man, a house guest of the Kendricks', from New

York, in poor Tom's coupé at the Labor Day dance, but no one was quite sure whether it had been Bea or that girl who had come from Old Lyme who looked like Bea. There was also the story about Bea diving into the swimming pool without a stitch on, not a stitch, but Bea herself had said that it had just been a hot summer night and she had just taken off her dress and nothing else — she was more covered than if she had worn a two-piece bathing suit. She hadn't even taken off her nylons. Still it was always an adventure, a slight step into the unknown, to dance with Bea. She was wearing a new black, sheathlike dress and the diamond clip that poor Tom had given her.

"Hello, darling," Bea said. "Have you read any good books lately?"

"I'm trying to read one called *Peace of Mind*," Charles said, "but I don't seem to be getting very far with it."

"My God," Bea said, "you're just like Tom. What do you need peace of mind for? Do you know what I've been thinking? I wish I were a Catholic. I wish that someone could tell me what to do."

"That's a great idea," Charles said, "but then you wouldn't do it."

"How do you know I wouldn't?" Bea asked, and then the music stopped. "Let's get out of here. Let's go outside."

This was not desirable because everyone always noticed who Bea's partner was when she left the dance floor. True, it was too cool outside to sit down and besides there were other couples on the terrace, but when Bea took his arm he knew that everyone was looking.

"Where's Tom tonight?" Charles asked.

"Where he usually is," Bea said. "In the office, working late, darling."

"I was late, too," Charles said.

"Yes," Bea said. "Well, here we are." Charles did not answer. It was obvious that they were out on the terrace.

"Darling, are you bored?" Bea asked.

"Why, no," Charles said, "of course I'm not."

"Well, I am."

"Never mind," Charles said, and he laughed. "In just a minute or two the music will be going around again."

"And it bores me to think of it," Bea said. "Everything goes around, right back to the same thing. Why can't you and I talk to each other like two sensible people? I don't mean about sex. You don't have that effect on me. To hell with sex."

Her voice had a rasping quality that could carry into out-of-the-way corners and tomorrow they would be saying that he and Bea Merrill had been talking about sex while poor Tom was working late.

"All right, Bea," he said, and he laughed. "Just remember I didn't bring it up."

Then Bea began to laugh.

"I don't have to remember. Darling, I don't suppose you've noticed, I don't suppose you've ever seen, the efforts I've made for years to make you bring it up."

That was why it was an adventure to dance with Bea Merrill. He could not very well help thinking of Bea Merrill in the coupé on Labor Day and of Bea Merrill in the pool.

"Why, Bea," he said, "don't give up. Please try again sometime."

"For years and years," Bea said. "You're completely unassailable, darling — but then it wouldn't work anyway, would it? Our loving friends here surround us with chastity."

"What?" Charles said. "How do you mean, with chastity?"

"You know what I mean," Bea answered. Her voice carried perfectly and he noticed that couples around them had stopped to listen unobtrusively. "This is the chastest place I know, but that isn't what I'm talking about."

"Well, what are you talking about?" Charles asked.

"I'm talking about you and me. Do we really know each other? Answer me that — do we?"

It was one of those conversations to which Bea was growing addicted lately, and he wished that the music would start.

"Why, you and Tom and Nancy and I have seen quite a lot of each other," he said.

"But do we *know* each other? Does anybody around here really know anybody else? We all call each other by our first names, we're a big happy family doing parlor tricks, but do we know each other? — and I don't mean getting into bed with someone, either."

It seemed to Charles that there were no other voices on the terrace and that the waiting couples were drawing closer.

"Well, that would be a basis for acquaintance," Charles said. "At least, that's what I've always heard."

"Well, it isn't," Bea said, and she gave his arm an impatient tug. "I don't know Tom. I don't know Tom at all."

Charles began to feel very much like Tom.

"Listen, Bea," he said, "perhaps you're expecting too much, perhaps nobody does know anyone else so very well."

"But, darling," Bea said. "How well do you know Nancy? Didn't there use to be a time — "

The music started and Charles was very glad of it, and he was glad, too, that Cliff Dunbarton had seen them and was hurrying toward them.

"Have you two about finished?" Cliff asked.

"Why, yes," Charles said. "We were talking about knowing people, and chastity."

"Well, let's dance," Cliff said, "in a chaste way."

Charles watched them move toward the dance floor. It was true, what she had said, that they all knew a lot about each other yet very few of them really knew each other. He would have to dance at least once more. Considering everything, it would be advisable for business reasons to dance with Molly Blakesley. There were probably rumors already about himself and Roger and if he were not seen dancing with Molly someone would be bound to notice it. Still he did not want to, because there were things about Roger's wife that made him very nervous, not the same things at all that stirred him when he danced with Bea Merrill. There would be no brisk innuendoes about sex when he danced with Molly, no disturbing mental pictures.

Roger had wooed and won Molly in Cambridge, Massachusetts, while he was a student at the Harvard School of Business Administration. She was the daughter of a Harvard Business School professor, had gone to a Cambridge progressive school, and was finishing her junior year at Radcliffe, where she was specializing in social science, when Roger had met her at her father's house on Coolidge Hill Road. She had been interested in the New Deal in those days and was writing a thesis on the Tennessee Valley Authority, a preparation which did not help her at those parties at Oak Knoll. Charles had thought of her first only as a plump, earnest girl with glasses and once he had made a particular effort to be kind to her, but now kindness was no longer necessary. Instead it seemed to him that of late Molly was the one who was being kind to him. Molly had made what she herself would have called a beautiful adjustment. She had given up long ago going to Boston for her clothes, and Henri in New York looked after her hair, and she only wore her glasses now for reading. She specialized in Japanese iris and columbine in her little back garden at Sycamore Park, but she did not call them iris and columbine. To Molly they were *I. Kaempferi* and *Aquilegia*. Once after a visit to that garden, Charles had suggested to Nancy that she might do more with flowers herself — she had always been good with flowers — but Nancy had said there was no time for flowers with children. There was no doubt that children were hostages to fortune. The thought flitted across his mind as he saw Molly Blakesley dancing with Walter Crumm.

The trouble with dancing with Molly Blakesley was that since that situation had arisen at the bank they each knew too well what the other was thinking. He suspected that her dress must have come from Bergdorf's and must have cost at least a hundred and fifty dollars, which Roger could afford because the Blakesleys did not have children. He wished that he did not keep putting their lives into terms of dollars and cents and that he did not always seem to be going over expenses whenever he danced with Molly Blakesley. It was necessary to be careful with her, too. She had a way of remembering everything one said, accurately and usefully. She was a very good wife to Roger.

"Well, well, Charley," Walter Crumm said. "Who stole Bea away from you?"

"She said she was bored," Charles told him. "She said I was unassailable."

"Well, well," Walter said. "He didn't look unassailable, did he, Molly?"

"Oh, were you out there too?" Charles asked.

"We certainly were," Walter said, "but we won't tell Nancy, will we, Molly?"

It was all good clean fun, a part of the spirit of Oak Knoll, and you had to take it that way. Yet at the same time, Charles knew that Roger would hear of it, and it was the sort of thing that Roger might be able to use with Tony Burton — all in good clean fun.

"Poor Tom," Molly said. "But it was awfully funny, Charley. You didn't look like a banker."

"Perhaps Roger won't either," Charles said, "if Bea gets him out there."

"Roger wouldn't let Bea get him out there. You know how Roger can side-step." Molly laughed brightly.

"That must be the Harvard Business School training," Charles said, and he smiled back at Molly.

"Charley," Molly said, "seriously, do you know what Roger was saying the other night, when we were just alone in the kitchen having a drink of beer?"

It was a time to be careful, but Charles still smiled.

"We were talking about you and Nancy, and Roger was saying how fond everyone is of you at the bank, Roger particularly. You know how full he is of everything at the bank. And he was saying how wonderful it was that we were all such good friends and he hoped we always would stay friends, no matter what happens at the bank. You know what I mean. It's so embarrassing, isn't it?"

"It needn't be embarrassing," Charles said. "Roger and I are grown-up. We can handle anything that happens."

"You know," Molly spoke more quickly, "I think the war did you a lot of good, Charley. Roger thinks so, too."

Charles did not answer. It was kind of her to say it, but he wished that he was not always searching for hidden meanings when he listened to Molly Blakesley.

"I think it was pretty splendid of you," she was saying, "with a wife and two children, to give up everything and go to the war. Roger thinks so, too."

He could not bring himself to care what Roger thought.

"It was a sort of compulsion," he said. "It wasn't wise, and I wasn't much use when I got there."

"How lovely Nancy looks," Molly said. "She always looks lovely in the simplest dress. That's what Roger always says. How are the children, Charley?"

"Why, they're pretty well," Charles answered, "except they keep turning on the radio."

"Do you know what Roger said the other day? He's so sentimental, sometimes. He said he wished they'd call him Uncle Roger."

He was balancing Molly's kindness against the possibility that she had heard something which he had not heard about the bank and Owen Martin cut in before he could answer. Neighbors always had to dance with neighbors' wives.

"I'll see you later, Charley," Molly called. "Perhaps we can do something Sunday. Roger would love it if we could."

Now that Charles had danced with Molly Blakesley, he felt that he had done enough, but it was still too early to be seen going home, even though he wanted to go home very much. His imagination was aroused by Molly Blakesley. Certainly Roger had thought it a fine thing that he had gone to the war. If he had not gone, if he had stayed put, there would have been no doubt about anything in the bank.

Out in the passageway that led to the men's locker room, he glanced at the plaque which must have been placed there in the early days of the conflict — the club's honor roll of members and employees, carefully differentiated, who had gone, as the plaque said, to serve their country. There were more employees than members, and three gold stars against employees' names with only one in the members' list. That was the Wilkes boy, Joe Wilkes's son. Most of the other members had been overage. The plaque itself was in the shadows, a good place for it now that the war was over.

Nancy was always saying that it was a bad thing for him to drink after dinner and he had always found that alcohol only exaggerated malaise. Nevertheless, as long as he could not leave, he wanted to get away from the music. There were two bars in the club, the women's bar, with new chromium furnishings and red leather-topped stools — he could hear the loud chatter from it as he passed — and the men's bar behind the men's locker room, a Teutonic looking place which had been built before prohibition and before women needed bars of their own.

Charles opened the locker room door and walked along the wood grating past the rows of green steel lockers. He was going to the men's bar because, though it was open to all male members theoretically, it had a clannish atmosphere that discouraged certain members from entering. In fact, Charles had never entered it until Mr. Forbush, who was still president of Oak Knoll, had once asked him why he never joined the crowd there. You could either stand up at the bar, or carry your drink to one of the locker room benches if you'd been playing golf, or else sit at the single round table.

The individuals sitting at the table that night all were drawn together by the common guilty bond of having made an escape. They all knew implicitly that they should be dancing, and they weren't. They all half apologized for being there, and they were just going to stay for a minute. They were hot and their feet were tired. Bill Forbush, who was sitting at the table, always said at every dance that he was only going to stay for a minute. He only wanted to drop in to see that everyone was behaving, and Joe Swiss was there, just for a minute, too, and Walter Crumm must have come in there after his dance with Nancy. And so had Christopher DeMille, just for a minute, and Roger Blakesley was there, just to take the weight off his feet for a minute. When they saw Charles they all greeted him heartily, as though his appearance salved their consciences for being there, just for a minute. Slim, the barkeeper, who was leaning over the bar listening and occasionally taking part in the conversation, also seemed glad to see him.

"What's the matter, Charley," Bill Forbush called, "are your arches falling?"

"Sit down and take your weight off your feet, Charley."

"All right," Charles said, "I will, for just a minute."

"What did you do with Bea, Charley?" Christopher DeMille called.

He was already getting tired of hearing about Bea.

"She left me for a handsomer, richer man," Charles said.

"Who's handsomer?" Christopher asked. "You're handsomer than Dunbarton. Look at him. Isn't Charley handsomer than Dunbarton?"

"What were you and Bea talking about?" Roger Blakesley asked. "Investments, Charley?"

"Come on and tell us everything," Joe Swiss said. "The rumor is that you were talking about chastity."

Charles did not like to think he was growing angry. He preferred to think that only an academic question of taste made him feel alone and aloof from all the group. Their faces looked alike, stupid, overweight and middle-aged, but at the same time it was all good clean fun.

"Slim," he said, "give me a double Scotch, please."

Then he saw that Roger was drinking ginger ale. He remembered that Molly had said that Roger had learned *never* to drink after dinner.

"Charley," Mr. Forbush said, "have you got your name down for a new car?"

Charles said that he and Nancy were worrying along with the old Buick and that he felt it had better stuff in it than most of the new cars, and Joe Swiss said he was absolutely right. Mr. Swiss had a close, personal friend from Detroit who had told him a thing or two about those new cars, a thing or two that Chris DeMille and these other word artists never wrote into their advertisements. The truth was that a lot of stuff that was going into those new cars was junk, pure junk, and it was not all labor cost, though a lot of the trouble was sloppy labor. No one wanted to do a day's work any more, no matter what you paid him. Yet putting all that aside, look what was going into the new cars. All this rumor about plastics and new gadgets was turning out to be eyewash. Look at the paint jobs. Look at the so-called chromium finish that rusted overnight.

It was a conversation Charles had heard often before and everyone else must have heard it too, yet they all listened as if it were a new discovery. Charles himself sat listening without having to put his mind on it. Perhaps this was why so many people enjoyed these conversations. You knew what was coming next. It might be communism. It might be the advisability of pouring money down the European rat hole. At any rate, you did not have to think. All those ideas had worn comfortable grooves in your mind.

But then you had to buy a new car sometime, Mr. Forbush was saying, and what happened then? You went to a dealer, didn't you, and could you get a new car at the list price? — not any more than you could get a piece of porterhouse steak. They made you buy accessories, extra bumpers, radios, heaters. Everyone was listening in silent agreement. Mr. Forbush was having a hell of a time with that new car dealer. Somehow it was agreeable to hear the details of Mr. Forbush's suffering. It was a sort of universal cosmic grief and it was a long way from actual want — and in the end you did not really have to listen.

Charles found his mind moving off at a tangent. He saw Joe Swiss close his eyes and nod. He saw Chris DeMille making designs on the table with burned matches. They were all caught in a current that jostled them and interfered with normal existence. All anyone could do was to try to adjust his life within the limits of a constantly changing frame. That was the difficulty. Even the limits were continually changing.

The limits of happiness itself, Charles was thinking, were continually changing. You got somewhere and then you wanted to move somewhere else, to another, larger bar, to better, brighter company. Charles could still remember how pleased he had been when Mr. Forbush had asked him why he did not drop in sometimes and sit at the round table. It had meant that he had made good, that he was a part of a small group within a group. It had never occurred to him then that Mr. Forbush could be dull or Mr. Swiss either, or that they were older men whose thought processes had slowed until

128

their minds ran in instinctive circles. He wondered if his own mind might be slowing also, because he did not give a continental damn what Mr. Forbush paid for a new car.

"Just wait, Bill," Christopher DeMille was saying. "There's a Ford in your future like the Ford in your past."

"I don't want a Ford," Mr. Forbush was saying. "I'm not talking about a Ford."

"It's only a figure of speech, Bill," Christopher was answering.

"You know," Roger Blakesley said, "in one way this talk is mighty interesting to me."

"In what way?" Christopher DeMille asked. "It doesn't interest Joe Swiss." Mr. Swiss was nodding, but he opened his eyes when his name was mentioned.

"It interests me," Roger said, "because it just goes to show we're in the same boat. No matter what happens, we're still in the same boat."

Charles moved uneasily in his hard oak armchair. Roger's voice was brisk and cheerful, full of sweet reason. Charles did not know why it should have annoyed him, except that it brought a disagreeable picture before him of himself and Roger in a small boat, each knowing that there was not room enough in it for two.

"You mean we've all got to pull together?" Charles asked.

"Now, Charley," Roger said, "don't be bitter. If we're not in a boat, where are we?"

"I don't know where we are," Charles said, "and neither does anybody else. But it doesn't do any good to oversimplify, Roger."

"What?" Mr. Swiss asked, and he woke up again. "How do you mean we don't know where we are?"

Charles saw from the way they were all watching him that he had introduced a new idea at an unpropitious time. He shifted his position again in his hard oak chair. He had not intended to get into an argument with Roger.

"I think we're in a pretty good boat," Roger said. "It rocks a little but it's the best boat in the world and I'm glad I'm aboard and I guess everyone else is."

From the way everyone else was listening, he was sure that they must have heard something about the bank. He could think of no other reason for their fascinated, strained attention.

"That's right," Charles said, "as long as we don't get tossed over board. Well, I've got to be getting along now. It's pretty late." He stood up and smiled and said good night and walked away through the open door of the bar and over the worn boards of the dimly lighted locker room. As he left he was aware of a silence behind him. As far as he could recall, he had said nothing unusual, and yet something must have been wrong or they would have started talking. In some way he had been a disturbing element back in the bar. They were not speaking. They were waiting carefully until his footsteps died away; and what would they be saying then? He did not know, and it did no good to tell himself that he did not care. He had not made good with his group. They were all like strangers to him. He had not fitted in.

It was now late enough so that no one would say they were leaving early, and it was early enough so that no one would say the Grays were always up late at parties. It was, in fact, the right psychological moment for going home, and Nancy was waiting for him, because, as Nancy often said, she had been a working girl herself. It did not take Nancy half a minute to get her wraps on, and she was even waiting at the steps of the club when he drove there from the parking space, instead of allowing herself to be drawn into conversation like other people's wives.

"Move over. I'll drive," Nancy said.

All he had to do was to thank her and to feel pleased that she not only knew he was tired but cared about it. Probably she also knew that the combinations of his day had not turned out very well, but she would not ask questions. She would wait for him to tell her, because she knew he would, eventually — but then, what was there to tell? There was only a premonition. There was nothing to explain, because the disturbance was inside himself.

"These parties," he said, "sometimes they're good and sometimes they're bad. Did you have a good time, Nance?"

"Well, yes," she answered, "in a sort of long-term way."

"How do you mean, a long-term way?"

"You know," Nancy said. "It's what I've told you before. I like feeling we belong somewhere. You know it's what I've always wanted."

"Well, so do I," Charles said. "So does everyone."

Nancy knew every turn on the road home, and she took each turn as unconsciously as a taxi driver.

"It isn't the same for a man," she said. "He always belongs much more than a woman, up to a certain point. A woman just has to tag along. It's nice, when she likes tagging."

"What did you do all day?" Charles asked.

"You always ask that. You don't have to."

"I know I don't have to," Charles said. "I just want to know."

There was a slight pause before she answered.

"I've had a good day, but you wouldn't understand why. It's partly being a woman. I took the car to the Acme place and got the choke fixed. Do you notice the engine goes better?"

"That's right," Charles said. "I notice now."

"Then I went to the A & P and bought some corned beef. Then I left Bill's shoes at that place below the drugstore, that new Italian place."

"I wonder why Italians always like to repair shoes," Charles said.

"Then I left that book of yours at the lending library. Then I bought some soap. I still keep buying soap whenever I see it. Then I came back and did the breakfast dishes. Then the man came to fix the unit in the stove, and while he was doing it the men from Hanson's came to wax the floor in the living room. I had to be there to see that they put everything back right. Then I went upstairs and made the beds and counted the laundry. Then I went over and had lunch with Polly Martin and helped her run up some new curtains, because she's going to lend me her sewing machine. I don't know why Polly wants everything in chintz — curtains, dresses, everything. Then I came back and worked on the bills."

"How were they?"

"They were terrible. There were two mistakes again on the Thaxter bill, always plus mistakes, never minus. I called him up about it, and then Bill and I glued the back of your old chair in the hall, and then I read to Evelyn for a while."

"What did you read her?" Charles asked.

"You'd be surprised. I read her Plutarch. Then there was their supper, and the Martins called, and we all went over to the club. That's all. I knew it wouldn't sound like much if I tried to tell it, but it was a very nice day."

"I'm glad you liked it," Charles said, "but I don't see why."

They had passed through the gates of Sycamore Park, up the blue gravel of their own short drive, and the car had stopped.

"I'll tell you why," Nancy said. "Because I'm married to a damn nice man. That's the only possible reason I can think of. Now get out and open the garage door and don't jerk at it."

That door had never worked well in wet weather. Charles opened it carefully and stood holding it so that it would not swing to while Nancy drove the car inside, close to the garden tools, and shut off the lights. Then she was beside him in the dark.

"And now you can give me a kiss," she said.

IX

A Fitting Place for the Enshrinement of Ancestral Relics

ONLY THE LIGHT at the top of the stairs was lighted, but the switch was just beside the door. There was a smell of fresh floor wax from the living room, and a moist smell in the dining room from Nancy's potted plants.

"Charley," Nancy said, "isn't it a lovely house?"

"Yes, it's a swell house," Charles said. Nancy had taken off her evening wrap and was straightening her hair by the mirror.

"I know it's got outs about it," Nancy said, "but don't forget one thing. You and I did this by ourselves, without any so-and-so to help us. I suppose you think it's a corny thing to say, but that's why it's a nice house."

Of course, the appearance of any house depended on one's state of mind, and now he was feeling more cheerful.

"And now come in and look at the living room floor," Nancy said. "Do you want a glass of milk before you go to bed?" The last thing he wanted was a glass of milk, but then Nancy had known that he had taken a drink after dinner.

The living room was always too neat for him ever to feel at home in it. The logs in the fireplace had a little paper fan beneath them, ready for a match, but the fire was too beautifully constructed for him to want to disturb the logs by lighting them, especially so late in the evening. Everything was dusted, every ornament on the tables was exactly where it should be. The picture of the ship above the mantelpiece, which had come from Clyde, had been cleaned and was bright with new varnish.

"I forgot to tell you," Nancy said, "it came back today from Jacobson's."

"They did a good job on it, didn't they?" Charles said, and he thought of that page in *Yankee Persepolis* about the lower upper family. The picture had hung in a shabbier room in Clyde. Here it was stiffly formal, the central theme of a self-conscious decorative scheme.

"We ought to use this room more, shouldn't we?" Nancy said. "I wonder why we don't."

"That's easy," Charles said. "Because we're afraid of it."

"Well, let's not be afraid of it," Nancy said, and she lighted a cigarette. "Charley, take off your coat and sit down on the sofa." Nancy kicked off her slippers. "Don't say we're afraid of this room. I don't like it."

"Why not?" Charles asked.

"Because I don't like being afraid."

She looked as though she were startled by her last words. She had a blank, embarrassed, provoked expression and she caught herself up quickly before he had a chance to answer.

"I don't mean that I'm afraid of anything. I only mean I don't like the idea. You know what I mean."

Every word only made a top-heavy structure destined eventually for a clumsy fall. It was like the match game so popular before the war, that late evening pastime in which you laid a match over the mouth of the bottle and then your opponent laid one upon it, and so it went until there was a tower of matches rising in the air. The loser was the one who put on the last match and tipped it over. Nancy had put on the last match. The room was uncomfortable and strange in an entirely new way; and he seemed to see it, and Nancy too, through a lens that had suddenly come into focus. Charles found himself passing his hand over the stuff on the sofa, half aware of its softness and of its light color, which, Nancy had said, would show every spot, though admittedly it was just the right shade. Now that the truth was there, now that the thing was there in the living room — the thing of which neither of them had spoken — it was a relief, in a way.

"Nance," Charles said, "we didn't use to be afraid."

She was sitting opposite him on one of those small upholstered chairs, very straight, just the way she had been sitting the day he had first seen her.

"Oh, are you afraid too?" she asked, and though his instinct was already preparing him to answer that of course he was not, he found himself nodding slowly.

"Well, you might have told me," Nancy said.

"It's all relative, you know, Nance," he said.

"What's relative?" She spoke impatiently.

"The more you get, the more afraid you get. That's all I mean," Charles said. "Maybe fear's what makes the world go round."

"Not love?" Nancy said, and she tilted her head sideways. "I used to hear that it was love."

It reminded him of the first night he had taken Nancy anywhere, when they were both obviously trying to impress each other. There was the same atmosphere of suspense, the same effort to be at one's best, and the same intense consciousness of each other. It was almost like falling in love, an unfamiliar sensation now — but they were talking about fear.

"Of course," Charles said. "Everyone's afraid of something — afraid of living, afraid of dying. Maybe it's better than being afraid of losing money. That's what the boys are afraid of downtown. Do you know what I wish?"

"What?" Nancy asked.

He was filled with a childish desire to show off before Nancy. It was almost like falling in love.

"I wish we weren't always being pushed around. I'd like for once in my life to be able to tell someone to go to hell."

She was smiling at him as he had seen her smile at Bill when he asked for an impossible Christmas present.

"Darling," she said, "basically you have the most expensive tastes. You'd better just tell me to go to hell, if you want to, and let it go at that."

"All right," Charles said, "but it isn't the same thing, is it?"

"Maybe it isn't," Nancy said, "but I'm awfully glad we're afraid

135

of the same thing. It's healthy to have things in common I'm awfully glad we're in the same boat, darling."

"That's what Roger said tonight," he told her.

"What else did he say," Nancy asked, "and what did Molly say?"

"She said you looked lovely in the plainest frock," Charles said, "and Roger thinks so too, and he wants the children to call him Uncle Roger and she wants us all to do something together on Sunday, and Roger does too. Wait a minute, there's something else I've got to tell you. I'm taking the plane to Boston first thing in the morning. I'm going up to Clyde for a day or two on business for the bank."

He saw Nancy's lips tighten. Then he saw her grind the end of her cigarette carefully into an ash tray.

"How did Clyde get into it?" she asked.

"It's funny the way things happen," he began. "When I got up this morning it was raining, do you remember? I looked out of the window at the trees. They reminded me of Clyde. Spring's always late at Clyde. No one ever admits it. Every year they only say that it's a late spring. Have you ever found yourself thinking about a thing and then finding later that something was happening about it?"

He saw Nancy glance uneasily about the room, as though she were afraid that someone might be listening.

"When something bad happens," she said, "you keep going back and wondering how it started."

"I don't see why you always get edgy whenever I mention Clyde," he said.

"You know very well why," Nancy answered. "Clyde makes you difficult. It's a queer place full of ingrown people, and you say so yourself."

It always made him sensitive when she began criticizing Clyde, even when her points were well taken. He had never expected her to fit into Clyde. He had never asked her to, and he knew what she thought about it without her telling him.

"I can't help it if I was brought up there," he said, and it occurred to him that he might say something to Nancy about upstate New

York and about Nancy's town with its gingerbread trimmings and its pseudo-Greek columns.

"Never mind," Nancy said. "You're always peculiar when you think about Clyde."

"Well, when I was at the bank," Charles began, "a man came in to see me and who do you think it was? I didn't recognize him at first. It was Malcolm Bryant."

"Oh," Nancy said. "You used to talk about him quite a lot once."

"That's the one," Charles said. "He wanted to marry Jessica Lovell once."

"Oh," Nancy said. "I always thought you were the one who wanted to marry Jessica Lovell." She said it in a very slow, disinterested way, as though Jessica Lovell bored her.

Charles spoke more loudly so that Nancy could not interrupt. "Then I went to the morning meeting, in the depositors' room downstairs by the vault . . ."

At last he was back where he wanted to be, telling her the details of that meeting and about the collateral on the loan and the stock in that company in Clyde. Then he told about Tony Burton's having called him later, and it was a relief to go into it fully. He never should have mentioned Jessica Lovell. Nancy was sitting up straight again, following every word.

"So you've got to go away for a day or two right now?" she asked. "At just this time?"

"Yes, it looks that way," Charles said.

"Why didn't you do anything about it? Why didn't you ask them to send someone else?" When it came to the bank, Nancy was always right there with him.

"I thought of it," he said, "but I think that anything I might have said would have made it worse. You'd have thought so too."

"If I'd been there, I'd have done something," Nancy said. "Something. Anything."

"No," Charles told her, "you just think so because you're here. If you'd been there, you'd have let it go. Besides" — he stopped and stared at the design on the Islamic rug — no animals, nothing but symbols — "I don't think it makes much difference. I think

Tony Burton's about made up his mind which of us he wants.

Suddenly Nancy stood up.

"Then for God's sake why doesn't he tell you instead of letting us — letting us — " Her voice choked on the last words and she swallowed.

"Because perhaps he doesn't like to do it," Charles said. "Tony's quite a nice guy, as far as anyone like him can be nice. I think we'll get the news when we go there to dinner. He almost said so."

Nancy stood looking straight ahead of her. She did not answer, and Charles went on.

"Besides, maybe it's just as well for me to be away. Tony knows Roger worked it, at least I think he knows. Maybe Roger will try a little too much. Tony's rather bright sometimes."

Nancy still stood there and he noticed that her hands were clenched.

"If he picks out that damn fool he isn't bright."

"I only said," Charles told her, "that he's pretty bright sometimes."

Nancy was no longer staring in front of her at nothing. She was looking at him in a level, appraising way, putting herself in Tony Burton's place, balancing his faults against his assets, wondering whether he had the personality and the broad-gauge ability to occupy one of the front desks.

"Listen," Charles said, "it doesn't do any good trying to look like a statue on a courthouse."

"If you'd only get mad," Nancy said.

"You were just saying it's a luxury," Charles said. "There's no use getting mad at a system. We're part of a system where there's always someone waiting to kick you in the teeth in a nice way."

"It's a rotten system," Nancy said.

"Maybe it is," Charles answered. "A lot of people have been saying so lately." He looked up at her and smiled, but she did not answer.

"Of course if I hadn't been away at the war there wouldn't be anything to it."

"You never should have gone," Nancy said. "I told you so."

"Yes," Charles said. "Yes. I remember."

Nancy sighed and sat down again.

138

"Haven't you any idea at all," she asked, "which one of you he's going to take?"

Then Charles felt a slight twinge of anger. It had been a long time since he had seen himself so clearly — tied down by little things. They were a steady accumulation of little things, innocuous in themselves, like the ropes the Lilliputians used to pin down Gulliver — the ship picture, the Islamic rug, the wax on the floor, the mortgage, the insurance policy, tiny half-forgotten decisions, words suddenly spoken.

"Charley," Nancy asked, "what's the matter?"

"Nothing," Charles said.

"Charley, what'll you do if he takes Roger?"

"Nance," he said, "let's not think about it now," but of course both of them were thinking about it now. The irony of it was that after years of work one became specialized, used to the ways of just one organization, too old to start again in a new one. He had seen plenty of men his age looking for a job.

"Charley," Nancy said, "if you'd ever done something about investing for yourself instead of for other people — "

"Nance, you know very well," he answered, "you don't do much of that when you're working for a bank."

Nancy sighed and stood up again.

"Well," she said, "I guess we'd better go to bed."

Charles stood up too.

"You go ahead," he told her. "I'll be up in a few minutes. Good night, Nance."

After he had kissed her, she buried her head on his shoulder. She made no sound but he knew she was crying, and it always gave him a completely helpless feeling when she cried.

"Don't, Nance," he said. "The show isn't over."

"I'm sorry, Charley," Nancy said. "I'm all right now. You always hate having me cry, don't you?"

"Yes," Charles said. "Go on up to bed, Nance. I'll be up in just a minute."

"Are you sorry you married me?"

"No," Charles said, "of course not, Nancy."

"I suppose I sort of made you marry me."

"Why, Nance," Charles said, "I never noticed that you did."

"Are you sorry we had the children?"

"No, of course I'm not," Charles said.

"They were my idea more than yours. Are you sorry we bought the house?"

"Listen, Nance," Charles said, "it happened, like the children. Now go on up and go to sleep. I'll be up in just a minute."

"What are you going to do?" Nancy asked. "Are you going to sit here and worry?"

"No, I'm not," he told her. "I'm not sleepy. I'm going to read for a little while."

"Because if you're going to worry, we might as well do it together."

"I'm going to read," Charles said. "I'm pretty well worried out tonight. Good night, Nance" — and he kissed her again, and walked with her to the foot of the stairs. "I'll be sitting in the library."

"Don't be long," Nancy said. "I won't be able to get to sleep till you come up."

Yankee Persepolis — A Social Study was lying just where he had left it earlier in the evening on top of his brief case on the table in the hall. As Nancy went upstairs, he picked it up because it occurred to him that, considering his mood, something absolutely new was better to read than something he had read before.

All he could do was to recognize his present state of mind as a definite malady like a cold or a fever and tell himself that it would pass. He knew the symptoms well enough. First there was a period of general uneasiness about nothing in particular, and then a growing illusion of being hemmed in, followed by a desire to escape, and finally an indescribable sense of loneliness mingled with a sort of deep self-pity which he particularly hated. He wished he had not mentioned Jessica Lovell, as she was always a part of the shadows which surrounded him suddenly and swiftly when he was in that mood. The only thing to do was to tell himself to behave, that he would be better in a little while. It was also time to consider the dangers of inheritance, and to remember his father.

"Charley," he could hear his mother saying, "don't bother him. He's in one of his spells again."

Charles himself had never particularly noticed his father's "spells" until the summer of 1916 but they must have been chronic because his brother Sam had often spoken of them as though they had been going on a long time.

There was always a brittle atmosphere in the house on those occasions. His father was usually in his room with his books, on the second floor, and the door would be locked. His mother and Dorothea would be talking in whispers in the kitchen. There used to be a tradition that everyone should ignore those periods of dejection, and all the family did, except Sam when he was alive. Sam never had any patience with them.

"We all know what the Old Man was doing up in Boston," Sam had told him once, "and now he wants us to be sorry for him. He ought to have a good shoot in the tail."

Sam was the only one who said such things and Charles believed him and he still could not escape that old impression that Sam had been a great man, although Sam could have only been about seventeen at the time.

"You can always tell when it's coming," Sam used to say. "It goes in a circle. It starts as soon as he gets a check."

Their Aunt Mathilda Gray's estate was being settled in 1916 and whenever a parcel of her real estate was sold, John Gray would get a check in the mail from Mr. Blashfield, the executor. First he would open the letter and look at the check, and then he would go down to the bank and deposit it in his special account, and then for a while a pleasant wave of prosperity descended on the household. He would come home each evening with a copy of the *Boston Evening Transcript* and everyone would watch him as he sat in the parlor after supper reading the *Transcript's* financial page. First he would only glance at it. Then in a few evenings he would read it when he thought no one was looking. Then he would read it openly. Everyone knew what John Gray was going to do, even if he did not know himself, and he probably did not know, because he had promised on his word of honor never to touch those things again.

He would be highly indignant if his wife or his sister Jane attempted to bring up the subject. It was better not to stir him up. Perhaps a week later he would say that he was going to take a day off and go up to Boston. He hadn't seen Boston for a long while.

When he came back from the day in Boston, he was invariably exuberant. He usually returned with a box of candy and some magazines, and generally he smelled strongly of bay rum, showing that he had been to the barbershop at the Parker House. Then he would begin to discuss scholarly subjects, especially the London of Samuel Johnson. He loved to re-create a world of coaches and sedan chairs and smoke-filled coffeehouses. You could never say that John Gray was not industrious or erudite. He could quote pages of Boswell, fitting them aptly into every occasion. Charles still winced at the sight of a Boswell's *Johnson,* and yet when he finally saw London for himself he knew many aspects of the city very well because of certain evenings back in Clyde.

"The Old Man's off again," Sam used to say. "You can tell it as soon as he starts on Mrs. Thrale."

Still it was not always a bad time when the Old Man was off again. It was a cultivated household for a while, after John Gray got back from Boston. There was no doubt that he was a delightful man.

"Your father might have been anything," his mother used to say, "anything."

The next week he would take another day off and go to Boston. This time he would return with a box of cigars and with a few French novels. The cigars were a definite part of a pattern, because John Gray usually smoked a pipe if he smoked at all. That was why Charles always hated Havana cigar smoke. At this period John Gray's thoughts would turn to Honoré de Balzac, his sleepless nights and his strange, frustrated love. Someday they must all go to Paris. It was ridiculous for Malcolm Bryant to have placed them in the lower-upper class. He should have seen John Gray when his brown mustache, usually dejected and drooping, was clipped like a British colonel's and when he had a new suit from Dunne's.

"By God," Sam used to say, "now he's upstairs juggling figures," and John Gray could do it, too. Charles had never seen anyone who could make mathematics as logical and simple. "He must be doing pretty well. Why doesn't the damn fool ever stop?"

Of course he never stopped. There would always be the last trip in the cycle, when John Gray came home from Boston with nothing to say at all. There would be a discreet silence in the house. There was nothing in the world quite like those silences. . . .

The library where Charles was sitting gave him a sense of not belonging anywhere. His mouth felt dry and his forehead felt moist and he was terribly alone.

"Charley." It was Nancy calling softly from the top of the stairs so as not to wake the children. "Charley, aren't you coming up to bed?"

"Yes, in just a little while, Nance," he answered. "I'm not sleepy."

"Oh, Charley," she called back, "please come up. It's after one o'clock."

"In just a few minutes, Nance," he said, and he opened the book he was holding.

Malcolm Bryant and his father had taken to each other from the very beginning and when Malcolm began dropping in at Spruce Street in the evenings years previously, Charles's mother was delighted. It was so good for Father, she said, to talk with an intelligent young man who could share Father's interests. They were interests which were boring to Charles because of constant exposure to them. To Charles, Samuel Johnson was a rude, untidy old gentleman with an itch, who had made a number of rash and not very brilliant statements, set down by an assiduous toady named Boswell, a snob who sucked up to the nobility and who had nothing better to do than to run after the old gentleman with a notebook. Charles could see nothing whatsoever in Johnson's heavy-handed prose. It was as slow as cold molasses, but now as he ran through the pages of *Yankee Persepolis,* he began to understand why Malcolm had been a Johnson addict and he understood at last what Malcolm had seen in his father. Malcolm had been attracted to John Gray not as an individual but as a social entity, an odd piece which he was trying to fit into the social puzzle of Clyde which had produced and tolerated him.

All at once it occurred to Charles that he was doing right now what his father had often succeeded in doing so magnificently. He was trying to forget the present by immersing himself in something else, by striving to identify himself with someone else. Instead of Samuel Johnson, he was using Malcolm Bryant. He did not care about Malcolm's ideas or his social worker's patter in themselves, except insofar as they took him away from his own ideas. If he could only concentrate on Malcolm, if he could only give him the attention that he had learned to give to papers at the bank, he could forget the bank altogether, he could forget the conference room and the antiseptic, oily smell of the vault, and Roger Blakesley and Tony Burton. He could forget the scene in the locker room and the queer, disturbing conversation by the window in the Whitakers' apartment, when that girl had made him think of Jessica Lovell. He could forget the knotty pine walls of the library which were enclosing him in impersonal mediocrity. Please, God, his mind was saying, get me out of this. Please get me out of this.

He was examining a chapter heading, "The Concepts behind This Survey." The words were as heavy as Johnson's words, without any of their waxy Chippendale polish. Social scientists were usually involved writers, who continually tripped over a jargon of their own invention. He again remembered Malcolm as the brain behind an agency of social spies, with an office force and card catalogues back in Boston.

Two of Malcolm's assistants, he remembered, had appeared one hot night at open house day on Johnson Street, a girl with dry brown hair and horn-rimmed spectacles, for whom he felt sorry because she was an outlander from the Middle West, and an undernourished man with an Adam's apple, who perspired beneath the armpits and only drank fruit punch. He never imagined that these two were a team of skillfully briefed probers who had been snooping innocuously through Clyde, standing away from it in a friendly way as though it were an ant hill, then worming their way deviously into the confidence of its inhabitants, sympathizing with frustrations, picking up gems of information, and rushing away secretively to an office to record those gems on charts of death and birth rates and of marriage incidence according to income groups. The investigative team operated according to scientific rules. They were directed to listen, when they buttonholed an individual, in a patient and friendly manner in order to discover the individual's approximate place in the society. They should only inject their own personalities in order to relieve fears or anxieties or to praise the interviewee. They should listen not only to what a person wanted to say but to what he did not say. All of this, according to Malcolm, demanded extreme flexibility. They must have done their work well, because Charles had seldom noticed it.

He remembered Malcolm Bryant and his team examining Clyde and occasionally descending to taste of its life, like minor gods and nymphs sporting with mortals. They were not interested in individuality, Malcolm was now explaining, but in social personality. It was clear now what Malcolm had been doing those evenings when he had called at Spruce Street and stayed for supper.

"Typical of a lower-upper family," Charles read again, "are the Henry Smiths — father, mother, son and daughter. Like other lower-upper families, they dwell on a side street ('side streeters'), yet are received on Mason Street. Mr. Smith, with investment interests in Boston . . ."

It was not fair to blame Malcolm, because it must have been confusing even for a god to know exactly what John Gray had been doing, but it was agreeable to remember that the god had fallen once.

"Charley." It was Nancy calling again from the top of the stairs. "Aren't you ever coming to bed?"

"All right," Charles called back. "I'll be up in just a minute, Nance, try to go to sleep."

"What are you doing down there?"

"I'm reading."

"Can't you read tomorrow?"

"I'll be up in just a minute," Charles said. "You'll wake the children up. Try to go to sleep."

His voice and Nancy's voice were only like the voices in a chorus. The interruption had not disturbed him.

"An upper-upper class family," he was reading as he spoke, "may be typified by the Johnsons, who live on the upper side of Mason Street in one of those fine, three-storied Federalist houses, capped by the delicate balustrade of the widow's or captain's walk."

Malcolm had let himself go at last. He was obviously describing the Lovells and their house on Johnson Street, studiously garbling the names, but as he had been writing, his memory of the Lovell house and of Mr. Laurence Lovell and Jessica must have blurred for an instant his concept of social personality.

"This gracious type of Federalist architecture is apparent here at its zenith. The gracious hallway of this mansion extends from front to rear, a fitting setting for the exquisite airy rising of its broad staircase . . ."

Yes, Malcolm Bryant for once had forgotten his social responsibility, now that he had turned from the Grays to the Lovells.

"A fitting place for the enshrinement of ancestral relics . . . a fitting frame for the rituals of the upper-upper class. . . . Mr. Johnson, a widower, suave and gracious, descendant of shipowners in the late eighteenth century, is a fitting head for the Johnson clan. Jacinth, his lovely only daughter, assisted by a maiden aunt, Miss Johnson, is eminently suited to give the family ritual an added charm. Her vivacity never quite conceals her seriousness or the impact of her social personality."

Yes, Malcolm Bryant had felt the impact of Jessica Lovell's social personality. He had forgotten that he was a social anthropologist, as he had penned those words. He had tried in a brief interval to be a poet in prose. He had contrived, within the limits of his talent, to express emotion and desire. He had called her Jacinth instead of calling her Mary or Molly or Miss X. In Malcolm's memory, Jessica was still there in the hallway, looking him straight in the eyes. She would never be Desdemona again and Malcolm would never be Othello, speaking of the habits of the Borneo head-hunters and the Zambesis or about that trip he would take some-day to the Orinoco.

"In the rear of the house," Charles was reading, "on a gentle slope rises the hundred-and-fifty-year-old Johnson formal garden, a verdant shrine of ancestor worship in itself, crowned by a delicate latticed summerhouse known as a gazebo." Malcolm Bryant would never sit in that gazebo again, but then neither would Charles Gray. Malcolm Bryant had shown without his knowing it that he had been impressed by austere beauty, a foreign interloper who could never have wholly grasped it. Through his own enthusiastic inadvertence, he had invoked a vision of Johnson Street — fantastic and beautiful on a dusky summer evening. Charles could see the broad uneven sidewalks of worn brick, pushed gently upwards by the roots of the elms. He could see the tall white fences with their urns and pineapples, and the houses rising behind them, disdainful of newer houses. He could see the cornices and the fanlights and the cupolas. The mere recollection of Johnson Street on a summer evening made this effort of Malcolm Bryant's a gross impertinence. It was still an impertinence when he thought of Spruce Street with its plainer picket fences, and of the moldering houses nearer the river inhabited by what Malcolm called the lower-lower class, the shanty Irish, not the lace-curtain Irish, and the Greeks and Poles. Malcolm Bryant and his team had seen them all and had checked them against their diagrams, but he and his team did not know Johnson Street or any other street in Clyde . . .

Yet, as he continued to turn the pages he could feel that his resentment was flagging, because momentarily, at any rate, time had dulled emotion, so that he could see the outlines of the Clyde of Malcolm Bryant, as he could never have seen them when he had lived in Clyde. He could see the passionless exactness of that scientific picture, stripped of sentiment's flattering lights and shades. The Clyde of Malcolm Bryant was a complex of instinctive forces and behavior. Its inhabitants moved into a pattern like bees in a hive, or like the Spartans under King Lycurgus. There was the individual's unknowing surrender to the group, the unthinking desire for order. He could see the Grays on Spruce Street and the Lovells on Johnson Street through Malcolm Bryant's eyes, and it was hard to believe that he ever could have lived in this arbitrary frame, illustrated by curves and diagrams, and now he was living in another. He could almost see the Stuyvesant Bank and that evening at Oak Knoll in a new revealing light — almost, but not entirely.

In spite of the years that had passed, in spite of all he had done and thought, he was still the likable Smith boy in the Bryant *Yankee Persepolis* striving to move on from the lower-upper, and still in mortal danger of dropping, of going down instead of up. He was still Charley Gray gazing wistfully at Johnson Street. . . .

"Charley." It was Nancy again. She was standing in the doorway in her quilted-silk wrapper. "It's two o'clock."

Her tone was definite, telling him that really this nonsense must stop, and he was very glad that she was there. He closed the book and pushed himself out of the leather armchair.

"All right," he said. "All right, Nance."

"Come on," Nancy said, "put out the light."

When he snapped off the light by the chair everything was pitch black for a second and then he saw her shadow against the dim light from the hall.

"The Martins will think we've been having a fight," Nancy said, "with a light on downstairs at two in the morning."

"All right, Nance," he said, and he put his arm around her and she raised her hand and touched his cheek.

"You shaved before the dance, didn't you? At least you won't need to shave again in the morning. If you're going to take that plane, I'll drive you to La Guardia."

"It's a pretty long way," Charles said.

"That's all right," Nancy said. "I'm going to miss you."

PART TWO

I

The Clyde of Alice Ruskin Lyte

CHARLES HAD NEVER THOUGHT of Clyde as having proud traditions of its own—it had only been a place which one accepted naturally because one lived in it and knew nothing else—until his mother, one hot August afternoon, read a paper before the Clyde Historical Society entitled "The Clyde of Alice Ruskin Lyte." Charles's hair had been brushed and his sister Dorothea had seen to it personally that he wore a clean white shirt and a bow tie. He had left the house with Dorothea and his Aunt Jane at ten minutes before three o'clock. His mother had left earlier. He was told that he must be quiet and must not fidget and that perhaps he would not understand all about Mother's paper but it would be a nice thing for him to remember. Actually, he was struggling with a keen sense of personal embarrassment, arising from his knowledge that no one else of his age was going to this gathering and that he might be singled out as a mother's boy and a sissy. He felt better when he found that his father would meet them there. All the family was going to hear Mother read that paper, except Sam, who was away on a visit.

He did not understand Alice Ruskin Lyte's significance, though he had heard her name mentioned more and more frequently in the evenings after supper. It was only later that he knew that Alice Ruskin Lyte was a poetess who had lived and died in Clyde and that she had been a dear friend of his mother's Aunt Sally Marchby. These two had, in fact, both been teachers at the Bedlington Academy in Lawrence. It was called the Bedlington Female Academy then. It seemed that Miss Lyte had corresponded freely with his Great-aunt Sally Marchby, after Miss Lyte had left her position at the Academy to live at her estate on the river, called Lyte's Castle.

Those packets of letters from Miss Lyte were now in his mother's possession and formed the basis of the paper.

Though Charles was not intelligently aware of these details, he had not missed the growing tension at home while the paper was being prepared. His mother had brought from the library a number of bound magazines in which Miss Lyte's verses had appeared, and also a small volume called *Stardust* by Alice Ruskin Lyte. Then he was told not to play catch with Jack Mason in the back yard because the noise disturbed his mother when she was writing. Then his mother began to worry about the paper. She did not know why she had ever said that she would do it. She never would have thought of doing it if Margaret Mason had not particularly asked her. She did not know a thing about writing.

"I wish you'd do it for me, John," she said. "You always write such nice papers."

"Now, Esther," Charles's father said, "if I were to do it, everyone would know."

"But they'll think so anyway," his mother said. "They'll know you helped me. You've got to help me."

"Esther, dear," his father said, "I wish you would try to be realistic. Let's grant that Miss Lyte was a dear friend of your Aunt Sally's. Let's go further and grant that she was a sweet old lady who never did anyone any harm intentionally except by writing jingles."

"Why didn't you tell me that you thought that in the first place," his mother asked, "and I wouldn't have said I'd do it? I wish I'd never promised, and now it's been announced."

"Poor Esther," his father said. "You'll get through with it. Your conscience will get you through."

"John, don't you think the idea's worth while?" she asked. "I mean — quoting from those letters?"

His father put his hands in his pockets and leaned against the parlor mantel. "This puts me in an embarrassing position," he answered. "I know your veneration for Miss Lyte and how your family have always felt about her. I have said she was a dear old lady. I can shut my eyes and see her now" — he made a gentle, expansive gesture as though he were conjuring up Miss Lyte -- "sitting there under an oak tree, looking at the river that she no doubt loved, with that niece of hers. What's her name?"

"Priscilla," his mother said. "And don't make fun of Priscilla. She was always sweet with her."

"I'm not making fun," his father said. "I'm only thinking of the old lady's bright character. As a human being she was intriguing because, given an ego and the industry to drive a feeble talent to the limit, she contrived to make something out of nothing," and John Gray cupped his hands together and gazed at the nothing his hands were holding. "It all goes to show what can be done if only you have a deep belief in self. That's what I would say if I were writing the paper. Think of her as a determined, industrious human being with charming intentions, but don't quote a line of her poetry, Esther. It would be unfair to her memory. She wrote like the sweet singer of Michigan."

Charles heard Dorothea giggle, and Sam was smiling. The gentle, precise way in which his father spoke was what made it funny, and he could see that his mother was only pretending to be annoyed.

"But, John," she said, "they published her poems in *Harper's Magazine*."

"And in the *Youth's Companion*," his father said. "Don't forget that mentor of our childhood, Esther, the dear old *Youth's Companion*. I tried to earn a pony by selling subscriptions for it once. Charles ought to have a pony."

"You used to say I ought to have one," Sam said.

"Well, well," John Gray said. "The main thing is thinking about ponies, Sam. Life is a series of ponies. I remember a story in the *Youth's Companion*, a Christmas story. A little boy wanted a Shetland pony more than anything else in the world. A little girl, a friend of his living in the big house on the hill, had one but his family was very poor, just like our family, Charles. His father, though he was hard working, was harassed by debts, just like your father, Charles, and Christmas was coming." John Gray spread out his arms. "Christmas was coming, and the shop windows were full of ponies."

153

"John," Esther Gray said, "what am I going to do about that paper?"

"Oh, yes, the paper." John Gray crossed the room to where she was sitting and put his hands on her shoulders. "We'll go through with it. We can't let the Historical Society down, can we? You and I will write that paper."

Everyone must have felt the same relief that Charles felt.

"John," his mother said, "are you going to be serious about it?"

John Gray laughed.

"You children go into the other room and close the door," he said, "and you read me what you've written, Esther."

Charles had already begun to mark off Dorothea's life into cycles identified with young men who appeared at the house, much as historians marked off eras by the names of monarchs. There was good reason for adopting this chronology because Dorothea's tastes, dress, and inclinations changed as her boy friends changed. At this time Frank Setchell was the most important figure in Dorothea's life. He was the eldest son of Mr. Setchell who owned Setchell's store, which sold ready-made clothing and haberdashery. Frank was hollow-chested, suffering from acne, and his appearance was never helped even by matching ties and socks.

Frank was going to take Dorothea to the beach that evening. She was to meet him at the corner of Meade Street because John Gray, whenever he saw Frank, asked him about his tie and always wanted to know whether he could get one like it, which was embarrassing to Frank and Dorothea. So Dorothea ran upstairs to get ready, and Sam went to the movies, leaving Charles to read *Guy Mannering* by the lamp on the dining room table, and it was difficult to read because he could hear his mother's and father's voices behind the closed door of the parlor. It seemed that whatever his mother had written was painful to John Gray.

"No, no, no," he could hear his father groan. "Oh, please, Esther, please."

"Can't you tell me what's wrong with it?" he could hear his mother ask. "It doesn't do any good to roar at me, John."

"I'm sorry," his father answered. "Go ahead and read it. I'll try to be quiet, Esther."

Then his mother's voice would go on half audibly, and then he could hear his father groan again.

"Oh, no, no. Why do you split infinitives? Why do you do it, why?"

"Because I thought it sounded better," his mother said. "How can I read if you roar at me, John?"

Then their voices died down again.

"John," he heard his mother say, "don't look as though you were swallowing castor oil."

"Go on," he heard his father say, "and don't start crying, Esther. Tears won't help it. Now don't interrupt me. Give me that paper."

Every evening for a week or so they all ate supper in strained silence and directly after supper the parlor door would close. His mother began to look pale and sleepless. She began to forget about the marketing, and when Dorothea broke the pressed-glass butter dish with the hen on top of it, she did not say a word — but finally the paper was finished. One evening after supper, his father rubbed his hands.

"Tonight Mother has a little surprise for us," he said. "Perhaps you've gathered that we've been working together. Come into the parlor and sit down and listen to Mother."

"John," his mother said, when Dorothea and Sam and Charles sat down in the parlor, "I feel so awfully silly."

"Of course you do," John Gray said, "and so do I. Now remember what I told you. I'm timing you. Stand up and look around, and don't keep looking at the pages. Look up at the audience and then find your place again."

"But I'll lose my place," his mother said.

"Not when you're used to it." John Gray set his watch on his knee. "We'll go over it and over it."

His mother looked red and hot and worried.

"Well, will everyone promise not to laugh?" she asked.

"It only makes it worse to talk, Esther," his father said.

"All right," his mother said. "Are you going to introduce me, John? Are you going to pretend to be Mr. Lovell?"

"I could if I wanted," his father answered, "but I don't want to be like Laurence Lovell, even in the realm of fantasy."

"Well, if you were more like Laurence Lovell — " his mother began.

"Don't get off the subject." His father tapped his watch with his forefinger. "I'm not like Laurence Lovell."

"Well," his mother began, and there was a silence. "Well." She looked at them over the top of her papers and began to read. "Every one of us here, I am sure, has seen a certain gray stone house with a mansard roof, known as Lyte's Castle. It does not in the least resemble a castle." She looked up. "I still don't see why you put that in, John. Everybody knows it."

"Everybody will know all the rest of it, too," John Gray said, "and it has to last for half an hour. Now you've spoiled it. Start all over."

"Every one of us here, I am sure, has seen a certain gray stone house with a mansard roof, known as Lyte's Castle. It does not in the least resemble a castle, but its name has been accepted through custom like so many names in Clyde and now no one would think of calling it anything else. No one would think, either, of calling its former chatelaine, known and revered by so many of us present, anything but a poetess, and the verse of Alice Ruskin Lyte, so much of which was penned within the gracious walls of Lyte's Castle, now stands to confirm our opinion of its writer."

His mother looked up again. "John, it doesn't mean what it says. It still doesn't."

"Esther, dear," his father said, "I've always loved your literal mind. It doesn't mean anything and yet it means everything, and you can go on from there. It's all you need to say about her until the very end. Now start it all over and don't interrupt again."

One thing was gained by all that preparation. All the Grays would always remember Alice Ruskin Lyte. Charles could see his mother standing straight and alone in the flowing dress of the period, looking like a full-length Sargent canvas. Her auburn hair was coiled and pinned together at the nape of her graceful neck. Her thin, eager face and her wide brown eyes were stamped with honest anxiety, because she wanted everyone to like her and that paper; and Charles could tell when the hard parts were coming from the way his mother swallowed and tossed up her delicate chin. John Gray must have enjoyed it all. Her words, the dress she wore, her pauses, and even the way she did her hair, were parts of his own creation.

It was one of those hot afternoons when the leaves on the trees were almost motionless and when everyone in Clyde hoped that a sudden east wind off the ocean might change the weather. One of the great beauties of summer in Clyde lay in that ever-present hope. The day might be stifling hot and suddenly the east wind, gratefully damp and cold and redolent of ocean salt, would make everything too cold — but in summer no one in Clyde ever believed this until faced by accomplished fact.

On his way to the Webster Grammar School, Charles always walked past the building of the Clyde Historical Society on Johnson Street, and he had often paused to admire the green brass cannon on the lawn, which had once been part of the battery of the Revolutionary War privateer *Eclipse,* built in Clyde and owned by Nathaniel Lovell, who had built the Lovell house. He had never been inside the building because when Charles had once tried to visit it, with his friend Jack Mason, Miss Hannah Smythe, the custodian, had told them that they had better run along. Little fingers had a way of getting into things, and little feet were always muddy. Nevertheless, he was already learning about Clyde, by listening to the words of elders. He already knew that the Historical Society had once been the Gow house, left to the Society by the will of old Mr. Francis Gow. He knew that the brick ell which had been added had been built by a contribution of Mr. Francis Stanley, who had come to Massachusetts to be the president of the Wright-Sherwin Company, and it was nice to have some money for an ell no matter where it came from. He also knew that the Historical Society was the repository of many valuable things left to it in wills and that it contained the collections of the Poseidon Society and the Captains'

Club, passed on to the Historical Society when those organizations had closed their doors forever.

"Charley," his Aunt Jane said, when they reached the corner of Spruce and Johnson Street, "remember not to touch anything."

She reminded him not to touch anything again as they crossed Fanning Street, where the iron horse fountain used to stand; and when they passed the Episcopal Church, with its carefully tended graveyard, Aunt Jane said she was glad she was a Unitarian.

"I hope your mother didn't eat much lunch, Dorothea," she said. "Your grandfather never liked to go to court on a full stomach."

"You mean she might vomit?" Charles asked.

"That'll be about enough from you, Charley," Aunt Jane said.

"My," Dorothea said, and she adjusted her butterfly bow, "isn't there an awful crowd. Poor Mother."

There was, indeed, an unusual number of people about the old Gow house, and it seemed that the history of Clyde's brave old days must have had a peculiar appeal for women, generally beyond the first bloom of youth. Only an occasional reluctant male was visible, except for three ministers, whose presence gave the gathering the appearance of a childless Sunday School picnic.

As Charles, his aunt and Dorothea neared the tar path leading to the front door, these three members of the clergy were standing outside on the lawn, each surrounded by the loyal members of his congregation. Dr. Morton Berry, from the Smith Square Baptist Church, stood in the shade of a catalpa tree, fanning himself with his straw hat. The Episcopal clergyman, the Reverend Gerald Pond, looked better fed and more professional in his lightweight black suit and reversed collar. In fact, Charles had heard Aunt Jane say that if he wanted to look like an Irish priest, he would do better to be a Catholic. The group around him also exuded an air of prosperity. Miss Lovell stood near him with her niece Jessica, a thin little girl in a white party dress, white socks and patent leather shoes. Mrs. Stanley was there, too, and old Miss Sarah Hewitt in purple crackling silk, and Mrs. Thomas. Dr. Pond bowed and smiled placatingly and cordially when he saw Aunt Jane, but Aunt Jane only nodded curtly. Dr. Pond had made the mistake that spring of stopping

Charles on his way to school and asking him whether he would not like to be a choir boy, and his Aunt Jane had not forgotten. Standing nearer the doorway, still lingering before entering and looking more like Puritans who had crossed the sea for faith, were the ladies of the Unitarian Women's Alliance, supporting their pastor, Mr. Henry Crewe, whose hair was not carefully trimmed and who looked like a pale ascetic compared to Dr. Pond.

"Well, this is a real occasion for you, Miss Gray," Mr. Crewe said to Aunt Jane. "Alice Ruskin Lyte. What a tempting subject for Mrs. Gray, and one I am sure she will handle beautifully."

"Well, we won't know till it's over," Aunt Jane said. "Charley, aren't you going to shake hands with Mr. Crewe?"

For some reason, some member of the family was always worrying for fear he would not shake hands with Mr. Crewe. He did not know why, because he always found himself trying to do it before he was told.

"How Charley's growing," someone said. "He has his mother's hair."

"And Charley won the fifty-yard dash at the picnic, didn't you, Charley?" Mr. Crewe said. "What did you do with the prize?"

"I ate it," Charles said. He was stricken, because his answer made everyone laugh, and he edged furtively away from the little group, while Aunt Jane began talking to Mr. Crewe about a candlelight service on the Isles of Shoals. Then, while no one was looking, he walked alone into the Historical Society.

The rooms were so crowded that he was allowed to wander unmolested from room to room and to encounter their confusion undisturbed. He did not realize until much later that it was a typical New England historical society, housing an odd assortment of things from garrets that combined to make an unscientific hodgepodge of the past. Yet its very disorder made so deep an impression on him that the unrelated, partially recognized objects in the hall and in the square rooms on either side occasionally appeared later in his dreams.

In the hall were two antique settles, three flintlock muskets, some powder horns and fire buckets, a blunderbuss, and a canvas done by a journeyman painter of an old gentleman in a wig. To the left was the room dedicated to the Captains' Club and the Poseidon Society and their collections from forgotten voyages. When he read *Java Head* some time later, he was strongly reminded of that room. Its walls were covered with paintings of ships, all bowling along under full sail, past lighthouses and Chinese pagodas, and between these pictures hung strange, rusted, rippling swords, and spears and clubs, a harpoon, and a few half models of the hulls of ships. He had seen most of those things before, in Mr. Burch's antique shop at the foot of Dock Street on Dock Square, but he had never seen so many of them at once. On a table in the center of the room, enclosed by a glass case, was an exquisite model of a ship, all carved in bone, with her standing rigging all intact. In another corner, on a black and gold lacquer table, was a miniature pagoda, with wind bells hanging from its eaves, and on still another table was a row of sextants.

Strangely enough, though the other rooms were becoming crowded, he was not conscious of people or of voices. The things there seemed to Charles to be wanting to return into the past, where they belonged. A soldier should have been wearing the moth-eaten Continental uniform that hung upon a clothing dummy. In another case, a bride should have worn the eighteenth-century wedding dress, and the Indian hatchet heads and gouges should have been back in a plowed field. They were all mixed together in those rooms — aboriginal arrowheads, muskets, candle molds, foot warmers, pine dressers, Chippendale sideboards, Lowestoft, pewter, and whales' teeth and four-poster beds. The elderly ladies of the Historical Society were drifting past them.

"That is a tooth extractor," one of them was saying.

"We have a better Chinese sewing box at home."

"We have some of that pink luster." It seemed that they all had something better or the same, and this made a visit to the Historical Society an occasion for personal triumph.

His Aunt Jane found him on the second floor, looking intently at a suit of Japanese samurai armor.

"Charley, where have you been?" she whispered, just as though they were in church. "We'll lose our place if we don't hurry." They moved downstairs, past more ship pictures, into the auditorium in the new brick wing. There was a buzz of voices in the auditorium and the slapping sound of folding wooden chairs, and the warm air smelt of cologne and talcum powder.

"We're sitting in front," Aunt Jane whispered. "There's your father. Move in beside your father."

John Gray was dressed in a gray flannel suit, and he raised his eyebrows slightly and patted the chair beside him.

"How would you like an ice cream soda — if you could get it, Charles?" he asked. He spoke in a needlessly loud tone and Charles was embarrassed. "Look at your mother." Then Charles saw that his mother was seated on a platform between Dr. Pond and Mr. Lovell. To Charles's way of thinking, Mr. Lovell was peculiarly dressed, in a blue coat and white flannel trousers and a soft shirt, and he especially noticed the mourning band on Mr. Lovell's sleeve — a sign, Charles knew, that Mrs. Lovell was dead. White flannels were still a novelty in Clyde, but they must have been correct if they were worn by Mr. Lovell. They made him look cool and aloof. His clean-shaven face was bronzed from the sun. He was smiling in a faint, embarrassed way and looking at his watch. Finally he put away his watch, rose, and walked over to a podium at the edge of the platform and glanced indecisively at a pitcher of ice water and two glasses on an antique candlestand. As Mr. Lovell stood up, the voices in the room died down, and he looked at the company in a tentative, agreeable way.

"If we are all here," he said, in a somewhat high but agreeable voice, "will the meeting come to order — not that this is one of our regular meetings but, rather, a delightful afternoon, or better still, an occasion." Mr. Lovell fumbled in the side pocket of his coat, drew out a small card, and stared at it. "We will begin, as is eminently fitting in this place, with a prayer from Dr. Pond."

As the clergyman rose, Mr. Lovell backed hastily from the podium as though he were afraid that he might be caught out of his chair before the prayer began, and Charles put his hand over his eyes.

"Oh, Heavenly Father," Dr. Pond began, "as we gather here among the relics of our forefathers and as our thoughts go back to the past of our town, we pray that our present may be as glorious as its past. We supplicate Thee to give us the courage of our fathers, who sailed the seven seas, and may our bread, too, return to us when it is cast upon Thy waters."

Charles heard his father cough gently. The prayer was long and Charles had lost the thread of it. There was a creaking of chairs and Mr. Lovell stepped forward again, groping in his pocket for the card.

"This, I think," Mr. Lovell said — "no, I don't think, I know — this is the twenty-seventh of our historical afternoons, and judging by the number present they are becoming increasingly successful. The other day" — he glanced at his card again — "I heard it said that New Englanders live too much in the past. It may be a bad habit, but whenever I come here, and I'm sure I wish we might all come here more often, I find it a rewarding habit. I think we are all better for realizing, as one must in a town like Clyde, that the present is a projection of the past, and I hope we will all grow increasingly to understand that this society is very much a part of Clyde, a piece of property to be shared equally by everyone who lives here. That is why I, and the other officers of this society, hope that you will all stay after our lecture for our tea party, supplied by our fellow member" — a frown creased his narrow, high forehead, and he glanced hastily at his card — "our fellow member Mrs. Jacob Plumm, so that we may all talk informally about Clyde as we have known it — and our future plans."

Charles heard his father cough again and he looked at his mother, who sat motionless in her armchair.

"Our speaker this afternoon" — Mr. Lovell paused and smiled — "is not an imported speaker. She is what we might call local talent" — he paused and smiled again — "not that I do not mean local talent is not very good talent. This building springs from local talent, from its fine cornices, carved by our shipwrights, down to the stone arrowheads, made by our first inhabitants. Now" — he cleared his throat gently — "I imagine that all of us here know the Grays. For generations a Gray has always appeared when he or she was needed. On the little monument by the First Landing Place, you will see the name of a Gray. A Gray was in the Civil War, and most of us here remember our late friend, Judge Vernon Gray. Now we have another Gray with us, Mrs. John Gray, whose aunt was a friend of Miss Alice Ruskin Lyte. She, too, answers our call in our time of need, and she will speak to us on" — he glanced again at his card — " 'The Clyde of Alice Ruskin Lyte.' Mrs. . . . Gray."

His mother stood up, and Charles felt his heart beat faster.

"Every one of us here," she began, "I am sure, has seen a certain gray stone house with a mansard roof . . ."

Charles saw his father draw a handkerchief from his breast pocket and mop his forehead. She was reading it more quickly than she had at home and her words seemed breathless and frightened by the discreet silence they encountered. They seemed to flutter one after the other about the room, lighting in corners, hiding behind pictures. The pictures, like the motionless rows of people, seemed very used to words. The portraits, by journeyman painters, of men who looked uncomfortable in stiff coats and of women sitting in startled erectness, seemed to be following the discourse as carefully as the living people on the chairs, but the pictures of the square-rigged ships, with their owners' flags flying in long streamers, kept on sailing, involved in their own navigational problems, bending before their artistic breezes, their bows cutting furrows through even regiments of waves.

She was getting near the end of it now. She was coming to the part that had a poem in it . . . "As Longfellow, Miss Lyte's old friend, expressed it so beautifully once — 'the beauty and mystery of the ships, and the magic of the sea.' " The ships in the Clyde Historical Society looked desiccated, devoid of mystery. There was nothing but a dry-as-dust accuracy in their realistic rigging and there was no magic in their painted seas — but now his mother's voice had stopped.

"Thank you," she said, and her voice sounded more natural. "Thank you very much for listening."

Then he heard the applause around him.

"Clap, Charley," his father said. "It's over."

"And I'm sure we are all most grateful to Mrs. Gray for a charming paper and a delightful afternoon." Mr. Lovell was calling above the rattling of the folding chairs, "And now shall we all adjourn to the Council Room for tea?"

Charles and his father walked to the edge of the platform.

"That was magnificent, Esther," John Gray said, "perfectly magnificent."

"It was," Mr. Lovell said. "It was a most interesting paper. Any time I want a good paper, I know where to go, John."

"And the introduction was even better," John Gray said. "It was superb. I ate up every word of it, Laurence. I don't believe you know my son Charles, do you?"

"Well, well," Mr. Lovell said, "I don't believe I do. And now we'd better get some tea."

"Let's go out on the lawn," his father said to Charles and his mother, "instead of getting in the crowd. Someone will bring us tea."

When they were standing on the lawn, just before the ladies came to tell his mother what a lovely paper it was, Charles heard her say to his father:

"You shouldn't have been so sarcastic, John."

"To you or to Laurence?" his father asked.

"John," his mother said, "you know what I mean, but perhaps he didn't notice. Here he comes. He's bringing us some tea."

"Oh, there you are," Mr. Lovell called. "I've been looking for you everywhere."

"Why, thanks, Laurence," John Gray said. "You keep that cup and stay with Esther. I'll get some."

"Why don't think of it, John," Mr. Lovell said. "It's a pleasure. Here."

"Well, thanks, Laurence," John Gray said. "It just goes to show I'm always right. I was just telling Esther if we came out here we'd get some tea."

The locusts in the elm trees were scraping out sad high notes which rose and fell in the still air, making a sound which Charles always associated with a hot summer afternoon in Clyde. More ladies, all holding teacups, were appearing on the lawn.

"Here they come," John Gray said. "Here's your public, Esther."

Then Charles saw Miss Lovell, and Jessica in her patent leather slippers and white socks, and Mr. Lovell saw them too.

"Why, Jessie darling," Mr. Lovell said, and he knelt on the grass and threw his arms around her. "How's my little girl?"

It did not seem right that Mr. Lovell should make such an abandoned gesture of affection right on the lawn of the Historical Society, and it made Charles feel sorry for Jessica because of what people might say. No one, however, seemed to feel it was in bad taste. Instead of being embarrassed, everyone stood watching the little scene with understanding sympathy.

"Isn't it sweet?" Charles heard someone say. "It's as pretty as a picture."

"Pa," Jessica said, "can't we go home now, please?"

"Yes," Mr. Lovell answered, "in just a few minutes, Jessie."

II

A Place for Everything

THE WAY TO LEARN about Clyde was to be brought up there. One learned who the Lovells were imperceptibly by a word here and there, and one grew up knowing that the Lovells could say what they wanted and do what they wanted and that they would always be right no matter what they said or did. One learned that there was a living plan in Clyde, without ever learning exactly what the plan was, for it kept growing as one grew, starting with Spruce Street and one's own back yard and spreading up to Johnson Street and down to Dock Street.

Everyone had a place in that plan and everyone instinctively seemed to know where he belonged. Its completeness reminded Charles of what his Aunt Jane said once when she was arranging the flat silver in the sideboard of her dining room — everything in its place and a place for everything. The Irish, for instance, had their place, and so had the French-Canadians and the new immigrants, like the Italians and the Poles, who naturally belonged close to the Wright-Sherwin factory and the shoeshops. There was a place for the North Enders, too. They lived in the North End and went to the North End Congregational Church and even if they lived in other parts of Clyde they were still North Enders.

The same sorts of people, he learned, usually lived in the same sections of Clyde; but you began to learn quite early, without ever knowing how, that certain people who lived on Johnson Street were not Johnson Street people, and hence, because you knew, their living on Johnson Street did not disturb the plan. For example, the Stanleys lived on Johnson Street. They had bought the old Holt house, and it was still called the Holt house though the Stanleys lived in it.

Mr. Stanley, everyone knew, was richer than the Lovells or the Thomases or old Miss Sarah Hewitt. You could tell this from his new greenhouse and from the number of men who worked on the garden and the lawns; and Mr. Stanley had a Cadillac automobile, driven by old Arthur Stevens, who had worked for the Holts and whose brother was a clam digger. Yet the Stanleys' prosperity was without the same face value as that of others. They lived on Johnson Street but they did not belong there.

You came to understand that the Holts, who had sold their house to the Stanleys and had moved to the North End, still belonged on Johnson Street. Miss Sarah Hewitt's house needed painting and Mr. Fogarty, who worked for her and for the Lovells too, only gave her one day a week, but Miss Sarah Hewitt belonged on Johnson Street. The same was true with the Lovells. They had always been on Johnson Street. You understood that Mr. Lovell was not very rich but his money somehow had the dignity of age. You heard it spoken of as the Lovell money. He was a director of the Dock Street Savings Bank and a trustee of the West India Insurance Company, which were both partially founded on Lovell money. He was a trustee of the public library, also partially founded on Lovell money. You came to understand that Mr. Stanley could do more generous things because he was richer, and anyone who was richer could do these things of course, but his contribution did not have the same value as a Lovell or a Hewitt contribution. You seemed to know these things implicitly.

The same was true with Spruce Street. The Grays belonged on Spruce Street and so, too, did the Masons, who lived next door; but when Vincent Sullivan, who was in the contracting business and who had the contract for the addition to the Wright-Sherwin plant, bought the house on the corner of Spruce and Chestnut, he still did not belong on Spruce Street. Everyone knew that Mr. Sullivan's father had been the Lovells' gardener and that Mr. Sullivan had driven a truck for the Bronson Shoeshop until he had invested his father's savings in the old livery stable on South Street. You could not get away from your past in Clyde and few wanted to get away from it, perhaps because it was not worth trying.

167

There were no secrets in a town like Clyde and so, of course, everyone knew all about the Grays. Everyone knew that John Gray was harder to place than some people because he was different from other people, and Charles must have always been aware of that unspoken difference. No matter what his father did or said, he had a right to be different because he was the Judge's son. He had always been a wild boy and had given the Judge a hard time, but everyone knew Johnny Gray. They could remember the time when Johnny Gray had a fight with Martin Donovan and when he stole a trolley car out of the carbarn and drove it down to the beach with a lot of boys from high school. It had been hard for the Judge to clear that one up, but everyone knew Johnny Gray. He was not lazy, but he never stuck to anything. He and Laurence Lovell had started out in Harvard together and they might have been friends but he didn't even bother to go with the right people. Still, Miss Hewitt always had a kind word for him and so had the Thomases.

It was all right for Johnny Gray, though it would not have been for Virgil Mason or Melville Summers, to join the Pine Tree Fire Company and to help man the Pine Tree machine at firemen's musters and to play poker at the Pine Tree firehouse, because everyone understood that he was different. He had been a wild boy but he was bright and he could have done anything he wanted if only he had put his mind on it. If only he had kept interested, he could have been a college professor or a lawyer. The trouble was, he was the only boy and the baby of the family and he had always been made too much of. Everything was too easy for Johnny Gray. He did not have to work hard, like other people, to get his learning. He could have gone through Harvard just as well as Laurence Lovell or Ralph Thomas. He was not a bad boy. He never got into a college-boy scrape, but he had not liked it there and after a year and a half the Judge had taken him out.

The Grays had always been solid people, not shipowners or warehouse owners like the old Johnson Street people, but solid people, and the Judge owned stock in the Crawford Mill. When Johnny Gray was tired of Harvard, it was natural for the Judge to put him in the mill and wait for him to settle down. It looked as if he would do it, too, when he began calling on Esther Marchby, old Dr. Marchby's daughter, and the Marchbys were good solid people, too. He was not getting on fast in the mill, but given time he would settle down. Yet perhaps the Judge himself was never sure. He had tied up Johnny Gray's share of the mill stock in trust when he died, though he let the girls own theirs outright. It was hard to fool the Judge.

Everyone knew who you were and what you were in Clyde and there was no need to guess. You always said kind things about everyone in the family and hastily dusted away discrepancies, but nothing was ever hidden because you could not help what other people said. Gossip always became in time a sort of mythology and lay before every inhabitant of Clyde like a long shadow on a summer afternoon. A word here, a word there, an embarrassed silence, a snatch of overheard conversation, an overelaborate explanation, an amusing anecdote — all those things finally could not help but make a picture. Everyone knew about John Gray, and so did Charles. Charles must have known when he was very young that John Gray was unstable, but he never could get to the bottom of this instability. When he tried to admire his father, even when he was a little boy, there was a gap somewhere, a total blank. The truth was, he often thought, that his father had been too busy with his own ideas, too involved with conflicting impulses, to have anything much left to give. John Gray was always too wrapped up in himself to have time for any of the children.

It was not the fashion in Clyde for parents to discuss each other before their children, but it was possible to hear bits of talk.

"It never does any good to nag John," he heard his Aunt Jane say once. "Father always said so."

"I never do nag at John," his mother answered. "I wouldn't dream of doing it."

"You mustn't ever let him see you're disappointed," his Aunt Jane said. "It's just as bad as nagging and it only makes him sullen."

"I'm not disappointed," his mother said. "I don't see why you say I am."

"Well, I never could have married anyone like John," his Aunt Jane said. "I couldn't have stood it."

"Well, I can stand it, Jane," his mother said, and she laughed in an exasperated way. "Maybe I like excitement, and you wait, John will do something someday. You wait, we'll all be surprised. I know he's planning to do something. Of course they don't understand him at the mill."

"What's he planning to do?" his Aunt Jane asked. "Whatever it is, don't encourage him."

"Why, I haven't any idea," his mother answered, and then she laughed again. "And if he never does do anything, Jane, I shan't mind. I love him just the way he is."

His father was the type of person whom women always loved. His mother was right, too, when Charles came to think of it later. John Gray finally did do something, and everyone was very much surprised.

Charles could at any rate start with a sense of having belonged somewhere. He had, at least, something from which he could revolt, and no one could very well revolt from anything as plastic as life in Sycamore Park. Bill would never see anyone like Miss Sarah Hewitt because Miss Sarahs simply did not exist in Sycamore Parks, or if they did they must have been pushed into corners where no one saw them. They never were elder statesmen, dominating the local scene. Active old ladies of eighty like Miss Sarah only seemed to flourish in towns like Clyde where climate, local biological selection, struggle for survival, and local respect rendered them indestructible. If personality were only strong enough, Clyde was the place for it. There would never be a base in Bill's background, Charles often thought, such as there had been in his own. The impermanence of a New York suburb with its shifting population of unrooted communities, with order that existed only on the surface, was as hard for a boy to grasp as it was for him to explain. He had been luckier than Bill in that in Clyde there had been so much to be accepted without argument.

One morning at about half past nine a few days after the meeting of the Historical Society, Mrs. Garrity, who was now Miss Sarah Hewitt's housekeeper and who had been in the Hewitt household ever since she had come to Clyde as a young girl from Ireland, pulled the glass knob of the front doorbell. The bell's tinkle in the front hall interrupted Dorothea's piano practice.

"You go, Charley," Dorothea said. "Someone's at the front door."

"Why don't you go?" Charles asked, and Dorothea tossed her head.

"Because you're not doing anything. You never do do anything."

Charles had been on the point of doing something. He had just made up his mind to see what Jack Mason was doing and to persuade him to go over to the Meaders' and see what the Meaders were doing and to find out if they couldn't go somewhere and do something together.

"You're not doing anything either," Charles said. "You're just drumming on that old piano."

"You go to the door," said Dorothea, "or I'll tell Mother," and then before Charles could move she began telling Mother. "Mother," she called, "Charley won't answer the doorbell. Should Charley or I answer the doorbell?"

Charles heard his mother's quick steps on the floor above them and he moved slowly into the front hall.

"You needn't start yelling," he called as he turned the brass knob of the front door. "I was going anyway."

Mrs. Garrity was standing on the doorstep, bareheaded, in her gingham dress but without her apron. She looked at him coolly but with kindness through her glasses.

"Young man, is your mother in?" she asked.

There was no need to answer. His mother was hurrying down the stairs.

"Why, good morning, Mrs. Garrity," she said.

She did not call her Ellen because only people who lived on Johnson Street would have dreamed of calling Mrs. Garrity Ellen.

"Good morning, Miss Esther," Mrs. Garrity said, and she stepped deliberately into the hall and glanced critically at the oblong mirror and at the steel engraving of Franklin at the court of Louis the Sixteenth and then at the colored print of the Clyde waterfront. "Miss Sarah sent me to wish you good morning." By calling his mother Miss Esther, Mrs. Garrity was obviously accepting her as a friend of Miss Sarah's — not just a calling acquaintance.

"I hope Miss Sarah is well, Mrs. Garrity," his mother said.

"Oh yes, she's well," Mrs. Garrity said, "and she wants to know if you would be at home this afternoon so that she might be dropping in for a cup of tea, Miss Esther, and to talk about the paper you've been reading."

"Why, tell her we'll be delighted," his mother answered in a new, bright voice. "Would she like to come at half past four?"

"Four," said Mrs. Garrity, "and she'll bring her own tea, and give her thin bread and butter only."

"We'd love to have her at four," his mother said, but Mrs. Garrity still stood in the doorway.

"I suppose you'll be getting Minnie Murphy in, Miss Esther."

"It isn't her day here," his mother said, "but yes, I'll see if I can get Mrs. Murphy."

"I'll tell her," Mrs. Garrity said. "Minnie will come if I tell her. Minnie knows how to do it. It would be best to get Minnie."

When the door closed, his mother looked worried.

"Oh, dear," she said. "Dorothea, stop playing the piano. Miss Sarah's coming to tea. Now let me see — Charles, I want you to go down to the mill and tell your father to be here at four o'clock, and then go and tell your Aunt Jane. Where's Sam?"

"He went fishing, off the breakwater," Charles said.

"Oh, dear," his mother said. "I suppose he'll come back all over fish. I think we'd better use the Canton tea set, don't you, Dorothea? Now run along, Charley. I wish we had more time."

Charles was the boy carrying the burning cross saying, Excelsior! Miss Sarah is coming to tea. At the end of Spruce Street, he turned right, past Gow's wharf and the coal pocket and then past the gasworks and then past the mill houses where River Street children were playing hopscotch on the sidewalk. The tide was low and he could see the black mud flats with their still pools of water. A humming came from the long brick mill building, a busy but drowsy sound that made him understand why Mr. Felch, the watchman, was dozing in the gatehouse. The windows of the smaller office building were wide open and so was the door, but inside everything was hot. The clerks behind the railings were in their shirt sleeves. He could see Mr. Stafford in his large private office reading papers and only Mr. Stafford wore his coat. Far down the hall, beyond the accounting department, his father sat in his small room, running over a column of figures.

"Mother sent me," Charles said. "Miss Sarah's coming to tea at four o'clock."

"Well, well," his father said, "if it isn't one thing it's another. Run along and tell her I'll be there."

When he left the mill Charles turned up Gow Street, still carrying the burning cross. Beyond the small and shabby houses, Gow Street made a crooked turn, by French's grocery store, and then widened and changed for the better the nearer one came to Johnson Street. His Aunt Mathilda and his Aunt Jane lived in the square yellow house with the plain picket fence in front and a small stable and garden. It had belonged to his grandfather and it still had his grandfather's name on the silver plate on the dark door. He opened the door without knocking but he closed it carefully because his Aunt Mathilda was sick upstairs, and he walked softly down the hall into the dining room which was dusky and cool because the wooden shutters were drawn.

"Where's Aunt Jane?" he called into the kitchen to Mary Callahan, who was sitting at the table peeling potatoes.

"Where would she be," Mary Callahan said, "except upstairs reading with Miss Mathilda? But don't go stamping on the stairs."

Even if he had stamped, the stair carpet with its heavily padded treads would have deadened the sound. In the upstairs hall everything was as dusky and cool as the dining room, with everything in its place and a place for everything. The brasses on the highboy shone in the faint light. Miss Trask, his Aunt Mathilda's practical nurse, was sewing in the hall bedroom, and further down the hall, in the square corner room, he could hear his Aunt Jane reading

poetry. She was reading it with pleasure because she loved declamation.

"*Shoal!*" he heard her saying. "*'Ware shoal!* Not I!"

His Aunt Mathilda was sitting in a Boston rocker and Aunt Jane
sat stiffly in a straight-backed chair.

"Why, Charley dear, where did you come from?" his Aunt
Mathilda asked.

Aunt Jane closed her book.

"Charles, I wish you wouldn't creep around," she said.

"You told him not to make any noise," Aunt Mathilda said. "I
heard you, Jane. Come here and kiss me, Charley."

He kissed her timidly because he knew that his Aunt Mathilda
was very ill.

"He doesn't have to creep around," his Aunt Jane said. "What is
it, Charles?"—and then he gave the message again. Miss Sarah
was coming to tea at four o'clock.

"Oh, dear," Aunt Mathilda said, and her thin white hands moved
restlessly over her dressing gown. "Is she coming here?"

"Of course she isn't, Mathilda," Aunt Jane told her. "She's going
there, to John's house, and I'd better go to help Esther. You know
how things are there, Mathilda."

"Charley, dear," Aunt Mathilda said, "I think your mother had
better get Minnie Murphy in. Tell her that I said so and we'll send
Mary Callahan over to help."

It was not the question of food, he remembered his mother saying,
it was the desire to have everything look right that made her
nervous. She was not going to have Miss Sarah Hewitt leave the
house and tell the Lovells and Thomases and other people that
Esther Gray had started as a careless, flighty girl and had not improved. When she had become engaged to John Gray, she knew
very well that Miss Sarah had said that it was a mistake and a pity,
that Esther was not the right wife for John Gray because she was
absent-minded; and Charles's mother did not want to have Miss
Sarah saying this again. She had never liked to sit behind a tea tray,
pouring hot water into cups and then pouring it into what was

called a slop basin — a horrid term, a slop basin. She had to admit that she did not understand tea. She wished that Jane would pour but Jane said that it was Esther's house. The main thing was to have the parlor and the hall picked up and to get rid of John's canes and umbrellas and the boys' fishing rods and John's and the boys' hats — and John's books should be taken upstairs and not left in piles upon the floor.

Charles had never seen the hall and parlor look so neat. Mrs. Murphy and Mary Callahan had washed the woodwork with soap and water. They had beaten the braided hall rug and the two parlor Persian carpets. They had washed the mirror; they had polished the Benares brass tray in the hall and the andirons and the fender in the parlor fireplace and the candlesticks on the mantelpiece, and the two Staffordshire dogs had been washed. The picture of the brig *Comet,* which had been sailed around Cape Horn by Charles's great-grandfather, had been taken down and Aunt Jane herself had wiped off the canvas. Cleanliness had transformed the parlor. Shine and polish made everything look almost new, and this was true also with the family.

They were all there except Sam, who was still on the breakwater. Aunt Jane wore her plum-colored silk dress, with a cameo brooch. His mother wore her best afternoon gown, with old lace on it. Dorothea wore her embroidered shirtwaist and her new skirt and her hair was done in her Sunday way. Although it was a hot afternoon, John Gray had put on his blue serge suit and stiff collar, and Charles was again in a clean white shirt and a bow tie. A cloth of Italian lace was placed over the tea table that stood in front of the Victorian horsehair sofa, and the Canton tea set was already on it. A fresh antimacassar had been pinned on the wing chair, partially concealing its soiled upholstery, and a candlestand had been placed beside it.

"Oh, dear," John Gray said. "Oh, dear me."

"Don't say, oh dear," Charles's mother snapped. "You haven't done any of the work. What time is it?"

She did not need to ask because she could see by the banjo clock, but John Gray took out his watch.

"The clock is two minutes slow," he said. "It's exactly three min·

utes before four. She'll be here in exactly three minutes. It's amazing how rejuvenating this is. Don't you feel young, Jane?"

"No, I don't," Aunt Jane said, "and I hope you're going to act your age."

"That's exactly it," John Gray answered. "I am. It's an intimation of immortality."

"I wish you wouldn't chatter, John," Esther Gray said. "I don't see why you like to talk when you're nervous. I don't."

John Gray sat down in one of the stiff ladder-backed chairs and folded his hands.

"I'm too young to be nervous," he said. "I've been washed behind the ears, like Charles. I'm as young as Charles, and Charles and Dorothea aren't born. They're back in the land of the unborn children, and Esther is Dr. Marchby's little girl and Jane is in pinafores."

It was difficult, sometimes, to understand his father. It gave Charles a very queer feeling when his father said he had not been born. When his father waved his hand slowly, as he did so often when he spoke, Charles could almost believe that he and Dorothea had been rendered invisible.

"I wish you wouldn't be so confusing, John," his mother said. "No one understands you and there isn't time to try."

John Gray sighed.

"That's true. No one understands me." A church bell was beginning to strike four. The church clocks in Clyde had never been synchronized, any more than the religions they represented. Another bell was striking. "That's the Baptist bell," John Gray said. 'You'll notice it's always behind the Congregationalist. Now, Dorothea." Dorothea looked at him doubtfully. "You and Charles are going to have a remarkable experience. Try to think of yourself as moving backward. I envy you. I wish I hadn't been born."

"Well, you are born," Aunt Jane said, "and here she is."

The bell in the hall was tinkling and his father and mother hurried out while the rest of them waited and Charles could hear their voices in the hall.

"Charley," Dorothea whispered, "your shirt is coming out." She seized him quickly, as though he were much younger.

"Let me alone," he whispered, and he was stuffing his shirt beneath his waistband when Miss Sarah Hewitt entered.

Charles had seen her often, but now she looked strange to him because his father had fixed it so that nothing seemed quite real. She looked as cool as though it were not a hot day. She looked so old that no weather could disturb her. Her brown dress of stiff silk rustled like autumn leaves, and the sound gave the artificial flowers on her small hat an incongruous, waxlike appearance. Her lips were set in an amused, determined line. Her hair was streaked with gray. Her eyes looked old and faded. There was a tremor in her thin, blue-veined hands that made the beaded reticule she was holding shake, but still she had a deliberate, airy way of walking. Her voice, too, had a quaver in it, but it retained a plaintive, musical note like an echo of a younger voice.

"Jane, dear, how do you do?" she said. "And these are the dear children, aren't they, Esther? I thought there were three. Isn't there an older boy?"

"Sam isn't here, Miss Sarah," John Gray said. "We had no way of reaching Sam. He's gone fishing."

"You needn't speak quite so loudly, Johnny," Miss Sarah said. "Fishing — and he should love the sea, shouldn't he? What are the other children's names? I've forgotten. There have been so many names . . . Dorothea, after her grandmother, of course. And Charles. Now who was Charles? Oh, I remember. Charles who went to the war. Where was it he was killed?"

"Fredericksburg, Miss Sarah," John Gray said. "Uncle Charles died at Fredericksburg. Won't you sit down? Try the wing chair."

"If you'll give me your hand, please, Johnny," Miss Sarah said. "Thank you. It was Burnside's fault, of course. There was a service, wasn't there — in the Unitarian Church, but then you wouldn't know. Esther, that paper at the Society was very good. I never knew you could write so well. It made me see her again. Dear Alice Lyte. And Laurence was so pleased with it. You know how particular Laurence is — a perfectionist like dear Nathaniel." She spoke with a conviction that was conjuring up the unseen, and the quick and the dead were moving about the parlor, mingling democratically together. "Dear, kind Nathaniel — but Laurence is more Lovell than Hewitt. I wish the children would move their chairs so that I can see them. So this is little Charles. He looks like Vernon. Do you know that your grandfather stole pears from the garden once, Charles? I didn't tell, but Father saw Vernon from the window. Did Vernon ever tell you, John?"

"Why, no," John Gray answered. "Father never told me that."

"We've all been friends for so many years," Miss Sarah said, "such friends, in such different ways, but do you know what's just happened? I mustn't forget to tell you."

"No, what's happened?" Aunt Jane asked.

"The Rose of Sharon bush is blooming again. The pink one. I saw it from my window, but it's not nearly as old as the lilacs. Grandfather brought the cuttings back from England."

"They're the most beautiful lilacs in Clyde," Charles's mother said. "I always stop to peek at them through the fence."

Miss Sarah had forgotten about the lilacs. Her expression had brightened, her glance had turned toward the mantelpiece.

"Why, there she is," she said. Everyone looked puzzled and John Gray cleared his throat.

"Who?" he asked gently. "Who, Miss Sarah?"

"I forgot you had a picture of the *Comet,* too," Miss Sarah said, "not that you haven't a perfect right to have one" — and then they realized that she was referring to the oil painting of the brig above the mantelpiece. "Grandfather always said that Captain Tom was his best captain," Miss Sarah said. "He always spoke so highly of him. Now he would be the children's great-grandfather, wouldn't he? And he had such bad rheumatism. You would never have thought he'd been before the mast. Grandfather always said so. Susan and I were brought downstairs to meet him. Grandfather wanted us to see what one of his captains looked like. Johnny, do you remember Captain Tom?"

"Why, no," John Gray said. "He was dead long before I arrived, Miss Sarah. He married after he was fifty."

"It's hard," Miss Sarah said, "to remember everything, but I did especially want to mention Captain Tom. There are more ship cap-

"tains' families left than shipowners', aren't there, but then of course there were more ship captains, and the owners have moved away."

"Yes," his father said. "Things are quieter along the river now."

"It was the fire," Miss Sarah said. "Grandfather always used to say that nothing was the same after the fire."

"You don't mean the fire of 1820," Aunt Jane asked, "when the waterfront burned down?"

"My dear," Miss Sarah said, "what other fire has there ever been? I can almost remember it — almost. There was so much talk of it when I was a little girl that I was afraid of candles. It started in the Higgins boat yard, a careless Negro boy with turpentine. The poor Holts never recovered from it. The sparks blew up to Johnson Street. We have the buckets that we used in the barn, the Pine Tree fire buckets."

"Have you really?" John Gray said. "I didn't know that."

"It always made me afraid of Negroes," Miss Sarah said, "even before the war. If it hadn't been for the fire those new people, the Stanleys, would never be in the Holt house. Nothing has been quite the same."

"Charles," his mother said, "will you please go out and ask Mrs. Murphy for some hot water?"

Mrs. Murphy herself was a creaky old woman with snow-white hair and a round, florid face. She was talking to Mary Callahan in the kitchen.

"Sure those were the days," Mrs. Murphy was saying. "Sure the Lovells had six horses."

"Six horses?" Mrs. Callahan said. "What would they do with them?"

"Six horses or ten horses," Mrs. Murphy said. "The Lord knows how many, and my own husband was the coachman, God rest his soul. What is it, young man?"

"More hot water, please," Charles said.

"Now see the manners of him," Mrs. Murphy said. "He has the manners of anyone on Johnson Street."

"And why shouldn't he have the manners, I want to know?"

Mary Callahan asked. "The Grays are as good as all your people on Johnson Street."

When he returned from his errand in the kitchen, Miss Sarah was sipping her tea, and her cup shook but nothing spilled.

"It's been a lovely tea party," she said. "What else was it I was going to say? I'm sure there was something else. I told you, didn't I, about the cemetery?"

"Why, no, you didn't, Miss Sarah," his mother said.

"Well, it doesn't matter at the moment. I remember what I wanted to say. That paper at the Historical Society — it reminded me so of dear Alice Lyte. She was such friends with the Marchby girls. Do you remember the colored woman?"

"What colored woman?" his mother asked.

"The one who was passing through to Canada before the war. She sewed a whole dress for Alice before they rowed her across the river, a whole dress in two days. She was very light colored. John?"

"Yes, Miss Sarah," his father said.

"I'm sorry that things didn't go so well at Harvard. It was such a disappointment to Vernon."

"So he told me," John Gray said. "I've been trying to do better since, Miss Sarah."

"And I know you will," Miss Sarah said. "You'll get hold of yourself in time. Let me see, there's something else I wanted to say. Oh, yes, do you know what's happened? The Rose of Sharon bush is blooming again, the pink one. And now I really must be going."

"Oh, please don't go," his mother said.

"No, dear, I must be going, if you'll give me your hand. It's been such a nice tea party. One should move out of one's orbit sometimes."

"May I walk back with you, Miss Sarah?" John Gray asked.

"Oh, no, Johnny," she said. "I can make my way quite well alone, if you'll see me to the door."

There was a silence after the front door had closed. The house was returning to its norm, but slowly, very slowly.

"Oh, dear me," John Gray said. "It was more nautical than I thought it would be, wasn't it?"

"I don't see why she came," Aunt Jane said.

"*Noblesse oblige*," his father said. "She was calling on the Captain's family."

"She's failing," Aunt Jane said. "She isn't what she used to be." Charles's father stood up and moved about the room restlessly, but there were still echoes of Miss Sarah's voice.

"Nothing's the way it used to be," he said. "Charley, did you ever have a telescope?"

"I don't see why you ask him that, just out of the blue," his mother said.

"Because my father gave me one," John Gray said, "a telescope or a spyglass. It's gone but it's around somewhere if I could only turn the clock back. It's back there in my mind, brand-new." Then Charles saw that he was smiling at him. The shadows were going from the room.

"I'm going to get you a telescope, Charley. Every boy ought to have one."

Charles did not want a telescope and it was just as well, because his father never kept those promises. Miss Sarah Hewitt was gone and the tea party was over.

III

Few Things Are Impossible to Diligence and Skill
— SAMUEL JOHNSON

MALCOLM BRYANT, who had come to Clyde as a complete stranger with a scientific preoccupation and only his boyhood in a small Midwestern town as a basis for comparison, had called Clyde a ghost town, as though it were like an abandoned Colorado mining settlement. It was true that Clyde had not changed much since the sailing days, because its harbor was now useless for heavy shipping. It had no water power as the mill towns further up the river had and it had little to attract summer tourists. It was a place to be born in and a place to leave, but it was not a ghost town.

There was a curtain, translucent but not transparent, between the present and the past. When you were young you did not bother in the least about it because there was too much present, and thus you accepted the older people and you accepted their deaths very easily, because you were so occupied with living. They disappeared behind that translucent curtain, which moved forward a little every year to cover up the year before. Charles knew, for instance, that Aunt Mathilda was going to die and when she did everyone said it was a mercy and so much easier for her poor sister Jane. She was gone and life went on, and she was hard to remember. Dorothea was too worried about Frank Setchell to remember much, and Sam was too occupied with problems of revolt, and Charles still had too much to learn.

He had to learn the new steps at dancing school and new jokes from the Meader boys and *The Bells* by Edgar Allan Poe for the declamation contest in the seventh grade. He had to learn why certain people thought the Catholic Church was a political menace, and what was difficult about the Irish, and why the boys on Johnson Street, the Thomases and the Stanleys, went away to boarding school when he and his friends did not. He had to learn why couples sat in back of the courthouse at night. He had to learn why Washington Irving's *Sketch Book* was worth reading, and he had to learn the dates and facts in the school history of the United States. Besides he had to follow Sam around when Sam would let him, and when Sam would not he had to talk things over with Jack Mason. It was hard to understand why Sam should have been discontented because Sam could come and go as he wanted, he was on the high school football team, and May Mason, who was the prettiest girl at high school, liked him better than anyone else.

One's ideas about everything underwent perpetual change while one was growing up, such as ideas of God and immortality and of wealth and poverty, and even one's family was not a constant quantity. You knew them better than anyone else, but suddenly something would happen and they were not the people you had thought they were. This experience was like seeing the back of a house for the first time when you had always been familiar with its front. You knew the lawn and the front windows, but in back were the clothes yard, the garbage pail, the woodshed, and the weedy garden. Nevertheless, it was still the same house. That was the way it was with the family, Charles used to think. Sometimes they turned their fronts to you and sometimes they turned their backs.

That was the way it was with Sam and his father and with Dorothea and all the rest of them. The scene that Charles remembered most clearly, the one that changed his ideas about them most, must have occurred when he was twelve and when Sam was seventeen. Dorothea must have been having supper with Olive Haskell, who was her best friend then, because he could not remember her being there at Spruce Street. It was obviously some months after his Aunt Mathilda's death, but the scene was unique and too vital to be confused with this or that.

His father had been in Boston all that day and Charles had been aware for some time that certain things happened, or were apt to happen, when his father went to Boston. Since his father had taken him with him to Boston several times, Charles could imagine his father stepping off the train, walking past the panting locomotive into the old North Station and through the dingy waiting room out to that street with the elevated railway overhead into a sea of sound and faces.

"I'll take you again sometime, Charley," his father used to say.

He was almost always too busy, but it was only fair to admit that those occasions on which his father had taken him to Boston must have represented a definite sacrifice, for they were antiseptic, useful and educational, consisting of a trip to the art museum or to the Old North Church, or a visit to the statue of the man who first used ether or to the brass letters on the sidewalk at the scene of the Boston Massacre. His father was conversant with all these conventional spectacles but Charles suspected, always, that when John Gray was alone he must have done other things.

"You're too young to understand what I have to do here, Charley," was all he ever said. "I have a few investments that I have to look out for on Congress Street. It's a very good thing to go to Boston or New York occasionally. I don't want you to pin me down to it, but sometime you and I will certainly go down to New York — sometime when everything is going right." It was only fair to remember, too, that John Gray did take him to New York, after Aunt Mathilda died.

It was a summer afternoon again and except for Mrs. Murphy in the kitchen no one else was in the house. Charles was reading *The House of the Seven Gables* in the parlor and had reached the eloquent passage where old Judge Pyncheon was sitting motionless in his chair. He heard the front door slam and then the sound of his father whistling in the hall. When his father entered the parlor, he was carrying a copy of the *Boston Evening Transcript* and the *Boston News Bureau* and the latest *Atlantic Monthly,* a box of cigars, and a pound box of candy.

"Well, well," he said. "Where's Mother?"

"She's out," Charles said. "I think she's at the Women's Club."

"Well, well," his father said. "So you're reading *The House of the Seven Gables*. Whoever thought it was a children's book was a very innocent person. Have you a knife in your pocket, Charley? That's right. A boy should always have a knife, to whittle things and carve his name. I think I'll open this cigar box." He sat down in the wing chair and lighted a cigar and the smell of the cigar smoke mingled with his words. "I think it's time, Charley, or about time, that we had a talk about your education. Hawthorne, Emerson, Thoreau, Whittier, Longfellow, James Russell Lowell, not to mention Irving and Harriet Beecher Stowe — they all have a place in the cosmos but it would be nice for you to know that there are other, better writers. These are only a twig on a great tree, but don't quote me as saying so, Charley." He smiled, leaned back in the wing chair, and blew a puff of cigar smoke at the ceiling. "I'm afraid you're having a wretched education — not that I'm against our public school system but it is a school of life, not letters. I wonder how it would be if you went to Groton next year? You'd be old enough to enter the first or second form. I wish I had gone to Groton."

There was no need for Charles to answer and he knew that his father did not want to be interrupted.

"I suppose Sam should have gone to Groton, but then the opportunity didn't exist for Sam. Well, suppose you did go to Groton, then a year at Harvard — I'd like you to meet Kittredge — and perhaps a year at Oxford." He flipped the ash from his cigar into the empty fireplace. "I wish we could all go abroad, but it's difficult with the war, even with Wilson keeping us out of it." He paused and looked at the smoke cloud above him. "If we can't go abroad, it might be a good idea for you to see a little of this country. We might take a trip in a week or two — Chicago, the Great Lakes, the Rocky Mountains, San Francisco." He paused again but his thoughts were moving in a swift, agreeable stream. "China. I don't see why it wouldn't be possible to consider a little trip to China. You've never read Huc and Gabet, have you? Or Lafcadio Hearn?"

He stood up and began pacing about the room waving his cigar

185

in broad arcs, not caring where the ashes fell. His freshly cut hair, the aura of bay rum and cigar smoke, his closely clipped mustache, made his face the face of a world traveler, unburdened by inadequate finance or by provincialism. It was unreal. Charles's common sense told him it was unreal.

"Have you read *Rasselas,* Charley? 'Few things are impossible to diligence and skill.' Now the next time I'm in Boston, I'll stop in at the American Express." Then they heard the front door open. "That must be your mother. Hello, Esther."

"John," his mother asked, "did you have a good day in Boston?" Charles always remembered her expression, both pleased and doubtful. "I wish you wouldn't drop those ashes on the floor."

"Oh," John Gray said, "I'm sorry. You know, Esther, I was thinking, coming back on the train, that it's time we got away from the heat. How would it be if we went for two weeks to Poland Spring?"

"You know how it would be," his mother said. "What would they say at the mill?"

Groton school and China were gone, but Poland Spring was there.

"Never mind the mill," John Gray said. "We could go there and sit quietly and drink Poland water. Rocking chairs, soft music, a little golf."

"But I can't play golf," his mother said, "and you can't play it very well."

"That's just it," John Gray said, and his mind had moved from Poland Spring. "There isn't a golf course here, but there's the Shore Club."

"But we don't belong to it," his mother said, "and if we did, it's twelve miles away."

"We ought to belong to it," John Gray said, "and we ought to have a car. Nothing expensive, Esther, but what would you say if we bought a small car? Then we could drive to the Shore Club. It's about time Sam saw some different people, and Dorothea, too — instead of Frank Setchell and his socks."

"And learn how to play golf?"

"And why shouldn't we play golf?" John Gray answered. "Sam

ought to learn a few skills before he goes to Dartmouth. It's nice of Jane to do this for us, but I don't know why she insists on Dartmouth."

"Well, as long as Jane's doing it," his mother said.

John Gray stared at the end of his cigar.

"Dartmouth," he said. "It is, sirs, a small college, and yet there are those who love it. His marks are bad enough and he likes football, but if he can't get into Harvard or Yale, why not Amherst or Brown?"

"I'd better help Mrs. Murphy set the table," his mother said.

John Gray began to laugh.

"All right," he said, "we can talk about the Shore Club later. Dear me, I'd better get washed."

After his father left the room, his mother still lingered in the parlor and her hesitation was novel and disturbing. She looked at the open parlor door and smiled. She looked younger and prettier than she usually did when she came home from a meeting of the Women's Club.

"Charley," she said, and she lowered her voice as though they were discussing something secret, "did he promise you anything?"

"No," Charles answered, "he didn't exactly promise anything."

She moved nearer to him and touched the back of his head gently.

"What were you talking about?"

"About a lot of things," Charles said. "School, and I guess about China."

"Oh dear," his mother said. "Did he get as far as China?" She did not want him to answer and she had something else to say. "Charley, we both love him very much, don't we?"

There seemed to be no reason for her question, since Charles had always believed that loving one's parents very much was an accepted principle, like asking God to bless them in one's evening prayers. She touched his head again and her voice was slower and softer.

"I want to tell you something about him, dear, something I think you're old enough to understand." She stopped and he could still feel her fingers stroking the back of his head very gently. "You mustn't feel hurt when he promises you something and then forgets. When he makes a promise and doesn't keep it, it means that he wants us to have the things that he wants us to have. Do you see what I mean?"

"Yes," Charles said, "I guess I see."

It was the first time that his mother had ever spoken to him in that way about John Gray or had ever admitted that in any way his father was different from other people. It was not a bad apology, either, for John Gray. Yet there was one thing that Charles could not understand then or later. Why should anyone promise something unless the means were there for making that promise good? That was the weakness behind it all, the insidious, deceptive plank which destroyed all the rest of the structure.

"You see we've got to believe in him," his mother said. "It would hurt him so if we didn't." John Gray was always escaping from hurts, he was expert at it. "My, it's getting late. I'd better set the table."

"Do you want me to help you?" Charles asked.

"Oh, no," she said, and she rumpled his hair. "Your fingers are all thumbs, Charley. And here's Sam. Sam always knows when it's mealtime."

Sam had attained his full growth when he was seventeen and he already had the build of an athlete. Instead of working that summer, Sam had been playing ball in the Twilight League, on a team made up of employees from Wright-Sherwin and boys who hung around the news store. He had barely passed his college board examinations and Charles had heard his father say that at least Sam might have done a few hours of daily reading instead of fishing or taking girls to the movies or lining out flies. Yet when Sam came in that evening before supper he was like a younger and slightly larger replica of John Gray. He had the same swinging walk, the same quick smile, the same sharply defined features and the same brown hair, though there was more of it and it was not as carefully brushed. He had his mother's brown eyes but Charles was the one who had inherited her auburn hair. Sam had his father's neatness, too. His suit was not well pressed, his tie was knotted carelessly, his soft shirt was rumpled, his low tan shoes were scuffed, but still in some way he looked neat.

"Why, Sam," Esther Gray said, "where have you been?"

"Oh," Sam said, "just wandering around, over at the Masons'."

"Oh. Seeing May?"

"That's right," Sam said. "I wouldn't be seeing Jackie or Old Man Mason, would I?"

"Well, I think that's very nice," Esther Gray said.

"What's there for supper?" Sam asked. "Fish?"

"Cold roast beef," Esther Gray said, "and we have ice cream." Then she left for the dining room.

Sam sat down slowly in the wing chair, raised his left ankle over his right knee and began tying his shoe.

"Hi, kid," he said.

"Hi," Charles answered.

"What you reading?"

"*The House of the Seven Gables,*" Charles answered.

Sam let his foot drop limply to the floor.

"That's about those old women," he said. "You're always boning up on books, aren't you, just like the Old Man?"

"I can read if I want to," Charles said.

"Sure you can if you want to," Sam answered, "but where does it get you? Look at the Old Man." Sam yawned and pointed at the ceiling. "Up there reading Boswell. Is the Old Man back from Boston yet?"

"Yes, he's upstairs," Charles said.

"How's he acting?"

"What?" Charles asked.

"How's he acting? Is he happy or is he sad? Is he sorry or is he glad?"

"He's happy, I guess," Charles answered.

"Oh, he's happy, is he?" Sam said. "Well."

"Well, what?" Charles asked.

"Well, nothing," Sam answered. "Listen, kid, you ought not to be sitting here alone pounding books. Get around and know people."

"I'm not snooty," Charles said.

"Well, that's fine." Sam leaned down and retied his other shoe. "There are a lot of snooty people in this town and there are a lot of guys here driving dumpcarts and clamming who are just as good as anybody else and nobody's going to tell me different."

"Who's been telling you?" Charles asked.

"Never mind who's been telling me. I stick by my friends."

"Has May Mason been telling you?"

"Listen, kid," Sam said, "there are lots of other girls around besides May Mason."

"Did you and she have a fight?" Charles asked.

"Who said May Mason and I had a fight?" Sam asked. "Did Jackie tell you that?"

"You just act mad about something," Charles said. "That's why I asked you."

"Well, it would be nice," Sam said, "if you and Jackie Mason didn't hang around and listen so much. I'm not mad. I'm feeling fine. And the next time you go over to the Masons' and you see May, tell her if she wants someone in lace drawers it's all right with me."

"So you did have a fight with her," Charles said.

Sam pushed himself out of his chair.

"Listen, kid," he said, "don't knock yourself out talking. That's all everybody does around here, talk, talk, talk. You shoot off your yap and then Dorothea and then the Old Man — everybody except me."

"What do you think you're doing now?" Charles asked.

"Listen, kid," Sam said, "you think you're funny as hell, don't you? I'm not going to sit around here all my life. I might go up to Canada."

"What would you do in Canada?" Charles asked.

"I'll tell you what I'll do," Sam said. "I'll join the Canadian Army and go overseas. You don't know there's a war, do you?"

Everyone knew there was a war in Europe and that Pancho Villa had been making trouble in Texas, but Charles knew that Sam was only angry about something May Mason had said.

"You're not old enough."

Sam laughed airily.

"That's the boy, kid," he said. "Go on and talk. It's catching" — but neither of them went on because they heard their father on the stairs.

"Hello, Sammy," John Gray said, and then he raised his voice. "Esther," he called, "is supper nearly ready?"

Supper would be ready now in just a minute.

"What are you two boys talking about?" John Gray asked.

"Nothing much," Sam answered. "Just talking."

"It seemed to me that I heard your voices raised in some sort of altercation. There's nothing more futile than shouting in an argument, Sam. It betrays a lack of intellectual resource."

"All right," Sam said, "maybe I haven't got any intellectual resource."

"That's the awkward thing about being seventeen," John Gray said. "Now when I was seventeen — well, I suppose I was like you. Well, it doesn't seem possible, Sammy, but I suppose I was."

Charles saw Sam's face grow red.

"I was madly in love when I was seventeen," John Gray went on, "and that may have made me worry about my personal appearance. Now, Sam, that suit you're wearing — it's time we began thinking about your clothes. I'll have to take you in to Boston, Sammy, and get you something new."

"When?" Sam asked.

"When?" John Gray repeated, and he raised his eyebrows. "Oh, almost any time. We've got to get you looking right for college, Sammy. I don't know exactly what the well-dressed young man wears at Dartmouth but we ought to be able to inquire."

"What's the matter with Dartmouth?" Sam asked.

"Nothing," John Gray answered. "It is, sirs, a small college, yet there are those who love it" — and then Charles heard his mother calling. Supper was on the table.

Charles wanted to say something that would break the sense of strain around him. He wished that his father would understand that Sam was hurt about something and that it was no time to make fun of him or to call him Sammy; but his father was in no mood, then, to notice anything but his own swiftly running thoughts. Sam sat down quietly at the table and every now and then Charles stole a glance at his face. Sam was looking stolidly at his plate.

John Gray was talking about the Poland Spring House again. He was saying that everyone was getting too much in a rut, and that was the trouble with Clyde. At the same time, his mind was back again on what had happened to him when he was seventeen. They used to have two horses then, he was saying, and one of them was a dappled gray named Skip. It was a pity they had no horses now, but it was about time he bought the boys a boat.

"Well, why don't you get one?" Sam said. "Joe Stevens's catboat is for sale."

"Is it?" John Gray asked. "I didn't know it was, but then I don't see as much of the Stevens boys as you do, Sammy. How much do they want for it?"

"I don't know," Sam said. "Around three hundred dollars."

"Well, Sammy," John Gray said, "you might go around and look at her and if she looks all right find what they're asking."

"You mean you'll buy her?" Sam asked.

"I don't see why I shouldn't," John Gray said. "We'll let Sammy negotiate it for us. It's about time Sammy learned a little about business."

"John," Esther Gray said, "three hundred dollars is a lot of money. Let's get the house painted first. Don't you think we ought to, John?"

The boat was safe at its moorings, and now the house was there.

"I'll have a little more cocoa, Esther," John Gray said. "I wish you'd tell Mrs. Murphy the cocoa's very good tonight. I don't know whether it's worth while painting the house. We ought to have a larger house — further back from the street, like the Weaver place, or something further out in the country. Do you know, I heard the other day that Lyte's Castle is for sale."

"Oh, John," Esther Gray said, and she laughed. "For mercy's sake, not Lyte's Castle. Why, it takes two men to take care of the garden and the lawns."

"Now, Esther," John Gray said. "Those things have a way of looking out for themselves. Dorothea needs a place to see the boys, and Sammy will be bringing friends from college, and Charley ought to have a pony. He ought to learn how to ride."

"Oh, John," Esther Gray said, and she laughed again, "let's try not to think of everything at once."

Then Charles heard Sam make a choking sound.

"What's the matter, Sammy?" John Gray asked.

"Nothing," Sam said. "I was just thinking about the pony."

"What about the pony?"

Sam looked carefully at his plate but his voice was hoarser.

"Nothing, except it's the same old pony I was going to get."

"Sam," his mother said. "Sam."

No one spoke for a moment. The rhythm of the talk was broken. They could hear Mrs. Murphy clattering the dishes in the kitchen and the rattle of a wagon and the clap of a horse's hoofs on Spruce Street. John Gray was looking thoughtfully at Sam, and something made Charles sit taut and motionless.

"I know," John Gray said slowly. "I'm sorry about that, Sammy."

Sam looked slowly up from his plate.

"If you're sorry," he said, "why do you go on with it?"

"Sam," Esther Gray said sharply. "Sam."

It was all new to Charles, new and unforgettable. Sam was not the person he thought he was, and neither was his father, as they sat there gazing at each other.

"Just exactly what do you mean," John Gray asked, "by going on with it?" Charles wished that nothing that was going on had happened and Sam must have wished it too, because he hesitated before he answered.

"The same old guff," Sam said. "That's all."

"I think it might be just as well," his father spoke very carefully, "if you were to leave the table, Sam."

In the silence that followed, Sam pushed back his chair and rose. "Sure I'll leave the table," Sam said.

"Sam," his mother called, "come back here and apologize to your father."

"Oh, never mind," John Gray said. "Leave him alone, Esther," and before he had finished speaking the front door slammed.

They were all intensely embarrassed. There was nothing left but the family responsibility for smoothing things over, for pretending that nothing had happened.

"Charley, do you know whether Sam is troubled about anything?" his mother asked. "I wonder whether he's been having some trouble with May Mason. Charles, will you go out and get the ice cream?" But before Charles could move, his father spoke.

"Esther," he said, "I think if it's all the same to you I'll go upstairs and read awhile. It's been a fine supper, but Charley will eat my ice cream for me, won't you, Charley?" and he clapped Charles on the shoulder.

"Oh, John," his mother began. "Sam didn't mean — "

"Oh, never mind it, Esther," John Gray said, and he rose and walked to her end of the table and bent down and kissed her. "There are some things I want to figure out upstairs and I can do it better without ice cream."

She followed him to the foot of the stairs.

"John," she called, "we might go sometime and look at Lyte's Castle."

Then he heard his father laugh.

"Well, perhaps not Lyte's Castle, Esther," he answered. "Let's trim it down a little. Perhaps Sammy was right about Lyte's Castle."

The house on Spruce Street was one of those two-and-a-half-story oblong dwellings which Charles came later to associate with New England seaport towns. It was plainer than anything on Johnson Street, but with the same architectural plan — the hallway running from front to back, the staircase with its landing, the spacious rooms on the second story and the lower-studded, smaller rooms above, hot in summer, cold in winter. Charles and Sam slept on the top floor, because there was not room for everyone downstairs, and the boys could do what they wanted with the rooms up there. They could use the spool beds and the old pine bureaus with the drawers that stuck. They could keep all their possessions upstairs, instead of leaving them in the rest of the house. They could pin pictures on the walls and arrange things in any way they wanted, but they had to make their own beds and look after the rooms themselves; and it was not such a bad idea, provided you had a sense of order.

When Charles went to bed that night, the moon was rising and the moon was large and yellow, almost full. He had been careful to move his bed so that the moonlight would not strike his face be, cause Mrs. Murphy had told him that moonlight on your face when you slept made you crazy, but from the shadow where he lay he could see the rest of the room, looking not the least as it did in daylight but indefinite and larger, as though there were no walls. This must have been why, when he awoke suddenly, he had the unpleasant sensation of not knowing where he was until he saw the windows and the trees outside. Then he saw a shadow which did not belong there near his bed and he heard Sam's voice.

"Charley, I didn't mean to wake you up."

"What is it?" Charles asked. "Is anything the matter?"

"I just looked in," Sam said, and he sat down on the edge of the bed. His voice was the only thing that was like him. The rest of him was shadow.

"What time is it?" Charles asked, and the bed creaked under Sam's weight.

"I don't know. After eleven o'clock."

"Where've you been?" Charles asked.

"Out, around," Sam said. "Walking around, thinking."

Neither of them spoke for a while and Charles knew that Sa did not want to be alone.

"If he hadn't shot his mush off," Sam said, "I wouldn't have shot off mine."

Again there was an interlude of wretched silence and Charles could hear the elm leaves rustle.

"I don't like him," Sam said. "By God, I don't like him."

Sam's voice sounded unreal and unpleasant in the moonlight.

"What's he ever done for us?" Sam said. "Not a goddam thing."

It was very unpleasant in the moonlight and it was very unsettling to Charles because he had a deep respect for Sam's judgment.

"It's always the same damn thing," Sam said. "First he shoots off his mush and then he ends by walking around his room like a squirrel, and it's never his fault when he's licked." Again the room was filled with an uneasy, awful silence. "Whenever he gets his hands on money, he goes up to Boston and loses it."

Charles did not know that Sam was discussing the eccentricities of a profit system or that it was his own first contact with a segment of living that he was later to know so well.

"How does he lose it?" he asked.

"You wouldn't understand it," Sam said. "Never mind how he does. You wouldn't understand."

There were a great many things about life that Charles did not understand but he could start with the assumption that his father was a highly intelligent man and that he must have known perfectly what the odds were. There was something which prevented men like him from stopping, something beyond the realms of ordinary reason.

"Listen, kid," Sam said, "if you ever get to doing what he does, if you don't take a hitch in your pants and behave like other people, I'll beat the pants right off you."

Sam still sat there and Charles could see his shadow as he leaned on his elbows with his chin in his hands.

"Charley."

"Yes," Charles said.

"If you're over at the Masons' tomorrow and you should happen to see May, I wish you'd give her this." He was holding out a folded piece of paper.

"Why don't you give it to her yourself?" Charles asked.

"You give it to her," Sam said. "That's a good kid, Charley." Then Sam was gone and Charles lay staring at the moonlight, still wondering why his father acted as he did in Boston.

Once Charles did ask him why — long afterwards, the year when Charles had left Wright-Sherwin in Clyde to work in the Boston investment house of E. P. Rush & Company.

"Now don't preach to me, Charley," his father had said. "I'm not going to stand any of your damn sanctimonious lectures."

Charles said he was not preaching, he was only asking why he never stopped when he had a profit.

"There you go preaching," John Gray said again. "All right, I'll tell you why — because I want everything or nothing."

If you kept on wanting everything or nothing long enough, particularly if you became too anxious for it, perhaps you always ended with nothing.

IV

Don't Let Anyone Tell You, My Young Friends, That There Is Any Such Thing as Luck . . .

CHARLES ALWAYS THOUGHT of the Masons when things went wrong at home. In periods of bitterness and frustration he found himself wishing that Mr. Virgil Mason were his father and that the Grays could be happy like the Masons, living in a well-painted house with everything in order, even if Mr. Virgil Mason was not as bright as his father and never read much or talked about books. Mr. Mason's father had owned the drugstore on Lyford Street and had once compounded a toothache remedy which had sold well locally. Mr. Mason himself was in the insurance business in Boston and when he came home in the evening he liked to work in his small vegetable garden when there was light enough, a form of relaxation that John Gray hated. In the winter he liked to make things down cellar or do odd jobs around the house which were never done in the Gray house next door. Mr. Mason could make beautiful toy boats or little windmills and he liked having children around. Mrs. Mason, Charles realized, long before he was interested in such things, must once have been as pretty as May, but she was too stout now and did not worry any longer about her looks.

"Anyway," he heard her say once, "I caught Virgil."

His own mother was much prettier but he was sure she was not as happy as Mrs. Mason. At any rate, he always had a good time at the Masons'. May was pretty but she was not stuck-up about it and she did not correct him the way Dorothea did, and Jack was his best friend.

Charles could never discover why Jack was discontented, too. He used to think that Mr. Mason was the best sort of father one could imagine, but Jackie said once, in one of those long and confidential talks they used to have, that he wished his father were more like Charles's father.

"I don't see what's the matter with him," Charles had said; but Jack had said there was plenty the matter with him. He was always in his shirt sleeves doing work that other people should do for him. On Sunday he would be hammering and sawing and tinkering outdoors where people could see him when they went to church. His father ought to go to church more often and not work on Sunday, even if it was only the Unitarian Church.

"But my father never goes," Charles had told him; but Jack had said that all the rest of Charles's family did, even if it was only the Unitarian Church and not the Episcopalian.

"Besides," Jackie had said, "my father never wants to do anything but sit around the house. He doesn't know the right people, and almost everybody likes your father."

Charles agreed with Jackie Mason that they were both going to be very different from their fathers. They were going to make more money when they grew up, and they weren't going to live on Spruce Street. Yet Charles could never understand why Jack worried because his grandfather had been a druggist and why he was always complaining about the Mason house and the furniture. He was always reading magazine articles about successful men. It didn't matter where you started — even if your grandfather had been a druggist — it was a question of working hard, Jack said, and of meeting the right people. Jack had won the composition prize in the seventh grade by writing a composition on the boyhood of Andrew Carnegie, and his mind was always on success. For example, he was deeply interested in the career of Mr. Sullivan, who had bought the house across the street, because Mr. Sullivan had started out as a laboring man and now he was in the contracting business, making a lot of money.

"The only thing wrong," Jack said, "is that he doesn't know the right people."

It was Saturday afternoon when Charles went over to the Mason house with Sam's note in his pocket, and he opened the front door without knocking because he was Jack's best friend, Mrs. Mason had said, and he could go out and come in any time he wanted. When he was in the hall, he heard Mr. and Mrs. Mason talking in the front parlor.

"It's the way he is," Mr. Mason was saying, "and it's none of my business, Margaret. There's no use arguing when it's the way he is."

"It's so hard on poor Esther," he heard Mrs. Mason say just before he reached the parlor doorway.

Mrs. Mason was darning a pair of Jack's stockings and Mr. Mason was in his shirt sleeves, sitting in front of a table covered with newspapers, mending a Canton china plate. His glasses had slipped down to the end of his nose and his heavy reddish face shone with perspiration and he held the broken pieces of china very carefully. It was remarkable that his heavy hands could do such delicate things.

"Oh," Mrs. Mason said, and she looked startled. "Why, hello, Charley."

"Hello," Charles said. "Is May anywhere around?"

"My, my," Mr. Mason said, "aren't you pretty young to be looking around for May?" and he smiled and pushed his glasses back to the bridge of his nose.

"Why, May's in the back room practicing, dear," Mrs. Mason said, and then Charles could hear the notes of the Masons' old upright piano, "and Jack's out in the shed splitting kindling, and there's some lemonade in the kitchen."

That was the way it always was at the Masons', lemonade, and everyone was happy. As he moved toward the back room, he heard May playing a waltz from *The Pink Lady*, not well, but he could recognize it, and he wished that Dorothea would ever play anything on the piano that he could understand. May's yellow hair was gathered up in a knot and she was wearing what Charles knew was her third-best dress, but still she looked very pretty. It might have been a perishable, Dresden china prettiness, but Charles was not aware of such things then. He never forgot May, sitting straight on the piano stool, her hands pounding the keys conscientiously. He remembered the curve of her white neck and though her head was turned away from him, he already had an impression of her blue eyes and her red, half-parted lips.

"Why, Charley," she said, "I didn't know you were there. You sneaked in like an Indian."

"I was making a lot of noise," Charles said, "but you were making more."

"It isn't nice to call it noise," May said. "I wish I played as well as Dorothea."

"You play better," Charles said. "I like it a whole lot better."

"Oh, Charley, you know I don't," May said, and she laughed. "I don't do anything very well. Where's Sam?"

"I don't know," Charles said, "but he wanted me to give you this," and he pulled the note out of his pocket.

"Oh," May said, and she snatched it out of his hand and tore open the envelope, and then she put her hand on his arm. "Don't go away, Charley. Please stay here while I read it."

As she read it, with her head turned away from him, he felt the warm grasp of her fingers on his arm and he wished she were his sister. Standing there beside her, so close that her shoulder touched his, he could have read the note if he had wanted, but he never knew what Sam had written. He only knew that May was crying. She had dropped the note. She had drawn him toward her as she still sat there on the piano stool. Her head was pressed against him and she was crying. He was still very shy with girls, particularly with girls of May's age, and besides he was madly in love with Miss Jenks, who had been his teacher in the seventh grade.

"May," he said, "don't cry."

"Oh, Charley," May said, "I'm just crying because I'm so happy. Tell Sam," she held him closer, "tell Sam it's all right."

He was relieved when May found her handkerchief and wiped her eyes.

"I guess I'd better go and see Jackie," he said.

"All right," May said, "but bend your head down," and before he knew what she was going to do, her arms were around his neck and she had kissed him.

"Charley," she said, "you didn't mind it, did you?" He had no idea what Sam had written or why any note of Sam's should have made May Mason cry.

Out in the woodshed, Jackie was splitting kindlings in a languid

201

way. When he saw Charles he dropped his ax and sat down on the chopping block.

"I don't know why an American boy has to split kindlings," Jack said.

"Oh, go on and split them," Charles told him. "Didn't Henry Ford split them?"

"I'll bet Henry Ford had a machine to do it," Jack said. "There ought to be a machine."

"Go on," Charles said. "Didn't Andrew Carnegie split them?"

"No," Jack said, "he had peat or something. He lived in Scotland."

"Well, hurry up and finish," Charles said, "and let's go over to Meaders'."

Jack pushed himself up slowly from the chopping block and pushed his hair from his forehead. He needed a haircut. He had yellow hair with a wave in it like May's.

"Are you going to the Lovells' party?" he asked.

Charles did not understand the question, until Jack explained. It seemed that Jessica Lovell was having a birthday party and Jack had been invited that morning and the Meaders were going.

"I thought everyone was asked," Jack said.

"Well, I'm not," Charles answered.

"Well, that's funny," Jack said. "I don't see why they asked me and not you."

Clearly Jackie was pleased that he had been asked and Charles not, but Charles was not worried in the least, in those days, about the Lovells or about Andrew Carnegie or about meeting the right people. He was still thinking of May Mason and Sam and he felt proud and pleased. He knew she was Sam's girl, and he always thought of her afterwards as Sam's girl. She was still Sam's girl when she finally married Jeffrey Meader. It was a secret which they always held in common. He knew and she knew that she would have married Sam if Sam had lived.

Memory had an erratic way of leaving some things clear and others blank. Those were the figures, the reference points, of his childhood. Somehow other people and things that he thought he would always remember were laid away in the partially open, dusty drawer of forgetfulness, but not those figures. There was a time when he had been out in a rowboat with the Meaders and the boat had been swamped in a squall and they had nearly been drowned in the river. He had once fought with a boy in grammar school whose name was Slavin and it must have been of great immediate importance and a full dress affair for it took place on Cedar Hill beyond the water tank, where one customarily went for serious fighting. No events like these, however, carried into the present as did the changing figures of those few people nearest him, his father, his mother, his Aunt Jane, Dorothea, and the Masons, and of them all Sam was by far the clearest, because he was a finished memory, distinct and beyond future alteration.

He always associated Sam with the end of childhood. When the music of World War I played, Sam was always there. It was a long way to Tipperary, and while you had a lucifer to light your fag, smile, boys, that's the style, I didn't raise my boy to be a soldier to shoot some other mother's boy. Sam always came back with those tunes, still not in uniform, but Sam had enlisted in the National Guard and was waiting to be called.

Sam was sitting in the City Hall auditorium where Charles's class at the Webster Grammar School was undergoing its graduation exercises. Pack up your troubles in your old kit bag, smile, boys, that's the style. This must have been at the end of Sam's first year at Dartmouth. At any rate, he could still sometimes see Sam, in a suit he must have bought at Hanover — John Gray or someone must have done something about his clothes — winking at him from the audience, twisting the whole left side of his face, as Charles sat on the platform in the second row, behind the girls.

Martin J. Gifford, who was going to run that fall for the state legislature, was delivering the speech customarily made to a Clyde graduating class. It was a speech containing all the doctrines on which Charles Gray and his contemporaries had been brought up and which so many of them tried in vain to reconcile with what they experienced later.

Martin J. Gifford was speaking in tender tones, in keeping with the tender age of his audience, but his discourse was keyed, too, to the mores of their parents, relatives and friends.

"Luck," Mr. Gifford was saying, in a quavering voice, "is a word that makes me laugh. Don't let anyone tell you, my young friends, that there is any such thing as luck. Do you think that you are here today, on the threshold of higher education, because of luck? No!"

At that moment Sam caught his eye and winked again. The faces of Dorothea, his mother, and Aunt Jane were blurred, but not Sam's.

"No, no," Mr. Gifford was saying. "You are here because of the sacrifices of your parents and the work of every citizen and the very fine achievements of the wonderful ladies and gentlemen on your school committee, your teachers, and of your great mayor, my dear old friend, Francis X. Flynn."

He did not intone the name of Clyde's great mayor but ended it in a shout, and then he waited for the fluttering of applause.

"And what made it possible for them to give you these advantages and to make their sacrifices and their dreams for you come true?" Mr. Gifford was asking. "Was it accident? Was it luck? No! I'll tell you what made it possible." And he walked to the edge of the platform before he told them. "It was possible because you live in the greatest country in the world, in the United States of America, where all men, I thank God, are free and equal, living in the frame of freedom, life, liberty and the pursuit of happiness, where each of us can look the other in the eye and say, 'I am as free as you are; no matter how rich you may be, I have the same chance as you, because this great land of ours is the land of freedom.'"

Mr. Gifford mopped his forehead before he went on with the credo of Clyde.

"Oh, no — there is no such thing as luck, my dear young friends, not for American boys and girls. As you sit here, not so far from entering the contest for life's prizes, you are all starting even because this is America, no matter what may be your religion or race or bank account. There is no grease for palms in America. The only grease is elbow grease. Look at our greatest men, born on small farms in small houses, boys without a cent to their names. Did they get there by luck? Oh, no. They got there by making the most of opportunities which are open, thank God, to every American boy and girl."

This credo was all a part of the air one breathed in Clyde. Later, if it did not jibe with experience, you still believed. If you heard it often enough, it became an implicit, indestructible foundation for future conduct. Even when Sam had winked at him, Charles was sure that Sam believed.

Charles was still sure that Sam believed when they were out on the sidewalk afterwards and when Sam clapped him on the shoulder. It was wonderful to be there with his older brother, who was in a fraternity at Dartmouth and who had been the captain of the football team at Clyde. It was wonderful to be walking down the street with Sam, where everyone could see.

"It was the same old bushwa, kid," Sam said. "He certainly could fork it out" — but Charles was sure that Sam believed.

The words of that speech were a tide that had carried him out of his childhood and there was no logical reason for associating them with his brother Sam but his memory always did. Johnny, get your gun on the run, we won't forget the memory of brave Lafayette, the Yanks are coming over there, you've got to get up in the morning. A long, long trail was winding to the land of my dreams, and how could you keep them down on the farm after they'd seen Paree. Sam had seen Paree one night, but there was no problem of keeping Sam down on the farm. He was going but he was not gone yet. Before the Twenty-sixth Division sailed, he had walked the streets of Clyde on leave from Framingham, in a uniform that was too tight around the neck. He had taken Charles with him to Winton & Low's jewelry store and he had bought a ring for May. It was getting close to autumn then, the year when Charles would enter high school. That was the year when he was first called Master Gray, and he was already madly in love with a girl named Doris Wormser, whose father was a foreman at Wright-Sherwin and who later married Willie Woodbury, when he got the farm machinery agency. Charles's head was already even with Sam's shoulder when they went in to Winton & Low's.

"She isn't going to wear it yet," Sam had said, "but she can tie
around her neck."

It seemed like a very good idea. Sometime he might buy a ring
for Doris Wormser to wear around her neck.

"Let me know how May's getting on, sometimes, will you?" Sam
had said.

He was getting almost old enough to be a friend of Sam's, right
there at the end. That was almost the last of Sam, but he was always
back with Charles whenever anyone played those tunes.

V

The Youth Replies, I Can

— RALPH WALDO EMERSON

CHARLES WAS THROUGH Dartmouth and he was working at Wright-Sherwin before he began to realize that no human problems are unique. He must always, though he only half knew it, have shared his father's discontent with what he had. He was very sure that success and happiness were the same thing, when he was twenty-three, and yet he could already see that different people had different ideas of success. It was a subject which he and Jack Mason discussed very often, for Jack had gone to work in Wright-Sherwin too, after he had graduated from Amherst. Naturally, they each would bring up personal examples, and this was the beauty of living in a place like Clyde, where the lives and careers of everyone were known to everyone else. Charles, who only knew Mr. Lovell academically then, did not consider Mr. Lovell a successful person, but Jackie said he was the most successful man in Clyde. Mr. Lovell knew the right people, not only in Clyde but along the North Shore and in Boston, and that was what success meant; but Charles said Mr. Lovell could not run Wright-Sherwin.

"That's exactly what I mean," Jack said. "He doesn't have to. He has everything that running Wright-Sherwin could give him."

There was a blind spot, Charles realized later, in everyone's line of reasoning. He could see that living on Johnson Street was not the end of everything and his nebulous ambitions were already larger than Jack Mason's. If you wanted to pick a successful man in Clyde, you could take Old Man Stanley, who ran Wright-Sherwin. He knew all the right people, too, because it was worth their while to know him. He was a director of the Clyde Fund, a trustee of the

Old Ground Cemetery, a director of the Dock Street Savings Bank and a director of the West India Insurance Company without ever having belonged in Clyde originally. He was in everything because of his ability and not because he lived on Johnson Street. He had taken over Wright-Sherwin when it was nothing but an unsuccessful brass foundry and now it made parts for the best precision instruments in the country.

Then, if you wanted, you could go on to Mr. Thomas, who was president of the Dock Street Savings Bank. He belonged in Clyde; his father had been head of the bank before him, but Mr. Thomas knew his business besides living on Johnson Street. The Dock Street Bank might be in a queer-looking building, but it was as sound as any in Massachusetts — or you could take Mr. Sullivan, who ran his contracting business and owned shares in a dozen small enterprises — or Mr. Levine, whose father had owned Levine's drygoods store and who suddenly had bought the shoeshop. Mr. Levine and Mr. Sullivan did not know the right people except in a business way, but it seemed to Charles that they had done pretty well in spite of what Jack Mason said.

From this gallery of Clyde's great men, Charles could turn to his own father, who, by contrast, was an habitual failure, though actually there were many like him in Clyde who were much worse off. If John Gray did not know when to stop when he started, at least he had his own ideas of when not to start, and there was no use starting, he wanted Charles to understand, unless you had some capital. In the summer of 1916 and the next winter, when he had inherited his share of Aunt Mathilda's estate, he would have succeeded if Hugh Blashfield had not doled out the money by degrees, a thousand dollars at a time. He could never feel afterwards that Hugh Blashfield had been a friend of his, not that he wanted to mention this to anyone but Charles. If Hugh Blashfield had let him have the whole twenty-five thousand dollars as he had asked, instead of handing it out to him in little driblets, the whole story might have been different, because you had to have capital. He had tried it once with the five thousand that was left him out of trust at the time of the Judge's death and he had tried it again with the thirty thou-

sand which had come to the family from Dr. Marchby, but this was
something that Charles only learned later from his mother. Then he
had tried it a third time with Aunt Mathilda's legacy. If Hugh Blashfield had not tried to stop it, it would have been a different story, but
Hugh Blashfield had no imagination. Hugh was nothing but a small-
town lawyer.

John Gray's appearance had changed very little since his reversals
of 1916. His hair was shot with gray and so was his mustache, but
he had retained his posture and he had not put on weight. He could
still read without glasses and he still had the appealing smile of a
younger man. As Aunt Jane used to say, John had matured beautifully, and Charles had even heard his Uncle Gerald Marchby admit
it once, on one of those rare occasions when he and Aunt Ruth
Marchby came to call. It meant a good deal when the Doctor, for
Uncle Gerald was a doctor too, like Charles's maternal grandfather,
had a kind word of any sort to say about his brother-in-law. He
said he did not know what John had done to keep so young.

John Gray answered that if he looked young it was because he
had not worried for years. He had no financial problems. Gerald and
Hugh Blashfield, not to mention Esther and Jane, would not allow
him to have them. He was referring, of course, to an agreement he
had made at the end of 1917 to let Gerald and Hugh Blashfield pay
the bills out of the proceeds of the Judge's trust. He had no financial
worries, and Jane had paid for Charles's education, such as it was —
he could never understand why Jane had wanted first Sam and then
Charles to go to Dartmouth. He did not have to worry about the
children. Charles was in Wright-Sherwin making twenty-five dollars a week, a miserable sum, even for a graduate of Dartmouth (a
small place but he loved it), and Dorothea, who never could seem
to find anyone suitable for a husband, although she had tried, was
comfortably established in the public library, and she still had someone keeping company with her. It was Elbridge Sterne now, who
had come from Kansas City and was doing something about metal-
lurgy in Wright-Sherwin. No, he had no financial worries, and besides, he had no vices. He smoked very little and he hardly ever
drank, except for an occasional glass of port in his bookroom up-

stairs, and he always walked to the mill, where he did not have to worry either. He could do the accounting with his eyes shut. If anybody worried about the mill, it ought to be Gerald and Hugh Blashfield. He had suggested that they sell the family's holdings, as cotton mills in New England were on the downgrade, but that was their responsibility since they were trustees for the Judge's estate. It was their blood pressure that ought to rise, not his.

Besides, he did not gamble. He was pained to see that Gerald and Ruth looked surprised but it was true, *he did not gamble*. He had attempted some investments occasionally in Boston, of a speculative nature, on the rare occasions when he had been allowed a little capital, but that was all over, now that Gerald and Hugh saw to it that he had no cash but pocket money. He did not mean to say that they were not generous. What they gave him, together with that wretched pittance that Stafford paid him for keeping the mill's accounts, would have been enough to have allowed him to do something at the race track, but there was one thing that they would all admit, Esther, Jane, and Ruth and Gerald, and Gerald could remove his gall bladder tomorrow morning if it wasn't true. He had never done anything with races. He had never approved of them and he hated the uncertainty of horse racing, and he did not like games of chance, dice, numbers or cards. He had never played them except for a little friendly poker down at the Pine Tree firehouse. He did not gamble. What was it Thomas Fuller said? "A man gets no thanks for what he loseth at play." Of course Edmund Burke took a wider view. What was it he said in his speech in the House of Commons? "Gaming is a principle inherent in human nature. It belongs to us all." Yet David Garrick put it another way. What was it David Garrick said? Oh, yes. "Shake off the shackles of this tyrant vice; Hear other calls than those of cards and dice." That would be a very good thing for Gerald to remember when he played auction at the Whist Club, but personally it did not apply to him.

He could not understand why certain people, particularly on Johnson Street, looked on him as a black sheep just because he had attempted to make a few speculative investments. He was faithful to his wife, and that was more than could be said of certain individuals on Johnson Street and on other streets in Clyde — but the trouble with Clyde was that Clyde never forgot. It remembered the indiscretions of youth as though they were yesterday and if you made one mistake in Clyde it did for you.

He still had a spring to his step when he walked down the street and he had what was commonly known as a cheery word for everyone. He and all the other John Grays Charles knew later were impulsively generous, always ready with a dollar when the hat was passed round, always ready to buy a tag, any sort of tag, on tag days. John Gray was the sort of man who would always stop when a child was crying in the street. When anyone was ill, he would always be the first to call. The people at the mill all loved him. He was the one they called on, when they were in trouble, to intercede with Judge Fanning at the police court or with Alf Jason, the truant officer, or with Miss Nickson, the visiting nurse. John Gray was exactly the sort of person who would give you the shirt off his back, impulsively and generously, if you needed his shirt.

It was true, as it sometimes occurred to Charles, that most people who said this about John Gray were not shirtless, and it was unfair to think that John Gray and people like him were tolerant and kindly because they were never sure when they would need such coin themselves.

Yet it was also true, as John Gray said so often, that no one forgot in Clyde, particularly about money. Everyone knew that John Gray had run through money, thousands and thousands of dollars of it. Everyone knew that Mrs. Gray and Dorothea would not have been able to afford even a part-time maid or a cleaning woman and that Charles could not have gone to college if Miss Jane had not helped out. If you were in the family you were always conscious of this, and though his father always treated those matters lightly when he mentioned them, John Gray was bitterly ashamed of his failures; but Esther Gray always understood his sensitivity, and Dorothea and Aunt Jane, and if the subject of poverty came up in the family it was always slurred over with great speed.

Charles first fully understood this family feeling from observing that his father was not put on the committee of the Clyde Fund after

Mr. Finch had died. At this time Charles had been working for more than a year at Wright-Sherwin. He had recently been moved into the accounting department under Mr. Richard Howell, one of those assiduous slaves of detail so useful in any office. The man whose place Charles had filled, and an older man, too, had been fired by Mr. Howell, who used to say that things were either right or wrong and that there was no excuse for not doing them right. When things were done right he accepted them without a word but he always blew up when there was a mistake. Charles had been checking over an inventory that afternoon and he felt tired and uncertain.

It was a dull September day and the wind was so high that he thought it was blowing up for a storm. He was wondering what he would do if he were fired from Wright-Sherwin. It was the first time that his future had depended on the whim of a single critical stranger. As he walked into the wind down River Street and into the square at Dock Street, he hoped that for once the family would not ask him how he was getting on with Mr. Howell. This was a question which his father invariably asked each evening. John Gray, it seemed, had been to Sunday School with Dickie Howell, who had been in charge of passing out the hymnbooks, and now Dickie Howell passed the contribution box. It all went to show, John Gray had said, what happened if you were consistent. Dickie had married a girl in the Sunday School class named Myrtle Snyder, who had a thin jaw and a button nose like Dickie's. They lived in the North End and you could see Dickie clipping his privet hedge every Saturday afternoon. He had the straightest hedge in Clyde. Details like these were always interesting to John Gray, but they had nothing to do with Charles's difficulties.

"It must be a beautiful relationship," John Gray said, "yours and Dickie Howell's."

"Can't you tell me what he's like?" Charles asked.

John Gray only said that it did not matter what he was like. He said it was the old master and man relationship. He only said it was fascinating that Charles was working for Dickie Howell, and that it was a small world and a just world.

"I used to kick Dickie Howell's shins at Sunday School," John Gray said. "I never dreamed that he would be kicking yours, Charley."

Dorothea and his mother were in the parlor when he got home, reading the *Clyde Herald,* which Tommy Stevens always threw on the front porch from his bicycle at five o'clock.

"I think it would be just as well not to speak of it at all," his mother was saying to Dorothea, who was darning one of her best silk stockings.

"Well, here's Charley," Dorothea said. "Ask him. He knows everything."

"I know how you got a hole in it," Charles said.

"How?" Dorothea asked.

"Running after Elbridge Sterne."

"Well, I'd rather run after Elbridge," Dorothea said, "than trot around after Mr. Howell."

"I wish you children wouldn't always bicker," Esther Gray said. "Charley, the Clyde Fund didn't take your father."

The Clyde Fund was one of those generous bequests which so many New England citizens have left for the benefit of towns in which they lived. It had started with a bequest of five thousand dollars in 1820 by a Mr. Clarence Fanning, the principal to be held for a term of years at compound interest and then the income to be expended on shade trees and on other street improvements, under the direction of five representative citizens, to be named by the Dock Street Savings Bank. The trustees met three times a year, in the Dock Street Savings Bank directors' room, and Charles's grandfather, the Judge, had been one of the first trustees.

"Why should they have taken him?" Charles asked.

"Oh, Charley," his mother said, "don't say that."

"That's just the sort of thing Charley would say about Father," Dorothea said.

"Well," Charles said, "you might as well mention it, because he'll find out."

Just at that moment John Gray came in from his work at the mill.

"Well, well," he said, "the wind's getting into the northeast. How's Dickie Howell, Charley?"

"Don't tease him, John," Esther Gray said.

"Now, Esther," John Gray said, "Charley and I have our own brand of humor, acrid, but it's humor. Well, so you're all reading the *Clyde Herald*."

"John." Charles's mother smiled brightly. "You didn't tell us that the Pine Trees were going to another muster."

"Are they?" John Gray answered. "I didn't see that, but I saw about the Clyde Fund. Don't look disappointed, Esther. I'm hardly the type. What would I do in a savings bank talking about shade trees?"

Supper was the time in the day when the family was always drawn closest together and Charles's pleasantest memories, as well as memories of quarrels and crises, all began with the supper table at Spruce Street. The old sliding shutters were always drawn across the dining room windows and for light there were four candles in brass candlesticks and a hanging oil lamp above the table, a strange and ugly Victorian contraption which let itself up and down on pulleys. There was a halo of light above the round dark walnut table but the fireplace with its mantel and paneling over it and the white dado of the dining room were always in shadow. The same willow ware pot of boiled cracked cocoa always stood by his mother's place. He had once told Nancy about that cocoa, which used to steep on the back of the stove for days, and out of curiosity Nancy had looked for some in New York but she could never find it. It only seemed to exist at Mr. Beardsley's grocery shop at Clyde. There were always a loaf of bread and a knife and a breadboard by Dorothea's place and a covered Sandwich glass butter dish at John Gray's end of the table. The napkins were neatly rolled in silver rings, each with its owner's initial. (Sam's ring was still in the Empire sideboard.) The chairs around the table were of the painted, Hitchcock type, and all these furnishings were so closely associated with the family that each thing in the room had an almost living relationship to each other thing.

Even if they were gossiping over the most humdrum events of

the day at supper, John Gray was always entertaining. He began that evening by touching lightly on the Clyde Fund. The Fund, he said, had a definite effect on the mental processes of all its trustees and being a trustee was a great responsibility. Should the income be spent to sprinkle Johnson Street in the summer or should it be spent for public hitching posts on Dock Street? It was still to dawn, he said, on a Clyde Fund trustee that it was more important to regulate motor traffic. Or should the money be spent in erecting a suitable drinking fountain for horses at the southwest corner of Dock and Johnson Streets to balance the Hewitt Memorial Fountain on the northwest corner, and, if so, how high should the fountain be? These were problems, John Gray said, that needed Clyde's best minds, and how could the birds be kept from the head of George Washington near the courthouse without discouraging the birds? He was sorry, very sorry, that he could not be there to help.

Then his mind moved on. The Dock Street Bank had closed its mortgage on the old Bingham house. Surely Charles must have noticed it, the square brick house that he passed every day on his way to Wright-Sherwin. Its fence was gone and its window sashes were rotted but it had a perfect doorway. Tony Leveroni, who worked at the mill, lived there, and John Gray had been in to see him when his boy was sick. The Leveronis lived in the old ballroom but their stove and sink and washtubs could not spoil it. It was one of the stateliest rooms he had ever seen. The molding was as light as lace. It was a privilege to sit with Tony Leveroni and look at the carved medallion below the mantel. If the Clyde trustees wanted to do anything they should buy that house and restore it, and then he shrugged his shoulders.

Usually after supper he went upstairs alone to his room to read and it surprised Charles that evening when he asked him to come up too.

"That is, if you have time, Charley," John Gray said, "or have you a round of engagements?"

The room where his father spent his evenings was almost square with two deep windows with window seats and, on either side of the fireplace, arches and two other windows. A battered sofa stood in front of the fireplace and a table behind it held a student lamp and the books and papers in which John Gray was currently interested. Two ugly Morris chairs by the sofa had come from the Marchbys and some older Windsor chairs had been sent over by Aunt Jane from the Judge's house, and the painted pine floor was partly covered with a worn Oriental carpet. The bookcases were filled with brown leather volumes from the Judge's library and others which John Gray had purchased. Among these were, of course, the works of Samuel Johnson and all sorts of other volumes of the period, all with elaborate dedications to their patrons. Tacitus, an early translation of the seventeenth century, stood beside Burton's *Anatomy of Melancholy,* and Boccaccio, with a broken back, leaned against Fuller's *Worthies.* The bookcases were far from adequate. Books stood in heaps on top of them and in piles on the floor near the table, like the broken columns of a ruined temple.

The room was never neat, because John Gray did not like to have the women dust it. He said he knew where every book was until people began to move them. Women never went with books. They did not understand why he did not want his print of London Bridge dusted, or why he liked the Landseer engraving of sad-eyed dogs. It might not be a good picture but he liked it, and he liked to have his shotguns leaning in the corner under one of the arches by the fireplace, and he liked to have his brass-bound box of old decanters on the floor, and the sea chest that had belonged to his grandfather, the Captain, cater-corner on the far side of the room, and he did not care whether the tall clock there kept time or not. He knew to the half minute how much time it lost during the week.

As Charles followed his father up the stairs, he could hear the clock ticking and then it made an asthmatic sound and struck the hour of three though it was half past seven o'clock. He could also hear the wind outside and a sharp spatter on the windows, showing that a northeaster was starting.

"You stand here by the door, Charley," John Gray said, "until I light the lamp. I don't want you tipping over books." There was a pungent smell of moldering leather and old wood and stale tobacco smoke as John Gray moved into the dusky room.

"Close the door, Charley," he said. "It's always better in here with the door closed." He had lighted the student lamp and had replaced the chimney and now he was turning up the wick and putting back the green glass shade. "Sit down in that Morris chair. That's right. Did I ever tell you that's the chair your Grandfather Marchby died in?"

"No," Charles said, "I don't think you ever did."

John Gray smiled and walked over to the fireplace and stood looking down at him.

"Well, don't look worried, Charley," he said. "He couldn't help it. There are a great many things we can't help, Charley, or do you think we can?"

"I don't suppose we can help dying, if that's what you mean," Charles said, and he was uneasy as always when he was alone with his father.

"You're at an age, I suppose, when you feel you can help anything by power of will," John Gray said. "How would you like a glass of port?"

"Why, thanks," Charles said, "if you want one."

"Open the decanter box, Charley, and hand me the right-hand bottle, filled with a purplish-red liquid, and take out two glasses. It's Jewish sacramental wine." His father was drawing a small tavern table in front of the sofa. "That's it. Moe Levine told me where to get it."

His father took the stopper from the decanter and filled two antique wineglasses. Nothing in his manner indicated that the occasion was in the least unusual, but Charles could not help wondering what he wanted. It was not a part of family custom to be sitting in his father's room. If his father wanted to talk he always came downstairs to the parlor.

"I suppose you've done a little drinking at Dartmouth," his father said. "But I'd have known it if liquor had ever passed your lips around here, Charley, above one fluid ounce," and he laughed and sat down on the sofa. "There would have been whisperings on the Rialto." His father raised his glass. "Try it, Charley, it won't hurt you."

217

The sacramental wine was heavy and unpleasantly sweet and its taste added to Charles's uneasiness. He felt, as he often did, that his father was laughing at him, and he was never sure whether the laughter was entirely friendly.

His father had half turned his head toward the window. "Listen to the rain," he said. " 'Neither coat nor cloak will hold out against rain upon rain.' Do you know who said that, Charley?"

"No, sir, I'm afraid I don't," Charles answered.

"Oh, dear," his father said. "Thomas Fuller said it in his *Gnomologia,* and I don't suppose you know what gnomologia is, either." He leaned forward and refilled his glass. "This is horrible wine. I wish you cared more about the polite adornments of the mind, Charley. 'Rain upon rain.' I've been through a lot of rains. Keep out of the rain, Charley." He smiled at Charles and seemed to expect him to make some reply, but when Charles talked with his father nothing ever seemed to be on a firm foundation.

"What does gnomologia mean?" Charles asked.

"Oh, dear," his father said, "didn't they tell you at Dartmouth?"

"I don't see why you keep picking on Dartmouth," Charles said. "It's a pretty good school."

His father raised his heavy, dark eyebrows. "I can't say it hasn't developed your mind," he said. "It seems to me that you have a retentive mind, neither receptive nor curiosity seeking, but retentive. Roughly gnomologia means a collection of sayings or proverbs. The word is obsolete."

"Then I don't suppose it will do any good to know it," Charles answered.

"That's an interesting way to put it," John Gray said slowly. "I suppose you mean that all knowledge should be useful, because someone has told you that knowledge is power."

"Well, I don't see any use in learning a lot of things that don't do you any good." He stopped and he felt annoyed at himself and his father. It did not help when John Gray laughed.

"Why, of course," he said. "Naturally, Charley. I'm not criticizing you for a single minute. You're only saying that you want to get on or get ahead. It's a very common objective around here."

John Gray leaned more comfortably back against the corner of the sofa. Perhaps it was the room or the rain on the windows or the sacramental wine or his uneasy annoyance that made Charles say what he said next.

"Didn't you ever want to get on?" he asked. The question was too personal and his father was no longer comfortable.

"Why, yes, Charley," he said. "Yes, I've wanted to get on, but I suppose you think it was a silly way, the way I tried, and I don't blame you. You'd be following a convention."

"Well, I don't know much about it," Charles said.

"Do you remember what Jonathan Swift said?" his father continued. "'Ambition often puts men upon doing the meanest offices: so climbing is performed in the same posture with creeping.'" Suddenly John Gray laughed and stood up. "I've never liked creeping. I suppose I could have crept and if I had I might be on the Clyde Fund."

He said it without much emphasis and for the first time Charles felt sorry about it. He wanted to say something, to tell him it did not matter, but he could think of no way in which to say it which did not sound stupid or gauche. He picked up his glass nervously between his fingers.

"Well, we weren't talking about that anyway," he said.

His father stood with his head tilted to one side, listening to the hissing rhythm of the rain against the window. The wind had risen in sharp gusts so that the rain splashed against the panes in wave-like surges, as though someone from outside were throwing it with a dipper. Something was making John Gray restless and he took a short turn around the room before he spoke again, moving as though he did not need to see any of the objects in it.

"I'm hardly in a position to give you any sound advice, Charley," he said suddenly. "'Advice, as it always gives a temporary appearance of superiority, can never be very grateful.'" From the sonorous tone of his voice, Charles knew that he was quoting again. He wished his father would not keep leaning on other people's thoughts. He was wondering whose words had been resurrected now, probably Samuel Johnson's. Yes, it was Samuel Johnson.

"And yet," John Gray was saying, "Johnson himself spent most of his time giving unsolicited advice." He paused and stared at the floor. "Now this subject of your getting on interests me. Of course, I know why you want to. You want to because I obviously haven't."

It was much better, Charles was thinking, not to answer. Instead of answering he found himself pouring another glass of that sticky wine.

"But I would like you to know, Charley," and he noticed that his father was speaking with an artificial, constrained sort of lightness, "that I've made what I consider several intelligent and rather vigorous efforts to get on, considering the handicaps, and without creeping, always without creeping — but I couldn't beat the system. The system is not fluid, and it's very hard to beat."

"What system?" Charles asked.

"Why, the system under which we live," John Gray said. "The order. There's always some sort of order."

He was speaking more rapidly and confidently and suddenly Charles understood that he was cutting the cloth to fit his faults, as everyone did at some time or other.

"There's always the bundle of hay out ahead, for any ass who wants to get on," John Gray was saying, "and They make it look like a very pleasant bundle."

"Who are 'They'?" Charles asked.

"That's an intelligent question," John Gray answered. "They are the people who own the hay. They are the people who run the system, and They have to toss out a little hay now and then to make the system work; and the curious thing about it is that They don't realize in the least that They are running the system. They are only acting through a series of rather blind instincts and that's about all there is to anything, Charley, instinct. They'll tell you there's plenty of hay for anyone who can get it, but the main thing, Charley, is that They don't really want you to get it. It might be some of Their hay."

Charles could follow his father's metaphor and he could tell from the bright look on John Gray's face that he was delighted with it himself. Voltaire had the same brilliant bitterness, the same cynicism, and a similar painful undercurrent of truth — and John Gray was still speaking.

"You can get so far by effort, Charley. You will find you can obtain a little hay but if you reach for more you'll get a sharp rap on the muzzle. I'm being very wise this evening, Charley, and I know I'm right because I've tried to get some of that hay. Don't worry. It's all over now. I won't try again. All I want now is to keep out of the rain and to manufacture a suitable waterproof. I'm tired of the system, Charley. I'm delighted to give up."

John Gray sighed and sat down again on the sofa. What he had said was the apologia of John Gray, an alibi, a distorted story of the talents and of labor in the vineyard — and now he was finishing his apologia.

"If I were you," he was saying, "I wouldn't try too hard for the hay. You might be disappointed, Charley."

It sounded like *Candide* and Charles was thinking that if everyone followed John Gray's philosophy nothing would happen anywhere and yet he could think of no reasonable ground for argument.

"Well," he said, "if you call it hay it seems to me that you've had a lot more hay than most people and more than I'll ever have."

That was where it ended. He did not think that he was speaking out of resentment until he saw the light leave his father's face.

"That's a detail, Charley," John Gray said, "and it doesn't alter the general picture."

"Maybe it doesn't for you," Charles said, "but it does for all the rest of us."

John Gray was silent for a moment. The talk was gone and the quotations with it. He picked up his empty glass and stared at it and put it back on the table.

"Don't be so hard on me, Charley," he said. "I told you I wasn't going to do it again. It's like liquor, I can take it or leave it alone, and besides" — he looked apologetic but at the same time he looked as though a cheerful thought had struck him — "it was a wretchedly small amount of hay."

VI

The Readers of the Boston Evening Transcript *Sway in the Wind Like a Field of Ripe Corn*
— T. S. ELIOT

SOMEHOW, AFTER THEIR TALK that evening, Charles and his father had arrived at a basis for friendship which prevented either of them from offending the other, though it was a little like the friendship between two lawyers who had argued in court and dined together afterwards. There was always something in their association that was like the mercury from a broken thermometer dividing and rolling about with the bits never really coming together. It was diverting when his father spoke about hay to remind him that there was still a little hay, in the shape of the mill stock left in trust under Uncle Gerald and Mr. Blashfield. They would not be able to live on Spruce Street if it were not for that hay.

"But it's getting moldy," John Gray said. "Mill stocks aren't what they used to be."

"But it's just as well it's in trust, isn't it?" Charles asked him. Somehow after that evening he could be as frank as that, and John Gray even seemed to enjoy it.

"But it ought not to be handled in Clyde, Charley," John Gray said, "not by a small-minded lawyer in a small-minded town."

If Clyde was a small-minded town, why had he stayed in Clyde? Had he not ever wanted to get out of it? Charles asked him, but he could never get a direct answer.

"The idea used to occur to me," John Gray said, "but where else could I have gone? Perhaps I was afraid. I'm aware of my deficiencies, Charley."

Being aware of his deficiencies, Charles sometimes thought, was a part of his stock in trade.

"I'll bet if you got your hands on some more money," Charles said, "you'd try it all over again."

His father was amazed, and not hurt at all.

"You know I never bet, Charley," he answered, "and it isn't so. I'm completely, magnificently aware of my deficiencies. I've learned my little lesson, Charley, and that's all over now." A part of his cloak was a garment of quiet puritanism, like so many other cloaks in Clyde. He was not an unregenerate figure of revolt with dangerous ideas. He voted a straight Republican ticket like everyone else in Clyde.

Dorothea was sure that he had learned his little lesson. As long as Charles could remember, Dorothea had been sure of everything. She had been sure that she would be a great concert pianist. She had been sure, when she had been sewing Butterick patterns, that she could be a successful dress designer; and now she was sure that she could tell Elbridge Sterne ways to advance himself at Wright-Sherwin. It may have been that sureness which had driven the other young men away, but Dorothea never admitted it. She was sure that Father was never going to do that again. She wished that Charles would not joke with him about it. No one had ever dreamed of speaking of it until Charles had and it was highly disrespectful. Charles ought to see that it hurt Mother to talk about bundles of hay.

His mother, too, was sure that Father would never do it again, but she did not think it was disrespectful to treat things as a joke as long as Father did not mind. It showed, she said, that Father was very fond of Charles. If he had not paid as much attention to Charles as he might have, one should remember that he had been so upset about Sam. Father always felt things very deeply. The main thing was to be kind and remember that he was a very remarkable person, quite different from other people. You could not judge him by other standards. For instance, when he joked with Charles about Wright-Sherwin he was really very proud of Charles. Father was beginning to depend on him just as she was and he was their only boy. They were all very proud of Charles, even Dorothea.

Aunt Jane was sure about it, too. Once she had harbored doubts but recently she had been sure that John had turned the corner. It was a little late, perhaps, but he had turned it. After all, he was only fifty-five and Michelangelo was still painting when he was ninety. She had deep faith in John Gray. She knew that he had been the spoiled baby of the family, twelve years younger than she and fourteen years younger than Mathilda — but at least he did not have what she called the Gray heart. The Judge had suffered with it and so had Mathilda and now she had it too. Yet, when his aunt spoke of the Gray heart, she always ended by treating it as a proud inheritance.

Charles could gather that the Grays did not have the past glories of certain other families in Clyde. They had only been country people, on the farm upriver, before the embargo of 1811, but they did have the Gray heart and it carried you off quickly when you had it. Gerald Marchby had told her so. Gerald's deafness was growing but he could hear her heart. It was because of the Gray heart and because he was deeply fond of her that Charles stopped to call on his aunt nearly every afternoon after leaving the office at Wright-Sherwin. Dr. Marchby had prescribed sherry for her, the only way you could get sherry in prohibition days, and she had arranged to obtain two quarts a week, one for her and one for Charles, because Charley ought to have something in return for coming to see her and the Judge had always liked sherry.

Those calls at the Judge's house on Gow Street were difficult to distinguish one from another, except for one on an afternoon not long after that talk with his father. There was a chill in the air in spite of the sunlight and the yellow elm leaves were beginning to drop on the sidewalks. When Charles opened the front door, his aunt was seated in her favorite bannister-back armchair in the Judge's study. Mary Callahan had already brought in the tea and the sherry decanter and had lighted a lump of cannel coal in the grate. His Aunt Jane had on her spectacles and was reading from a piece of foolscap written in the Spencerian penmanship which she had learned long ago at the female academy. Charles knew at once it was one of those lists of personal effects she was always making. For the last two years she had been arranging for their distribution but the arrangements were never final. She wanted everyone to have something and she did not want any friend of hers to be out of sorts when she was dead.

"I told Mary to light the fire to take the chill off," Aunt Jane said. "Charley, I'm going to give Mary the Sheffield teapot and a thousand dollars."

There was no use trying to deflect her from this subject because she liked it, and he had learned it was best to fall in with her mood.

"I thought you were going to let her have the tray," Charles told her.

"I know," she answered, "but I asked her this morning. She thinks Dorothea ought to have the tray."

Of course, she had asked Mary Callahan. Mary had told him only the other day that she was going simply crazy being asked about every stick and plate in the house and being told about the Gray heart. In Mary's opinion, it was stuff and nonsense. Miss Jane, in Mary's opinion, was just as spry as ever she was, up and down stairs and all over the place, emptying out trunks and bureaus, her heart and all. In Mary's opinion Miss Jane was only being contrary to draw attention to herself, and Miss Jane had always been contrary.

Though his aunt's demise was a grim subject, Charles had grown used to it and somehow it was not as grim as it sounded in the Judge's study. He had never seen his grandfather but Charles could feel his presence in the room his grandfather had remodeled in the most unfortunate decorative period of the eighties. He could feel the Judge's precision and his love of order in the golden-oak bookcases and the shining brass about the black marble fireplace. He could feel that nothing was entirely gone, least of all his aunt, sitting as straight as she ever had, in the room's most uncomfortable chair.

Her mood usually changed for the better when she took her sherry. She always drank it in delicate sips and she always coughed.

"It's just as well I never touched it until now," she said. "Charley, I hear you're doing very well."

"Where did you hear that?" Charles asked.

"At the Women's Alliance."

"Where?"

"You heard me," Aunt Jane said, "and it's about time that someone in the family was successful. I think John would have got on if he had gone to Dartmouth instead of Harvard. Charley, do you think Dorothea's going to marry that factory man she brought in here, the one who squints?"

"Who?" Charles asked. "Elbridge Sterne?"

"Yes. He knows all about brass. He kept looking at the andirons. Is Dorothea going to marry him or isn't she?"

"I don't know," Charles said. "She's never taken it up with me. She'll probably get discouraged with him. You know — after a certain time she always gets discouraged."

"She's only particular like me," Aunt Jane said. "Esther thinks she's going to marry him."

"Mother always thinks she's going to marry someone," Charles told her.

"If she does," Aunt Jane said, "she can have the tea tray and the dining room chairs besides the five thousand dollars."

The cannel coal snapped viciously and a piece of it fell on the carpet. Charles rose hastily and kicked it back on the hearth.

"Charley," Aunt Jane said, "you look exactly like the Judge. Did I tell you I'm leaving you five thousand dollars?"

"Yes," Charles said, "you did tell me."

"Well, you might at least say thank you," Aunt Jane said.

"But I have thanked you," Charles told her, "and I've told you you ought not to do it after sending me through college."

"Well, I'm going to," Aunt Jane said, "and Esther's going to have ten thousand and the Queen Anne mirror and my bureau. It's time Esther had something. That's twenty thousand, isn't it? Charley, how do you think your father seems?"

"Why, Father's all right, I guess," Charles said.

The door opened and Mary Callahan came in with a glass and a bottle of pills. It was six o'clock.

"Thank you, Mary," Aunt Jane said, and she looked hard at her back and did not speak until the door closed softly. "Do you think she stands outside and listens, Charley?"

"No, Aunt Jane," he said, "I don't really think she does."

"Well, I don't want her to hear this," Aunt Jane said. "Charley, I've been thinking about your father. You don't know him as well as I do. I'm worried about his self-respect."

"His self-respect?" Charles repeated.

"Yes," Aunt Jane said, "and I'm not going to leave the rest to him in trust. It will hurt his self-respect."

The cannel coal snapped again with a sound that was like a punctuation mark. Charles had heard about the furniture and the silver and the rugs and about a bequest to the Unitarian Church, but she had never told him this before.

"I think it's a mistake, Aunt Jane," Charles said.

"I'm not asking your opinion," she answered, but of course she was asking his opinion. "I don't want to have anyone unhappy after I'm gone."

He felt sorry for her because he knew that she only half believed what she was saying, but it did not seem possible to discuss the subject, when he was still so young that his loyalties were confused.

"Charley," she asked, "aren't you going to say something?"

"No," Charles said. "There isn't any more to say if that's the way you want it."

She reached toward him and put her hand over his. "We have to trust him. He's your father, Charley," and then there was a quaver in her voice. "Charley, I'm so proud of you. Now turn on the lights. Isn't it nice to have electric lights?"

Until he pressed the switch by the door, he had almost thought that his aunt was dead already, but when the ceiling light was on in the old gas chandelier the brilliance of the room erased all that talk of death.

"Well," she said, "that's settled. Charley, I wish you saw more girls."

"Why, you're my only girl," Charles said, and he laughed.

"I wish you saw some nice girls," his Aunt Jane said again. "Why don't you ever see Jessica Lovell?"

"Jessica Lovell?" Charles repeated. "Why, I hardly know her." His aunt should have known he belonged in a different group from Jessica Lovell and that groups hardly ever mingled in Clyde.

When Charles arrived home after his talk with Aunt Jane on death and testaments, Dorothea was playing the phonograph. The family were sitting in the second-best parlor and Elbridge Sterne was with them, in an inconspicuous pepper-and-salt suit and a stiff collar. He had asked Dorothea if she would go to the movies that evening and if he could take her somewhere to supper, and Dorothea had asked him to come home to supper because there was no place to eat in Clyde, unless you wanted a sandwich and a soda at the Sweet Shoppe or a meal in a booth that smelled of fried clams in that restaurant of Nicky Demetrios's on Dock Street. A log fire was burning, which showed that Elbridge must have lugged the wood in from the shed outdoors, because Charles had not brought any in and his father disliked doing it. His father, he saw, was reading a newspaper by the big table lamp, not the *Clyde Herald* but the *Boston Evening Transcript,* and his mother was darning a sock. She had thrust her darning egg well up into the toe and she was bending over her work with an intent and puzzled look. She always said that she hated sewing.

"Hello, Charley," Elbridge said. "You weren't in my part of the shop today, were you?"

Elbridge was exhibiting the classic desire, shared by all Dorothea's other callers, to be agreeable to the younger brother. When Charles shook hands with Elbridge he had the younger brother's conventional feeling of amusement and slight contempt for anyone so weak as to put himself in the situation of calling on Dorothea, and Dorothea was looking at him suspiciously, as though she were still afraid he would blurt out some crude remark or play some practical joke on her and Elbridge Sterne. Elbridge in many ways looked like a shipwrecked sailor among strange natives. His voice was heavy and Midwestern, and he had not lost the hopeful breeziness of more open spaces.

"That's right," Charles said, "I was in the office all day."

"Well, come out into the plant sometime and meet some of the fellows," Elbridge said. "That's a fine crowd of fellows in Shed Two."

"Elbridge could show you a lot about the plant," Dorothea said, "if you'd only let him."

"Who said I don't want to let him?" Charles asked. "But I'm not supposed to leave the office and be wandering around."

"Well, as long as you know everything about everything," Dorothea said.

His mother looked up from her darning.

"I wish you two would stop arguing for just a minute," she said. "It can't be very interesting for Elbridge. How do you think Aunt Jane seemed, dear?"—and Charles said he thought she seemed very well.

"Was she still talking about the furniture?" Dorothea asked.

"Yes," Charles answered, "most of the time."

"That reminds me," Elbridge said, "I dropped into Burch's antique shop and I saw a desk there. It's got a sort of a curved front. I was thinking of buying it for a Christmas present for Mother. I wish you'd look at it, Dorothea, and tell me if it's any good."

There was a pleasant rustling sound and Charles saw that his father had lowered his newspaper.

"From my experience, Elbridge," he said, "I conclude that most attractive fronts should curve."

Then they all saw that the *Boston Evening Transcript* was open at the page of transactions on the New York Stock Exchange.

"The market's still going up, isn't it, Mr. Gray?" Elbridge said.

John Gray smiled faintly and his glance met Charles's for a moment and then he looked away.

"I suppose it is," he answered, "but I only buy the *Transcript* for the Notes and Queries. Do you ever read them, Elbridge?"

"Why, no, Mr. Gray," Elbridge said.

"You really ought to," John Gray said. "Sometimes you encounter the most unworldly queries — and then there's the genealogical column, and the department called the Churchman Afield. That's a fine active name, isn't it? It always makes me think of clergymen running about in riding boots blowing horns. Esther, dear, is supper nearly ready?"

Yes, supper was nearly ready, but his father had not been reading the Notes and Queries. Charles knew it when he continued speaking.

"That phonograph," he said. Dorothea had risen to put on another record. "It's about time, isn't it, that we changed it for a radio? I know what you're going to say, Dorothea. I know the house isn't wired for electricity but it ought to be. We ought to keep in touch with the times. Your Aunt Jane has had her house wired. Esther, we ought to get a radio for Jane."

Charles saw his mother close her sewing basket and she also must have known what John Gray had been reading.

"John," she asked, "have you been to see Gerald?"

"Gerald?" John Gray's forehead wrinkled. "Oh, yes. I had a nice talk with Gerald."

"What did he say about Jane?"

She must have forgotten that Elbridge Sterne was there.

"He said Jane's heart is doing very well," John Gray said. "He says we're all worrying too much about Jane." He stopped and began folding the paper carefully, as though he hoped the noise might distract everyone.

Charles saw Dorothea glance up quickly and uncertainly and his own eyes met Dorothea's for an instant. Dorothea also knew what John Gray had been reading. In spite of what had been said at Gow Street that afternoon about trusting, Charles knew that nothing could change.

"What do you think of this holding company Electric Bond and Share, Mr. Gray?" Elbridge asked. "The way the market's going, I don't see any use in keeping money in the bank."

John Gray had rolled the paper into a neat and careful cylinder.

"Elbridge, I really wouldn't monkey with anything like that," he said. His speech sounded elaborate and self-conscious and he went on with an unnatural haste. "Oh, by the way, Charley."

"Yes, Father?" Charles said quickly.

"There's going to be a muster tomorrow afternoon," and he must have noticed the blank look on Charles's face. "A muster, a firemen's muster. The Pine Trees will be there and there will be eight hand tubs and two hundred dollars in cash prizes. Why don't you watch me make a spectacle of myself, Charley? It's Saturday." The tension in the room had eased. His father had tossed the paper on the floor. "They don't have firemen's musters in Kansas City, do they, Elbridge?"

"Exactly what is the purpose of a firemen's muster, Mr. Gray?" Elbridge asked him.

It often seemed to Charles that Elbridge knew nothing about anything except the composition of brass, but John Gray was very patient.

"The purpose of a muster, Elbridge," he said, "aside from social relaxation, is to see which of these antiquated fire engines can squirt the longest stream of water from its tank — an athletic contest, Elbridge. You should come with Dorothea and see us, and, Charley, I want you particularly."

"I don't know whether I can get away in time, Father," Charles said.

"Charley," his mother said, "if your father wants you to, of course you can."

Charles could not understand why that homely conversation should have depressed him or why its humdrum quality should have made it so indelible. It had been as dull and quiet as everything in Clyde, and yet, when he was in his room that night, the words kept running back and forth in his mind and details kept cropping up with the words. He was again shaking hands with Elbridge Sterne, listening to Elbridge's anxious conversation, and again his mother was darning the sock and again he saw her half-startled look. He saw his father folding and rolling the *Boston Evening Transcript* — oh, no, he was not following the transactions of the financial page — he was only searching for Notes and Queries.

The door of Charles's bedroom was closed but it could not shut out those thoughts and every object in the room helped to give them emphasis. The framed picture of Sam in his uniform, standing on his bureau, was a part of them, and so was the silver cup he had won at freshman track in college and so were the books he had purchased, standing in the mission bookcase that he had brought from Hanover. The casual volumes from Everyman's Library, his copy of *Lord Jim,* his books on economics, his Channing's *History of the United States,* his Shakespeare, his *Oxford Book of English Verse,* and even the volumes of accounting and salesmanship — all of them were a part of what he was thinking.

At least everything in his room was neat, not like his father's room. When he hung his coat on the hanger in the narrow closet beside his extra suit and his evening clothes, it was a relief to see that his black pumps and his other shoes were in a straight and even row and that his blue suit of pajamas and his dressing gown were hanging tidily above them covering the illustrated list of morning physical exercises tacked inside the closet door. The Bible his mother had given him and a volume of Emerson's *Essays* lay on the candlestand beside his narrow spool bed. He could see all those objects suddenly as belonging to someone else and he could read the character of the person who owned them almost as though it had nothing to do with himself. It was a small, cold, narrow room, but at least it was not like his father's. When he thought of it afterwards, he knew it was a priggish room, an accurate reflection of early attitudes, but still it had shown something of which he was never ashamed. No bedroom of his was ever quite like it afterwards, never as simple, never as serene.

He had yet to buy T. S. Eliot's poems, and Adam from the Sistine Chapel was not yet hanging on the wall, and Pliny's doves in white marble sitting on the edge of their little yellow fountain were not yet on his bureau in front of Sam's picture, between two wood-backed military brushes. Jessica Lovell had not given them to him yet. There was no trace of Jessica in that room, no hint of lightness or humor, no sign at all of love.

VII

When We Ran with the Old Machine

"CHARLEY," Jessica said to him once, "it was all so funny, wasn't it? You being there, and me, when we neither of us wanted to be there at all" — they were talking, of course, about the firemen's muster and it always seemed curious that neither of them had wanted to go there at all — "and if it had been anywhere else we'd have both been different. Do you remember the fife-and-drum corps?"

Of course Charles remembered.

"And your father in that red shirt," Jessica said, "standing on top of the machine?"

Naturally Charles remembered his father, in his helmet and his red shirt with "Pine Tree" written on the front in white letters, in his blue trousers and his belt with its ornate brass buckle. For years Charles had been deeply embarrassed whenever his father had appeared in that make-believe fireman suit. To Jessica Lovell it was only another Currier and Ives print, an amusing rustic scene, while he was close enough to it to feel that his father's standing on the tub and giving orders had an indecorous, discordant quality. Jack Mason's father, for instance, would not have dreamed of being in the Pine Trees, but his father enjoyed the organization and persisted in speaking of it on unsuitable occasions.

"I don't see why Father likes it," Charles said.

"Because he has a good time," Jessica told him. "He was having a wonderful time."

Charles never could understand the release of being dressed in an absurd costume and of pretending, even briefly, that he was not himself.

233

"And we had a good time too," Jessica said. "We had a wonderful time."

Still it was an impossible sort of time. He had not drunk hard cider in the Stevens barn and yet he had behaved as though he had.

"Charley, why did you get into that wrestling match?"

"You know why," Charles said.

"I know, but tell me why."

"Because you wanted me to. You shouldn't have been there in that crowd."

"But I was," Jessica said. "It couldn't have happened anywhere else, could it? It was all — " but she did not finish what she was saying . . .

Luncheon that Saturday afternoon had consisted only of a little cold meat and cracked cocoa and his father ate it hurriedly. He might not have been elected to the Clyde Fund but he had been elected captain of the Pine Trees, in a very close election, with Wesley Adams, the undertaker, running against him. As John Gray ate his cold meat he kept glancing critically at Charles and finally he told Charles that he had better put on some older clothes, that his business suit might get wet. He was really saying in a nice way, Charles knew, that Charles would look out of place if he came there all dressed up and in a white collar.

His mother was not going to the muster. If John had to pretend he was a fireman, she often said, he could go to those things alone. She had to draw the line somewhere. When Charles started upstairs to change his clothes, he heard them discussing the time-worn subject.

"I know, Esther," he heard his father saying. "It's a weakness of mine and I appreciate your indulging me, but you miss a lot. It's always quite a sight."

"I suppose it is," his mother said, "if it's a sight to see tipsy men pretending they're boys, running around bellowing at each other, squirting water."

Charles was wearing his gray flannel trousers, his old sneakers and his old tweed coat when he and John Gray walked out of the front yard and down Spruce Street. It was all very well to tell himself that everyone condoned his father's eccentricity, but nothing could reconcile Charles to the way his father's whole manner changed whenever he wore that red shirt and helmet. They turned him into a River Streeter. His father's voice had already assumed a nasal tone and he walked with a slight swagger that reminded Charles of members of the American Legion gathering for the Decoration Day parade. His father was glancing anxiously at the clear sky to gauge the breeze as it blew off occasional yellowing leaves from the elm trees.

"The wind's certainly calming down," he said. Charles noticed that he said "calming" in a flat way that was more River Street than Spruce Street. "I don't want any downdraft blowing the spray sideways before it hits the paper."

On one occasion some years ago, his father said, when he was pumping with the Pine Trees, right out on the old training field where the tubs were going to pump today, a puff of wind caught the spray and though the Pine Trees had never pumped a longer stream, that puff blew it sideways and the Eureka tub from Salem beat them. It was a fluke, because the Eureka tub was never as good as the old Pine Tree. Its stroke was too short.

It was going to be a small muster this afternoon but the Eurekas would be there and the Excelsiors from Smith's Common, and the Nonpareils were bringing their machine down from north of Kittery. They were already at the training field, and so was the old Blairtown pumper. There would be eight machines, and they had better hurry because the Pine Trees always pulled the old machine themselves. They didn't depend on a truck like the Lions and they ended up in a run, with the bell going.

As his father walked he continued worrying about the weather and the wind, as he always did on muster days. He had been to the training field already to see where the stand for the tubs would be placed. He and Wesley Adams had selected the spots for the tall bamboo flagpoles. The elms on the edge of the training field made a tricky downdraft, a draft that you had to watch on those wind flags before you gave the boys at the brakes the signal to turn it on and let her go. They had watched the long strips of paper being laid in the roped-off enclosure on which the stream from the hose would fall. He hoped that the crowd would not get too near the paper. That summer they had lost to the Haviland Protectors at the July muster because, he suspected, Haviland backers spat upon the paper, thus making the furthest drops appear to have come from the Protectors' hose.

Then he discussed the strengths and weaknesses of the hand engine that the Pine Trees owned — the old Pine Tree tub. Charles knew she was a beautiful machine, made by Button in 1878. He knew, or at least he had been told, that the Button machines were better than the Borgs or the Lyles. The tub had a new coat of paint and a new pressure gauge and the ropes for pulling her had been stitched with clean white canvas. Everyone always recognized the Pine Tree tub right away at musters.

The Pine Tree firehouse was the same shed which had sheltered the machine when Clyde actually relied on volunteers and hand pumps to put out fires. It stood on the water side of River Street in a vacant, weedy lot, not far from the gas tank and the coal pocket and the mill. Behind it was a good view of the old wharves and warehouses of Clyde. It was a shabby building outside but the Pine Trees had fixed it inside into a pretty comfortable club-house. A "salamander" stove warmed up the shed nicely in winter and there were tables and benches for cards and checkers and a big sandbox. The most striking feature of the firehouse was the rows of buckets hung on pegs along the walls, the decorated fire buckets which pre-Revolutionary Clyde firemen had once kept handy in their houses, with the dates and names of their former owners painted on them. The old shed was an amazing survival, but Charles had always accepted its history automatically because Clyde was full of other survivals. He was only wondering why the Pine Trees still enjoyed being Pine Trees and persisted in being Pine Trees when their usefulness was over.

There was a big crowd waiting outside the firehouse, old Pine Trees and young Pine Trees drifting in and out through the open doors and eddying about the weedy lot. Mr. Elmer Swasey, who

236

must have been over eighty, was standing with his helmet tilted back on his head and his white beard cascading over his red shirt. He had led a useless, unregenerate life, but he had run with the Pine Trees in his youth and he was still a Pine Tree. Mr. Wesley Adams was there too, in his red shirt, and so were the fathers of a lot of boys Charles had known in high school, town tradesmen and mill foremen, and many of his former schoolmates were there with them. There was Earl Wilkins. They had played football together on the high school team and Earl was now a helper for Mr. Wesley Adams. There were Johnny Leveroni and young Vincent Sullivan and Andrew Garvin, and any number of little boys ran yelling around the legs of their elders, and the Pine Tree fife-and-drum corps was already beginning to play "The Gang's All Here."

His father was an integrated part of the Pine Trees but Charles was an outsider who had come to look on and who had no real part in the ceremony.

"Hi, Earl," he said, trying to get in the spirit of it. "Hi, Johnny." And they all said, "Hi, Charley. How's it going, Charley?" but they all knew he was not one of them. He belonged on Spruce Street, not on River Street. Charles was an outsider but somehow, by some strange alchemy, his father had bridged the gap.

"All right," John Gray was calling. "Now wait a minute." The fife-and-drum corps had stopped and his voice had filled the space of silence. "We're going to roll her out in a minute. This is going to look right, by God. And don't forget what happened at Smith's Common." Charles did not know but all the Pine Trees did. "We don't want anybody winded before he pumps. Now we all know there's a barrel of hard cider down cellar in Stevens's barn and you get into the cellar by the back way. Now, if the Excelsiors or the Lions want it give it to 'em, but no one on the Pine Tree brakes gets it till it's over. All right, boys, bring her out."

The tub clattered out into the sunshine, an antiquated hand-pumping mechanism with its long pump bars, called brakes, its brass and its bright red wheels and its name painted on the center bar, *Pine Tree, Clyde* — a beautiful, shiny, obsolete thing. The fife-

and-drum corps started playing "The Gang's All Here" again and the procession moved down River Street. Heads appeared in the windows and the mill whistle blew.

The training field was conditioned to musters of firemen and others. It had been the training ground for the militia in the Revolutionary War. The company sent by Clyde to the Civil War had performed its first drill there. For a hundred and fifty years, the elms on the edge of the field had cast their shadows over similar gatherings and over the South End ball games. Some of Clyde's oldest houses bordered the field, making a Colonial group not noticed by anyone in Clyde but eliciting the enthusiasm of strangers, who often turned their cars off the main highway and down Training Street to see their low sloping roofs and small-paned windows. Those windows so often shattered by baseballs now looked upon the crowded green and the roped-off area over which the hoses would play and the flag-draped booths from which chances were sold on useful articles, or which dispensed balloons, hot dogs, popcorn and tonic. It was always tonic, not soft drinks, in Clyde, but there was also a hint in the actions of certain citizens that something stronger was available.

The crowd had lined Training Street and covered the field as the hand tubs marched past, but Charles had dropped from the procession as soon as the Pine Trees reached Training Street and finally he found himself, when the pumping contest started, by the old tubs at the far end of the field. This was the more disorderly end where the pumping teams were congregating to await their turns on the tub stand, far back from the hose nozzle and the paper where most of the crowd had gathered. This was the spot where there was always quiet drinking and where the fife-and-drum corps played to encourage the pumpers and where individuals performed small, competitive feats of strength. The Excelsior machine was on the stand; the Excelsiors had lined the pump bars and their captain stood holding a handkerchief in his upraised hand, watching the wind flag and waiting for his assistant to tell him the pressure. As Charles watched the captain's arm drop, the pumpers moved into unified action, creakingly and slowly, and the fifes and drums began playing "Stars and Stripes Forever." It was hard for the captain to make himself heard above the squealing of the fifes.

At this moment Charles heard a girl somewhere behind him humming "Stars and Stripes Forever." Established custom made it unusual for many girls, or at least many nice girls, to be at that corner of the field, where it was necessary to shout crude Anglo-Saxon exhortations as the pumpers increased the beat.

"Come on, you bastards," the pump captain called.

At this exact moment Charles turned to see who the girl behind him was and he was very much surprised to find it was Jessica Lovell.

"Hello," she said. "I was wondering when you'd speak to me."

She was as tall as he was. She was dressed in a gray tweed suit tailored so that it seemed to add to her height. A tight red felt hat was pushed over her soft black hair and she was smiling at him, not in the cool way that she had smiled on other occasions when she had met him, but as though she were glad to see him.

"Oh, hello," Charles said. "They're really working now."

He could not think of anything else to say. Though he had always thought of her as Jessica Lovell, he could not very well call her Jessica and yet it would have sounded silly to call her Miss Lovell. "The Excelsior has a good pump team, at least that's what they say."

"I suppose you know all about this," she said. "Your father's in the Pine Trees, isn't he?"

It was not surprising she should have known, since everyone in Clyde knew his father.

"Yes," he said, "my father's crazy about the Pine Trees."

"Well, it must be fun," she said.

"He thinks it is," Charles answered, and then there was silence and it was just as though they had not spoken at all. He was thinking that she should not have been in that corner of the field, and then it occurred to him that she did not have to bother. Everyone knew who she was. She was Jessica Lovell.

239

"You haven't seen a queer sort of a man around, have you?" she asked.

Charles laughed and looked at the crowd. The Excelsiors were mopping their brows and panting after their first try.

"There are lots of them around here."

"But not like this one." Her voice had a confidential note, as though they were old friends. "He's been studying the head-hunters from Borneo. He was at the house for lunch. He's here to make a survey."

The captain of the Excelsiors was exhorting his pumpers and the crowd was helping.

"What sort of a survey?" Charles asked.

She gave her head a quick, impatient shake.

"Why, I don't know," she said. "Some sort of social survey. He wanted to see this thing and now he's gone away and left me."

"Do you want me to help you find him?" Charles asked.

"No," she said. "I'd rather stay here and let him find us, that is if it's all the same to you, Charley."

He was startled when she called him by his first name, but then nearly everyone in Clyde referred to him as Charley Gray.

"What are they going to do now?" she asked.

"They're going to pump again," he said. "They have three tries."

"It's nice to be here with an expert," she said. "Let's go over there and listen to the music."

The music had stopped. The fifes and drums had gathered in a sunny spot on the edge of the road opposite the Stevens barn.

"I wouldn't go over there," Charles said. There was always a tough crowd around the Stevens barn, but then everyone knew she was Jessica Lovell. She was moving over toward the tough crowd before she answered.

"Come on," she said. "I've never been to one of these things before."

Obviously no one would as much as whistle at her It was only a question of convention and he was surprised that she did not realize it. Of course, she could join the fifes and drums and all the visiting firemen lounging on the edge of the road if she wanted, but she might have noticed that there were no other girls there. She should have understood that being there would cramp everyone's style.

Loud voices trailed off into whispers, the fife-and-drum corps, who had been to the Stevens barn cellar, gazed at both of them in a way that made Charles shift from one foot to another, but the lull did not last, because they had all been drinking cider. As soon as they saw that Jessica had not made a mistake and that she enjoyed being there, the red-shirted firemen and all the hangers-on reminded Charles of small boys showing off before a friendly adult. They were stealing timid glances at her, and Charles could only smile, like a guide who was taking a tourist to a corner of some foreign carnival.

"Aren't they going to play again?" Jessica asked.

Of course, the fifes and drums heard her and they were delighted to show how well they could play. They began playing "School days, school days, dear old golden rule days," and then with hardly a pause they began playing "Marching Through Georgia." Someone touched a cigarette to a balloon and it exploded in a very humorous way.

"You see, they've all been at the hard cider," Charles said.

"What hard cider?"

"In the barn over there. In the barn cellar."

In the warmth of the cider and group companionship, he and Jessica were beginning to be forgotten. There was a tightening circle around the fifes and drums. A heavy, florid young man, with short yellow hair that looked as if it had been cut by the old bowl method, shoved inside the circle. Someone tripped him and he fell down and it was just the thing that everybody needed to make the gathering a success. The young man took off his frayed coat sweater and began asking who had done it, while the fifes and drums played "School Days" again and a chorus began bellowing, "You wrote on my slate, I love you, Joe, when we were a couple of kids."

"Who is he?" Jessica Lovell asked. She had to lean close to him before he could hear her. "The one who got tripped up."

"He's a North Ender," Charles answered. There were always jokes about the unregenerate qualities of North Enders. It seemed unnecessary to tell her that he was Hughie Willis and that almost every Saturday Hughie Willis got into trouble.

A Smith's Common fireman pushed Hughie and one thing led to another. They were not fighting, they were wrestling. They were rolling over and over on the grass, and when the fireman's shoulders touched the ground everyone was delighted that Hughie had got the Smith's Common fireman down.

"Who else wants a try?" Hughie shouted. "Where the hell are all the wrasslers?"

"He's pretty good, isn't he?" Charles said, and he had some childish desire to impress Jessica Lovell. "I'd like to take him on myself."

He could certainly have had no serious intention of doing it. He could only have meant to explain to Jessica that he had gone out for wrestling at Dartmouth.

"Why don't you?" Jessica Lovell asked.

"Because it would be silly," he said.

"Then why did you say it?"

"I just said it," he answered.

"Oh," Jessica said, "you just said it."

He looked straight at her and she looked back, and she was telling him without words that she knew he would not do it.

"I don't suppose you think I would," he said.

"No," she answered, "of course you wouldn't."

"All right," he said. "All right."

So many things were always in a balance and so often before you knew it, it was too late to stop. When he was in the open space he wished to heaven it were not too late, but while he was wishing he was taking off his coat.

"What do you know?" somebody was saying. "It's Charley Gray" — and they were already taking sides, yelling for him and for Hughie Willis. He wished he were not there, but there was no time for wishing. Hughie was reaching for him as he dropped his coat. They were swaying together, holding each other's arms, when Hughie lunged for the back of his neck and Charles sprang forward into the old cross-buttock hold and it was good luck and nothing else that Hughie was off balance. It was simply the application of force at just the right moment that made Hughie fall. It was over so quickly that Charles was not out of breath. He was getting into his coat before Hughie could start to say it was not fair, but the Pine Trees were going to pump and no one was interested in wrestling any longer. The crowd was moving back to the hand tubs when he reached Jessica Lovell and by then reaction was setting in.

"Well," he said, "do you want to watch the Pine Trees?"

"Why, yes," she said, "I'd love to. Your tie's all on one side."

"Oh," Charles said. "Thanks. I hadn't noticed."

"I don't know why we've hardly ever seen each other before," she said. "It's queer, isn't it?" And it did seem queer, as they walked across the grass.

"Would you like some cold root beer?" Charles asked.

"No. Would you?"

"Not very much," and they both laughed.

"Oh," she said, "that's your father, isn't it, on top of the machine?"—and Charles saw his father, holding up a white handkerchief.

"Yes," Charles said, "that's Father."

"It's awfully funny," she said.

"What is?" Charles asked.

"Oh, everything," she said. "Oh dear, here he comes."

"Who?" Charles asked.

"That man." An angular-looking stranger was coming toward them.

"Jessica," he said quickly, "can I come to see you sometime?"

Jessica began to laugh.

"What are you laughing at?" he asked.

"It sounds so funny," she said. "Wait a minute. Can you drive a car?"

"No," Charles said. "We haven't got a car."

"Well, I can," she said. "We'll go driving tomorrow. Come

around at three o'clock. Oh, hello, Mr. Bryant. What happened to you?"

Jessica Lovell was speaking to the stranger, an untidily dressed man in his middle thirties, with a bony face and deep-set eyes.

"This is Mr. Gray," Jessica was saying, "Mr. Bryant."

It seemed to Charles that Mr. Bryant looked like a teacher or a college professor. He had the stooping posture and the studious look, but his face was tanned and something in his manner was not entirely like that of a professor. It was sharper and more inquisitive.

"I'm glad to meet you, Mr. Gray," he said, and his speech reminded Charles of Elbridge Sterne's. "Do you live here in Clyde?"

"Yes," Charles said, "I live here."

"Well, that's fine," Mr. Bryant said. "Let me see now, you must be one of the Grays on Spruce Street."

"Yes," Charles said, "we live on Spruce Street."

"I'm still trying to orient myself," Mr. Bryant said. "It's a little hard to get the general structure straight. I suppose Miss Lovell's been telling you about me."

"Why, no," Charles said, "not much."

"Well, you see we're considering doing a little job on this town," Mr. Bryant said. "My God, it's a wonderful town, a beautiful, static, organized community."

Charles looked questioningly at Jessica Lovell. He could not understand what Mr. Bryant meant and he wondered if she did.

"Mr. Bryant is doing a survey," Jessica said. "I told you. Some sort of a social survey, and he's just back from Borneo."

"That's right," Mr. Bryant said, "just back from a call on the head-hunters."

The fifes and drums began to play again and the Pine Trees were putting their backs in it to beat the Eurekas. "Hail, Hail, the Gang's All Here," the fifes and drums were playing.

"What are they like?" Charles asked.

"What are they like?" Mr. Bryant said. "They're people, just like you and me. All men are basically alike. What's your first name, Mr. Gray?"

"It's Charles," Jessica told him. "Charley Gray."

"Well, why don't we all get on a first-name basis?" Mr. Bryant asked. "I'm Malcolm, and you're Charley and Jessica. God, this is a wonderful town."

"Charley and Jessica are awfully glad you like it," Jessica said. "Aren't we, Charley?"

"And, my God, this thing"—Malcolm Bryant waved his arm in a gesture that embraced the training field—"this beautiful, tribal ritual. It's like the Maori war dance. I'm just beginning to get it straight. It doesn't include the whole tribe, does it?"

"Jessica and Charley don't know what you're talking about," Jessica said.

"I mean it's a folk custom," Malcolm Bryant said. "Of course, you think of it as a thing called a firemen's muster, but obviously, deep down inside, it's the survival of a tribal rite. But the whole community isn't in it, not all the classes. I mean your father wouldn't be in it, Jessica. It's more of a folk custom."

"Charles's father is," Jessica said. "He's right up there now on the machine."

"My God." Mr. Bryant turned around. The Pine Trees were pumping again. "That's interesting. Now let me get this straight. You're a college man, aren't you, Charley?"

"How did you know?" Charles asked.

"Because it's my business to know social groups." Malcolm Bryant rubbed his hands together. "Look at Jessica. She has Smith written all over her."

"Vassar," Jessica said, "not Smith."

"Is your father a college man, Charley?"

"He went to Harvard for a while," Charles said.

"And there he is up there," Malcolm Bryant said. "Now, that's very interesting. Up there and out of his group. It's going to take me quite a while to get this structure straight."

"It's four o'clock," Jessica said. "I'd better be going home. Are you coming back to the house, Mr. Bryant?"

"Well, if it's just the same to you," Malcolm Bryant said, "I'd better stay right here. Somebody says there's going to be a raffling off and I'm just beginning to get a picture of the cliques. You don't mind, do you, Jessica?"

"No," Jessica said, "I don't mind. Charley can take me home. He understands the cliques."

"My God," Malcolm Bryant said, "this is a wonderful town, and I certainly want to meet your father, Charley."

"Well, have a good time," Jessica said. "These head-hunters are going home. It's time to lock up the virgins. Come on, Charley."

VIII

Not That I'm Not Very Glad You Found Him

I⊤ WAS FOUR and Charles had left the Pine Tree clubhouse at one
o'clock but the gap of time seemed much greater when Jessica
Lovell and he turned off Training Street to Johnson Street. They
had left the hose players and the balloons and the sounds of the
crowd on the training field, but Charles Gray had left more than
this behind him. He had left a part of his gaucheness and shyness
and some of the bewilderments of youth. He had stepped across a
boundary into another land. He had reached one of those turning
points, those unperceived corners, which everyone rounds at some
time or other without knowing that there has been a corner — but
he was not conscious of any of this. His thoughts were moving
to that refrain of Malcolm Bryant's. By God, it was a wonderful
town.

All of Johnson Street looked on them kindly as he and Jessica
Lovell walked along it. No earlier memories of the sunsets across
the river, gilding Clyde's white church spires, no memories of the
waves on the beach by the river mouth, could compare with his
present receptiveness. The chilly autumn air and the clear northern
sunlight and the color of the turning leaves gave all of Johnson
Street a friendly brilliance, and the Federalist façades of its houses
behind their delicate white fences were no longer austere or untouchable. He was a part owner of all of Clyde that afternoon, of
Johnson Street and the side streets, of the courthouse and the elms
and maples, of Dock Street with its shops, of River Street by the
river. He was like his father, able to move anywhere and to
understand anyone in Clyde. By God, it was a wonderful town.

Jessica was talking about Malcolm Bryant. He had just appeared
in the house one day with a letter from someone. He was working

247

for some kind of foundation, like the Rockefeller or the Carnegie. Something, she could not tell what, had made her father like him. It must have been because he liked foundations and societies. Then when he had heard that Malcolm Bryant was doing a survey which might be published in some sort of book, he seemed to feel that Malcolm Bryant was his personal responsibility.

"You see," Jessica said, "Father feels he's the world's greatest living authority on Clyde."

"My father's an authority, too," Charles told her.

"Does he keep going on about it?" Jessica asked.

Yes, Charles said, he kept going on about it.

"Well, you and I don't have to, do we?" Jessica said.

They were at an age, of course, when they could condone kindly the errors of their elders. She was wondering what it was that made people in Clyde, especially as they got older, talk more and more about the place, as though it were the most remarkable town in the world. As Jessica wondered, she would occasionally turn her head toward him, giving him appraising little glances as though she hoped that he agreed with her. She was wondering whether he had noticed that living in Clyde made people different from other people. Whenever she was back from Westover or later from Vassar College, she was always very conscious of this. She always thought that people in Clyde were like bees in a beehive, concentrated on their own errands without knowing there were any other beehives. She wondered if Charles knew what she meant, and strangely enough Charles had never thought that anyone else had been bothered by those ideas, but then he had been away himself a good deal. She knew he had been, Jessica was saying. He wasn't all tied up, well, by invisible strings. He did not have any of the prejudices or any of the queer little, well, hesitations. Had he ever noticed that living in Clyde was like walking through spiderwebs without any spiders? There were always those invisible strings, getting around you, brushing across your face — and strangely enough Charles knew exactly what she meant.

There was a boy, she said, who knew Charles and who came to call on her sometimes and he was always all covered with spiderwebs. He never could be natural for a single minute and he made her feel, too, all spiderwebby. Charles knew whom she meant. His name was Jackie Mason. At least she always called him Jackie to herself.

"Now he's always worried," Jessica said, "because his grandfather was a druggist. That's one of his spiderwebs." If he had not kept alluding to it, she would not have given it a thought but now it worried her, too. "I'm sure," she said, "he reads the book of etiquette."

He wanted to do the right thing, Charles told her. It was wonderful that she did not put him in the same category with Jackie but with her on an emancipated plane.

"People ought to do the right things naturally," she said, "without reading them in books."

And this, too, was what he had often thought.

She could see how Clyde must look to an outsider, she said, because she was partly an outsider herself, and so was he, since they had both been away to college. She only hoped that Malcolm Bryant did not think that she and Charles were like the rest of the natives — and she was afraid he did.

"Did you notice the way he looked at us?" she asked. "It made me feel as though you and I were on a microscopic slide."

Charles laughed, and then they both were laughing. He was sure that he was not like Jackie Mason.

"I suppose there's something eccentric about every family," she said. "I suppose" — she hesitated and then looked at him as though she were telling him a secret — "I suppose some people think Father's a little eccentric."

"Well," Charles said, "so's mine, I guess."

He had never dreamed of saying such a thing to anyone before, but Jessica Lovell's mind was on her father — not his father.

"Of course," she was saying, "Father's the dearest person in the world. I love him because he's so shy."

Charles had never met Mr. Lovell, except long ago at the Historical Society, but he had seen him often enough, walking down Dock Street to the bank or to the post office. He had never struck

Charles as being shy. Jessica must have been preparing him for an inevitable meeting, but he was not concerned with it then.

"Do you know what I think sometimes?" Jessica was saying. "When anyone comes to see me, I think Father's a little jealous, not that he really knows he is."

Charles had been so absorbed by the conversation that the dwellings on Johnson Street had passed by him in a pleasant blur — until he saw the pineapples on the wooden fence before the Lovells' house and the border of autumn chrysanthemums. The gate stood open and a brick path lay before them, leading to the Corinthian portico of the Lovells' front door, and he saw old Mr. Fogarty slowly and rheumatically raking leaves on the front lawn.

"Well," he said, "I'll come around tomorrow if you haven't got anything better to do."

"Aren't you coming in now?" she asked.

"I guess I'd better not," Charles said. "It's getting pretty late."

"Why, it isn't late at all. It's just time for tea."

He heard the leaves scrape noisily together under Mr. Fogarty's rake.

"I look pretty shabby," he said, "to go anywhere for tea." As a matter of fact, those old clothes of his were exactly the ones he should have worn, because his tweed coat and baggy flannel trousers showed that he did not consider calling on the Lovells a great occasion.

When they were in the hall, Jessica closed the front door noisily behind her and it made a cheerful, booming sound that echoed along the length of the hall and up the broad, airy staircase. She had pulled off her red felt hat and had tossed it on a Chippendale chair and now she stood before the dusky glass of a great gold hall mirror, giving her head a quick impatient shake and pushing her soft wavy dark hair from her forehead. He could see his own reflection as he stood behind her and their glances met in the dark glass.

"We look like the portraits, don't we?" she said. "That's the trouble with this mirror."

He saw two portraits in the hall, dimly lighted by the arched window at the head of the staircase and by the fanlights above the front and back hall doors. It was true. The gold frame of the mirror was almost like the portraits' frames and for a moment they were both as still as portraits before he followed her down the hall.

Jessica was leading him, as Charles learned later, to what the Lovells called the wallpaper room. "This room," he read later in one of the many architectural accounts of Clyde, "is a triumph of Federalist interior. The windows set in deep paneled reveals are fitted prettily with mahogany window seats. The dado is a wide, clear board of pine. The baseboard is high, contrasting nicely with the door architraves, descending plinthless to the floor. It is as though the room were consciously built to house its greatest treasure, a magnificent wallpaper from France, showing, through the eyes of a French artist, a romantic interpretation of European merchants visiting a Chinese waterfront. The ships, the pagodas, the pavilions, blend most happily with the mantel and the few pieces of Chinese Chippendale which fit in the room as if they, too, were built for it." Charles read this later but he was only conscious then of the spaciousness the paper gave the room and of the dancing fire beneath the Chippendale mantel and of Jessica's aunt, Miss Lovell, who looked like his own Aunt Jane as she sat on a Hepplewhite sofa behind a low mahogany tea table, working on a panel of embroidery.

"This is Charley Gray," Jessica said. "I've brought him in to tea. You know Charley Gray, don't you, Aunt Georgianna?"

Miss Lovell inserted her needle in her embroidery and laid it down beside her and looked up at Charles. Her eyes, which were dark like Jessica's, gave her thin, pale face an expression of suspicious watchfulness.

"I don't know Charles," she said, "but of course I know all about him," and she held out her hand.

"Aunt Georgianna knows about everybody," Jessica said.

"Ring the bell, Jessica," Miss Lovell told her. "It's time for tea. You look as though you'd been walking."

"Well, not exactly walking," Jessica said. "We were at the firemen's muster."

"Oh, yes," Miss Lovell said. "What became of Mr. Bryant, Jessica? Did you get tired of him?"

"No," Jessica said, "he got tired of me. He's down there still."

"I'm sure I'd have been tired of him if I'd been you," Miss Lovell said. "His voice goes right through my ears. How is your Aunt Jane, Charles? Did I ever tell you, Jessica, that Jane and I went to the academy together? We used to call her Lady Jane Gray."

"Aunt Jane's pretty well, thank you," Charles said.

"All we can be at our age is pretty well," Miss Lovell said. "Jessica, I do wish you'd do something to your hair so it doesn't blow."

The tea on a silver tray was being carried in by Mrs. Daniel Martin, an old friend of Mary Callahan's, whom Charles had often seen in his own aunt's kitchen, but Mrs. Martin looked unfamiliar to him now in a black dress and a white apron. In another day everyone on Johnson Street would know who had been to the Lovells' that afternoon.

"Hannah," Miss Lovell said to Mrs. Martin, "will you please tell Mr. Lovell that tea is ready? How do you like your tea, Charles?"

"Oh," Charles said, "why any way at all, thank you, Miss Lovell."

Charles heard a footstep behind him and he turned to see Mr. Lovell, holding a folded newspaper.

"Well, well," Mr. Lovell said, "I didn't know we were going to have company."

"You know Charley Gray, don't you, Father?" Jessica asked him.

"Of course I know Charley Gray, Jessie," Mr. Lovell said, "or *of* Charley Gray. Where on earth did you find him, Jessie? Not that I'm not very glad you found him."

Then Jessica was explaining again that she had found him at the firemen's muster.

"This is quite a coincidence," Mr. Lovell said. "Only a day or two ago I heard Francis Stanley say that you are at Wright-Sherwin. Thank you, Georgianna," and he took his cup of tea.

Charles could not see why Jessica had said that her father was shy. He looked very much as he had there at the Historical Society. His voice had the same high but agreeably resonant ring. He had the same careless way of standing, even when he held his teacup.

The lines in his face were deeper and his hair was grayer, but that was all. He did not look shy at all, as he stood in the wallpaper room, raising his teacup to his thin, straight lips and glancing at Charles over the edge of it.

"That was not a happy remark of mine when I asked where Jessica found you," he said. "I'm delighted to have a Gray in the house. Now let's see. You went to Dartmouth, didn't you? How's your father, Charles?"

"He's out on the training field with the Pine Trees," Charles told him.

"When we were boys he was always running to fires. Jessica, what became of your other friend?"

And Jessica told again where Malcolm Bryant was.

"Well, he'll be back for supper, won't he?" Mr. Lovell said. "We always call it supper in Clyde, don't we, Charles? But Jessie likes to call it dinner."

"Charley," Jessica said, "have you ever seen the garden?"

Charles shook his head. He said he had never seen the garden but he would like to see it.

"What do you want to show him the garden for?" Mr. Lovell said. "It's October."

"There's still the boxwood," Jessica said, "and the chrysanthemums."

"Well," Mr. Lovell said. "Well. I'll say good-by to you now, Charles, in case I don't see you again, and give your father my regards."

The wallpaper room was silent as Charles and Jessica walked down the hall together but before they reached the back hall door Charles heard Mr. Lovell's voice.

"Well," Mr. Lovell was saying. "Well."

"Come on, Charley," Jessica said quickly, and they stepped outside onto a long path bordered with boxwood. The formal garden of the Lovells so often described in Garden Club lectures lay before them, rising gradually to the top of a gentle slope, with its box borders casting long shadows across the gravel paths in the setting sun.

"You know," Jessica said, "I really think Father likes you."

"I don't see why you think so," Charles told her.

"Because he talked so much," Jessica said, "and you didn't do anything wrong."

He wondered exactly what she meant. They were following the path up to a summerhouse on top of the rise, past the terraced flower beds where everything was cut down ready for the winter. At any rate, nothing in the Lovell house had made him uneasy and perhaps that was what she had meant when she said he had done nothing wrong. Perhaps she had meant that he had been neither impressed nor disturbed by her aunt or father and that they had not seemed to him in any way extraordinary. He was even thinking that there was nothing so extraordinary about Jessica, either. He could still see her as she was, before whatever drew them together became too strong for him to see her in any true perspective. She was not strikingly beautiful. She was too tall and her chin and nose were both a little too long and her eyebrows were too black and heavy, but those defects were vanishing already as she walked beside him up the path. The open fire had made her cheeks glow and her eyes were bright and her lips, which were rather like her father's, were relaxed. Once they reached the summerhouse, it was cool and almost chilly in the shadows.

"Well," she said, "there's the garden."

They stood leaning on the summerhouse railing, gazing at the garden, which had been laid out by a French *émigré* more than a century before, and back at the house with its high-arched windows and its balustrade and cupola.

"You can see the harbor from the cupola," she said, and then she said it was strange to think of staying at home with no more college and nothing to do but just be there.

"I don't know what I'm going to do," she said, and Charles was telling her that there were all sorts of things to do in Clyde.

"Well," she said, "I'm awfully glad you think so." She had been moving her fingers idly, making little patterns on the summerhouse railing.

"Oh dear, here he comes. God, this is a wonderful town." Malcolm Bryant was coming toward them up the path.

"Jessica," Charles said, "you won't forget about tomorrow, will you?"

"No," she said, "of course I won't," and her hand touched his. "Good-by, Charley."

IX

All the World's a Stage
— SHAKESPEARE

CHARLES KNEW there would be talk, because gossip always eddied through Clyde like smoke from the burning piles of autumn
leaves, and it also usually assumed fantastic shapes. It was only to
be expected that everyone would know by Monday of his encounter with Hughie Willis, but instead of looking on it critically
people seemed in general to approve of his action. His father,
when he mentioned it, appeared to be amused and only said that
he must have had quite a time that afternoon at the muster. His
mother, of course, was not amused. She had heard, both from Mrs.
Mason and from Mrs. Gow, that Charles had got into a fight with
a North Ender, and she could not understand why Charles had
done such a thing, and it did no good to tell her and Dorothea that
it was not a fight, because they could not understand the difference.
Charles's main fear had been that someone would say that he and
Hughie Willis had been fighting over Jessica, but he concluded that
this was absurd.

As a matter of fact, his encounter with Hughie Willis did him no
harm at all. Groups of his old school friends began calling to him
in Dock Square with a new sort of familiarity. In fact there was a
warmth about everything which made him imagine that people
were saying that Charley Gray was not stuck-up because he had
been to college. He had taken off his coat and pitched right into
Hughie Willis. At Wright-Sherwin on Monday morning, it seemed
to him that the girls in the accounting department smiled at him
more brightly and nobody there appeared to disapprove, except
possibly Mr. Howell who told him that it was Monday morning

and time for fun was over, but even Mr. Howell was interested. "That Willis was always a bad boy," Mr. Howell said. "When he was a kid, he was always putting cannon crackers in my hedge." It even seemed to Charles that Mr. Stanley looked at him in a different way, when Charles met him in the hall.

"Good morning, Charley," Mr. Stanley said. "How are you feeling this morning?" Mr. Stanley had never asked him before how he was feeling and it seemed to Charles that Mr. Stanley was examining his face for possible contusions — but even Mr. Stanley's manner was not disapproving.

Of course, Jackie Mason knew all about it. All morning Jack kept looking at him across the room, trying to catch his eye, and when they met at the water cooler around eleven o'clock Jackie immediately brought up the subject.

"Charley, you ought not to do that sort of thing," he said.

"What sort of thing?" Charles asked.

"You know as well as I do, Charley, that someone always sees what you do around here — and wasn't it true that Jessica Lovell was there?" Jack Mason looked worried and his anxiety was friendly. "What I mean, Charley, is that a girl like Jessica Lovell won't forget a thing like that. It simply means she'll never have anything to do with you. What are you laughing at?"

"She never had anything to do with me anyway," Charles said.

"But she might have," Jack said. "She's going to be here all the time now and you've simply lost your chance of ever seeing anything of Jessica Lovell."

Those remarks of Jack Mason's came as a great relief because they showed that perhaps after all everyone in Clyde did not know everything immediately, but someone would have seen Jessica's new Dodge phaeton, with its top down, as it crossed the intersection of Dock and Johnson streets on Sunday afternoon. There was no way of escaping facts in Clyde and, indeed, he did not care much what anyone would say. He only felt concerned that the offices at Wright-Sherwin where he was earning his twenty-five dollars a week already seemed smaller since the firemen's muster and he was already beginning to realize that it would take years for him to get anywhere in Wright-Sherwin — years and years.

Before long it began to be recognized, of course, that he was seeing a good deal of Jessica Lovell, but on the whole it was an acceptable fact. The Grays did not live on Johnson Street as the Thomases or the Stanleys did, but his father was the son of old Judge Gray and had married Dr. Marchby's daughter and so it was not markedly unusual for Charles Gray to go around with Jessica Lovell.

"Going around" was the expression which was used in Clyde when a boy and girl saw a good deal of each other. It was not the same as the more vulgar expression "going with" or "keeping company" which was employed when speaking of River Street couples and which had a more definite connotation. It was not even the same as saying that Charles was "attentive" to Jessica Lovell, which was more serious. His relationship in those months might have been better expressed as one of being "seen around" with Jessica Lovell, which was not even quite as strong as "going around" with her.

Since Jessica was fourteen she had spent her summers in Maine and had been away to school at Westover and then at Vassar College, so that now she was really back in Clyde for the first time in years, and Mr. Lovell had told several people that he wanted very much to have Jessica "show herself" in Clyde. It was exactly, she told Charles once, as though her father wanted her to go trotting up and down Johnson Street every afternoon, but of course he really meant that she should take part in Clyde activities, such as attending the Harvest Supper at the Boat Club and the Boat Club monthly dance and Pound Day at the Episcopal Church.

Her father had also told her that he did not want her to act as though she were just at home poised for flight to somewhere else. He wanted Jessica to show herself, and if she had to show herself obviously she had to be seen. She was seen with Charles but she was also seen with Hewitt Thomas, when Hewitt was not busy somewhere else. She was occasionally seen with Lester Gow, who was studying at the Harvard Law School, and now and then with Jackie Mason. She was even seen once or twice with Melville Meader, but if Mr. Lovell discouraged this everyone could understand why. The Meader boys were nice boys but Mr. Meader's father had been in the grocery business and Mr. Meader, though he was in real estate, often worked, himself, with the plumbers and carpenters, improving the buildings he owned. Besides, Jessica Lovell also had young men from Boston as guests sometimes for the week end. Thus if she was seen with Charles it did not mean that they were going around together.

When Jessica joined the Clyde Players that winter, it was natural for Charles to take her home because the other members of the theater group were married, except Jackie Mason who was the property man and who had to stay after the others. There was no reason for anyone to know that Charles had joined the Clyde Players only because Jessica had asked him to. Everyone believed that Charles enjoyed amateur theatricals.

It must have been an evening early in December when Jessica called Charles up, something which she did very seldom in those days. His Aunt Jane had been ill for two weeks with the grippe and his mother had gone to Gow Street to see how she was doing. When the telephone in the hall rang, his father was reading Boswell by the fire and Dorothea and Elbridge Sterne were playing backgammon and Charles was looking over a catalogue of surveying instruments which he had brought home from the office. Everyone stopped to count since it was a party line.

"Go and answer it, Charley," Dorothea said.

"It will only be for you," Charles told her. "It always is."

"I don't know why it should be," Dorothea said, "at this time of night."

The telephone was under the stairs in front of a line of coat hooks and it was necessary to bend one's head when one took the receiver off the hook.

"Is that you, Charley?" It was Jessica's voice. "You haven't gone to bed yet, have you?"

"Why, no," Charley answered. "It's only nine o'clock," and he heard Jessica laugh.

"Everybody's gone here except Father, and he's asleep in the library. Charley, would you mind coming over for a few minutes? I won't keep you any time at all."

It was only a step to Johnson Street. It was the most natural thing in the world, he was telling himself, for Jessica suddenly to ask him to come to see her at nine o'clock. He only thought of it as peculiar when he came back into the parlor with his overcoat to say he was going out.

"But why are you going out?" Dorothea asked. "Who called you up? Was it Jackie Mason?"

"It was Jessica Lovell," Charles said. "She just wants me to come over for a few minutes."

"Now?" Dorothea said. "At nine o'clock? I didn't know that you knew Jessica Lovell as well as that."

"I don't see why it shows that I know her very well," he answered.

"Oh, doesn't it?" Dorothea said, and she and Elbridge smiled at each other and his father looked up from Boswell's *Life of Johnson*.

"Now that I think of it," he said, "Jessica has been gracious to me lately. She stopped me in the street and asked me about fire engines. Her looks have improved, too. Her chin is still a little long and her eyebrows are too heavy, but she's improved."

When Charles walked up Spruce Street, the clear coldness of the December night air reminded him of new dark ice on a pond, just frozen thick enough to bear one's weight. His pulses danced with a strange elation, not because Jessica Lovell had called him up, certainly not because of that, but because of the beauty of the evening and the nearness of the stars. He seemed to have Clyde entirely to himself. The house lights were already going out on Spruce Street. It was absurd, he was thinking, for Dorothea to have made any comments when Jessica had called him up. It only showed that he and Jessica Lovell were not bowed down by small stupidities.

Jessica must have been waiting for him because she opened the front door herself and his idea that it was natural to be dropping in there at nine o'clock was contradicted by the soft tones of her voice and by the gentle way she closed the door.

"We'll have to sit in the wallpaper room," she said, as Charles was taking off his overcoat. "The library's the only comfortable place but Father's asleep in it. There's a little room upstairs — " She sighed. Of course they could not go to a little room upstairs. "We'll have to sit and look at the Chinese junks."

She asked Charles to put a new log on the dying embers of the fire and then she curled up on a corner of the Hepplewhite sofa. She was wearing a very simple, purplish woolen dress that fell just below her knees. She gave it a careless pull over her silk stockings and then she pushed her dark hair away from her forehead with both hands. His father may have been right in his remarks about Jessica. Her eyebrows were too heavy and her chin was too long and so were her legs, but she looked very well in the wallpaper room. She had none of the self-consciousness of other girls he knew, no fear that her hair looked untidy and she made no fluttering efforts to conceal her knees.

"Charley," she began, "the most awful thing has happened. I've got to join the Clyde Players. Father says I have to," and she let her hands drop helplessly on her lap.

"Oh," Charles said, "has Mrs. Smythe Leigh been to see you?"

"She just went away," Jessica said. "Who is she, Charley?"

It showed how little Jessica really knew about Clyde that she had never heard anything about Mrs. Smythe Leigh.

"She's pretty energetic," Charles told her. "She likes art and she's one of those people who like to run things."

"Charley, give me a cigarette," and she pointed to a box on the table. "Light it for me, will you?" He leaned close to her as he lighted her cigarette, and she pointed at the table where the cigarette box had stood. "Look at that thing, Charley, look at it."

"What thing?" Charles asked.

"That thing," she repeated. "That play. Tell me, how did she ever find it, Charley?"

She was pointing to a small volume covered with yellow paper and Charles picked it up. It was entitled *Lord Bottomly Decides, a Farce-Comedy*.

"Did she leave it here?" Charles asked.

"Of course she left it here," Jessica said.

"Well," Charles said, "it's just one of her ideas," and then he told Jessica about Mrs. Smythe Leigh.

Mrs. Smythe Leigh had come to Clyde about ten years before and she lived on Gow Street and was very active in women's organizations. Mrs. Smythe Leigh — she did not like being called plain Mrs. Leigh — had organized the Women's Club pageant in 1920 and she coached in dramatics at the high school and she sometimes even hinted that she had been on the stage herself. She had also organized the Clyde Players, and there were a number of people who liked that sort of thing. Dr. Bush, who was the osteopath, liked it, and so did Mr. and Mrs. Knowles, and there were always a few people who liked to paint scenery. It was not strange at all that Mrs. Smythe Leigh had asked Jessica to take part in a play. She was always asking everybody. All that you had to do was to say that you could not do it and then she would ask someone else.

"But Father says I ought to do it," Jessica said. "I know it's silly, but things like that make me sick."

She was serious about it — the whole idea really frightened her. She was saying that once she had tried to be in a play at school and that she had begun walking in her sleep. She had tried again at Vassar and she had been taken ill.

"Look at me, Charley," she said. "I'm all arms and legs and I trip all over myself and it's such a God-awful play."

It was one of those plays that started with a monologue by the engaging British hero. He was in a most frightful fix. His aunt, Lady Ponsonby, had made him her heir but just this morning she said she would cut him off with a shilling if he did not marry a hideous girl whom she deemed a suitable match instead of allowing him to marry lovely Lucy Clive, the curate's daughter, whom he loved to distraction. He was in a terrible fix.

"Father's making such a point of it and look at me, Charley," Jessica said. "Do I look like lovely Lucy Clive?"

She was wretchedly unhappy, curled up there on the corner of the sofa, and no consolation, only austere disapproval, came from the wallpaper room.

"Why don't you tell him you really don't want to?" Charles asked.

"Oh, Charley," she answered, "I can't do that. I simply can't."

"Why can't you?" he asked. "Why not just tell him how you feel?"

She passed the back of her hand across her forehead and she looked as though she were about to cry.

"Oh, Charley," she said, "nobody understands about Father and me. I can't."

Charles could only sit there baffled. He wanted to touch her hair softly and tell her that it was all right. He wanted to put his arm around her and draw her close to him, but the idea still seemed preposterous.

"Jessica," he said, "it isn't going to be as bad as all that."

"I don't know what you'll think of me," she said. "I haven't any right to ask you, but if I have to be in this thing, will you be in it too?"

He could still view it all aloofly. He had never until that moment thought that Jessica Lovell might need him for anything.

"All right," Charles said, "if you want me to, Jessica."

Then she smoothed her dress carefully over her knees and her voice had changed. She was Jessica Lovell again, back in the wallpaper room.

"Thanks ever so much," she said, and suddenly everything was completely settled, and he was saying that it was about time to be getting back home. He rose and put the paper-covered play back on the table.

"I wish you didn't have to go," Jessica answered.

When he was in the front hall, getting into his overcoat, he could hear the tall clock ticking on the landing; and when he saw Jessica glance behind her, toward the closed door of Mr. Lovell's library, his call suddenly became a clandestine meeting. Her voice had dropped almost to a whisper and he was sure that she was very anxious to have him on the other side of the great front door, walking down the path. When he put his hand on the heavy bronze latch and turned to say good night, she pulled his hand away.

"Let me do it," she whispered. "Don't wake up Father," and

she opened the front door very gently. It was clear to him that she did not want Mr. Lovell to know that she had asked him to be in the Clyde Players.

When he arrived at Gow Street a few nights later for what Mrs. Smythe Leigh called a preliminary get-together of the group, Charles knew by the number of hats and coats in the hall that he was late. He had hardly seen Mrs. Smythe Leigh since his senior class in high school had done *Officer 666* and then Charles had only helped take in tickets. Now Mrs. Smythe Leigh squeezed his hand, holding it tight in both of hers. She was wearing a flowing gown of green velvet and on her right wrist was a Navajo bracelet.

"Why, Charley Gray," she said. "I hardly dared think that you would join us. Come right into the living room. Everybody's here."

The scene in Mrs. Smythe Leigh's living room, Charles sometimes thought afterwards, was one which must have repeated itself continuously in other places. Mrs. Smythe Leigh's living room was an intellectual fortress and it stood for the larger world. As Mrs. Smythe Leigh told him later, there was no reason to get in a rut because one lived in Clyde. Clyde was a dear, poky place, full of dear people, but one could always open one's windows to the world. One could bring something new to Clyde, and this was what she always tried to do . . . a few reproductions of modern pictures, a bit of Chinese brocade, a few records of Kreisler and Caruso, and the *American Mercury* and the *New Republic* and of course *Harper's* and the *Atlantic,* and the *New Statesman* and *L'Illustration.* All one had to do was open one's windows to the outer world — and the surprising thing was the number of congenial spirits who gathered if you did it. Sometimes, frankly, she had thought of giving up the Clyde Players. There was always the inertia, but the old guard, Dr. Bush and Katie Rowell, always rallied around her and would not *let* her give up. Once you had the smell of grease paint in your nostrils, you could never get away from it, and there was always that joy of getting out of oneself by interpreting character on the stage. Charles was a newcomer, but someday he might be the old guard, too.

The newcomers and the old guard were all seated in the living room. There were not enough chairs so some were seated on the floor.

"This is Charley Gray," Mrs. Smythe Leigh said, "but then of course everybody knows everybody" — and of course everybody did, in a certain way.

"And of course," Mrs. Smythe Leigh said, "you know Jessica Lovell?"

She obviously asked the question because she was not quite sure. Jessica was sitting on a piano stool and her face had the same strained, self-conscious look of all the other faces, but she smiled at Charles in a friendly, distant way.

"You'll have to sit on the floor, Charley Gray," Mrs. Smythe Leigh said. "It's your punishment for being late," and everyone laughed politely. "And now I'm going to begin by giving my usual little talk. It's an orientation talk. Some of us know it already but perhaps it won't hurt to hear it again."

When the first meeting was over and Charles took Jessica home, this was something everyone understood, including Mr. Lovell. In fact, when Jessica asked him in, Mr. Lovell seemed pleased to see him. As they stood in the front hall, they could hear voices from the library and Jessica put her hand on his arm.

"Wait," she whispered. "Let's see who it is." Then she recognized the Midwestern voice, that sounded almost foreign at the Lovells'.

"It's Malcolm Bryant," she whispered. "He always keeps dropping in," and she gave her head an exasperated shake. It occurred to Charles that he had heard other people saying lately that Mr. Bryant kept dropping in on them unexpectedly, and he should have known better since no one ever made sudden descents on anyone in Clyde. By this time, everyone in Clyde knew who Malcolm Bryant was. He was the professor who was writing some sort of book and he had rented two rooms from old Mrs. Mooney in Fanning Street, where he stayed when he wasn't in Boston and Cambridge, and he had his meals at Mrs. Bronson's boardinghouse. It was time he knew better than to be dropping in suddenly on people.

"Oh dear," Jessica whispered, "Father's telling him about the family again," and they stood for a minute side by side listening.

"I'd like to get this straight, Mr. Lovell," they could hear Malcolm Bryant saying. "It's a way of life that has just the continuity I'm looking for. Now when was it that your great-grandfather lived on River Street?"

"That was before he built the house here," they could hear Mr. Lovell saying. "Of course, River Street was different then. Johnson Street was hardly opened. My great-great-grandfather, Ezra Lovell, built and improved the house on River Street, before the Revolutionary War. The land ran down to the river, approximately where the gas company is now. There's nothing left but one of the old warehouses. Webley's blacksmith shop is in it now, and of course the wharf is gone."

"Oh dear," Jessica whispered. "Why does he want to know about it?"

"Ezra Lovell was in the coastal trade," Mr. Lovell was saying. "It was an old gambrel-roofed house, torn down after my grandfather sold the property. The countinghouse was in the ell, and then there were the slave quarters."

"What?" Malcolm Bryant asked. "Did they have slaves?"

"Only in a small way, I think," Mr. Lovell answered. "I came across a paper just the other day with Ezra Lovell's signature liberating a Negro he owned named Pomp, but that was before the Revolution."

The Lovell library was a large, paneled room, with mahogany bookshelves all around it, designed by the order of Nathaniel Lovell. The same gold-tooled sets of books must have always been on the shelves, and now, though age was making their backs shaky, Charles could imagine that many of them had never been read. A celestial and a terrestrial globe stood on either side of the fireplace and above the books were more Lovell portraits and two pictures of Lovell ships and also the well-known engraving of the Clyde waterfront. There was a comfortable sofa in the library, as Jessica said, the only comfortable sofa in the house, and there were some reasonably modern leather armchairs. Mr. Lovell was seated in one of these with a stack of papers on the floor beside him, and Malcolm Bryant was seated opposite him with a notebook on his knee.

"Hello, Jessie," Mr. Lovell said, and he held out both his hands to her and Malcolm Bryant stood up. "Back so soon? Why, hello, Charles."

Mr. Lovell gave him a questioning look, as though he could not understand his sudden appearance.

"Charley took me home," she said. "Charley's in the Players."

She gave a little exasperated laugh as though she were telling her father that there was no reason for her to explain everything.

"Why, of course, Jessie," Mr. Lovell said. "I'm delighted Charles is in the Players. I told you you'd find friends there. You know Mr. Malcolm Bryant, don't you, Charles? Jessie, why don't you bring us some milk and a little cake, or some crackers and cheese?"

"Oh, not for me, thanks," Malcolm Bryant said. "Please don't bother."

"No, please don't bother," Charles said. "I've got to be going home."

It seemed to him that Mr. Lovell looked relieved, although he said that it would be no trouble at all and that Jessica would love to get them something.

"Then how about a cigar?" Mr. Lovell asked. "Will you smoke a cigar, Charles?"

"Oh, no, thank you, sir," Charles said.

"You know Charles can tell you a good deal about Clyde, Mr. Bryant," Mr. Lovell said. "Charles is born and brought up a Clyde boy, aren't you, Charles? More of a Clyde boy than Jessica is a Clyde girl, I'm afraid. How were the Players, Jessica?"

"They were terrible," Jessica said. "I told you they would be terrible."

"Now let's see," Malcolm Bryant said, "I must have missed the Clyde Players. Where do they fit in?"

"Fit in?" Mr. Lovell repeated.

"I mean in the general picture."

"Don't you ever get tired of asking questions?" Jessica asked.

"Now, Jessie," Mr. Lovell said, "Mr. Bryant is here to ask questions. I should say that the Clyde Players is an ordinary community effort. Jessica is in it, and she should be, and Charles is in it. Why did you join the group, Charles?"

"Because he must be weak-minded," Jessica said quickly.

Malcolm Bryant was leaning back in his comfortable leather chair with his hands laced in back of his head. He was the outsider, enjoying that little scene and evaluating it, while his deep-set eyes kept shifting from Jessica to Charles and back to Mr. Lovell.

"And then there's Dr. Bush, the osteopath," Mr. Lovell said. "I believe he's very active in it. That shows it's a cross section — Jessica and then an osteopath. I had a stiff shoulder once and I got Bush in and he fixed it, just by pulling."

"Down in Borneo," Malcolm Bryant said, "I had a stiff neck once and I was treated by a tribal doctor. He killed a bird and put it on my neck, after cutting it open with an obsidian knife. There was an interesting ritual connected with it."

"Did it help your neck?" Mr. Lovell asked.

"I don't really remember." Malcolm Bryant was smiling at Jessica. "But I have some pictures of it. I'd love to show them to you sometime. Charley Schwartz, one of my assistants, took the pictures. He's at Johns Hopkins now. Men are about the same everywhere." Malcolm Bryant smiled again at Jessica. "Well, I mustn't keep you up too late. I always have a lot to think about after an evening here."

"I wish I knew what you thought," Jessica said.

Malcolm Bryant rose and Charles stood up too. It was time to be going.

"Grateful thoughts," Malcolm Bryant said. "This has been a really challenging evening."

"Good night," Mr. Lovell said, "and good night, Charles. It's good news you're in the play. We all have to take part in things, don't we, and I'm glad there's someone to take Jessica home."

Charles understood what Mr. Lovell meant — that it was better for him to take her home than for Dr. Bush. As long as they were both in the Players, engaged in a common community effort, there was no reason why he should not be seen with Jessica, no reason at all. In fact Charles could imagine later what Mr. Lovell must have said to Jessica.

"Jessie," he must have said, "I think it's very nice that Charles Gray is in the Players, and it's very nice if you see something of Charles Gray, as long as you don't take him too seriously, Jessie. You'll remember, won't you, that a young man like Charles Gray has no prospects, or hardly any."

Perhaps he spoke differently later, for there was a time, just for a little while, when he may have thought that Charles did have prospects — when John Gray bought a Cadillac car and when the market was going up.

By the time Charles and Malcolm Bryant left the Lovells' house that evening, the other houses on Johnson Street were dark except for an occasional light in their upper windows.

"By God," Malcolm Bryant said, "this is a wonderful town. It all fits together without a blur in the pattern. By God, I was lucky to discover it. How well do you know the Lovells, Charley?" It was an impertinent question and Charles felt annoyed.

"Not very well," he answered.

"Oh, I thought you did," Malcolm Bryant said. "You seem to be great friends with Jessica."

Charles caught his breath in astonishment, and then he was angry.

"Suppose you mind your own business," he said, and he stopped walking and stood facing Malcolm Bryant. Malcolm Bryant had stopped too. They were only two dark shadows standing face to face on Johnson Street, but all at once Malcolm Bryant's voice was placating and soothing.

"That's just the right thing for you to say," he said. "I had it coming to me. I'm sorry."

"All right," Charles said.

Charles could not understand why his resentment was ebbing but there was a disarming quality in Malcolm Bryant's voice.

"It was rotten investigative technique," Malcolm Bryant was saying. "If one of my team had done that, I'd have fired him. I just forgot myself. Don't get mad, Charley. It wasn't a personal question. I was just thinking about your groups, and the Lovells aren't quite in your group — are they?"

"No," Charles said, "I don't suppose they are."

"Now, Charley." Malcolm Bryant put a hand on his shoulder. "This is scientific — none of it is personal. Look at me as a father confessor — just an old man you can talk to. It won't go any further. You're not mad any more, are you?"

"No," Charles said, "that's all right. Good night."

Malcolm Bryant held out his hand and patted his shoulder again.

"Well, that's fine," he said. "We'll be seeing a lot of each other, Charley. My God, this is a wonderful town."

Malcolm Bryant walked whistling down the street of the wonderful town and Charles walked home, but Malcolm Bryant's hasty words were still running through his mind. He had never encountered anyone like Malcolm Bryant and he could not tell whether they were friends or not, but then perhaps a man like Malcolm Bryant never could be friends with anyone. Sometimes he was not sure that Malcolm Bryant had the same capacity for likes or dislikes that other people had. He was always thinking of everyone from a viewpoint which he called mass instinct. It was Charles's first contact with pedantries.

X

The Procedural Pattern

THE CONFESSIONAL CLUB, the men's club to which Charles's father belonged, met at the Grays' home that year in January. Annually each member of the Confessional Club entertained all the other members for supper and for the evening. Charles remembered the occasion especially, because Malcolm Bryant had been invited.

He had not known that his father knew Malcolm Bryant until a week before the meeting and already the house was in a turmoil, because John Gray always wanted to entertain the club properly. Until it was his turn to receive them, he was apt to make fun of the members of the Confessional Club and the club itself, although Charles was sure that he was proud to be in it. He used to say that the Confessional Club was only another of those blatant, self-conscious groups that had always cluttered up Clyde with preposterous, useless discussions. He used to say that those evening clubs were just like boys' clubs except that they were formed by men and that no one had anything to say in Clyde that was worth listening to for half an hour — yet people in Clyde always had wanted to gather around and listen to dull papers.

It showed a lack of personal resource, John Gray always said, and women, too, as well as men, were infected by the germ. No one ever really learned anything from these intellectual outpourings, but everyone wished to try to be improved, during the long winter months. The Women's Club continually met to hear lectures on French fans or on Mount Vesuvius, and the ladies of the Garden Club were always gathering to learn about cutworms or means of eradicating poison ivy. The Knights of Columbus kept listening to travelogues, the Rotary Club would hang on the words of someone who told about sewage disposal. The only organization, John Gray said, that had never wanted to be improved was the Pine Tree Association of Veteran Firemen.

Think of the geysers of words, John Gray used to say, that were spouted forth each winter in Clyde. Every two weeks the Monday Club had met, since 1787, and the Thursday Club had met every two weeks since it had broken away from the Monday Club before the Civil War. He could not imagine, he said, why he had ever joined the Confessional Club, unless because of local contagion. Why had the Confessional Club ever started? It had started thirty years ago because of hurt feelings and merely because there were certain people who were not included in the Monday Club and the Thursday Club; and now two more groups of men who could not get into these three clubs had formed other clubs, and they all met every two weeks in winter and some member always read a paper.

Think of the papers, John Gray said, to which he had been compelled to listen in the Confessional Club alone. Fortunately most of them went in one ear and out the other, but there were details in some which had an adhesive quality that awakened him at night and gave him nervous indigestion. There was the gallstone, for instance, which was removed from the interior of Samuel Pepys, the subject of a paper by Gerald Marchby. Gerald had read it ten years ago but it was very fresh in John Gray's memory. Then there was "The Story of the Mammoth," a paper which had been read by Willard Godfrey. The juvenile quality of this paper had caused John Gray to consult reference books in the public library and to discover that the whole thing had been cribbed from a children's encyclopedia. He might also mention that scholarly work entitled "Certain Old Teaspoons" written by Mr. Norton Swing, a retired official of the Wright-Sherwin Company. This was a double-header, because you not only had to hear about the certain old teaspoons but you had to examine them afterwards one by one. He could go further. If he wanted, he could describe that hour-and-a-half long paper by Hugh Blashfield entitled "Certain Personages in Bench and Bar of Massachusetts," but he was not even going to think of it. He would never even consider the hours of common suffering in the Confessional Club except with the belief that they may have drawn its members together into a sort of perverse bond of friendship.

Nevertheless, whenever it was John Gray's turn to entertain the Confessional Club, he appeared to forget the bitter things he had previously said. He wanted to have as good food as anyone else. The members could wait on themselves, but he wanted tables arranged on which they could eat comfortably and he always provided cocktails made by mixing medical alcohol procured from Gerald Marchby with distilled water and juniper. The main thing was to be sure that the members all had enough cocktails so they could endure the paper but not so many cocktails that they would become noisy or fall asleep during the paper's progress.

"Now, Esther," he said, "I'm not at all sure that you and Dorothea and Mary Callahan can do everything in the kitchen."

"Don't start worrying already, John," she told him. "Jane isn't well enough to let Mary come over, but all sorts of people like to come in and help. They like to sit at the top of the stairs, you know, and listen."

This was exactly what John Gray meant, he told them, when he said everyone wanted to be improved in Clyde.

"And don't forget to get the Wedgwood plates and the silver from Jane," he said, "and glasses. Plenty of glasses."

There was no reason to worry about it. Everyone in the house understood about the Confessional Club.

"And you can come, of course, Charles," John Gray said. "Someday you may be in the club yourself, if you don't get gallstones first. It's something to live for."

Then Dorothea asked if he was not going to ask Elbridge Sterne, and John Gray said that it would be unwise to ask Elbridge Sterne, that he might never come to the house again.

"But I am asking that professor," he said, "the one who's writing the book. He says he knows you, Charles."

"The one who says, 'My God, this is a wonderful town'?" Charles asked.

"Yes, that's the one," John Gray said. "I took him over to the Pine

Trees. He kept talking about the aborigines in Borneo, and then we went to see the cemetery."

"Why did he want to see the cemetery?"

"We were talking about the cult of the dead," John Gray said. "He has some interesting ideas, but I'm afraid he has the unselective curiosity that goes with a closed mind. I don't know why people who know too much already are the only ones who keep trying to learn more."

Malcolm Bryant arrived at Spruce Street early. John Gray was still arranging cocktail glasses and struggling with the top of the large shaker he had borrowed from Dr. Marchby. Malcolm stood by the open fire examining the room and stealing glances into the dining room, where everything was on the table except the hot dishes.

John Gray poured the contents of a bottle into the cocktail shaker and gave it a few brisk shakes.

"Try some of this, will you," he said, "and tell me how it tastes?"

"There should either be liquor at a social function," Malcolm Bryant said, "or a few men beating drums. You'd be surprised — good drumming has nearly the same effect. Now a year or two ago I happened to be out with the Ojibways in the lake region of Ontario. I went out with Clarence Spinner from the Sykes Foundation. I don't suppose you've read his papers on the Ojibways. He has the gift of tongues, but he exaggerates."

Charles could see his father straighten up alertly. He always liked something new.

"It was a very unspoiled tribe," Malcolm Bryant went on. "Beautiful birch-bark wigwams and very fine canoes. They were completely out of liquor, but one evening they began beating a drum — four or five delightful old gentlemen around a big drum, beating with a quick syncopation that was more subtle than the African, I think, and singing a soft falsetto chorus. Just after sundown all of us began dancing in a circle, men, women, and children, quite slowly. Thank you, Charley." Malcolm Bryant held out his glass and Charles poured him another cocktail but he held it absent-mindedly without drinking it. "There was a compulsion in that drumming, a mass, hysterical compulsion. By God, it was a wonderful group. I've seen the same thing in Africa but not as well expressed. Oh yes, it was a beautiful exhibition. That drumming made you forget who you were. We danced until two in the morning. We all loved each other at two in the morning."

"Really," John Gray said, "it must have been a delightful party. I wish you'd brought a drum."

The paper that evening was read by Mr. Virgil Mason and Charles knew from Jackie that Mr. Mason had been working on it for weeks. It was entitled "Old Streetcar Lines in Clyde." Mr. Mason read it haltingly after supper, perspiring freely. He dealt with the river line that used to run up Johnson Street and with the Dock Street line that used to go to the beach. Instead of listening attentively, Charles found himself glancing at Malcolm Bryant, wondering what he might be thinking as he sat with his heavy hands clasped about his right knee staring fixedly at a corner of the room.

When the paper was over Dr. Marchby announced the reading time. It had taken Mr. Mason exactly twenty-seven and a half minutes to finish the paper and John Gray said it was a delightful paper. All of them there remembered when the first electric cars had come to Clyde and most of them remembered the horsecar lines that had preceded them. Then John Gray spoke of various motormen and conductors, dealing with their eccentricities. Mr. Blashfield, who followed him, said it was a delightful paper, too, but he was sure that Moses Wilkins had never been a motorman on the old Beach line, but on the other hand Dr. Marchby was sure that he had been, and when Mr. Crewe said he was sure he had not been, everyone said that Mr. Crewe had not been in Clyde long enough to remember. The argument became more heated as other motormen were discussed, but every member had said his say by ten-fifteen and it was time to be going home.

"Charley," Malcolm Bryant said, after he had thanked Mr. Mason for letting him hear the paper and after he had thanked John Gray for allowing him to be there, "why don't you walk back with me? It's still pretty early."

Actually Charles was glad to be asked and he could see that his father was glad that Malcolm Bryant had asked him, for obviously his father wanted very much to know what Malcolm Bryant might say about the Confessional Club.

There had been a heavy snowfall two days before and Charles could remember the walls of snow on either side of the cleared path, as they walked up Dock Street, and the penetrating chill that came from the ground. Though they spoke very little on the way Charles did not mind the silence.

"I'm trying to get it straight in my mind," Malcolm Bryant said after Charles asked him what he thought of the evening.

"I don't see what there is to get straight," Charles said. "There were just a lot of old men there, talking about streetcars."

"Don't interrupt me, Charley. There's a great deal for me to get straight. It was a wonderful occasion, a very wonderful occasion."

"Why was it wonderful?"

"Don't interrupt me, Charley. You're wonderful and none of you know what you're living in. By God, this is a wonderful town. Its crystallization is nearly perfect."

They passed the dark façade of the public library, and the barred windows of the Dock Street Bank with its single night light burning, before Malcolm Bryant spoke again.

"These male groups are always the same," he said. "They are simply the projection of the old men's council. They have the same taboos and the same drawing-together habits. Now out there with the head-hunters there were three councils. They all discussed their tribal exploits, just like the streetcars, exactly like the streetcars."

"I don't see how the head-hunters in Borneo have anything to do with the Confessional Club," Charles said.

"They have everything to do with it," Malcolm Bryant told him, "but you're too involved with this locale to understand. Actually I wish I could take time off someday to belong to a social group. It's just one thing after another with me, the Zambesis in those beehive huts in Africa — the elongated skull Zambesis, not the Pygmy off-shoot — and then the head-hunters, and then this job, and next the upper Orinoco, that is if I can get old Smythe in the Foundation sold on the idea of sending me to the Orinoco. It's just one damn thing after another."

"Are you really going to the Orinoco?" Charles asked him.

"Oh, I suppose so," Malcolm Bryant said. "There's been very little first-class work in the area. There's a rumor that they have a very interesting way of getting rid of old people there, but not a line of documented investigation. These damned explorers are all exhibitionists. Thank God, I'm not an explorer." Malcolm Bryant was walking more rapidly. "Now the women were hidden tonight, weren't they? It's a characteristic pattern, that hiding of the women."

"What women?" Charles asked.

"It's the same with the Sicilian peasants," Malcolm Bryant said. "I mean your women."

"My women?"

"Your mother and your sister." Malcolm Bryant was speaking patiently. "I saw them flitting about but they didn't dare to show their faces, Charley, not before the old men's council, and they ate in the women's hut. It's always the same thing."

"It wasn't a hut," Charles said, and he laughed. "They were eating in the kitchen. Where else would they eat?"

"Nowhere else," Malcolm Bryant said. "It was absolutely perfect. Now don't interrupt me, Charley."

They did not speak again until they came to the rooms that Malcolm Bryant had rented on Fanning Street and then Malcolm Bryant only repeated himself.

"I wish I could give it up and be in a group," he said.

He had rented a bedroom and a sitting room on the second floor of Mrs. Mooney's house. The rooms were plainly furnished and Malcolm Bryant had done little to improve them. He had only brought in a draftsman's trestle table and two battered army lock trunks. When he turned on the light Charles saw that a blueprint map of Clyde, marked with colored crayons, was tacked on the drafting table and that there was a large pile of yellow paper beside the blueprint.

"Just a few notes," Malcolm Bryant said as he took off his overcoat and dropped it in a corner of the room. "All the real work is in the Boston office."

Malcolm opened a tobacco jar, filled a pipe and lighted it. Then he took off his jacket and unbuttoned his vest and began pacing up and down the room while Charles sat down in a rickety rocking chair and watched him.

"You know, I'm just beginning to get this town straight," he said. "I'm just beginning to get a pattern. That's the first thing you have to do on a job like this, create a procedural pattern, and once you get it everything fits into it."

"I don't exactly know what you're talking about," Charles said.

"Of course you don't," Malcolm Bryant answered. "There are only a very few people who can understand what I'm talking about."

"Then why did you ask me up here?" Charles asked.

"Because you interest me, Charley." Malcolm Bryant put his hands in his pockets. "You're in tune to the beating of the drums."

Charles leaned back in the creaking rocker. He had a picture of himself and everyone else in Clyde dancing to a tune that Malcolm Bryant was playing.

"All right," Charles said, "what is your procedural pattern?" He was not as much interested in the idea as he was in Malcolm Bryant himself, and Malcolm went on slowly, patiently, from the platform of his erudition.

"I am managing to get this whole town into a grouping," he said, "and to separate the cliques and classes. It's a wonderful town because its structural cleavages are so distinct and undisturbed and so unconsciously accepted. You see, it goes this way" — Malcolm Bryant raised his hand and began counting on his fingers: "there are three distinct social groups, the upper class, the middle class and the lower class, but each of these can be divided into thirds — the upper-upper, the middle-upper, and the lower-upper; the same way with the middle class — the upper-middle, the middle-middle, and the lower-middle; and the same way with the lower class — the same three categories. Everyone in Clyde falls into one of them. That's the procedural pattern."

"Well, I don't see why it's so remarkable. I could have told you that myself," Charles said, and then Malcolm Bryant became a kindly instructor in a lecture hall.

"Of course it doesn't seem remarkable to you, because you're integrated in the group. Look at yourself, Charley — not that you can possibly see. You have a suitable education, you understand your taboos and your rituals, you're working happily under an almost immobile system, and the beauty of it is you're perfectly happy."

The assumption that he was happy annoyed Charles.

"How do you know I am?" he asked.

"Of course you are," Malcolm Bryant said. "You've got to be. You have the greatest happiness vouchsafed any human being, you're an integrated, contented part of a group. You don't know how I envy you. You see — I'm personally not contented, Charley."

"Why aren't you?" Charles asked him. "You can go anywhere you want and you must like what you're doing."

"That's the trouble," Malcolm Bryant said. "I'm tired of moving. By God, I might settle down and do a little quiet writing and give up this Orinoco thing. Don't try to move away, Charley. Don't break out of your group."

Charles had not been sure of Malcolm Bryant's seriousness before, but now he was obviously saying that he was lonely and that he wanted friends. Charles heard the bell of the Baptist Church striking.

"Well," Charles said, "I guess I'd better be going. It's getting pretty late," and it occurred to him that this was what he was always saying in Clyde.

Malcolm had pushed himself from the table and was standing up again in his shirt sleeves and open vest and he looked uncertain.

"Wait a minute, Charley," he said. "There's something I want to say to you. As a human being, not as a social entity . . . frankly, just how interested are you in Jessica Lovell?"

Charles felt his back stiffen and his face grow red. The question was impertinent and a cold wave of caution descended on him.

"I don't know how much I am," he said, and his voice sounded hoarse and awkward. "I've told you that I don't really know Jessica Lovell very well."

"You don't?" Malcolm Bryant repeated, and he pulled his hands out of his pockets. "Well, that's fine. It makes everything easier. This is a sort of hard thing for me to say, but I believe in being honest, Charley. I've had the damnedest thing happen to me. Let's put it down squarely as a biological fact. Frankly, I've fallen in love with Jessica Lovell."

Malcolm looked at Charles questioningly as though he wanted Charles's opinion of the biological fact and for a moment Charles's mind was as vacant as his face must have been. It did not seem possible to him that Malcolm Bryant could have said such a thing and yet he had heard the words distinctly, and now Malcolm Bryant was going on more rapidly.

"I don't know how in hell it ever happened and I may say it comes at a damned inconvenient time and I'm afraid any sort of adjustment is going to interfere with my work, but there it is, and I thought I ought to tell you, Charley."

Charles's mind was still a blank and the palms of his hands felt moist.

"Why did you think you ought to tell me?" he asked, and Malcolm moved his feet restively on the carpet.

"Because I thought it was the honest thing to do. I know it sounds silly, and of course you're in no position to marry her. You're just a kid, but I thought you had a right to know."

It sounded silly and yet at the same time Charles, in spite of a hollow feeling in the pit of his stomach, realized that not everyone would have been so honest.

"Who ever said I wanted to marry her?" he asked. "I've never thought of marrying her."

It was true. He had never thought until that moment of marrying Jessica Lovell and now his mind was running on tribal customs and beating drums. The worried look had gone from Malcolm's face.

"Well, that's fine," he said. "Of course, I haven't much to offer her but there's some talk about something in the museum at Harvard or there might be a permanent fellowship on the Sykes Foundation. I could give up that Orinoco thing. You know, I think I might make her quite happy."

Charles found himself standing up without ever remembering that he had risen from the rocking chair. He knew that he was smiling because his face felt stiff and contorted.

"Of course, she may throw you down."

"Oh, yes," Malcolm Bryant said, "she may."

"And of course" — his voice sounded louder — "I'll go on seeing her if I want to. Well, good night."

XI

And You End with a Barrel of Money

IT DID NOT DEFINITELY DAWN on Charles until the spring of 1928 that he was in love with Jessica Lovell. Then suddenly he was so much in love that nothing else seemed to matter and everything seemed possible. When all the reticences of caution or barriers of common sense, or whatever you cared to call them, broke, it was plain that this situation must have been developing for a long while without either of them having consciously perceived it. The slow growth of such an involvement, he sometimes thought later, made it something that left a deeper scar than any sudden flowering of passion. Yet it was possible that he would never have fallen in love with Jessica or she with him if it had not been for the irritating stimulus of Malcolm Bryant.

Malcolm was dedicating his life to the study of social relationships but when it came to the people around him, he displayed the unskillful ignorance of most dwellers in academic ivory towers. On the one hand he was a dispassionate analyst, a synthetic recording angel, employed by a learned institution to classify the inhabitants of Clyde according to their incomes and their prejudices; on the other, he was an absent-minded professor who had been shielded from many ordinary drives of living. As soon as Malcolm Bryant had confessed his interest in Jessica — because it was an honest thing to do — every day or so he would drop in to call at Spruce Street or ask Charles up to his rooms at Mrs. Mooney's.

It was easy for Charles to converse with Malcolm Bryant because he was always more like a doctor or a lawyer than a friend. Charles found himself telling about Sam and how he had been killed in the war, and about Jackie Mason's worries about his grandfather's drugstore, and about his Aunt Jane and the Gray heart. He was no longer annoyed when Malcolm asked him questions. He was glad to tell about himself in return for learning more about Malcolm and before long Charles was familiar with Malcolm's complete dossier.

It seemed that some wealthy individual or some university or some institution had always supported Malcolm. Thus, although Malcolm worked hard for the support, he had never been obliged, except when he had sold papers while he was a high school student in Kansas, to earn his living like other people. Instead, someone was always paying his expenses to places barely mentioned in school geography. He was always getting a Guggenheim grant or doing a piece of work for a museum or an institute. Ever since his father, a Kansas farmer, had sent him to the state university, Malcolm had consistently been receiving scholarships. His father, plus a scholarship, had helped him get an A.M. at Wisconsin, and other scholarships, plus instructing jobs, had helped him to his Ph.D. at Harvard. Then he had gone with a museum expedition to Polynesia and had written his paper on the knotting of fish nets, which tended to support certain theories on Polynesian migrations — a paper which gave Malcolm the beginning of his reputation. It seemed that social anthropology was not as crowded a field as it might have been. At least there were not so many brilliant social anthropologists who could get along with academic groups. As far as Charles could gather, besides having the requisite academic background it was also necessary to be assiduous and polite to the right people to achieve true anthropological success. Malcolm said that he had always been able to get on with heads of museums — it was a gift.

"Besides," Malcolm said, "I get on with primitive people. Put me anywhere and I can make friends with them."

Besides, Malcolm said, he was a good lecturer and he was good at raising money. They always liked him around when a money raiser was needed, even though he might be forgotten when they were passing around honorary degrees.

"Put me anywhere where there's money," Malcolm said, "and I can dramatize myself," and this was important, Malcolm said, if you wanted to get anywhere. He could tell good after-dinner stories about curare and shrunken heads in the Oriente, and besides, Malcolm said, he knew how to organize an expedition.

Charles was never tired of hearing about Malcolm's expeditions, though he sometimes thought if he were a rich man he would not finance one, and when he once told Malcolm so, Malcolm told him he was not the type. Malcolm said that most people who financed expeditions were frustrated and only wished to project their egos.

Charles preferred having Malcolm talk of his academic ambitions to listening to his ideas on love, but Malcolm frequently brought up the subject. As a rule, he said, he was too busy to think about love and he never approved of women on expeditions. Wives inevitably interfered with progress, and the women who did go along were a type it was hard to fall in love with. There was a time in central Africa when he had met the daughter of a British medical missionary, but it might be just as well to skip that; and once, when he was with the Persian nomads in Luristan, there was an archaeologist named Alvira Small, who wore shorts. He had always intended to look up Alvira in California sometime. There was also a girl in Kansas, but that was a long while ago. On the whole, women interfered with work, and there was seldom time to fall in love when you were always writing a report or getting organized for a trip. He could not understand why this had hit him all of a sudden, up there at the Lovells'.

"It happened late one afternoon in the wallpaper room," Malcolm said. "She was standing by the fireplace. Abruptly it came over me."

It was the room's fault, Malcolm said, that beautiful, frigid, restrained room, and then her lips and the way she narrowed her eyes when she smiled.

"And her figure," Malcolm said.

Until that moment Malcolm had never been conscious of her figure, and Charles hoped he would leave it at that, but Malcolm did not. She was wearing a silk dress that was too long and badly cut and suddenly something reminded him of "The Road to Mandalay."

"I don't know why the devil that dress made me think of an

erotic dance in Burma," Malcolm said. "It was the damnedest thing to think of in that restrained and sterile room."

Charles wished that Malcolm would not go on with it, but Malcolm went right on.

"You know," Malcolm said, "her figure's Balinesque. I don't know where she got it. I don't usually mentally undress women."

That wasn't all, either, Malcolm said. She was so lonely, so unfulfilled, in front of that fireplace, so hopeless in that ugly dress. It all made him feel his own loneliness and that nothing he had done had amounted to anything and that until then he had never lived.

He had tried for several weeks, he said, to get Jessica out of his mind. He told himself that he did not like the Lovells. Mr. Lovell was frankly a desiccated stuffed shirt with an absurd approach to everything and Miss Lovell was a perfect tribal type, except that there were few virgins in primitive societies. He had tried, but he could not get Jessica out of his mind. He supposed it was love. He had once read half of Freud's *Interpretation of Dreams* in the South Atlantic, but he had lost the book when he came down with malaria in Kenya. He had learned enough, however, to realize that Jessica's father was in love with her. He wanted to do something about Jessica. He wanted to save her. He supposed that this was love. The only thing to do, he supposed, was to tell her frankly how he felt, but he never could find an opportunity. She did not seem interested in what he was doing, and she never wanted to talk about herself. It never should have happened and it was destroying his perspective, but he supposed that it was love.

It was embarrassing for Charles to listen but at the same time it gave him a perverse satisfaction. He was relieved to discover that when he saw Jessica at the Players she talked about herself very often and frequently asked him what he had been doing lately. It was wonderful when she told him once that his necktie did not match his suit and nothing was more wonderful than when she told her once that she wished Malcolm Bryant would not always keep popping in and out of the house. She wished he would stop telling her about Africa and Borneo and would stop comparing everyone in Clyde to the head-hunters. Charles was very much relieved when she said she liked to be with someone of her own age for a change. There began to be something new about Jessica every time he saw her. He did not know enough that winter to suppose that it was love.

Charles met Jessica Lovell in the Dock Street Savings Bank un-expectedly one Saturday morning near the middle of April. He had asked Mr. Howell at Wright-Sherwin for permission to go there before the bank closed in order to cash his pay check and deposit a part of it, and Mr. Howell had told him that it would be all right if he would hurry.

Malcolm would probably have called the regular visits of citizens to the Dock Street Bank a ritual, similar to a primitive temple offering, and Charles would not have disagreed with him. At birth his Aunt Jane had presented him with a five-dollar deposit in a savings book, entered in beautiful Spencerian writing, and this was the beginning of his financial biography. Charles had been taught, not by his father but by the women in the family, that regular, persistent saving was essential for successful living.

Among his earliest memories was one of those little scenes so dear to bankers. His mother had led him up the steps of the Dock Street Bank, holding a small coin receptacle, supplied by the bank, in the shape of a barrel, upon which was written the slogan, "Put in a coin and you'll soon have a barrel of money." Though he was scarcely tall enough to see over the dark walnut counter, he could remember being propelled gently forward by his mother and placing his barrel of money and his savings book in the hands of Mr. Gregg, the cashier, and watching Mr. Gregg open the barrel with a little key. Mr. Gregg always made some wise remark about thrift as he counted the nickels, dimes and pennies and he used to say that this was the way to make It grow but the slow growth of It was sometimes discouraging to Charles, even when he was conversant with the wonders of compound interest. He had learned what would happen if you left a small sum in the Dock Street Bank a hundred years undisturbed, in the care of its kindly officers. Every year you got four cents on a dollar and the four cents, too, would begin making money too if you left it long enough, but a hundred years was a long time. Mr. Gregg explained that the start was the slowest part of it but wait until Charles had a thousand dollars, then he would have forty dollars a year and think what a boy could do with forty dollars.

Now when Charles was twenty-four, his account had risen to a hundred and fifty dollars and the pages of his savings book told their own story of general self-denial and occasional indulgence. More through habit than through any faith in accumulating a large sum he was back again at the Dock Street Bank on that Saturday in April.

Mr. Gregg, now a frail, elderly man, was still behind the broad counter. There was still the old reassuring smell of oil and ink and ledgers, and still the same small pyramid of coin barrels that would give you a barrel of money. There were still the same rustle of paper and clink of coinage, and Mr. Thomas, also older, was still visible in the distance at his black walnut roll-top desk beyond the rows of bookkeepers; and beyond Mr. Thomas yawned the open doors of the Dock Street Savings Bank safe, an up-to-date addition, with its time lock and tumblers glittering in the light that came from the tall windows. Everyone in the space behind the counter seemed to move in his own stream of time, impervious to anything except geologic change.

Outside on Dock Street the pallid April sun had been dodging in and out behind low, wind-blown clouds. The trees were still bare and front yards and lawns were as brown and sodden as they had been when the winter's snow first melted. It was a gusty morning and the air had a reluctant touch of winter, but inside the bank there was a uniform climate. Charles had cashed his check and had just given Mr. Gregg five dollars and his deposit book when Jessica Lovell came in, and when Mr. Gregg saw her, he pushed his spectacles more securely on his nose.

"Good morning, Miss Lovell," Mr. Gregg said. "I'll be with you in just a moment, and it *is* a good morning, isn't it?"

Jessica, too, was holding her savings book. Her cheeks were red and fresh from the April wind and she was wearing a short coat of gray wombat, a sensible, inexpensive fur, and one of her tight felt hats was pulled down close over her unruly hair.

"Hello, Charley," she said, and she spoke in the low, serious tone which one always used in the Dock Street Bank. "Don't go. I'll be through with this in a minute. It's my Wright-Sherwin dividend. Father likes to have me bring it in myself."

She was entirely at home, friendly and confiding, as she should have been, in the Dock Street Bank. Her voice, though it was low, carried pleasantly through the banking room and Mr. Thomas when he heard it rose from his roll-top desk and walked to the counter.

"Good morning, Jessie," he said. "Are you getting on all right?"

"Oh, yes, thanks, Cousin Ralph," she said. She was just endorsing a check, and Mr. Thomas nodded pleasantly to Charles and asked if his Aunt Jane were feeling better.

"Tell her not to overdo," Mr. Thomas said. "We all forget we're growing older."

Jessica snapped her bag shut and thanked Mr. Gregg and Charles held the door open for her.

"It's like church, isn't it?" she said as they walked together down the steps. "I always want to whisper in there. Where are you going, Charley?"

He told her he was going back to the office.

"But it's Saturday," Jessica said. "What are you doing this afternoon? Suppose we go for a drive?"

She asked the question as though she were sure he would have nothing else to do and he understood, when she asked him where they would meet, that it would be better to have it seem like an accidental meeting.

"How about the courthouse at half-past two?" she said. "It's so much easier."

It was much easier than meeting at the Lovells' front door and going through explanations because there would be nothing underlined or portentous about it.

When Charles arrived in front of the courthouse at half-past two and while he stood with the wind whipping at his coat, watching the cars go by, the realization that there was a secret element to the meeting scarcely dawned upon him, because it was all connected with the Dock Street Bank. The bank had become a symbol of the way he felt about Jessica Lovell, a symbol of integrity and of serious intention. When he saw Jessica's black Dodge phaeton glide around the curve of Johnson Street, he actually considered it a delightful sort of accident. It seemed like an accident, too, that Jessica should see him and slow down and wave her hand.

"Why, hello," Jessica said. "What are you doing here? Can't I give you a lift?"

"I was just walking around," Charles said.

"Well, get in if you're going my way," Jessica said.

"Are you sure it won't be too much trouble?" Charles asked.

"Oh, no." Jessica shook her head slowly. "Not a bit of trouble."

Neither of them laughed until the Dodge was moving again and then they both laughed at once and though they each must have known most of what the other was thinking, they never explained their thoughts and actions of that afternoon. The sun kept trying to come out from behind the scudding clouds and it was still like winter as they drove through town, but when they were on the edge of town the sun was brighter and the brown fields seemed warmer. Where the roads forked at the small common where the Civil War monument stood, the Union soldier, too, with his visor cap and overcoat, standing on his pedestal flanked by pyramids of cannon balls, looked almost warm. Jessica turned to the right at the common and they crossed the river at the third bridge and drove over the hilly road that led to Walton Spring. There were farms on either side of them, old houses with their outbuildings attached, each with its apple orchard, its pastures and its hayfields. Charles was aware of stone walls and of weathered barns and piles of wood in woodsheds, but he noticed nothing in detail. He and Jessica were talking as though they had not seen each other for a long while and when they were silent they still seemed to be talking.

She was wearing the same gray suit and the same red hat that she had worn at the firemen's muster and though her eyes were on the road she would glance at him now and then in a quick, amused way. She asked what he had been doing since she had seen him last, and she was thankful that the winter was over. It was the longest winter she had ever spent. Granted she had been to New York and she had been in Boston quite often for the symphony, still it had been a long winter. It had been a long winter for Charles, too, though he had been working. He could tell her a good deal about brass and precision instruments, but he was not going to tell her.

"No," Jessica said, "don't. Let's not talk about anything constructive. I'm tired of being constructive."

The land around them also seemed tired of being constructive. The frost was seeping out from it, leaving it moist and weary. The further they went, the further they were away from anything that was constructive.

"I'm tired of sitting around and being nice, too," Jessica said. "I wonder how nice anyone is, really."

"Everyone has to pretend," Charles said.

"That's the trouble," Jessica said, "and so you never know what anyone is really like."

He never could remember how Malcolm Bryant's name came up but it must have been Jessica who spoke of him first because he never would have. She was saying that Malcolm Bryant was always dropping in and giving travel talks about central African beads and life in beehive huts. She never could keep her mind on what he was saying, and she always felt as though she were sitting in a lecture hall.

"But he's pretty interesting sometimes," Charles said. "He's been around a lot."

"Everybody acts as though I ought to like him," Jessica said. "Charley, did you really think I liked him?"

It was the most beautiful question that anyone had ever asked him. They were crossing a culvert, over a piece of swampy land, and there was a row of old willows on either side of the road.

"Did you really?" she asked again, and then before he could answer she slowed down the car and asked him what that singing noise was.

"It's the peepers," he said, "the frogs"; and the high notes of the singing frogs rose all around them.

"Sam used to take me out to catch them," he said, "but they were pretty hard to catch."

If you came near where they were they always stopped their sing-ing, but if you stood still long enough you could see them, some-times. They blew their throats up like balloons. You had to wait a long while, absolutely still, before they began to sing again.

"Sam could make the best willow whistles," he said.

This was just the time for whistles, now that the sap was running in the willows and the twigs were growing yellow. You could always tell by looking at the willows when spring was coming.

"Can you make a whistle?" she asked — but he was not good at making whistles. He never had been good at doing things with his hands. He never could carve boats or do any of those things in the *American Boy's Handy Book*.

Once long ago, she said, one spring in Clyde, she had gone out picking wildflowers in a place called the High Woods. She always remembered them coming through the dead leaves and she had always wanted to go again but somehow there had never been a chance.

"Do you suppose there are any flowers yet?" she asked him.

It was just the time of year when you thought of such things, whether you cared for flowers or not. He told her that the grape hyacinths were out by the front door at Spruce Street and this meant that there might be hepaticas in the woods — not liverwort, he hated the name "liverwort." It had been a cold, late spring, but still there might be hepaticas on a southeast slope. They would be pushing up through the leaves. He liked hepaticas, he said, better than any other flower, because they were the earliest.

The road was winding up into the hills again. They were not far from Walton Spring and he was thinking that it sounded innocent and artificial, talking so much about frogs and telling her that he liked hepaticas.

"I don't know why it always sounds flat when you talk about flowers," he said.

"No, it doesn't," she said. "It sounds all right to me," and she slowed down the car again. "Do you suppose there are any in those woods?"

She had stopped the car and she pointed to the woods on a hill above a pasture, and when he said there might be, that he didn't know, she said they might walk up and see. There were bars in a gap in the stone wall and he pulled the bars down carefully so that she could step over them. They walked quickly up the rocky, grassy slope and he held up a strand of a barbed-wire fence so that she could crawl under. There was a stand of oak and hickory on top of the hill and when their feet rustled through the dead, sodden leaves there was a musty smell, half of winter and half of spring, but there was not a single hepatica.

The buds on the branches above them were as tight as though it were still winter, because oaks were suspicious trees, never coming out until they were sure it was spring. There was not a sign of life in those woods, not even a trace of green, except for some rock ferns growing in a crevice of a granite ledge. Nevertheless, they kept on walking. If she started to climb a hill, she said, she always liked to get to the top and they might as well get there. The hill was higher than it looked and when they reached the crest and turned around they could see a wide expanse of country below them through the bare branches of the trees. They could see the curve of the river and the third bridge in the hazy distance and further off to the left the roofs of Clyde, a long narrow town on its bank. Afterwards whenever he saw journeyman paintings, he always thought of himself and Jessica standing on that hill, looking at the toylike town.

They were both a little out of breath, both looking into the distance down the hill, and they both must have turned toward each other at the same moment. He stared straight at her and she had a grave, startled look and her brown eyes were opened very wide.

"Oh," she said, in a dry, matter-of-fact sort of voice, and then the next moment they were in each other's arms.

"Oh," she said again, and he kissed her and they clung to each other, their eyes closed, not speaking. When she turned her head away and let it rest a second on his shoulder he dropped his arms, but suddenly she pulled him close to her again and they stood side by side, looking into the half-defined distance.

"Well," she said, "there's Clyde." It was just as though nothing had happened.

"Yes," he answered, "there it is."

"I didn't know we could see so much from here." She was not looking at him.

"It's because the leaves aren't out," he told her.

The sun had broken through the clouds again, the slanting sun of late afternoon. It was just as though nothing had happened when Jessica and he walked down the hill, as though they had never stood locked in each other's arms and had never kissed, except that she put her arm through his while they were still in the woods.

"It's always harder walking downhill," she said, but she drew her arm away when they were out in the open pasture.

"I always like juniper in a pasture," she said. "Listen. You can hear the frogs," and they stood for a moment listening, with their shadows long on the brown turf. They walked across the pasture without speaking. It was almost as though it had never happened, but not quite.

When they were in the car, she pulled a gold compact from her pocket, opened it, stared at herself intently in its little mirror, put a dab of powder on her nose, and snapped the compact shut. Then she pulled down her hat.

"I wish my hair didn't always blow," she said.

"I like it when it blows," he told her. It was almost as though it had never happened, but he never would have said such a thing before they walked up the hill.

"Do you?" she said. "Well, I'm glad somebody does."

The truth was that so much had happened that it was better not to talk about it. It was better to sit quietly as they were driving home, conscious only that they were near each other.

"Charley," she asked finally, "have you ever been abroad?"

Once he had thought of working his way abroad on a cattle ship, while he was in college. Some of the boys in his fraternity had talked of it, but he had never done anything more than talk. It was different with her. She had been to England and France with her father last summer and before that she had been with some of the girls from school on a tour arranged by one of the teachers, one of those queer schoolgirl tours when you walked in a small procession through the cathedrals and the galleries. They had gone to Rome and to Florence.

"I brought back Pliny's doves," she said. "Everyone seems to buy Pliny's doves."

As soon as you got home it all seemed a long way off in the distance. It was hard to believe that you'd ever been to Florence. It was like coming home after a dance that year her father had made her come out in Boston. She used to come down from Vassar in her coming-out year and stay at her Aunt Rachel's on Marlborough Street. She was always doing things, she told him, that she did not want to do particularly.

"I wish," she said, "we didn't always have to do things. Charley, tell me what you have to do."

He told her that he would have to go to Wright-Sherwin on Monday morning. He began to tell her about the office and about Mr. Howell, but when he started he had a desperate feeling of everything closing around him because they were back in Clyde again and Clyde was as orderly as the houses on Johnson Street, everything in its place and a place for everything.

"I might as well get out here," he said, when they came near the courthouse.

"Well, all right," she said, "I suppose it's better."

Everything was in its place and there was a place for everything.

"Thanks ever so much," Charles said when the car stopped. "I had a wonderful time."

"So did I," she said, and then she smiled. "I loved every minute of it."

"Did you?" Charles asked.

"Yes," she answered, "every minute of it. If it's a good day, let's do it again next Saturday."

"Why, that would be fine," he said.

She waved her hand to him when he took off his hat, and when the Dodge rounded the curve on Johnson Street he wondered what she would tell them at home of how she had spent the afternoon.

XII

In the Spring a Livelier Iris . . .

— ALFRED LORD TENNYSON

CHARLES COULD occasionally see himself through the perspective of elapsed time. His mind still worked in much the same way as that of the Charles Gray who must have existed that spring in Clyde. He still had a desire to accept what was around him and to develop according to established rules. Not even in those days, he realized, did he wish to change the rules, although he could see their unfairness. He had never been a revolutionary, he had never possessed the reformer's urge, but still that spring he could perceive in himself undercurrents of discontent. He was acutely conscious of his own deficiencies and of his inexperience, but it was a healthy sort of discontent and at least he knew what he lacked and what he wanted. He wanted, of course, to be more like Jessica Lovell. He studied, that spring, as well as one could in the Clyde library, the Italian primitives and Del Sarto and Da Vinci. He read the autobiography of Cellini. He learned the difference between Gothic and baroque architecture and he read Hare's *Walks in Rome* and *Florence.* It was probably Jessica Lovell who stopped him from being a small-town boy, Jessica Lovell and possibly Malcolm Bryant. He never attempted to conceal his cultural deficiencies from Malcolm Bryant. In fact he must have felt instinctively that Malcolm presented intellectual opportunity.

"Listen," Malcolm said, one evening in May, "why are you always picking my brains about Europe? You wouldn't like it if you got there. You want to learn to cultivate contentment, Charley. It's a wonderful thing, contentment. Look at me."

"Why are you contented?" Charles asked.

"I'll tell you," Malcolm said. "If you want a frank answer, I think I'm doing better with Jessica. I used to have the idea that she didn't like to have me around, but now all of a sudden she really does."

There was a maddeningly inartistic lack of reticence in Malcolm's discussion of Jessica. He could not understand, Malcolm often said, what there was about her that attracted him in such a blind, irrational manner. Sometimes he could see very clearly that he was on the verge of making a fool of himself. It was a problem, he admitted, of his own emotional instability aggravated by the forces of biological selection. Did the things he seemed to see in Jessica exist in fact or were they manufactured out of his own imagination? Love was a biological disease, Malcolm said, and once you contracted it you could never be sure of facts. This was hard for anyone who believed in the empirical approach.

He liked to think, quite frankly, that he was a trained, scientific observer — and quite frankly he was a very good one. His training showed him what was wrong with the Lovells — wealth and tribal ritual had a limiting effect that ended in atrophy. He had never previously been in a position to observe such ritual, aside from the South Sea taboos, and the Lovells were what he termed *kapu ali'i,* meaning that ritual removed them completely from reality. They lived in a world of antiquities and were actuated by ancestor worship and cultism of the dead. He could see this with painful clarity, only to forget it whenever he saw Jessica. It was emotion triumphing over reason. And what would he do with Jessica Lovell if he ever got her? It would have been amusing to tell Malcolm Bryant that he need not bother to worry, but of course Charles never did and actually he could agree in principle with many of the things that Malcolm Bryant said.

Charles, too, could see that the Lovells were shut off from most of the rest of Clyde by their own elaborations, but this was not strange because Clyde had made them what they were. Furthermore, he could see that though Jessica Lovell was touchable she was still unattainable, because they had different positions in the plan of Clyde. Though their clandestine meetings that spring had occurred in fact, they still held elements of the unreal and consequently their moments together were the more vivid. He also knew that this situation was bound to change eventually and that the reticences between them would have to break.

This happened on a warm day in May when the trees were all a soft green. They had driven along the Spring Road again to the same pasture and they had left the car and had walked up the same hill. They had spoken much as they had before as they walked across the pasture, shyly and uncertainly as though neither of them could be sure of what would happen when they reached the woods.

"It's been such a late spring, hasn't it?" Jessica said. "I was afraid it was going to rain today."

"So was I," Charles said.

"But if it had, we could have driven in the rain."

"Yes," he said, "of course we could have driven in the rain."

That meaningless conversation carried them across the pasture and into the woods.

"I like that coat of yours," she said. "It's old but it looks nice." It was the old tweed coat, he remembered, that he had worn at the firemen's muster. "You always look so nice, so self-possessed."

"So do you," he said. "You always do."

It did not seem possible that the same thing might happen again that had now happened several times before. It did not seem possible that he had ever touched her, because she was unattainable.

"I'm getting pretty good at walking up this hill," she said.

"Yes," he said, "but it's good exercise" — and then the same thing happened, the same impossible thing.

"Darling," she whispered, when he held her in his arms, "darling," and then he told her that he loved her. He could not have said it if she had not spoken first.

"Yes," she said, "I know."

It was still too immense to talk about intelligently, but suddenly it was fact, now that they had put it into words.

"Oh, Charley," she said, "what are we going to do?"

"I don't know," he said, "but I don't mind right now."

"I always wondered what would happen if we said it," she said. "Do you still love me?"

"Yes," he said.

"Darling," she said, "everybody's going to find out "

"Yes," he said, "I suppose they will."

"I wish they'd let us alone." She stopped and rested her head on his shoulder. "Charley," she asked him, "are you happy?"

Yes, he had never been so happy.

"It's so different," she said, "from the first time."

"It's because we said it."

"Well, let's not think about anything else."

"What else?" he asked.

"Oh, everything. What we're going to do next. All those silly things."

"Everything's going to be all right," he said, but all sorts of things that should not have mattered were already gathering around them when they walked back down the hill.

"I don't think Father will mind so much," she said, "if he gets to know it gradually and not all at once."

"You mean your father won't like it," he said. "I don't suppose he will."

"I wish he could just see more of you without its disturbing him. You're not cross, are you, Charley?"

"No," Charles said, "I'm not cross."

"Charley, don't look so unhappy." She took his arm and pressed it tight against her. "If we had only met each other somewhere else. Do you see what I mean?"

She was saying, of course, that everything would have been all right if he had only lived on Johnson Street. She was saying, without saying it, that everything would have been all right if the Grays had been better off or even if he had not been a Clyde boy, and it made him angry. It might have been better if his name had been Marchby, but at the same time he was Judge Gray's grandson. He was thinking that if Jessica had been Priscilla Meader or one of the Latham girls everything would have been all right.

"Oh, Charley," she was saying. "Charley, please."

He had forgotten until she spoke that she was still close beside him.

"Oh, Charley, I don't care what anyone's going to say."

"If you think I'm as bad as all that," he began, "why did you ever have anything to do with me?"

"Oh, Charley," she said, and they stood there in the pasture and she began to cry. It made him feel hopeless and desperate but there was nothing he could do about it. "I only said I didn't care."

"Then don't say it again," he said.

They stood there without speaking, and Jessica Lovell was still crying.

"Lend me your handkerchief," she said. "I haven't got a handkerchief."

"All right," Charles said. "Just stop crying, Jessica. It's going to be all right," and then something made him laugh.

"What are you laughing at?" she asked.

He was laughing, he told her, because it might have been Jackie Mason and what would she have done then, or it might have been one of the Meader boys, he was saying, or it might have been a North Ender. She should not have been allowed to wander around so much.

"You see what happens," he told her.

It was then that the idea came to him that changed so much of his life. It came to him suddenly, but perhaps it had been back of his mind for a long while.

"Jessica," he said, "I guess I'd better make some money."

He was thinking of Mr. Howell, who had been all his life at Wright-Sherwin and now was almost ready to retire, but Jessica still thought of Mr. Lovell.

"He'll like you, darling," she said, "if he only gets used to you little by little." She did not say how Mr. Lovell would get used to him little by little but she stopped the car about a half mile from the third bridge. "Aren't you going to kiss me again," she asked, "before we get into Clyde?"

When Charles arrived at Spruce Street, his mother was in the dining room in her oldest gingham apron polishing the flat silver. Charles wished he had never heard Malcolm speak of women in

Clyde going through various phases of household ritual. The spoons and forks had come from the Marchby family. They had been the wedding silver of his Great-grandfather Marchby, and now his mother referred to them as "the Marchby Silver." The spoons were plain and very thin, each with a Spencerian *M* faintly engraved upon it. The forks were equally plain and their tines were worn and rounded from nearly a century of family use, but for his mother, and for Dorothea too, they had a spiritual value that made them are and beautiful. They were The Marchby Silver. His mother was bending over the spoons now, handling each one gently, rubbing it lovingly with a soft cloth. Her hands were gray from dried silver polish and drops of it had fallen on her apron.

"Hello, dear," she said. "Where have you been all afternoon?" He remembered telling Dorothea that he was going to mow the lawn on Saturday and Dorothea had an uncanny ability for getting to the bottom of everything, but his mother only asked him curiously, not sharply or attentively.

"Oh," Charles said, "I've been for a walk in the country. Where's Father?"

His father was upstairs working on the paper which he was to read at the next meeting of the Confessional Club.

"He always puts it off," his mother said, "and now I suppose he'll have to work all night and all day Sunday. He wants coffee for supper instead of cocoa."

"Do you want me to help you?" Charles asked.

"No," she said. "I love to do the silver. Run along, dear." Children were always told to run along. It was just as though he were ten and could run along to the back yard and look for Jackie Mason.

Though he knew his father disliked being interrupted when he was writing a paper for the Confessional Club, Charles went upstairs to see him. John Gray had pulled up the leaf of the table that stood behind the dilapidated sofa and he had pushed off the books which usually stood on it. He was sitting in shirt sleeves and suspenders, writing with a pencil on sheets of yellow paper.

"Well, well," he said, "what's the matter? Are you lonely, Charley?"

His dropping in was so unusual that Charles realized how seldom there had been anything he had wanted from his father.

"Oh, no," Charles said. "It's just a question about something I'm thinking of doing."

His father tilted back in his chair and stroked his closely clipped mustache.

"In my experience," John Gray said "— not that my experience isn't almost completely without validity — it's usually a great deal better to think of doing something than to do it. Sit down on one of the Windsor chairs. They're uncomfortable and you'll have to leave soon. Now take this paper for this confounded Confessional Club. It was much better thinking about it. It's the action that's painful. Do you know how many tugboats there used to be in Clyde in the year 1902?"

"No," Charles said, "why should I?"

"Not the slightest reason," John Gray said. "But actually there used to be four tugboats tied up between the Nickerson Cordage Company and the old coal pocket in the year 1902, and their names were" — John Gray folded his hands behind his head and looked up at the ceiling — "the *Lizzie K. Simpkins,* named, I think, after the wife of Captain Simpkins who ran her, although he was living with another lady at the time, the *H. M. Boadley,* the *Indian Chief,* and the *Neptune.* Well, they're all gone now and the coal barges and the lumber schooners they used to tow are gone and I don't suppose you remember any of them."

"No," Charles said, "I don't remember."

"I don't know why it is," John Gray sighed, "I really don't know why, you and your generation care nothing about the river. When I was your age I was on it all the time in my catboat, and if I wasn't in my catboat I was in my canoe. I knew every rock in the river."

"I never had the chance," Charles said. "You were always going to buy a catboat and teach me to sail and you never did."

"That's true. I was," John Gray said. "Why didn't you ask me more often?"

"I asked you and asked you," Charles told him, "but you never got around to it."

"Well," John Gray said, "the river isn't what it was. It's better to sit on the shores and weep." He sighed and stared up at the ceiling. "Now downstairs your mother is polishing the Marchby spoons, while I sit up here blowing the dust from the pages of my lexicon of youth."

"Are you writing about tugboats?" Charles asked.

"No, no," John Gray said. "About the river, and the fish, and the boys who used to swim in it, and the golden plover, and, frankly, it's too good for the Confessional Club. Frankly, I'm too good for it too, Charles. I'm a little depressed this afternoon — and now you'd better not interrupt me any longer. Just run along and close the door behind you without stumbling over the books. I want to sit beside the river and weep."

"But I wanted to ask you a question," Charles said.

John Gray pushed his chair forward until its front legs came in contact with the floor.

"I was thinking of getting a job somewhere in Boston. I don't believe I'm going to get anywhere if I stay at Wright-Sherwin, not for years and years."

"You mean, Charley," John Gray asked softly, "that there isn't enough hay in the bundle?"

"The truth is," Charles said, "I'd like a chance to make some money."

John Gray said nothing for a moment.

"Why, Charley," he said, "you couldn't be thinking of a brokerage office or a bond house, could you?"

"As a matter of fact," Charles began, "I was just thinking that if you know anyone — if you wouldn't mind speaking to someone — "

"Why, Charley," his father said, and Charles had never seen him look so pleased, "I never thought our minds could ever work in the same way. It's about time you realized you can't get anywhere without money. It's queer that so few people ever see it clearly. It's the sophistries that catch them, the opiates."

The words had an ugly, materialistic sound and it was not fair to bring his thoughts of Jessica and all the ideas that were confusing him down to such unattractive terms.

"I didn't mean that money's everything," he said.

John Gray's forehead wrinkled and he shook his head slowly.

"Oh dear," he said softly. "Oh dear me, of course it isn't, but this is what always happens if you fall back on maxims. That was the trouble with Marcus Aurelius. He meditated in maxims. Naturally, money isn't everything, but money, it seems to me, helps most situations. Perhaps you can look down on it when you have it, but let's admit it does help, Charley, and let's try not to live by maxims."

There was no doubt that it helped but he hated to admit that it did. He did not want to have his mind work like his father's and he was fighting against the thought that it ever might.

"I don't want to get anything for nothing," he said. "If I make any money, I want to earn it."

John Gray sighed and shook his head again.

"Oh dear, there we go again," he said. "Those maxims. I don't blame you, Charley, but do you think anyone who's accumulated a large sum of money has ever actually earned it? I doubt it, in the literal sense. It's so much easier when one faces fact but then all life is largely based on an avoidance of fact, and I admit I try to avoid them. I try to turn them and twist them. Everybody does. I suppose you're implying that I have occasionally tried to get something for nothing." John Gray raised his eyebrows and waited for Charles to answer.

"I was just saying that I don't see how I can get ahead at Wright-Sherwin." Charles was speaking more loudly than he had intended, almost impatiently. "I was just asking you if I couldn't get something to do in Boston, and I don't know much about Marcus Aurelius."

He rose from his Windsor chair but his father was looking at him in a level, disconcerting way.

"Do you mind if I ask you a question, Charley? How did this idea ever get into your head?"

Charles looked straight at his father and tried to speak casually. "It just came over me."

"It couldn't have anything to do with Jessica Lovell, could it?"

"How did you know?" Charles asked. "Yes, it does have something to do with her."

"And you're in love with her?"

"Yes," Charles said.

John Gray pushed his chair back from the table.

"Well now, this really does me a lot of good. I wonder what Laurence Lovell will say," he said. "You and I have certainly got to do something about this, Charley. We had certainly better go up to Boston on Monday."

"Not Monday," Charles said. "I'd better tell them I'm through at Wright-Sherwin on Monday, but I guess they'll let me take the day off Tuesday."

"Do you want to do that before you get another job? I never thought you'd do a thing like that, Charley."

"I'll find something else," Charles said.

He was through with Wright-Sherwin but he had no way of knowing that the whole course of his life was changing, and his father's too — what was left of it. He had no way of knowing that they were both moving for good out of that dusty room.

"Charley," John Gray said, and put his hand on his shoulder. "If you want her, I'll see you get her, Charley." John Gray walked to the sofa and picked up his coat. "And now I think I'll go downtown and get the *Transcript*. It ought to be in now."

"Charley?" He heard his mother's voice calling from the hall downstairs. "Where are you?"

John Gray opened the door.

"It's that Mr. Bryant, Charley. He wants you on the telephone."

Malcolm wanted him to come over at eight o'clock that night.

"Tonight," Charles said. "Let's see." He disliked using the telephone as an offensive or defensive weapon.

"I wish you'd come as a special favor," Malcolm said. "I want you to meet the team."

"What team?"

"My team, of course." Malcolm's voice sounded sharper. "My investigatory team. They're starting in on Clyde on Monday. We're just talking over the field and I'd like to show them one firsthand exhibit." Suddenly Malcolm's voice was placating and exuding charm. "You don't mind co-operating, do you, Charley? Now don't argue over the telephone but come on over at eight o'clock and meet the team."

It was a relief that Malcolm did not want to talk about Jessica Lovell, such a relief that he was glad to go, and besides he was curious to see Malcolm in his own environment.

There were eight or ten people in Malcolm's room that night who all looked somewhat like Malcolm. Their faces were sharp with eager perspicacity and at the same time complacent with hidden knowledge. It was the peculiar look, of course, of the professional investigator which, he often thought later, was worn by people trained to interfere in other people's business, whether they were social workers, bank examiners or income tax examiners.

Malcolm Bryant's team sat on the couch and on Malcolm's trunk and on chairs which must have been brought from Mrs. Mooney's kitchen. Malcolm himself was perched on the drawing table with two glass gallon jugs of sacramental wine beside him and all the members of the team were holding cups and glasses.

"Well, here he is," Malcolm said. "Thanks for coming, Charley. This is Charley Gray, everybody, and I think Charley will be as much of a help to you tonight as he's been to me. This is Evangeline Scroll. Evangeline's back from Yucatán. And here's Bill Horsley. You've heard me talk about Bill."

As Malcolm mentioned the names of the team he waved his arm at each one but Charles did not remember them distinctly because he was not trained to associate names and faces then. Malcolm and all the rest of them, he imagined, were trying to put their subject at ease, but he could see them anxiously making mental notes of his skull, of his tweed coat and his flannel trousers. They made him feel as a Polynesian on an atoll must have felt when he suddenly encountered a boatload of strangers from a whaling ship. He remembered what Malcolm had said, that it was hard to fall in love with girls who were anthropologists, and he agreed with Malcolm as he gazed at Evangeline Scroll, fresh from Yucatán.

"Sit down in the rocking chair," Malcolm said, "where everyone can see you, and have a drink," and Malcolm raised his voice.

"Now, my idea is for you and me to talk as though no one else were here. It's a new method, but you don't mind it, do you Charley?" Malcolm smiled at him ingratiatingly and Charles sipped his glass of sacramental wine.

"No," he said, "I guess I don't mind it."

Everyone laughed in a way which indicated that they had all been waiting for something to laugh at. It only showed again that Malcolm had a lot of good ideas but did not understand people.

"Let's think of Clyde," Malcolm said, "as a big aquarium, and, by God, it's a wonderful aquarium, and I scooped you out and put you in a globe to show the team."

"I hope the team likes it," Charles said, and again everyone laughed.

"Now, Charley, here, lives on Spruce Street. Spruce Street runs into Johnson Street and yet Charley is not a side streeter, in the broader sense of the term. He has an upward and downward mobility that is very interesting. He is able to touch, without belonging to, the cliques on Johnson Street, and yet at the same time he can move downward. His societal mobility is emphasized because he was brought up in the Clyde public school system. He has rubbed shoulders with all the groupings. He may not have the middle class mobility but he has mobility, the downward trend of which has been checked somewhat by a college education. The first time I laid eyes on him I knew he was a beautifully conditioned type."

Malcolm Bryant paused and Charles sat there staring blankly at the team.

"I think Mr. Gray is a very nice type," Miss Scroll said. "Don't let Malc disturb you, Mr. Gray."

Charles's face flushed and he looked around him uneasily. "Well," he said, "what do you want me to do for you — sing a song?"

"Nothing," Malcolm said. "That's the beauty of it, Charley. I just want the team to see you react. You're being a great help, Charley."

"Give him another drink," Miss Scroll said. "I think Charley's wonderful. You don't mind if I call you Charley, do you, Mr. Gray?"

"No," Charles said, "not if it makes you feel any better."

They laughed again in the same hearty, mirthless way, and their curiosity was too impersonal to be unpleasant. He was a Greek letter in a quadratic equation representing Clyde. He could even forget Jessica Lovell and his other problems as he sat there, because he was a part of Clyde. They were strangers invading his town and all at once he was anxious to have them understand it. It may have been the second glass of wine he drank that made him want to speak.

"All right," he said, "I'll tell you something about Clyde. I'm pretty tired of all this talk about classes and about Johnson Street and Spruce Street. It doesn't matter. Nobody thinks about classes because everyone in Clyde knows he's as good as everyone else. This is a free country and Clyde's a free town."

He was surprised at himself for having said so much. His words were like those of that grammar school commencement speaker.

"Listen to him," he heard Malcolm say. "You see he has great mobility."

He did not care what Malcolm Bryant said. He could see all of Clyde in one piece. Johnson Street, Spruce Street, Dock Street, River Street, the North End, the South End. You could pull it apart and classify it, as these preposterous strangers would try to do, but all of it fitted together and it fitted beautifully and there was no reason to disturb it. Everything was in its place and there was a place for everything.

"You ought to be here," he said, "for Decoration Day. It's coming pretty soon. And for the Fourth of July. That's when you'll see what I mean. Everyone's as good as everyone else."

"You see," Malcolm said. "The feast days — the mingling of the classes."

"But it isn't the classes," Charles said. "Everybody knows everybody else."

"There you are," Malcolm said. "It's beautiful conditioning. But you wouldn't marry a North Ender, would you, Charley?"

His thoughts went back to high school and Doris Wormser. She was surprisingly clear in his memory. He could see her as she walked in ahead of him in the assembly room in high school.

"No, not at the moment," he said.

"You see what I mean," Malcolm said. "By God, this is a wonderful town."

That evening in Malcolm's room was a most peculiar ending for a peculiar day. Charles had never thought of himself as convertible into diagrams and geometric curves and a mass of static, regimented fact. What was the social position of the Grays — in Clyde in the eighteenth century? In the nineteenth century? How often did he go to church? Were there cliques in the Clyde High School, and to what extent did the cliques mingle? A part of the survey, and a very important part, would cover the lives of the minority and racial groups that had found lodgment, as Malcolm put it, in the growth of that predominantly Anglo-Saxon community. Did Charles know any who had worked their way into the upper-middle? What about the politically-minded Irish-Catholic group? Did the French-Canadians exhibit adaptive capacities?

As time went on and as they continued drinking sacramental wine, the team itself began dividing into groups and cliques, arguing about charts and graphs and questionnaires and methods of cataloguing. None of them was thinking of him as a person, except possibly Evangeline Scroll, who asked him to sit next her on the couch. She was a thin girl, with straight, short hair and horn-rimmed spectacles. As they talked, her knee inadvertently kept touching his. Once when he saw Malcolm Bryant looking at them curiously, he was quite sure that Evangeline Scroll was not thinking of him wholly in a scientific way but he could not keep his mind on her, he had too much to think about.

"Do you go around much in Clyde?" she asked.

"No, I'm pretty busy. I don't go around much," Charles told her.

"Aren't you in a crowd?"

"What sort of a crowd?" Charles asked.

"Weenie roasts, or dances. That sort of thing," Evangeline said. "You know. I wish you'd introduce me to your crowd."

The last thing he wanted to do was to introduce Evangeline Scroll to anyone and he was glad when Malcolm Bryant interrupted them.

"Come on, Charley," Malcolm said. "Bill Horsley wants to ask you a question. This isn't a time for sexual selection."

"Now, Malc," Evangeline said, "you told me he was mobile."

That was the word, mobility, an awkward word. He could move either up or down, and when he thought of Jessica he could see that she could move nowhere at all. She must remain exactly where she was. If things had been slightly different, if he had not gone to college, it might have been Doris Wormser, and now the thought made him shudder. It was dangerous to have mobility, but at the same time if he had not possessed mobility nothing that had happened that afternoon would have happened.

It was after eleven when he left but it was a beautiful night and he did not want to go home at once. Nearly all of Clyde was sound asleep. There was a faint smell of lilacs in the air, although the lilacs were not in bloom. They always bloomed on Decoration Day. There was also a scent of new leaves and grass and a touch of salt from the sea. Spring in Clyde, the soft darkness of that starlit night, and the halo of the street lights with the May flies fluttering about them, were things that Malcolm Bryant and his team would never put in their cross-reference catalogues. There were still a few couples on the benches on the green by the courthouse and now and then a car would whirl by it, going you could not guess where. The last show at the movies was over. The last soda fountain had closed, but there were still lights in the pool parlor at Dock Square and there were lights in the firehouse. Its doors were open and a few men were sitting by the engine. Peter Murphy, who was on the police night shift, was standing in front of the darkened news store, staring up Dock Street.

"Hello, Mr. Murphy," Charles said. "It's a nice night, isn't it?"

"Why, hello, Charley," Mr. Murphy said. "What are you doing up this time of night? Are you in love?"

It was a beautiful night and he did not want to go to bed. Down on River Street, he could see the harbor lights and the light from the stars on the calm black water. The Wright-Sherwin plant was a grim black shadow on River Street, with the street light shining on its blind brick façade. A radio was blaring and a dog was barking, but when he walked up Dock Street and turned left to Johnson Street there was no sound except his own footsteps on the brick sidewalk. Johnson Street was sleeping in the starlight. The trees made black patches on the Lovells' lawn which hardly could be called shadows, but the fence and the house itself looked very white indeed, as he stood there for a minute looking at them. The night light was burning in his Aunt Jane's room on Gow Street. He had never felt the unity of Clyde as he felt it then. It all belonged to him that night, because he was in love with Jessica Lovell.

XIII

How About It, Charley?

THE WRIGHT-SHERWIN COMPANY was the oldest of the three or four small industries that furnished work for the inhabitants of Clyde and nearly everyone knew its history and origins, simply because they had always heard about them. Ezra Wright, who in 1795 had started a small brass-and-iron foundry on the river, must have been one of those ingenious artisans who could turn their hand to anything. He invented a new type of blacksmith bellows. He made certain improvements, too, on the Franklin stove, and for a time he made clocks and andirons, which were still in existence, but his main interest was in metals, especially brass. Then a newcomer to Clyde named Samuel Sherwin had purchased the company and had obtained valuable contracts during the Civil War, and it kept going in a modest way down through the turn of the century. In 1912 Mr. Francis Stanley, a modern entrepreneur more concerned with business methods and salesmanship than invention, came to Clyde and acquired the property, and he obtained several large subcontracts in World War I for the manufacture of precision instruments.

Thus Wright-Sherwin was a tidy, aggressive little company when Charles Gray worked there, with complicated inventories and a plant that was thoroughly new. Mr. Francis Stanley, though he made a good thing of it, had not drained the profits but had plowed most of them back into brick and mortar and modern machine tools. He hated to raise wages, but he was willing to pay generously when necessary for metallurgical designers and a salesmanager — and whatever one thought of Mr. Stanley, more than five hundred people were employed at Wright-Sherwin that Monday morning in May 1928 when Charles left Wright-Sherwin forever.

The plant always opened at eight and Charles could hear a pleasant humming sound when he walked up the granite steps of the administrative building. The clock on the wall opposite a cadaverous looking portrait of Ezra Wright showed that it was twenty minutes before nine and Daisy Glover, who ran the telephone switchboard, smiled at him and checked off his name when he pushed open the little gate that led to the offices. Typewriters were clattering in the sales and promotion departments and the safe in the accounting department was already open, and he noticed a smell of freshly scrubbed linoleum in the passageway between the ground-glass partitions.

The desks of the accounting department occupied a large room, the rear windows of which looked over the foundry roofs to the blue water of the river. By the time Charles opened the door of the little closet where he hung his coat, Jackie Mason had arrived and nearly all the girls as well. Though they were always called girls, they were all middle-aged except Lottie Barnes, the secretary, who had been a classmate of Charles's and had taken the business course at high school. On the other hand, Miss Rosa Follen, who handled the petty cash and all the data that came to the office, and Miss Winona Pearson had been school friends of Charles's mother before Esther Gray had gone to the Academy. Charles said good morning to them all in a gentle tone because Mr. Howell always kept the door of his small office open.

"Good morning, Jack," Charles said, and he pulled back the chair of his own desk across the aisle from Jackie Mason.

"Hello, Charley," Jackie said. "Where were you yesterday? I thought you were going over to the Meaders'." Jackie Mason had been checking up on him lately and he wondered whether Jackie knew how much he had been seeing of Jessica. He even wondered why he had never spoken to Jack about Jessica, because technically Jack was still his best friend though for a long while he had not seen much of him. When Charles saw his yellow hair still moist from its careful morning brushing and his sedulously knotted tie with its unduly brilliant colors, he was so conscious of Jackie's limitations that he had a guilty feeling. They were growing away from each other and it was not Jackie's fault. Charles knew it was he who had changed in the last six months and not Jackie Mason. Jackie was a small-town boy. It was the first time Charles had used such a term about anyone, even in his thoughts, and it was ridiculous since he was a small-town boy himself, but there was something too aggressively brown about Jackie's suit, something about his manner that made Charles know all at once that they could never talk unreservedly again. Still he should have told Jackie on Sunday that he was going to leave Wright-Sherwin.

Charles opened the drawer of his desk and took out the inventory figures which he had been transferring to the Boston account book on Saturday morning. It seemed like a year ago that he had started checking the final list in Shed Three against receipts.

"I had to mow the lawn," Charles said. "I couldn't get over to the Meaders'."

"What are you doing Decoration Day?" Jackie asked. "The crowd is going down to the beach."

Jackie meant, of course, that Jeffrey and Melville and Priscilla Meader and Sally Bolton and Olive Rowell and all the rest of them were going for a picnic on the beach.

"I don't know," Charles said. "I will if I can make it."

"You'd better come along," Jackie said. "Don't be a stranger." It was what the old crowd always said if you did not see enough of them. They had started saying it when he went to Dartmouth.

He should have told Jackie on Sunday that he was going to leave Wright-Sherwin, but actually, there was still time to change his mind about leaving. He had never before faced the fact that by saying a few words security could be irretrievably ended. He would be leaving Jackie Mason and the old crowd forever when he left Wright-Sherwin. He would see them but he would not be a part of them.

"Let's have lunch at the dog wagon," Jackie said. He was referring to the new luncheon place across the street where the Wright-Sherwin office ate if they did not go home. He could tell Jackie then that he was going to leave Wright-Sherwin — but nothing would amount to anything until he had done what he had to do.

It was impossible to keep his mind on the inventory figures. Charles twisted in his swivel chair so that he could see Mr. Howell's room behind him. Mr. Howell was at his desk, unlocking the red leather general ledger, that contained all Wright-Sherwin's financial secrets. He had already put on his black alpaca coat and his green eyeshade, relics from bookkeeping days at Wright-Sherwin before Mr. Stanley had bought the company. Charles drew a deep breath, rose from his chair and walked down the aisle, even though he knew Mr. Howell did not like to be disturbed early in the morning.

Mr. Howell pushed up his eyeshade when he saw Charles and the green shade made Mr. Howell's gray hair rise in an untidy wave.

"Do you mind if I close the door, sir, for a minute?" Charles asked.

Mr. Howell straightened his bent shoulders and his pale lips tightened. If anyone closed the door it indicated, of course, that there would be some sort of trouble.

"What's happened now?" Mr. Howell said. "Don't just stand there looking at me."

Charles just stood there because there was not an extra chair in Mr. Howell's office. If other people wanted to see Mr. Howell, they sent for him, and so there was no need for a chair.

"I just wanted to tell you," Charles said, "that I want to leave, sir."

Mr. Howell took off his steel-rimmed reading glasses.

"What's the matter?" he asked. "After I've been losing my patience teaching you and you're just getting to be useful you want to leave? Don't you like your job?"

"Yes, sir, I like it all right," Charles said.

"Then, by godfrey," Mr. Howell said, "why don't you use your head? You're in the best place in Clyde and you're doing all right. Why do you want to leave?"

"Because I don't think there's much future here, sir," Charles said.

"Don't you?" Mr. Howell said. "What do you know about a future if you haven't got a past? How do you mean there isn't any future in Wright-Sherwin? Look at me. I've been here for forty years. I've got a house of my own and money in the bank."

"Yes, sir," Charles said.

"And how did I get it? By sticking to one job and not changing.

That's the way to get ahead. You want to get ahead, don't you?"

Charles had never thought that Mr. Howell would be sorry to have him go. Mr. Howell had never said a word to him about his work unless it was incorrect and each day he had made some acid remark about penmanship.

"I'm leaving because I want to get on."

Mr. Howell closed his general ledger carefully.

"What in hades," he said, "do you think I've been training you for? Do you think I'll live forever?"

Mr. Howell took his long-view spectacles from his waistcoat pocket and snapped open the case. It was a tremendous statement, because it was the same as saying that he was offering everything he cared for most. It was the same as saying that Charles could be the head of the accounting department someday. The unvarnished simplicity of it was what made it pathetic. Charles could see himself, his hair thinner, growing older, sitting at Mr. Howell's desk unlocking the red control ledger.

"I'm glad if you think I've done all right."

"I didn't say you've done all right," Mr. Howell said. "I said you might do all right. Now get out of here. It's nine-fifteen."

"It isn't as though I were leaving you without anyone," Charles said. "There's Jack Mason and he's just as good as I am. I'd like to leave in two weeks, and if it's all right I'd like tomorrow off."

"Oh," Mr. Howell said, "so you don't believe what I've been telling you, do you?"

"I didn't say I didn't believe you," Charles began again, but he had to make it clear that he was going to leave.

When he was back at his desk he thought of himself for the first time as a possible asset or as a piece of human material that could be sold at a price and it gave him a feeling of confidence. Mr. Howell emerged from his office a minute or two later and walked down the aisle between the desks and there was a quiver of excitement because it was obvious that Charles had done something to disturb him. When Charles heard that Mr. Stanley wanted to see him, he knew that he really must have been spoken of as a possible new head for the accounting department someday, but he also knew that nothing short of unforeseen accident would ever take him out of the accounting department if he was useful there.

Charles had only faced Mr. Stanley once in a brief interview when he had applied for work at Wright-Sherwin although they always had exchanged greetings when they met outside the office; but even this superficial acquaintance was enough to show Charles that Mr. Stanley carried on his shoulders the cloak of a larger world. Unlike most other Clyde businessmen, he attended out-of-town conventions and once or twice a year took trips about the country calling personally on his customers. Mr. Stanley was stout, bald, and wore rimless glasses. He had a plump face, hard and yet jovial, which was always to remind Charles of the photographs of successful executives which appeared on the *New York Times* financial page above the announcement of a large company's change in management. As he sat in his comfortable corner office, behind his leather-topped desk, surrounded by prints of sailing ships, Mr. Stanley looked deceptively approachable. He smiled and waved his hand at Charles as though they were old friends and, in the same gesture, waved to a green leather armchair beside his desk.

"Sit down. Take your weight off your feet, Charley," he said. "Will you have a cigarette? It's all right. You can smoke in here and I won't tell anyone," and he pushed forward a silver cigarette box.

"No, thank you, sir," Charles said. Something told him that it was not a good idea to accept anything from Mr. Stanley then, even a cigarette, and it was a habit to which Charles always adhered later. He never liked that easy, disarming business of taking a cigarette and looking for a match. If you refused when you were asked to smoke, it always put a burden on the other person. Instead he sat down, neither too stiffly nor too casually, and waited for Mr. Stanley.

"You get a great view from this room, don't you?" Mr. Stanley said, and he waved his hand to a long window with a view of the river and the harbor mouth. "I had that window especially cut for it."

Charles wondered why Mr. Stanley should take the time to offer him a cigarette and show him the river, which he knew as well as Mr. Stanley did, but Mr. Stanley was going on.

"When I'm down in New York, up in one of those tall buildings overlooking the Hudson, I like to tell my friends about our river here. When they ask me why I bury myself in a little one-horse town like Clyde, I tell them they ought to see our river; and that isn't all I tell them. I tell them there's no place like Clyde for contentment. I tell them they ought to see my house, or your father's house on Spruce Street, Charley. They don't have houses like those in Rye, New York, or Short Hills, New Jersey. They don't know what houses are or what living is. They forget that money doesn't buy everything." Mr. Stanley shook his head sadly. "They don't know what it means to be in a town with — " Mr. Stanley waved his hand, groping for a word — "with a Yankee historical tradition. They don't know what a good snowstorm means or looks like. They don't know what it means to be in a business a hundred years old and going strong, with men in the works who are there because they like what they're doing and wouldn't do anything else if you paid them maybe a little more than I can. They don't understand pride of craftsmanship or pride in a community. The longer you live here, the more you know that there's nothing like a small town for happiness. Maybe we don't make millionaires here, but what of it? This is a wonderful town."

Charles was obviously not expected to answer. He was wondering whether Mr. Stanley had picked up the wonderful-town phrase from Malcolm or whether everybody who came to Clyde and settled there thought that it was a wonderful town, and Mr. Stanley was going on.

"If I were young and had to start all over again, I'd want to live in a place like Clyde and never get out of it. I can talk all night when I get started on Clyde, but then we know it, don't we, Charley?"

"Yes, sir, I guess we do," Charles said. He thought that Mr. Stanley looked at him sharply. He almost thought that Mr. Stanley guessed what he was thinking — that Mr. Stanley was an outsider who did not belong in Clyde.

"We ought to get together and talk about this again sometime," Mr. Stanley said. "I've been meaning to tell my boy Norman to ask you up to the house sometime. Well, we'll make a point of it now it's getting on to summer and things are easing up. By the way, what's all this that Dickie Howell's been in here telling me about you, Charley?"

Mr. Stanley smiled, picked up a silver letter opener from his desk, and stared straight at Charles. It was obvious that Mr. Stanley wanted him to stay.

"What's he been telling?" Charles asked. Even then he had the right instincts. It was always better to let the other person talk when possible.

Mr. Stanley laughed indulgently.

"You've got Dickie Howell all upset. You don't want to do that, Charley. There's no one more valuable to this plant than old Dick. You and I mustn't stir him up."

"I'm sorry if I stirred him up," Charles said. Mr. Stanley smiled and shook his head.

"All this talk about your leaving us. You're not leaving us, are you, Charley?"

"Yes, sir," Charles said. "I told Mr. Howell I was."

"Well," Mr. Stanley said, and he laughed but Charles saw that Mr. Stanley still watched him carefully. Then he stopped laughing but he still smiled and tapped the letter opener softly on the desk. "We've got to have a little talk about this, Charley. Maybe you think I don't watch you boys when you come in here. Well, I do. That's my business. We have to have young blood here. Now Dickie Howell — this is between you and me — Dickie isn't as young as he used to be. He needs someone to take the weight off his shoulders. We need a new system here and something besides Boston ledgers." Mr. Stanley laughed again. "Now I've been turning over an idea in my mind. I'd like to send you to a school of accountancy for six months, Charley."

Mr. Stanley stopped but Charles did not answer. Mr. Stanley hitched himself forward in his chair and lowered his voice.

"Confidentially, Dick Howell and I have been talking about this. How would you like to head the accounting department of Wright-Sherwin in about two years? How do you think that sounds?"

It was necessary, Charles knew, to pretend that he was thinking.

"It's very kind of you, sir," Charles said.

"Kind of me?" Mr. Stanley looked grave and shook his head definitely. "I'm never kind when I do business. My job is picking people, and maybe I know more about you than you think, Charley. You've got a good mind and you keep your mouth shut. I've never seen you when you haven't been working. How about it, Charley?"

It was time to say no, but he did not want to say no in the wrong way.

"Thank you, but I'd rather not," Charles said.

"Why not?" Mr. Stanley had laid down the letter opener and sat motionless. It was better to answer frankly.

"If I got the accounting department, I'd always stay there," Charles said. "I don't think I'd be useful anywhere else."

"Wouldn't you want to stay there?" Mr. Stanley's voice was gentle but it had changed.

"No, sir," Charles said. "I'd like to get higher in the business than that someday."

"Let's see." Mr. Stanley picked up a small sheet of paper. "You're getting twenty-five dollars a week. How would you like it if I gave you fifty?"

"No, thank you, sir," Charles said. He would have been delighted a little while ago at such an offer. If it had not been for Jessica Lovell, he might have stayed in Wright-Sherwin.

"You're pretty ambitious, aren't you?" Mr. Stanley said.

"Yes, sir, I suppose I am," Charles answered.

"It doesn't pay to be too ambitious. There's much more to life than money. Fifty dollars here is the same as a hundred and fifty in New York. Money isn't everything. Have you got any other reason, Charley? Any personal reason?"

Mr. Stanley watched him intently and smiled in a warm, engaging way. If Mr. Stanley had heard so much about him, he wondered if he had heard about Jessica Lovell.

"Yes, sir," Charles said, "but I can't very well discuss it."

Mr. Stanley was silent for a moment. Then he straightened his heavy shoulders and cleared his throat and Charles knew that the interview was over.

"Well, we'll be sorry to lose you," Mr. Stanley said. "What are you going to do?"

"I think I'll go to Boston," Charles said, and he rose.

"Well, we'll be sorry to lose you," Mr. Stanley said. "If you change your mind come around and see me."

Sometimes Charles considered that interview a model of its kind. Neither Mr. Stanley nor he had said too much but they had said enough. He often wondered whether he had learned more of Mr. Stanley than Mr. Stanley had of him. He often wondered whether Mr. Stanley had thought of offering him anything more, but this was hardly possible because he was too young. He often wondered whether he would have stayed if he had known Mr. Stanley better.

XIV

The Gambling Known as Business Looks with Austere Disfavor upon the Business Known as Gambling

— AMBROSE BIERCE

CHARLES HAD OFTEN HEARD his father speak at length on the old days of downtown Boston. Those were the days, he used to say, when Boston's alleys all led to dignified bars and secluded restaurants which served the best food in the world. In those days, Boston had a respect for the male, particularly in the State Street district, and Boston was a comfortable, civilized town. Woodrow Wilson and the income tax had begun to send it downhill, John Gray used to say, and the World War and prohibition had done the rest. The old places were closing, like the New England House, with its fat dog and its gray African parrot in the upstairs dining room. The bars with their free lunches had vanished. The old oyster houses around the market were not what they used to be, now that there was no ale. You could still get tripe at the Parker House, but no Parker House punch in the spring. To put it another way, Boston was becoming contaminated by New York and the rest of America. It was, John Gray hated to say it, losing its fine isolation and its proud provincialism. Even the shoes of Boston women were not as sensible as they used to be.

John Gray repeated all this to Charles on that Tuesday morning in 1928 but Charles was too concerned with the future to bother with the past. The narrow sidewalks of Washington Street and the old State House, the Old South Church, Milk Street, and Congress Street seemed to Charles completely modern that morning. He could only accept Boston in a contemporary way, as one accepted everything when one was twenty-four. He never dreamed that the time would come when he, too, would speak of the old Boston he had known in the bond department of E. P. Rush & Company, the old pre-depression Boston of marble corridors and black walnut woodwork, of leisurely elevators moving upward through their shafts like giant spiders on webs of looped cables, the Boston of trustees and real estate trusts and well-trained barbers who came to clip the gray hair of trustees and lawyers as they sat in their offices gazing at the tombs in the Old Granary Burying Ground or into the dingy streets off Post Office Square.

"Dear, dear," John Gray said. "There used to be a time when everything was static here. I hate this sense of change."

He was always cheerful when he was back in Boston after a longish absence. He was wearing his best tailored suit, which he very seldom wore in Clyde, and his newest brown felt hat.

"It makes me feel old and even sordid to be taking a son of mine down here, but I suppose we have to start sometime."

As they turned left on Congress Street he began to whistle a snatch of an old waltz.

"Did you say this place is on Congress Street?" Charles asked.

"Yes," John Gray answered. "Congress Street, and on a third floor. Old E. P., the father of the present Mr. Rush, Charles, said an upstairs office stopped the riffraff from dropping in."

"Don't you think," Charles said, "if you're going to introduce me to Mr. Rush you'd better tell me a little more about him?"

"I'm not introducing you to E. P. Rush," John Gray said. "E. P. Rush is dead and perhaps it's just as well because I'm afraid he didn't approve of me. It's his son — not E. P. Rush — whom I met during my brief sojourn at Harvard University. We played poker and did other things together."

"I know, you've told me that" — his father was in one of his most exasperating moods that morning — "but you haven't told me what he's like."

"It doesn't matter," John Gray said, "because he'll probably make a different impression on you from any he has made on me. I wonder how the market's opening."

E. P. Rush & Company occupied half of the third floor of a building on Congress Street. It was a curiously planned office which seemed to have grown like a living organism, producing small clusters of desks and typewriters, throwing out new railed enclosures and rearing new counters and pieces of grillwork and acquiring, as an afterthought, a few leather armchairs and cuspidors grouped in front of a board on which were listed in abbreviations some but not all of the stocks on the New York Exchange. Two tickers near the board stamped quotations upon reels of tape which poured into tall wicker baskets. The exchange had not opened yet so the tickers were almost silent. The bookkeepers were already at work and the young men in the bond department were reading prospectuses and making their morning telephone calls. Charles did not know then that the studied, dusty carelessness of E. P. Rush & Company was an effect deliberately cultivated to create a sound atmosphere.

This impression of casualness was also reflected in the clothing of the young men in the outer office. They wore soft shirts and their clothes were not aggressively pressed. They slouched easily in their swivel chairs, and yet they were always ready to come courteously to attention. The secretaries, who were still called stenographers at E. P. Rush & Company, were gathered in a small paddock of their own, and they, too, fitted perfectly with the spirit, most of them approaching middle age, none of them endowed with disturbing beauty.

Behind this outer office, which smelled of creosote and paper and stale cigar smoke, was a railing guarding the ground-glass doors of the partners' rooms. A switchboard operator, a plump, cheerful looking girl, guarded the railing gate. John Gray, with Charles following him, walked across the room and bowed to her and she said that Mr. Gray was quite a stranger lately.

"Yes," John Gray said, "lately, but my thoughts are often here, Miss Swift. Is Mr. Rush in yet?"

"Oh, yes," Miss Swift said. "He's just reading the papers. I know he'll be glad to see you."

Mr. Rush sat at a shabby roll-top desk working on a crossword puzzle by the light from a single unwashed window. Mr. Rush was wearing a blue serge suit, which was shiny at the knees and elbows. The morning mail, opened and in a neat pile on the desk before him, was weighted down by an Indian hatchet head. In the corner behind him, like a leafless tree, stood a mahogany hatrack on which hung Mr. Rush's leghorn hat. The lenses of his horn-rimmed spectacles gave his light blue eyes a surprised look which did not fit with his mouth.

"Hello," he said. "Where did you drop from?"

"Don't let me interrupt your train of thought, Moulton," John Gray answered. "This is my son Charles."

"He looks the way you used to," Mr. Rush said.

"But he isn't like me," John Gray said. "Charley wants to get on."

"What class were you in?" Mr. Rush asked Charles.

John Gray sighed and spoke before Charles could answer.

"My sister Jane wanted him to go to Dartmouth. Don't hold it against him, Moulton. It's a small place but we love it."

"Does he want a job?" Mr. Rush said.

"Why, Moulton," John Gray answered, "why do you think we're here?"

Mr. Rush pulled a thick gold watch from his waistcoat pocket.

"It's five minutes after ten," he said. "Why don't you go out and see the opening, Johnny?"

After John Gray had left, Mr. Rush looked at Charles for a moment without speaking.

"Your father is a remarkable man," Mr. Rush said.

"Yes, sir," Charles said, "I suppose he is."

Mr. Rush stood up.

"Well, I suppose I'd better introduce you to Mr. Stoker. He runs our bond department."

They walked down the partners' row to Mr. Stoker's office. Mr. Stoker was younger, a barrel-chested man who looked like a football coach. In fact Charles learned later that Lawrence Stoker had once been a line coach for Harvard.

"Lawrence," Mr. Rush said, "this is Charles Gray. He comes from Dartmouth but I'd like you to find something for him to do."

It astonished Charles that Mr. Rush had not asked him a single question, but later when he knew the office better he approved of that method. Mr. Rush had known who he was and had passed on his personal appearance and this was about all that was necessary. As in Victorian England younger sons once rushed to join the Church and the army, so in those days on America's eastern seaboard they crowded into reputable investment houses. There were so many nice young men in those days that they were expendable material. Their energy and resilience could be used to the limit until almost inevitable disillusion made it evaporate. Not one in twenty of these young men, Charles heard Mr. Rush say later, ever developed a permanent value. They entered the Boston offices, in the late twenties, only to disappear eventually no one knew where. It was not the policy of Rush & Company to expend much time on their education. It was a matter of sink or swim, and there were always lots more waiting.

That was how he started with E. P. Rush & Company and though he sometimes wondered what would have happened to him if he had gone to sea or into publishing or if a little later he had gone with Malcolm Bryant to the Orinoco, he found the order and the relentless flow of forces at E. P. Rush & Company satisfying and congenial. Besides, as his father had said, he wanted to get on. He wanted to wear the right clothes and do the right things. He wanted to do well as quickly as he could, because he was in love with Jessica Lovell.

He had been a very nice boy, that day when he went up to Boston, devoid of disillusion, indoctrinated in all the right creeds. He had believed everything that Mr. Stoker told him. He was entering the finest investment house in Boston, a firm whose backing meant that any issue in which it participated was as sound as a nut. Everybody who worked for E. P. Rush was hand-picked. It was like being in a club to be in Mr. Stoker's crowd. Everyone had a chance to earn his letter. E. P. Rush & Company was a gentlemen's firm, with gentlemen's ethics. There was money enough in the firm to build an office that would look like an Italian palace, but E. P. Rush did not want the type of customer who was attracted by upholstery. Its partners were broad-gauge public-spirited men who were there not for window dressing but because they understood the investment business and were personally interested in most of the companies whose securities they handled. In fact it was all one big happy family and now Charles was in the family. Charles already realized that it might be just as well if he did not talk much about Dartmouth.

When Charles returned to Clyde at six o'clock, his manner was already changing. He was in the old-line house of E. P. Rush & Company and someday he would be a partner. The prospect was a long way off but already its charm was working. If he had not been in E. P. Rush he would not have called up Jessica Lovell that evening after supper. As a matter of fact, he might not have telephoned her if the family had not been so pleased.

"The funny thing about it was," his father said, "that I've never known Moulton Rush very well, Esther. It was Charles who did it. Moulton just took one look at him."

Charles saw his mother take one look at him too, a proud, possessive look.

"I don't see how Charles ever got in it," Dorothea said.

"Through accident, Dorothea," Charles told her. "They weren't thinking what they were doing."

"Well, see you stay in it," Dorothea said. "At least they must think he's honest, Mother," but she said it kindly. She even said it as though she were proud of him.

"I think I'll go over to see Jessica," he said. He was fully aware, from the pause at the supper table, that this was the same as announcing to the family, as it was said in Clyde, that he was attentive to Jessica Lovell.

"Why, Charley," his mother said, "I think that would be very nice, but don't stay too late."

Of course they were all listening when he went into the hall to telephone — but then he was in E. P. Rush & Company.

"Why, Charley," Jessica said over the telephone. "Of course I'm not doing anything. We'd love to see you." He was disturbed by the coolness of her voice until he remembered that the Lovells' telephone, too, was in the hall.

It was eight o'clock though it was still light and all of Johnson Street was bathed in a misty, mysterious afterglow that gave the Lovells' house a remote look, but a sense of never having been there before vanished when Jessica opened the front door herself. Her silk afternoon dress was a grayish-green color very much like the color of the new leaves in the fading light. The hall in back of her was dark and the light from the open door of the wallpaper room made it hard to see her face. She clasped his hand very tightly, and her own hand felt cold.

"I've been wondering where you've been," she said. "We're all in the wallpaper room." He walked slowly in behind her and shook hands with Miss Lovell and Mr. Lovell.

"We've been reading *Jane Eyre*," Miss Lovell said. "That is, I've been reading it. Do you like *Jane Eyre*, Charles?"

"How do you do, Charles?" Mr. Lovell said, getting up from the sofa.

"Please don't get up, sir," Charles said. "I didn't mean to interrupt you."

"It's just as well you did," Mr. Lovell said. "*Jane Eyre* is the most improbable book I know and, at the same time, the truest."

Charles wished he could remember more about the Brontë sisters.

"How's your Aunt Jane, Charles?" Miss Lovell asked.

"I'm afraid she hasn't been so well lately," Charles answered.

"Let me see" — Mr. Lovell was speaking — "I don't think I've set eyes on you, Charles, since the Players were finished. How is everything going at Wright-Sherwin?"

"I'm leaving there at the end of next week, sir." Charles tried to speak as though he were speaking about the Brontë sisters.

"Oh," Mr. Lovell said, "I'm sorry. Was anything the matter?"

"No, nothing was the matter," Charles answered. "Next week I'm starting work in Boston at E. P. Rush & Company."

A change had come over Mr. Lovell. He was looking at Charles for the first time as though he were not a Clyde boy who had come to call.

"Why, Charles," he said, "how did you ever get into E. P. Rush?"

"Father knows Mr. Rush," Charles said.

"I didn't know John knew Mr. Rush."

"Yes," Charles said, "he knows him."

Mr. Lovell still looked at Charles as though he had heard something incredible.

"Why, that's splendid," he said. "Well, well. Congratulations."

Charles wanted to look again at Jessica but he restrained himself, and then Miss Lovell spoke quickly.

"Charley, I'm awfully glad for you," she said. He always liked Miss Lovell after that.

"E. P. Rush & Company." Mr. Lovell was speaking again. "Well, well, well. If you hear of anything interesting in the way of securities, Charles, be sure you let me know."

"Jessica," Miss Lovell said, "why don't you show Charles the tulips in the garden? It's still light enough."

"It's getting damp tonight," Mr. Lovell said. "Jessica's the only girl I have and I don't want her catching cold. Well, just walk around the garden, Jessica, and then come back."

When they were opening the door at the end of the hall, Charles could still hear Miss Lovell's voice.

"Laurence," he heard her say, "try not to be so ridiculous."

The tulips made a beautiful show in the beds on the lower terrace and above them on the second terrace the peonies were just ready to bloom. Though there was no strong scent of flowers, the air was filled with that strange repressed vigor of a New England spring.

"I can't stay out long," Jessica said. "You understand, don't you, dear?" She was walking quickly up the gravel path, climbing up the steps to the third terrace. "Father hates seeing me grow up. He always has." She sounded as though she were talking to an imaginary person, much as Charles in his thoughts had often spoken to her. "I wish I weren't the only thing he had."

Her coat was over her shoulders with its sleeves hanging loose, for she had not bothered to put her arms through it before she left the house. Her bare head and the loose sleeves and the way she talked made him think of Jane Eyre, hurrying away from something in the house, afraid that it might follow her or afraid that it might call her back.

The third terrace, a level, close-cropped lawn called the bowling green, was shut off from all the rest of the garden by a high, carefully clipped spruce hedge and she seemed uncertain that he was beside her until they were in that dusky green enclosure.

"Oh, darling," she whispered, "I've missed you so," and her coat slipped off her shoulders. She said she had missed him until she could not believe any of it.

"I've missed you, too," he said. "We've got to see each other, Jessica." It did not seem possible that they could be making love in that formal garden.

"Yes," she said, "we've got to. Everything's going to be all right, isn't it?"

"Of course," he said. "Everything's all right."

"Darling," she said, "I love you so that everything goes to pieces." He kissed her without answering.

"I'm so proud of you," she said. "You're so honest and you never are afraid, are you?"

"What's there to be afraid of?" Charles asked.

"Oh," she said, and she turned her head away, "of something happening to spoil it all. I keep waking up in the night and thinking something's happened." She shook her head very quickly. "Darling, wasn't Aunt Georgianna sweet? She wanted us to see the tulips."

"Have you told her anything?" Charles asked. She shook her head quickly.

"Not exactly. I've talked about you. I have to talk about you, dear, and there's no one else."

"Have you told your father anything?"

"Of course not," she said. "That's a silly question. Darling, you can see, can't you? It's got to come over him by degrees. We'd better be going back now."

"Yes," Charles said, "I suppose we had," and he wrapped her coat around her.

"And now you're in Boston we can see each other there sometimes, too. Darling, everything's so wonderful. I've got to forget it's so wonderful." She seemed to be forgetting already as they walked back. "Look how black the box border looks. None of it was winterkilled."

She only said one thing more before they reached the house. She said it just as she put her hand on the heavy brass latch of the outside door.

"We've got to keep believing."

Nothing else mattered if you could keep believing, and nothing was left if you stopped.

Charles never considered that his or Jessica's manner, aside from all appearances, might indicate the probability of what had happened in the garden because they took great pains to walk into the room decorously, far apart and entirely unconcerned with each other.

"Hello," Mr. Lovell said. "So you're back."

"You were right," Jessica said, and she bent down and kissed his high forehead. "It was very cold out there. You're always right."

"Charles," Miss Lovell said, "would you mind getting my knitting? It's on the table."

"Patrick's doing pretty well with the garden," Mr. Lovell said. "None of the box border was winterkilled."

"I suppose it's pretty far north for box, sir," Charles said, and Mr. Lovell gave him a searching look.

"Virginia's the place for box, Virginia and England. Were you ever in Virginia, Charles?"

"No, sir," Charles said.

"You must go someday . . . Jessie" — Mr. Lovell smiled at her — "I've just been thinking you and I might go abroad again this summer."

"This summer?" Jessica repeated.

"I was just speaking of it to Aunt Georgianna," Mr. Lovell said, "Why, don't you like the idea, Jessica?"

There was nothing for Charles to do but to listen. Jessica sat with her hands carefully folded.

"I thought you wanted me to get used to Clyde," she said, "and now I'm getting used to it you want to go away."

"Now, Jessie" — Mr. Lovell laughed — "Clyde's always an easy place to come back to and don't look so upset. We couldn't possibly leave till toward the end of June. I'll want to go to Class Day and there are all sorts of odds and ends I have to attend to. I think it would do us a lot of good to get a change."

"But you were just saying yesterday — " Jessica began, and she stopped.

"When we get back, Charles may be a partner at E. P. Rush, but I'm afraid it's dull for you, Charles, our talking over plans," Mr. Lovell said.

It was clearly time to be leaving, but he did not want it to look as though he were hurrying away.

"I hope you have a good trip, sir," he said.

"Don't go, Charles." Mr. Lovell smiled at him, but Charles knew when it was time to go. He said good night to Miss Lovell and shook Mr. Lovell's hand.

"Good night, Jessica," he said.

"Oh, Charley," she said, quite loudly, when his hand touched hers, "don't forget tomorrow night," and she turned away from him before she dropped his hand. "Charles is going to take me to the movies tomorrow night."

He certainly had not asked her, but she said it so convincingly that he almost thought he had.

"Why," Mr. Lovell said, "that's very nice of Charles to take you," and his words rang with complete conviction. "Good night, Charles, and come in any time."

"Yes," Miss Lovell said, "any time. Good night."

He must have been thinking more of the way he had behaved than of anything else in the first few minutes after he left. He hoped he had shown no surprise or resentment; he even found himself admiring the way in which Mr. Lovell, with his flat, agreeably modulated voice, had contrived to show him that he had stepped into a region where he did not belong, gently, delicately, and yet in a way you could not possibly mistake. What lay between him and

Jessica was now an incontrovertible fact or it would not have occurred to Mr. Lovell that it might be nice to take her abroad that summer.

He had never asked her to the moving pictures and perhaps everyone had known it. Nothing had been as wonderful as the moment when Jessica had said, still holding his hand, "Don't forget tomorrow night," for she might as well have said that she cared for him no matter what anyone thought. She might as well have stood beside him and have said that she would see him any time she pleased and that no one could prevent it. Perhaps Jessica actually did say so, after she had brushed her lips against his cheek in the dark front hall and had closed the door behind him.

When he returned to Spruce Street, his father was sitting alone downstairs openly reading the financial page of the *Boston Transcript*.

"How was it at the Lovells', Charles?" he asked.

"It was all right," Charles said.

"I suppose they were all sitting in that room with the wallpaper," John Gray said. "How did Jessica look?"

"She had on a grayish-green dress," Charles said, and he went on because he had to tell someone. "Miss Lovell was reading *Jane Eyre* aloud."

"Oh dear me," John Gray said, "the Brontës. Did you all read aloud?"

"No," Charles said. "Miss Lovell asked whether Jessica and I wouldn't like to go out into the garden and see the tulips."

"Oh my," John Gray said, "what did Laurence say?"

"He said it was getting cold outside."

"Well, well. How long were you in the garden?"

"Not long. Jessica thought we ought to get back."

"Well, well," John Gray said. "What happened when you got back?"

"Mr. Lovell said it had just come into his mind that he and Jessica might go abroad this summer."

John Gray smiled and passed his hand over the back of his head.

"There's nothing like a small town, Charley. Of course, everyone is going to guess why the Lovells went abroad."

Charles felt his face grow deep red, and his father leaned forward and put his hand gently on his knee before he could answer.

"I never did like Laurence Lovell, Charley." The intensity of his dislike must have had its roots deep in some past of which Charles knew nothing.

"Charley," John Gray continued, "this is a very small town, smaller than a smaller town and someday you'll see what I mean."

XV

Laugh, Clown, Laugh

"You're always on time, aren't you," Jessica said when he called for her the next evening in time for the late show. "Do I look all right for the movies?"

Naturally he told her that she did though it was obvious that she would not have been wearing a semi-evening dress and a short, dark velvet cloak if she had gone often to the movies in Clyde.

"I suppose you know that everyone will see us there," he said.

She moved closer to him before she answered and put her arm through his.

"I want everyone to see us," she said, and her hand was trembling. "You don't mind, do you?"

Of course, he said, he did not mind who saw them.

"It's been a dreadful day," she said. "It isn't anything Father says. It's the way he looks. You might think I was going to run away with you because you're taking me to the movies — but he's really trying to be sweet. It isn't you, you know, it's me. Do you know what he said at supper?"

Charles wished that he did not have the helpless feeling of an innocent bystander.

"No," he answered, "what did he say?"

"He said to be sure to ask you in when you took me home. He didn't want me to catch cold walking around outside. Oh, darling." He heard her catch her breath. "It has to be all right. As long as he sees there's nothing he can do."

They had turned down Dock Street and they were passing the Dock Street Bank.

"Do you remember the bank?" he asked her. "You had on your red hat." It had only been that spring.

Two years before, the only moving picture house in Clyde had been called the Acme Theater. It had been built in the days when there had been vaudeville acts and illustrated songs between the pictures. It had been renovated at about the same time the new soda fountain and the uncomfortable little booths had been installed in Walters's Drugstore, around the corner from it on Dock Street. The Acme Theater was called the Savoy now and was equipped with new soft seats and Romanesque decorations and an electrically lit marquee which cast a harsh halo of bright light on the sidewalk. Lon Chaney in *Laugh, Clown, Laugh,* was on that night, and the customers for the late show were already entering, while the new manager, Mr. Dupree, who was soon to sell it to a theater chain, stood by the ticket booth watching an out-of-town blonde making change.

Though it was now the Savoy and not the Acme, and though its lights were brighter, the whole scene reminded Charles of high school days when he used to take Doris Wormser to the same late show. The faces were different but there were the same crowds of adolescent boys and girls. They must all have been in grammar school when Charles had taken Doris there. There were all sorts of familiar faces, too, faces of older people and old schoolmates. First he saw Earl Wilkins, who had been tackle when he had been left end on the high school team, and Earl was with Lizzie Jenkins, one of the Wright-Sherwin girls.

"Hi, Earl," he said.

"Hi, Charley," Earl answered, and looked at him as if he had not seen him for a long while.

Then he saw Doris Wormser with Willie Woodbury, who was working in the Clyde Grain and Implement Company. Both Charles and Doris must have looked startled, but they called out to each other, and then he saw Melville Meader and Jackie Mason and Priscilla Meader.

"There's Jackie Mason," Jessica said.

335

He did not want it to seem unusual for him to be there with Jessica Lovell. He told himself that it was perfectly natural for him to be taking Jessica to *Laugh, Clown, Laugh,* and that it was only his imagination that made him feel that everyone was staring at them. At the same time, there was no reason why they should not have stared, because he would have been equally surprised to see a friend of his with Jessica in her velvet cape. It was a relief when he was in the dark theater, holding Jessica's hand, until he saw that Priscilla Meader was beside him and then he dropped her hand hastily.

"I thought you never went to the movies any more, Charley," Priscilla said.

"I don't often," Charles answered. "You know Jessica Lovell, don't you, Priscilla?" It would have been much better if he had not asked, since it indicated that perhaps Priscilla did not know her.

"Oh, yes," Priscilla said, and there was no need for Jessica's having been quite so cordial. There was a cloying effort at politeness as they both leaned across him to talk during the short comedy.

"I haven't seen you for a long while," Jessica said.

"It was when the gardens were open, wasn't it?" Priscilla said. "I don't see how you ever got Charley to the movies."

"I had to ask him. He wouldn't have thought of it," Jessica said.

Tomorrow everyone would know that he had taken her to the movies and that she had asked him.

"How about going to Walters's after the show?" Charles asked. "How about it, Jack?" If he was going around with Jessica Lovell, they might as well go around to Walters's.

Everyone always went around to Walters's for ice cream after the pictures but Jessica looked foreign there in her velvet cape. They had divided decorously, like changing partners at a dance, so Charles looked across one of the little booths at Jessica sitting beside Jackie Mason. They were all speaking above the giggles and whistles of the high school crowd.

"This place is dreadfully crowded, isn't it?" Priscilla said. "But at the same time, I can't count how often I've been here. Can you, Charley? Do you remember Saturday nights at high school?" She beamed across the table. "You ought to have been with our crowd at high school, Jessica. You don't mind my calling you Jessica, do you?"

"I don't see what else you could call me," Jessica answered.

Jackie Mason was looking at his ice cream. It was a strawberry nut sundae and Priscilla was speaking again.

"We've seen each other around enough to be on a first-name basis, I guess. You honestly ought to have been with us at high school, Jessica. We used to have more fun. Gosh, it seems like a long time ago. Jackie, didn't we have fun?"

Jackie Mason looked up hastily from his plate.

"It was quite a long while ago, wasn't it?" Jackie said, and he smiled feebly.

"Everybody sort of drifts apart, don't they?" Priscilla said. "It doesn't seem like we could ever have been like all those kids over by the fountain. I don't think we ever behaved like those kids."

"They're just having a good time," Jessica said. "I wish I had gone to high school. Charley, have you any cigarettes?"

"Here, let me," said Jackie Mason.

"Look, Jackie's got a silver case," Priscilla said. "Who gave you the silver case, Jackie?"

"The family," Jack Mason said. "Just the family."

"Oh," Priscilla said, "it wasn't you-know-who? We had more fun in high school. We all paired off. There was Jackie and you-know-who — "

"There's Earl Wilkins over there now," Charles said.

"Oh, Earl," Priscilla said. "Just because Earl used to take me to the movies . . . What about you and Doris Wormser, Charley?"

Charles laughed. He had almost forgotten Jessica. He was back with the old crowd again.

"What about you and Wilkins in the physics laboratory?" he said, and then he remembered Jessica. "You ought to have been in high school, Jessica. If you'd been there, I wouldn't have worried about Doris Wormser."

"He never did worry about her much and I ought to know," Jackie Mason said.

"You don't want to believe him," Priscilla said. "Jackie's always sticking up for Charley. I'm just being funny. I never meant it was anything serious at all. Why, Charley and I played post office. Do you want a letter, Charley?"

Charles wondered what it would have been like if Jessica had been there, playing tag in the Meaders' back yard. He felt almost sorry for her because he knew she had missed a lot although he had moved a long way from it himself.

"I wish Priscilla hadn't talked so much," Jackie murmured, after they had paid the check at the cigar counter. "I'm afraid she gave a wrong impression." Jackie always worried about impressions. Priscilla and Jessica were waiting for them on the sidewalk.

"There's nobody like Charley," he heard Priscilla saying. "I've always been crazy about Charley, Jessica."

When he and Jessica were walking up Dock Street, he remembered thinking that he must not apologize for any of it — that she was the one who had asked to go.

"Priscilla Meader," she said, and obviously she had no previous recollection of Priscilla Meader at all. "Is her father the one who has the real estate and insurance office?"

"Yes," Charles answered, "that's the one."

Then they were silent again.

"I wish I'd been to high school," she said. "I wouldn't feel so far away and I wouldn't have worn this damn dress."

Charles at this time did not understand that there was a purpose behind many social gestures. As long as Mr. Lovell had especially asked that Jessica invite him in afterwards, Charles believed that Mr. Lovell might end by liking him after all. As early as a year later, however, Charles was able to appreciate Mr. Lovell's motives.

It happened that Mr. Rush had called Charles into his office to explain some details concerning the bond issue of the King Wassoit Textile Company to a trustee named Mr. Garvin, but when Charles entered they were talking, in that informal way they did in Boston, about their children and especially about Mr. Rush's daughter Ruth, whom Charles had never met but whose picture in riding clothes stood on Mr. Rush's desk.

"She met him somewhere," Mr. Rush was saying. "I never saw him until she brought him out to Brookline for Sunday dinner. God knows where girls pick up men nowadays."

"It's a phase that girls go through," Mr. Garvin said. "You've got to put up with it. Just don't let her see you don't like him, Moulton. That's the worst mistake you can make, you know."

"Yes," Mr. Rush answered, "that's what Alice and everyone keep saying."

"Let it run its course," Mr. Garvin said. "They're always crazy to do some damn fool thing that you don't approve of and as soon as you approve of it they forget it. Have him around to the house. Give him your whiskey and cigars."

"They all smoke cigarettes," Mr. Rush said.

"Just let her see you like him," Mr. Garvin said, "and she'll be tired of him in two weeks."

"But I don't like him."

"Well, don't tell Ruthie so."

Charles never knew what had happened to that boy of whom Ruth Rush had been fond but he understood then why Mr. Lovell had told Jessica to be sure to bring him home that night and why Mr. Lovell had asked him to drop in sometimes in the evening, in those few short weeks before he took Jessica abroad. It was, of course, before John Gray was at leisure and began taking the eight-two regularly to Boston and before the Grays bought the Cadillac and finally joined the Shore Club.

Everything had seemed possible that evening. Those minutes at Walters's drugstore had a reassuring quality that carried even into the wallpaper room. Charles no longer worried about the creases in his trousers when he sat beside Jessica on the sofa. The Chinese junks and the pagodas on the wall and the studied elegance of that English furniture had a homelike, welcoming quality, as though it were natural and proper for him to be there with Jessica. They talked for a while about those arid days when they had hardly known each other. He told her about Earl Wilkins and about the Thanksgiving Day football game with Smith's Common High. He asked her whether she remembered Sam. Jessica was the only person with whom he ever talked freely about Sam, except of course with May Mason. He must have told her about Sam's going to the war and that he still could not believe that Sam was dead. He surely must have told her what he had said to Mr. Howell and Mr. Stanley at Wright-Sherwin, because it was possible to tell her everything or almost everything. He must have laid his whole life, such as it was, before Jessica Lovell in a magnificent, prodigal gesture and Jessica did the same.

There was nothing more lonely than being an only child, Jessica said, particularly in a place like Clyde. She always knew she belonged there without any sense of belonging, if you could understand what she meant. If she had been a boy she would have belonged more to it, because she could have moved about. She could have gone everywhere, as Charles had. Her father had often said that he would have sent her to school in Clyde, at least for a year or two, if she had been a boy, because the Lovells belonged to Clyde and they had always played a part in it. His own father, Grandfather Lovell, had sent him to school there for two or three years and he valued that experience more than any other. He was always saying that it had taught him to get on with all sorts of people, though Jessica had never seen this side of him. He often said that he was disturbed at how the school system had changed. It was run now by politicians and so many foreigners had entered Clyde that there was not the background of good Yankee stock in the schools that he had known. He had never wanted Jessica to learn the habits of some girls, particularly foreign girls, at grammar school. Though girls from nice families went there, from all sorts of solid, self-respecting Yankee families, they usually ended by speaking ungrammatically in high, nasal voices.

It was not that he was snobbish in the least. If her mother had lived, instead of dying so suddenly when Jessica was six, her father might not have wanted her to be so perfect. As it was, there had been a governess for her until she went to school in Boston and she never belonged anywhere at all. She used to watch the children, sometimes, going along Johnson Street to school. She used to see them at her birthday parties. (She was sure she did not know why Charles had never been asked to her birthdays, because Jackie Mason had been.) They used to play together sometimes but she never really knew them and no one, or hardly anyone, in Boston knew about Clyde. Her father always brought her home for week ends when she was at school in Boston. He never wanted to be away from her too long, after her mother died. He had always given up so much for her. It was the same way at Westover and Vassar. He was often at Poughkeepsie for week ends and they were always together at vacation time.

"I sound like Emily Dickinson," she said.

She did not mean that she had not seen other men but there had always been something, something. It was just as though she had been asleep, or almost asleep, until that day at the firemen's muster.

"I don't know why it happened then," she said. "I don't see why you liked me."

"I guess it was your red hat and your hair," he told her. "I don't exactly know how it was. You seemed to be looking for someone and there wasn't anybody else there but me."

"I wasn't looking for you," she said. "I was looking for Malcolm Bryant."

"No, you weren't," he said. "You were really looking for me. It couldn't have been anyone else, and you couldn't have been anyone else. And there's another thing."

"What other thing?"

He found himself staring at the molding of the room, thinking of the time it had taken to saw and chisel its intricate design. There was just the faintest irregularity, something a machine could never duplicate.

"It wouldn't have happened if we'd known each other too well." And then he thought of Malcolm Bryant and he began to laugh.

"What are you laughing about?" she asked.

"About that chart of Malcolm Bryant's," he said. "It wouldn't

341

have happened if we had both been upper-uppers. You'd have seen too much of me and we wouldn't have had anything to wonder about."

They were sitting together on the sofa so close that her hair brushed his cheek, but she moved closer to him.

"Darling," she said, "you don't really think that way about me, do you? It's so damned silly. You don't really?"

"Not right now," he said, "or I wouldn't have told you."

"Darling," she whispered, "don't let anyone ever put us on a chart"; and then she drew away from him because Mr. Lovell was calling from the top of the stairs.

"Oh, Jessie."

At least they did not spring guiltily apart; her hand was still on his shoulder when she answered.

"Yes, Father."

"Is Charles there?"

"Yes, Father."

Her hand dropped noiselessly from his shoulder and rested on his hand.

"You'll excuse me for not coming down, won't you, Charles?" Mr. Lovell called. "What was the name of the picture you went to see?"

"It was *Laugh, Clown, Laugh,*" Charles called back.

"Well, Jessie," Mr. Lovell said, "when Charles goes, don't forget to put out the lights."

There was no need to read the news notes in the *Clyde Herald* to find out what had happened to anyone in Clyde. The news notes dealt with engagement showers, illnesses, and the trips of citizens to visit close relatives, but the more vital matters never appeared on the printed page. These were retailed by word of mouth with bewildering speed, edited and exaggerated, cut and lengthened. This interest in other people's business was unmalicious in Clyde compared with what went on in any large office, for people in Clyde usually wanted to know about each other simply because there was human consolation in others' misfortunes, and at worst a mild envy in others' small successes, Charles had only told Jack Mason the whole story of his interviews with Mr. Howell and Mr. Stanley because Jack was his best friend and also because he wanted Jack to know that they were looking for someone to run the accounting department eventually. Jack had declared that he would say nothing about it, and Charles was sure that Jack had not, because they were friends and because Jack wanted a chance at that job himself; but in two days people were stopping Charles on the street to say they had heard he had left Wright-Sherwin and that it was fine that he had such a nice job in Boston.

Still, no one except Jackie Mason ever brought up with Charles his trip with Jessica to the movies. Actually all that Jackie ever said was that if *he* had invited Jessica Lovell to the movies he would certainly not have taken her to Walters's drugstore afterwards. He would have been afraid that she would have thought it was cheap of him or that he was trying to show her off. It would have been better to have taken her to the Sweet Shoppe on Dock Street. It was quieter at the Sweet Shoppe and the booths were more comfortable.

"You ought to think about those things," Jackie said, "when you take someone like Jessica Lovell anywhere. Somebody around here always sees everything you do."

He wanted to ask Jackie what someone had seen him do, but he did not want to talk about Jessica.

"I don't care what anybody sees," he said.

"But you ought to care," Jackie told him, and he looked very worried. "Now I never asked Jessica to the movies myself, Charley. I thought of it, but I knew how it would have looked. You know, I've been to call on Jessica sometimes, and you know what people began to say."

"What did they say?" Charles asked.

"Oh" — a faint touch of color came into Jackie's face — "you know. How is it up there? That sort of thing. Of course, it isn't the same with you, Charley, as it is with me. They wouldn't say just that about you, but you know how people talk."

All he had to do was to ask another question to learn what they were saying and it might have been better if he had, but the worries of Jack Mason were too like an exaggeration of some of his own worries for him to be comfortable with them. Besides, he had other things to worry about that May.

His Uncle Gerald Marchby had said as recently as the beginning of May that there was no reason to be concerned about his Aunt Jane. Dr. Marchby had been practicing medicine in Clyde for years, as his father had before him and as his son Jerry, who was now in the Harvard Medical School, might very well do after him, and Dr. Marchby had seen a lot of people live and die. There was no reason to feel that his uncle was wrong when he said that the Gray heart was only a cardiac condition common in older people and not serious in itself. At some time or other, he had entered the sickroom of nearly every house in Clyde, carrying his black bag with him and dealing imperturbably with shocking sights and sounds. That experience had given him the patient, inscrutable look which sets doctors apart from other people. There was no way to tell how much Gerald Marchby knew. You had to put your trust in inscrutability, but Charles as a layman could see that his Aunt Jane was not as well as she had been six months before. Still, Gerald Marchby only said not to worry, that Jane was in fair physical condition, that it was good for her to lose a little weight, and that everyone looked peaked after a hard winter. She liked attention, that was all. If she talked about making her will, so did a lot of other people after they reached a certain age. If she wanted her bed moved downstairs into the parlor and it made her feel easier, why let her. You only had to remember that people acted in certain ways when they got to be a certain age. They loved medicine and they loved attention.

Yet in spite of this reassurance when Charles called on her the Sunday before he started to work at E. P. Rush & Company he was disturbed by the thinness of her hands and by her general frailty.

"Charley," she said, as soon as he had kissed her, "are you going to remember those letters in the right-hand drawer of the desk or had I better burn them now?"

344

Of late she had often brought up the subject of letters and once he had asked her what was in them and she had told him they were just old letters. She wanted them burned because she did not want parts of herself drifting around after she was gone. She wanted to go, when she was gone, and not have the family prying into everything.

"Why, no, Aunt Jane," he said, "I wouldn't burn them now," and then she began again about the silver.

"I wish I could get the silver settled once and for all. I had Mary bring it in here this morning and here's the list." It seemed to him that her hand shook more than usual when she picked up the list. "I can't ever seem to get it settled because everything keeps changing."

"Why don't you just leave it?" Charles said. "Everything can't be exactly right."

"I don't know why everything shouldn't be," she answered. "Everything used to be. Now, Charley, come closer." He moved his chair next to hers and took her hand. "Now, tell me once and for all, is Dorothea going to marry that Elbridge Sterne or isn't she?"

"I guess she is, but you know Dorothea, she never talks," Charles said.

"I don't see why she can't make up her mind," she said. "Do you want that teapot, Charley?"

"Dorothea ought to have it," Charles said, "even if she doesn't marry Elbridge Sterne."

"You can have it if you want it, and Dorothea can have the spoons."

"Don't worry about it," Charles said. "Dorothea's used to the idea of getting the teapot."

She sighed and put down the silver list.

"It's a Burt teapot. . . . Charles." She was sitting very straight in her stiff-backed chair with her head half turned toward him. "Are you attentive to Jessica Lovell or aren't you?"

The word "attentive" as she spoke it had a delicate, half archaic sound.

"Yes," he said, "I suppose I'm attentive."

"Well," she said, "I'm glad that someone tells me something. . . . Charles?"

"Yes," he said.

"It isn't anything to be excited about. I'm not excited at all. I hope she is a nice girl, but there's no reason to be excited. Charles." And she picked up the silver list from the table.

"Aunt Jane," he said, "don't bother about the silver."

"I'm not bothering about anything," she answered. "I wish you'd go to the kitchen and call Mary. She never brings my medicine on time. And then you can read to me if you want to."

"All right," Charles said. "What do you want me to read?"

"Why, anything," she answered, "as long as it's reading."

She might have asked so many questions but that was all she ever said and somehow it gave him a warm and pleasant feeling. She said again before he left:

"You might have told me without my asking . . . but I'm not excited at all."

XVI

Shake Off the Shackles of This Tyrant Vice

— GARRICK

WHAT WAS IT that he saw and thought in those last years of the twenties? He must have been oblivious then to nearly everything outside himself, and Clyde had become a background which he had no time to examine. There was no sense of leisure in his recollections, not a single memory of a careless day swimming with the Meaders, no helping Earl Wilkins take his automobile apart, no long dusky evenings talking with Jackie Mason. These and all the other diversions that once made up a Clyde summer were lost to him for good. Everything was still around him in certain fixed positions, but there was no time for content or discontent, because he was too busy living to think of much except immediacy. Everything was just around the corner when once everything had been ahead of him and he had no way of knowing that this would continue to be so. He was already beginning to say to himself that he would not always be so busy, that sooner or later there would be an opportunity to do a few things he wanted to do.

Obviously he must have tried too hard, but at least he was not a prig because he did not have time for priggishness. He was already becoming externally a type which he was to know too well, but at least he always knew it was a type. It was just as well that Jessica was abroad. If she had been in Clyde that summer, he could never have concentrated so fully on E. P. Rush & Company — and what he had learned there was still valuable. The way one earned one's living had little to do with love and all the things one hoped for that were just around the corner. It was better never to take the office home with you. The people one knew in a business way might mingle

347

sometimes with that other life, like oil and vinegar, but they never really mixed. There could be mutual respect and liking and loyalty, but it was safer never to let these merge into friendship if you wanted to get on downtown.

On his way home in the train Charles often reread Jessica's letters. She was in London, darling, and she wished he were there in large, scrawling strokes. She was in Paris, darling, looking over the Place de la Concorde, and she had bought an old book for him and she wished that he were there. She was in the *châteaux* country, darling, and in Rome, darling. She could not wait to get home, but they were staying a little longer. They were coming back in September — no, in October. Truthfully, there was not much time to remember Jessica, but she was safe around the corner. There was so much else without Jessica that he sometimes wondered how things would have turned out if she had come home later than she did.

His Aunt Jane had died suddenly in her sleep that summer. The Crawford Mill, where his father had worked so long, had folded up, and John Gray was going into Boston every day when October came around. The house had been painted and equipped with electric lights and there were cigars in the parlor. Dorothea was definitely engaged to Elbridge Sterne. In August Charles had been moved into a new department at E. P. Rush designed to give investment advice to clients and to compete with the investment counsel services which were becoming popular.

Mr. Blashfield had nearly settled the details of his aunt's estate. The furnishings at Gow Street had been sold or divided. He and his father were wearing mourning bands, although his Aunt Jane had especially asked them not to. The legacies had been paid, and John Gray was the residuary legatee. His aunt had died less than a week after hearing the news that the mill was closing, but no one could say that the news had upset her. She had spoken of it, Charles remembered, one of the last times he had seen her.

"It's just as well I sold my shares," she said. "John always said it would happen."

It was, of course, what his father had been saying for years.

He would have sold out his mill stock long ago if it had not been held in trust, and he had asked Hugh Blashfield again and again to sell it — but John Gray had not lost his temper when the mill went into receivership.

"There isn't anything to say, Hugh," was all he said. "Dorothea's getting married and Charles is working and I suppose Jane can give Esther and me a small allowance, but you might admit that I was right."

It was not fair or just to pry into his father's thoughts when his sister died. There was always something indecent about thoughts at such a time, because they were too much like the cool, bland passages of a Victorian novel, but at least there was no hypocrisy in the way his father took the news. He said that Jane always did the right thing at the right time, but his voice broke when he said it.

"I'll look after the funeral," he said. "I'm always good about funerals, Esther, and I don't mind undertakers," but his voice broke again. "Do you remember what Jane was always saying? She doesn't want any artificial grass around the grave."

She had wanted "Sunset and evening star" and she did not want gladiolas if she died in summer.

Charles wished that she had not discussed her will and arrangements so often for somehow all that discussion made him more conscious of her now that she was gone than he had been when she was living. She still seemed to have duties to perform before she could step back decorously into the past, and she still seemed to be watching to see whether everything was being done the way she had wanted it.

He was sure that she had been there at Gow Street when he had gone with Dorothea to the house to look over the furniture. Everything was still in its place, arranged by Mary Callahan exactly as Miss Jane had wanted it, and Mary herself was crying in the kitchen. He had the lists with him, but he hated to think of tagging things with other people's names, he hated to touch anything. He was sure that she was there, telling him not to be silly but to burn those

349

letters as she had told him and to destroy those other things of hers that no one else would care about — the pincushion and the sachets in her bureau that her sister Mathilda had made for her one Christmas when they were little girls, and the boat that Johnny had once whittled for her, and her dolls in the attic. She had always said that she did not want parts of herself drifting around after she was gone.

"Don't just stand here," Dorothea said, and she spoke more loudly when he did not answer. "Aren't you going to say something?"

"Let's not start arguing," he said. "She never liked it when we argued."

"We're not arguing," Dorothea said. "What's the matter with you, Charley?"

"Nothing," he said. "Can't I just stand here for a minute?"

"We'd better start with the dining room," Dorothea said, "and leave the study till the end."

The Judge's portrait was looking down at them in the study and Aunt Jane's pills were on a candlestand by her chair.

"Don't be so fussy, Charley," he remembered Dorothea's saying. "You're beginning to act just like her."

And so was Dorothea. She was handling the silver so as not to leave marks on it. She was putting everything she touched back exactly in its place.

The illusion of her presence was even stronger when the family had gathered in Mr. Blashfield's office. His aunt had worked very hard over that will. If the dead ever could return this would, of course, have been the time when she would have insisted on a visit.

Mr. Blashfield had stood on the formality of reading every word of the will instead of simply telling what was in it, as John Gray had suggested. John Gray had said that wills, especially the ones that Hugh Blashfield drew, were becoming constantly duller and correspondingly incomprehensible. He would have enjoyed hearing it if Jane had written it, but if Hugh was going to insist on reading his original composition, they would all come to the office. He could not stand one of those conventional tableaux with the family lawyer sitting in the parlor.

Although John Gray must have known everything that was in

the will, he kept looking at his watch to see what time it was; and when Dorothea suggested that Elbridge Sterne go with the family, he said that Elbridge had been at the grave and that was about enough for Elbridge, considering they weren't married yet.

"Only the four of us are going," he said, "and there's no reason to make a procession of it. Esther, it's five minutes before ten. You and I will go first, and, Charles, you take Dorothea along at ten o'clock."

"What do you mean by Charles's *taking* me?" Dorothea asked.

"I mean that Charles will accompany you," John Gray said, "to 76 Dock Street and upstairs to the first floor. You will turn to the right and open the door marked Hugh Blashfield, Counselor at Law. You're not married to Elbridge Sterne yet."

"There's no reason why you should be horrid about Elbridge," Dorothea said. "You're always making fun of Elbridge."

"Is it making fun of Elbridge," John Gray asked, "to say you're not married to him yet? I'm not even thinking about Elbridge." He pulled out his watch again.

Even if they did not go all four together, everyone who saw them must have known why they were going to the brick building at Number 76.

Number 76 Dock Street was a dingy Romanesque building which must have been constructed in the nineties. Its ground floor was occupied by Setchell's Toggery Shop and by Stevens's hardware store, divided by a flight of stairs that led to the upper floor. Charles nodded to the Toggery Shop, with its window display of ties and summer suiting.

"Do you think Frank Setchell still loves you?" he asked.

"Oh, shut up," Dorothea said, and he could almost believe that Aunt Jane was telling him not to tease Dorothea. She was tired and nervous. Engagements always upset a girl.

The names of the tenants of 76 Dock Street were painted on the wall at the head of the stairs large enough to be easily read in the ill-lighted hall, and pointing fingers were painted after them so that the directory looked like a signboard at a crossroads. If you turned to the left you could visit Dr. J. I. Brush, Dentist, and the whole hall had that sinister odor characteristic of dental parlors; or if you went further to the left you could visit E. C. Meader, Real Estate and Insurance, or further still, the Minnie Persepolis School of Dancing. To the right was Estelle's Beauty Shop and then the office of Hugh Blashfield, Counselor at Law.

Lawyers in Clyde, like the local doctors and dentists, all had their individual public ratings. Hugh Blashfield did work for Johnson Street, such as searching titles and other odd jobs for which it was not necessary to retain someone from Boston. Even if you did not live on Johnson Street but wished to draw a will, Hugh Blashfield was the one to do it, and besides he was the one who handled trust accounts which were not large enough to go to Boston, and who assisted Boston counsel in routine work for Wright-Sherwin and the banks. He was a sensible, reliable family lawyer, to whom you could safely tell family troubles which were not too bizarre or extreme, but he was no good at all on his feet in front of a jury. If you wanted any fighting done or if you were really in a scrape, it was better to keep away from Lawyer Blashfield, as he was called when he was safely out of earshot. The man to see was Martin X. Garrity. Mart was the one who might fix it out of court or if it got into court you could depend on Mart to see you safely through. On the other hand, Counselor Cooker was the one to handle a dignified damage suit, and the senior of them all, Judge Morby, could represent you in arguments before the probate court. There was a lawyer for each contingency, and each of them knew his place.

Katie Rowell, who had been with Hugh Blashfield for twenty years, was alone in the outer office. Her faded yellowish hair and her freckled nose looked like her golden-oak desk and the yellow shades and the yellow painted woodwork. Both the doors of the tall safe in front of her were open and she kept staring fixedly at the black japanned boxes inside it as though she were afraid that one of them might disappear if she shifted her glance. Charles had seen her at rehearsals of the Clyde Players last winter but Katie, when she greeted them, appeared to have forgotten this and to have forgotten, too, that she and Dorothea were in the same study club, because business came first during business hours.

"Hello, Miss Rowell," Charles said. "Have you been doing much acting lately?"

"No," Katie answered. "Not enough were interested in a summer group. Mr. Blashfield is expecting you and you can step right inside."

In Mr. Blashfield's office, his law books, his diploma and his engraving of the Clyde waterfront all had a confidential veneer which indicated that nothing that might be said would go farther than the room and that plenty had been said in it. Mr. Blashfield was seated in a golden-oak chair at the head of a long table with Charles's parents on either side of him. He was holding the will, a blue-bound document, informally but respectfully in his left hand. When he saw Dorothea and Charles he pushed back his chair noisily on the battleship linoleum and stood up and patted his double-breasted suit into place as though he were going to address a meeting.

"I don't believe I've had an opportunity to congratulate you on your happy news, Dorothea," he said. "Elbridge Sterne is such a fine young man, and how is everything going in Boston, Charley?"

There was an odd moment of hesitation as they all gathered around the table. Though he obviously wanted to read the will and though they all wished to hear it, at the same time it did not seem correct to be too precipitate.

"That last paper of yours at the Confessional Club was first-rate, John," Mr. Blashfield said. "I think it is one of your best."

"Why, thank you, Hugh," John Gray answered.

"A good reminiscent paper is a whole lot better than something cribbed from the *Encyclopædia Britannica,*" Mr. Blashfield went on. "I suppose we all have a weakness for reminiscence, especially as we grow older. Now before we start I should like to say, aside from anything professional, how touched I am that Miss Jane wanted me to carry out her wishes. I remember her so well when we were boys, John, though of course we were younger."

"Yes," John Gray said, "we were, but I think Jane would like you to get on with it. She would tell you so if she were here."

Mr. Blashfield smiled in a kindly way to show that he remembered the definiteness of Miss Jane and Charles found himself looking at the empty chair at the other end of the table.

"Well, I suppose she would," Mr. Blashfield said, and he opened the blue-covered document. "Stop me if there are any questions . . ."

"I, Jane Gray, of Clyde, Massachusetts, in the County of — " His quiet voice was the only sound in the room. It was like the reading of a Clerk of the Court, which was probably what Mr. Blashfield intended. It was dull, as John Gray said it would be, but anyone could understand it — two thousand dollars to Mary Callahan, ten thousand dollars to Esther Gray, five thousand to Dorothea and five thousand to himself, and the remainder to John Gray.

Charles was thinking of the power of money and the respectful way one always spoke of it when sums above a certain amount were mentioned. It could arouse jealousy and dislike and all sorts of other small unpleasant thoughts. It was only decent to have gratitude, but the will, as Mr. Blashfield read it, had no human quality. It was Mr. Blashfield, not his aunt, who had been speaking. It was only Mr. Blashfield's pedantic interpretation of all her worries, consolidated into rotund legal phrases. Charles straightened himself in his chair and looked across the table at his father. He was disturbed by his father's expression. It was one of deep, almost indecent relief.

"Good old Jane," he said.

"It's a simple will," Mr. Blashfield answered. "Now if you have any questions — " Charles saw his father lean forward.

"Just one question, Hugh," he said. "I am right, am I, in understanding the remainder is left to me without any strings attached?"

Charles found himself gripping the arms of his chair nervously. He saw his mother's head turn sharply, and Mr. Blashfield's pale, rather dull face had a stiffer look as he glanced up from the paper.

"Yes, that's right, John," he said. "Miss Jane wanted it that way" — he cleared his throat — "though I advised her differently."

"I suppose you did," John Gray answered. "Good old Jane. Can you give me some idea of the amount?"

Mr. Blashfield cleared his throat again.

"I called on Mr. Thomas yesterday. After the legacies, debits and taxes, I should say approximately seventy-five thousand dollars, at the present market." He mentioned the sum diffidently, trying to hedge it around with words.

"Well, well," John Gray said. "I didn't know Ralph had done as well as that. When can I expect to get any of this, Hugh? Perhaps you know the Gray family is short of cash. The mill, you know."

"As soon as it goes through probate, John," Mr. Blashfield answered.

"That may take a year," John Gray said, "but I suppose I could raise a slight loan?"

Charles felt a faint shiver run up his spine. He hated the sound of his father's voice. It was his first close experience with such a sum of money. It was small compared with sums in customers' accounts at Rush & Company, but it had a peculiar value because they were all involved. It was something to be guarded and not to be spoken of with levity. It was nothing on which one should raise a slight loan.

"Why, yes," Hugh Blashfield said, "I suppose I can advance you something, John — or the bank can. I'll speak to Ralph Thomas."

"I shall want a very substantial sum," John Gray said.

"Oh, John," his mother said suddenly, "please don't try to borrow anything."

"Now, Esther," John Gray began. "Now, Esther," and Hugh Blashfield cleared his throat again.

"I know I'm not the one to talk, John," he said, "but don't you think — "

His father shook his head.

"I know, Hugh," he answered, "but I've done quite a lot of thinking myself, for quite a term of years. If you could arrange for me to have something this afternoon, I should appreciate it very much, and we can discuss then methods of paying me the balance." He paused and lowered his voice. "Remember, Hugh, I always wanted to sell that mill stock."

Charles felt himself sitting rigidly, still gripping the arms of his chair. John Gray looked at his watch.

"I think we've covered everything for the moment," he said. "I'll be in again this afternoon, Hugh. I'm always glad to hear your ideas, and thank you very much."

He must have forgotten that they should not look like a delegation because they all walked down the stairs of 76 Dock Street in a body and out into the hot summer sunlight.

"It was so sweet of Jane," Esther Gray was saying to Dorothea. "I'm glad she told me first and I'm glad I thanked her."

"Well, well," John Gray said. "These wills. I wish the lawyers could write testaments in verse like François Villon."

"Father," Charles said, "there's something I'd like to talk to you about when we get home."

It was absolutely necessary to take up the subject of that money. The money which had been left them was a product of self-denial and steady planning, something which had been saved and earned, something to be treated with decent respect.

"That is, if you don't mind," he said.

It was a hot summer's day and through the open windows of his father's room he could hear the drowsy sound of a lawn mower in the Sullivans' yard and the patient plodding of a draft horse and the rattle of one of the Mullins Company ice wagons on Spruce Street. The room, with its untidy collection of books and unrelated objects, was like his father's mind. John Gray was already moving about, searching for something in much the same way he ransacked his memory for an apt and comfortable quotation.

"Now wait a minute," he said. "Where the devil is it? Oh, here it is." He had found the case and the decanters of his port wine under a pile of newspapers. It was obviously an occasion for him.

"I know it's early in the day," he said, "but I think I'll have a glass of port. It's sweet and sticky but I need some sort of mild stimulant to get over Hugh Blashfield. Will you join me, Charley?"

"No, thanks," Charles answered, "only don't let me stop you," but John Gray was absorbed in his own ideas.

"All right," he said, "I don't blame you, Charley. Of course, Hugh Blashfield and all of this"—he waved his hand in a vague, expansive way—"doesn't have the same effect on you as it has on me. Going to a lawyer is like going to a doctor. No matter how well or how long you know them personally, they always put you at a disadvantage because of their specialized knowledge. I'd rather have a good, dry chat with a clergyman. He may know about God and sin, but God and sin are a sort of public domain and no one knows definitely about them. But a lawyer always knows about law and a doctor knows exactly where your spleen is and there's nothing whatsoever that one can do about them except sit respectfully and listen. Now I know all about Hugh Blashfield personally."

It was obvious that he was annoyed by Hugh Blashfield and that it would be impossible to divert him from the subject.

"I couldn't help thinking as I sat there this morning that Hugh Blashfield was a painfully small-minded man. I must have told him twenty times to sell that mill stock. He's plodding and rudimentary, without a single broad, long thought. I used to help him with his Latin and his algebra, and he always has trouble with women. I know all his frailties, and yet there he was, reading my sister's will. There's something queer about a lawyer in his office, but never mind it," and then a taste of the sacramental wine distracted his attention. "You know, I think it might be a good idea if we bought some Scotch whisky. Mel Stevens keeps running it in. I don't know why I shouldn't go around and see Mel this afternoon — we ought to have electric lights, and we really ought to have a car, Charley. I don't know why we shouldn't have a car now."

He paused and in the silence Charles could hear the lawn mower.

"Father," he began, and John Gray sighed.

"Oh, yes," he said. "You wanted to ask me about something, didn't you?"

Charles cleared his throat, but even so his voice was hoarse.

"Father," he said again, "what are you going to do with Aunt Jane's money? Are you going to play the market with it?"

His father looked watchful. It was bluntly stated, but it was an issue, and his father had always been skillful in avoiding issues.

"How about a cigar, Charley?" he asked. "Let me see. There must be some around somewhere. If there aren't, I'll have to go down to the news store, but they haven't got Havanas."

"Father," Charles said, "are you or aren't you?"

John Gray finally faced the issue, and as he did so a film of cloud passed across his sun.

"It's rather like the old question of whether you have stopped beating your wife, isn't it?" he asked. "Everybody who makes an investment plays the market. I suppose I might tell you it's none of your business. I'm tempted to, but I won't."

There was another silence, a long, unpleasant silence.

"I don't like to talk to you this way," Charles said, and his father nodded and his voice was warm and kind again.

"I know you don't," he said. "That's all right."

"You know it's everybody's business," Charles began. "I don't care about myself, but what about Mother and Dorothea?"

He saw his father's face flush and then he saw him fold his hands.

"Well, go ahead and tell me why I shouldn't. Do the best you can."

Charles could only say what anyone would have said. The market was like a wild river, that year, breaking through all the dams of prudence and common sense. Prices of common stocks had already discounted all conceivable earnings in any foreseeable future. The market might still go up, but it was already dangerous. It was time to invest in sound bonds, preferably governments. There was bound to be a break. It was only a question of when.

"You put it very clearly, Charley," John Gray said. "Do you know what I begin to think? You may be a good investment man someday. You're dead right, but it's all a matter of self-restraint. I know when to stop — but you don't believe that, do you?" He was going to be careful. He was watching the market, and he knew the market. He was going to get in and out.

Charles did not answer. There was no use saying aloud that he did not believe him.

"Let's leave it this way. You can watch me, and I'll be careful, Charley."

When it came to money, everyone always promised to be careful. In fact, it often seemed to Charles that most of his subsequent life had been spent in a series of timid, hedging precautions, in balancing probable gains and losses in order to keep sums of money intact. The probity, the reliability and the sobriety that such a task demanded were to make his own life dull and careful. Except for a few brief moments, he was to face no danger or uncalculated risk.

He was to measure his merriment and hedge on his tragedies. He was to water down elation and mitigate disaster, and to be at the right place at the right time, and to say the right thing with the right emphasis. Yet whenever he thought of himself as a dull, deluded opportunist, compared with other people, he always remembered the intensity of his own feelings when his father had been speaking. There had been a hideous sense of inevitable disaster, and no possible way to stop it.

There was no point in pleading, because his father was growing angry, and Charles could hear their voices, each rising against the other.

"All right, Charley," his father said. "I understand you perfectly and you needn't shout. How are you going to get anywhere if you never take a chance? What is life but a chance, Charley? After all, what is seventy-five thousand dollars? Do you expect me to live on the income, at four per cent?" He shrugged his shoulders. He opened his hands and closed them. Did Charles really want his mother to live on three thousand dollars a year? And what was it Samuel Johnson said?

"A man who both spends and saves money is the happiest man, because he has both enjoyments."

That was what he was going to do, both spend and save. As soon as he made a profit, and any fool could make a profit in this bull market, he would put the original sum in a bank, he swore he would, and he would go on with the rest. And what was that quotation in Thomas Fuller's *Gnomologia* about its being better to have a hen tomorrow than an egg today?

"A hen," John Gray said. "You can't stop me, Charley. It's the first chance I've ever had, the first real chance, to beat the system."

It was not worth while trying to stop him, now that he was talking about the system.

"When is Jessica coming back, in October? All right, we'll have a Cadillac by October. Don't look as though I were hurting you, Charley. I'm going to spend and save and it's perfectly possible."

There was no use in being angry, there was no use in being hurt.

"There was always that pony," Charles said.

"Oh, yes," John Gray said. "I'd forgotten about the pony. Well, he's growing now, Charley. I've given this a great deal of thought, but it might be just as well if you didn't mention this to your mother."

"Don't worry, I won't," Charles said.

"Come to think of it," John Gray said, "I might as well go up to Boston tomorrow, and, Charley, I wonder whether you would do something for me now, that is if you don't mind? Would you mind going downtown and seeing if the *New York Times* has come in yet and would you please stop at Southern's and buy me a small account book? I'm the one who's going to do the worrying, Charley."

Then, just before Charles reached the door, his father called him back. He had settled himself comfortably in his Morris chair, with one knee crossed over the other, and everything he had said seemed to have been erased already. The magnificence of his thoughts made him look like a New York customer of E. P. Rush & Company. He looker richer than Mr. Thomas at the bank and more distinguished than Mr. Laurence Lovell.

"Charles," he said, "I've just thought of another quotation, which won't ever appear in a gnomologia. You'll like this one. 'Everybody's doing it now.' "

Charles must have known that morning that his aunt's legacy was as good as gone. There was no use going to anyone for advice and it was pointless to tell his mother and Dorothea what he knew. He walked out of the front door and stared for a long while at Spruce Street, at the elms with their leaves drooping in the summer heat, and at the heat waves shimmering on the shingles of the Masons' roof. While he stood there at the front yard gate, he conceived a fear and contempt for certain aspects of finance, but it was a respectful contempt. He was afraid of money and he never lost that fear, and it was not a bad attitude, either, if you had to deal with investments — caution and contempt held together by respect. He was thinking of his mother and Dorothea in the house. He was trying, for the first time in his life, to cut a loss. He was thinking of the five thousand dollars his aunt had left him, an immense sum in one way and so insignificant in another, and someone had to do something. At least he was sure that he knew when to stop.

That was his only reason for playing the stock market that next year, a desperate and feeble reason. Circumstances forced him and he did it without satisfaction, as though he were engaged in a secret vice. It was interesting, sometimes, to imagine what would have happened to his mother and indirectly to Dorothea if he had not, or if he had not known when to stop, but it was hardly worth the time. Nothing could have altered what happened in Clyde, though he did not know it then.

XVII

If You Can Dream — and Not Make Dreams Your Master . . .

— RUDYARD KIPLING

NEARLY EVERYONE in Rush & Company was in the market and it may have been just as well that he was in it too, for it afforded a common ground on which to meet all those others who had come there to learn what was called finance. It was an era of apprenticeship, when most people preferred to pick up their knowledge by firsthand experience, backed only, perhaps, by a course in Economics I at Harvard. Finance still had the aura of a gentleman's profession, particularly in Boston. All those young men in Rush & Company, whom Charles knew and whose manners he studied so carefully once, were there because gentlemen handled the broader aspects of money. They did not count it or set it down in figures as the tellers did and the bookkeepers, who, whatever their abilities, could only by the most outside accident rise out of these departments to compete with the young men in the open spaces. In military terms, these latter were the officer class, who might be partners and bank officers some day.

They were a class not trained to realities and they were not, he often thought, well fitted to cope with the depression. The early thirties made gaps in their ranks, as though they had been hit by round shot and canister, and he still knew the crippled casualties of those days, the limpers, the spiritually legless and the armless. The truth was that finance, using that inclusive term for partners, bond salesmen, and bank presidents, was not entirely a gentleman's game, though it demanded as a rule the code of ethics and morality associated with a gentleman. However, all the temptations and spiritual stresses and strains which came later with the depression were negligible when Charles worked in E. P. Rush & Company with what Lawrence Stoker, the head of the bond department, called the Team.

Football men and crew men were somehow the most desirable material at E. P. Rush & Company and it seemed to Charles that all of the team came from what were known as final clubs at Harvard. He only learned these facts gradually but later he realized that they were important in a business way and he faced them without rancor. He had nothing in common with the team, except the market and the routine of the office, but he was sufficiently one of them so that he might listen when they talked to each other and about each other. His position on the team reminded him of the story of the man who maintained that the Harvard crew was democratic because after three years everyone in the boat spoke to him except number seven.

They were nice — the boys on the team at E. P. Rush — and they seemed to accept cheerfully the fact that he had to be more ambitious and brighter than the rest of them, much as Charles himself had accepted the same thing with a Chinese or a Japanese student in a college class. They even seemed pleased that he was getting on. There was none of that sense of competition and knifing in the back that he was to know later. They were nice boys and they began calling him by his first name — after a decent period.

Although he looked like most of the team, he knew that he would always stand out from them, and it had been just as well, even in E. P. Rush. He was not too different from the rest to have that difference disturbing, but he was different enough sometimes to be noticed. If he had not been a little apart, Arthur Slade would never have noticed him that time when Mr. Slade came on some errand from New York, and he told Charles so long afterwards.

"I saw you right away," he said, "and I said to myself, how did he ever get in here? But I said it in a very nice way. I wondered if you could be a Yale man, but that could not have been possible in E. P. Rush. It explained everything when you said you came from Dartmouth."

* * *

363

There was every reason to remember his first meeting with Arthur Slade, for had it not occurred he might never have gone to New York. Certainly he would never have been given his chance in the Stuyvesant Bank at the time when banks were firing instead of hiring. There would have been no Nancy, no children, no house in Sycamore Park. Instead, he might have stayed on in Rush & Company and married some girl in the Newtons, perhaps, and have been living now in one of those tapestry-brick Colonials, forgotten by people like E. P. Rush partners after business hours. Finally he would have been like all those other useful Boston wheel horses who knew the business like the palms of their hands and came through in a pinch and who disappeared daily behind a curtain of suburban life. He would have been Charley Gray, an agreeable and reliable person, whom you could trust to do anything. Mr. Rush would have invited him to his lunch club now and then, but never in the world would he have become a member. It would have been a pity that he did not have quite the background or connections to have made him partnership material. There was every reason why he should have remembered every detail of his meeting with Arthur Slade.

Charles's desk was about midway in the center of the open office and one September morning when he was reading market letters he heard Mr. Rush speaking, but he did not look up.

"It will only be what you've seen already," Mr. Rush was saying. He had brought a stranger with him to the investment advisory department.

"Oh, Gray," Mr. Rush called. "Mr. Slade wants to see everything we have on —" and he gave the name of that foreign stock which later was to make so many people poorer. "Gray will get you everything, and you can read it here if you want to."

"Yes, sir," Charles said, and he hurried to the files for the folders.

"I think there are a few rather frank office notes on it," Mr. Rush said. "Go ahead and read them, but don't quote us."

Mr. Rush walked away, leaving the stranger from New York. Mr. Slade must have come in from New York on the "Owl" but he did not show it. He was, of course, an imitation of Tony Burton, like everyone else in the Stuyvesant Bank. His dark hair, appropriately gray at the temples, was closely clipped, like Tony Burton's. His dark gray flannel suit had the style of Tony Burton's tailor. His face had Tony Burton's authoritative alertness. His whole appearance was like that song parody which Charles wrote later about walking and talking and dressing like Tony Burton. The Stuyvesant Bank was printed on Arthur Slade, indelibly, magnificently, an imprint distinguishable from anything in Boston.

"Wouldn't you like to use my desk, sir?" Charles asked.

"Oh no," the stranger said. "Go on with what you're doing," and he sat beside the desk reading, while Charles went back to the market letters. Mr. Slade did not speak again for three quarters of an hour.

"Dear me," he said, when he had finished, and Charles saw he was holding a memorandum in Mr. Rush's handwriting, "you certainly have a personalized investment service."

"Yes, sir," Charles answered.

"Well," Mr. Slade said, "I'm much obliged to you. You'd better put that away and lock it up." He was smiling and Charles did not like the suggestion because it somehow seemed to reflect on Rush & Company.

"You know I was told to show it to you," Charles said.

"I know you were," Mr. Slade answered, "but I hope you won't leave it around."

"We don't leave things around here much," Charles said, and he sat up straighter because he was a member of the team.

"It's about time for lunch, isn't it?" Mr. Slade said. "How about your coming over with me to the Parker House?"

Arthur Slade must have been curious about Rush & Company, because he asked a good many questions, Charles remembered, and Charles answered them as he should have, politely and loyally. When Arthur Slade asked him about himself, he told him that he lived at Clyde, and Mr. Slade had never heard of Clyde.

"I suppose you're in this market like everyone else," Arthur Slade said.

"Yes," Charles answered. "It's all a question of when to stop, isn't it?"

He said that the market did not interest him as it did his father, and he began talking to Arthur Slade about his father, a safe subject because Arthur Slade would never meet him. Perhaps he spoke with the clumsy confidence of anyone his age, but whenever he thought of that lunch at the Parker House, he was never entirely sure that he had been clumsy. There was no reason to show himself in any sort of light or to strive to make a good impression, and besides he did not feel like a callow young man from Rush & Company.

"There's no such thing as unbiased advice from an investment house that markets securities," Arthur Slade had said. "It's a little like selling patent medicine that can be used externally and internally, for baldness, dandruff, muscular pains, and stomach-ache. Now in this investment advisory thing of yours, doesn't Rush recommend its own securities? Of course it does. It can't help it. All bond houses recommend Telephone and Tobacco B and General Electric and some railroad bonds and then they slip something of their own into the package."

It was true, of course, but Charles was loyal to Rush & Company.

"If you believe in what you're selling," he said, "why shouldn't you recommend it?"

"Now, it's different in a bank trust department. We haven't got anything to sell." Arthur Slade took a thin gold cigarette case from his pocket and opened it and laid it on the table.

"Don't you ever get stuck with anything in a bank?" Charles asked.

"Not usually," Arthur Slade said, and he smiled. "Not in our bank. Did you ever think of working in a bank?"

Charles shook his head. "No, I've got too much else to think about where I am."

It never crossed his mind that Arthur Slade might be offering him a job. As he looked about that solid, conventional room, the face of Arthur Slade stood out from all the other faces and Charles wished that he could ever manage to be like him. There was irony in the recollection, but a pleasant sort of irony for there at the Parker House it was like seeing himself mirrored in the future. He was not so far now from being like Arthur Slade, though without his money and without his game of tennis and without his place on Long Island, but he, too, could dress and talk like Tony Burton. Perhaps you always picked a hero when you were in your twenties, and Arthur Slade was the best trust officer he had ever known. Yet back there at the Parker House, Arthur Slade was still an impeccable stranger from New York, whom he would never see again, and lunch was nearly over, like all those other workday luncheons which he was to know so well later. It was time to get back to Rush & Company. No one liked it if you stayed too long for lunch.

"Some people think that banking's dull," Arthur Slade was saying, "but I've never found it dull. It's a matter of perspective. There's only one trouble about it." He stopped and lit a cigarette. "You get pressed from the bottom and the top. Something always hems you in."

As Arthur Slade was speaking, Charles saw his father walking toward them between the tables, with his hair and his mustache freshly clipped, and Charles's attention wandered.

"Oh," he said, "there's my father."

"Where?" Mr. Slade asked, but his father was already at the table and they both stood up. John Gray smelled pleasantly of bay rum and he was smoking a cigar. He remembered Arthur Slade's smile as they shook hands and he had that fear one always had about one's parents — that his father might say something startling or out of place.

"Won't you sit down and have coffee with us?" Mr. Slade asked.

"That's very kind of you," John Gray answered, "but I'd better be getting back to work. Perhaps I'll see you on the five-twenty, Charley."

John Gray smiled and nodded and walked away. He had said nothing significant, but Charles was always glad that Arthur Slade had met his father.

"He looks happy," Arthur Slade said.

"Yes," Charles answered. "Father is usually happy."

"It's curious how few people are," Arthur Slade said. "Have you ever thought of working in New York?"

Charles grew familiar enough with those luncheons later. It had been his duty, especially just before the war, to look for promising material and to size up individuals as candidates for minor executive positions in the Stuyvesant Bank, just as Arthur Slade must have been doing then. The technique was always the same. The Stuyvesant at its executive level was very much like an exclusive club, requiring of a candidate certain definite standards for admission. You watched his hands as he held his knife and fork, the expression of his eyes when your glances met. As you listened to the inflections of his voice, you tried to think of his possible behavior under the strain of exasperation or temptation. Discretion, loyalty and trustworthiness were, of course, among those standards, but there were others less susceptible of definition, such as his attitude toward money. He could not have the businessman's greed or anxiety for profit if he was to be in the crowd. He could not covet money, but at the same time he must respect it in an impersonal way, as an astronomer might think of light-years in interstellar space. It was hard to tell, even after long acquaintance, whether someone would fit into the Stuyvesant, but the method of selection was always the same.

"Have you ever thought," Arthur Slade had asked him, "of working in New York?"

Later Charles knew the technique perfectly, because afterward he had been in the position of both the watcher and the watched. In later years, just before and just after the war, he was used to being asked to lunch by someone from the City or the Chase or some other bank, and there was always that aimless conversation about how busy one was, what one did on Sunday, the Securities and Exchange Commission, anything at all. Then, if everything went well, just at the end of lunch there was always that question. Had he ever thought of moving over to some larger bank like the Chase, or whatever bank it might be, where there was a real future? Frankly, without mentioning names, a lot of the crowd had been talking him over. He was just the material that they wanted. Of course, if he was happy where he was, think no more about it, but at the same time, this was a real chance and it was not offered to everyone. They were not advertising in the papers; they wanted a particular man named Charley Gray and, if he wanted, he could write his ticket. He had better think it over.

He was used to those offers and they always made him happy and he always knew what to say. The Stuyvesant was a small bank, but he was used to it. He knew the office politics. He wouldn't know his way around anywhere else, and of course they wanted him because he was not available. You always wanted someone who was doing well and who was loyal to his crowd.

Had he ever thought of working in New York? He must have told more about himself to Arthur Slade than he could remember and perhaps that glimpse of his father had rounded the impression — but there was no appeal at all in the idea of going to New York.

"No, I haven't thought of it," he said. "I like it pretty well where I am, but thanks ever so much for the lunch. I've had a very good time."

"Well," he remembered that Arthur Slade answered, "if you should be in New York, stop and look me up. Just tell Joe inside the door you want to see me."

His father was keeping a seat for him in the smoking car of the five-twenty. He had evidently been shopping after the market had closed because there were a few carefully wrapped packages on the rack above his head.

"I happened to see two silver gravy boats in an antique shop," he said. "Your mother has always wanted a pair, and then I saw a small radio. Who was that Mr. Slade you were having luncheon with, Charley?"

"He came to see Mr. Rush about something," Charles said. "He comes from New York."

"Of course he comes from New York. Anyone can see he does. You know, if things would quiet down a little, Charles, and if you could get away for a day or two, we ought to go down to New York. There's nothing like the night boat — a good dinner and a quiet sleep and there you are. He was a banker, wasn't he?"

"How did you know that?" Charles asked.

"Because they're as easy to tell as clergymen. They have a slightly antiseptic, sanctimonious look, and yet they don't look like lawyers."

"How did things work out today, Father?" Charles asked.

John Gray tilted his hat away from his forehead.

"Oh," he said, "everything went very well."

The smoking car of the five-twenty was an old car with uncomfortable seats and painfully creaking woodwork, and its worn wheels made it sway on the rails with a rhythm of its own. Three million share days and the Parker House and especially Arthur Slade had nothing to do with the stale tobacco smoke and the pitch players and the elderly brakeman who was always watching the card games.

"If we only had a good car and a chauffeur," his father said, "I don't see why he couldn't drive us back to Clyde in good weather."

"We haven't got a car or chauffeur," Charles said.

"I didn't say we had," his father said. "I was just saying we might get one. Charley, you're looking rather tired." His father was looking at him not impersonally, as he did so often, but in a kindly, interested way. "If I were you I wouldn't push too hard."

"How do you mean?" Charles asked.

"It doesn't pay. It isn't worth it," his father said. "You can't beat the system that way, Charley." Sooner or later John Gray's mind was always back there.

"You can't beat it your way either," Charles said. "I hope you're being careful."

His father laughed and slapped him on the knee.

"As careful as a banker," he said. "I'm as sound as Electric Bond and Share."

It was strange to think how little seemed unusual in those days, perhaps because nothing seems peculiar in any present. Lindbergh had flown the Atlantic. Human flies were scaling the exteriors of office buildings. Flagpole sitters were perched on their poles like Simeon Stylites, and marathon dancers were fainting in the clinches. They were all phenomena which one could accept. Nothing was ever very peculiar at the moment when it happened.

Charles was not particularly surprised, for instance, at an extraordinary episode that occurred one Sunday at church, shortly after he had met Arthur Slade; or if he was surprised at least it was appropriate to the contemporary scene. For years he had gone to the Unitarian Church with his mother and Dorothea. It was a habit of childhood, something which was expected of him and a part of Sunday, but his father seldom went with them. His father always said that church was a very good thing and that he approved of it entirely. He would have been glad to go to church if it had not been for Mr. Crewe. It might be all right for Esther and Dorothea and for Charles to listen to Mr. Crewe, but it always gave him an unholy reaction. He did not want to have Mr. Crewe telling him how to be good in a Unitarian way. He was not at all sure that Mr. Crewe knew much about goodness, because Mr. Crewe did not know anything about badness. He was not able to visualize the powers of evil.

Besides, he used to say, what was Unitarianism? He was in no position, not for a minute, to embark on a theological discussion or to criticize the tenets of a religion embraced by Emerson, Channing, and Samuel McChord Crothers. As a religion it was an obvious and enlightened outgrowth of the New England Congregationalist faith which had attracted his ancestors to these shores. He was willing to admit, too, that his own father had been a Unitarian and so had the Marchbys. He had been to Sunday School himself in the room behind the organ loft, and he had been married in the church. He realized also that a belief in the brotherhood of man and in the general progress of mankind, onward and upward forever, was a stabilizing influence, good for him and for everybody else, particularly for the children. He would have been glad to consider this mild dogma every Sunday and even listen to the asthmatic sound of the organ and to swelter with cold feet beside the hot-air stove in winter if it had not been necessary to have Mr. Crewe tell him about it. He simply could not follow Mr. Crewe's train of thought and instead of trying to follow it he found himself thinking instead of all sorts of things that had nothing to do with church or the possibilities of immortality. The best thing about Unitarianism was that there was no compulsion about attending its services — none at least for him. When it came to Charles and Dorothea it was different. If their mother wanted them to go to church, they had better go.

When John Gray came down to breakfast that Sunday morning, he was wearing a new double-breasted suit.

"I think it looks rather well, don't you, Esther?" he said. "Why are you looking at me in that critical way, Charles? Is there anything wrong with it?"

There was nothing wrong with it except that its impeccable newness and the careful tailoring of the coat gave his father the disconcertingly streamlined appearance of a figure in a fashion plate.

"Why, John," Esther Gray said, "you didn't tell me you'd bought a new suit. You look as though you'd stepped out of something."

"It's a surprise," John Gray said. "A new leaf, Esther."

"You're not going to church with us, are you?" Dorothea asked.

"I don't see why I shouldn't," John Gray answered. "It's been in the back of my mind." He sat down and stirred his coffee slowly. "It just occurred to me that a morning in church might do me good. You never can tell till you try."

"But, John," Esther Gray began, and her forehead wrinkled. "Why did it come over you this morning?"

"I'm sure I don't know why, Esther," John Gray said. "It must be some sort of compulsion."

"John," she asked, "why are you going?"

Charles could understand his mother's uneasiness. There was something unstable and bizarre about the morning.

"I'm sure I don't know," his father said again. "Let's say I have a new sense of spiritual responsibility this morning that demands direct action. After all, why shouldn't I go to church? I do believe in the institution, Esther."

It would have been like any other Sunday if John Gray had not been with them. The church was a hundred years old, a beautiful church, and its white woodwork with the delicate moldings, consciously devoid of all clerical richness, gave a sense of repressed peace and of serene plainness that must have been a part of an older, Puritanical tradition. The bell was ringing but Charles was more conscious of its vibrations than of its sound, which only accentuated the stillness and the cool, white light that came through the tall, plain windows. There were not more than fifty persons in the box pews, distributed unevenly, with large areas of unoccupied space between them. The church had been built for a larger congregation but its very vacancy added to his general sense of peace. He found himself thinking, as he had as a boy, of invisible presences in the vacant gallery and in the empty pews. The past and the present always seemed to meet when the bell was ringing.

A spareness and a graceful restraint in all its detail, which reflected the old, deliberate attempt of its builders to eradicate any hint of papacy, gave the building its own peculiar sense of freedom and gave to Charles a feeling of personal loneliness that somehow was not disturbing. He always seemed to be drawn inside himself in those first silent moments, and his mother and Dorothea and his father were like strangers to him, cloaked in a sudden aloofness. The Meaders, three pews in front, and the Masons, to the right, and Mr. and Mrs. Howell, just below the tall white pulpit with its double winding stairs, did not look like weekday people. Though they were together, they were all alone with their thoughts. Mr. Crewe had climbed the stairs to the pulpit and now he stood, a small figure, high above them.

"Let us unite in singing," he was saying in his reedy voice, and the service began, an unadorned, rational service which had little beauty except in its plainness and which relied on little else to bring conviction.

"When two or three are gathered together," Mr. Crewe was saying, and Charles glanced at his father, still incredulous that he was there. Later he heard his father repeating the Lord's Prayer, in a voice which seemed to him unduly loud, and when they came to the responsive reading he was conscious again of his father's voice, more deliberate than the other voices, not to be hastened by others' haste. He saw Dorothea glance up nervously from her book. His father was enjoying the words of the Psalms for their own sake and he clearly did not care how rapidly others might slur over them. In church, as everywhere else, he was unwilling to conform and this did not disturb him in the least. He was reading the Psalm the way he wished it read and not the way the Masons or the Meaders or anyone else cared to read it.

"The lines are fallen unto me in pleasant places; yea, I have a goodly heritage."

His father spoke the last words, serenely and unabashed, long after everyone else had finished, and Charles knew that everyone there would speak of it later.

"Dear me," Charles heard him whisper as they sat down, "how they mumble."

When it was time for the offering, the organ in the loft played wheezily while Mr. Howell, Mr. Meader and Mr. Blashfield walked to the table in front of the pulpit. Each of them picked up a wooden contribution box, holding it gingerly by its long handle, and each walked down the aisle with self-conscious precision, their shoes and the boards beneath them both creaking. There was the usual furtive rustling sound above the music. His mother and Dorothea were opening their purses and he saw his father draw a wallet from inside his new double-breasted coat. It was a pigskin billfold, aggressively new, and his father flipped it open carelessly. Mr. Blashfield, conscientious and perspiring slightly, halted at the pew and pushed the box impersonally in their direction. Then Charles saw Mr. Blashfield's back stiffen. His father had taken a bill from his wallet and had dropped it in the contribution box. It was a hundred-dollar gold treasury note. Then he leaned back, gazing upward at the American flag and the service flag which hung suspended from the balcony. Mr. Blashfield paused uncertainly before he took the box away and at the same time Charles heard his mother draw a sharp, indignant breath. In a little while, perhaps even before the sermon was over, everyone would know about the hundred-dollar bill.

Outside the church, in the September sunlight, everyone spoke to everyone else agreeably.

"Well, John," Mr. Blashfield said, just as though he had not passed the contribution box, "it's nice to see you in church."

"I suppose I should go more often," he heard his father answer. "I really suppose I should."

"John," he heard his mother say, "we'll have to be going now or dinner will be late." She did not speak about the hundred-dollar bill

374

until they were on Dock Street. "If you wanted to do that," she said, "at least you might have put it in an envelope."

"I know, Esther," John Gray answered, "I know. It was vulgar ostentation. I apologize to everybody. I'm sorry."

"You're not sorry," she answered, "because it's why you came."

"That's true," John Gray said. "Of course, that's perfectly true. I've always wanted to do that, Esther, ever since I was a little boy, I know it's childish of me, but I don't suppose I am sorry."

Everyone must have wanted to do that at some time. Charles could, of course, deplore many sides of his father, but usually his memories ended with a faint, reluctant admiration. His father had never tried too hard. He had never grown measured and tired by trying. He must have had a very good time in those months and this might have been worth the rest, and when the good time was over he paid for it in his own way. It was not a way that Charles could respect. It was all a gesture of supreme egotism, a futile, deplorable sort of selfishness, but vaguely Charles could understand it.

Most of Charles's life was dedicated to being as unlike his father as possible and yet he could not lose all sympathy because John Gray must have been a very sympathetic person. He had to be or no one would have tolerated him. Those dreams of his were like a boy's dreams. That desire of his for getting something for nothing and for beating what he called the system was shockingly immature, and yet immaturity lay often at the root of desire.

Whenever Charles heard the expression "wish fulfillment," he always thought of that bill in the contribution box and also of the expression on his father's face after luncheon that Sunday. The doorbell rang before the dishes had been cleared away and he remembered his mother's dismayed look. It was early for Sunday callers and people very seldom dropped in in Clyde, but his father must have been expecting the interruption because he pushed back his chair at once.

"I'll go, Esther," he said, and then they heard him calling. "Esther, Dorothea, Charley, will you come out here for a minute?"

There must have been a new note in his voice. At any rate, it was all like a dream, the Great American Dream. They were all gathered in the doorway staring out at Spruce Street and beyond the fence stood a long maroon phaeton shining in the sun and Mr. Robert Sweet, the Cadillac agent, was standing beside it.

"How about taking a ride this afternoon?" John Gray asked. "Robert will drive us, won't you, Robert?"

They must have all guessed before he told them that he had bought the car.

"Don't worry, Esther," he said. "We really needed a car."

Somehow it was inevitable, somehow the Great American Dream was not tawdry.

"Get in, Esther," John Gray said, "and we'll all go for a ride. Take us along Johnson Street, Robert."

"John," his mother said, "it's too big. Why didn't you get a little one? You know what everyone will say."

"Yes," John Gray answered, "of course I know. That's exactly why I bought it, Esther. I don't want a little one. A heavy car holds the road. What's the matter, don't you like it, Charley?"

At the moment, the car fitted in with nothing. It was simply there, glittering and preposterous, at the curb in Spruce Street, like the bill in the contribution box.

"I don't know," he said, and his father laughed, and Charles never forgot what his father said next.

"You'll learn to like it. You'll be surprised how fast you'll learn, and we'd better start in learning now."

It was remarkable how quickly one could adapt oneself to change. It must have been that same evening that his father told him that he was almost two hundred and fifty thousand dollars ahead of the game. That was the way he put it, as they sat upstairs.

"There's no reason to tell the women yet, Charles," he said. "It would only make them difficult and I'm not through just yet."

The sum that his father had mentioned was as implausible as the Cadillac. It only had an academic meaning.

"Isn't that enough?" he asked.

"Now you let me do the worrying, Charley," John Gray said. "The market will be going up after election, and I'll know when to stop"

— but of course he did not know when to stop because wish-fulfill-ment people never did.

"Now," John Gray went on, "just remember, any time you want some money, Charley. There are a lot of things I want to do, but just ask me any time."

It was like the pony all over again. Of course, Charles should have asked him for a large sum but he never did. Instead he talked about a trust fund for his mother and Dorothea.

"We'll attend to that later," John Gray said. "There are a lot of things we've got to do" — but of course he never did any of those things.

XVIII

When I Was One-and-Twenty, I Heard a Wise Man Say
— A. E. HOUSMAN

CHARLES MUST HAVE CONCEDED, at least in a measure, that his father had some pretty good ideas, for even in Clyde they were beginning to buy common stocks that autumn. Mr. Thomas, everyone knew, had begun, in a cautious way, and the word came from Wright-Sherwin that Mr. Stanley was doing the same thing in a more dashing way; and if these men, who knew all about business, were doing it, it was all right for everyone else. His Uncle Gerald Marchby had bought some General Electric, with results which were growing happier all the time. Hugh Blashfield, they were saying, had bought some Electric Bond and Share for himself, and Mr. Sullivan had said that United Gas Improvement was a good thing, and Mr. Levine, everyone knew, had subscribed to a market service which sent him the name of its favorite stock every week by wire. Mr. Walters, at the drugstore, had bought just a little McKesson and Robbins, because he was in the drug business. If everyone else was doing it, it was silly to leave your savings in the bank and miss cashing in on an era of prosperity. Even Jackie Mason had bought some International Telephone and in three weeks had made a hundred and fifty dollars. Everyone knew, or thought he knew, how much everyone else was making, and of course the figures became exaggerated, as everything did in Clyde.

It seemed that John Gray must have had a hidden talent and that he had been waiting for just this time. He might not have done so well previously but he had obviously learned from old mistakes and now he owned a Cadillac and the Grays had joined the Shore Club and there weren't many people from Clyde in the Shore Club. Somehow, somewhere, Johnny Gray had developed a head for business and he was getting rich and even Mr. Thomas had asked him about the market when they had been waiting for the morning train. Johnny Gray was doing so well that he did not have to go into Boston every day. Everyone knew, because he said so himself, that he could often do as well by sitting at home and calling up his broker, and everyone knew that he had a telephone of his own upstairs in his study for just that purpose.

He knew so much about the market that he still had time to enjoy himself. He still played poker at the Pine Trees and he had bought the Pine Trees a new pool table and he had even had the building painted at his own expense. He still had time to find out when anyone was hard up or sick or needed a little financial help. It was too bad that other people weren't more like him. Though Johnny Gray was getting rich, he still was just the same and he would stop and give anyone a lift in his Cadillac car, just as though it were not a Cadillac. He did not have to squeeze nickels because he knew there were more where they came from. He wanted everyone to share that pleasure denied to most, of easy-come and easy-go, and you had to respect anyone like Johnny Gray. That was what they must have been saying in Clyde.

Charles, too, had bought his own small list of stocks with the money his aunt had left him but he never had his father's flair or his father's careless courage. He only possessed a good capacity for reasoning. He did not have the temperament and his conscience always hurt him because he was sure you could not get anything for nothing. Once or twice, he remembered, he asked his father for advice and it was good advice, too, for a time when the market was running wild.

"Don't be too anxious," he remembered that his father told him. "Play it high, wide and handsome"; but he never had the temperament, and this may have been why he knew enough to stop in time. At least he was able to get out and stay out and he was never proud of any part of it and he never wanted to speak about it later.

Nevertheless, he must have learned a great deal. When Jessica and Mr. Lovell came back to Clyde in the middle of October and when

Charles had bought Radio and Celanese on margin, he was not the same person he had been that spring. Jessica had called him after supper on the day they had arrived and had asked him to come over, and his father had suggested that he take the Cadillac for the evening, but his common sense had told him that it would need too much explanation if he were to drive up to the Lovells' in a Cadillac. He was wearing a new suit of herringbone worsted, a brownish-gray English cloth with a faint pinkish thread running through it, the sort of suit that looked very well at Rush & Company, and he was not a Clyde boy calling at Johnson Street.

The lights from Johnson Street shone dimly on the façade of the Lovell house and the railing of its widow's walk and its cupola possessed an airy, half-substantial quality, but it seemed to Charles that the house exhibited a pompous, fussy quality which he had never observed before. It was old and brittle and supported by a charitable sort of pretense, and to appreciate it fully you had to accept certain manners and traditions which no longer possessed validity. When he met Jessica in the front hall she did not look the way he thought she would though he was not sure how he had expected her to look. He was not exactly disappointed, but it seemed to him that her tweed skirt, her low-heeled shoes and her light brown camel's-hair sweater were too much like the country. She had not acquired as much veneer by taking that trip abroad as he had by staying at home.

"Why, Charley," she said, and they stood for a second or two looking at each other uncertainly. He had an unexpected feeling of constraint until he took her hand and then when she grasped his hand very tightly the constraint was gone and everything was just as it had been.

"I was so frightened," she said later, when they had a chance to talk. "I was afraid you didn't love me any more."

There had been an instant, just before he touched her hand, when everything must have been ready to fall one way or the other, a moment of concealment, a queer blind pause when everything was in balance. If Mr. Lovell had been there in the hall with her, denying them those few moments together, it might have been worth his while to have taken her abroad, but now it might have been better for Mr. Lovell if Jessica had stayed in Clyde.

He knew that Mr. Lovell and Miss Georgianna were waiting for them. Although he did not hear a sound, he was sure that they were in the wallpaper room listening.

"I loved your letters," Jessica said softly.

"I loved yours," he answered.

"Well," she said, "come on. Father's dying to see you," and the corners of her eyes wrinkled as she smiled.

Miss Georgianna looked nervous as she sat in a corner of the sofa. Mr. Lovell stood by the fireplace and their glances met before either of them spoke. Then he looked hastily at Jessica.

"Good evening, Charles," Miss Georgianna said. "I've just been telling them how thoughtful you've been, coming so often to call while I was here alone."

"Hello, Charles," Mr. Lovell said. "You look as though the summer had done you good."

"Well," Charles answered, "it's been quite a summer."

"I was sorry to hear of your aunt's death. I hope your father got my letter. He didn't answer it."

"He spoke of getting it," Charles said. "I didn't know he hadn't answered it. My father's been pretty busy, with one thing and another."

"There's no reason why he should have written and perhaps his letter never caught up with us. I think we gave Brown, Shipley too many forwarding addresses. It's better to let all letters stay at 123 Pall Mall, London. It's a perfect address, isn't it? 123 Pall Mall, London."

"Yes, sir," Charles said. "It's easy to remember. I suppose Brown, Shipley must have thought of that."

"I don't believe they ever did," Jessica said. "It was probably ordained."

Mr. Lovell turned his back to the fire and clasped his hands behind him.

"It's good to be home again," he said. "One of the beauties of going away is getting back, the feeling that everything's been waiting. Sit down for a minute or two, Charles. What s the news? I don't suppose there's any chance of our friend Al Smith's winning the election?"

"The betting's against him," Charles said.

"I imagined so." Mr. Lovell smiled. "And the market's still going up, isn't it? I'll have to go into Boston tomorrow and see if my list of things is up to date."

He was the one who had changed, not Mr. Lovell. He knew that Mr. Lovell disapproved of him but he was no longer disturbed by his disapproval. He could see that Mr. Lovell was typical of certain customers of E. P. Rush. Banks, lawyers and trustees were especially made for people like Mr. Lovell, and Charles's attitude was already what it would always be toward Mr. Lovell's type, courteous and watchful but devoid of real respect.

"It's better not to try to do anything with the market, sir," he said. "All the trustees are moving very slowly."

He was older than Mr. Lovell already and infinitely wiser than Mr. Lovell but he knew enough not to show it unduly.

"They always do, don't they?" Mr. Lovell said, and he laughed. "March Associates take care of my things — the details. In the last analysis I like to rely on my own judgment and I don't think I've done so badly, either, by and large, have I, Georgianna?"

"No, you haven't," Miss Lovell said. "You have very good judgment, Laurence."

"I think I have a little of my grandfather's business instinct," Mr. Lovell said, "an instinct for survival," and he laughed again. "I'm still feeling the motion of the ship. It was rough the last day out. An unexpected squall, the captain said. Well, we've had a long, hard day. I thought that customs inspector was slow and disagreeable, didn't you, Jessica?"

"He was cross because you put down everything," Jessica said, "instead of just saying souvenirs."

"I only obeyed the instructions, Jessica. Well, I think we ought to get a good night's sleep. You should, especially, Jessie. There's always a letdown after an ocean crossing. You've been very nervous all today."

"I wasn't nervous," Jessica said. "I was just anxious to get home. I'm not tired at all."

"It's been very nice to have had a glimpse of Charles," Mr. Lovell said, "but I have an idea that Charles will keep and I know that Charles will understand."

"Oh, yes," Charles said. "That's all right, Mr. Lovell."

"Oh, well," Jessica said, "all right. What are you doing tomorrow, Charles? I'll be rested tomorrow."

"Tomorrow isn't a holiday," Mr. Lovell said. "Charles will be in Boston."

"I know," Jessica said, "but he'll be back in the evening. Let's do something tomorrow evening, Charles."

"Now, Jessie," Mr. Lovell began, and stopped.

There was a brief, heavy sort of silence in the wallpaper room and Charles was aware of everything that caused it.

"Would you like to go out to dinner, Jessica?" Charles said. "We could motor somewhere."

"Now, Jessica," Mr. Lovell said, "I don't want you driving the Dodge at night and Charles hasn't got a car. Have you, Charles?"

"No," Charles answered, "but my father will let me take his."

"Oh," Mr. Lovell said, "has your father bought a car? What sort of a car?"

"A Cadillac," Charles said. He had hoped not to have to mention it but he could not help enjoying the silence that followed. "We might have dinner at the Shore Club, Jessica."

"The Shore Club?" Mr. Lovell looked startled. "You're not a member, are you, Charles?"

"No, but my father is."

Mr. Lovell did not ask in words how John Gray happened to be a member of the Shore Club but the question was written on his face.

"My father knows a good many people," Charles said, and he hoped that he spoke politely.

"Why, I'd love to go," Jessica said.

"The dining room will be cold," Mr. Lovell said. "No one ever goes there for dinner in the autumn if he can help it."

But Mr. Lovell could do nothing.

"We can start early," Charles said to Jessica. "If it's all right, I'll call at half past six."

"I'll wear something warm, Father, and remember what we decided." Jessica's voice was sharper. For a second there was another blank silence.

"Well, well." Mr. Lovell sounded as though a valuable piece of bric-a-brac had been broken. It was all right. It did not matter, at least not before company. "I feel quite out of touch with things. Quite a lot must have been going on since we've been away."

"Not so much," Charles answered. "Everything's about the same."

The differences were only superficial. Everything between them was basically the same except that everything was better than it had been. When Jessica Lovell sat beside him on the front seat of the Cadillac, wrapped in her new polo coat from London, the lights on Johnson Street did not matter. It was a starlit October night and the headlights cut sharply into the coolness in front of them. There was that old smell of burning leaves and toward the end of Johnson Street there were wisps of autumn mist.

"There's no month as beautiful as October," Jessica said.

"It's the best month there is."

They spoke as though they were strangers because they were still on Johnson Street.

"Let's drive around the training field first," she said.

They were silent as they drove around it, but they both must have known they would stop awhile when they were back on the main road, where the houses ended.

Beyond the Royall farm on the main road there was nothing but the black of wind-swept fields and she moved closer to him as he brought the car to a stop. It was like the hill again, that spring. They were clinging to each other and they did not speak for a long while.

"Darling," she said, "aren't you going to say anything?"

"I don't need to say anything," he told her.

"I know. Darling, I've missed you so." That was when she said she had been afraid last night, just for a moment when she first saw him in the hall, that he did not love her any more.

"There's nothing to be afraid of," he said.

"No, I know there isn't," she said, "not any more, but we mustn't ever let ourselves get away from each other again. If you see me getting away, you'll tell me, won't you? And I'll tell you." She was thinking of the way things had been, before she had gone abroad, and now there was not the same sort of gap between them.

"I suppose we'd better go on," she said. "I wish we didn't always have to be going somewhere or saying good-by."

When he started the car again she was still close beside him with her head on his shoulder and with her arm through his as he held the wheel. There was so much to say that it was hard to know where to start. She had missed him every minute, she was saying. She had never been so wretched or unhappy as when they had sailed away and he had been on her mind every minute, or almost every minute. It was no fun seeing all those places alone if you were in love. She had never known how much she loved him. All those places had a sterile sort of blackness which she could not describe.

"It was awfully hard on Father, but he was awfully sweet," she said. "He kept trying so hard not to notice when I couldn't keep my mind on anything."

He did not answer her directly. They were in the car and they were going away from Clyde and he wished that they were going away for good right now, alone together, but he did not tell her that. There were all sorts of other things he wanted to tell her about what he had been doing and what he had been thinking. He had to tell her all about Rush & Company and about why he liked what he was doing there.

"If you want to get on there, you have to see things in a special way," he said, "and I'm trying to find the way."

If she could understand what he was trying to do, everything else he had to explain would be much easier. He had to tell about John Gray and it seemed very necessary that she should see his father as he did, what was wrong and what was right with him. He had never told anyone so much about his father and he had never spoken so many of his thoughts.

"Of course, I don't know much about him myself," he began. "We don't speak the same language, or at least we use different dictionaries. The same words don't mean the same thing."

Then he told her about the system and the ass and the bundle of hay and how his father was going to beat the system. The only trouble was that he did not seem to know when he had beaten it enough. People like him never knew. It was like walking outdoors into the sunlight being able to say those things to someone without being too careful how you said them.

"He thinks I'm the ass following the bundle of hay," he said, and then he laughed. "He doesn't care much about work. Sometimes I think everybody works but Father."

Of course his father was making a lot of money, money on paper, and he kept trying to persuade his father to get some of it off of paper, but sometimes when he was with his father he felt as though he were the tail of a kite, he said. Had she ever flown a kite? He and Sam used to fly them. If you did not put enough tail on to balance it, then the kite would begin darting from side to side and finally it would come crashing.

"Of course, when you're the tail of a kite," he said, "you've got to follow it. That's why we're in this car. We're both tied to the kite."

"It's nice, being tied to something."

She had always been tied to something, she said, and she supposed a girl always was, but all of this was new.

Yes, all of it was new and it would always stay so in memory. The car, he supposed, if he were to see it now would look antiquated and clumsy, and the dress she wore that night would be ludicrous if he could see it now, but the Cadillac, her dress, and everything they said always would be new and they always would be young, in memory, riding through an October night.

He was the tail of the kite and he was gambling as hard as his father, he told her. He had no right to criticize.

"You see," he said, "someone's got to beat the system. You're my system," and she laughed and her arm tightened through his.

"Darling," she said, "you don't have to beat me, and besides, I'm not much to beat."

He knew then that he would ask Jessica Lovell to marry him. The idea of its being possible was like the Cadillac. It was there, but it might not be there permanently. It might, and yet it might not, be illusion. It was just as his father had said — it was surprising how quickly you got used to things — even to impermanence.

The Shore Club, in spite of its name, was two or three miles inland from the water. It was old, for a country club. Its wooden verandas were pockmarked by the hobnails of more than a generation of golfing shoes. Its walls were decorated with mementos of great bygone events and with comical English prints of riders being tossed by their mounts into ponds and hedges. Antiquated drivers and tennis rackets, all suitably labeled, were hung upon the walls, together with whips, a few hunting horns, and the puckered, sad masks of foxes, for there were still a few foxes on the Shore, carefully watched by the owners of the estates on which they took refuge. The tables were decorated by large silver cups and bowls won by club teams and of such a cumbersome size, perhaps, that no one wanted to take them home and so left them where they properly belonged, at the Shore Club. All these objects gave the whole place an atmosphere of violent out-of-door activity, so it did not seem right to be there unless one had reached a state of suitable physical exhaustion.

The members must have been resting at home that evening because the club, when Charles and Jessica arrived there, was empty, and their footsteps echoed in a reproachful sort of silence. A fire was burning in the main room and the chimney must have still been cold for the room was drafty and smoky. They stood there for a moment uncertainly and then Jessica began to giggle.

"I guess nobody's here," she said. "It's like something in *The Green Fairy Book* or *The Purple Fairy Book,* isn't it?" The log snapped sullenly in the fireplace.

"What do I do now?" he asked her.

"Why, you ring the bell for Clarkson."

"Who's Clarkson?"

"I don't know," Jessica said, "except he's always been here."

Clarkson was the club steward and Charles supposed he should have known it, but then Jessica was used to the Shore Club and he had only been there once before.

"Where's the bell?" he asked.

"I'll ring it," Jessica said. "That's the way you can tell a college girl. They always ring bells when they're with a man."

Clarkson was a thin, elderly man, who of course knew Jessica and who accepted Charles when he explained who he was. It even seemed to Charles that Clarkson looked at him approvingly, as though Clarkson understood that he was on the team at E. P. Rush & Company. It was strange how quickly everything was changing. If they wanted, Clarkson said, he could set a table for them in front of the fire, and if they wanted something before dinner there was something in Mr. Gray's locker. He was sorry it was so lonely tonight, but then perhaps they did not mind. They could have a Martini cocktail, if they wanted.

"Oh," Charles said, "I didn't know my father had a locker."

Though he did not need the drink — he seldom did in those days — it was just as well to have one, but even without the cocktail, even with the smoking fireplace and the cold air about their ankles, the room would have been warm and friendly simply because Jessica and he were alone in it.

"I never knew what this place was good for until now," she said. "I wish we could do this all the time."

Then she told him it was the first time she had not been afraid of the Shore Club. She had been there for golf lessons and she had been there for dances but she had always felt uneasy because she did not live on the Shore.

"I know what the trouble was," she said. "I never had anyone who belonged to me — and you don't mind it at all. I never thought of your being able to get on everywhere. What are you laughing at?"

"Malcolm Bryant once said I had mobility," he told her. "I do feel awfully mobile. I guess Father and I both have it."

"You were mobile at the firemen's muster," she said. "Do you remember?"

There was so much to remember that belonged only to them. Did he remember, she asked at dinner, that Saturday morning at the Dock Street Bank? Did she remember the frogs and the swamp, he was asking, and she asked if he remembered the hepaticas. They had never found a single hepatica.

"We'll find some next spring," he told her.

"It was like playing hide-and-seek, wasn't it?" she said — "always pretending to hide what we thought about each other and yet not wanting to hide it, and now we don't have to hide anything any more."

It was not exactly so, because no one would ever tell anyone else everything, but there was the illusion that there was no concealment. When you were in love, all the cards seemed to lie face upwards on the table.

After dinner, they walked out to the parking place where they had left the car. It was the only car there and they did not drive away for a long while.

"I never thought I'd be in just this place under just these circumstances," she said.

"It's probably happened before," he told her, "but then I wouldn't know."

"Darling," she said, "I'm so happy. I'm not sorry about any of it, except one thing, just one thing."

"What one thing?"

He was not thinking attentively of what she was saying, because they had said so many other things, the things perhaps one always said when one was in a parked car when one was in love.

"It's Father," she said. "Poor Father. You like him, don't you, darling?"

There were still things it was better to conceal. She had raised her head from his shoulder. She was looking at him, trying to see his face through the dark.

"I'm afraid he doesn't like me much," he said, "but I don't blame him. Why should he?"

389

"He does." It hurt him because she was no longer happy and he wished that Mr. Lovell had not come into it. "He likes you as much as he can anyone who likes me, don't you see?"

"Yes," he said, "I guess I see."

"It's my problem anyway," she said. "You don't have to mind as long as you understand the way he feels. It's just waiting until he gets used to it." She was always saying to wait until he got used to it. "I wish I weren't torn in two pieces whenever I see you both together . . . Darling?"

"Yes," he said.

"He really does like you. At least, he tries to like you. He always says nice things about you, or at least he tries to. I've got to love you both at once. That's all I mean."

It was a time when nothing was a problem. When one talked of cold facts at such a time, they were like the roseate clouds of a summer sunrise, drifting like gilded islands across one's thoughts. If they were so large that they temporarily obscured the sun, you knew that the sun would burn through them. There had to be a happy ending, or you could not be in love.

He put his foot on the starter of the Cadillac and at the same time he switched on the lights. The sound of the motor was strong and reassuring. He did not speak as he backed the car and started it down the drive because he still had to give the gears his full attention. The car moved deliberately and slowly until it was in second, and then it was in high and the crunching of the gravel beneath the wheels was louder than the sound of the motor.

"Jessica," he said, "will you marry me? I wish you would."

"Why, Charley," she said, and there was a catch in her voice. "What made you think of that just now?"

Johnson Street and Spruce Street and all of Clyde seemed to be around him as he had proposed to Jessica Lovell.

"Why, I've been thinking about it all the time," he said.

"Well, so have I," and there was that catch in her voice again. "Oh, Charley, of course I will."

He felt the blood rush to his cheeks. He could never have described everything he felt but relief must have been a part of it, deep relief that the waiting was over. It had been bound to happen and it was over and now they could go on from there, anywhere they wanted, he and Jessica Lovell.

"But we can't get married right away."

"No," he said, "not right away."

"We wouldn't have anything to live on, would we? That's what Father keeps saying."

"No," he said, "not now, but we will have by spring."

At least he had offered her everything once. He told her that he was only making thirty dollars a week at Rush & Company but he would get a raise on the first of the year. He might be getting fifty dollars a week by spring. Besides, there was the five thousand dollars his aunt had left him, and now it was twenty thousand. He would not be afraid to marry her now, if she were not afraid, but he hoped to have fifty thousand by spring and if he did he would stop. The income from fifty thousand dollars, safely invested at five per cent, would be twenty-five hundred dollars, and if he were making fifty dollars a week that would be five thousand dollars a year. The prospect had a desperate quality, but with Jessica there listening he could believe in it implicitly.

"And Father will give me an allowance," she said.

"He doesn't have to," Charles told her. "I can take care of you, Jessica."

He could take care of her, now that his thoughts were moving on. He knew that he was doing well in Rush & Company. He might be a partner some day. He could see life stretching out before him like the dark road beneath the headlights.

"Of course, it won't be much to start with," he said, "and we don't have to live in Clyde." He must have known even then that they should get away from Clyde. Everything he was saying would be truer if they were somewhere else.

"Of course we have to live in Clyde," she said. "All our families are there."

They were already talking as though everything were settled.

"Charley," she said, "you like children, don't you? We'll have the nicest children, two boys and two girls. No, three girls"; and then she laughed. "And we can buy one of those little houses by the river, and we can do it over . . . Why, we're talking as if it had already happened."

When she said it, the house of cards fell down and for a moment he could see every fallacy of its flimsy structure.

"Well," he said, "it's got to happen. Jessica, please go on and keep believing."

"Of course I'll keep believing, but, darling," and there was a doubtful sound in her voice, "we'd better not tell anyone — and certainly not Father yet. He might stop me from believing."

By the time Charles had left the Cadillac in Rowell's Garage, the lights were out in the house on Spruce Street except in the front hall and in his father's room at the head of the stairs. The door to the upstairs room was half open and he could see his father sitting in front of his table adding a column of figures beneath the light of his old student lamp which had recently been wired for electricity. The sofa had been reupholstered in green velvet and there were glazed chintz curtains around the windows and a new green carpet, but no one had touched the books. Though the room was swept now and freshly painted, it was still like his father's mind, full of odds and ends for which he had never found a place.

"Oh, there you are, Charley," his father said. "You didn't smash the car, did you?"

"No, sir," Charles said, "nothing happened to the car."

"How was Clarkson — and the Shore Club? Did you see Clarkson?"

"Yes, sir," Charles said.

"You know, I rather like Clarkson. I'd like to have someone like him looking out for me. I'm tired of carrying my own clothes down to Dock Street to be pressed."

John Gray leaned back in his chair and pushed away his papers and opened the mahogany humidor which he had recently purchased.

"We really ought to have a man here to pass us things. We ought to have a couple to look after us, a nice woman who's a good cook and her husband. What we really need is two Filipinos, but I'm afraid your mother wouldn't like them. Perhaps we'd better look for a French couple and have some French cooking and a little wine at dinner. There's no reason to have these old Irishwomen in by the day. Mary Callahan when she comes in is more like my nurse than a maid. We'll have to find a couple."

His cigar cutter made a sharp incisive sound, and he struck a match.

"The devil of it is, we'll need another bathroom if we have a couple. We need more bathrooms at any rate. We can put two of them up on the third floor, one for the couple and one for you, and I suppose Dorothea ought to have one, too, but then she's going to marry Elbridge. Still, we could use it for a guest bathroom, couldn't we? — but then if you get married there will be another vacant bathroom. Well, we'll get three new bathrooms. I'll get Sid Stevens in here to measure them up tomorrow. There's always plenty of room for them in an old house. Now, how did my mind get on plumbing?"

"You were talking about a couple," Charles said.

"Oh, yes. I wonder how many bathrooms the Lovells have."

"I don't know," Charles said.

As he had told Jessica, if you were the tail of a kite you had to follow the kite. His father was glancing again at the papers on which he had been working.

"I always wonder why I'm doing so well, Charley, until I remember this is the first time I've had any real working capital," he said, and he puffed on his cigar and blew a cloud of that heavy, permeating smoke of expensive Havana tobacco. Charles would always associate cigar smoke with brokerage accounts and working capital. "You see, I'm pretty well up in the system now. Just between you and me — don't tell the women yet, it will only make them nervous — as of today there's three hundred and fifty thousand in the kitty."

"I don't like being out at sea in a canoe with just one paddle," Charles said. "When will you have enough, Father?"

John Gray's thoughts must have been winging happily over

393

broader fields and it must have annoyed him to be brought up short.

"Dear me," he said. "There we are again. Don't you know, Charley, that once you're up in the system you have leverage? They'll find it hard to shake me down."

"Who are They?" Charles asked.

His father picked up a pencil and tapped it on the paper.

"I'm damned if I know who, but somebody's running this show."

"It isn't somebody," Charles said, "it's everybody. Why don't you call your system a common state of mind?"

Later he was to read the debates and the dogma of economists and weigh the theories of the orthodox against those of the disciples of John Maynard Keynes. Those people with their set conventions always reminded him more of theologians than philosophers. They were the high priests of materialism, constantly trying to establish their creeds and trying to give unbreakable definitions to acquisitive forces, and yet in the end it was nothing more or less than what he had said that night at Spruce Street.

"Maybe you're right," his father said. "Maybe it is a state of mind, but states of mind change, don't they? You know — I'm going to say something that may relieve you, Charley. I've been seriously thinking that there's an end to everything — you can't carry a good thing too far, can you? You know, I really think that perhaps I ought to make a limit. I think I'll stop all this and cash in — when I have a million dollars." It was the ultimate end, the mathematical symbol for security and happiness. "Well . . . good night, Charley."

XIX

"Give Crowns and Pounds and Guineas, but Not Your Heart Away"

— A. E. HOUSMAN

THERE WAS ONE GOOD THING about Clyde. People there might know everything about you but they still had respect for individual privacy. No one, except his immediate family, ever asked Charles directly about Jessica Lovell. If you lived in a place like Clyde, you were keenly conscious of public approval or disapproval. Though Charles was too busy most of the time that winter to go around much, as the expression went, he still realized that he was a figure of interest. At the railroad station or when he went to the post office or to the news store or to Walters's drugstore, he could perceive an atmosphere of veiled expectancy. Jackie Mason, he thought, was always waiting for him to say something and he seemed hurt when Charles did not allude to his private affairs. The girls he knew had grown sedulously impersonal, as though he were no longer a part of any of their plans. They would smile at him brightly and say, "Why, hello, Charley. You're quite a stranger these days"; and friends of his, like Earl Wilkins and the Meaders, would say, "Hi, Charley. How's everything going, Charley?"

It was what one always said, but when they asked the question it seemed to him that other people would turn and look and listen for his answer. Everyone, of course, must have been talking about the Grays that winter, including Mr. and Mrs. Meader and the Masons and all the family's particular friends. They would all say when they met him, "Why, Charley, we haven't seen you for a long while. I suppose they're keeping you busy in Boston" — but they were not thinking about Boston. They were thinking of what was

395

keeping him busy in Clyde. They were saying, in private, that he was "attentive" to Jessica Lovell and his own friends must have been saying that he was "crazy about" Jessica Lovell and down on River Street they were probably saying that Charley Gray was "going with" Jessica Lovell.

Everyone was watching the Lovells, too, and someone must have heard the Thomases and the Stanleys and other people on Johnson Street say that Mr. Lovell did not like it. He wanted Jessica to do better. After all, she had come out in Boston and the Lovells were always down on the Shore, but then he could not do much about it if Jessica liked Charley Gray. The Grays were doing very well. They had a couple working for them and a Cadillac and the house on Spruce Street had been redecorated and they had put in three new bathrooms and Wallace Brooks, who had done the painting for them, had said that the interior decorator himself had come from Boston to hang the drapes, and Mary Callahan, who now did the cleaning, said that Esther Gray had bought the loveliest new china and new sheets and blankets and candlewick bedspreads, and that Elbridge Sterne did look plain beside Miss Dorothea in her new dresses and her fur coat. The Grays were doing very well. Besides, Charley was getting on well, too, in Boston. Mr. Stanley had said that he had the makings of a businessman and that he wished he had him back in Wright-Sherwin. There was nothing that Mr. Lovell could do about it, and Jessica might have done worse.

This was what everyone must have been saying and Charles did not mind whatever repercussions he sensed of it because he was almost sure it was all said in a kindly, friendly way. Those rumors about himself and Jessica Lovell gave everyone a vicarious sort of satisfaction for it looked as though Jessica might marry a Clyde boy who did not live on Johnson Street and Mr. Lovell, in spite of all his talk about the Lovells and Clyde, thought the Lovells were too good for Clyde.

No one could say anything definite. The Grays had not been asked to the Lovells' for a meal and Laurence Lovell and Miss Georgianna had not been to call on the Grays, but then Clyde was never a hospitable place. However, when his mother finally asked her,

Jessica Lovell did go to supper at Spruce Street, in spite of implications, and there was nothing Mr. Lovell could have done to prevent it.

Charles had somehow been reluctant to talk things over with his mother because he had felt that she knew enough of what was happening without his having to explain it. She knew that he and Jessica were always calling each other up and she knew how often he went to see her, and she had seen the marble Pliny doves on his bureau and the photograph of Adam from the Sistine Chapel and later a pair of silver-backed military brushes. He had told his mother immediately when she asked about the brushes that Jessica had given them to him and his mother had said they were perfectly lovely brushes and that Jessica had very good taste. A curious sort of pride had prevented his saying anything more to anyone until it could be more definite, but one December evening when he came home from Rush & Company, his mother and Dorothea were waiting in the parlor and something in their expressions told him that they were waiting for him particularly.

"Where's Father?" he asked, because his father had not gone into Boston.

"Just where he always is — upstairs reading the papers," Dorothea said.

"You can see him later, dear," his mother said. "Why don't you just sit down and talk to us?"

"Is anything the matter?" Charles asked. His mother and Dorothea exchanged a meaning glance.

"I don't know why you're so nervous lately, dear. Why should anything be the matter? Dorothea and I just like to visit, now that we don't have to get supper. It's awfully queer to sit here in the afternoon and have Axel and Hulda doing everything. Did Axel press your other suit nicely, Charley?"

"Yes," Charles said. "Axel's all right."

"I can't get used to having a man in the house in the daytime," his mother said, "and Dorothea was just saying Axel's lazy. He makes Hulda do his work and he sits in his room all afternoon reading *True Love Stories.*"

"*True Love Stories?*" Charles repeated.

"Yes," Dorothea said. "There are such things as true love stories, in case you haven't realized it."

"Well," Charles said, "you ought to know. Where's Elbridge?"

"You ought to know, too, and never mind about Elbridge."

"Charley" — his mother smiled at him very sweetly — "Dorothea and I have just thought of something that we think might be nice. Don't you think now that we have the couple, Charley, it might be nice to ask Jessica Lovell for supper on Saturday?" The expectant way they watched him explained the uneasiness he had felt the moment he entered the parlor.

"I don't see any particular reason for it," he said. "Why should you suddenly ask her to supper?"

"But she's never been inside the house, dear, after all this time."

"After all what time?" Charles asked.

"Oh, Charley," his mother said, and she looked hurt.

"We know about these things better than you," Dorothea said. "It looks queer not having her. Don't you know that everybody's talking?"

"If anybody so much as looks at a girl around here," Charles said, "everybody starts talking."

"Now, really, Charley," Dorothea said, "have you only just been looking at Jessica Lovell?"

Charles felt his face grow beet-red.

"Oh, Charley" — his mother still looked hurt — "don't you see it looks as though you were ashamed of us? You're not ashamed, are you, Charley?"

"I didn't say I was ashamed of anyone," Charles said. "I just don't see any reason to underline things."

"Charley, dear," his mother said, "there's nothing to be so upset about. We all think she's a very nice girl and we're all very happy about it."

"I'm not upset about anything at all, Mother," Charles began. "I only think — "

"Then don't you think, dear" — she was speaking in a soothing tone she had used when he was much younger — "that it would be nice to have her for supper on Saturday night, just so we could all see each other? I'd love to ask her myself."

Charles shrugged his shoulders.

"Oh, all right," he said, "if you have to have her, if you all want to look at her, why go ahead and ask her." He did not mean to sound ungracious but he hated to think how it would be, with the family knowing everything and yet not saying anything.

As a matter of fact, it was not nearly as bad as it might have been. Everyone tried to behave as though it were the most natural thing in the world for Jessica Lovell to come to supper. The new silver candlesticks and a new Canton china dinner set were on the table — his father loved Canton china — but there was no reason for Jessica to have thought that a special effort was being made. In fact, it was almost like a family meal — just the family, Esther Gray had told Jessica over the telephone, just a family supper.

The worst of it was waiting for Jessica. Elbridge Sterne was there, just to even out things, as Dorothea said, and everyone gathered in the front parlor, which looked very well with its fresh curtains and with the new furniture from Gow Street. Everyone tried to talk about ordinary things, but his mother and Dorothea, in their dresses from Hollander's in Boston, kept moving about straightening ornaments or going out to the dining room to take a last look at the table. Elbridge Sterne was kind to him, almost like an elder brother. His father had a bland, noncommittal look.

"I'm sure Jessica won't mind if Axel brings in the cocktails," John Gray said, and then he went into the hall and called loudly. "Oh, Axel." He always loved to call to Axel, and Axel and Hulda were always saying what a fine gentleman Mr. Gray was. John Gray seated himself on one of the Martha Washington chairs from Gow Street and examined complacently his new shoes which had been made to order in London.

"I've just been rereading Ignatius Donnelly's *Atlantis*," he said. "Have you ever read it, Elbridge?"

"No," Elbridge answered. "What's Atlantis?"

"Oh, dear me," John Gray said. "That's another hiatus in a Kansas education, Elbridge. I know they only teach useful things in Kansas and Atlantis is perfectly useless — a mythological concept based on a geological fact. A body of land somewhere near the mouth of the Mediterranean actually did sink beneath the sea in the tertiary epoch and the rumor is that it was the cradle of civilization with beautiful cities and palaces, a dream world, perhaps the basis for the universal flood legend. Oh, here come the cocktails. Thank you, Axel."

"Now, Father," Dorothea said, "there's no reason to give us a free lecture. Why should Elbridge know anything about Atlantis?"

"I don't see why I shouldn't give one while we're waiting, Dorothea," John Gray said, "and it's very good for Elbridge, and Charles too. Ignatius Donnelly, though brilliant, is doubtless inaccurate, but think of Atlantis, the cradle of beauty and wisdom, and then a slight quiver of the earth's crust and then in comes the sea. Only the Azores are left, according to Mr. Donnelly. You know, I don't see why we shouldn't go to the Azores sometime. They have wild canaries in the Azores."

The doorbell rang.

"It must be Jessica," John Gray said. "You'd better let her in, Charley."

Her cheeks were glowing from the cold and she spoke a little breathlessly, saying she hoped she was not late. She must have been hoping, too, that she did not look nervous and that everyone would like her. She wore a new green dress, and he wished she had not walked into the parlor as though she were going to a formal dinner, but actually everything went very well. At first, Charles had a sinking feeling, but when she stood beside him in the parlor he suddenly felt proud and happy and glad that she had come.

"Would you like a Martini, Jessica?" John Gray said. "We were just talking about Atlantis."

"Oh," Jessica said, "the book about the lost continent?"

"Yes, Jessica," John Gray said. "I always keep it beside the *Origin of Species* and *The Voyage of the Beagle*. Atlantis is really a state of mind. Everybody is always on his own Atlantis sometime. We must learn to jump when the earth shakes. I suppose Charley talks to you about states of mind."

Jessica shook her head, the way she did when her hair blew across her forehead.

"I wish he would talk about Atlantis instead," she answered.

"Well," John Gray said, "here's to Atlantis, Jessica."

It was just as though he had said, Here's to Jessica and Charles. Everyone knew that they belonged to each other, as they stood side by side in the parlor.

"What is it, Axel?" his mother said. Axel was standing silent in the doorway to the dining room. She never could get entirely used to Axel's announcing supper.

It was something he would always remember, the dining room and everyone around the table. There was an irony to his father's having mentioned Atlantis, for the waves were to flow over all of that era and it was buried long ago, fathoms deep — but the echoes of it were still with him, like the church bell that rang beneath the sea.

"Your father and I don't see as much of each other as we ought to, Jessica," his father said, as he carved the leg of lamb, "but we know each other very well. Did he ever tell you that we studied together for our entrance examinations before we went to Harvard? I was a very bad boy. I didn't last there long."

Then he was telling what things had been like in those days and about his sisters and the Judge.

"Esther, do you remember the first time I ever called on you? I'd just been excused from Harvard."

"I don't know why you should think of that now," Esther Gray said.

"It just passed through my mind," John Gray said. "If I hadn't come to call, if I hadn't quoted Shakespeare — " He stopped and looked at the carving knife. "Do you know what I wish?" He stopped, but no one answered. "I wish Sam were here."

It must have been years since his father had mentioned Sam and it was strange that he should have spoken of him with Jessica there.

"Charley has told me about him," she said. "Do you remember that time you told me about making whistles, Charley?"

"Yes," Charles said. "I never could make one, could I?"

"When did you two try to make whistles?" Dorothea asked, and Jessica laughed.

"Oh, that was a long time ago," she said. "Well, it was only last April, but it seems like a long time ago."

When he walked home with her, she said she loved the family. She loved his mother; she was so pretty and she seemed to be so happy. The whole place was so alive, she said, and she liked the way he and Dorothea kept arguing, without ever really getting angry. He would never know, she said, how lonely it was to be an only child. She liked Elbridge Sterne, too, though he had not said much.

"No one says much," Charles told her, "when Father starts talking."

"I hope he likes me," Jessica said. "Charley, do you think he does?"

"Didn't you see him showing off?" he said. "Of course he likes you."

"Darling," she said, "it seemed so, well, so ominous when I was standing ringing the bell, and now I'm awfully glad. I feel just the way I ought to feel," and then she sighed.

The wind was waving the bare branches of the elms in front of the Lovell house. Though it was late in December there was no snow on the ground yet, but the air felt like snow.

"Father's got to get used to it," she said, but it seemed to make no difference then whether Mr. Lovell was used to it or not. Jessica had gone to Spruce Street and though the Lovells did not ask Charles to dinner, Miss Lovell, a week later, asked his mother and Dorothea to tea.

Memories of that winter in Clyde had little or none of the continuity of his recollections of former winters. There was not the usual sensation of endlessness or the interminable waiting between the melting of the snow and spring. December and January were considered possible in Clyde but as long as Charles could remember he had heard people say each winter, as though it were a new thought, that February and March were the worst months in the year. He had always felt this monotony in his school days and in his days at Wright-Sherwin, but those early weeks of 1929 possessed a staccato quality which he had never experienced before or since. They had the rhythm and the irregularity of dots and dashes in a telegraphic code — a dot for the fenced-off desks at Rush & Company, another dot for the board room and for Mr. Rush taking off his arctics, a dash for hurried, furtive luncheons with Jessica when she came to Boston, a break in the cadence and two quick dots for Spruce Street.

Early in January, John Gray had said that he could see no earthly reason why they should congeal slowly in Clyde if it was not necessary. February and March were the hardest months and at least they could get away for a week or two. He could put things in shape and leave them for that long. Winter in Clyde did something to people's faces, particularly to women's. Charles could stay, he had to since he was following his bundle of hay at Rush & Company. Axel and Hulda could look after him, but his mother needed a rest and so did Dorothea.

By the middle of the month he was reading the travel folders, usually aloud, and the rich, glowing texture of their language kept setting his mind off on cruises of its own. They would sail to the Caribbean on one of those ships which was your hotel while you were in port, and it had better be an English ship because the English knew how to do things properly and English crews did not rush to the boats first when there was an accident. They stood at attention and sang "Nearer, My God, to Thee" — not that any ship would sink, not on a voyage of enchantment to the dreamlike Windward and Leeward Islands, to dark Haiti with its brooding citadel, to Yucatán with its Mayan ruins, to Cartagena, a topaz in a setting of old Spain, or to quaint, neat, varicolored Curaçao, a bit of old Holland, adrift, but charmingly, on a turquoise sea. What ho, for the Spanish Main, with its memories of pirates and buccaneers, its century-old frowning ramparts and cathedrals, its islets like emeralds surrounded by reefs of purple coral. Esther needed a change and so did Dorothea. They all needed to get out of themselves, and there was no reason why they shouldn't, for a week or two.

Another year, when things were quieter, they could take a longer trip — the Riviera, Monte Carlo. Even though he did not gamble himself, he had always wanted to watch those improvidents at Monte Carlo and there was no reason why he shouldn't. Egypt, up the Nile, India, the Taj, Japan, China, islands of the Pacific, Hawaii — they could do it, another year. In fact, there was no reason why they should stay in Clyde in the winter at all. Eventually they could get a house at Pinehurst or Sea Island or Palm Beach. Palm Beach might be best, because he could drop in at Bradley's and watch other people lose their money.

There were other dots and dashes that winter — a dot for the New Year's dance at the Shore Club — it was Jessica who suggested the New Year's dance — another dash for a call at Johnson Street when Mr. Lovell was away and when Miss Georgianna went up to bed and left them alone; but one of the longest dashes of all, of course, was his triumph at Rush & Company.

In England there was the New Year's Honors List and that custom of granting favors and distinctions applied also to American business. First, at E. P. Rush, there were the Christmas bonuses, a carefully prorated largesse expected of financial houses at the end of a good year and primarily intended for the clerical force, the boys and girls behind the grating, and not for the team. The raises at New Year's, however, had a different, more permanent value, not to be discussed as openly as bonus money.

Charles was not surprised when Mr. Rush sent for him on the afternoon of January second. First they talked about the weather, and then Mr. Rush shifted the papers on his desk and looked embarrassed. He always had a hard time with personnel relationships. The partners, he said, had all been having a talk about everybody, a routine, end-of-the-year talk, and they had all agreed that Charles was getting to be part of the family, and he hoped that Charles liked the family. He did not want to encourage Charles too much, Mr. Rush said, but it was beginning to be plain that there was an eventual future for him in E. P. Rush and he wanted Charles to feel happy and contented so that the good work could go on, particularly the investment advisory work. Of course, he said, Rush & Company was not noted for paying large salaries, but Rush & Company looked after its own. It was a two-way loyalty. Employees were loyal to the firm, and the firm to the employees. He had not been with them long, but Mr. Rush was willing to forget length of service. As of the first of the year — Mr. Rush looked wretchedly embarrassed and drew circles on his memorandum pad — Charles's salary would be sixty dollars a week, a pretty large salary considering his age and experience, and Mr. Rush hoped that Charles would be happy about it.

There was never again in his life anything else exactly like that moment. He had been vaguely thinking of a possible fifty dollars and secretly he had felt it was a presumptuous hope although Mr. Stanley had offered him as much. For a second he struggled with a dizzy sort of incredulity and then instinctively he knew that he should not show it.

"Thank you very much, sir," he said. "I'm very much obliged."

"That's all right," Mr. Rush said. "Well, that's all now."

At the moment, he would gladly have died for Mr. Rush, that simple man who always wore a last year's hat and had his suits turned by his tailor to avoid buying new ones. As of that moment he was making three thousand dollars a year. It was possible, barely possible, that he could marry Jessica Lovell on three thousand dollars a year.

He must have still been riding on the wave of that elation when he met Malcolm Bryant in a snowstorm one night after a call on Jessica. It was another of the dots and dashes of that winter, extraneous, because Malcolm was already like a shore line that he was leaving far behind. Yet the memory of Malcolm always formed a part of the design of that winter, a reminder of the things he had missed and of the way things might have been if he had done this or that.

Jessica had told him that she really thought her father was getting used to it. He had recently fallen into the habit of sitting in the library with the door open when Charles came to call instead of sitting in the wallpaper room and joining in the conversation, and this may have proved that he was getting used to it. It even was possible to sit together on the sofa, though it was better always to talk brightly, without any gaps of silence, or Mr. Lovell would grow restless. Charles had said good night to her at ten and they had not lingered in the hall except long enough for him to buckle his overshoes, but it did not matter because she would be with her aunt in Boston over the week end and they were going to spend Saturday afternoon together and go to the theater on Saturday night.

It had started snowing at eight o'clock and now the wind was rising and the small, hard snowflakes eddied and swirled with it and beat against his face. Since it was early he decided to walk down Dock Street before he went home, just to see the storm. The snow made a hissing sound, gentle but very persistent as the wind drove it against the brick walls of the public library. He was just passing beneath the light by the Dock Street Bank and by the blank, dark windows of the notions store when he saw a figure coming toward him, head down, moving noiselessly against the wind. He slowed his steps to see who it was, as one always did in Clyde, and it was Malcolm Bryant.

"Hello, Charley," Malcolm said. "Come on back with me. I haven't seen you for a long while." Malcolm had not been to call at Spruce Street for months. "I've been up in Cambridge," he went on, "getting all the material whipped into shape. We ought to be cleaned up here by March or April. God, this is a hell of a town."

"You always used to like it," Charles said.

"I know . . . I must have been crazy," Malcolm said. "At least it's warm where you get anopheles mosquitoes. Well, how has everything been going with you, Charley?" There was a vague note in Malcolm's voice. "Are you still with that stock-and-bond job in Boston?" He had once been a collected specimen of Malcolm's and perhaps he was somewhere in a card file now but obviously Malcolm's interests had moved on and so had his. "I'm damned if I know why you do it," Malcolm went on. "Where have you been? Calling on Jessica?"

"Yes," Charles said.

"My God," Malcolm said. "I suppose I have a mercurial disposition. When I first see a thing, I love it, and then when I get it worked out I'm ready to move on — but I've done quite a job here, if I do say so, and it ought to get me an honorary degree somewhere if anyone has any sense. God, the prejudices you run into, the small minds, but I'm not a prima donna. Thank God, I'm not a prima donna." Charles never felt at home with Malcolm Bryant's weakness for frank personal revelation, but obviously something had happened. Obviously Malcolm was disturbed. "And I'm not a politician, either, and I'm not interested in publication. After all, my job is field work. I don't know what ever put it in my mind to ask for the G. Price Fellowship."

"What's the G. Price Fellowship?" Charles asked.

"It's one of those stupid lecture fellowships." Malcolm laughed airily. "Well, if they don't want me, they don't have to have me. Frankly, Harvard's a damn provincial place and I should have known it. Thank God, I'm not a time server or a prima donna."

When they reached his rooms at Mrs. Mooney's, Malcolm switched on the light above his drawing board. The room had a crowded, restive appearance. His locker trunk and bedding roll, always closed before in neat readiness for departure from Clyde, were both opened. A rubber poncho and a mosquito net were draped across the couch and a collapsible rubber basin, a desert water bag and a pair of binoculars lay on top of them. All sorts of things had emerged from the tray of the locker trunk, small articles distributed in neat rows and piles on the floor like lead soldiers taken from a box — flashlights, medicines, camera film, and a great many other things that experience had taught the traveler were essential for a long journey.

"I'm just checking up on everything." Malcolm waved at the locker and bedding roll as he wriggled out of his snowy overcoat and dropped it on the floor. "There won't be many stores along the Orinoco."

He reached under the couch and drew out a whiskey bottle and told Charles to wait while he got a pitcher of water from the bathroom. As Charles stood there alone, he felt his own restiveness growing. In some ways Malcolm Bryant must have had a wonderful life and its design was right there in front of him, drawn with sheath knives, fishhooks, and mosquito netting. There was no need for careful, long-term planning in that life, because someone else did all the planning for him. Someone else supplied the money and the steamship tickets. If he did not like it where he was, Malcolm could move on, always supported by some learned foundation. He could go and he could return to tell his tales in his own strange, scientific jargon. He was returning now with the florid hot-water pitcher from a Victorian chamber set.

"There isn't any ice," Malcolm said, "but if you want it cold just open the window and scoop in some snow."

He leaned over the drawing board, poured a tumbler a third full of whiskey, and pushed it toward Charles. It was much more than Charles would have thought of consuming, yet Malcolm Bryant was escaping from Clyde and from whatever else it was that bothered him, and Charles felt, with the aid of that glass of whiskey, that he too could escape vicariously. He did not know from exactly what he wished to escape, but curious uncontrolled desires were pulling at him.

"I'm sorry you're going away, Malcolm," Charles said.

"Are you?" Malcolm's deep-set eyes had a kindly look. "That's nice of you to say so, Charley. You're a nice kid, Charley." Malcolm had tossed off his glass and was pouring himself another drink. "This whole thing is going to have repercussions, it's going to make a noise."

"What whole thing?" Charles asked.

"This whole survey and its ultimate conclusion." Malcolm waved his arm vaguely. "You see, I've been able to prove something."

"What have you proved?" Charles asked.

Malcolm pulled a pipe and a tobacco pouch from his pocket. He reminded Charles, as he filled his pipe, of a detective, explaining to an appreciative audience, in the last chapter of a mystery story, just how he caught the criminal.

"It's a little hard to clarify for a layman," Malcolm said, "but it can't help but get recognition when I get time to get it into print.

Not that I want recognition. I'm against the whole theory of honorary degrees — but let me put it in one-syllable words. Man is essentially the same, whether he's in G-strings or plus fours, and I ought to know. After all, what is man?"

There was no need to answer the question. Malcolm Bryant was standing up. He was on the lecture platform, preparing to address a wider audience, fortifying himself first with a few swallows from his glass.

"What is man? Nothing but a very recent evolutionary form of mammal with a surprisingly adaptive brain. He tries to cloak himself with dignity. He's a self-conscious, worrying mammal, but he is only a small link in the chain of life. And what is life?"

Charles found himself groping cautiously through the maze of Malcolm's verbiage and he was thinking that Malcolm in his way sounded like a market letter, which also endeavored to prove something.

"What is our planetary system? Only an insignificant unit in a galaxy among other galaxies. There must be other planets, millions of them, billions of them, supporting life. What is man? To hell with him. Why should I worry?"

"But you are worrying," Charles said.

"Now when I get to the Orinoco — " He had dismissed the planetary system. His gaze had traveled to the mosquito netting and the bedding roll. "Charley, how would you like to get away from all this and come with me to the Orinoco?"

"That would be fine," Charles told him, "but I don't see quite how I can work it now." He was using that placating tone one customarily employed in dealing with a drunk, and perhaps Malcolm recognized it.

"What are you going to do if you don't, Charley?" he asked.

"I guess I'll just have to try to get along," Charles said, "in my planetary system."

He did not like the way he sounded. He sounded like an old man or like a schoolbook, smug and reasonable. He was thinking of Jessica Lovell and Rush & Company, of a house and children of his own, of Jessica meeting him when he came home. If one could go beyond those thoughts at least those wishes were universal, but their ultimate purpose evaded him just then.

"The biological urge," Malcolm was saying. "I suppose you realize you're a victim of the urge."

"Yes," Charles said, "I suppose so."

"Oh, my God," Malcolm said. "Excuse me, Charley."

His meaning was perfectly clear. Malcolm was asking what a pedestrian life amounted to, a material plodding through the years — but then there was always Jessica Lovell, and there was nothing plodding about Charles's life. Then he thought of Malcolm's life — as much as he knew of it. It seemed to be spread out on the floor, between the foot locker and the bedding roll.

"Malcolm," he asked, "what will you do when you're through with the Orinoco?"

"Oh, hell," Malcolm said, and he stared at the floor for a moment and then he rubbed the back of his head. "You sound like the *Saturday Evening Post*, Charley. Don't bother me any longer. I'm not conditioned to environment. I'm not societal and I can't take punishment. I'm drunk and I guess I'd better go to bed, but there's one thing I'll say for you. You're a damned good type and you've got a lot of guts."

Charles was shaking hands with him. It was one of those aimless conversations, questions and no answers, but he had always liked Malcolm Bryant and somehow he felt that this might very well be his last talk with him.

He knew when he was outside in the storm again that he had been drinking too much whiskey and that he would have a headache in the morning, and yet it had been worth it. With every step he took on Fanning Street, he seemed to be leaving something further and further behind, some possibility, but something of what he was leaving must have been with him always or he would not have dropped everything years later, he would not have left Nancy and the children and the Stuyvesant Bank and have gone to the war when he was overage — and not the type.

XX

No Time for Jubilation

— MR. LAURENCE LOVELL

LATER, during long evenings in New York in which he used reading as a means of self-forgetfulness, Charles read a book on the Orinoco which he had borrowed from the public library but there was nothing in its pages resembling what he had hoped to find. Later still, he had seen a part of that country from the window of a C-54 on his way to Cairo, where he had been ordered during the war for no reason he could ever discover. From the height of eight or nine thousand feet he had looked down on the closely packed, tufted tops of trees, silvery gray like the olive, or angry green like a squally ocean, depending on how the clouds and the rainstorms happened to be passing over them. In the midst of this endless, regularly billowing carpet of treetops, he had seen winding stretches of muddy water, tributaries to the Orinoco or the Amazon, no one had told him which.

Malcolm Bryant had asked him, though perhaps he had not been serious, to go away from Clyde up a tropical river. He was young enough to be stirred by this invitation, but he knew the idea was preposterous. At that time in his life, he had no real desire to escape from what lay around him. If one wished to put it obviously, Clyde and E. P. Rush & Company made his Orinoco, and what lay between him and Jessica Lovell was as new and fascinating a country as any on a map. There was no premonition of failure, no sense of doubt. Everything grew consistently better as the days grew longer. There were no Cadillacs in the Orinoco, no Boston theaters, no walks like that one across the pasture, no spring sunsets above the river, and no savage chiefs more difficult to placate with beads and bangles than Mr. Laurence Lovell. There was no need to go to the Orinoco.

All the elements of his life were moving as they should that spring and he did not have the sense to pray that eventual compensation should be light. He knew that luck had entered into it, but also his own perspective and a maturing, instinctive judgment had achieved a result which he knew was above the average. He had wanted something and he had set out as intelligently as he could to get it and he was ending by getting it.

First there had been that raise at E. P. Rush & Company, which was something due entirely to his own efforts and there was no luck about that; then there was his brokerage account, starting with the five thousand dollars he had received from his aunt. Like other members of the team, he had done his trading through E. P. Rush, since it would have been disloyal and deceitful to have placed his business elsewhere. Also, he had had the good sense to speak to Mr. Rush about it personally. Mr. Rush told Charles he would probably lose it all, but if he did it would be a lesson to him. It was not his business what Charles might do with his money, but it was his business when employees used office time worrying about their own affairs and standing around the ticker and looking at the board. Charles was careful never to use the office time. He only watched the quotations during the lunch hour. It was his own judgment that put him into Radio and a few other equities that were being purchased without any regard to earnings but because of future prospects. The future was boundless that spring, in the light of mass hysteria.

Charles did not believe in this future. He was sure that buying power would not continue with inflated credit and he sold out in May, during one lunch hour, just as he had told Jessica he would, in the midst of a rising market. His account with E. P. Rush, less commissions, showed a balance of fifty thousand dollars. He had started on a shoestring, he had pyramided, he had been cognizant of every risk, and he had increased his money tenfold. He had not believed in what he was doing and he had hated every minute of it, but at least he had known when to stop.

He felt almost weak with relief that noon in May. In his way he had beaten the system, as he had told Jessica he would. Ever afterwards when he saw Radio among the stock quotations he always winced and saw himself standing on an unsubstantial pyramid already beginning to topple. Now that the profit was no longer on paper, he wanted it absolutely safe. He did not even like the risk of five per cent — it was ironical to think they used to call it five per cent and safety then. He bought Government 4's, and when they were delivered he rented a box for them in the State Street Trust Company and then he did something he had never done while he was in Rush & Company. Though he had always disliked the way certain members of the team chatted indiscriminately over the telephone, he had called Jessica from his extension during the noon hour and had told her.

He could walk now with Jessica anywhere in Clyde without pretending that they had just happened to meet. When he called on her he would no longer imply that he just happened to call because he had nothing else to do. They would not have to talk furtively about meetings in Boston, nor would they have to think that they were seeing too much of each other in public, considering everything. There was no reason for any of this any longer.

There was no reason, either, why he should have felt grim in his triumph, except that he instinctively never wanted to be too happy when things were going right. He went straight upstairs before supper and put on his blue suit, though it was heavy and though it was a warm May day. When he saw his face in the mirror, as he brushed his hair very carefully with the military brushes that Jessica had given him, he was surprised that his face did not look older after everything he had been through; instead it still looked young and there was the cowlick in his hair which Jessica always spoke about and there were the usual freckles on his nose.

"Charley," his mother said at supper, "has anything gone wrong in Boston?"

"No," he said. "Why do you ask?"

"You look so stern and efficient, dear," his mother said.

His father, at the head of the table, asked Axel for a bottle of Moselle wine that he had just brought home.

"Look at Charley," Dorothea said. "Why are you all dressed up?"

413

"Are you going to see Jessica tonight, dear?" his mother asked.

"Yes," Charles said, "I've been thinking of it."

Then he noticed that his father was looking at his new blue suit with a sudden, lively interest.

"Would you like the car?" he asked. "You could go to Rowell's and get it. We won't need it tonight."

When he met Jessica that evening, he was Jason back with the Golden Fleece, and at one and the same time, he was the small-town boy who had made good and the embarrassed young man who would have to speak to Her father. He was also the gilded youth of the Jazz Age, in his high-powered car, and Jessica, bareheaded, in her print dress, was a part of the age too, and so was the spring evening.

"Charley," she said, "don't drive so fast," but he knew that she did not really mind it.

They drove down Johnson Street to the main road and then over the causeway to the beach, because she said she would like to see the ocean, and they stopped where the road ended, just between the sand dunes. It was still too early for the small houses along the beach to be occupied so they were all alone, looking at the sea that grew continually darker in the twilight. When they were not speaking, there was no sound except the somnolent pounding of the surf and the bell on the buoy at the mouth of the river, tolling with the rhythm of the waves.

He could not help thinking that it was a queer place to be mixing love with bookkeeping, to be so conscious of the sea and of Jessica in his arms and at the same time to be talking about the Radio Corporation of America. He remembered that he told her that he was tired of hiding in corners with her, and she had said that she had liked it in the corners.

"But then, you know," he said, "everybody knows we're hiding."

"But I like to pretend," she said. "I like to think it's all just our secret. I don't know what it will be like when it isn't."

"It will be better," he told her, "much better."

"We've been so awfully happy the way it was," she said. "It's all

414

going to be 'Is it wise? And how much will everything cost?' We never had to think about any of that before."

"But you don't mind thinking about it, do you?" he asked her. "I hope you don't mind, Jessica."

"Oh, darling, of course I don't really," she said, "it's just — "

"Just what?" he asked.

She was silent for a moment, looking at the dark sea.

"I know the way you feel," he said. "Everything seems to be happening all at once but you mustn't let it worry you, as long as you still love me. You do still love me, don't you?" It was only a rhetorical question.

"Oh, darling," she said, "of course I do. It's only — only that I used to think we couldn't be married for years and years and now it's so queer to have it happen. I don't mean I don't like the idea," and she laughed. "I'm crazy about it, really, darling, but so much else goes with it."

"Jessica." He stopped. He wished he did not sound so portentous. "I suppose I ought to speak to your father. We can't go on like this."

It had not occurred to him until then how necessary this was or how unendurable any further waiting would be.

"Oh, Charley." He heard her draw a sharp, quick breath. "We don't have to tell him just yet."

"We'll have to do it sometime," he said. "We'd better do it now."

"Oh, darling," Jessica said. "Suppose he — " Her voice trailed off into a wretched silence but it was too dark to see her face. "Charley, why are you starting the car?"

"Because I'm going to take you back," he said.

"Charley, you're not going to speak to him tonight?"

"I'm going to get it over with."

"Oh, Charley, I wish you'd let me talk to him first. It's — it's going to hurt him," she said.

He was thinking of himself, of course, and not of her, and for some reason the idea that it might hurt Mr. Lovell came close to making him angry. At any rate, it eliminated all feelings of diffidence.

"I don't know what you think is the matter with me," he told her. "I'm not as bad as all that. You must have known I'd have to see him sometime."

Of course he was really telling her without saying it that he lived on Spruce Street and not Johnson Street and that there had been ample opportunity for her to have faced those facts. It was something he could not say, but though Jessica was crying it was not a quarrel.

"It's not what's the matter with you, dear," she sobbed. "It's what's the matter with me."

"There's nothing the matter with you," he said. "It's going to be all right, Jessica."

It was not a quarrel, and he was stronger than she was once his mind was made up. It was one of those rare moments when he was not impressed by Jessica, and at least she had stopped crying.

"I wish you'd let me talk to him first," she said. "You don't understand him, Charley."

"No, I'll have to do it, Jessica," he said.

"Well, at least I've got to be there with you, and if he says anything don't be cross or I won't be able to bear it."

She did not seem to be beside him in the car. He was planning what he would say to Mr. Lovell and it did not do much good to plan. Experience was seldom present when you needed it, and it was always too late when you had gained experience.

"Back so early?" Miss Lovell called to them from the wallpaper room when they entered the front hall, and Mr. Lovell in the library said the same thing.

"Back so early?"

Mr. Lovell folded his newspaper carefully.

"Why are you closing the door, Jessica? I like the draft. It's a warm evening."

Mr. Lovell was sitting in one of the heavy leather armchairs, leaning backward comfortably, but he had dropped his newspaper when the door closed. Somehow Charles was not able to introduce the subject gracefully. Standing in front of the empty fireplace, he did not see the books or the ship pictures, but only Mr. Lovell's thin and rather handsome face and Mr. Lovell's hands gripping the arms of his chair.

"Mr. Lovell," he said, "I want to marry Jessica."

After all, it could not have been news to Mr. Lovell that he wanted to marry Jessica, yet suddenly Mr. Lovell looked deathly ill and raised a trembling hand to his forehead.

"Jessie," he said, "would you mind getting me a glass of water, please?"

"Oh, Father," Jessica began, and she ran to him across the room.

"It's all right, Jessie," Mr. Lovell said, and he smiled at her. "Just a glass of water."

Charles heard the door close as Jessica left the room and for a second neither he nor Mr. Lovell spoke.

"I'm sorry you feel this way about it, sir," Charles said, "but I thought I ought to tell you."

Mr. Lovell pushed himself forward and spoke in a steadier voice, as though he were rallying from the shock.

"Of course you should tell me, Charles, but someday, perhaps, if you have an only daughter who is everything in the world to you, perhaps you'll know a little of how I feel. I have to apologize, Charles. It's no reflection on you at all." He sighed, but before he could go on Jessica was back with a tumbler of water.

"Thank you, Jessie dear," Mr. Lovell said. "Sit down, Jessie. Sit down, Charles. We'll have to talk this over, won't we?" He took a sip of water and placed the glass carefully on the candlestand beside his chair. "I've just told Charles I'm very glad he told me."

"Father," Jessica said, "are you sure you feel all right? We don't have to talk about it any more."

"I feel splendidly now," Mr. Lovell said. "It had nothing to do with Charles, who did absolutely the right thing." Mr. Lovell smiled wearily. "Now don't interrupt Charles and me, Jessie. If there ever is a time to be frank, I suppose this is it. I hope you won't mind, Charles," and Mr. Lovell smiled again.

"No, sir," Charles said. "Of course not."

"I want to say first," Mr. Lovell began, "that I know what you're going through. I remember when I had to see Jessica's grandfather — even though everyone expected it. Jessica, as long as you're here why don't you get Charles a cigarette?"

"I don't care for one, thanks, sir," Charles said.

"Well," Mr. Lovell said, and his voice reminded Charles of that day years ago at the Historical Society. He was marshaling his thoughts, preparing to make a graceful speech. "I've naturally known for some time, Charles, that you and Jessica were interested in each other, but I never believed it would quite come to this. Naturally, I've always known that Jessica would marry someday and I've always hoped — well, of course I'm prejudiced. This is no reflection on you, Charles. I know how well you've done and I can see your romantic side, through Jessica's eyes, and I can see how Jessica must seem to you. At least you and I have that in common. You and I love Jessie, each in our own way."

He stopped again and took a sip of water, like a speaker on a platform.

"You young fellows, Charles," Mr. Lovell went on, and his voice was mild and playful, "always think we old dodos don't see things from your point of view, but I do know Jessie, perhaps a little better than you do. Now you say you want to marry Jessie. How long have you wanted to marry her?"

"For quite a while," Charles said. "I guess for about a year now."

"And a year is quite a while," Mr. Lovell said gently, "when one is — how old are you now, Charles?"

"Twenty-five, sir," Charles said.

"Well, well," Mr. Lovell said. "You've done very well, and I respect you for it, Charles, but we must both think of Jessie."

"Yes, sir," Charles answered.

"Now don't interrupt us, Jessie," Mr. Lovell said. "To me Jessie is one thing, Charles, and to you undoubtedly quite another. You mustn't blame me for wanting Jessie to have everything she's been used to. She wouldn't be the same in another setting. Now we'll have to think what you can do for Jessie, Charles. I know you're doing well at Rush & Company but how much are you earning there? You don't mind my asking, do you?"

"No, sir," Charles said. "Sixty dollars a week."

"Well, well," Mr. Lovell said. "That's splendid, but you can see, Charles, that a girl like Jessie — "

418

"Yes," Charles said, "I know."

Mr. Lovell looked at him triumphantly but kindly.

"Now, Charles," he said, "you know that wouldn't be enough for Jessie. It's hardly a time to talk about marrying Jessie, really, is it? Let's leave it the way you began. You want to marry Jessica. Let's leave it there."

"I have fifty thousand dollars besides that," Charles said, "in government bonds."

It sounded strangely primitive, as though he were buying Jessica, and Mr. Lovell suddenly looked blank. There was no longer any kindliness in his glance.

"Well," Mr. Lovell said, "well. Did your father give it to you?"

"No, sir," Charles said.

"Did you make it on the market, Charles?"

"Yes, sir," Charles said.

"I can't say I like that," Mr. Lovell said.

"I don't either," Charles answered, "but I wanted to marry Jessica."

"Money is one thing," Mr. Lovell said, "and stock-market money is another."

"There may be a difference," Charles said, "but as long as you don't lose it, it's money."

"It's not the same," Mr. Lovell said, "as inherited money."

Charles did not feel impatient. It was a pathetic intellectual quibble.

"Everybody has to start sometime," Charles said. "I suppose your family did once, Mr. Lovell."

"Father," Jessica said, "it really doesn't make any difference, does it?"

"Jessie" — there was a new edge on Mr. Lovell's voice — "please be quiet."

"Unless you have some other reason, sir . . . ?" Charles began. Mr. Lovell sat quietly without answering.

"Father," Jessica said, "we had to tell you, didn't we?"

"Oh, be quiet, Jessica," Mr. Lovell said. "If I had thought there was any chance of this happening . . . If things have gone this far,

I suppose — " Mr. Lovell pushed himself slowly out of his chair. "I can't say that I like this, Charles. I don't like being presented with an accomplished fact."

"Oh, Father," Jessica said, "you sound as if Charley and I — Father, please!"

"I'm sure I don't know how I sound," Mr. Lovell said, "but I expected a rational discussion and instead it's an accomplished fact. Very well, you can be engaged, but I don't want any public announcement until we get to know each other better. And now I'm feeling very tired. Good night, Charles. Good night, Jessie, dear."

"Oh, Father," Jessica said, and she threw her arms around him. "You know you'll get used to it in time."

It was hard to place events in order after all that time. They kept standing out irrationally by themselves, like sentences removed from the context of a carefully written page, but it was only a short time after this conversation that Jessica had shown him all through the Lovell house. It was a Saturday afternoon and Mr. Lovell must have been away playing golf at the Shore Club, as he usually did on Saturdays, and Miss Lovell had been out paying calls on Johnson Street. It was one of those days in Clyde when you wished the furnace were still going but felt it self-indulgent to have a fire in the cellar because it was after the first of May. The house was a little damp and the dampness brought out those smells one always associated with old Clyde houses, the scent of old leather, old carpets and of dust that could never entirely be swept away.

"It's awfully funny," Jessica said. "I don't believe you've ever seen the house. I don't believe you've ever been upstairs."

It struck him as strange, too, knowing Jessica so well, that he had only seen the front hall, with the portraits and the dusky mirror, and the little parlor with the Aubusson carpet which had been made for it in France, and the wallpaper room and the dining room with its highly waxed English table.

"You know all the rest of me," she said, "and the house is a part of me."

They walked up the broad staircase hand in hand to the landing and from there, where the stairs divided, to the upper hall, lighted by its two beautiful arched windows. The tall clock, which he had heard tick and strike the hour but which he had never seen, was standing near the landing and its ticking only emphasized the cool silence. The bedrooms were just as they should have been, each with its four-poster and its canopy, each with its bureau or its highboy. Jessica's room was the smallest, next to Mr. Lovell's large front room. She had slept in it as long as she could remember and her father's feelings were always hurt when she wanted to move the furniture because her mother had arranged the room herself, even down to the china dogs on the mantel above the little fireplace. Its windows, each with a window seat, looked over the formal garden where the tulips were already pushing up through the black earth of the box-bordered bed.

It was an enormous house, much too large for the Lovells now. No one occupied the third floor any longer, but all the rooms were still furnished as they had been when there were more Lovells. Finally there was the storeroom, containing generations of trunks and hatboxes. A narrow flight of unpainted pine stairs, redolent of pitch and dried by hundreds of summers, led upwards from the storeroom to the cupola. The cupola, enclosed by arched windows with old, uneven panes of glass, rose above the slate roof and above the elaborate railing of the widow's walk and looked across the town to the river.

As he stood there holding Jessica's hand, a little out of breath because they had hurried up the stairs, it seemed to him that they had traveled a long way together and that together they had reached a height where nothing could touch them. The leaves of the elms were still that soft, yellowish green and the trees rose plumelike above the roofs and the yards of the other houses. It was a dull day, because of the east wind, and the river had a leaden color and the sea was misty.

"There's your house," she said.

He could see the line of Spruce Street beneath them and he could see a corner of the house through the trees.

"There's the Meaders' yard," he said, and then they were in each other's arms. They were above everything and all alone.

"I like it here," he told her. "You and I are all that matter here."

They did not stay long because it was cold and drafty and they never went there again; yet whenever he thought of that spring and summer when he was engaged to Jessica and ever afterwards when he smelled seasoned pine, he was there in the cupola again, above the new leaves of the elms with Jessica, safe from what Mr. Lovell thought and safe from what other people were thinking and saying. They should have run away and got married, but neither of them could have thought seriously of such a thing. There seemed to be so much time that summer and everything seemed settled, and so it was, until the autumn, and so it should have been and might have been.

Mr. Lovell said that night in the library that it was still a tentative matter and that no one should be told except immediate members of the family. He supposed that Charles should tell his mother, his father, and his sister, but there was no reason to tell the Marchbys yet. He did not want any family jubilation, because there was no immediate reason for it. It was an ordeal for him, because Jessica was his only daughter and all he had in the world. He would face the ordeal, but at least he could expect reasonable consideration. There would be no engagement teas, no rounds of calling, and no other jubilation until matters were more definitely resolved than they were at present. Marriage, in case Charles did not know it, and Jessie too, was a serious matter. When two people were infatuated — he knew it was a graceless word, but one which he really thought described the situation — they could not be said to know each other or the complications of each other's backgrounds. Any engagement was a severe emotional strain and this whole affair's coming so suddenly was more of a strain on him than it was on Charles. He had not asked for it or expected it, but now they must share this period of strain together as best they could. They must bear and forbear and it was no time for jubilation.

Nevertheless, it seemed to Charles that there was an undercurrent of illicit jubilation. When he and Jessica had told Miss Georgianna, after Mr. Lovell had gone to bed that evening, she did not need a glass of water. Instead, she kissed Jessica and then Charles, and she told Charles that he must call her Aunt Georgianna now. She sounded like his own Aunt Jane when she told Jessica that she could have the silver tea set.

"And what did Laurence say when you told him?" she asked.

"It was dreadful," Jessica said, "but he was awfully sweet. Wasn't he sweet about it, Charley?"

But Miss Lovell said of course he was not sweet about it. That would be more than could be expected of him.

"You'll have to learn to put up with him, Charley. You'll get used to him in time. And now you'd better run along home. Jessica must be tired."

Jessica did look pale and tired, but she told him in the hall that she was very happy. She never knew that she had loved him so much. It was dreadful knowing what the two people she loved most in the world must have been going through.

"I feel just as though I had been cut in two, darling," she said, "and now I'm growing together again. Everything will be better now. You wait and see. Father didn't hurt your feelings, did he?"

There was a strange egocentric quality about being in love that created an acute perception but clouded any rational judgment. He was profoundly touched that she had been able to see that he might have been hurt. She was the gentlest, kindest, most understanding person in the world.

"He can't hurt me," he said, "as long as you understand."

"Oh, darling," she whispered, "I do understand. More than you think, so much more than you think."

It was past the family's bedtime when he left the car at Rowell's Garage, but even so they were all still sitting in the parlor. He knew at once from the quick, alert way they all turned toward him that they had been waiting for him.

"Charley dear," his mother said, "aren't you going to tell us what happened?"

"Charley," his father asked, before there was any time to answer, "did you see Laurence Lovell?"

"Yes," Charles said, "I saw him."

"Charley." His mother looked hurt. "Aren't you going to tell us what he said?"

All at once he was very glad they were all there waiting, because they were on his side and they would be no matter what.

"All right," he said. "I'm engaged to Jessica, but I'm only to tell you. It isn't to be announced yet."

It sounded as dry as dust when he told it but he never forgot how happy they looked. Dorothea hugged him, a very unusual thing for her to do, and his mother began to cry, but it was only, she said, because she was so happy, and his father shook hands with him.

"Oh, dear me," he said, "I wish I'd seen Laurence Lovell."

"Charley" — Dorothea hugged him again — "tell us what he said."

Suddenly he was very glad to tell them everything.

"I don't think he liked it much," he began. "First he asked Jessica to get him a glass of water."

"Oh, dear me," John Gray said. "A glass of water."

"I don't think he thought it was serious at first," Charles went on, "until we began talking about money."

He had never told them about his brokerage account and they were asking him why he had been so secretive and he found it hard to explain. He could only say there were some things he did not like to talk about, but there it was. He and Jessica were engaged, although it was not to be announced.

"And I don't want anyone to do anything about it," he said. "I don't want anyone to tell anybody."

"I can't quite fit this all together," his father said, "but it seems to me that Laurence Lovell was mildly insulting, Charley."

"I told you he didn't like it," Charles answered.

"And that's one part of it that I don't like," John Gray said. "I think I'd better go and see Laurence Lovell myself tomorrow."

It was the last thing that Charles had expected or wanted and it was utterly uncalled-for but he was not able to dissuade him.

"Can't you leave him alone?" Charles asked. "What did he ever do to you, Father?"

John Gray smiled and stared straight at the wall in front of him.

"That's just it," he said. "He never did do anything."

"Now, Charley," his mother said, "of course your father must have a talk with Mr. Lovell if you and Jessica are engaged and I think it would be very nice if we asked Mr. Lovell and Miss Georgianna here to dinner. Don't you, John?"

"No, Esther," John Gray said. "I don't think it's necessary to ask Laurence Lovell to dinner."

His father was playing poker at the Pine Trees when Charles got back from Boston the next evening. It was the Pine Tree get-together night, an annual occasion on which they all met at the firehouse and ate steamed clams and hamburgers, so Charles did not see his father until later. His mother and Dorothea both told him that his father had been to see Mr. Lovell that morning but when he came home he had been very busy telephoning Boston — something to do with some sort of auxiliary schooner — and that he had not mentioned Mr. Lovell and they had not wanted to ask him.

Mr. Lovell, however, had spoken of it himself when Charles had gone to see Jessica after supper.

"Your father dropped in this morning, Charles," Mr. Lovell said.

"I told him I wished he wouldn't," Charles said.

"There was no reason at all, under the circumstances, why he shouldn't have," Mr. Lovell said. "We had a very pleasant talk — largely about financial matters."

"I'm glad it was pleasant, sir," Charles said, but he could not very well ask Mr. Lovell what financial matters had been discussed.

His father never told him either. He was in his room upstairs later, reading *The Anatomy of Melancholy,* and he called to Charles to say good night.

425

"Oh, there you are, Charley,' he said. "I had a little talk with Laurence Lovell this morning."

"What did you talk about?" Charles asked.

"Oh, this and that — financial matters. Do you know what I think, Charley?"

"What?" Charles asked.

"I think I'll get out of this market. I haven't been sleeping well lately. I had to go to Gerald's last week to get some pills. The market's getting on my nerves." He closed *The Anatomy of Melancholy* and placed it on the table. "I don't see why I shouldn't live on my money like the Lovells, for a while, and let someone else worry."

"You're not serious, are you?" Charles said.

"I don't see why you never believe me, Charley," John Gray answered. "I've never liked doing the same thing all the time. There's too much else going on. Dorothea's getting married in June and you're engaged. I've been using my mind too much. Now what I really need is a little sea air. Look at this, Charley."

He picked up a photograph from the table. It was a picture of a schooner.

"It's the *Zaza*. It's a damned funny name, isn't it? People who own yachts and horses never have much imagination. The *Zaza*. Sixty-five feet overall. Three in the crew. You'll like the captain, Charley. He says garlic cures indigestion, but he bunks forward with the crew. She'll be in the river tomorrow."

"You mean to say you've bought that thing?" Charles asked.

"I wish you wouldn't jump at conclusions," his father said. "I know my place, Charley. That's what I told Laurence Lovell this morning. I've just chartered her for a month. I need some relaxation."

"I wish you'd have some sense of proportion," Charles said.

It must have been a part of Clyde folklore still — his father and that schooner-yacht called the *Zaza* — but at least he only had her for a month.

"Father," he asked, "did you do this because you were going to talk with Mr. Lovell?"

His father did not answer him specifically.

"That's a very sensible question, Charley. I won't say yes and I won't say no. I admit it has its juvenile side." His father was enjoying every minute of it. He was having a wonderful time. "I'm sorry if it embarrasses you, Charley," he said, "but aren't you glad I'm getting out of the market?"

"If you're out, you won't stay out," Charles said. "You can't."

"I don't know why you're so sure of everything," his father answered. "I might stay out."

He was still holding the photograph of that schooner-yacht, a ridiculous plaything with its full white billowing sails. Everything had gone too far, Charles was thinking. Nothing could end in defiance of the laws of gravity.

"I wish I could believe it," he said.

He was thinking of what Sam had said long ago, that it was all a lot of guff. His father had assumed his old look of composed displeasure.

"That's not very complimentary, Charley," he said.

"Why don't you set up a trust fund for Mother?" Charles asked. "Then I'd be very complimentary, Father."

He had asked the same question again and again lately and his father's reaction was always exactly the same. "How many times have I told you," he asked, "that I agree with you? Of course, I'm going to do it, but Hugh Blashfield isn't going to handle it and there isn't any hurry. Don't be so worried, Charley."

Charles never liked to think about that schooner in the river and he only went aboard her once or twice. He told Jessica that he was ashamed of it and that he wished his father would keep her at Marblehead and not in the river. He always had a feeling that he ought to apologize to everyone and explain, but he could not very well explain that the boat was symbolic and a gesture, and after all no one seemed to be as upset about this as he was. Jessica was only amused and said it was just like his father and that it was nice he had something to play with. Dorothea said that of course it was silly and ridiculously extravagant, but then he was only going to have it for a month and it probably did not cost much more than that winter cruise to the Caribbean. His mother was more definite, because she always accepted everything that John Gray did. If he had earned the money — that was the way she put it because she always thought of money as being earned — there was no reason why he should not use it. There were all sorts of other, bigger yachts everywhere and it was not as though he were not sharing it with everybody. He was taking everyone he knew for a sail and there was no reason why he should not have some pleasure himself for once. He had worked so hard for years at the mill and no one had appreciated him and now that he was a success, as she always knew he would be, it was not fair to be so critical. He deserved to have a good time and she wished that Charles could see what a very remarkable man he was. She wished that Charles understood him as well as Dorothea.

"Charley," she said, "you're getting as fussy as Jackie Mason."

XXI

A Formal Announcement Will Be Necessary

A HAZE OF UNREALITY surrounded that summer and this may have been the reason why Charles found himself seeking Jackie Mason's company again. Jackie was still what he had always been — a constant quantity. When Charles told Jackie Mason that he hated to think what everyone was saying about his father's spending and extravagance, Jackie was reassuring.

"Of course," he said, "there's a certain amount of talk, but I wouldn't take it too seriously. You see, your father has a certain position, Charley, and if you have a position no one talks so much." Jackie frowned and patted his yellow hair carefully. He was always worried for fear his hair would not stay in place. "Now if Mr. Sullivan or Mr. Levine put a hundred-dollar bill in the contribution box, it would be different. It would be different with my father, or me too, Charley, because, well, my grandfather was a druggist and your grandfather was a judge. That gives position, and if you have it you can be more eccentric, Charley. It's the same way with you. You have more position than I have. Let's admit it."

Jackie Mason was looking at him wistfully, as though their positions were far apart already and as though he felt privileged that they were still friends. Charles wanted to tell Jackie to stop, that they were just the same as they ever were, that they had lived next door to each other and had known each other all their lives, but before he could speak Jackie was going on.

"You can really go anywhere now," Jackie said. "It must be nice to be so secure."

"But I'm not secure," Charles told him. "Don't you see, with Father nothing is secure?" But Jackie shook his head.

"That isn't so, Charley," he answered, "Really it isn't. I used to think you were hurting your position when you left Wright-Sherwin, but you knew what you were doing."

"I wonder if anyone really knows why he does anything," Charles said.

"Now, Charley," Jackie said, "we know each other well enough to be frank. I know you don't tell me everything, you don't have to." It was true. You never had to tell much in Clyde. "You can get anywhere you want." Jackie Mason sighed. "You'll be a director of the bank someday, and there's no reason why you shouldn't be a trustee of the public library." Jackie was always loyal. He was loyal to the end. "It doesn't even make any difference if Dorothea marries Elbridge Sterne, and furthermore, don't you see, Charley — " and Jackie stopped as though he were going to say something indiscreet.

"Go ahead," Charles told him. "What don't I see?"

"Don't you see that Mr. Lovell can't do anything about it, in spite of his position?"

Jackie had lowered his voice when he mentioned Mr. Lovell's name. They had been standing in the dusk talking in the Masons' yard as they had ever since they were children, and Jackie looked half-apprehensively toward Johnson Street. It was as close as he ever came to mentioning what everybody knew, that Mr. Lovell could do nothing but accept what lay between Charles and Jessica. Mr. Lovell could do nothing about the accomplished fact. Mr. Lovell himself was a part of Clyde.

If there were anything in the theory that the past remained intact, he and Jessica Lovell must still have been somewhere, with the other ghosts of Clyde. Perhaps all of that summer might have returned to him again and again if he had stayed in Clyde. If he had never seen Jessica Lovell again except in the distance, he would have seen the shadows of Jessica and himself around every corner and on every country road. If he had walked down Dock Street, he and Jessica might still have been standing in front of the window of Stowell's furniture store, talking of living room curtains. She had wanted green monk's cloth curtains. Down at the foot of

430

Gow Street, they might still have been gazing at the For Sale sign on the Pritchard house, for old Miss Pritchard had died that summer. It was in bad condition, but they could have fixed it up if they had bought it. If he had gone to the beach in the moonlight, he and Jessica would have been there with their picnic supper. Their two shadows would have been everywhere, because they had been everywhere in Clyde together. By God, it was a wonderful town.

They would have been talking still about the things they were going to do. There would have been the same surprise that they liked so many of the same things. They had been so very, very practical. Jessica was going to learn how to keep a budget and he was going to learn how to work in the garden. They were going to read together in the evening. They both loved to read aloud. At last it was possible to talk of all those practical things. She could buy him neckties now and she could go with him to Boston in the morning, if she wanted, and of course they were going to have a car, a Ford or a Dodge, perhaps — but they only looked at cars in Boston, because their engagement was not announced.

He could buy her a gold bracelet now and a moonstone pin, but not a ring because their engagement was not announced. They could not very well look at rings in Marston's Jewelry Shop but they could look at them in Boston and if anyone who knew them should happen to see them it would not matter much because they were engaged, although it was not announced. They could even go to Jessica's aunt's summer place at Cohasset for the night, because the family knew they were engaged. There were all sorts of things that they could do and say that summer. It was strange how few of them he could remember. It must have been because he had pushed them so relentlessly aside. That summer was now covered up by so much that was more actual — that summer and all of Clyde.

The summer and those shadows of himself and Jessica, and Clyde too, were like the Atlantis upon which his father had discoursed that night when Jessica came to supper. Elbridge Sterne had not known about Atlantis, but that was natural. Elbridge was an ex-

431

ceflent metallurgical chemist, so excellent that a few months later a larger company from Kansas City had sent for him. He was too good for Wright-Sherwin and anyway it was a chance to get back home. Elbridge did not care about lands beneath the sea or sunken shoals that jutted above the water when the tide was very low.

Dorothea and Elbridge Sterne were married in the Unitarian Church that June. May Mason, who had married Jeffrey Meader and who already had two children, was matron of honor, though she said she was too old — still, she was not as old as Dorothea — and Elbridge had asked Charles to be best man, instead of his brother, who came on with Elbridge's mother from Kansas City. Dorothea had wanted Jessica to be a bridesmaid but they had not asked her in the end — because it had not been announced.

Nevertheless, the Lovells did come to the church, probably because Mr. Lovell had thought it would be more conspicuous had he stayed away. All that made the Lovells conspicuous was that they were placed up in front, just behind the Marchbys, and everybody saw them during their long walk up the aisle. If Charles had known of this arrangement he might have been able to stop it, but he only knew when he walked out with Elbridge from the minister's room under the pulpit stairs.

It was a very large wedding and John Gray wanted everyone to be in silk hats and cutaways and he would have been very glad to have paid for the clothes himself. He was hurt when Dorothea did not want this. He only had one daughter, he said, and he wanted it to be a good wedding, but instead the ushers wore blue coats and white flannels and the bridesmaids were dressed in pastel organdy.

"The bride," the *Clyde Herald* said, "wearing her mother's wedding veil, a family heirloom, was exquisitely gowned in a white satin dress from Bendel's, the well-known New York dress house . . . the flower girls were the Misses Edwina and Malvina Meader, daughters of Mrs. Meader, the matron of honor . . . the gifts to the bridesmaids were exquisite gold compact boxes and to each of the ushers was given a gold cigarette case . . . the music for the reception was furnished by the fife-and-drum corps of the Pine Tree Veteran Fire Company . . . refreshments and a buffet luncheon for the numerous guests at the Gray residence on Spruce Street were supplied by the J. E. Crowell Catering Company from Boston . . . the bride and groom left for the wedding trip in a Duesenberg convertible automobile — a gift of the bride's father."

His father had not succeeded with the cutaways but at least he had insisted on buying the compacts and cigarette cases and he had persuaded Dorothea to accept a foreign car instead of a check because he had always wanted a Duesenberg himself.

His future in the Duesenberg convertible disturbed Elbridge more than the crowd in the church as he waited with Charles beneath the pulpit stairs. Charles had always thought of Elbridge as being literal and phlegmatic, but instead he was perspiring freely.

"I don't know why we have to drive that thing," he said, "after all the rest of this."

It gave Charles a fraternal feeling when Elbridge spoke about "that thing." They were both creatures of circumstance, being moved without their own volition, there beneath the pulpit stairs. "Charley, it doesn't tie in with anything else."

"That's right," Charles said. "It doesn't really."

"Do you remember" — Elbridge mopped his forehead — "when I used to come to Spruce Street and Dorothea and I dried the dishes after supper?" Elbridge mopped his forehead again.

"I know, Elbridge," Charles said. "I know."

"We're like a lot of kids playing," Elbridge said, and he put his hand on Charles's arm. "It doesn't make sense." Charles often wondered what they would have done if Elbridge had not married Dorothea.

The reception was so large that there were tables in both their own and the Masons' yards. The fife-and-drum corps made too much noise and all the people he had known all his life seemed like actors in a play, crowded simultaneously onto the stage and half forgetting their parts. The Meaders, the Masons, the technicians from Wright-Sherwin, Mr. and Mrs. Howell, the Thomases, the Stanleys, the Lovells, the Sullivans, the Levines and the Walterses were there

433

and so was everyone else. John Gray had insisted on inviting everyone and everyone had come, and no doubt they must still be asking each other if they remembered Johnny Gray before the crash and that wedding of Dorothea's; and Charley Gray and Jessica Lovell standing on the lawn and city waiters pouring champagne right where everyone could see from Spruce Street. When he had it he could spend it. It made Clyde look like a seafaring town again. That was quite a party, they must still be saying, quite a party, and did they remember the speech that Johnny Gray gave? It was too bad, they must be saying, too bad about the Grays, too bad about Charley and Jessica, but then he was a banker now, holding an important position in New York. It was too bad, they must still be saying, that the Grays had moved away. Easy come and easy go. Charley Gray was a nice boy, and Esther Gray was a Marchby and the Marchbys were good people. It was too bad that the Grays were gone.

Of course, Charles had the Lovells on his mind and it would have looked peculiar if he had not seen that Miss Lovell was comfortable and that Mr. Lovell had ginger ale when he refused champagne, but he had to be at the bride's table, too, and he could not be in two places at once and it annoyed him when Jackie Mason said, "Charley, I think you ought to be seen with the Lovells." He was going to be seen with the Lovells, but they could not have been at the bride's table. The fife-and-drum corps was playing "Put on Your Old Gray Bonnet" because they were running out of tunes. Miss Lovell was in rust-colored silk, with a parasol. Jessica was in green organdy. She always loved green, and she was wearing his moonstone pin.

"Well, Charles," Mr. Lovell said, "this is quite a day for all of you, isn't it, and quite a day for Clyde. This is really a most original wedding party."

It was unnecessary for him to have been quite so amused and tolerant — it was a time to be loyal to the family.

"I hope you're enjoying it, sir," Charles said.

"Of course, I'm enjoying it." Mr. Lovell smiled. "Especially the fife-and-drum corps."

"You know how father is about the Pine Trees," Charles said.

"Yes, indeed, I know," Mr. Lovell answered.

A minute later Charles was standing alone with Jessica and they were each holding a glass of champagne. At least it seemed to him that they were alone, in spite of the crowd on the lawn.

"You're not angry with Father, are you?" she was asking. "He's never nice in crowds."

"Angry?" and he laughed at her. "I'm glad you wore the pin."

"It's a lovely party. Dorothea looks so sweet and your mother is so darling. I love your father. He's so happy. He's so young."

"Look at poor Elbridge," Charles said. "I wish it weren't so noisy."

"He's wanted to marry her for a long time, hasn't he?"

"It took them a long while to make up their minds," Charles said.

Jessica smiled at him over the rim of her glass.

"I'm awfully glad we've made up ours. Where's Father?"

"Over there, talking to Mrs. Thomas."

"He always tries to talk to everybody. He's really awfully sweet. Charley, I really think he's getting used to it."

"To you and me?"

"I keep saying 'It,' don't I? You and me, everything."

The fife-and-drum corps had started again. The corps was not used to champagne and the drums were off beat.

"Charley," she asked, "does all this make you think of something?"

"What?" he asked.

"Why, the firemen's muster. . . . Charley, what'll we do tonight? Let's go somewhere and be alone."

It was wonderful to think that such a thing was possible.

The reception was growing more and more like a firemen's muster. The Pine Trees and the hand tub, with its brasswork shining in the sun, had suddenly appeared on Spruce Street. It was a surprise thought up by the Pine Trees and the Pine Trees were going to follow the bride and groom when they went away. Earl Wilkins and some of the boys had thought it up all of a sudden, perhaps because John Gray had sent six cases of champagne down

435

to the firehouse. He would never forget Elbridge Sterne's stricken look. It was something that could only have happened in Clyde.

Later on other bright June days when the weather was cool, Charles would think of himself and Jessica standing there in the crowded Spruce Street yard, alone and not alone, and he could always recall those obvious words they both had said. Somehow everything they meant to each other, their beginning and their ending, was explained in that brief conversation. It was one of the glittering fragments of the summer and it was indestructible. The truth, of course, was that she had never grown used to it any more than Mr. Lovell. There was no reason why she should have, because she could not love them both at once, but she did not know this then and neither did he.

It was strange in the light of the present to recall that a period existed in his life's span when the only clouds on the horizon were the roseate prophecies of an even more roseate future. You could call it a fool's paradise or a debauch or all the other hard words the economic experts and the planners called that summer later, but Charles was never sure that most of them at the time had not been fooled by it even though all the sinister symptoms which everyone recognized later were already apparent. The low-pressure areas and the storms were already assembling behind the pellucid sky. There were inequities and there were greed and social blindness. It was a hectic, materialistic, egocentric world, along the lines of boom and bust, but it sometimes seemed to him, though he seldom said it, that no prophet had succeeded in making a securer society — not Mr. Roosevelt or his Brain Trust, or Hitler or Mussolini, or Hirohito in Japan, or Stalin, or even Mr. Attlee. This was a reactionary thought but his profession was investment which in the purest sense was only an endeavor to cut the cloth according to the situations which radicals and liberals created.

There were no wars or rumors of war that summer. Instead there was a sense of peace and almost of good will. There were no threatening, saber-rattling ogres and few confusions of thought. It was ironical to remember that the cost of government and general taxation were considered too high, and of course there were the gang wars and prohibition, but it was quite a world that summer. There was going to be enough for everyone, a standard of living that would grow always higher, a general advance in science and culture. The country was only dimly becoming aware of its resources and potentialities. Business and enlightened competition would take care of any contingency. It was a great place, the United States, and a great world, that summer.

You could not help but catch some of that contagion. There was freedom from want and freedom from fear for a little while that summer. He and Jessica were going to get married and live happily ever after, and perhaps even Mr. Lovell began to believe this.

It honestly did seem to Charles that Mr. Lovell was really trying to get used to him, but Jessica and Miss Georgianna were trying so hard to get them used to each other that they may have tried too hard. Miss Georgianna was always asking Laurence if he would mind entertaining Charles for a few minutes while she and Jessica went upstairs to look for something; and Jessica, if she and Charles were going out somewhere, was always saying that it would take her a few minutes to get ready but that Father would love to see him.

"Darling," Jessica said once, "what were you and Father talking about when I was upstairs?"

They had just been talking, he told her, and Mr. Lovell had said it was too bad — it was a great pity — that he had not gone to Harvard.

"He didn't mean it the way you think," Jessica said. "You mustn't be hurt about it."

"Why should it hurt me?" Charles asked. "It's a common point of view in certain groups. Mr. Rush said the same thing to me yesterday."

"What did you say to Father when he said it?"

"There wasn't much to say," Charles answered. "I just said that there are a lot of schools besides Harvard."

"You didn't call it a school, did you?"

"I don't remember," Charles said. "I think I called it a school."

437

"Darling" — she sounded bright and determined — "Father wouldn't have said that if he weren't interested in you. He really is. He's beginning to quote some of the things you say."

"I suppose he is," Charles said, "and I'm interested in him. I guess we both have to be."

"What did you talk about after that?" Jessica asked.

"About painting the house," Charles told her. "He had some estimates."

"Why, darling," Jessica said, "why didn't you tell me that first? If he told you how much it's going to cost it means you're almost in the family." She shook her head and pushed her hair back from her forehead. "It's awfully funny . . ."

"What's so funny?" Charles asked.

"If it weren't for me," Jessica said, "if it weren't for Clyde, why you're just the person he would like. He's always talking about people who make their own way, and he'd be doing nice things for you and giving you advice and he'd be just the way he was with Malcolm Bryant and you'd be having a good time together."

"I wish you wouldn't worry about us," Charles said. "We're getting along all right. I understand the way he feels. Honestly, I don't blame him. He just feels disappointed."

"Darling," Jessica said, "how many times must I tell you that he's getting over it. Every day, every minute, he's getting over it. His point of view hasn't got anything to do with you. You're just a general subject. Charley, he's trying so hard and you've got to try. I can't bear it, I simply can't, if you don't like each other."

It was that pressure. He sometimes found himself being almost sympathetic with Mr. Lovell, but he knew they would not have liked each other even had they met in a casual way. Both of them had tried yet neither of them knew the art of placation. Neither of them was the agreeable person, bearing gifts and little favors, and both of them were proud. Yet there always was that pressure. They were always circling about each other, seeking for some common ground, and the only common ground was Clyde, not the town of the present but the town of the past, and even in that past the Lovells had been shipowners and the Grays had been ships' captains — the Lovells had made money out of shipping while the Grays had only worried along. Yet both of them had tried.

The time had come when Mr. Lovell had to face the inevitable fact that there could not be an indefinite *status quo*. It must have been in late August, because Charles could remember the singing of the crickets. He was sitting with Jessica in the summerhouse in the garden, because Jessica had said that Mr. Lovell had recently asked her why they were always leaving the house to go somewhere when they could have the house and the garden all to themselves. It had been sweet of him. He had asked Jessica why Charles did not feel more at home. It did not look well, he said, always going some-where else.

They often loved to sit without talking, and they were not talk-ing when Mr. Lovell called to them from the house.

"Oh, Jessica, are you and Charles out there?"

"Yes, Father," Jessica answered. "Don't you want to come out with us?"

"No, Jessie," Mr. Lovell said, "but I wonder whether you and Charles would mind coming in. I'd like to speak to you both for a minute."

Mr. Lovell led the way to the library, which meant that he had something serious to say. Though Charles was gradually beginning to discover that Mr. Lovell had never read and probably never would read many of the old leather-bound English editions on the shelves, Mr. Lovell seemed to draw from the physical presence of Fielding, Sterne and George Eliot, Maria Edgeworth, the British poets and all the rest of them, a vicarious and genuinely deceptive erudition. Perhaps they all gave him an assurance which he may have lacked in other places. Perhaps they afforded him the back-ground for being the person he wanted to be but never could be — the man of cultivated taste and tradition, who, through fortunate circumstances, had ample leisure in which to gratify those tastes. He did not possess, Charles was beginning to learn, the energy, the persistence, or the curiosity ever to become what he thought he was, but then few people like him ever did, outside of the novels of Jane Austen, and besides Charles admitted that he was overcritical of Mr. Lovell. As he stood with the books behind him Charles had an idea that Mr. Lovell must have been rehearsing what he was going to say while they were sitting in the summer-house.

"Jessie, dear, I wish you'd sit down, and you too, Charles," Mr. Lovell said. "You're so used to my habits, aren't you, Jessie, that you won't mind my standing up? Jessie dear, the time has come — I did hope it wouldn't come so soon — to talk seriously about you and Charles."

"Oh, Father," Jessica said, "has anyone said anything?"

Mr. Lovell seemed surprised that Jessica should have guessed. He nodded and cleared his throat again and raised his voice.

"Yesterday afternoon I happened to run into Francis Stanley on Dock Street when I was on my way to the library meeting and he asked me, out of a clear sky" — Mr. Lovell lowered his voice — "if I were to be congratulated. Of course, I've always known Francis Stanley — I've always known the Stanleys were not real friends of ours, in spite of the amenities — but there you are."

"But Father," Jessica said, and she laughed feebly, "I don't see anything so bad in that. It's just the way Mr. Stanley always says everything."

"I suppose it is," Mr. Lovell said. "I know Francis Stanley very well, Jessica, and I've never been impressed by him or the Stanley money. He's a good businessman, but there are other things besides business, Charles. Now don't" — Mr. Lovell raised his hand " — don't interrupt me, Jessie. Let me make my point. It does show where we have drifted. If Francis Stanley felt himself free, and he did feel himself free, to ask me such a question even jokingly, it shows what other people must be saying. I don't mind about myself, Jessie, but I can't have your name becoming a byword."

Mr. Lovell paused and seemed to be looking back over what he had said.

"Now this is every bit as embarrassing and as difficult for me as it is for you, more so because this involves my daughter, my only daughter. I can see by your expression, Charles, that you think

I'm overemphasizing this, but perhaps your friends and family have a different view. I'm sure I don't know."

As always he was facing the situation honestly and fairly.

"In the first place, Charles — and I must address this to you rather than to Jessica, because I have never thought that any of this, well, this imbroglio, was ever primarily your fault, Jessie dear. It is the man who takes the initiative — well, in the first place, I feel in justice to myself — and I do think I have to be considered — that I should say frankly and without malice that none of this is my fault, any more than it was yours, Jessie dear. If I had been consulted in time, we would not have this problem. Instead, I had to condone it, because it was an accomplished fact. I had hoped if you were thrown together you both might have seen some of the things that are so painfully obvious to me . . . but no. This is where we've drifted." Mr. Lovell's face had reddened. He pulled a fresh white handkerchief from his breast pocket and blew his nose.

"Father dear," Jessica said, and her voice broke a little, "I've told you and I've told you you won't lose me. Charles doesn't want to take me away from you. Don't be so unhappy, dear. It makes us all so miserable, just when we all ought to be so happy. Don't you see?"

"I know, Jessie darling," Mr. Lovell said softly, "and I'm sorry if I've said too much. I'm trying to face the situation and it can't go on the way it is much longer." Mr. Lovell blew his nose again. "There's only one thing to do. Jessie, if you feel by the middle of, well, November as you feel now, I'm afraid a formal announcement will be necessary, a tea or something. This will have to be clarified somehow."

Mr. Lovell had a stricken expression. He folded his handkerchief and put it carefully back in his pocket.

"Father dear," Jessica said, "you're awfully sweet," and she threw her arms around him. It made Charles feel like an intruder when Mr. Lovell kissed Jessica's forehead gravely and softly.

"I'm glad if you're happy, dear," Mr. Lovell said, "and, Charles, I'm glad we've had this talk. Shall you and I shake hands?" It was hard to be elated in the face of Mr. Lovell's deep sorrow but he honestly tried to put himself in Mr. Lovell's position when he shook hands.

"And now, Jessie," Mr. Lovell said, "why don't you take Charles out to the garden again? I'd like to be alone, just for a little while."

Jessica closed the door softly and tenderly behind her, leaving Mr. Lovell standing on the hearthrug, resigned, head bent, alone with no company but his shattered dreams. If it seemed to Charles over-theatrical, it was not his place to say so. Instead he owed it to Jessica to show a decent, measured sympathy.

"Darling," Jessica whispered, "it's so hard for him. I wish he didn't love me so much," and then she began to cry.

"Don't, Jessica," he said, and he put his arm around her and gave her his handkerchief.

"I wish everything wouldn't hurt him so," she sobbed. "I wish he had ten children and every one of them a girl . . . Charley, he wasn't nice to you at all."

"He can't help it," Charles said. "I don't mind as long as you love me, Jessica."

"Darling, if I didn't I couldn't stand it," she said. "Do you still love me?"

"Of course I do," he said.

"In spite of everything?"

"All the more."

"That's why it's so terrible," she said.

"I don't see why you say it's terrible," he told her.

"I don't know why I did either. I didn't mean it," she said. "And, Charley, it won't be so long till November, will it?"

It would not be long. The goldenrod was out and they could hear the crickets and soon it would be time for the asters, the small white ones and the large purple ones. There was nothing but security, now that she had stopped crying. If their engagement was announced in the middle of November it would not be a long engagement. That was what Jessica was saying. There would be no reason for it. As soon as their engagement was announced they could buy the Pritchard house. They could start doing everything they were talking about. They could really start doing it now — almost.

XXII

That Gale I Well Remember . . .

— OLIVER WENDELL HOLMES

DURING ALL of his later business experience, many otherwise reasonable people kept resurrecting the details of the crash of 1929. They discussed it, apparently, for the same reason that old ladies enjoyed describing surgical operations and sessions with their dentists. There was a snob value in boasting of old pain. Instead of wishing to forget, they kept struggling to remember. The older men would talk about Black Friday in the nineties and the more technical panic of 1907 as though all these debacles were just alike and sanctimonious members of the Securities and Exchange Commission who had had nothing to do with that market would discuss the immoralities of the moneychangers in the temple and cast sharp aspersions on entrenched greed. There were even people, who should have known better, who seemed to be imbued with the fixed idea that the crash of 1929 caused the depression. They could no longer see it as a symptom or as an extreme example of mass hysteria. Only unattractively strong individuals should have been allowed to dabble in that market.

Most people never seemed to see what Charles saw in the crash — a sordidly ugly exhibition of the basest of human fears. They had forgotten the desperation that made cowards and thieves out of previously respectable people, and the fear evolved from greed which had no decency or dignity. Instead, they always harked back to the spectacular — the confusion, the lights in downtown New York burning night after night while clerks were struggling to balance the brokerage accounts; and sooner or later they always asked Charles where he had been working then and whether he too had been long on the market on that particular day in October. He had learned long ago to answer accurately, with only part of the truth. He always said that he had been in Boston with E. P. Rush & Company and nothing much had happened to him. He had made some money out of the market the year before and had put it into government bonds. His mother was living on the income derived from her late husband's estate. His mother was living next door to his sister Dorothea in Kansas City. His sister had married a man, a metallurgical chemist, who had a very good job in Kansas City.

He never told the whole truth to anyone, except to Nancy and to Arthur Slade, and Arthur Slade may have told some of it to Tony Burton at the Stuyvesant Bank but Charles was never sure. Naturally his mother and Dorothea and Elbridge Sterne knew part of the truth, and Jessica Lovell knew some of it. There were some things which were better not told, and there was no use digging up what was so completely finished. His own illusions and everything he had planned had crashed in that common crash, but then millions of lives and plans had been crashing ever since. It did no good to imagine what he might have done to have prevented it. Actually he could have done nothing. Everything was what Mr. Lovell would have called an accomplished fact before Charles had been permitted to face it. He was always glad he did not have to blame himself, at least not very much.

When the drop occurred in September, that minor break which nearly everyone considered a normal readjustment considering the market's phenomenally unbroken rise, he had seen it for what it was — the first rumblings of a landslide, an ominous shift of stress and strain that would never strike a balance until the whole structure broke. He knew this was the beginning of a greater break even before Mr. Rush, after a partners' meeting, called him in to help compose a letter advising customers of Rush & Company to sell their holdings of common stocks. While he was waiting for the letter to be typed, Charles wandered over to the row of leather armchairs before the tickers and the board. Although Rush & Company was essentially an investment and not a brokerage office a large group

444

was there, as there had been all that summer. He was just looking at the last quotation for Telephone when he heard his father call him and saw his father standing near the tickers with his hands in his pockets and with his felt hat pushed back from his forehead.

He was surprised to see his father because John Gray had never done his trading at Rush & Company. He had always said he liked a bigger office and a bigger board and besides Moulton Rush was always disapproving.

"I've been feeling a little lonely, Charley," his father said. "I thought I would drop into the cloisters here. There's an atmosphere bordering on hysteria down the street. I'm seeking conservatism. There doesn't seem to be a rally yet, does there?"

"No, not yet," Charles said. "I thought you were staying at home on the side lines."

"I thought I was until I telephoned," his father answered, "and then I got Will Stevens to drive me in, just to see the show. Is the ticker much behind?"

"I don't know," Charles said. "I've only been here for a minute." He was not a customers' man and he had given up all interest in the mechanics of the market.

"Well, well." John Gray took his hands out of his pockets. "I think I'll see whether Moulton's busy. Willie can drive us back home if you'll be at Post Office Square around five o'clock."

"Father," Charles began.

"Don't say it," his father said. "Don't say it. We'll talk about it driving home." He walked away between the rows of chairs toward the ground-glass doors of the partners' offices.

Mr. Rush's door was open, as it usually was in the late afternoon, so Charles did not knock when he brought in the draft of the form letter half an hour later. Mr. Rush was using the bottom drawer of his roll-top desk as a footrest and he sat tilted back in his swivel chair. John Gray was still there with him.

"All right, Johnny," Mr. Rush was saying. "I only know what I think. If you're out, stay out. Go home and read Boswell."

"And three days from now it will be up again," his father said.

445

"Do you want to bet me, Moulton?" — and then Charles gave Mr. Rush the draft of the letter.

He never told anyone but Nancy what happened that afternoon and he only told her about it at the time of the bank closing, in 1933. She awoke at two in the morning and found him staring at the floor without any idea what time it was, and he had to tell her why to prevent her from worrying. He had been thinking about his father and about that afternoon at Rush & Company and about the ride home in the Cadillac.

It had been hard to talk because the top was down and Willie Stevens began to drive over fifty once they were out of the traffic. John Gray had always loved fast driving and it had seemed as if they were hurtling through space. It was easier to tell Nancy than he thought it would be. She knew all about the Grays and she had formed her own opinion of Clyde, although she had never seen it. Besides she knew all about places like Rush & Company. She felt exactly as he did about board rooms and she shared his own ideas about getting on in the polite free-for-all of downtown offices.

"Pull up your socks and forget it," Nancy said. "You couldn't have done a single thing about it. It had to happen and you know it."

She sometimes told him to pull up his socks when she argued with him and it was partly affectionate and partly malicious. She was usually so austere and correctly cynical that it was always as surprising as though Psyche in the White Rock advertisements had said "Damn."

"It might have made some impression if I'd got mad at him," he told her, "but it was hard to get mad at him. He could always rise above everything."

"It wouldn't have made any difference," Nancy said. "You couldn't have done anything, not with all your piety and all your wit. Those boys are all just the same."

"You didn't know Father," Charles told her. "He had a lot of charm and he could shed things, consequences and everything."

"I wish you'd listen to me," Nancy said. "I didn't know him, but

446

they're all alike. They have a congenital and insidious charm. They have to, to get away with what they do, and they don't want to be reformed. I know, because I tried to reform one once. You couldn't have done anything about it."

"When did you try to reform one?" Charles asked.

"When I was younger," Nancy said, "before you came along. Didn't I ever tell you?"

Actually she had said the same thing about John Gray that Moulton Rush had said that September afternoon.

After John Gray left, Mr. Rush went over the typed pages very carefully. He disliked market letters and he did not want anything from Rush & Company to sound like one and neither did he want to hedge behind provisos. He wanted a letter that said something and then stopped, but when they were finished Mr. Rush asked Charles to wait a minute.

"It's none of my business," Mr. Rush said, "but I'm worried about your father." The springs of Mr. Rush's swivel chair creaked. "He's intelligent, but I can't do anything with him. They're all alike, you see, the whole lot of them." He nodded toward the open door. "There are five or six of them in the board room now. They're all alike."

The Cadillac was parked in Post Office Square in a space where there was supposed to be no parking, because his father had learned that the traffic officer on duty there was interested in common stocks.

"Thank you, Tom," his father said to the policeman, "and don't forget what I told you. This is my son Charles."

"Pleased to meet you," the policeman said. "Just leave the Caddy here any time, Mr. Gray."

"Tom is very reasonable," his father said as they drove off, "but I wish he wouldn't call it a Caddy."

He leaned back on the red leather cushions and half closed his eyes. He had perfect confidence in Willie Stevens's driving and looked with relaxed trust at Willie's clean-shaven neck. Willie was wearing his best clothes but he refused to wear any sort of uniform

447

and John Gray had sympathized with him It was hard talking with the top down but also it was difficult for Willie to hear much of their conversation. His father had enjoyed his talk with Moulton Rush. He had always liked Moulton. He had a very human streak considering his type.

"He's a Puritan," John Gray said, "and I have more catholic tastes, but then I'm glad I'm not a Catholic."

"You're not really anything, are you?" Charles said.

"I have religious prejudices," John Gray said, "and I read a chapter from the Bible nearly every night."

"But you only read it for the English," Charles said.

"Charley" — his father pulled his hat down hard, because it was windy with the top down — "why do you imply that I'm a pagan?"

"I don't know what you are," Charles said. "You're too complicated, Father."

"I know. I have a lot of ideas, too many ideas." John Gray took his cigar case from his pocket and put it back again. It was too windy to smoke in the rear seat of the Cadillac.

They had reached the open road and Willie Stevens was driving faster. They did not speak for a while and his father closed his eyes.

"Father," Charles said, "haven't you done enough about beating the system?"

"Now, Charley." John Gray looked hurt. "Let's not spoil this drive."

"All right," Charles said, "but what about that trust fund?"

"I'll attend to it next week," his father said. "Now drop it. I really don't know why I like you, Charley."

Charles did not drop it although he had to speak so loudly in the car that his voice became hoarse and dry. What was the earthly use in taking any risks, he was asking, when his father had everything, enough, too much of everything? The market was shaky. Anyone could see there would be a break. It was egotism, it was childish, it made no sense. If he had set up that trust fund and then he wanted to be a fool, he could go ahead and lose the rest of it.

Charles said all that was on his mind for once. It was utterly selfish, he was saying. His father might for once grasp the idea that everyone was involved. It was not as though he had earned the money to start with. He was losing his head because of a streak of luck. He had said himself he was not sleeping well. What was the use in going on with it if he did not need any more? There would be only one end to it.

His father folded his hands when Charles had finished and was silent for almost a minute before he answered.

"You've always said all that, without saying it, Charley," he said. "This must be unpleasant for you. I'm very sorry, but we can't help how we're made, can we? I suppose I'd better tell you the truth. I like what I'm doing, and what under the sun would I do if I stopped?"

Then his whole face brightened. It was what Charles had said to Nancy later. His father could always shed things.

"You're quite right about the trust fund, too, Charley. I'll attend to it right away. You remember that ten thousand dollars of your mother's and that five of Dorothea's? Well, they wanted me to do a little something with it. I thought perhaps I'd better not tell you, but I've done something, quite a lot, and it really is time I saw about that trust fund."

He undoubtedly was planning to attend to it. The papers were even drawn, as Charles found later, for a fund of a hundred and fifty thousand dollars. The papers were all there upstairs in his room, but his father had never signed them. It was one of those details to be taken up when he had the time.

The day when the market first broke in October must have started for everyone the way it did for Charles, as a part of the ordinary routine of living. He remembered reading later, in a brochure published by a banking house: "In years to come the 1929 crash will doubtless be remembered merely as a summer thundershower." When this was written prosperity was still just around the corner and happy days like those old happy ones would be here again if you were not a bear on the United States. When the storm did break, in

449

a cloudless sky, work went on that first day without much interruption in conservative offices like Rush & Company. It was only when the drop went on the next day and the next and when the tickers lagged further and further behind the trading that Charles began to observe that all the faces in the office were stamped with an expression that began to erase individuality.

Jessica had come to Boston on the morning of the break and they were to have had lunch together but he had called her up at her aunt's house to say that, although it had nothing to do with his own department, he felt he had better stay at the office on general principles. Yet at home for the first day or so he could not notice any change and there seemed to be no more connection between home and E. P. Rush & Company than there ever had been. Back in Clyde he could forget the crowd around the board and those sickly individual attempts at indifference and composure.

That first evening before supper, his father said it would be nice if Axel were to mix some Martini cocktails because it had been quite a day in Boston and Dorothea and Elbridge were coming to dinner. Elbridge had something particular to tell them and he hoped that Elbridge had not been monkeying with the market. It was impossible to read anything on his father's face but as soon as they had a moment alone together Charles asked him if everything was all right, and his father looked very cheerful.

"I wish you wouldn't try to look like a doctor," he said, "and I wish you wouldn't think of me as a widow or an orphan. Hasn't everybody been expecting this? Of course I'm all right."

He was like all the rest of them. They were already beginning to say that they had seen it coming, but Charles felt deeply relieved. His father drank two Martinis, which was unusual for him, but he did not speak again about the market. Instead they talked about the announcement of the engagement in November and who would be coming to the tea. Miss Lovell had called that morning to go over plans for the tea.

When Dorothea and Elbridge arrived, John Gray was describing the next paper he was going to write for the Confessional Club. It would be about the South Sea Bubble, starting with Charles Lamb, and he was going to put it in one-syllable words so that it would not be over the heads of his audience.

"And, Elbridge," he said, "please don't ask me what the South Sea Bubble was, because it's nearly time for supper."

"Elbridge doesn't care anything about a bubble," Dorothea said. "He wants to tell you our news."

Elbridge fidgeted in his chair and asked for another cocktail.

"I don't know how you'll take it," he began, "but Dorothea thinks we ought to do it."

He liked Clyde, Elbridge said. He had always thought he was going to stay on in Clyde in Wright-Sherwin.

"But Charley knows how things are there," he said. "You get in a rut at Wright-Sherwin." Maybe he had been getting into a rut. Maybe he was more ambitious now that he was a married man. You had to think about the future. Perhaps they might have children.

"Oh, Dorothea," Esther Gray said, "I really think you might have told me."

"Axel," John Gray called. "I think we might have some more cocktails, Axel. Well, well. This is quite a day."

"Mother," Dorothea said, "I wish you wouldn't jump at things. Elbridge only said that we *might* have children."

Confidentially, Elbridge said, he had received an offer, quite a big offer, from a concern in Kansas City to be the head of their research department. It did not mean that he did not like Clyde.

"Well," John Gray said, "I'm sorry we can't start knitting garments, but maybe you're right, Elbridge. I never got very far here myself."

They discussed Elbridge and Dorothea and Kansas City all through supper and just before they left the table John Gray said that he had always wanted to go down the Mississippi — ever since he had read *Huckleberry Finn*. There was that musical play *Show Boat*. He wished that showboats were still running. There was no reason at all why they should not all charter a yacht next summer and go down the Mississippi. When Charles left to call on Jessica, his father was still talking about the Mississippi.

No one at the Lovells' discussed the break in the market for a moment. If the engagement was to be announced in November, Mr. Lovell could not put off certain mechanics and formalities. As long as they were going through with it, and it seemed as though they must, it was a time for everyone to stand together. Jessica would have to have a new photograph taken. Also, an announcement must appear in the Saturday edition of the *Boston Evening Transcript,* and Mr. Lovell had been engaged all day in preparing it.

"Mr. Laurence Lovell," the announcement began, "of Clyde, Massachusetts, announces the engagement of his daughter Jessica to Mr. Charles Gray, also of Clyde, Massachusetts." Mr. Lovell's face had a set, determined expression as he read on and he sighed resignedly when he finished.

"I wish I could think of more to say about you, Charles," he said, "but I did mention your grandfather and I did say that you come of an old Clyde family. And now, Jessie, I hope you and Charles will go over this carefully. I've given my day to it. At least you can give half an hour."

The next afternoon Charles left Rush & Company for an hour to go with Jessica to look at engagement rings and whenever he saw a diamond in a platinum setting from then on he thought of the faces and the tickers. You could no longer tell what you might get for a common stock when you sold it. Quotations had no meaning because the ticker was so far behind. Yet there was not a flurry at home that evening. His father's one interest seemed to be Jessica's engagement ring. Charles did not want too large a stone, but John Gray wanted it large enough. All through supper he discussed the theory of diamond cutting, and after supper he suggested that they all read aloud. He was reading from *The Three Musketeers* about the Duke of Buckingham and Richelieu when Charles left to call on Jessica.

The third day was terrible but it was reassuring that his father had not bothered to go to town. He said there was no use going until things cleared up, and of course he was quite right. He did not want to answer any questions, he said. He would be glad to go over details with Charles when everything was brushed up and in order again. Short covering would cause an automatic rise — no matter what happened later. He was more interested in his new velvet smoking jacket of a deep Burgundy color which had come by mail that morning than in the news, and he wore his jacket to supper.

"Why, John," his mother said when she saw it, "you never told me about it."

"I still like to surprise you, dear," John Gray told her. "You always look so pretty when you're surprised. I hope you won't mind if I ask Axel for cocktails, and I've asked for champagne at supper."

"I don't see why it should be a party," his mother said. "It's just an ordinary supper."

"Charley looks tired," John Gray said. "You don't want to take these things too hard, Charley. Everything goes up and down." Charles felt deathly tired that night but his father did not seem tired at all.

"John, dear," his mother said, "I'm so glad you got all through with everything before this happened. Do you know what he's been doing all day, Charley? He's been at the library reading about the South Sea Bubble."

"You know, Esther," John Gray said, "I think perhaps we made a mistake not going abroad this summer instead of chartering the schooner. It's funny neither you nor I have been abroad, but there's always next summer. We can stay at Claridge's in London and I really don't see why we shouldn't take the Cadillac with us, and perhaps Charley and Jessica can meet us over there and we can go over to France. That reminds me — I haven't bought Jessica an engagement present, Charley. . . . Do you think she would like pearls?"

Charles was always up by seven in the morning in order to be in time for the eight-three train and the family usually had breakfast together at twenty minutes past seven. His father always said that he never could sleep late, because of those years at the mill. His mother was already at the table and the coffee was there too, in the new silver coffeepot, when Charles came down next morning.

"Charles, dear," his mother said, "I wonder whether you would mind going up and knocking on your father's door. He always likes to be with us at breakfast."

"If he's asleep," Charles said, "perhaps he'd like to sleep."

"No," his mother said. "You know he always likes to be down for breakfast."

There was no sort of warning or premonition. The sunlight had begun to creep through the fanlight above the front door. As Charles walked upstairs he heard the sound of a horse's hoofs and the rattle of wheels on Spruce Street. It would be the ice company. The ice company still used horses.

For years his father had slept in the small room to the right of the stairs, because he liked to go to bed when he pleased without disturbing anyone. Charles remembered the freshly painted panels and the brass latch of the old thin door. The latch was brightly polished, because Axel liked to polish brass. When he knocked, the ice wagon was still rumbling down Spruce Street.

"Father," he said, "are you awake?"

There was no sound on the other side of the door and he opened it instead of knocking again. The window was open and a cool breeze was blowing the new chintz curtains. His father was lying on his narrow spool bed. The bed had come from Gow Street and he had especially liked its hard mattress. His Bible was on the bedside table and beside the Bible was the bottle of sleeping pills which his brother-in-law had given him. There was nothing to explain the spasm of fear which shook Charles except his father's utter stillness. He was out in the hall again, closing the bedroom door very softly, before he faced the full realization that his father was dead.

A moment later he was in his father's study and he had closed the door behind him before he had consciously thought what to do next. His actions were automatic but at least they were correct. He could never admire himself for anything he did that day or the days following. He was only conscious of certain things he had to do and when he saw his father's private telephone he must have given the operator his Uncle Gerald Marchby's number from instinct rather than reason. It was still early and his uncle would be at home. He told him to come to Spruce Street as soon as he could, to open the door without ringing, and that he would be waiting in the hall.

Instinct again rather than reason told him that his mother had better not be in the house when Dr. Marchby called, that it was better for him and his uncle to be alone for a few minutes. There was that dreamlike feeling of hurrying without being able to hurry, but he called up the Masons' house and asked for Mrs. Mason. He wanted her to call up his mother and to think of some reason to ask her to come over and to please keep her there for a while. He must have said that something serious had happened and that he would tell her later. He may have said that his father had died suddenly, or that his father was very unwell. He was never sure. Then he walked downstairs to the dining room.

"Here's your coffee, dear," his mother said, "and Axel will bring you your eggs right away. Was he asleep?"

Yes, he must have answered, he was asleep.

He remembered the taste of the coffee. He wanted to drink it in a gulp but instead he drank it slowly. He must have said something else, but he could not remember what. He had not finished the coffee when the telephone rang, and his mother said not to bother, that she would answer it.

"It's Margaret Mason," she said. "I'm sure I don't know what she wants so early in the morning."

"She probably wants to talk," he heard himself saying, "but it is early, isn't it?"

He was waiting in the hall when his Uncle Gerald came. He was not aware of any lapse of time. He remembered his uncle's heavy, stooping figure and his baggy trousers.

"Father's dead," he said.

"All right," his uncle answered, "let's go up."

Charles followed his uncle up the stairs but not into the room. He waited on the landing until his uncle called to him. Again he was aware of no lapse of time. He only knew that he had done the best he could and that the rest of it was up to his uncle.

"Charley, you can come in now," his uncle said. His uncle was standing by the bed holding his black bag and the pill bottle on the table was gone.

"He died in his sleep," his uncle said. "It was a heart attack. The Gray heart, Charley."

"Yes, sir," Charles said.

"Are you feeling all right?"

"Yes, sir," Charles said.

"Where's your mother?"

"She's over at the Masons'."

"Does she know?"

"Not yet," Charles said.

"How did she get over there?"

His voice was hoarse when he answered.

"I asked Mrs. Mason to ask her."

Their glances met and neither of them spoke for a moment.

"I'm glad you thought of that," his uncle said. "I'll go and tell her. I guess you'd better call up Hugh Blashfield, Charley."

"Yes," Charles said. "I guess I'd better, Uncle Gerald."

A time like that was a period of inevitable selflessness. Certain things which had to be done were cropping up successively and he was the only one who could possibly have done them. There was no time for deep subjective feeling. In all the rest of his days in Clyde, there was no time to think of himself and Jessica Lovell until the very end, no time to analyze his feelings about his father. It was only when he left Clyde that all the things he repressed and controlled came over him in dark, disorderly waves, and he could handle those moods by then, because he was away from Clyde. He was like someone who stood on the stern of a ship — by then — watching a vanishing cloudy shore line. Dreadful, half-believable things had occurred ashore. Those things had marked him, but now he was moving on, leaving the ruins of them behind.

It was possible at length to begin deliberately forgetting a great deal of what had happened there, not all but a great deal. It was better to make a clean break and to leave regrets behind, and feelings of hidden guilt, and thoughts of how one might have said and done things differently. There was not much he had consciously avoided. He had not run away from anything. There was nothing left to run away from except memory by the time he had left Clyde, and of course he had taken unavoidable elements of it with him. Yet even so his memory of that time was singularly devoid of pain. Something in that morning seemed to have killed desire or some capacity for feeling and he had been shaken by deep emotion only once or twice. His self-control was with him through all of it, perhaps because it was starkly obvious what everyone would say and do after his father's death.

Neither Charles nor his uncle ever spoke again of that moment when they had stood at the head of the bed inside his father's room; and as far as he knew no one ever heard anything about it. No one ever heard, but certain people must have guessed. At least he was sure that his mother and Dorothea had never learned the truth. His father had died of a heart attack, brought on by strain and worry, and perhaps it was just as well. He never liked to think of his father trying to face what was left.

A note came from Jessica that same morning. It was delivered by old Mr. Fogarty, who still sometimes did a little work in the Lovells' garden, and Charles could still remember the heavy blue paper.

"Charles, dear, I feel so sick and sorry for what you must be going through, and please come and see me, dear, as soon as you feel you can."

He telephoned her himself that afternoon and told her the family needed him and he knew she would understand. His mother and Dorothea were not seeing anyone just yet.

The doorbell was beginning to ring. He never forgot the sound of the doorbell. He never forgot the hours in that room of his father's with Mr. Blashfield and Elbridge Sterne, the closed door, the opening of drawers, and the stacks of papers. There was no way of keeping Elbridge out of it and he was glad he had not gone through with it alone with Mr. Blashfield.

When he called up Boston, he said he would come in at once with his father's lawyer, but even before they left, they had some idea of the figures and realized that the fewer people who knew, the better. They might already be saying that John Gray had left his affairs in a mess.

"Charley," Elbridge said, "I don't see why he did it."

"He couldn't help it." That answer explained everything, but excused nothing. "And no one must ever know."

"I don't see how you're going to stop it," Elbridge said. He was hopelessly at sea. Elbridge may have known all about brasses and bronzes but he always was confused when he had to separate liabilities from assets.

Of course, there was one way to stop a part of that inevitable talk. He could put his own government bonds into the assets. He would have to tell Hugh Blashfield and he would have to tell the Lovells and Elbridge would know, but there was no reason why it should go any further. There was no reason why his mother and Dorothea need ever hear of it. He could never give himself much credit for his decision, because it was the best way out and it was something he owed to the family.

"I'll get along all right, Elbridge," he heard himself saying. "Mother will have to have something and we can get her to put it into a trust."

All he wanted, all he could do, was to have everything look as well as possible. His father had said that he was being conservative and careful and he had expressed that conservatism by protecting himself with what he considered a ridiculously large margin. When he had been sold out at the market the previous day the account had come close to breaking even. It was even possible that it might be slightly in the black when the final figuring was completed, but even so there was almost nothing left.

Mr. Crewe had come to call. Charles could still see himself sometimes talking to Mr. Crewe in that upstairs room of his father's, which already was losing its character. Though it was a parochial duty, Charles was sure that Mr. Crewe was conscious of inadequacy. He could not draw upon ritual or upon *The Book of Common Prayer* and he must have known that John Gray had never liked his sermons. He said he had come to call, not to discuss the details of the service, because they could talk of that later. He had come as a friend, in the hope that he might be of some help in an hour of deep bereavement, and he looked very helpless when he said it, a thin, pale little man, struggling with abstract periods.

"I feel deeply for your mother and sister and you too, Charles," he said. "I wish there were something I could say which would bring comfort. Do you remember that '*in my Father's house are many mansions: if it were not so, I would have told you'?*"

Charles remembered. The word "mansion" always made him think of lawns and a driveway and of a white-pillared portico. His father would love to dwell in such a mansion. Mr. Crewe's glance had moved to the papers on the table and to the private telephone and Charles was sure that he wished to express the hope that his father had left his affairs in order.

"I knew him for a long while," Mr. Crewe said. "I've always admired the richness of his mind. We always depended on his spirit at the Confessional Club to lift us over hard places. You would be touched to know how many people have spoken of him to me today, many different sorts of people. There is a broad sense of loss, the loss of a generous friend."

"Yes," Charles said. "Everyone always liked Father."

"And memory continues much longer than life," Mr. Crewe said, "so very much longer. He is living still in memory. Your father was very proud of you, although he never expressed it in a conventional way, perhaps."

"I hope he was," Charles said. "No, Father was never conventional."

"At a time like this," Mr. Crewe said, and he glanced at Charles and then stared at the floor, "one feels, doesn't one, very keenly the presence of an outside power, of a guiding spirit, of — of God. I'm sure you feel it, Charles."

Mr. Crewe was doing the best he could, because it was his duty, and Charles felt anxious to help him.

"I know what you mean," he said, "but right now I don't seem to feel much of anything. I only know it's there."

Mr. Crewe coughed.

"A great deal has been said and written about the efficacy of prayer," he said. "I sometimes feel we speak too little of it. I think it might help us both if we prayed, that is if you don't mind."

"No, sir," Charles said. "It's very kind of you to think of it, Mr. Crewe. You're being very kind."

He had not anticipated Mr. Crewe's suggestion. It was a very awkward moment when Mr. Crewe left his chair, one of the old Windsor chairs, and sank abruptly to his knees upon the new green carpet. It was awkward, yet there was something that was beyond grotesqueness. For once that day everything was simple.

"I think we will both feel better for it," Mr. Crewe said before he began, and they shook hands when the prayer was over.

"Thank you very much, Charles," Mr. Crewe said, "and please remember that I'm always here to help."

He called on Jessica that night, just for a few minutes, because he did not want to leave his mother or Dorothea too long. When he reached Johnson Street it was late and he was glad that Mr. Lovell had retired. Somehow all the day was still with him and there was still so much to do that he felt strangely impersonal when he kissed her. It was what he had said to Mr. Crewe — that it was hard to feel anything, but he hoped that he said the things he had to say properly. She knew, of course, how he had felt about his father but he hoped that she did not think that he sounded cold and practical. He might have put off until later telling her about adding his bonds to his father's estate but it seemed to him that she should know right away.

"You see, don't you?" he remembered saying. "It's the only thing to do."

"Oh, Charley dear, of course it is," she said, and they did not speak for a while. They sat there in the wallpaper room, holding hands.

"You and I can get on," he said. "We can be married just the same."

"Darling," she said, "of course we can. I'll never marry anyone but you."

"I'm awfully glad you're with me," he said. "I don't know what I'd do without you."

"Of course I'm with you, dear," she said. "I'll always be with you."

"You see why I don't want anyone to know," he said, "but I suppose you ought to tell your father."

They kissed again in the front hall before he opened the door, and it never occurred to him — there was no possible way he could have told — that he would only see Jessica Lovell once again.

His mother and Dorothea were in the parlor when he reached home and Elbridge Sterne was with them and his mother said it was time they faced things. She could not stay in Spruce Street alone. There were too many memories in Spruce Street, and she could not go on alone in Clyde.

"Charley," she said, as she said so often afterwards, "why didn't he ever tell us he wasn't well — but it was just like him, wasn't it? He never wanted any of us to worry."

Then for some reason she asked him if he remembered that paper she had read long ago at the Historical Society about Alice Ruskin Lyte. Charles was only a little boy then but he must remember. Did he remember those evenings they worked over it together? John had been so patient and he always had loved words so, and Sam was alive. She could not live in Spruce Street any longer and Dorothea and Elbridge wanted her to go with them to Kansas City.

He had never thought of Clyde without his mother. It was only later that he was glad she felt as she had. It was better that she had left before the Cadillac and the house and the furniture were sold. It was better that she had gone to Kansas City instead of living on in Clyde. If she had stayed, he would have had to stay himself and that would scarcely have been possible with Jessica still there.

XXIII

I Think That Frankness Has Been the Basis of Our Previous Relationship

— MR. LAURENCE LOVELL

ONCE, as a step in that long process of advancement at the Stuyvesant Bank, Arthur Slade had asked Charles if he could arrange to come out for the week end to his summer place on the beach at Wainscott, Long Island. Everyone knew that there were going to be some changes in the trust department and this obviously was the reason for the invitation. It was a week end in the summer of 1937 and Charles had said he would be glad to go if things were all right at home in Larchmont.

Arthur Slade had met Nancy but it was too early even to consider whether Nancy would be a help or a detriment as the wife of an officer at the Stuyvesant. It was only a question of the trust department upstairs. He had told Charles that they would love to have his wife too, but Charles had refused for Nancy because obviously there was no place to leave the children.

"I hate to ask you without her," Arthur Slade said, "but I hope you can manage to come yourself. I feel like sitting on the beach and talking."

Nancy understood perfectly what the invitation meant.

"He wants to see how you use your knife and fork and whether you're housebroken," she said. "They don't care whether I chew gum or not yet, but if you go and behave yourself, around next year they'll begin to care."

Nancy helped him pack his suitcase. She pressed his dinner coat. She brushed his tweed jacket. She made him take both white flannels and gray slacks, and his new crepe-soled shoes and the pullover

462

sweater that went with his tweed jacket and four soft shirts and four assorted ties. She checked and double-checked everything in the suitcase.

"Don't let them get you into any games," she said. "You're rotten at golf and tennis, but play bridge if you want to. You're not bad at bridge."

"I wish you were going," Charles said. "It isn't fair to leave you."

"It's life," Nancy told him. "Drink two cocktails before dinner and don't drink anything afterwards unless you have to, and you'd better take a good book along. Take *Mathematics for the Million.* It will show them that you think."

He knew that Arthur Slade wanted to see how he would act on Long Island but he had not been self-conscious. He was devoted to Arthur Slade and he knew that Arthur liked him. When Arthur Slade had asked him if he would like to play golf, Charles told him he had better not. He had once taken a few lessons from a professional at the Shore Club north of Boston but he had never been good at golf. He had always worked too hard — no time for golf and no time for any bad habits either. He was not much at athletics. He had played a little football once. He had gone out for track at Dartmouth and he had been on the wrestling team, but that was all quite a while ago.

On Saturday evening there was a buffet supper, ten or a dozen people, a lawyer and his wife and some men from downtown who reminded him of Rush & Company. There were two tables of bridge afterwards and he played at a table with Elsie Slade and a couple named Murchison and when the rubber was over Elsie Slade sat with him on the steps of the piazza. They drank ginger ale, because, he told her, Nancy had warned him not to drink anything after dinner unless he had to. He told her about Nancy and about life in Larchmont, where they had moved because of the children instead of staying in town, and Elsie Slade talked about her two boys who were away at camp and she called him Charley because she felt she knew him very well. Arthur had said so much about him.

Obviously Arthur Slade had asked her to talk to him — certainly he wanted her reaction — but Charles did not mind in the least. In fact he found it surprisingly easy to talk about himself. Once, she said, Arthur had told her that he had met his father for just a second, in Boston at the Parker House.

"Oh, yes," he said, "I remember. Father was a big-time operator then."

He found himself speaking of it lightly, aware that it fitted well with the evening party and the cottage on the dunes and the cool air from the ocean. He told her about the Cadillac and the Shore Club and the *Zaza*.

"It was quite an adjustment for me," he said. "You see, I was a small-town boy. I'm still basically small-town."

Then Arthur Slade came out of the dark, manifestly to see how they were getting on. He sat on the steps beside them for a moment and asked Charles if he wouldn't like some Scotch.

"Don't ask him," Elsie said. "Nancy doesn't like him to drink after dinner."

Elsie Slade must have liked him or she would not have referred to Nancy by her first name, never having met her. He said he would like a thin drink of Scotch after all, as long as it was Saturday night, but it was not because of this, it was because he felt she was genuinely interested, that he told Elsie Slade about Clyde. It sounded like an amusing place, as he described it that evening.

She said that she had always lived in New York, except in the summer; her family had always spent their summers on Long Island, right here in Wainscott. She had met Arthur at a debutante party and here they were, still in Wainscott. It was a small-town life in itself, she said, but of course in a different way; and then she asked him the inevitable question. Why had he ever left Clyde? It sounded like a wonderful place.

He took a swallow of his thin drink of Scotch. Those days were so far away that he could see their amusing side, at least he could that evening sitting on the steps by the beach.

"It's a small-town story," he said. "It's the difference between Spruce Street and Johnson Street. I should have remembered we were Spruce Streeters. Both Father and I should have remembered."

He had never told Arthur Slade about Jessica Lovell but he did not in the least mind telling Elsie Slade that night. They had first really become acquainted, he told her, at a firemen's muster. She had never even heard of a firemen's muster so he told her about his father and the Pine Trees. It was the difference between Spruce Street and Johnson Street. They used to meet surreptitiously by the courthouse and go riding in her car — and then he had left Wright-Sherwin and gone to work in Rush & Company.

"Her father never did approve of it," he said, "but then why should he? He was always trying to break it up, and he did, when my father died. It was a strain for her, you see, divided loyalty, Spruce Street, Johnson Street. She couldn't go on with it. Her father took her away to forget."

He took another swallow of his whisky. It was just what he had called it, a small-town story. All one had to do was change its emphasis to make it humorous.

"And what did you do?" Elsie Slade asked.

"Why, I left too," he said. "I was hurt, but it made me ambitious."

"Are you still ambitious?" she asked.

This made him laugh. He had never realized until then how little Jessica and the struggle for Jessica meant to him any longer.

"Of course I am," he said, "or I wouldn't be here now, Mrs. Slade."

"Aren't you going to call me Elsie?" she asked.

This made him laugh again. It was wonderful to be so wholly free from Clyde and he was thinking of Nancy and the suitcase and the four neckties and the crepe-soled shoes.

"No," he said, "not yet, but I love to have you call me Charley. Please don't stop. And I'd love to call you Elsie someday, when I'm a little further ahead at the bank, but not right now. You see, I know the difference between Spruce and Johnson streets."

Then Arthur Slade was back again.

"Arthur," Elsie Slade was saying, "Charley won't call me Elsie, but he'd love to sometime later. He's made a very favorable impression on me, Arthur, and you must be sure to get him to tell you the difference between Johnson Street and Spruce Street."

* * *

The Lovells were at the funeral but they sat in the back of the church, not near the family, and Charles had no opportunity to speak to them afterwards. After the service at the grave at the old North Cemetery, Jessica sent him another note by Mr. Fogarty. Her father was going away to New York for a few days, she told him, and he especially wanted her to go with him and she really felt she should. They would be back on Monday or Tuesday. She would call him the minute they were back and she would be thinking of him all the time.

He wished that he might have seen her before she left and he was as much surprised as one could be at such a time that she had not asked him to stop at Johnson Street instead of sending a note, but it was a very sensible thing for her to go away. There would have been no chance for them to be alone together. He was much too busy putting things in order.

Elbridge Sterne had left Wright-Sherwin and the sooner they could all move to Kansas City the better, now that they had definitely made up their minds. Still there were all those final farewells and repeated explanations. His mother could not be expected to leave immediately. She could not cut the ties all at once, but Elbridge's job in Kansas City could not wait indefinitely. It was as though she were leaving the house to go on a visit and always returning for some odd object she had forgotten.

In the end Charles was the one who had to make the decisions. They confronted him in every waking moment and they plagued him through the nights. He never realized until later how tired he must have been though it was not a physical weariness. Mrs. Mason and all his mother's friends kept telling him they did not know what his mother and Dorothea would have done without him, and his mother and Dorothea were always saying the same thing. He was the head of the family and in every detail he had to represent the family. Besides Mr. Blashfield and a lawyer from Boston, who were always giving him papers to sign and wanting to see him for half an hour, there were all sorts of extraneous questions. There was the stone in the North Cemetery, what furniture his mother and Dorothea wanted to take to Kansas City and what was to be done with the 1est. What was to be done about the Cadillac, and what about the couple and the bills and the donation his father had promised to give the hospital? His mother was so relieved that he had left enough so that she could have her independence. She wanted to give a little of it to the library as a John Gray Memorial Fund. The books that would be purchased from it could have a note in them saying that they were bought by the John Gray Memorial Fund, and the library could have all his books, except the ones Charles wanted.

He was tired of seeing people. They were continually calling at Spruce Street and whenever he was not talking to Mr. Blashfield his mother was sending word for him to come downstairs and meet them. She had never known how many friends they had and how kind they all could be. Everyone had been to call except the Lovells, but then Jessica and Mr. Lovell were out of town.

He was tired of seeing people. They were always seeking a private word with him in the house, and they stopped him on the street whenever he went outdoors. They were very kind but they seemed to be saying something they had learned by rote — and he suspected that they were covertly scrutinizing him, seeking from him an answer to a question they did not care to ask. Yes, it was very sudden, he would reply. Yes, his father had been very well, but the crash had been too great a shock. At any rate there was no sign of financial embarrassment for anyone to see. The bills were being paid and twice he deliberately had Willie Stevens drive him in the Cadillac to Boston, and there was the John Gray Fund at the library. He was glad that his mother had thought of it. By the time the Lovells were back, he had been through so much that Mr. Lovell was only another problem — at least he always hoped that he had given Mr. Lovell that impression.

Charles and his mother and Dorothea and Elbridge were in the parlor discussing everything in an aimless way, saying the same things over and over — it was like a clock running down from lack of winding — when Axel had knocked on the door and had said that Mr. Lovell wished to speak to Mr. Charles on the telephone. Axel, in his black alpaca coat, was a false note in the house. He had never really belonged in it, but he had done very well. No doubt he wanted a good reference and was hoping for a financial present.

"Do you mean Miss Lovell?" Charles asked.

No, it was Mr. Lovell, and the telephone was still in the hall below the stairs.

"Good evening, Charles," Mr. Lovell said.

"Good evening, Mr. Lovell," Charles answered. "When did you and Jessica get back?"

"This afternoon," Mr. Lovell said. "I wonder if you would mind coming over for a little while, Charles — that is if you're not too busy."

Of course he was not too busy and he had thought that Jessica would surely be at the door to meet him but instead Mr. Lovell opened it himself. The house was very still, but he was used lately to portentous stilted silence.

"Good evening, Charles," Mr. Lovell said. "Shall we go into the library? There's a fire there."

"Where's Jessica?" Charles asked.

"Upstairs," Mr. Lovell said, "but she'll be down in a few minutes. Charles, I haven't had the opportunity to tell you how sorry I am for you and for everything."

Mr. Lovell seemed relieved as he always did when he reached the reassurance of his library.

"Have a comfortable chair, Charles," he said. "Take my chair, over by the lamp."

Charles did not sit down, as Mr. Lovell asked him, because as soon as they were in the library he had some premonition of what Mr. Lovell was about to say and he could feel some force within himself gathering to meet an immediate shock.

"Don't you really want to sit down, Charles?" Mr. Lovell said.

"No, thank you," he answered. "I've been sitting down all day."

"I don't exactly know how to begin," Mr. Lovell said, and it occurred to Charles that Mr. Lovell usually did not know how to begin, "but I think that frankness has been the basis of our" — he paused, groping for a word — "our previous relationship, don't you?"

"You've been frank, sir," Charles said. "Maybe I should have been franker myself." He was always glad that he said it in just that way.

"Now, Charles," Mr. Lovell went on. "Nothing that I have to say, please believe me, reflects on you personally. You have behaved magnificently. Everyone is saying so. Everyone has more than sympathy for you. They have respect."

It was a handsome speech. He must have been thinking of it and thinking of it, and now he was waiting for some adequate and grateful reaction, and Charles was always satisfied with what he answered.

"Perhaps you'd better tell me what you have on your mind, Mr. Lovell," he said. He would never have spoken in such a way if it had not been for what he had been through.

"Now, Charles," Mr. Lovell said, "I want to be kind, but I wish I did not have to be cruel to be kind." Mr. Lovell sighed. He was having a very unpleasant time, but then this was true of both of them.

"Jessica told me what you have done, Charles, toward settling your father's affairs. It was what a generous and dutiful son should have done, and I respect you for it, but, Charles, there's a change, and an unavoidable change, in the whole situation, and I am not referring to its financial aspects. I wish I didn't have to be so frank." Mr. Lovell cleared his throat. "I don't mean there's anything verging on, well, scandal, but there's a shadow, Charles. In a way, there will always be a shadow of doubt as to whether something was not concealed."

Charles did not answer. He never would be able to allay that doubt. There was always a shadow but it never would have been as deep if the Lovells had stood behind him.

"I've thought this over carefully, Charles. I've been over it thoroughly with Jessica," Mr. Lovell was saying. "We've been most unhappy. It's an impossible situation, Charles. We must end it. It can't go on."

He had been ready for it but he was thinking that Jessica should have been the one to tell him, not Mr. Lovell.

"Jessica," he began, and his voice was hoarse and he hated to have

469

Mr. Lovell see him so upset. "Does Jessica want it this way?"

"Jessica's very unhappy," Mr. Lovell said, "but I wouldn't have spoken to you if she did not want it this way. It's only fair for her to tell you so herself, fair for both of us. If you'll wait a moment I'll get Jessica."

He must have stood alone in the library for a minute or two but he was not conscious of any period of waiting until he saw Jessica in the open doorway with Mr. Lovell just behind her.

"Oh, Charley," she said. "Charley." Her voice shook him because she seemed to be crying out to him as though she were hurt.

"Don't cry, Jessie dear —" Mr. Lovell had his arm around her — "it's only fair to tell Charles how you feel yourself."

He had told her not to cry but she was crying.

"Oh, Charley," she said, "I'm so ashamed of myself. I'm not fit to marry anyone."

"Now, Jessie," Mr. Lovell said very gently. "Just control yourself for a minute and tell Charles and then it will be over, Jessie dear."

He seemed to have been waiting for a very long time before she spoke.

"Charley, darling," she said, "I can't go on. I can't marry you with both of you feeling the way you do."

Of course, it was the final truth and it had hung between them all the time. She was almost asking for forgiveness, and she was hurt as much as he was. He wanted to tell her not to cry, he wanted to quiet her with her head on his shoulder. He wanted to tell her not to bother to explain, but she was still speaking through her sobs.

"I'm so, so torn, Charley," she was saying. Though her father's arm was still around her, she was talking as though he were not there at all. "You see, don't you, that he's given up everything for me. I have to do what he thinks best." He wished that she would stop and her tears did stop her for a moment.

"Now, Jessie," Mr. Lovell said, "it's all right. It's all over, Jessie dear"; but it was not quite all over.

"Oh, Charley," Jessica sobbed, "it doesn't mean I don't love you. I do still love you."

It was long ago, but nothing that had happened since had ever put it in clear perspective. There was too much of him and Jessica in those next few seconds; they were always vibrant and alive with their own peculiar triumph and their pain, and, for just a moment, he believed she always would still love him. It was like that time that spring when they had spoken the words that had made everything different. Nothing else mattered, not Mr. Lovell or Johnson Street or Spruce Street or the shadow of John Gray's death. It was himself and Jessica, and that was all, and never mind the rest.

"Jessica," he said, "I love you too, and that's all there is to it, isn't it?" Although he did not expect an immediate answer, he waited and he did not go on until he was conscious of the silence. "Jessica . . . do you remember what you said one night . . . if I saw this happening to you . . . you wanted me to tell you?" At least this was what he always thought he said, but words had no great value as they stood there facing each other.

"Charley," she said. "Oh, Charley."

She called his name across the space that divided them and he always remembered the happiness and the relief in her voice. She pushed herself away from Mr. Lovell, gently but definitely, and moved toward him. He was always sure that if they had so much as touched each other they would never have left each other, and he was always sure that Mr. Lovell, and Jessica too, knew this as well. As she stretched out her arms to reach him he had a glimpse of Mr. Lovell's face, startled and stricken, and their hands never touched because Mr. Lovell made a gasping, strangled sound and Jessica turned when she heard it.

"Oh," Mr. Lovell said. "Oh." His face was alarmingly white. He took two wavering steps and slumped brokenly into a chair and covered his face with his hands. Jessica fell on her knees and put her arms around him.

"Father," she asked, "oh, Father, what is it?" and Mr. Lovell straightened himself and reached unsteadily for her hand.

"It's nothing, Jessie dear," he said. "I'll be all right in just a minute, my darling. I'm sorry to make such an undignified exhibition of myself. If you want it this way, my dearest, please forget about me, please."

Mr. Lovell's voice was gentle and controlled and he looked over Jessica's shoulder at Charles.

"Please forgive me, Charles, and please, my dearest dear," he said again, "don't think about me if you want it this way."

Then Jessica, still kneeling by Mr. Lovell's chair, looked up at Charles too and her voice was shaken with tears.

"Oh, Charley, I can't . . . Don't you see I can't? . . . I can't bear it any more."

It was natural and yet it was unnatural. To Charles there was something faintly repellent in that conjugal scene. The memory of it was always mingled with old reflexes of pain. They used to say in Clyde that a cat had nine lives and that a snake would live till sundown, but all at once Charles did not want to go on with that scene. As long as he lived he did not ever want to see Jessica or Mr. Lovell again.

"That's all right, Jessica," he said. "Please don't cry." There should have been something more for him to say, some sort of farewell speech, but he could not think of any. "Well, I'd better be going now."

This was what he had always said in the old days, when he first came to call on Jessica, and now he never even wanted to see the Lovell house again. He knew at last that Jessica could never be separated from it and in some vague way he wanted her to be sorry and to show her how wrong she was. He had no desire to stay in Clyde any longer, and perhaps the main reason why he went to New York was because he wanted Jessica to be sorry.

There were, of course, other reasons, all combining into an urge or drive the force of which he could not combat. The shadow of Clyde must have always lain behind his subsequent actions. He would never have had such a strong desire to get ahead or to make the necessary sacrifices if it had not been for his father and the Lovells. There was a negative force, a combined revelation and above all humiliation that needed to be surmounted. He must have always been seeking to assuage the pain that those few last weeks in Clyde gave him.

* * *

"It was all very good for you," Nancy said once. "It's made you into a very nice guy. Maybe it's made you too nice."

He told her this was not so. In many ways he was self-centered and perhaps they had both tried too hard to get ahead, though Nancy did not think so.

"You see, I'm like the Old Man," he said. "I'm just trying to beat the system in a different way."

"Everybody's trying to beat some sort of system," Nancy said, "but most people don't know it. It's nice that you and I know it and that we don't fool ourselves. It makes everything all right."

She had always loved that effort to beat the system because she possessed a quality of combativeness. She liked what they did together, she told him once, because there was no one to help them. It was always the two of them against the world.

"We'll show them," she used to whisper to him sometimes in the night.

She never had to explain whom she meant by "them" or what it was they were going to show. It was always himself and Nancy against the world and against all the systems in it, against Tony Burton and the Stuyvesant Bank and American Tel & Tel, against the furnace and the doctors and the bills. It was always himself and Nancy striving for security, and they never needed anyone to help. It was always himself and Nancy, striving within the limits of free enterprise if you wanted to put it that way.

"You see, I was looking for a man," she told him once. "That's what every girl is looking for and don't let anyone tell you differently. I suppose I might have married old Jessup if you hadn't come along." She was referring, of course, to Mr. Clive Jessup in the firm of Burrell, Jessup and Cockburn where she had been working when Charles went downtown that time on his errand from the bank.

"Well, you'd have beaten the system, Nance," he said, "and you could have had a box at the opera."

"Being a kept woman doesn't beat any system," Nancy told him. She always said what she thought.

Her father ran a real estate and insurance business up there in

New York State and it was a relief that Nancy did not like her family much. It meant that they could always speak the same language. She had moved away from there as soon as she could, because she had wanted to go to college. She had gone to Barnard for two years and then to the Katharine Gibbs secretarial school because her family were always telling her about the sacrifice they were making. She was not going to go back home ever if she could help it. When he went up there with her just before they were married, he was reminded of his brother Sam and May Mason.

"You know," he told her once, "you're really a Spruce Street girl."

"I wish to God," Nancy said, "you'd get over thinking about Spruce Street."

But she really was a Spruce Street girl. It was always himself and Nancy against the world.

XXIV

One Big, Happy Family

CHARLES came to New York early in January in 1930. He had taken the midnight from Boston and he had checked his suitcase in the parcel room at the Grand Central Station, the one beneath the stairs that led to Vanderbilt Avenue. He had eaten breakfast in the restaurant on the lower level, not at the counter but at a table, staying there as long as he decently could, reading the *New York Times*. He knew almost nothing about New York but he did not feel either lonely or confused. He felt that he was in a new country.

Outside the station, the streetcars and the traffic were already running in a steady stream under the ramp at Pershing Square. The shops on Forty-second Street, the drugstores, the optical stores and the haberdasheries, were already opening for the day. When he reached Fifth Avenue the lions in front of the Public Library looked white and cold and those old buses with the seats on top were moving in lines on the Avenue, but New York was sleepy still. New York had the appearance of having been up very late, and everyone on the streets had a patient, complaining look of having been routed too early out of bed. As he walked up the Avenue the city seemed to him as impersonal as it always did later and he loved that impersonality. Now that he had left his bag at the parcel room there was nothing to tie him. The tides of the city moved past him and he was part of the tide. His own problems and his own personality merged with it.

The Stuyvesant Bank would not be open for two hours, so he walked up Fifth Avenue to the Eighties, then down Park Avenue and then along Madison. Looking in the shop windows there was like carelessly turning the pages in a book while waiting some-where. The depression had not fully gripped New York as yet. There was still a sort of shining plenty. Soon the sun began to break through the morning cloudiness and a fresh cold wind blew through the cross streets.

His impression of the Stuyvesant Bank was not very different from all his later impressions except that the details had more depth and breadth than they ever had again — the converted brownstone front, the illusion of leisure, the small fire near the front door burn-ing in the open grate. There was none of the untidiness of E. P. Rush & Company. Everything was spick-and-span in a polite, aggres-sive way, as offices were in New York. It all had something of the present, amply able to compete with new trends but the more confi-dent because of an established, dignified past.

Gus, the doorman, looked younger then but he already presented the appearance of a trusted chauffeur in a wealthy but dignified family, as well he might. Until a few years before, Gus had driven the black limousine of Mr. Mortimer Waldron, one of the largest clients of the bank, and at Mr. Waldron's death the bank had administered Gus as it had the rest of the Waldron estate. As the vanguard of the Stuyvesant service, he felt responsible for anyone who turned from the sidewalk to the bank's front door.

"Morning, sir," Gus said.

He was the first person who had said good morning to Charles in New York City and it had not been wholly necessary and this was undoubtedly the reason that Charles went to the hospital every few days to see Gus after Gus had slipped once on the icy sidewalk and had broken his hip while hurrying to open a car door for a depositor. The gesture had not hurt Charles because Tony Burton called at the hospital himself, and so had nearly everyone else, after Tony Burton went, but Charles had gone there first. He had never thought of any favorable impression it might make. He had gone because Gus had said good morning to him that first morning.

Joe was there, too, and Joe, too, looked younger. It was not long before that he had left the detective division of the police force, but

Joe fitted there already. He was already part policeman, part greeter, and part club doorman.

"Are you looking for someone?" Joe did not call him sir but it was a polite, interested question. Joe was already classifying him and Joe never made a mistake, or hardly ever.

The gilded tellers' cages and the high tables with the pens and blotters and deposit slips only looked like additional ornaments in a large comfortable room. He saw the roll-top desks of the officers by the front windows and then the green carpet with the two large flat-top desks upon it and next the other smaller desks grouped more closely together on the uncarpeted floor. He saw the small marble staircase that descended unobtrusively to the vaults, and he saw Mr. Cheseborough at his inconspicuous desk in the comfortable nook near the open fire, ready to help old ladies with their checks and to lead them to the ladies' tellers. He saw all the Stuyvesant Bank just as he always saw it later.

"I wonder if I could see Mr. Arthur Slade," he said, "if he's not oo busy."

He always remembered that Joe did not tell him to wait, or that he would see whether or not Mr. Slade would see him. Instead he walked with Charles across the room toward the edge of the green carpet. Arthur Slade was seated behind one of those two assistant vice-president desks, firmly on the green carpet — at the same desk which now belonged to Charles himself.

"I don't know whether you remember me or not," Charles said, but Arthur Slade remembered him.

When Arthur Slade asked him if he would like to walk around upstairs and see the trust and the tax and the statistical departments, nothing had been said about his working at the Stuyvesant. Charles was already experienced enough to know that it was wise not to be too eager. When Arthur Slade introduced him to Walter Gibbs, who was one of the key men in the statistical department at the time, and then excused himself because there was something he had to attend to downstairs, still nothing definite had been said.

The statistical department occupied what had once been the rear bedroom on the second floor of the brownstone house, with more

desks in the dressing room and more in the hall. It was a compli
ment, though he did not know it, to be left in the statistical department talking to Walter Gibbs, but even when Arthur Slade returned
and took him back downstairs and introduced him to Mr. Burton
and Mr. Merry nothing was said directly. The whole problem of
personnel was handled in a rather haphazard manner in those days,
except in the statistical department. Arthur Slade must have vouched
for him because the conversations were all general and no one asked
him anything definite about his previous experience. An hour must
have elapsed before Charles said he must not take any more of
Mr. Slade's time and thanked him for showing him around. It was
only then that Arthur Slade asked him whether he would like to
try it in the statistical department.

"You can't tell," Arthur Slade said. "It might be worth trying.
How much were you getting at Rush & Company?"

Of course they could not pay him what he had been getting at
Rush & Company but there was a future in the statistical department. You were a part of the family. It was like E. P. Rush & Company again — one big happy family, as though all families were
necessarily happy.

Yet the Stuyvesant may have been more like a family than many
other business organizations. There were the same jealousies, the
same incompetent poor relations, the same feuds. There was also a
sort of loyalty, as much as there could be loyalty to as cool and grim
an institution as a bank — but the Stuyvesant Bank was a force
beyond the control of any individual or group. The president and
officers might fix the rules and policies under the general advice of
the directors' board but those rules and policies themselves had a
way of changing in a manner no individual could anticipate. They
were swayed by practices and theories of other vanished personalities,
by economic laws of loan and interest that stretched into the hazy
past of the goldsmith guilds in the Middle Ages.

The Stuyvesant was the aggregate of the character of many individuals, who merged a part of their personal strivings and ambitions into a common effort. It was like a head of living coral rising
above the surf, a small outcropping of a greater reef. He only knew

that in the end it was stronger than any one person. In the end, no matter what the rewards might be, a part of one's life remained built into that complicated structure. They were all asses following their bundles of hay, the clerks, the tellers, the department heads, the vice-presidents, the president and the directors, and Gus himself standing on the Avenue. They were all on an assembly line, but you could not blame the line. It was too cumbersome, too inhumanly human for anyone to blame. At least he and Nancy knew they were part of the blueprint. They would never have met if it had not been for the Stuyvesant Bank, not that the bank knew or cared. They would never have had the children. They would never have built the house at Sycamore Park.

They must have both been thinking of this one spring before the war just after they had moved to Sycamore Park. It was a Saturday afternoon and Charles was mowing the lawn. His son Bill was raking up the short grass in little piles and Nancy was sitting under a tree sewing and Evelyn was reading *The Purple Fairy Book*. He had just reached a difficult place near the recently planted rhododendron bushes when Nancy called him, and when the whirring sound of the mower stopped her voice sounded unusually distinct.

"Charley."

"Yes," he said, "what is it?"

"Why was it they sent you down there?"

"Down where?" he asked.

"Down to Pine Street. Down to Burrell, Jessup and Cockburn."

He stared at her blankly before he understood what she had in mind.

"It had something to do with that fund," he said, "that Burrell School fund and the trust report. It was the Burrell estate, wasn't it? I don't exactly remember."

Nancy dropped the shirt she was mending.

"It's funny," she said. "I can't remember either."

They both must have been thinking that there would have been no lawn mowing or shirt mending or mortgage or Evelyn or Bill, they would never even have known each other, if it had not been for that trip downtown. It could not have been an important errand because he was new in the bank and yet they had not sent one of the regular messengers.

"It's funny," Nancy said again, "we can't remember."

That evening after supper when Nancy was upstairs hearing the children say their prayers, Charles did remember some of it by thinking but not trying too hard to think.

Charles had been like a mountain climber clinging to a precarious foothold up there in the statistical department. As there were no extra desks he had been stationed at a table in the corner of that converted bedroom, and one day Arthur Slade had come up from downstairs, which was unusual. He would not have noticed what Arthur Slade said to Mr. Gibbs if he had not felt at the time very dependent on Arthur Slade. Arthur Slade was a little like a commissioned officer that morning, entering the orderly room to speak to the sergeant major.

"Oh, Walter," he said to Mr. Gibbs, "where's the analysis?" Charles was beginning to realize already that Walter Gibbs had lapses and moments of forgetfulness.

"I've just finished checking it," Walter Gibbs said. "I was just going to send it down. I didn't know you wanted it in a hurry."

"Where is it?" Arthur Slade asked. "Those lawyers are meeting us tomorrow. It should have been in the mail last night. That's all right, it's my fault. I should have told you." It was probably not his fault because he never slipped up on things but Arthur Slade was always careful never to blame anyone when it was not necessary.

"Jessup's just been telephoning," Arthur Slade said. "It ought to be given to him personally. Is there anyone here you could send down to Pine Street?"

"Why, yes," Walter Gibbs said, "there's Gray."

All law offices, particularly in New York, Charles often thought, had a self-conscious atmosphere, which was very much like their stationery. Their pictures and chairs and tables and the personnel of the outer offices were all selected to create an air of erudition, security and ponderous judicial calm. The boy who greeted Burrell, Jessup and Cockburn visitors noted Charles's name and that of the partner he wished to see on a memorandum pad. Then he rose slowly and walked down a corridor, leaving Charles seated by a round mahogany table with his brief case on his knees gazing at a steel engraving of Chief Justice Marshall. Charles found himself thinking of all the other people who must have sat in that waiting room, rearranging their thoughts. He felt as if he were in the hands of Burrell, Jessup and Cockburn and that he must tell the truth and nothing but the truth. The office boy came back and led the way down a corridor to the partners' offices.

"You can go right in," the boy said.

It was obviously Mr. Jessup's office because his name was on the door, Clive W. Jessup, but when Charles opened the door he was in another outer office, lighted by a single window that looked across a few low roofs to the blank wall of a tall building. There was a new leather couch and a stiff armchair and a Burgundy-red carpet and behind a mahogany secretary's desk Nancy was sitting typing a letter.

Charles stood watching her because she did not look up when he came in. Her eyes were on her open shorthand book. Her fingers moved over the typewriter keys easily, almost contemptuously. She wore a plain silk shirtwaist. Her light brown hair was done up in a knot. Her lips were pressed in an even line and her whole face looked cool and aloof. Her skin was as clear as her white silk waist but there was a faint natural touch of color in her cheeks. There was no lipstick. Nancy never used it in business hours.

She did not look up until she had finished the paragraph she was typing and then she looked straight at him, but she did not smile. Her eyes were greenish-gray and they were wide, almost too wide, apart.

"Do you want to see Mr. Jessup," she asked, "or do you want to leave something for him?"

"I'm from the Stuyvesant Bank," Charles said, and that was the first thing he ever said to Nancy. "They sent me over with some papers. I'm supposed to hand them to Mr. Jessup."

"You're supposed to," Nancy repeated, and she sounded as though she were faintly amused but there was no way of telling. "What are they about?"

"They didn't tell me," Charles said. "They don't tell me much up there."

"Well, Mr. Jessup's busy now," Nancy said. "You can leave them with me and I'll see that he gets them."

"I'm afraid I'd better wait," Charles said.

"Haven't you got anything else to do back at that bank?" Nancy asked. "I'll see he gets them. I'm pretty good at handing people papers."

"So am I," Charles said, and he smiled.

"Mr. Jessup's in conference," Nancy said, "and he won't be free for half an hour."

"I'm supposed to give them to him personally," Charles said.

"What are you in that bank, a messenger?" Nancy asked.

"No," Charles said. "I'm in the statistical department."

"Have you been there long?"

"Of course I haven't," Charles said, "or they wouldn't be sending me on errands. This is the first important job that's been offered me."

Then she smiled. It was the first time he ever saw her smile.

"Well," she said, "take off your overcoat and sit down, if you want to waste your time."

She was much further along than he was then. She was Mr. Jessup's executive secretary and she was being paid forty-five dollars a week and they could never have been married if she had not kept that job.

"If I bother you waiting here," Charles said, "I can wait outside."

"You don't bother me," Nancy said. "This is my last letter."

He never bothered her, she always said, right from the beginning, and most men did. There were a great many maladjusted junior partners in that office.

"You didn't seem to have me on your mind," she told him once. "We just sat there and talked. And sex didn't seem to enter into it, but I suppose it did. It was all perfectly natural. God knows why it was so natural"—but then everything always was with him and Nancy.

PART THREE

I

Please Leave No Articles

THE CARS on the subsidiary line that led to Clyde were always anti-quated, relegated to the branch for their final tour of duty. As they rocked and rattled on the uneven roadbed, you could tell from the sounds exactly where the train was, especially as it was approaching Clyde. There was a stifled roar as the train passed through the cut that came just before Brainard's Crossing. Then came the hollow rumble of the trestle that spanned Whiting's Creek. After the train crossed the low farmlands just outside of Clyde there came the louder roar of the short tunnel and with it an instant of darkness, always startling no matter how often one had experienced it, and the brakeman's voice mingled with the roar and the darkness.

"Clyde," he always shouted. "Clyde"; and if it was the three-thirty train out of Boston he always added, "Please leave no articles in the car," an admonition that was never heard, as far as Charles could remember, on any other train.

Charles had taken the three-thirty because he had stopped for a while in Boston to do what Roger Blakesley would have called sweetening certain contacts. It was an expression which especially revolted him, but he recognized it as an essential part of business to drop in, now that he was in Boston, on a few old graduates of Rush & Company and on other acquaintances. He always did so on his rare visits there because you never could tell when it might help to have a working relationship with someone on State or Congress or Milk Street. Besides he was the only executive in the Stuyvesant with much of a firsthand knowledge of Boston. When any Boston problem came up at the Stuyvesant, as it did occasionally, Charles was always called in to help with it. It was only recently that Roger

485

Blakesley, too, had been making himself helpful with Boston problems, and in the last few months Roger seemed to have considered himself something of an authority, going so far as to tell a few of those quaint stories about Boston trustees that always went so well in New York and even giving the impression of knowing the subjects of those anecdotes.

It occurred to Charles that in his talk with Tony Burton and Stephen Merry when he got back he might say casually that he had dropped in on Tommy Sage at the First National, that they had known each other since those days at Rush & Company, and that some of the boys at the Boston Safe Deposit had been talking about United Fruit and that he had asked Bill Jenkins at the Old Colony about United Shoe. Bill was an old Rush & Company graduate who was a director. It would be possible to make these allusions without any undue emphasis. As a matter of fact, his hours in Boston had been very useful in a business way.

When he stopped by at Rush & Company, old Lawrence Stoker had been surprisingly glad to see him and had asked him to lunch at the Union Club. Everybody had been glad to see him and everybody had regarded him in that polite, embarrassed way that they often reserved for old friends who had done well in New York and who must therefore be very prosperous. As always there was a suspicion about prosperity that came too easily.

It would not hurt at all to tell Tony Burton about his lunch at the Union Club with Mr. Stoker. The invitation in itself made Charles realize the long distance he had traveled since the old days. Though Mr. Stoker called him Charley and he still called Mr. Stoker mister, they were almost on an equal basis because of the Stuyvesant Bank. He was both an assistant vice-president of the Stuyvesant and a bright graduate back on the college campus. They had old-fashioned cocktails, and this in itself showed that Lawrence Stoker felt that the occasion demanded a special effort. There was a warm, mellow glow about their meeting and they spoke first of old times at Rush & Company and then edged gradually into the present.

"You boys who go away to New York," Lawrence Stoker said, and he looked across the table at Charles as though he were someone who had lived for a long while in a foreign country, "you go and you never want to come back." Charles believed that Mr. Stoker's words had a tentative, suggestive note. "Of course, we can't offer you enough to get you back. You boys get used to high living in New York."

"And low thinking," Charles said, and he laughed. He wondered how much Mr. Stoker thought he was earning. Obviously, Mr. Stoker was judging from appearances, as they always did in Boston.

"Of course," Mr. Stoker said, "money doesn't go as far in New York as it does here."

"It doesn't go far anywhere if you have a wife and two children," Charles said.

"Two? I didn't know you had two, Charley," Mr. Stoker said. "I thought you only had a boy. That boy must be growing up."

"Yes," Charles said, "Bill's getting to be a big boy now."

"Where's he going to school?" That was a question they always asked in Boston.

"He's going to one of those suburban country day schools now," Charles said, "but he wants to go to Exeter."

"It doesn't matter so much where he goes if you're going to send him to Dartmouth," Mr. Stoker said. "I hope you're not going to send that boy to Dartmouth."

You were always placed in Boston by your beginnings and Mr. Stoker had never forgotten that Charles had gone to Dartmouth.

"But you never acted like a Dartmouth man," Mr. Stoker said. "Moulton always said so. He always said he shouldn't have let you go."

If he had stayed there would have been nothing much for him at Rush & Company and both of them must have known it, but it was very reassuring to be there at lunch with Mr. Stoker toying with the impossible.

"You wouldn't have wanted me, you know," Charles said. "I couldn't have been a partner."

"I wouldn't say that," Mr. Stoker said. "The war would have made a difference."

His having gone to the war would have been a gesture that could have erased the educational stigma. It would have been almost as good as having been on a Harvard team.

"Three boys from the office were killed," Mr. Stoker said.

"I was just on an air strip," Charles said. "I should have stayed at the bank."

"Well," Mr. Stoker said, "it wouldn't have hurt you one damn bit at Rush & Company. It's too bad about Arthur Slade. Are they going to move you up?"

He had not thought that Mr. Stoker knew enough about him to connect him with Arthur Slade. He sounded as though he were asking Charles if there had been an injury on the football field and if the coach were going to call him from the bench.

"Of course I hope so," Charles said. "You never can tell what's going to happen, can you?" Sitting with Mr. Stoker in the Union Club looking at the bare trees of Boston Common, it was pleasant to conjecture that he might actually become a vice-president of the Stuyvesant Bank.

"Mr. Stoker," he said, "have you ever heard of anything over-the-counter called the Nickerson Cordage Company? They sent me up here to ask about it. The company's in Clyde. I'm going to take the three-thirty train down there. It's funny, isn't it, to be going back to Clyde." He wished he had not said it was funny going back to Clyde . . .

"Clyde," the brakeman was calling. "Clyde. Kindly leave no articles in the car."

He had been looking out of the window. He had seen the sodden April brown of the fields. He had seen the muddy banks and the low tide of Whiting's Creek. He had put on his overcoat and had pulled his suitcase from the rack above him. In a way it was just as though he were coming back from Boston after a day at E. P. Rush & Company and yet he was startled when the name was called. Even when he saw the drab station and the platform and the baggage trucks and the river and the old houses and the lunchroom across the street from the station, he could only half believe he was in Clyde again. It was all so entirely unchanged. It seemed

488

only to have been waiting for him through a long hard winter instead of for almost twenty years.

He had always been as sure as one could be of anything that someday he would return to Clyde. It was an assurance based on a sense of dramatic fitness and a suspicion, that must always have been in back of his mind, that something there needed to be finished and that he must finish it someday. For years he had not avoided thinking of it. He often spoke of Clyde to Nancy and rather enjoyed it, and Bill and Evelyn often asked him to tell stories about the Webster Grammar School and the Meaders and the Masons and old Miss Sarah Hewitt and Grandmama and Aunt Dorothea and his older brother, Sam. He had never brought them to Clyde but at least they knew its folklore. It never hurt him to tell about it. He even told Evelyn about Jessica Lovell, a little girl with filmy dresses and patent leather shoes who lived in a fantastic house with a widow's walk and a cupola and who played in a garden with box-bordered edges and flower beds stamped out in amusing shapes like cookies out of dough. He felt no pain any longer. He was completely free of Clyde. It was deep beneath the waters of experience.

His thoughts of returning to Clyde had usually been in the form of fantasies. His stay in Clyde was always brief, in these fantasies. He might be motoring north with Nancy during his summer vacation from the bank on their way to spend a few days together in Maine. They would be driving up from Boston in a new convertible with red leather seats and curiously enough the car would always be a Cadillac and he would say to Nancy, as though the idea had struck him suddenly:

"Let's turn off Route 1 and drive through Clyde."

Nancy would be wearing a new tailored broadcloth suit, the color of which was never definite, and Nancy would say:

"Why not, if we're going past it?"

They would drive down Johnson Street very slowly and they would never once get out of the car in that fantasy, but he would actually stop the car in front of the Lovell house and they would sit there commenting on it, as strangers often did who motored through Clyde.

"That's where she lived," he would say. "It's perfect Federalist architecture, but it's sterile, isn't it?" And she would say:

"Sterile as a test tube. Maybe she's in there now." And he would say:

"Possibly, but it isn't as bad as those Currier and Ives temples in upstate New York." And Nancy would say:

"You're the one who said it was sterile. All right, I've seen it. Check" — and she would tap the road map with her finger. She always loved to read the road map — "We can't stay here all day if we're going to spend the night at Poland Spring. What else is there to see?" And he would say:

"Well, there's the Webster Grammar School and the courthouse and the cemetery." And she would say:

"Let's skip the courthouse and the cemetery."

Then he would start the car and they would go down Dock Street and up Spruce Street so that she could see where he had lived and she would say when she saw the house:

"What, haven't they got a bronze plaque on it?" — and if there was time he would show her the Judge's house on Gow Street, and she would say:

"Yes, dear. Light a cigarette for me, will you? I know why you're so peculiar now. I'll tell you what you can do. You can give them a tower someday with chimes in it. What's the best way back to Route 1?"

Then they would be leaving. He would toss away his cigarette and pull down his Panama hat. Somehow in this fantasy he always thought of himself in a Panama hat.

When he was in England he had often daydreamed his way through another fantasy. In this one he would find himself traveling on Route 1 in an army car with the Air Corps insignia on the door. He would be alone in the back seat, just home from overseas, and a technical sergeant would be driving, and he would say, just on the spur of the moment:

"Turn right at the next crossroad, Sergeant. I want to go through Clyde," and when they reached the corner of Dock and Johnson streets he would say:

"Drive ahead, Sergeant, and I'll tell you when to stop. I want to get out for a minute. I haven't been here for quite a while."

The army car would stop in front of Walters's Drugstore and he would get out and stand on the sidewalk and light a cigarette. No one would speak to him but there would be a group of three or four people a few yards away whom he had known once but whom he could not remember. He would glance toward them in pleasant half-recognition. Then he would toss away his cigarette and turn back to the waiting car, and he would hear someone say in a low voice:

"Isn't that Charley Gray — and isn't he a lieutenant colonel?"

He would give no sign of having heard.

"All right, Sergeant," he would say, "let's go," and the army car would be moving down Dock Street.

It was strange, in spite of those occasional rehearsals, that he was not prepared at all for what he saw when he got off the train. He must have thought of Clyde in terms of climax instead of anti-climax, but instead Clyde was like the churchyard in Gray's "Elegy." When the train moved away from the station it was like the lowing herd winding o'er the lea.

He was standing on the platform holding his suitcase, an out-lander now, a stranger, but at the same time nothing was strange to him at all. There was the same smell of coal smoke from the train, the same damp in the air, the same chill of frost in the ground and the same dull, forbidding April sky that he had known. It had been raining and the roofs were wet and the wind made tiny ripples in the puddles in the street and the clouds still hung sullenly over the town. It was going to rain again. The cars were parked about the station in the old disorderly way and a single car was waiting for passengers in the taxi space but everyone was walking home. The driver, a gangling boy of about seventeen, reminded Charles of Earl Wilkins but of course he was not Earl because he was too young to be.

"Taxi, sir?" he asked, and his voice sounded like Earl's.

It never occurred to Charles until he heard the driver's voice that he would not be walking home to Spruce Street, now that he was off the train. He had been thinking of himself and Clyde without ever planning what he would do when he arrived there. Now he did not know where to go and he did not want to go anywhere. He wanted to be alone but he could not stand there holding the suitcase.

"Taxi, sir," the driver called again. The taxis at the station had always called strangers sir.

His cousin Jerry and his Aunt Ruth Marchby were in Clyde, as far as he knew, through his mother's letters from Kansas City. They might be hurt if he did not stay with them but it seemed abrupt and almost rude to appear unexpectedly when he should have telephoned that morning from Boston. No one ever dropped in suddenly on anyone in Clyde.

"Yes. Just a minute," he said.

There were the Masons. He knew they still lived on Spruce Street, also from his mother's letters, and the Masons, too, might be hurt if he did not stay with them, but Mr. and Mrs. Mason would be very old and it might be upsetting to them.

"I guess I've got to go somewhere," he said, and he found himself staring at the driver again. "Are you any relation to Earl Wilkins?" — and the driver said that he was Earl Wilkins's son.

"Let's see," he said. "I haven't been here for quite a while. Is the Clyde Hotel still running?"

In all his years in Clyde he had hardly been inside the Clyde Hotel. It was where drummers stayed and visitors who came to do business with Wright-Sherwin and the mills.

"You mean the inn," Earl Wilkins's son said. "They call it the Clyde Inn now."

"Tell your father," Charles began, and he felt self-conscious and unsure of himself, "tell him Charley Gray was asking for him. We used to go to school together." He had never thought that he would have to introduce himself in Clyde. "I guess you'd better take my suitcase and take it up to the hotel, I mean the inn. Tell them at the inn I'll be along in a little while. I think I'll walk around." He took a dollar out of his pocket though he felt awkward about tipping Earl Wilkins's son. "Just take the bag and keep the change."

"Thanks," Earl's son said. "Thanks a lot."

"And don't forget to tell your father Charley Gray was asking for him."

"I'll tell him all right," Earl's son said, "and thanks a lot." At least he no longer called him sir.

It was not at all like those stories he had read of persons returning to the scenes of their childhood. He was not Rip van Winkle after a twenty-year sleep. He was simply back in Clyde on an earlier train than usual.

There were a few places that he did not want to see — the part of Johnson Street where the Lovell home stood, the Judge's house on Gow Street, and Spruce Street; so he walked up Fillmore Street from the station, not along Chestnut, as he would have if he had been going to Dock Street and then home. First there were the shabby rooming houses near the station, where the workers in the shoeshops and Wright-Sherwin lived, and then came the larger houses as Fillmore approached the northern end of Johnson Street, but he was not thinking of the street. The wind and the dampness of the air were so characteristic of reluctant spring that he might have been waiting in front of the courthouse again for Jessica to come by, just by accident, in her Dodge car. It was too late for snowdrops already but in a flower bed with a southern exposure blue grape hyacinths and a few crocuses might be blooming, flaming orange, white and blue. He saw none and he did not look for them but he was as certain that they would be there as that there would be robins in the budding branches of the lilacs. The willow branches would be turning yellow and on some wooded slope beneath fallen oak leaves there might even be hepaticas. Spring was like autumn, except that everything was coming to life instead of dying. In the country the peeper frogs would be singing in the puddles that could not yet soak through the sodden, frosty ground. Clyde, unhindered by its ghosts, was approaching its annual resurrection.

The Episcopal Church, with the flat tombs in its small churchyard, was on the corner of Fillmore and Johnson streets. He did not look up at its steeple and its cross but he remembered that his Aunt Jane always said as she passed it that she was glad she was a Unitarian. She had said so on the hot summer's day when he had walked past it with her and Dorothea on their way to the Historical Society to hear his mother read her paper. He was walking in the same direction now and soon the Historical Society was in front of him, behind its cast-iron fence on its moist brown lawn, but there were no groups of people waiting for a meeting. "Clyde Historical Society," a new sign by the old brass cannon read. "Open weekdays, 2 P.M. to 5 P.M., except Saturdays." It was a quarter before five.

A bell clanged when he opened the front door, like an old shop bell. There was the same disorder in the hall, the same two antique settles he remembered, and the flintlock muskets, the fire buckets and the blunderbuss. The light in the hall was gray but somehow strong, because the days were growing longer.

The custodian of the Historical Society, he remembered, had always been Miss Smythe, but it was a Miss Smythe of the present who appeared to answer the bell. She had the same grim, watchful expression — she was just the age Miss Smythe had been — and she wore a shabby buttoned sweater because the place was cold. She was looking at him with Miss Smythe's lack of welcome and he would not have been surprised if she had told him to run along as Miss Smythe had when he and Jackie Mason had called there once.

"We close at five o'clock," she said.

"Yes," Charles said, "I know. I just wanted to look around for a few minutes."

"There won't be time to see much before five o'clock," she said.

"Yes," Charles said again. "I just wanted to look around." He was simply another of the objects in that indiscriminate mixture of things in the Historical Society which all belonged somewhere else and to some other age.

"The admission is twenty-five cents," the custodian was saying. "The South Sea ornaments and the ship models are in the room to the left and there are collections upstairs, too, but we close at five o'clock."

The white bone ship still stood in the center of the room to the left. The Chinese pagoda with its wind bells and the sextants were still on the tables and the ship pictures were still on the walls, still plowing under full sail through their conventional canvas seas. The chairs were in rows in the assembly room, facing the same stage on which his mother had stood, and he could almost hear his mother's voice. He could still remember the opening of that paper.

"Every one of us here, I am sure, has seen a certain gray stone house with a mansard roof . . . As Longfellow, Miss Lyte's old friend, expressed it so beautifully once — 'the beauty and mystery of the ships, and the magic of the sea.' "

Nothing was ever entirely over.

"I'm sure we are all most grateful to Mrs. Gray for a charming paper and a delightful afternoon," he could hear Mr. Lovell saying.

Nothing was ever entirely over, but he still wondered why anyone should have brought a suit of samurai armor from Japan and why it should be resting upstairs now in the Historical Society, meaninglessly and yet with some hidden meaning.

Before he left he walked to the lawn in back where tea had been served that summer afternoon. He knew the exact place where he had stood with his mother and father and he remembered exactly where Mr. Lovell had knelt on the grass and had thrown his arms around Jessica. He could almost hear the locusts in the elm trees.

"Pa," Jessica was saying, and he could see her lacy white dress and her white socks and her patent leather slippers, "can't we go home now, please?"

The clock in the Episcopal Church was striking and then he heard the other bells. He remembered the deeper timbre of the Baptist Church and the almost nasal ring of the Unitarian bell. It was five o'clock and the Historical Society closed at exactly five.

Home Free

IT WAS STILL TOO EARLY in the season for raking up front yards and too early for ball-playing by the courthouse. Though the stores on Dock Street were open until six, everyone was hurrying home without lingering on the corners. There were a good many people on Dock Street but for some time Charles recognized no one, though 'hey all had types of features he remembered, and the whole appearance of the street was just the same. The Dock Street Bank had its old grim, evening look. There was a display of seeds and gardening tools in the hardware store, a promise for the future that did not apply to the present. The North End bus was moving up the street and a few mud-spattered cars were following it. There was the same slow sound of traffic that he had always known, and the gentle, splashing sound of overshoes upon the wet brick side-walks. All of Clyde was going home to supper.

It was just the time in the evening when everyone used to gather in the Meaders' back yard. The light was much the same as Charles remembered it. The shadows would be deeper downstairs in the barn and behind the carriage shed and you could run and hide behind the cordwood or behind the pung in the corner of the barn while the voice of whoever might be It counted five hundred by fives. You would hide where you could watch Home, which was the Meaders' back porch, or else you would sneak around the carriage house and wait until the coast was clear. There was always that uncertain moment for deciding whether to risk everything and run or whether to wait longer and risk being seen. Then there was that dash across the yard and the sharp, triumphant moment when you touched the steps of the Meaders' back porch first and shouted, "Home Free!"

In a way, Charles thought, Dock Street was like the Meaders' yard, now that he was walking down it. He was back at the start of everything, among the hidden reasons for everything, but he was not yet home. He saw the window display in Walters's Drugstore that had always been created for April, pyramids of bottles containing assorted spring tonics — Beef, Iron and Wine, Sulphur and Molasses, and also remedies that were guaranteed to break up a cold in twenty-four hours, all connected together by paper streamers which led to a colored cardboard cross section of the human nose and throat.

Beyond the bottles he could see the soda fountain and the booths, all newer than they had been but in exactly the same position. He could see a boy, wearing a Clyde High School sweater, and a girl, with a scarf tied over her head and wearing a green-and-white mackinaw, standing by the fountain. He should have known who they were, but of course he did not. He had stopped in front of Walters's Drugstore without realizing that he had stopped.

A woman was walking toward him holding a bag of groceries and it seemed to him that he should have known her, too, though there was nothing distinctive about her except that her face belonged to Clyde. He remembered thinking that she was too old to be wearing one of those silk scarves tied over her head and that it was not becoming. The scarf was too bright for her gray coat and its worn fur collar and for her blue mittens. Suddenly Charles recognized her — when the light from the drugstore window struck her face, making it look less worn and tired. They had been to Walters's Drugstore together. They had stood by the fountain just as that boy and girl were standing now, and he had often worn a maroon sweater with "CHS" lettered on it. It was Doris Wormser. Her yellow hair was darker, there were deep lines on her face, but it was Doris Wormser, and she recognized him, too, at almost the same moment.

"Why, Charley Gray," she said, and her voice was high and nasal,

497

although he remembered that it had sounded delightfully musical once.

"Why, hello, Doris," he said.

"Well, of all the people I didn't expect to see," Doris Wormser said. "It's the funniest thing. I can't believe it, Charley."

"Well, I can't either. How about a soda, Doris?"

"Oh, no," she said, "I couldn't. I've got to go home and get supper on," and then she laughed. "But it's funny, right in front of the drugstore. You look like everything's agreed with you. You look just the same."

"So do you," he said. "Exactly the same."

"Oh, you go on, Charley," Doris Wormser said. Her voice rose as it did when he used to tell her in high school that she was awfully pretty. "You wait till I tell Willie."

Then he remembered that Doris Wormser had married Willie Woodbury.

"How's Willie?" he asked her.

"He still has the farm machinery agency. Let him know if you want to buy a tractor," Doris said. "We've got three children now, all boys. We're living in the old Adams house. You know, on River Street."

"Oh, yes," he said, and he was glad that she took it for granted that he knew. "I'd like to come and see Willie and the boys."

She smiled at him and held out her left hand because she had the bag of groceries in her right.

"I wish you would," she said, "if you get time, Charley," but she obviously could not ask him then because she had to get supper on and there was a place for everything in Clyde and everything was in its place.

"I've only got two children," he said. "A boy and a girl."

"Yes," she said, "I know. I always knew you'd get ahead, Charley."

He knew what she was saying. She was saying that their lives were entirely separate and that everything was in its place in Clyde, but she was saying it without bitterness or rebuke.

"If you get time, come down and see us," she said, but at the same time she was saying that she would understand if he did not,

Just because they had been to high school together was no reason why he should go down to River Street. She was saying it without saying it and of course he understood. "But it's funny, isn't it, right in front of the drugstore, just as though we were meeting for the picture show."

She looked away from him up Dock Street and he knew what she was thinking. She was thinking that people would be wondering to whom she was talking so long in front of Walters's Drugstore. She was thinking that everyone would have noticed that she had met Charley Gray, not that it mattered any longer, not that it had ever mattered.

"Well," she said, "I've got to be getting on. It's been nice seeing you."

"Tell Willie he's lucky," Charles said.

"Oh, you go on," Doris Wormser said. "Good-by now, Charley."

In Charles's recollection, the Clyde Inn had been a dingy hotel that one passed thoughtlessly on one's way to the public library. He remembered that strangers sat on its porch in summer, their chairs tilted back, their feet on the railing, staring in a bored way at Dock Street and already abysmally convinced that Clyde had no recreational possibilities. There had been no service during prohibition for transporting liquor to a lonely drummer's room and there were certainly no merry girls on call for an informal evening party, because the hotel was right on Dock Street and everyone would have known about it. It had always been a place where one took a compulsory one night's rest and ate a mediocre meal and passed on to somewhere else.

That was the way it was when Charles had lived in Clyde but things were different now. The hotel had been transformed into one of those jolly little taverns, a delightful place for a weary motorist to drop in for the night. Everything had been done to bring back its Georgian lines and its new porch was solid and substantial, behind a thick grouping of evergreen shrubs. Its doorway and blinds were painted Colonial smoky gray and there was a pretty sign with a stagecoach and also the approving stamp of the American Automobile Association and the Lodging-for-a-Night Association. "The Clyde Inn," the sign read, and beneath it in smaller letters, "The Fife and Drum Taproom, A Murgatroyd Hotel."

Each detail contrived to give a gentle hint that the Clyde Inn was a suitable place for a sophisticated, urban visitor compelled to stay in a provincial town. It was a Murgatroyd Hotel, and the inference was that Mr. Murgatroyd knew how to make you comfortable with a foam-rubber or an innerspring mattress and a private bath. Then, too, there was the Fife and Drum Taproom. It was disturbing to enter the Clyde Inn after his meeting with Doris Wormser. Its bright upholstered chairs and the mushroom-like ash receptacles that could not tip over did not belong to Clyde. Neither did the clerk behind the informal, semi-Colonial desk. He was not a Clyde native, he was trained by the Murgatroyd chain.

"We've been waiting for you, Mr. Gray," the clerk said. You could tell it was a piece of the Murgatroyd thoughtfulness that made that nice young man immediately catch his name and realize that he came from a larger world. "We were afraid you might have lost yourself somewhere," and he laughed in a way that indicated that one could hardly lose oneself in Clyde.

"Oh, no, I was just walking around," Charles said.

"Well, we're glad you didn't get lost," the clerk said, and he laughed again, "because you're only our fifth guest today. Things are slow this time of year, but you ought to see us in summer. How long are you staying with us, Mr. Gray?"

"Just overnight, I'm afraid," Charles said.

"I suppose you're making business calls," the clerk said. It was a natural question. Obviously he was not a tourist or he would not have been stopping there in April.

"Yes, a few calls," Charles said. "I'm just passing through."

"Mr. Jaeckel's here, calling on Wright-Sherwin," the clerk said. "He's from the Henderson-Wilckes Pump Company, the New York office. Perhaps you're acquainted with Mr. Jaeckel."

"No," Charles said, "I don't know him but I know the company." The clerk did not belong to Clyde and plainly he was lonely.

"We have some nice little industries here in Clyde," the clerk said.

"There's the shoe business. Clyde's an old shoe town. We have some nice ship pictures in the taproom. Mr. Murgatroyd collected them personally. We still build boats here, runabouts and cabin cruisers, and then there's Wright-Sherwin, brass precision instruments."

"Yes," Charles said, "I've heard about Wright-Sherwin."

"It's a fine company," the clerk said, "but that isn't all there is to Clyde. I wish you could see us in summer."

"Ought I to see you in summer?" Charles asked.

"You really ought to, Mr. Gray," the clerk said. "There's a lot to do in Clyde in summer."

"Is there?" Charles asked. "What is there to do?" He was interrupted by a distant strain of music and he recognized the tune. "Have you got a juke box here?"

"Yes," the clerk answered. "In the Fife and Drum Room. You have to have something these days," and he laughed apologetically. "Some of the local boys and girls come to the Fife and Drum Room for beer in the afternoons but they don't disturb anyone. You were asking what there is to do in Clyde? It isn't fair to Clyde to see it in April. I know how I felt when I came here a year ago myself, right from the Stars and Bars at Atlanta. Did you ever stop at the Stars and Bars, Mr. Gray?"

"No," Charles said. "I never stopped in Atlanta."

"Well, it's quite a shock to come from there to here," the clerk said. "I didn't think I was going to be able to stand it. I didn't realize the charm this place has, or the quaintness. It doesn't quite come through in April."

He was right, it did not quite come through in April.

The clerk reached beneath his counter and produced a small, narrow booklet. It was entitled *Stop Awhile in Clyde*.

"Take it with you, Mr. Gray," he said, "and read it when you have time. Clyde is really a lovely, unspoiled place. There are some very fine old homes here and beautiful gardens. There are several homes here owned by the Society for the Preservation of New England Antiquities, and then there's Johnson Street — I don't know whether your walk took you along there. Authorities say it is the most beautiful street in America — of its kind, of course."

501

The clerk paused and Charles looked at the title of the booklet in his hand, trying to imagine what Clyde would seem like if he had not lived there.

"You really ought to take five or ten minutes in the morning and walk up Johnson Street and especially you ought to see the old Lovell house, even if it isn't open to the public. It's in the Federalist style and there's a description of it here in the book. I'll mark it for you and I'll mark it on the map."

"Thanks very much. That's very kind of you," Charles said.

"It's just an unspoiled Yankee town, Mr. Gray," the clerk went on, "and the natives are friendly. Peculiar and ingrown, some of them, but friendly. And then there are plenty of recreational facilities."

"What sort of recreational facilities?" Charles asked.

There was an inviting pause before the clerk described them.

"There's a fine bathing beach and boating on the river and deep-sea fishing. We have a native here, Captain Willie Stevens, who knows where the big ones are, and there's another native, Captain Earl Wilkins."

"Are they both captains?" Charles asked.

The clerk laughed sympathetically.

"Well, you know how natives are. We call them captains here at the inn anyway . . . And then we're in easy motoring distance of some of the sportiest golf courses in America and we can issue cards to most of them right here at the desk to guests — most guests."

But he was tired of hearing about Clyde and he put the booklet in his pocket.

"Well," he said, "it sounds like a wonderful town."

"It is a wonderful town," the clerk said, "if you get the spirit of it, a wonderful town with lovely people, although most of them don't seem to come here much except for the Rotary Club luncheons. They all seem to like to eat at home and they're pretty tight with money, Yankee types. Well, the dining room opens at six-thirty and the Fife and Drum Room's open now, and if there's anything I can do for you just let me know, Mr. Gray."

"Thanks," Charles said. "Thanks very much. Can you tell me where the telephone is?"

"There's a booth down the hall to the left, on the way to the dining room," the clerk said, "but if you want to make a call from your own room, I can put you through on the switchboard."

"Thanks," Charles said, "the booth's all right."

It was time to face the situation. It was time to find who was alive and who was dead and in the course of it he knew he would have to hear about the Lovells. At least he knew from his mother's letters that the Masons were all alive. He wanted to call them and tell them he was here. He could not bear the thought of being alone with the juke box or alone at a table in the dining room.

When he put his five cents in the telephone coin box and gave the number, he kept the narrow booth open for air. He was sure that he had found the correct number — Virgil Mason, Spruce Street — and he remembered that it was their old number, 693. He could hear the ring at the other end of the line, not the steady, automatic signal of the city. There was an interminable wait and a long, dull silence between the rings but he was sure the Masons would be at home, unless there was a Unitarian supper, because it was six o'clock by then.

As he sat crouched in that narrow booth he tried to picture what was going on in the Mason house at Spruce Street. Mrs. Mason might be out in the kitchen doing something about supper, but certainly Mr. Mason would be in the parlor. Jackie might be upstairs in his room fixing himself for supper. Jackie never thought it looked well to get careless at home. Charles remembered that his mother had written not long ago that Jackie was still at Wright-Sherwin and a great comfort to his mother. He began jiggling the hook.

"Operator," he said, "will you ring them again, please?"

"What number are you calling?" the operator asked.

"The same number you're ringing, I hope," he said. "The number is 693."

"I'm ringing 693." The operator's voice sounded exactly like Doris Wormser's.

"Yes, I know," Charles said, "but would you ring it again, please?"

There was a silence and a very long and vicious ring on the other end of the line. He and the operator were both annoyed by then. His struggle with the telephone was as frustrating as both that walk down Dock Street among the unfamiliar faces and the Clyde Inn under the Murgatroyd management.

Then someone was answering and he closed the door of the booth very quickly although he could not imagine why he should be so anxious for privacy.

"Hello," he said, and he tried to sound bright and cheerful. "Is this Mr. Mason's house?"

"No, it isn't," a woman's voice answered. "What number did you want?"

"I wanted 693," Charles said.

"Well, you have the wrong number." The voice was acid and triumphant. "This is 603."

"Oh," Charles said, "I'm sorry," and he began jiggling the hook again.

"Operator," he said, and he had a strange feeling of defeat and hopelessness, a feeling that he would not get anywhere in Clyde and that nothing would come out right. "You gave me the wrong number. You gave me 603. I asked for 693."

"Oh," the operator said, "well, I'll try them again."

"Don't," Charles said, "don't try them again, Operator. Try 693."

He was extraordinarily grateful when he heard Mrs. Mason's voice. Enclosed in that telephone booth, he had felt like a disembodied spirit, speaking through a medium, but at last he had got through to earth from the spirit world. He was as far away as that. New York, the bank, and Nancy and the children, and life, all lay between him and the Masons' house on Spruce Street.

"This is Charley, Mrs. Mason," he said. "Charley Gray."

She asked him where he was and where he had come from, and he could hear her calling, "Virgil, it's Charley Gray on the telephone."

He said that he was staying at the inn and Mrs. Mason told him to come right over — there was plenty of supper and Jackie was at home. He had hoped that she would ask him but he had known

504

enough not to invite himself. You never dropped in suddenly on anyone in Clyde.

It was a little like looking through a box of old photographs when he reached Spruce Street, almost but not quite. It was nearly dark but some of the long spring twilight was left in the sky and the easterly breeze was dropping. He would not have been surprised in the least if he had seen himself running through the dark toward Gow Street to tell his Aunt Jane that Miss Sarah Hewitt was coming to tea or if he had seen his father walking up from the mill on River Street or if he had heard his mother calling. Nothing on Spruce Street hurt him as he thought it would, yet he did not want to look at the family's house. Nevertheless, he had to stop and turn toward it deliberately and when he did so, it was still their house, though plainer than he had thought it would be behind its uncompromising fence. The house looked as shabby as it had when he was growing up, just as it was meant to look. Some other family lived there now, with other boys and girls, perhaps, all with their own problems, but he could feel no resentment toward its present dwellers, whoever they might be, and he could still think of it as Our House. The yard was untidy again and it looked as though children had been playing in it. He reached and touched the white wooden fence, damp and cold from the rain, and then he turned his head away.

The Masons' house looked neater, as it always had, because Mr. Mason was good about doing things around the house. There was the porch, with its thin turned columns and its jigsaw decorations, and all that was new was an electric light with a milky globe fixed on the ceiling of the porch. There was the same bell in the center of the front door, a bell with a handle that you turned to make it ring, and it gave out the same sound that it had when he and Jackie used to play with it.

Jackie Mason opened the door and for a second each of them looked involuntarily but not impertinently to see what had happened to the other. Jackie was wearing a blue double-breasted suit with a fraternal button. His hair was faded but it was still yellow and it still had a natural wave, though it was thinner and receding from his temples. His face was heavier, but his eyes still had their old worried look.

"Why, Charley," he said, "I'd have known you anywhere."

"Hello, Jackie," Charles said, and then something told him that Jack Mason no longer liked to be called Jackie. "I'm awfully glad to see you," and for a moment it all was the way things used to be. They had been best friends once and they still were friends, without having anything in common.

"Come in," Jack said, "and give me your hat and coat. The old hooks are still under the stairs. I wish you'd let us know instead of going to the hotel, I mean the inn, but of course I understand exactly why you did it. If you'd stayed with us the Marchbys might not have understood, and it's quite an inn, isn't it? I go there Tuesdays to Rotary."

"I didn't know you were in the Rotary," Charles said, and Jackie looked worried.

"I can't say I'm a conscientious Rotarian, but the crowd down at Wright-Sherwin all sort of felt that there should be more Wright-Sherwin representation. Seeing you is going to be a thrill for Mother and Father. They're right in the parlor, Charley" — but Mr. and Mrs. Mason were no longer in the parlor. They were already crowding into the hall. Mr. Mason was in his shirt sleeves, as he always was before supper.

"Charley, dear," Mrs. Mason said, and she kissed him. "You haven't changed at all . . . except you look more like Sam. Virgil, I think at least you might put on your coat for Charley."

"Charley's used to it," Mr. Mason said. "Charley isn't company. I want to show him what I'm making," and they all went into the parlor.

The center table of the parlor was exactly as Charles remembered it, covered with something that Mr. Mason was making. It was now a model stagecoach. The pieces were sawed out but you had to smooth them down and put them together from the diagram.

"Now look at this damn thing," Mr. Mason said. "It says the front axle should go here and when you try to fit it there isn't room. I bet I'm the only person who ever got as far as trying to fit in the axle."

"May and Jeffrey are coming over right after supper," Mrs. Mason said. "It will be just like old times. Sit down, dear, and I'll see what's happening in the kitchen. We have Lucy Slavin working for us."

"Lucy Slavin?" Charles repeated.

"You know, dear," Mrs. Mason said. "She's Mary Callahan's niece — and you must go and see Mary tomorrow."

Jackie Mason cleared his throat.

"There are all sorts of people Charley ought to see tomorrow. Would you care for an old-fashioned cocktail, Charley?"

"Why, Jack," Mrs. Mason said, "I'm afraid we haven't anything in the house."

Jackie Mason cleared his throat again.

"It's locked in the sideboard, Mother," he said. "There was some left over, you know, from the time when Mr. Lovell and Jessica were here to dinner. There's quite a lot left over."

There was a short, sharp silence and Jackie Mason seemed startled by it. He cleared his throat again and his face looked redder.

"There's so much for all of us to catch up with," Mrs. Mason said, "but we have all night. You must tell us your news, Charley, and I'll tell you our news, and Jack will tell you his news, that is if it is news."

"Life has just been going on," Jackie said. "I'll go and fix those old-fashioneds," and he went out into the kitchen.

"Nothing's been the same," Mrs. Mason said. "I still keep thinking that the Grays are there next door — but Esther keeps writing me the news and I write her the news and she sent us some pictures you sent her, Charley, of Nancy and the children and that lovely home of yours. We're all so proud the way you're getting on — the president of a bank — " Charles found himself laughing nervously.

"Mother exaggerates things," he said. "She's showing off to you. I'm not the president of any bank. I'm just one of those boys who are trying to be and an awful lot of us are trying."

"We know you will be, dear," Mrs Mason said. "Shall I tell about Jackie, Virgil? Or shall I let Jackie tell Charles?"

"I don't know what you want to tell him," Mr. Mason said, "but you might as well if you want to, Margaret."

Charles found himself sitting up straighter.

"Jackie's the head of the accounting department at Wright-Sherwin," Mrs. Mason said. "They had a new man from out of town after Mr. Howell died but he didn't get on with Norman Stanley. Jack gets on beautifully with Norman Stanley."

"Well," Charles said, "that's wonderful. That's more than I could have done — get on with Norman Stanley."

Then Jackie was back with a tray and three old-fashioned cocktails.

"Father," he said, "would you mind moving some of the stage-coach so I can put this down on a corner of the table?"

"Put it on another table," Mr. Mason said. "If anything moves here, the whole thing will go."

"Jackie," Mrs. Mason said, "I've just been telling Charley your news."

"Now, Mother," Jackie Mason began, "I especially asked you — "

"Not that news, dear," Mrs. Mason said. "The other news, that you're the head of the accounting department at Wright-Sherwin."

"Oh," Jackie Mason said, and he looked relieved. "It isn't much, Charley, but the company's bigger than it was when you were there."

"I think it's wonderful, Jackie," Charles said, but of course it was not wonderful. Jack Mason was made to be the head of an accounting department someday in a small-town factory.

"You'll have to come down tomorrow and see the boys," Jackie said, as he handed him his cocktail. "I hope I haven't put too much bitters in it."

"And there's another piece of news," Mrs. Mason said. "Jackie's in the Shore Club now."

"It isn't anything," Jackie said, and he looked worried again. "It isn't what it used to be, since the war. It's a good place to take customers now and then. Well, here's looking at you, Charley."

"Yes," Mr. Mason said, "here's looking at you. Here's to the old days, Charley."

III

Second Man in Rome

When they sat down to supper Charles felt almost as if he were back at home in the family dining room on Spruce Street. Mrs. Mason was not unlike his mother as she sat behind the cocoa cups, and it was the same cracked cocoa they were drinking, clear and bittersweet. It was hard to get now, Mrs. Mason said, and they had done without it during the war, but Mr. Mason had found some in Boston recently. Mr. Mason was going to write a paper about cocoa for the Confessional Club.

"It's a funny thing to be writing about with the world the way it is," Mr. Mason said, "but it might just as well be cocoa as communism." Surprisingly enough there was quite a lot about cocoa and chocolate in the public library and it would start right with Cortez and the Aztecs. Their ruler, Montezuma, drank cocoa, and he ate small babies, too, that were cooked in a kind of chafing dish.

"Now, Virgil," Mrs. Mason said, "you're not going to put that in about the babies, are you?"

He could almost hear his father and mother speaking.

The room had almost the same proportions as the old Gray dining room. There were the same plain chairs, a pressed-glass butter dish, and a breadboard with its loaf of homemade bread. The wooden shutters had been drawn and now they shut out a distracted world. His father, Charles was thinking, would have loved to discuss Aztecs eating babies. He could see his mother's incredulous but patient look and Dorothea's expression of horror and his father's delighted smile, and if Elbridge Sterne had been there of course he would never have heard anything about Montezuma or Aztecs either. It was hard to realize that his father was not there, when Mr. and Mrs. Mason began talking about him.

"He was always saying he was going to beat the system," Mr. Mason said.

"Yes," Charles said, "I remember."

"Well," Mr. Mason said, "maybe he did beat the system, in his own particular way."

"Yes, perhaps he did," Charles said, and he saw that Jackie looked nervous, "but he never did get me that pony," and they all laughed just as though his father were not dead. He seemed to be with them in the dining room, pleased that they were speaking of him.

"Perhaps Charley would rather we talked about something else," Jackie Mason said.

"Oh no," Charles said, "I don't mind at all."

"Of course he doesn't, Jackie," Mrs. Mason said, "and, Charley dear, you know what people used to say about John Gray's running through money — people who didn't know him as well as we did?"

"Yes," Charles said, and he found himself smiling, "but then Father never cared."

"Well, no one has ever been able to say that he didn't leave his wife and daughter comfortable. He didn't mind about himself but he always thought of other people."

"Yes," Charles said, and he found himself sitting up straighter and speaking more carefully. All the Masons were looking at him and he took a sip of water. "Yes, I know what you mean."

"We're all so proud of him," Mrs. Mason said, "and then there was that fund for the library."

He could not get away from the idea that his father was there with them, and if he were, Charles knew that he would have been very much amused.

"I don't believe you've ever seen the bookplate for the John Gray Fund," Jackie Mason said. "The library trustees had one designed especially. By the way, I was made a trustee last year." He mentioned the news casually and modestly but Charles had not forgotten its value.

"Jackie's in everything these days," Mr. Mason said. "Why, he's even a director of the Dock Street Bank."

Jackie looked worried. He folded his napkin carefully.

"Charley will get wrong ideas about me," he said, and he laughed. "What's a local savings bank to Charley?"

For a moment it all was a little like one of his daydreams of coming back to Clyde. As he sat there with his herringbone suit still neatly pressed, he must have looked to them much as Arthur Slade had once looked to him, the aura of a city bank still about him, polite and measured, with all his edges smoothed.

"Charley, dear," Mrs. Mason said, "tell us where you live and what you do. Tell us about everything."

He folded his napkin, forgetting that he was a guest. They were all waiting for him to speak. He was a rich and glittering visitor from a strange and foreign land.

"Well," he said, "I'm in the trust department in the bank and that keeps me pretty busy. I don't ever seem to have much time to see Nancy and the children, but perhaps I will get time if everything turns out right. Nancy's an awfully nice girl."

It seemed very necessary to say that Nancy was a nice girl.

"We've always wondered," Mrs. Mason said, "why William wasn't named after his grandfather."

"Nancy named him," Charles answered. "I wanted to name him Sam." He stopped and for a second it seemed as though Sam were with them too. "But Nancy said let's make a clean break of it and call him Bill. Well, we live in a place called Sycamore Park . . ." He found himself speaking more quickly, more easily. He was laying out his whole life on the dining room table, just as though he were dealing from a deck of cards, and it sounded rather well.

"There's a good country day school for the children, but I want Bill to go to boarding school next year. And then there's a good country club; and then there are, well, my business associates. Nancy and I have a lot to keep us busy."

"We have a picture of the house," Mrs. Mason said. "It looks so new and lovely with your car standing in front of it on the driveway."

"Of course, there was that gap while I was away."

"You mean at the war?" Jackie Mason said.

All at once his going to the war was an action which he wanted to explain and justify. The Masons were almost the only people who could have understood all his reasoning.

"I shouldn't have gone," he said, "at my age and with a wife and two children. It's the sort of thing that doesn't help you in a business way. Nancy didn't like it and I don't blame her much." He was not sure himself why he had gone to the war but he was almost sure. "Sam went, and you know I always thought a lot of Sam. And then — well, maybe I was tired of beating the system." He laughed, but only because he felt it would be a good idea to laugh. "When I got there it was just the bank all over again with a different set of rules."

He had dealt the cards of his little game and they were in order on the table.

"Well," Mr. Mason began, "I think it was a mighty fine thing," but he did not finish because the doorbell rang.

"That's May and Jeffrey," Mrs. Mason said. "I guess they thought we'd be finished supper."

"Charley," Jackie Mason said, "would you care for a cigarette? Or would you rather have a cigar? They're right in the sideboard."

"No, thanks," Charles said. "Just a cigarette."

May and Jeffrey Meader came into the dining room and everyone was standing up and the room seemed very crowded, with those who were there and those who were not. The moment he saw May Mason he thought of the summer afternoon when May had been sitting alone in the back room trying to play "The Pink Lady" on the old upright piano and he had brought her that note from Sam; and he knew that May, stoutish, middle-aged and gray-headed, remembered, too.

"Charley," she said, "I guess I've got to kiss you." He could tell from the way she spoke that it was an impulsive break from what she had planned to do or say. "You look like Sam."

"I've thought of you a lot, May," he said. It had a brittle, banal sound and he wished he could have thought of something better. "I'm awfully glad if you think I look like Sam." It was a very public, awkward moment, because everyone was listening.

Jeffrey Meader was pudgy, with horn-rimmed spectacles, and almost bald. He looked like someone in a small real estate and insurance office, but then this was exactly the way he should have looked.

"Why, Charley looks like a good prospect," he said. "Hi, Charley."

"Hi, Jeffrey," Charles said.

"And here's Edwina," May went on, as though she had not heard Jeffrey. "You remember Edwina, don't you? She was Dorothea's flower girl." May's daughter was standing in the doorway, looking just as May had once looked except that her blond hair was cut in a page boy bob instead of being long and tied up in a knot, and she, too, must have been the prettiest girl in her class at high school.

"Why, I'd know Edwina anywhere," he said. "She hasn't changed at all."

"Malvina's married," May said. "She's living in Brockton and as long as we're just the family I'll tell you Malvina's news. What do you think — she's expecting, Charley."

"May means Malvina's going to have a baby," Jackie said. "I wish you wouldn't put it that way, May. It sounds local."

"All right, all right," Jeffrey Meader said. "No matter how it sounds May's going to be a grandmother any time now and that sounds pretty funny, doesn't it?"

"Now you're here," May said, "how long are you going to be here, Charley?"

He was a visitor again, that successful visitor from the city who had left them long ago, and his voice sounded polite and assured when he answered.

"Only over tomorrow, I'm afraid. I'll have to be taking the midnight from Boston tomorrow. I'm sorry I can't stay longer but perhaps some other time — "

"There are certain people that Charley ought to see before he goes back," Jackie said, "and there'll be talk if he doesn't. I'll make a list and go over it with Charley."

They all trooped back to the parlor, now that supper was finished, and when Charles took part in the conversation it was like speaking a language which he had known well a long time before and which he could still speak, although he was unfamiliar with the latest idioms and his tenses might occasionally be confused. In his absence Clyde, aloof and indestructible, had been drifting through a turbulent sea, but Clyde was made for trouble. Nothing could entirely alter its values. Everyone still knew his place and there was a place for everyone.

Charles had forgotten that everyone went to bed early in Clyde until he saw Mr. Mason yawn and then he said he would have to be getting back to the hotel, he meant the inn, and that he had had a wonderful time; and they all said it was like old times, seeing him, and they would see him again tomorrow.

"I'll go back to the inn with you," Jackie said.

"Oh, no," Charles told him, "don't bother, Jack. You'd be surprised. I know my way."

"Why," Jackie Mason said. "I'd really like to, Charley. You and I have a lot to talk about and there won't be time tomorrow."

Charles had begun to speak that forgotten language of Clyde so fluently that he and Jack Mason seemed to have picked up something which they had both dropped years before; when they began walking up Spruce Street, there was that old realization of having been friends, and it was still completely usable. There was a persistent quality in Jackie Mason's loyalty and he knew that Jackie admired him for the same reasons he previously had, and he liked Jackie, too, with the same old reservations. Their friendship was on a different footing from other, later friendships. It was deeper, it was unavoidable, and he felt very grateful for it. He seldom gave way to impulse. His training was all against it, but almost without thinking he slapped Jackie softly on the back.

"Well, Jackie," he said, "here we are on Spruce Street," and he knew that Jack was pleased.

They were walking toward Johnson Street and the houses were growing larger and more imposing. He did not want to see Johnson Street but if he had to he was glad that Jack Mason was with him.

"I guess it's going to rain," Jackie said. "We've had a lot of rain lately. It's nice to see you again, Charley."

"The same here," Charles said, and they walked for a while without speaking, now that each had said what he had meant to say.

"The old place hasn't changed much," Jackie said. "It's still about the same. Charley, I wish you'd never gone away."

It was not what Charles would have wished and he thought of what might have happened if he had stayed in Clyde. They had turned right at the corner of Spruce and Johnson streets and there was the Hewitt house, all dark, and the Lovell house diagonally across from it. He made a deliberate effort not to look at it, though common sense and his knowledge of human relationships told him that he could not blame the Lovell house or Johnson Street for what had happened to him and Jessica. Still he did not want to see it.

"I couldn't have stayed," he said, and it was a great relief that he had not a single doubt about it.

"Of course, it might have been a little difficult at first — " Jackie Mason hesitated — "but nothing would have affected your position. For instance, take the library," but he did not go on about the library.

It was very natural to be walking down Johnson Street with Jack Mason talking about position. Jackie did not mention that his grandfather had been a druggist but it was still on Jackie's mind.

"Or take the bank," Jackie said. "You would have been in just the right position, the first time there was a vacancy on the board."

If he had stayed in Clyde, he might certainly have been a director of the Dock Street Bank. He might even have been president of it if he had done the right things at the right time.

"Well, never mind it," he answered. "You're the one who's got position now."

"Oh, I haven't done anything much," Jackie Mason said, "except in a small-town way."

A sad note in Jackie's voice made Charles realize that Jackie wanted him to be impressed with everything he had done, and, after all, he was a trustee of the public library and a director of the bank. He had gone a long, long way.

Charles had to answer properly and he could not sound patronizing.

"Everything you do depends on where you are," he said. "Do you remember what Julius Caesar said" — he was like his own father, groping for an apt quotation — "about preferring to be the first man in Ostia to the second man in Rome? I'm sure it wasn't Ostia but let's call it Ostia." He could not see Jack Mason's face in the dark but he was sure that he had said the right thing, neither too little nor too much.

"That's awfully nice of you to say that, Charley," Jackie said.

"It isn't nice," Charles said quickly, "it's the truth," and he thought of something else, because it was an occasion when one could say anything. "What is that line in the Declaration of Independence — or is it the Constitution? 'Life, liberty, and the pursuit of happiness.' Well, I suppose everybody's pursuing happiness, and you usually lose your liberty when you do, and the best part of your life. Maybe that's what everything's about. Maybe. I don't know."

They had turned down Dock Street and it was a radical statement to have made in front of the Dock Street Bank and it had no reference to anything except that he was thinking of Jackie Mason and also of himself.

"I know what you mean," Jackie said. "You mustn't try to crowd your luck." It was not what he had meant but he was glad that Jack had misunderstood him.

"Maybe I am crowding my luck a little but everything does seem to be coming my way all of a sudden." Jackie stopped and sighed. "But it's taken a lot of time, a lot of time. Maybe it's just that somebody has to take hold and I seem to be elected . . . let's see, did I tell you I was in the Tuesday Club?"

"Why, no," Charles said, "you didn't. That certainly is something, Jack."

"It isn't anything really," Jackie said. "Everybody's dying pretty fast, but it's funny, isn't it, being in the Tuesday Club with Mr.

Stanley and Mr. Lovell and everybody? I thought you'd be amused."

"It isn't so funny," Charles said. "You have what it takes, that's all."

They had crossed the street and they were in front of the Clyde Inn before Jackie spoke again.

"Don't think I look on myself as the first man in Ostia. I'm a long way from it — er — Charley, do you mind if I come up to your room with you? There's something else I want to tell you." Jackie looked worried again. "Something I hope you won't mind."

"Of course I won't mind," Charles said. "What is it, Jack?"

"I'll get it off my chest in just a minute," Jackie said, "but I can't tell it in front of everybody."

There was no one to tell it in front of at the inn except the clerk, who still sat behind the desk and who looked surprised to see them enter the place together.

"Oh, hello, Edgar," Jackie said. "Mr. Gray wants his room key. I hope you've given Mr. Gray a good room."

"Good evening, Mr. Mason," the inn clerk said. "I didn't know you were acquainted with Mr. Gray."

"It would have made all the difference, wouldn't it?" Jackie said, and he laughed. "I'll tell you what you can do for me, Edgar. Just get me a bottle of rye, the kind I bought for Mr. Jaeckel, and put it on my bill. You like rye, don't you, Charley?"

Charles said that it did not matter, he did not care for anything particularly, and Jackie may have been sorry for his impulse, because he was careful to conceal the bottle beneath his overcoat as they walked upstairs.

"Life, liberty, and the pursuit of happiness," he said. "I'm afraid Edgar was a little surprised. I don't do this sort of thing very often except in a business way, but seriously, it does mean a lot to the town having an inn like this, and this isn't a bad room, is it? I'm glad you have a quiet one that opens on the back."

Charles's room had a country, chintzy look, and was furnished in yellow Colonial maple, with an imitation spool bed and a bedside

517

table with a telephone on it, a writing table, one small upholstered chair and one straight chair. The room was stifling hot. He had forgotten that the heat was on, and when he opened the window he found himself looking over the old back gardens toward the houses along Fanning Street.

"Yes, it's going to be quiet here," Charles said.

Jackie had put the bottle of rye on the writing table.

"Here, let me pour the drinks," he said. "This is my party, Charley. There ought to be some glasses in the bathroom. Dear me, I should have ordered up some ice."

"Oh, never mind the ice," Charles said.

It was rather like the war, sitting in an unfamiliar room with a bottle of rye whiskey and tepid water. It was not at all like Clyde.

"Well, now we're here," Charles said, "what is it you want to tell me, Jack?"

Jackie cleared his throat and his worried look returned.

"Well," he said, "all right," and he cleared his throat again. "Charley, I think I ought to talk to you about Jessica Lovell."

Charles knew, of course, that he could not erase his memory of Jessica Lovell and that at some time while he was in Clyde he would have to meet the past face to face, but so far he had heard nothing except that talk about cocktails and the remaining ingredients which had been left at the Masons' when Jessica and Mr. Lovell had been entertained. He was seated on the stiff chair by the writing table and he was conscious of many little things, of a draft on the back of his neck from the open window, of a soft hiss from the valve of the radiator. He had leaned forward as though he wanted to hear better and now he leaned back because he did not like that display of eagerness. Still the palms of his hands were moist and the room felt very stuffy. Mentioning Jessica was like opening a box filled with things you would never use again but which could not be thrown away.

"I'm glad you brought up Jessica," he said. There was nothing revealing in his voice. It had just the right note of friendly interest — exactly as he wished it. "I've been meaning to ask about her. How is Jessica?"

"Oh, she's very well," Jackie said. "Very well and busy. She has that same interest in things, but then you know Jessica."

"I don't know her now," Charles said, and he smiled agreeably at Jackie and everything he said was just as he wanted it. "I've been pretty busy, too."

"I know how you feel," Jackie said. "I don't want to bring up any painful memories."

"Oh, my God," Charles said. Jackie's manner made him impatient. "Don't call them painful memories, Jackie. They're too old."

"I'm awfully glad you take it this way," Jackie said, "but of course I know how you must feel."

"No, you don't," Charles said, "because I don't feel anything," and he smiled. He was saying just what he wanted to say. "I hope Jessica's well and happy and I'm glad we didn't get married because it wouldn't have worked — and that's all there is to it, except I always supposed she'd find someone else. Why didn't she ever marry?"

Jackie looked at him reproachfully as though he had not assumed the serious attitude the circumstances demanded.

"She just never did, Charley," he said, and his voice was reproachful, too.

Charles rubbed his hands softly on his knees and he had an absurd notion that Jackie Mason was blaming him for Jessica's being unmarried. It was like those stories of old Clyde spinsters keeping a night light always burning in the spare-room window for lovers who had disappeared at sea.

"Well, I don't see why she didn't," he said, "unless it was her father again."

"No," Jackie said, and he sighed. It seemed to Charles an elaborate, overdramatized sigh. "I don't think it was entirely that."

Charles did not answer. Instead he stared at the yellow maple bed with its bright chintz cover. The conversation was reminiscent of a weeping willow above a suitably inscribed tombstone in an old memorial print.

"I think she always hoped that you'd come back sometime."

He could see that Jackie Mason believed it and he almost believed it too, because at one time she must have thought of him often — but it was not the way things were. There were no lights nowadays burning in lonely windows. The room was very hot and there was still that draft on the back of his neck.

"Maybe she did for a year or two," Charles said. "She knew I'd married, didn't she?"

"Yes," Jackie said. "Jessica's a wonderful girl. She's always wanted you to be happy, Charley. She's always wanted to hear about you."

"Well," Charles said, "I think I'll have another drink."

When Charles went into the bathroom to fill his glass with tap water he glanced at himself in the mirror above the washbasin, as he did usually at the bank. His tie was straight, his soft collar was smooth. He looked as he should have, like someone from New York, and suddenly he realized as sure as fate that he could have come back to Clyde, he could have married Jessica Lovell. Her father could not have stopped them, nothing could have stopped them if he had come back, but until this moment the idea had never crossed his mind. He walked out of the bathroom holding his glass and sat down again in the uncomfortable chair.

"Well," he said, "I never did come back."

He never would have. He would have been too proud.

"I thought I ought to tell you, Charley," Jackie said. "I thought you ought to know." He still could not understand why Jackie thought he ought to know except that Jackie had always found it hard to keep things to himself.

"Did Jessica tell you this?" he asked. "It doesn't sound like Jessica" — and for a moment he had a proprietary feeling, as though Jessica still belonged to him.

"Well, you see — " Jackie Mason looked too large for the small upholstered chair in which he sat. His face looked moist and he pulled out a neat handkerchief from his breast pocket. "It's awfully hot in here, isn't it, but it will cool off given time. . . . You see, Jessica had to talk to someone and I suppose I was elected — just because I knew you. She still talks a lot about you, Charley. Jessica was in love with you for years. She really was."

"I wonder if I could have another of your cigarettes?" Charles asked. He did not want to consider Jessica Lovell's having been in love with him for years.

"Oh, excuse me," Jackie said, and he snapped open his silver cigarette case. "You know, there's something about women — " his face was redder — "I think that women seem to stay in love longer than men, once they fall in love."

"Maybe they do," Charles said. "It's possible."

It was possible but not probable. Jessica Lovell, as Jackie Mason saw her, was an unreal character. Girls did not stay in love indefinitely unless there was some outside compulsion. He was glad that he was able to tell himself that this was so.

"You see" — Jackie was still speaking — "I thought you ought to know this so that you won't misunderstand Jessica."

"My God, Jackie," Charles said, "I don't misunderstand Jessica. It's all over and, I told you, I'm glad I didn't marry her and that's all there is to it"; but Jackie was going on.

"I'm glad you take it this way, Charley. You see, I've been seeing a lot of Jessica." He laughed deprecatingly. "I guess Mr. Lovell thought I was pretty harmless, but things can't help changing and that's what I want to tell you. I want to tell you that Jessica and I are engaged and are going to be married in June."

Somehow Charles had thought of everything else but not of that. He was reconciled to Jackie's being a library trustee, a director of the bank, a member of the Tuesday Club, but he had never thought of his marrying Jessica Lovell. He could not think that he resented it or that it was jealousy he felt, or envy. He was mainly disturbed because of something in the whole picture that was malformed, something that should not have been. He was thinking of what Jessica used to say about Jackie Mason, but as Jackie said, things changed if you saw someone long enough — and it had taken a long, long time. It was all as dry as dust, almost repellent, and for once he did not say the proper thing.

"Why, Jackie," he said, "it looks as though you have everything," and he heard Jackie's nervous laugh.

"Oh, I wouldn't put it that way," Jackie said, "and I know that

Jessica and I are a little old to take this step, but then we've known each other so long."

The radiator hissed again and Charles still did not know how he felt.

"I wish you'd tell me," he asked, "how Mr. Lovell took it."

"Well, I was a little surprised," Jackie said. "He didn't seem to mind. It's funny, when I had my talk with him, he kept calling me Charles. Of course, his mind isn't what it was before he was ill last winter, but he's really a grand old gentleman, and we'll all be living there together. He couldn't live without Jessica."

At last Charles said the right thing. He said he thought it was splendid and he knew they would be happy.

"I'm awfully glad you think so, Charley," Jackie Mason said, "and now there's one thing more. I hope you'll call on Jessica tomorrow. She knows you're here, you know."

Charles picked up his glass and was surprised to find it empty. He set it carefully back on the writing table and rose.

"No," he said. "No, I don't think so, Jack. It — " His voice was unexpectedly hoarse. "It wouldn't help anything."

"But, Charley" — Jackie looked deeply hurt — "I wish you'd think of Jessica. Everyone will know you didn't see her."

It was that old phrase again, everyone would know, but it was something he could not do, something he would not do, even though everyone would know.

"I can't," he said, and his voice was still hoarse. "I suppose I ought to, but I can't . . . I'm sorry, Jackie."

No matter what Jackie Mason said, he would not go to the Lovells'. Jackie Mason was still his friend and Jackie was always loyal, but he did not have to see Jessica or Mr. Lovell or the Lovell house again.

"Why, Charley," he said, "if you really feel that way . . . But just think it over and we'll talk about it again tomorrow."

"All right," Charles said.

"And now I'd better be going. It's getting awfully late."

"Wait a minute," Charles said, and his mind was back to where it should have been. "Just a minute before you go, Jackie. There's something I've been meaning to ask you. What do you know about the Nickerson Cordage Company?"

His voice at last sounded the way it should have through all that conversation.

For a minute or two after Jackie Mason closed the door and after the sound of footfalls disappeared, Charles Gray had the illusion that he was in a hotel room somewhere else and that Jackie Mason had appeared unsubstantially and that their conversation had been still another fantasy. Although the place had the impersonality peculiar to any hotel room and though the presence of people who had occupied it could be erased from it as one wiped chalk off the surface of a blackboard, the imprint of Jack Mason's posterior was still visible upon the cushion of the small upholstered chair. The bottle of rye was gone, because he had insisted that Jack Mason take it back with him, under his overcoat if necessary, but the two bathroom glasses were on the table — his own empty and the other only faintly colored and still three quarters full, showing that Jackie Mason very seldom did that sort of thing.

Charles took his thin gold watch from his waistcoat pocket, the unnecessarily expensive watch that Nancy had given him just before they were married. Nancy had never liked wrist watches in an office because, without meaning to, you always glanced at them. It was very late for Clyde, almost half past eleven o'clock. He picked up the two glasses automatically and walked into the bathroom, where he rinsed them out carefully, but rinsing glasses could not change his frame of mind. He could not get his thoughts away from Jack Mason and the career of Jack Mason. A sense of emptiness and futility hung darkly over him. It was late, but he wanted to call up Nancy. He had never wanted so much to speak to anyone and he felt better already when he had given the number at Sycamore Park.

"Ring me when you get it, will you, please?" he said.

Then he walked to the single window and opened it wider and stood breathing the cool night air. There was the sound of a train in the distance. It would be the eleven-thirty going north to Portland.

The timetable had not changed. It was a dark, cloudy night but the sky was lighter than the earth and he could see the blurred shapes of the elms and the houses on Fanning Street. The town was asleep but it was still alive and as full of blind instinct as a beehive. Malcolm Bryant had perceived this once and he had tried clumsily to translate it into the pages of *Yankee Persepolis,* so named because the Persians had worshiped memories there.

He thought again of Jackie Mason, beset by this instinct and wanting to get on according to the rules, and he had seen the result that night, a preordained and sterile ending. The worst of it was that it partially reminded him of his own career. He had been living carefully according to other rules. Someday he might be a vice-president of the Stuyvesant Bank in New York City, and Jackie Mason was engaged to Jessica Lovell. He wished that the night were not so dark. He wished that everything were not so deathly still. There was not even a sigh of wind in the branches of the trees.

The sharp ring of the telephone broke into those thoughts and he was relieved to hear the low and sleepy sound of Nancy's voice.

"What are you doing? Where are you?" she asked.

"I'm here in the hotel in Clyde," he said, and it sounded like the beginning of a letter — Clyde Inn, Clyde, Massachusetts. "Did I wake you up?"

"Yes, you did," Nancy said. "Never mind it. Are you all right?"

Nancy always hated wasting money talking aimlessly on the long distance and he disliked it too, but nothing could have made him stop talking.

"I'm fine," he said. "Are you all right? Are the children all right?"

"There's no perceptible change," Nancy said. "Molly Blakesley came to call."

"Oh," he said. "What did Molly Blakesley want?"

"She didn't want anything, damn her."

"Molly's all right," he said. "What else has happened?"

"Well, Bill cut his lip. A baseball hit him. And that man you called to see about the roof, he never came."

"Well, never mind," Charles said. "How about the Buick?"

"Why do you want to know about the Buick?"

"I don't know," Charles said. "I'm just feeling lonely for you and the Buick."

"It's a nice association of ideas," Nancy said. "How lonely are you?"

"Very lonely." he answered. "There are too many ghosts up here."

"Well, when are you getting back?"

"The midnight tomorrow," he said.

"What about that company?"

"I'm attending to it tomorrow."

"Well, what have you been doing?"

"Just talking," he said. "I had supper at the Masons'."

"Oh," she said. "The Masons — those people who lived next door?"

"Yes, they're the ones," he answered.

"Well, what about that Lovell girl?" He knew that Nancy would ask about the Lovell girl. "Have you seen her yet?"

"No," he said. "She's going to marry Jackie Mason. What do you think of that?"

"You mean the boy next door is marrying the girl in the big house?" Nancy said. "I've never seen him, so how should I know what to think?" It was wonderful to hear the indifference in Nancy's voice. "Now wait a minute. Is that why you're lonely?"

"No," he said, "it isn't. I wish you were here."

"Well, I'm glad you do," Nancy said. "Now listen, we're not getting anywhere and we've been talking more than three minutes. Come home as early as you can on Friday, and don't worry about anything."

"About what?" he asked her.

"You know what . . . the bank . . . And Charley, I didn't really mean what I said — about its not being much but its being the only thing we had. It was a silly thing to say."

"Just a second." At least he was no longer thinking about Clyde. "Have you heard anything?"

"No," she answered, "I didn't mean it that way, darling. Don't sit alone there worrying. I'll see you on Friday. Good night, dear."

He set down the telephone and stood up, conscious of a new sound which he had not noticed while they had been talking. It was the rushing sound of rain. It was pouring rain outside.

The rain had a finality that reminded him of the mechanical whir of the curtain in a theater falling inexorably upon the last line of a play. Random, undisciplined thoughts were with him again and there were voices in the persistent beating of the rain as clear as though they had been real. His mind was wandering off in aimless reminiscence as it had just the night before in his knotty-pine library at Sycamore Park. For no good reason, he was thinking of the time he had sat on the stage in the Clyde City Hall for the graduation exercises of his class at grammar school. He remembered exactly how his stiff collar had chafed the left side of his neck and Jackie Mason had been beside him, in a stiff collar, too. Jackie's hair was slicked smooth with soap but soap could never straighten the wave in it. They sat bemused in the second row behind the fluffy dresses and the big bow hair ribbons of the girls, while Mr. Martin J. Gifford, who was going to run that fall for the state legislature, was addressing the graduating class. His voice came back with the rain.

"Don't let anyone tell you, my young friends, that there is any such thing as luck . . . no, no . . . The wonderful ladies and gentlemen on your school committee, your teachers . . . your great mayor, my dear old friend Francis X. Flynn . . . The greatest country of the world . . . the United States of America, where all men, I thank God, are free and equal, living in the frame of freedom, life, liberty and the pursuit of happiness . . . Each of us can look the other in the eye and say, 'I am as free as you are . . . I have the same chance as you.' "

The voice was in the patter of the rain, mingling with other voices, and Charles could hear his father's voice beside it.

"The system, Charley. You have to beat the system."

The sound of the rain was growing louder. It was tapping out its own refrain on the sodden earth and on the sidewalks and on the roofs of Clyde — life, liberty and the pursuit of happiness.

It was true — the harder you pursued happiness, the less liberty you had, and perhaps if you pursued it hard enough, it might ruin you. His father had died pursuing it. No one had told the school children that freedom of choice was limited. He could see himself hurrying, always hurrying, and he would be hurrying again tomorrow, back to Nancy and the children and back to taking care of other people's money. It was not what he had dreamed of, there in Clyde, but if he had to start all over again he would not have acted differently. He would not have stayed at Wright-Sherwin. Inevitably he would have gone to Boston in that pursuit of happiness and he and Jessica Lovell would have pursued it for a little while together, but he would have used the same judgment and he would have made the same mistakes.

"But there is no such thing as luck," he heard Mr. Martin J. Gifford saying, "not for American boys or girls," and he remembered what Sam had said.

"It was the same old bushwa, kid," and so it was, but in a certain sense Martin J. Gifford was nearly right. It was not due to luck that Martin J. Gifford had been there to address the boys and girls.

The drumming of the rain was slackening, changing to the gentle, persistent sound of steady April rain, and again he was acutely conscious of the weather. Weather was a part of living again as it used to be long ago and he remembered how he had once hoped for northeast storms, wild enough and heavy enough to make the sirens blow in the morning, signaling no school. The brooks, already swollen, would spill over parts of their banks by morning, and the tufted grass on the swamp would be covered near the bridge on the road to Walton Spring. The peeper frogs would be singing their thin, plaintive song there in the morning. Jessica had not known what it was when she had heard it on the road that day . . .

IV

I Suppose She'll Wear a Long Dress

CHARLES might have reserved a bedroom on the midnight back from Boston. It would not have been out of line and it would have been sensible, because he had not slept well that night in Clyde. The cost would not have exceeded that of a hotel room and no one would have dreamed of questioning the expenditure, but he was always very careful about expense accounts. His training in handling other people's affairs had made him absurdly meticulous in spending money that was not his own. He had taken a lower berth in what might have been the same grim and antiquated car that he had boarded at Boston when he left Clyde for good in 1930. He checked his suitcase in the morning at the Vanderbilt Avenue checkroom, just as he had checked his suitcase when he had arrived from Clyde that other time. There was the same sleepy emptiness in the Grand Central Station. He was in New York again following a familiar procedural pattern.

It was a quarter before eight when Charles arrived at the bank, too early for anyone to be there except Martin, the night watchman, and his assistant, Francis. Martin opened the side door carefully and spoke softly, like the sexton of a church.

"Good morning, Mr. Gray," Martin said, and his hand was on the emergency button, just where it should have been. "You're pretty early, aren't you?"

"Hello, Martin," Charles said. "I'm just down from Boston."

"How is the weather up there?" Martin asked.

"Rainy," Charles said.

"Is that so?" Martin said. "It rained here yesterday but it was fine last night."

528

"It certainly is quiet here," Charles said.

"It's spooky until you get used to it," Martin said. "You always keep waiting for an alarm to go off." There was no reason why Martin should not have been used to it. He had been in charge at night for over fifteen years.

The banking floor was very still and all the curtains were drawn over the windows so that the light reminded him of a bedroom in the morning. The officers' desks beside the windows all had their tops closed tight and his own desk and Roger Blakesley's stood side by side on the edge of the green carpet, impersonal and bare. Charles laid down his brief case and took off his overcoat.

"Well, it's nice to be back," he said. "I feel as though I've been away for quite a while."

He opened his brief case and pulled out his notes. The yellow scratch pad and the pencils were in his upper right-hand drawer and Miss Marble always saw that his pencils were sharp. He began to write his memorandum to Mr. Burton in clear, very legible handwriting. He could thank Miss Jenks, his teacher in the seventh grade, for that readable script, and once he had tried very hard to please Miss Jenks.

Another day was starting. First the bookkeepers and the tellers appeared, laughing and talking until their voices were lost behind all the preparatory sounds in the cages. He was conscious that the room around him was filling up but he kept persistently on with his writing. If he could get his memorandum finished before he was interrupted the whole day would run more smoothly and on schedule. He did not realize how late it was until he felt a hand on his shoulder. It was Roger Blakesley, with his rimless glasses, still in his overcoat, carrying his brief case. All the desks were occupied and Miss Marble was there. It was almost half past nine.

"Well, well," Roger said. "Did you blow in on the midnight?"

It was exactly the way Roger would have put it, "blowing in."

"Hello, Roger," Charles said. "That's right. On the midnight."

"Well, it's nice you're back, fella," Roger said. "How are things up north?"

"Fine," Charles said. "It was a nice trip, Roger."

Roger's grasp on his shoulder relaxed and they smiled at each other, like old friends, aware that they were being watched.

"Well, everything's just the same here," Roger said, "the same old rat race," and he lowered his voice. "Damn it, I wish they'd get this thing settled, Charley. It's getting on my nerves."

It was the first time either of them had mentioned the Thing to the other.

"So do I," Charles said. "It's on my nerves too, Roger."

"Anyway," Roger said, "it's nice to see you back, fella."

It was no time to look at Roger too sharply. He could only wonder whether anything had happened while he was away to make the Thing get on Roger's nerves.

The three-two local for home was a slow train, stopping at nearly every point along the line. Charles could tell where he was by counting the stops, and instead of looking out of the window he read the *World Telegram* and the Kiplinger *Washington Letter* and *Time* magazine. It was a beautiful, bright, sunny afternoon, not a reluctant New England April afternoon but more like mid-May. When he stepped off the train the station platform gave off a warm, tarry smell and the air was cool but languid. The waters of Long Island Sound in the distance had a blue that was almost like the blue of summer. It was suburban New York weather and so warm that he did not need an overcoat.

When he saw the Buick he knew that Miss Marble must have called Nancy or that Nancy had called Miss Marble at the bank. At any rate, she was there waiting for him and Bill and Evelyn were with her.

"Why, Nance," he said, "I didn't expect to see you all here."

This was not exactly true, because he had half expected them, and the best of it was they looked just as they had when he had left them, Nancy in her greenish tweed suit, Evelyn with her braids and her low-heeled shoes and Bill in his gray long trousers and his coat that was too short in the sleeves. It was time to take Bill into town and buy him a new suit. Perhaps they could all go to town and have lunch at Longchamps and see some sort of show, if there was anything on the New York stage that the children ought to see. It had been a long while since they had been to town together. All sorts of other plans came to mind as he saw them but there was no opportunity to sort out those plans because they were all so glad to see him.

"I called up Marble," Nancy said. "She said you were going to take the three-two."

"Here," Bill said, "let me carry that for you," and he took his suit-case.

"Hello, Evvie," he said. "Do you know what I did in Boston? I bought a bottle of that after-shaving lotion."

"Evelyn, get in back with Bill," Nancy said, and then she held his hand for a moment as they walked to the car. "I've got to pick up my dress at the cleaners'. That's all we have to do."

"What dress?" he asked.

"The almost new one," she said, "with flowers on it, for tonight."

"Oh, yes," he said. "Tonight," but there was a long while until evening. He felt pleasantly tired and he could not be worried about that dinner at the Burtons'.

"It's funny," he said. "I feel as if I'd been across the ocean. The climate's different here."

"I know," Nancy said. "It must be very difficult to pick up all the threads, but don't try too hard . . . just give yourself time."

"It isn't so hard," he said, and he laughed.

"It's nice to know it," Nancy said. "The first thing for you to do is to get to know the children all over again. I can come later and more gradually. We all may be a little shy with each other at first but we can all adjust together."

The grass was beginning to turn green and forsythia was out already and there were tomato plants and forget-me-nots in baskets in front of the hardware store.

"Mother," Evelyn said from the back seat, "I don't know what you're talking about. Daddy's only been away two days."

"Oh, put on another record," Bill told her. "Don't you know when Mother's being funny?"

"Don't try to put your feet into the front seat, Bill," Charles said, "and don't sit on the back of your spine. They won't approve of it when you go to Exeter."

He had not intended to mention Exeter. He did not want to talk about anything in particular. He felt relaxed and tired, but pleasantly tired.

"We ought to buy some garden hose," he said. "I wonder whether they have any decent hose this year."

"Oh, never mind it now," Nancy said. "Let's just go on home and maybe you and Bill had better rake the lawn, or perhaps we might just sit around and do nothing for a while. I'd rather like to do nothing." She glanced at him quickly. "How did it all look when you got back?"

"Oh," he said, "the general situation?"

"Yes," she said, "that God-damned situation."

"Now, Nancy," he said. "The children."

"It's all right," Nancy said. "The children know I swear sometimes," but of course neither of them could speak fully of the general situation in front of the children.

"It looks about the same," Charles said. "I only saw Tony Burton for a minute. He came in late and he was busy but he said he was looking forward to tonight, that he had something on his mind."

"Is that the way he put it, looking forward?"

It was awkward, talking in that veiled way in front of the children. "Nance," he said, "there isn't anything more I can do. Let's try to forget it, shall we?"

"Just as long as it gets over," she said, "one way or another. You haven't forgotten about that payment on the mortgage, have you?"

He could understand this association of ideas. They were turning into the gateway of Sycamore Park and he could see the whitewashed brick of their house already.

"No, I haven't," he said. "Can you name one time when I've forgotten about the mortgage?" The lawn had never looked so green and the house had never looked so well. "Do you know what I think?" He raised his voice because he did not like to think of Bill and Evelyn in the back seat trying to piece their words together as children always did. "I think it's about time Bill and Evvie learned to sail." The idea must have come to him both from thinking of the products of the Nickerson Cordage Company and from that glimpse of the Sound from the station platform.

"Learned to sail?" Nancy repeated.

"I don't see why not," he said. "Here we live right near the water and we've never had a boat. I don't see why we shouldn't — an eighteen-foot knockabout or something" — and then he checked himself before he said any more. He sounded exactly as his father had and even the words were almost the same.

"Do you really mean that about a sailboat?" he heard Bill asking.

"I don't know why not," he said. "We'll have to think about it, Bill."

The car had stopped and Bill and Evelyn were on the graveled driveway.

He and Bill and Evelyn were still talking about that hypothetical sailboat when Nancy opened the side door and called him. The idea of the boat kept interfering with other things he was thinking and while they raked oak leaves from under the rhododendrons, everything he thought was also mingled with the persistent rustling and crackling of the leaves. It was a sound like the lapping of small waves.

He had put on sneakers, and a pair of khaki trousers from one of his old uniforms, and a white shirt with a frayed collar which Nancy had saved for him for working around the place. It would be torn up for cleaning rags after he had used it once or twice. He and Evelyn raked and Bill packed the leaves into a bushel basket and carried them to a shady place by the side of the garage where they were going to make a compost heap. He had never made one but Nancy had been talking about compost heaps for a long while and this year they would start one. The Martins had a compost heap, Evelyn was saying, and it was wet and soggy and it smelled, but it was meant to be wet and soggy, he told her, and when she asked him what they would do with it after it was made he told Evelyn to ask her mother, who knew about those things. Evelyn was getting old enough so that she ought to learn something about gardening. Lots of people liked it and it was good exercise, and it made no difference that he did not know much about it. He had always been too busy, but when he was Evelyn's age he had always cleaned up the back yard.

"Did Aunt Dorothea use to clean it up too?" Evelyn asked.

Yes, her Aunt Dorothea did sometimes, when he did not do it well enough. Her Aunt Dorothea always liked to have things picked up.

"You know," he said, while he raked the leaves, "we might all go up to Clyde this summer. I've always been thinking of taking you there. We really ought to get around to it. I don't see why we shouldn't just take the Buick and drive up there, if I can get some time off. It might be a new Buick. I've got my name down for one."

"Never mind about the Buick," Bill said. "Let's talk about the boat."

"If we went up to Clyde," he said, "we might go on to the White Mountains. I've never seen Mount Washington."

Some of his senior class at high school, he was thinking, had taken a trip to Mount Washington once, with Mr. Flanders, the physics teacher, but it had been one of those times when there was not much money and he had not gone with them.

"Never mind about Mount Washington," Bill said. "Let's talk about the boat."

"All right," he said. "It won't do any harm to talk about it."

"If we got it, where would we keep it?"

"Don't spill all those leaves," he said. "We could moor it some-where. My father was always talking about getting us a boat and a pony but he never did and maybe I won't either."

"Well," Bill said, "we could get a magazine and look at pictures."

Yes, they could look at pictures, and perhaps no one believed en-tirely in the boat. But then Evelyn was saying that Mr. Swiss had one, with an auxiliary engine. But then he was not Mr. Swiss and he did not want to be Mr. Swiss.

"You see," he said, "you can't be anything very different from what you are."

They were all still talking but his attention was wandering. He

534

was thinking about security, a popular word still, even when nothing was secure. The foundation of everything was shaky and yet there were always plans on top of those shaking foundations, pathetic plans, important only to an individual. Nothing was certain. Yet he felt contented and at peace doing nothing but raking leaves on the lawn, he and his two children.

"Now, listen," he said, "let's stop all this about a sailboat. We'll probably never have one. I don't know what we'd do with one if we had it."

"You said it wouldn't do any harm to talk about it," Bill said.

"It doesn't matter what you talk about or think about," he said, "as long as you know what's real, and it's pretty hard to learn what's real and what isn't. A lot of people never learn." He rubbed the sleeve of his frayed shirt across his forehead. "This is a pretty tough world, Bill."

Bill and Evelyn looked at him with that half-astonished, half-bored expression that always came over children when grownups spoke of the hardness of the world. He could see that they did not believe him and it was just as well. No matter what might happen, all he could do was give them an illusion of security.

"Why don't you go in and get a baseball and a mitt, Bill?" he asked. "I'd sort of like to toss a ball around."

It was an effort to escape. It reminded him of his father reading *Candide* aloud — the part about digging in one's garden.

"Why is it such a tough world?" Bill asked. "You're doing pretty well, aren't you?"

"Well," he said, "there's always room for improvement."

Then Nancy opened the side door and called him.

"Charley," she called, "you'd better come in now if we're going to get there on time." They always got everywhere on time, they both felt the same way about punctuality, but for the moment he had completely forgotten about the dinner with Tony Burton.

Upstairs in their room Nancy pulled at the zipper of her housecoat and looked critically at the long flowered silk dress spread out on the bed, fresh from the cleaners.

"I suppose she'll wear a long dress," she said.

535

She was referring, of course, to Mrs. Anthony Burton, and Nancy had the same watchful, determinedly pleasant expression that she always assumed on those semiannual occasions when the Burtons asked them out to Roger's Point, near Stamford. It was quite different from the expression she assumed when they went to the Merrys' or when they had dined with the Slades.

"Nance," he said, and he put his arm around her.

"Don't kiss me," she said. "You'll muss my hair and I've got on lipstick."

"All right," he said. "All right."

"I put your studs in for you," she said. "It's your new shirt. I've laid out everything."

"Well, don't sound like an undertaker," he said.

"I don't sound like anything," she said, "but I wish you'd hurry, Charley."

Everything was laid out, as she said it was, on the fresh candlewick spread of his twin bed.

"I don't see why I should wear a stiff shirt," he said.

"Because you're going to the Burtons', that's why," Nancy said. "He never wears a soft shirt, Charley."

"You mean he expects it of me?" he said. Everyone always dressed like Tony Burton.

It was a small matter and he could not understand why he should have given it another thought but he had pulled open his second bureau drawer. Nancy had her flowered dress over her head but she heard the sound.

"Charley, what are you doing?" Nancy asked. "Everything's laid out."

No matter what she said, he was going to wear a soft shirt to the Burtons'.

There was no problem about the children's supper because Mary was back from Harlem and she would get it. The Buick was by the front door, where they had left it after the trip from the station.

"I'll drive," Nancy said.

"Let me drive over," Charles said. "I'd like the kids to remember that their father can drive a car."

Bill and Evelyn were standing at the end of the walk. The rhododendrons by the front door were budding and there were small soft dots of yellowish green on the tips of the yews. It was seven o'clock, the right time to be leaving for the Burtons', with a little leeway in case there should be heavy traffic on the Post Road. He stepped on the self-starter and the engine still sounded smooth and quiet. It was still a good car and it showed how long you could keep a car if you took care of it. People might not be changing cars every other year as they had before the war and this might affect motor stocks if Ford and Chrysler and General Motors ever caught up on their production.

"Good-by," he called. "We'll be back early, I guess."

"Wait a minute," Nancy said. "Evelyn, will you please water the begonias in the dining room, and, Bill, be sure to close the windows if it rains. Mary always forgets."

"Is that all?" Charles asked.

"Yes," Nancy said, "that's all," and she opened her white bead bag to be sure she had not forgotten her lipstick, her compact, and a clean handkerchief.

They were alone and there was a change in tempo because there was always a slight façade, a different set of manners, when they were with the children. Now they would have to talk about facts, plain contemporary facts. They were on that twisting road with all the driveways. Obviously they were each waiting for the other to speak and neither could wait too long or else the other might think there was a sense of strain.

"Well, tell me about everything," Nancy said.

What he wanted to say to her might have been possible in their room just before she had told him not to kiss her because of lipstick and her hair but it was not possible in the car on their way to the Post Road. Though there was a proper time for everything, opportunities were very rare when he could appropriately say what he really thought without its sounding simple and banal. She was asking him to tell her everything. It was a set speech, like a phrase in a book of etiquette. He wished to God he could tell her everything. At that moment, for example, he wanted to tell her that he loved her. He wanted to tell her that she and the children were all that mattered and that he had wanted to tell her so when he had called her up from Clyde, but it was not the time or place.

"Charley," she said, "don't drive so fast."

"All right," he said. "Nance, we've been through a lot together, haven't we? One damn thing after another."

"I always have that feeling after you've been driving for a while," she said. "Aren't you going to tell me about everything?"

"Well," he said, "it was queer going back to Clyde. It was quite an experience." He paused. They were coming to the intersection with the Post Road.

"You don't have to slow down," Nancy said. "The light's turning green."

"Well," he said, "anyway Jackie Mason's got everything," and he turned left on the Post Road.

"Who?" she asked. She was evidently thinking of something else and there was no reason why she should not have been because she had nothing to do with Clyde. Nevertheless, it was exasperating when she asked him who.

"Jackie Mason," he said. "You know, Jackie Mason."

"Oh, yes," she said. "Of course. Well, what about him?"

He was passing an oil truck on the Post Road. On the rear of it was a sign in chalk, "If you can read this, you're too damn close." He could not look at her but he knew she was looking at him and he could tell from the effort in her voice that she was trying to enter into the spirit of what he was trying to tell her.

"Well," he said, "there isn't much more except that he's got everything. He's a director of the Dock Street Savings Bank, and he's a trustee of the public library and he's in the Tuesday Club and he's going to marry Jessica Lovell, but I told you that, didn't I?"

"Well," Nancy said, "you could have done that too. I always told you so."

"Well," he said, "I'm glad I didn't." He took his right hand from the wheel and put it over hers.

"Darling," she said, "I wish you'd look where you're going."

"All right," he said, "I'm looking," and he took his hand away.

"But at the same time he hasn't got anything, that's what I'm trying to say."

"Who hasn't got anything?" Nancy asked. She could not keep her mind on anything he was trying to say.

"Jackie Mason," he said. "I was telling you, Jackie Mason."

"Well, to hell with Jackie Mason," Nancy said. "There isn't any reason to shout. He hasn't made a touchdown. Besides, I thought you said he had everything."

"All right," he said. "Never mind it, Nancy."

It was well after seven o'clock and cars on the road were switching on their lights. She moved closer to him and she patted his hand as he held the wheel.

"I'm sorry, Charley," she said. "I just can't concentrate. Let's stop trying to talk as though we weren't both thinking about the same thing."

"Yes," he said, "I know." In just a minute they would have to slow down for Stamford, then right, then left at the first stoplight, and then a right turn at the underpass about a mile beyond.

"Charley" — her voice was sharper — "what's the matter?"

There must have been something in his voice, but then they knew each other too well for either of them to conceal anything.

"Oh, God," he said, "I wish everything weren't so contrived."

They were right back where they had been that morning when she had taken him to the station.

"Contrived?" she repeated. "How do you mean, contrived?"

"I mean what I say." He had not intended to sound so bitter. "I mean it's all so superficial. The bank president and the big job, and what will happen to Junior, and whether a boiled shirt will help. The values of it are childish. It hasn't any values at all."

"I know." Her voice was softer. "You've said it before."

"Nance," he said, "I wish you wouldn't be so tense. This isn't as important as all that."

"Charley." She sounded steady and controlled, a great deal too controlled. "Don't say it. I can't stand it if you say it."

"Don't say what? What do you think I'm going to say?" he asked.

"Don't say — " her voice became harsh and strident — "don't say we have each other. We *have* got each other but I don't want to hear it and you're just getting ready to say that, aren't you? It's been in your mind all afternoon. I knew it when you were out there on the lawn being sweet to the children. Say it later but don't say it now."

"Nance," he said, and his own voice was edgy, "I've done everything I can. Let's change the subject."

"You're acting licked already," she said. "I hate it when you act that way."

"All right," he said, "maybe I'm licked, and maybe I don't give a damn."

"I suppose you're going to say I've always been pushing you because I want us to get on," she said.

"I wish you'd stop telling me what I'm going to say," he answered.

They were through the underpass and now that they were approaching the Sound the places were growing older and larger. Houses with mansard roofs and newer Colonials were standing on broad lawns.

"You shouldn't have gone to that damned war."

It seemed to him that he was driving too fast and he glanced at the speedometer but the speed was only thirty miles an hour.

"Yes, you told me so at the time," he said. "You were right, but at least — "

"At least what?"

"I don't know," he said. "Let's not talk about it now."

"Can't we talk about anything?"

"No," he said, "let's not talk about anything."

It had been a long while since his nerves had been so on edge but even so they were almost at Roger's Point. He could see where the public road ended at a wooden booth where a watchman stood to exclude unwanted visitors. It was like entering a military installation when you went to dinner with the Burtons.

"I don't see what they see in him. Any fool ought to know you're ten times as good as he is."

"Who?" he asked.

"Blakesley. I wish you'd listen to me. Blakesley."

"Oh, yes. Well, Roger's pretty quick on his feet," he said.

"Charley, if —" She stopped and started again. "If . . . what are you going to do?"

He did not answer. He felt as though everything were hanging on a few threads and as though anything might break them. They were passing walls of dressed granite and carefully raked driveways. He and Nancy did not belong there. They were like intruders in a larger world.

"Haven't you even thought what you're going to do?"

"My God," he said, "I'm sick of thinking."

The threads had broken and he saw that she was crying. It was the worst possible time for this to have happened, just as they were approaching the private road to Roger's Point. He stopped the car.

"It isn't fair," she sobbed. "It isn't fair."

"Never mind, Nance," he said, and he put his arm around her. "We've got lots of time and it doesn't matter if we're late."

She was already opening her beaded bag.

"I'm all right now," she said. "I didn't mean to let you down."

"You haven't let me down," he said.

"I'm all right now," she said. "Start up the car. This wouldn't have happened if I'd been driving. Don't look at me, don't say anything, and to hell with everybody."

V

Fate Gave, What Chance Shall Not Control . . .

— MATTHEW ARNOLD

IT WAS GOOD BUSINESS to learn unobtrusively all one could about one's superiors and through his years at the Stuyvesant Bank Charles had collected a considerable amount of information about Mr. Anthony Burton and his background. He had picked this up gradually, a little here and there from occasional remarks that Mr. Burton had made when there was general conversation, and more from Arthur Slade. In the course of time, Charles had been able to sift fact from gossip and to make his own evaluations, until now, if necessary, he could have written from memory a biographical character sketch of Tony Burton, and he could have filled in any gaps from his own firsthand observations of Tony Burton's habits. He knew that Tony Burton was both typical and exceptional — a rich man's son with inherited ability and with ambition that had somehow not been dulled by his having always been presented with what he had wanted. Though Charles knew that he would always observe Tony Burton from a distance, it was fascinating to speculate upon his drives and problems.

His life and Tony Burton's were actually two complete and separate circles, touching at just one point, and they were circles that would never coincide. Though they each could make certain ideas comprehensible to the other, the very words they used had different meanings for each of them. Security, work, worry, future, position, and society, capital and government, all had diverging meanings. Charles could understand the Burton meanings and could interpret them efficiently and accurately, but only in an objective, not in an emotional, way, in the same manner he might have interpreted the meanings of a Russian commissar or a Chinese mandarin. He could admire aspects of Tony Burton, he could even like him, but they could only understand each other theoretically.

When Tony Burton said, for instance, as he was recently fond of saying, that the neighborhood where he lived on Roger's Point was running down, it was not what Charles would have meant if he had made the statement. Tony Burton did not mean that any place on Roger's Point was growing shabby or that crude parvenus had pushed in on Roger's Point. He only meant that several places during the war had changed hands rather suddenly — nothing along the shore, of course, but in back. He did not mean that the new owners of these places were financially unstable or made noises when they ate their food. He only meant that one of the owners was the president of an advertising agency and that another controlled the stock of a depilatory preparation. Though these people were agreeable and wanted to do better, their having been allowed to buy into Roger's Point indicated that the general morale was running low. It would not have happened, for instance, when Mr. Burton, Senior, was alive. That was all he meant.

This did not sound serious to Charles, but it was to Tony Burton and Charles could understand it, intellectually. What was more, Tony Burton must have known he understood it, for he discussed the situation quite frankly with Charles, just as though Charles owned property on Roger's Point — not on the inside but on the water side. Yet they both obviously knew that Charles could never afford to live there. A backlog of inherited wealth was required to live there, unless one made a killing on the stock market or invented a laxative or a depilatory. There was no way of telling what might happen to Roger's Point. Anyone might live there in time, and Tony Burton could laugh ironically about it, and Charles, too, could laugh, sympathetically and intellectually, without ever fully savoring the suffering behind Tony Burton's mirth.

Tony Burton's father, Sanford Burton, had bought all of Roger's Point in 1886, when there were no houses there, and he had built the Burton house in 1888. He had already formed the brokerage firm of Burton and Fall, and the Point had been a profitable real estate investment. It had not been difficult to sell off parts of it around the turn of the century to the proper sort of person. Simpkins, a director of U. S. Steel, had bought the cove, and the Marshalls, the Erie Railroad Marshalls, had bought the place next, and the Crawfords, the Appellate Justice Crawfords, were there also. Charles could remember most of the owners' names. It was good business to know them as many of them had accounts at the Stuyvesant Bank. In fact Charles knew the names as well as did the watchman at the beginning of the private road.

"I'm going to Mr. Anthony Burton's," he said, and he could even employ the proper tone, intellectually. "Mr. Burton is expecting me for dinner."

"You needn't have told him all the family history," Nancy said. "Why didn't you tell him you're forty-three years old and show him our wedding certificate?" She was telling him indirectly that she was feeling better, that she was all right now.

"Oh, my God," she said, "here it is, and they've put on the lights."

She was referring to lights in the trees along the drive, a recent innovation of Tony Burton's, inspired by a winter's visit at the place of a friend of his in Fort Lauderdale, Florida. If they could have lights in coconut palms, Tony Burton said, there was no reason for not having them in the copper beeches at Roger's Point, but those new lights did not go so well with the house. Lampposts and gaslight would have fitted the whole scene better. The building had been designed by Richardson, the Romanesque architect — another fact that Charles had learned and filed away. It was too dark to see the detail of the slate roof, the brick walls and the arched doors and windows trimmed with old red sandstone, but its vague outline still looked indestructible. The light beneath the brick and sandstone porte cochere shone on the iron and glass front door and on the potted hothouse azaleas in rows beside the steps.

The doors had swung open already and Jeffreys, the Burton butler, had stepped outside — but not as far down as the lower step — and was saying good evening.

"You go in, Nancy," Charles said. "I'd better put the car somewhere."

"There's no need to move it, Mr. Gray," Tony Burton's butler said. He was wearing a dinner coat with a stiff shirt. "There's no one else this evening."

"Oh," Charles said, "if you're sure it's all right." He had never been able to speak even an intellectual language with Tony Burton's butler. "It's a beautiful evening, isn't it?"

"Yes, sir," Tony Burton's butler said. "It's balmy for this time of year," and then Charles saw that a maid was behind him, relieving Nancy of her cloak.

It was impossible to forget Tony Burton's house once you had been inside it. In summer or winter the air in the hall was balmy like the evening and fragrant with the scent of hothouse flowers. It was a huge oak-paneled hall, with a double staircase and a gallery and a Romanesque fireplace. For a second he and Nancy stood in the shaded light of the hall almost indecisively. There was an especial feeling of timidity when one went there, a furtive sense of not belonging. Yet in another way he was perfectly at ease for at those semiannual dinners Tony Burton had always made them feel most welcome. Besides, each summer there was always that all-day party for everyone at the bank, with three-legged races and potato races and pingpong and bridge for the wives. Mrs. Burton, too, always made the bank wives feel comfortable. The bright light from the open parlor door shone across the dusky hall and Tony Burton was already in the oblong of light, a white carnation in the lapel of his dinner coat, holding out both hands, one for Nancy and one for him.

"Home is the sailor, home from sea," Tony Burton said, "and the hunter home from the hill. I wish you wouldn't always surprise me, Nancy my dear. Why are you more beautiful every time I see you, or do I just forget?"

"It might be that you just forget, mightn't it?" Nancy asked.

Tony Burton laughed. He had a delightful laugh.

"We've really got to do something about seeing each other more often," he said. "It's been too long, much too long. Why don't you come to work some morning instead of Charley? I'm getting pretty sick of seeing Charles around." He laughed again and slapped

Charles on the back and they walked behind Nancy into the drawing room.

Charles knew all about Tony Burton's drawing room, too, both from Tony Burton and from Arthur Slade. Mrs. Burton and the girls, before the girls had been married, had made Tony Burton do it entirely over. The enormous Persian carpet had come from the Anderson Gallery and so had the two Waterford chandeliers. Charles remembered them very well because Tony Burton had sent him to the auction to bid them in on one of the first occasions that Tony had ever paid any attention to him, and this did not seem so long ago. He also remembered the huge canvas of a mass of square-rigged ships — the British fleet at anchor. Mrs. Burton was always buying new things for the living room and besides Tony always loved boats. The cup he had won in one of the Bermuda races was standing on the concert grand piano. You could roll up the carpet and clear out all the furniture. It had been a great place for dancing before the girls had married.

"Althea," Tony Burton said, "I told you Nancy Gray would be wearing a long dress."

"Oh, my dear," Mrs. Burton said, "I should have called you up. Tony's getting so absent-minded lately. He spoke of it as supper. There should be set rules for short and long. Now just the other evening at the Drexels' the same thing happened to me. I thought it was dinner and it was supper. But the men thought this up. We didn't, did we?"

"Charles should have told me," Nancy said. "Why didn't you tell me it was supper, Charley?"

"It's always some man's fault, isn't it, Charley?" Tony Burton said.

"That's one of the truest things you ever said, sweetheart," Mrs. Burton said. "Everything that happens to a woman is always some man's fault."

"Jeffreys can bring us almost anything," Tony Burton said, "from sherry and a biscuit to Scotch on the rocks, but Charley and I will stick to dry Martinis, won't we, Charley? What will you have, Nancy my dear?"

"A Martini," Nancy said, "and if I don't like it I can blame it on the men."

"But not on Tony," Mrs. Burton said. "Blame it on Jeffreys. Tony mixes terrible Martinis. Don't you think so, Mr. Gray, or have you ever tried one of his Martinis?"

It was characteristic of that relationship and perfectly suitable that Mrs. Burton should call him Mr. Gray. It meant that he was a business friend of Tony Burton's, or associate might have been a better word, who had come to supper on business with his little wife. She knew how to put Tony's business friends and associates at their ease, but there were certain limits and certain degrees of rank. They were not on a first-name basis yet and he was just as glad of it. It would have embarrassed him acutely, it would have seemed like a breach of etiquette, if he were to call Mrs. Burton Althea. He knew his place and they could meet on common ground by his calling Mr. Burton Tony and by Mrs. Burton's referring to Nancy as "my dear."

"I'm not in a position to say what I think of Tony's cocktails," Charles said, "except that Tony is always right."

"You all lick his boots so," Mrs. Burton said. "That's why he's so impossible when he comes home. Sherry, please, Jeffreys. Is Mr. Gray impossible when he comes home, my dear?"

"Usually," Nancy said. "Normally impossible."

"I wonder what they do at the bank," Mrs. Burton said. "I have a few vague ideas. That blond secretary of Tony's . . . we can compare notes after dinner." The oil of small talk soothed the troubled waters, if there were troubled waters. Mrs. Tony Burton was putting Nancy at her ease. It was necessary business entertaining, household duty, and one of these suppers that must have helped in some vague way.

Everything moved so smoothly that when Charles tried to discover anything revealing in Mrs. Burton's voice or attitude, he could hit upon absolutely nothing. He could discover no new flicker of interest or no new warmth. She was simply being as nice as she could possibly be to one of the younger men whom Tony had to have around sometimes and to the little thing the younger man had married. She had even dressed thoughtfully for the occasion in an oldish gown, with no jewelry except a simple strand of pearls, yet you could not say that she was dressing down to Nancy. Charles remembered Arthur Slade's saying that she was a good ten years younger than Tony, that she was one of the Philadelphia Brines, and Charles knew from the size of the Brine estate, which the bank was handling, that, like Tony Burton, she had always been free from want. He could tell it from the tilt of her head, from her confident happy mouth, and even from the tint of her hair. There was a single lock of gray in it and perhaps all of it should have been gray but he could not be quite sure.

"I love that little house of yours, my dear," she was saying, and he could see Nancy smiling at her with elaborate enthusiasm. "That whitewashed brick, and everything so compactly arranged. It must be a comfort to live in it instead of in a great barn, but Tony insists on the ancestral mansion."

"The only good thing about a small house," Nancy said, "is when the maid leaves."

"We've been marvelously lucky," Mrs. Burton said. "Ours keep staying on with us, I'm sure I don't know why."

Jeffreys, the butler, was passing round pieces of toast with cream cheese and recumbent anchovies on them, and a maid followed Jeffreys carrying an icy bowl of celery, raw carrots and olives.

"I hear that raw carrots are good for the eyesight," Charles said to Tony Burton.

"That's one of those new ideas," Tony said. He looked bright and alert as he always did before dinner. "It's on a par with the one about alcohol being good for hardening of the arteries. Have you heard the new one about Truman?"

Tony Burton always enjoyed those stories. Formerly it had been Franklin D. Roosevelt, though Tony was hardly what you would call a Roosevelt-hater, and now it was Truman.

"I don't know," Charles said. "I've heard a good many new ones lately." He had almost called Tony Burton sir but he had checked himself in time.

"I know just what you mean, my dear," he heard Mrs. Burton

saying. "These country day schools are never quite right. Now when the girls were growing up — "

"Always remember it might have been Wallace," he said to Tony Burton. Everything considered, Tony was surprisingly tolerant about politics and politicians. To him politics was like the weather. You could make occasional forecasts but you could not control it.

"I'd like to know what those playboys are going to try next," he said. "And that's a good name for them, playboys. Did you ever read the Van Bibber stories by Richard Harding Davis?"

"The Van Bibber stories?" Charles repeated. "I'm afraid I must have missed them."

"Well," Tony Burton said, "they belonged to my flight more than your flight, Charley." This must once have been a shooting term, Charles thought, used when one foregathered in a gunroom after a hard day on the moors. "They typified a certain era — the period when I was a playboy myself. There used to be a fashionable character, believe it or not — the gay blade about town, the white tie, the silk hat, we won't get home until morning. He's an extinct type now, of course, a product of a different social scene. Dick Davis hit him off rather well in the Van Bibber stories. Dick Davis was quite a playboy himself. I used to try to model my conduct after his, in a small way. Here comes Jeffreys. How about another cocktail?"

"Oh, no, I don't think so, thanks," Charles said. He did not want to refuse too quickly or too eagerly, and of course Tony Burton must have known that when urged he would take another.

"It won't hurt you to relax and tomorrow's Saturday and I'm going to have another."

"Well, thanks," Charles said, "if you are. They're very good cocktails."

He wished that he could relax as Tony Burton suggested, instead of trying to read a meaning into every simple action. Tony Burton would never have taken a second Martini if they were going to talk of anything seriously after dinner. It meant that everything was settled in one way or another.

"Now, Henry Wallace," Tony Burton was saying, "and all the rest of the New Deal crowd are the playboy type. They have the same power and the same privileges expressed in different terms. They're all Van Bibbers."

Tony smiled at him triumphantly but it was hard for Charles to discuss the subject intelligently, not being familiar with the works of Richard Harding Davis.

"It's an interesting thought," he said, "but it might be that you're oversimplifying."

Tony Burton looked at him in a fixed, cool way that made Charles think that perhaps he had said too much. It was necessary not to forget just who he was and what he was. It was necessary to assume a convivial attitude and yet not too convivial, to be familiar and yet not overfamiliar.

"Sometimes you have a cryptic quality, Charley," Tony Burton said. "I never seem to know lately whether you're laughing at me or not. Sometimes you're an enigma."

"Well," Charles answered, "sometimes you're an enigma to me."

When he heard Tony Burton laugh he knew that he had been familiar but not too familiar.

"Oh, Jeffreys," Tony Burton said. "How about another one, Charley?"

"No, thanks," Charles said.

"Definitely not?"

"Definitely," Charles said. "You might start talking about books and authors again and I want to understand everything you say tonight."

It might have been too familiar but at least he had made a point. He waited smiling, watching Tony Burton, and he put his glass back on Tony Burton's butler's tray. He was thinking of what he had said to young Mrs. Whitaker in the apartment on Park Avenue when she had offered him a drink. He had told her that he did not think she would take one if she were in his place and she had said they were both very good for what they were. He watched Tony Burton and smiled an innocent friendly smile. He and Tony Burton were both very good for what they were. They had both been trained in the Stuyvesant Bank and they had the same veneer and discipline. He had come a long way from Clyde.

550

"Tony," Mrs. Burton called, "if you can stop talking business with poor Mr. Gray we might all go in to dinner."

"Now, Althea," Tony Burton said, "Charley and I have a lot of other things to talk about. I wish you would get it out of your head that I always talk business with the boys."

The dining room with its heavy oak chairs, and an English leather screen placed before the pantry door, and its ornate Tiffany silver upon the massive sideboard, was also a long way from Clyde. The table, set for four, beneath another Waterford chandelier, looked too small for the room but imposingly beautiful with its Venetian tablecloth, its water and wine glasses and its bowl of tulips. He was glad there were only four of them because the conversation would be general and he would not have to talk to Mrs. Burton. He saw Nancy glance at him quickly as he sat down and he smiled at her. It was better to let the Burtons start the conversation. It was better not to say what a beautiful tablecloth it was or to speak about the tulips. It was better to make no remark about the surroundings that would show how little one was used to them, but there was no reason to worry, because Mrs. Burton was already speaking.

It was so nice, she was saying, to have them drop in like this instead of coming to a large dinner. Eight was the limit for general conversation and four was better than eight, and she was thinking, just the other day, about the first time she had ever heard about Mr. Gray — from poor Arthur Slade. She did not think she had seen Mr. Gray since that accident. It was tragic and so unnecessary. They had both been so fond of poor Arthur, but then she knew that Mr. Gray knew all about flying. The conversation was moving very pleasantly. It was not necessary to think carefully of what he was saying, now that they all were talking. Tony Burton was asking Nancy about the children, as though he knew them very well, and while they talked the plates were changing. There were soup and guinea hen and then a salad and then dessert. He was glad that it was not a long or complicated dinner. There was no obvious sense of strain but all the while he felt that Tony Burton was watching him.

"I wish," Tony Burton said, "there weren't so many words, or it may be because I'm getting old that they confuse me more than they used to. Somehow they keep having more shades of meaning. Now even with Charles and me it's difficult. I say a word and he says a word and we can look it up in the dictionary, but it doesn't mean the same thing to either of us and it would mean something a little different to Nancy and it would be a little different even to Althea. I don't suppose this is a very new thought of mine, but it's a thought."

"I can't imagine what you're talking about, Tony," Mrs. Burton said.

"But Charley knows," Tony Burton said, "don't you, Charley? We all may be worrying about the same thing but we worry about it in different ways."

It was startling to find that Tony Burton was thinking during dinner exactly what he had been thinking earlier.

"Yes," he said, "I know just what you mean."

He saw that Nancy looked startled too and he saw Tony Burton glance at her and then look back at him triumphantly.

"I wish we could all get together," Tony Burton said, "and we might do something with the world, but of course we never can get together. That's the exasperating thing about it."

"Really," Mrs. Burton said, "I don't know what you're talking about, Tony."

Charles himself could not gather what this was leading up to, but as he watched Tony Burton he could see that Tony's face was set in the expression he always wore when he was about to say a few graceful words before a group of people.

"Perhaps I'm being cryptic now," he said, "but all I'm saying is that I wish we might all be friends. I really hope we can be, in spite of anything that may happen in the future, and the future isn't as clear as it used to be. That's all I'm trying to say. And now if you girls will excuse us, I'm going to take Charley into the library, Charley and I want to have a little talk tonight but we'll be back as soon as we can."

Mrs. Burton stood up and as Charles rose he felt a slight wave of nausea. He could only put one interpretation on that hope for friendship. He guessed the final answer to their little talk already.

He felt the back of his chair biting into the palm of his hand but he still had to say the right thing.

"Why, of course," he said, "we'll always be friends, Tony." He said it automatically but he knew that they never had been and they never would be friends. They might wish it but it would never work for either of them, no matter what might happen.

"Don't stay too long and get too interested," Mrs. Burton said. "I don't see why Tony can't ever get through his business in New York."

Charles was no longer thinking clearly as he walked with Tony Burton from the dining room. What he desired most was to behave in such a way that no one would have the satisfaction of seeing how deeply he was hurt. That desire was partly discipline and partly human instinct for concealment. His own reaction was what shocked him most because he had believed that he was prepared for bad news and that he would not consider bad news as complete a disaster as was indicated by the sinking feeling in the pit of his stomach. Yet after that first moment the shock was giving way to relief. He suddenly felt free and a weight was lifted from him. There was no reason for him to try any longer, not the slightest reason. He did not know what he would say or do in that final interview but there was nothing more that he could expect from Tony Burton. He would never have to be obsequious and careful again. He would never have to go through anything like that dinner. If Tony wished that they could still be friends, this meant at least that Tony liked him personally, but that was inconsequential. There was no room for personal likes in a corporation.

It was not far from the dining room to the smaller room where men customarily gathered. They both walked across that gloomy hall without speaking and space had lost its significance. He was actually walking also over the road of his career, a feeble little human track like the progress of a sea creature in sand. It stretched all the way from the day on the stage at the City Hall to the accounting department in Wright-Sherwin, to Johnson Street, to Rush & Company, to the day his father died, to New York, to the day he met Nancy downtown, and now the track was ending in that walk across the hall. There would never be the same hay in the bundle again. The ass would never have to walk after it so assiduously. He might still be useful, but in a business way his career was as good as over. He had gone as far as he would go.

It was amazing that his thoughts could move so far afield in such a short space of time. He was like a defeated general withdrawing to a prepared position. He could sell the house at Sycamore Park. Suburban real estate was still high. They could move to a smaller place. There would be funds enough to educate Bill, and there was that trust fund of his mother's which would revert to him eventually. He would never have his present reputation but he would have the commercial value of an educated wheel horse, if he knew his place. He would never have to try so hard again.

"It's over," he said to himself as he walked across the hall. "Thank God, it's over." It was the first time he had felt really free since the moment he had met Jessica at the firemen's muster.

Tony Burton's room had always reminded him of the corner of a men's club. It was filled with the mementos of the travels of Tony Burton, gathered on that trip to Bagdad and on two world cruises. There was a gilded Chinese Buddha on the mantel above the arched fireplace, and a Chinese ancestral portrait and other things, but Charles was no longer obliged to be interested in them. He seated himself in a comfortable armchair without waiting to see if it was Mr. Burton's chair or not. He no longer had to bother.

"Sugar and cream, sir?" Mr. Burton's butler asked.

"Just coffee, thank you," Charles said.

"And brandy, sir?"

"No, thanks," Charles said. "No brandy."

"Try it, Charley," Tony Burton said. "It's some of my father's brandy. There isn't much like it left."

Tony Burton was still standing up. He should have waited until Tony sat down but he no longer had to try so hard.

"Nancy always says I shouldn't drink after dinner," he said, "but all right if you're going to have some, Tony."

"Why not break down all the way and have a cigar?" Tony Burton said.

"Why, thanks," he answered. "I'd like one."

"Now that I think of it, I've never seen you smoke a cigar, Charley."

"I don't often," Charles said, "but I'd rather like one tonight."

Tony Burton was still standing and again he wore the look he customarily assumed when he prepared to say a few graceful yet pointed words.

"Close the door, please, Jeffreys, when you go out," Tony Burton said.

It was like a meeting in the bank directors' room when someone who came in with papers was told to close the door when he left. Charles leaned back comfortably in his chair. It was up to Tony Burton and he did not have to try. He was thinking of other talks in other libraries, the Judge's library at Gow Street and that hypocritical library of Mr. Lovell's and his own library at Sycamore Park. Thank God, it was all over, but he still had a detached, academic sort of curiosity. He was waiting to see how Tony would handle the situation. Tony was sometimes slow and fumbling with decisions but when he made up his mind he carried them through cleanly.

"This friendship in business — " Tony Burton said. "It's always bothered me. They shouldn't be mixed together." He must still have been thinking of that speech in the dining room.

"They don't mix together," Charles said. "Don't try to make them, Tony." It was the first time he had ever spoken to Tony Burton exactly as an equal and it was a great relief. He flicked off the ash of his cigar and picked up his brandy glass and waited.

"And yet they must mix," Tony Burton said. "None of us can help it, Charley. If you see somebody every day, if you have any human instincts at all, you get interested in him. You're bound to like him, or things about him. I like everybody at the bank. They're like members of my family. Now take Blakesley. What do you think of Blakesley, Charley?"

It was not a fair question and there was no reason to give a fair answer and besides it did not matter what he thought of Roger Blakesley.

"What do you want me to think?" he asked, and he was glad to see that Tony did not like the answer.

"It isn't what I want." Tony Burton gave his head an exasperated shake. "You and I are alone here, and you don't have to be so damned careful. There's no necessity for it any more. I want your opinion of him. Do you like him or don't you?"

"All right," Charles said, "as long as it doesn't matter any more, Tony. He's conscientious, energetic, and well-trained, but I don't like him much. Why should I?"

"I rather like him," Tony Burton said. "He's been on my conscience lately. He's been so damned anxious, so damned much on his toes. He's always in there trying."

"I don't know what else you could expect," Charles said, and he was almost amused, now that there was nothing to gain or lose. "I've been trying pretty hard myself."

He had never realized that it could be such a delightful moment, to sit sipping Tony Burton's brandy, entirely free, entirely without thought control.

"Not in the same way, Charley." Tony Burton shook his head again. "You're subtler. You've developed, you've matured. You don't fidget mentally — not in the same way, Charley."

"Thanks," Charles said, "but I wouldn't say that I've been very subtle, Tony."

Tony Burton shook his head impatiently as though he were being diverted from his train of thought.

"Of course I'm out of touch with things, being where I am," he said, "but I've been getting an idea lately . . . and maybe I'm entirely wrong. I wish you'd tell me, Charley. You're more in touch with the office than I am and you're in a position to know Blakesley. . . . It seems to me that he has some idea that we're considering him for Arthur Slade's place. Do you know anything about this, Charley?"

"My God," Charles said. "My God"; and he had a hysterical desire to laugh and then he found that he was laughing. "What did you think that Roger was considering?"

"I didn't give it much thought until about ten days ago," Tony

Burton said. "I'm glad if it amuses you. It doesn't amuse me. When anyone gets ideas like that it's a problem what to do with him later. You never thought that any of us were considering Blakesley seriously, did you? He was useful while you were away but he is not the right material. Of course, there had to be a decent interval after Arthur died but it never occurred to me that you'd have any doubts about it. Your name's coming up before the directors on Monday. Now what do you think we'd better do about Blakesley?"

Suddenly Charles felt dull and very tired.

"You'd better tell him something, Tony," he said, "instead of teasing him to death."

"I suppose I'll have to on Monday. I don't suppose I can put it off on anyone else," Tony Burton said. "I should have discouraged him long ago. I'm sorry about the whole thing but perhaps he had better resign."

It was like the time at Dartmouth when he had won the half mile at freshman track. He felt dull and very tired.

"That was all I meant in the dining room." Tony Burton shook his head again. "Now that we'll be working together more closely, Charley, I hope that we'll always be friends."

Tony's voice seemed to come from a long way off. There was a weight on Charles again, the same old weight, and it was heavier after that brief moment of freedom. In spite of all those years, in spite of all his striving, it was remarkable how little pleasure he took in final fulfillment. He was a vice-president of the Stuyvesant Bank. It was what he had dreamed of long ago and yet it was not the true texture of early dreams. The whole thing was contrived, as he had said to Nancy, an inevitable result, a strangely hollow climax. It had obviously been written in the stars, bound to happen, and he could not have changed a line of it, being what he was, and Nancy would be pleased, but it was not what he had dreamed.

"Well, Tony," he said, "I guess that means I can send Junior to Exeter," and Tony Burton was asking why Exeter? He would not send any boy of his to Exeter.

They were on a different basis already, now that he was a vice-president. Automatically, his thoughts were running along new lines, well-trained, mechanically perfect thoughts, estimating a new situation. There would be no trouble with the directors. There were only five vice-presidents at the Stuyvesant, all of the others older than he, most of them close to the retirement age, like Tony Burton himself. For a moment he thought of Mr. Laurence Lovell on Johnson Street but Mr. Lovell would not have understood, or Jessica either, how far he had gone or what it meant to be a vice-president of the Stuyvesant Bank. Nancy would understand. Nancy had more ambition for him than he had for himself. Nancy would be very proud. They would sell the house at Sycamore Park and get a larger place. They would resign from the Oak Knoll Club. And then there was the sailboat. It had its compensations but it was not what he had dreamed.

"A week from Saturday there'll be a little dinner. It's customary," Tony Burton said. "You'd better be ready to make a few remarks."

"All right," Charles said, "if it's customary."

"And now we'd better go back and see what the girls are doing, unless you have something else on your mind."

"Oh, no, Tony," he answered, "I don't think there's anything else."

They would have to turn in the old Buick as soon as he could get a new one. There were a great many things to think about but they could wait till morning.

Nancy and Mrs. Burton were sitting together on a sofa in the living room and he thought they both looked relieved to see the men come back.

"Well," Mrs. Burton said, "I hope you two have settled the affairs of the world. You look as though you have, and poor Mr. Gray looks tired."

He saw Nancy look at him and Nancy looked tired too. He wanted very much to tell her the news but it would have sounded blatant. Then Tony Burton must have noticed that there was a sense of strain.

"I don't see why you keep on calling Charley Mr. Gray," he said, "when Charley's in the family — or at least he will be on Monday," and then he must have felt that he should explain the situation

558

further because he turned to Nancy. "I don't suppose this comes as any great surprise. Why should it? It's hardly talking out of school. Charley's name is going before the directors on Monday, but I've spoken to them already. There won't be any trouble."

If it meant more to Nancy than it did to him, it made everything all the better, and he was very much impressed at the way she took it. She looked as though she had known all the time that he would be the new vice-president, that nothing else could possibly have happened. She was fitting into her new position more than adequately.

"I can't say I'm surprised," she said, "but it's nice to know definitely . . . Tony."

A minute before she would never have dreamed of calling him Tony, but it sounded very well.

"As long as we're all in the family," Tony Burton went on, "I was just telling Charley that I've been worried about Blakesley lately. Do you suppose he really may have thought that he was being considered?"

"Now that you mention it," Nancy said, "I think perhaps he did — a little."